ZIG ZAG

TONY FOSTER

ISBN 0-89343-051-x

Editorial: Ronald F. Patrick

Ermine Publishers, Inc.
6253 Hollywood Blvd.
Suite 312
Hollywood, CA 90028
(213) 461-3256

ZIG ZAG

TO ARMAGEDDON

TONY FOSTER

'Z' is a zigzag path I know
Through the woods where bluebells grow.

:from a child's nursery rhyme

" . . . if a great number of countries come to have an arsenal of nuclear weapons, then I am glad I'm not a young man and I'm sorry for my grandchildren."

Dr. David Lilienthal
First Chairman of the Atomic Energy Commission
speaking to the U.S. Senate Committee Hearing
in January 1976

AUTHOR'S NOTE

In August 1976 I commenced a fifteen month sentence at the Terminal Island prison in San Pedro, California. The sentence was received after a conviction for smuggling almost a ton of marijuana into the United States from Mexico by aircraft the previous Fall. Upon arrival at prison I was lodged in a two-man pink cell where I remained between August and October, 1976. For some reason the Bureau of Prisons believes pastel shades of pink, green and brown provide an interesting variation on the sterility of color found outside prison walls, although from my own experience a seven-by five-foot, two-man cell equipped with sink and lidless toilet can hardly be considered the ideal location from which to offer a valued judgment. It was during the *pastel* period I began to write *Zig Zag*, using a pencil and paper provided by the Bureau of Prisons; later graduating to a ballpoint pen which I managed to steal from one of the guards. From that moment on it was all downhill.

During late October I was released into what is euphemistically referred to as *population*. This particular graduation ceremony takes a prisoner from the solitary luxury of a private cell where time weighs heavy, to a hundred-man dormitory and prison yard, where time weighs heavier. However, I discovered the main advantage of being in *population* was the access to a typewriter, in addition to the variety of interesting people I met among the thousand odd souls—both men and women—who were sharing my fate. Pimps, prostitutes, drug addicts, smut peddlers, tax evaders, bank robbers, smugglers, con men, swindlers and embezzlers with an assortment of warped idealists, lesbians and homosexuals, plus the insane. Some of them noble and quite innocent, some not so noble and guilty as hell, but all of them very real human beings. To them I am grateful, for they taught me to understand a part of life I never knew; each of us is really after all the sum total of our own experience, no matter what we choose to pretend.

Without belaboring the point, I'd like to thank my wife Helen, who, with our three children, endured the coldest winter on record in Canada while I endured the California sun, and who had the courage to wait until the nightmare ended; my lovable loyal Lorraine, who spent those long lonely hours typing this manuscript during the winter months in Toronto, deciphering my cramped scrawl initially, then later, my badly typed copy, and who had the steadfastness to wait until the dawn. Finally, my thanks to the staff and prisoners at Terminal Island, without whose help and comments this book could never have been written; the inmates, because they cared enough to understand—the staff of 'F' Unit, because they understood enough to care. This story is dedicated to that villain who dwells deep within us all.

Terminal Island F.C.C.
San Pedro, California

March 30, 1977

PROLOGUE

Canadian nuclear power started in 1945 at Chalk River, Ontario, near the deepest part of the Ottawa River, 125 miles west of the nation's capital. ZEEP (Zero Energy Experimental Pile) was the British Commonwealth's reply to the United States' independent nuclear energy program. While the beneficiaries of the technology produced in the Manhatten Project at Alamogordo, New Mexico, shared their idealistic philosophy and information to develop atomic power for peaceful purposes, Canada joined Britain to produce its own unique nuclear reactor—CANDU.

The U.S., after a brief examination of the ZEEP system, decided on an alternative type of reactor technology. Britain abandoned its program based on ZEEP out of prudence and political common sense, realizing the long term dangers inherent in such a system. Canada, mistress of international vacillation and compromise, proceeded on its development alone.

In 1968 the first commercial production of this Canadian Brain Child commenced operations on the shores of Lake Huron at Douglas Point. Government plans called for one hundred and twenty of these reactors by the year 2000. With future power problems organized to its satisfaction, the Canadian government then turned to sell the progeny to foreign markets.

In keeping with the policy decisions made by Prime Minister Lester B. Pearson in 1962 to provide Canadian assistance in developing countries, a full scale CANDU reactor was presented as a gift to the government of India between 1964 and 1972. It was built in Rajastan and called RAPP 1. Pearson, a Nobel Peace Prize winner and compromising civil servant turned diplomat, sensitive to the Indian government's desire to avoid losing 'face' by having inspection teams from Canada control the use of CANDU, settled for a 'gentlemen's agreement'. This agreement provided that India would never use the technology of CANDU for anything other than peaceful purposes. The tree planted in Rajastan by the Canadian government bore a terrible fruit.

On May 18, 1974, India exploded her first atomic bomb, using plutonium fuel supplied by the Canadian government for RAPP 1. The CANDU reactor, like the U.S. Light Water Reactor (LWR) 'breeds' its own plutonium through use. The fuel required to make a bomb is simply removed from the CANDU reactor a little earlier than is usual and reprocessed with natural uranium and radioactive wastes. Common chemical solvents are used to separate the plutonium from these raw wastes.

Obtaining plutonium of a standard capable of producing a bomb from the U.S. reactor is a much more difficult problem. In the LWR, made by the U.S., the important Plutonium (Pu 239) is contaminated with another isotope of Plutonium (Pr 240), creating a lot of heat, light and radioactivity with no explosion. In addition, the LWR requires enriched uranium to operate. Russia and the U.S. are the only two world suppliers of this commodity.

CANDU eliminates all these annoying problems by providing the ability to use world-wide supplies of natural uranium and breed its own plutonium. However, instead of moving swiftly to chop down the offending tree, when the nature of the first harvest had been perceived, Canada moved its gardening efforts elsewhere.

Pakistan, the unplacated enemy of India, was also provided with a Karachi version of the CANDU reactor called Kanupp. Next, Taiwan, the armed island fortress with unfulfilled dreams of reconquering mainland China, collected the same reactor used by India to make her bomb—another gift from Canada. Six weeks before the predicted overthrow of the constitutionally elected government of Argentina by a group of army officers, a CANDU reactor was supplied to that country. South Korea, crouching at the bottom half of the Korean peninsula awaiting the opportunity to spring to the North, is to be the next recipient of Canadian generosity, together with several other nations in the dictatorial areas of the free world which aspire to nuclear membership. No enforceable treaties, safeguards or inspection agreements have been obtained from any of these countries. To date, the government of Canada has not made a single penny from any country to which it has provided CANDU. Payment, when it comes, will be the terrible harvest.

This story concerns one small country in the Western Hemisphere which used its CANDU reactor to build a bomb, and some men and women in various parts of the world who made it possible. They are the heroes and heroines of the story. The villain—and every story must have its villain—is the Bomb. The Bomb that will explode tomorrow morning at dawn, ending all our illusions.

1

THE PRESENT

Ottawa, Canada: The digital clock radio on the bedside table clicked at exactly seven a.m.

"The World at Seven," the announcer intoned ponderously. "Good Morning. From CBC news, here is the world at seven with Rex Corning and Owen Bogden."

Corbin's mind began its journey into consciousness. He rolled over in the bed, dragging the sheets with him. His wife, familiar with the morning procedure, clutched her half of the linen defensively.

". . . . explosion of the thermonuclear device occurred several miles offshore from the small Latin American Republic with no prior notification to shipping in the immediate vicinity. Authorities here state the device was in all probability a dirty type of atomic bomb in the 20 kiloton range and that any fallout should drift well out to sea with prevailing westerly winds before settling on the ocean. Ships in the anticipated fallout area are being warned . . . ."

Corbin was wide awake now, sitting on the edge of the bed.

"That sonofabitch!" he said aloud.

" . . . .the Canadian CANDU nuclear reactor was installed in the Republic under an aid program to provide nuclear energy for underdeveloped countries. Officials from the Atomic Energy Commission, the authority responsible for ensuring the reactor was used for peaceful purposes, have refused to comment on the situation until they have studied it further. The last CANDU reactor violation took place in 1974 when the Republic of India exploded a nuclear device . . . ."

The telephone cut across the newscast. Corbin plucked it off the cradle.

"Corbin here."

"Chuck. Have you heard the news?" Don Affleck's voice was excited, worried.

"Yeah. I'm listening to it now. What's happening?"

"The Minister has scheduled a meeting at nine. He told me to call you. You may have to go down to the Republic yourself. It's a real baddie."

"Okay, Don, thanks. See you at nine." He slammed the phone back on the side table, then looked angrily at his wife. "El Chirlo. That sonofabitch. He's done it!"

Caracas, Venezuela: Sitting in the transit lounge of the international air terminal at Maiquetia, Galal Jamil also heard the news. He was waiting for Hassan to bring him an English newspaper from the kiosk, when he heard two American businessmen on the seat behind discussing the affair. He smiled to himself, as he listened to the sketchy details and outrage from the two voices.

The DC-10 VIASA direct flight from Madrid had left him numb with jet-lag by the time it landed at the Caracas airport in Maiquetia. He had been tired of looking at Hassan's stupid face and close-set Libyan eyes, ever since clearing customs and immigration with their forged Kuwaiti passports. The Libyans had insisted Hassan accompany him to the Republic. Well, it was their right. They were paying the bills.

The short swarthy Libyan returned to the seat beside Jamil and sat down, handing him a copy of yesterday's Miami Herald, then folded his arms and stared vacantly into space. Jamil ignored him as he glanced through the thin overseas edition, waiting for the flight announcement of the *Lineas Aereas Republica* departure to take Hassan and himself on the last short leg of their trip.

San Ramon, Cosecha Rica: The big man sitting behind the plain burnished mahogany desk pushed the pile of telex sheets and telegrams aside. It was noon, and already thirty-seven countries had wired their displeasure. The messages had not been addressed to him directly, of course, but to the President. It amounted to the same thing. The old doctor left everything for him to look after anyway. The President had known nothing about the test firing fifty miles off the coast that dawn. There was no reason to concern him now with the resulting flurry of international disapproval.

He stroked his well-formed Spanish beard absently, toying with the envelope dagger on the massive desk. His not-quite handsome face crinkled into a grim smile. It was a lopsided facial movement, as the muscles in his left cheek had been sliced in half many years before. For as long as he remembered he had been called "El Chirlo—Scarface." Sometimes it was said with awe, sometimes with fear—sometimes with love.

The door at the far end of the terazzo opened. The uniformed guards standing on the lawn just outside the open window behind his back, appeared suddenly, their machine pistols at the ready. They had been covering the room through the reflection of the open pane, adjusted to the right angle to see without being seen. He waved them aside without turning his head, as Paco, his aide, slipped into the chamber, closing the door softly.

"They have arrived, Colonel," he announced in a stage whisper.

El Chirlo nodded and stood up, buttoning his khaki field tunic. It was devoid of insignia.

"Show them in," he commanded. His voice bounced around the high marble walls.

He crossed to the center of the floor to greet the two visitors. Paco bowed into the room. He waited until the aide had left, shutting the door behind him, before speaking.

"Again, welcome to the Republic, Mr. Jamil." He switched to English, inclining his head courteously.

Jamil turned to the Libyan. "Colonel. May I introduce Major Hassan of the Revolutionary Council."

Hassan stepped forward, saluting. He looked ridiculous in his wrinkled grey gabardine suit.

"Major Hassan." The head nodded courteously again, the eyes ignoring the salute. He led his two guests over to the soft leather lounge chairs grouped around a low circular table near his desk, out of earshot from the open window. The table, a thick cross-cut mahogany log removed near the base of the tree, was polished to a clear glass finish. He stood until they were seated.

"I have Arabian coffee, or do you wish to dispense with formalities?"

He picked a tiny gold bell from the table to signify a willingness to observe traditional courtesies as host. He held the bell silent.

Jamil waved away the suggestion. "The gesture is appreciated, Colonel, but we have traveled far. Perhaps later?" The bell was returned to the table.

"As you wish." He waited for the Arab to speak, keeping his own face a mask while he examined the hawk-like features across the table. It was to be a chess game. El Chirlo was very good at chess.

"Colonel. We heard of your success this morning when we landed in Venezuela. You have provided the proof Major Hassan and his associates required. The rest is now a matter of concluding our earlier agreements. Unless there is something else . . ." Jamil let his voice trail off. The opening gambit.

The big man shrugged indifferently. "We agreed on five bombs for a price. It was your decision to explode the first to see if the others would work. I obliged you. Now, you have four. I still expect payment for five."

"But surely, Colonel, you would not expect full payment for a test?" The hooded eyes glittered.

"The test was your idea, not mine."

"Even so, Colonel, do you not agree some consideration should be made in the final price—some adjustment where we share the cost of the test?"

Jamil's voice was oily smooth.

"No."

"Perhaps only a small reduction—let us say ninety-five million instead of one hundred? Surely a five million adjustment is within reason?"

El Chirlo laughed. A dry barking sound. "Jamil! We made a deal—no papers—no treaties—your word and mine. You've changed the deal once and now I've got everyone down my back. If you want a change again, it's no deal at all. I'll keep the bombs."

He was beginning to enjoy the game. The next attack gambit should be a suggestion of individual purchase instead of lot consignment. He formed the defense argument swiftly in his mind.

Suddenly, Hassan spoke up, interrupting the game. "The bullion will be shipped from Tripoli this week, Colonel. I guarantee it!"

Startled, they both looked at the intruder on their game. El Chirlo seized the advantage quickly. "Splendid! When I see the bullion arrive and sitting on the dock, you can load the bombs, Major."

"Two weeks, Colonel. The ship will be here within two weeks. I guarantee it."

Jamil looked at the Libyan without changing his expression.

Goat herder! he thought. They had told him that Hassan would keep his mouth shut, allowing him to finalize the negotiations. *The mother's whoreson has just given away twenty million dollars on the first bomb!* Jamil was incredulous at the man's stupidity. He had been certain El Chirlo could be talked down on the cost of the test firing and settle for a lesser amount than the original one hundred million. Perhaps not the full price of the twenty million dollar bomb, but certainly a portion of its cost. His Arab sense of bargaining was outraged. The opportunity of negotiating the point had been thwarted by the dim-witted Libyan. Jamil felt powerless.

If Hassan were a member of the Jimaz al Rasad instead of the Libyan Council, he would have been eliminated years ago. The Black September Movement within Al Fatah executed idiots like Hassan, swiftly. What he had done was criminal. He swung his eyes back to El Chirlo.

"One hundred million dollars in bullion at the London Fixing price on the day of delivery then? I take it we are agreed?"

It was not so much a question as a flat statement of fact. Jamil's eyes flickered in defeat as El Chirlo smiled and reached down on the table for the little bell. Its tinkle reminded Jamil of the delicate Dresden doll he had seen dancing on its pedestal in a shop at Munich shortly before the Olympic games.

2

1960

"Mayday! Mayday! Mayday! This is eight one seven zulu. I'm a C 45 on VFR flight plan out of Miami for Salvador. I've just lost my second engine and am going in. Does anyone read me?"

Gunnarson had been working a crossword when he heard the voice over the ship's radio. Normally he kept the 121.5 emergency frequency turned so low that it was barely audible, but this call was very close. He picked up his microphone stand, turned the volume up on the receiver and flicked the switch onto the distress frequency.

"Aircraft calling Mayday, this is tanker Sonderstrom. I read you loud and clear. Over."

"Hello, Sonderstrom. Eight one seven zulu here. I'm at five thousand gliding into the Gulf. Could you please contact the Coast Guard? I lost my first engine about ten minutes ago, then the second started overheating and swallowed a valve, I guess. Aircraft is a twin-engine Beechcraft C 45. I have a raft and rations. My position is—wait a minute . . . ."

Gunnerson stopped writing and looked at the radio speaker, waiting for the position report. He watched the brass encased wall clock as its second hand swept through two complete revolutions. When the voice returned, it was very faint. *He's almost to the sea,* he realized.

24

"Tanker Sonderstrom. Eight one seven zulu here. Near as I can figure, I'm about half way across the Yucatan Channel on a dead reckoning—got that? Half way!"

The voice was barely audible by the end of the transmission.

Gunnerson replied quickly. "Roger. I have that eight one seven zulu and will advise the Coast Guard immediately. Please keep transmitting for an ADF fix."

For a few moments he listened to the crackling of the speaker. There was no further contact. He picked up the telephone at his elbow on the desk and pushed one of the white buttons.

"Bridge." He recognized the second officer's voice.

"Gunnerson, Sir. I just picked up a Mayday from an aeroplane going down in the Gulf. He's fairly close by I think, judging from the signal strength. About forty or fifty miles away, no more."

"Did you get a position report?"

"Yes sir. Said he was halfway across the Yucatan Channel, heading for the mainland."

"Stand-by. I'll call the captain. See if you can raise a Coast Guard vessel in our area."

"Aye Sir." He replaced the phone and reached for his copy of the Coast Guard radio frequencies, flipping it open at the tab index marked 'CARIB'. He ran his finger down the page, stopped and picked up a pencil. He wrote down the frequency numbers, then spun the dials on his radio set and picked up the microphone.

"Coast Guard, this is tanker Sonderstrom calling Coast Guard. How do you read?"

Colley still could hear the voice of the tanker's radio operator when he yanked the earphones off his head and slung them over the hook above the side window in the cockpit. The altimeter showed the aircraft passing through two hundred feet towards the water. He held it steady until he estimated he was fifty feet over the waves, then leveled off, pushing both engine throttles back to cruising power. He adjusted the propellor synchronization until the sound of engine beats matched exactly, then swung the aircraft into a slow turn almost due west. When the Beechcraft settled on its new course, Colley switched to autopilot, then slid out of the seat and went back into the cabin.

He released the safety locks on the cargo door and pulled the folded panel inside the fuselage. Warm moist air rushed past the dark opening, sucking bits of paper and debris out into the night. Quickly, he picked up pieces of Beechcraft rudder, wingtip, tailwheel and flung them out at the bottom of the open door, pushing them down to avoid hitting the tailplane. He then slid three cardboard boxes across the floor and shoved them out in sequence to splatter their contents across the sea. He replaced the door, locked it and made his way back to the cockpit.

Five hours later he saw the yellow flickering lights of Tampico on the horizon. Colley altered course to parallel the Mexican coast, heading north. Twenty miles further along the shore the lights from the next town, Altamira, came into view abeam the wingtip. He edged the plane closer to land until he was well clear of the Tampico shipping lanes then tightened down his shoulder harness until the straps bit into his flesh. He reduced engine power to a slow idle, patted the top of the instrument panel affectionately, then switched off the main fuel selectors. Seconds later the port engine stopped, its carburetor starved. The starboard engine idled a few moments longer, then it too was silent, its propellors windmilling idly. The aircraft slanted towards the water.

Colley flared out a few feet above the blackness, checking his descent. He held the control yoke steady as the speed fell off, then gradually pulled the control column back, keeping the nose high as the remaining flying speed dissipated. The Beechcraft settled onto the waves, tail touching first, then the propellors, finally the fuselage. There was a slight bump, the machine skipped once, then ploughed the water abruptly and started to sink.

He unhooked his harness and went back to the cabin swiftly to release the emergency escape window, and poked the raft in its bright yellow kitbag out through the opening. It dropped onto the wing. Colley scrambled out the hole after it. Only the trailing edge of the wing was underwater. He dragged the kitbag up on the dry leading edge and shook the lifeless raft out onto the dull aluminum. The small air bottle attached to the folded dinghy blew it into life. He threw the empty kitbag into the bottom of the boat and cast off.

Using the small hand paddle to circle the dying airplane, he paused at each of the fuel ports along the wing to remove the gas caps, then moved alongside the engine cowls to pull the dipsticks with their attached caps from the oil tanks. Finally, he paddled to the fuselage cargo door, now partially submerged, and turned the handle. The door was pushed back suddenly by the rush of water carrying the raft into the opening. Colley shoved himself away from the flooding and paddled strongly until he was well clear. He paused to watch the final plunge. It took longer than he had anticipated. The top of the fuselage seemed to be resting on the water, air trapped in the roof of the cabin, holding it afloat. Bubbles from the empty gas tanks streamed up from the submerged wings as they filled with seawater. Gradually, the aircraft sank until only the double tail fins were visible. Then, they too slipped under the dark surface. A few phosphorescent bubbles continued to burst above the water, then all was still except for the waves.

Colley sighed. "Goodbye, old girl. Thanks." He spoke the words softly with love and started to paddle for the shoreline three miles away.

He covered the distance quickly, helped by the onshore night breeze from the water. He dragged the raft well up from the waterline, then cut the canvas with his pocket knife and stamped the hissing yellow sides flat on the sand. He pushed the remains back into the kitbag and tied the drawstrings. then dropped to his knees on the sand and began scooping out a grave. When he had finished, he checked his watch. It was twenty-seven minutes to three. Colley adjusted the moneybelt under his shirt to make it more comfortable, and started walking along the beach towards the lights of Altamira. He kept close to the wet sand along the water's edge. It made walking easier.

The glow from the small fire behind the low banks of sand dunes was almost invisible until he was abreast of it. He stopped as two Mexican peasants in white cotton pants and chemises left the fire and their friends to greet him. Both were carrying long machetes.

"Que Tal." The taller of the two spoke, smiling.

Colley nodded to them. "Que Tal."

"A donde va?"

"To Altamira," he answered them, speaking Spanish. Colley's Spanish was perfect, without a trace of Gringo accent. He had learned it as a child from his nurse at the Residence where his father had been Charge d'Affairs in Santiago, Chile, during the early forties.

"Are you a Gringo?" the Mexican asked, puzzled by the big, black-haired man in the lovely boots who looked like a Gringo, yet spoke like a Latin.

"Do I sound like a Gringo my friend?" He laughed. He knew he didn't, which was why he was here instead of Corbin.

The Mexican laughed too; his friend joined in, uncertainly. They spoke to each other briefly in low tones. Colley caught the words 'tourist' and 'hotel' and guessed they had probably decided he was visiting one of the local resorts, a businessman from Mexico City out for his late evening stroll.

"May we offer you a share of our beans?" the shorter man

asked.

The taller peasant joined in the invitation. "It is a poor meal suitable for poor people like ourselves, but we share it with you gladly." He stepped back a pace, ushering Colley to the fire with a wave of his machete and a bow.

"Gracias, Senor. But my wife will be expecting me back at the hotel. I have been strolling to digest my evening meal." He started to walk on.

Like a cat, the smaller man jumped in his path, the machete raised.

"Mentirosa! Liar. We have been on this beach all night and no one has passed. Are you too proud to share our humble beans?"

Colley stopped, his senses alert to impending danger. Out of the corner of his eye he saw the other three leave the fire and saunter down the slight dune to the flat beach. He edged towards the water, keeping his rear covered. He cursed the fact he had left his .38 on the Beechcraft, but he had agreed with Corbin—no identification; just his wristwatch, penknife and the money belt.

"Little man, if you don't get out of my way I'll break you in half!"

He spoke evenly, unhurried, then moved towards his antagonist. He almost reached him when the machete swung. He flicked his head sideways and saw the dark blade for an instant out of his left eye as it glided down his face. Colley thought it had missed him until he saw blood dripping onto his shirt, then felt his cheek with anger. It was numb; his fingers unknowingly went through the slit touching his back teeth. With a roar of surprise he leaped at the little swordsman, who impaled him through the side of his waist as both fell to the sand. He saw the peasant face twist in terror as he thumbed the man's cartoid arteries, watching the eyes pop. It was the last thing he remembered. A driftwood log smashed the back of his skull and the lights went out.

The terrified peasant scrambled out from beneath the big unconscious body and withdrew his machete from the bleeding side.

"Puta Madre! He's a mean one!" He wiped the long knife on the sand, grinning nervously.

"Strip him," the taller one ordered the other three. The man that had wielded the log tossed it aside and went for the boots.

"The boots are mine Miguel. Bring them here!"

Miguel complied, grumbling. They were far to big for his feet anyway. It was while the tall one was trying the boots on over his bare feet the other two found the money belt with the fifty thousand dollars that Colley and Corbin had so quietly put aside over the past four months. They carried the belt over to the tall one, sitting on the sand.

"Dinero, Pablo. Mucho dinero!" they told him excitedly.

He seized the cotton waistband, glancing through the pockets briefly, then stood up quickly.

"Vamos! Strip him of everything. You, Chico, put out the fire. Vamos Caballeros! Vamos!"

They left Colley naked and bleeding near the water and disappeared over the dunes to their village.

Dr. Luis Artega de Cordoba watched his daughter standing on the flying bridge of the deep sea fishing schooner. The boat was rolling lightly in the mid-morning swell, not uncomfortably. Two tall fishing rods, locked to either side of the cabin, nodded with the motion of the boat. They had left the marina in Tampico at dawn, carefully skirting the big oil slicks trailed by the small tankers leaving the PEMEX refinery in the bay, then headed up the coast past Altamira, keeping close to the shoreline. A day's fishing was just what he needed to take his mind off politics for a few hours. His daughter had been quite right. Felina was always right. He regarded her lithe figure on the bridge with affection.

"What's the use of having a lovely boat if we never use it?" she had argued persuasively over dinner the previous evening. "Let's take a day off and go deepsea fishing, Papa. Please. It will be good for you. You need a change, doesn't he Ruis?"

Even Ruis hadn't objected to the proposal. Perhaps he was too tired of planning the endless permutations of political intrigue necessary to re-install a deposed president. *Perhaps he is sorry now that he followed me into exile.* He switched his gaze from Felina to his old friend standing on the wing of the platform, scanning the shore with his binoculars, looking for birds. Ruis was an avid ornithologist and had catalogued over a thousand species in his spare time. He saw Ruis wipe an arm across his eyes, then raise the glasses, pausing to hold their image. He lifted the binoculars from around his neck and called to Felina at the wheel. Artega could not hear their voices above the throaty muffled roar of the engines at the stern. Felina studied the beach with the glasses a few moments, then handed them back and said something to Ruis as she spun the chrome wheel, turning the schooner towards shore.

Ruis stepped down the short gangway from the bridge and joined Artega on the afterdeck.

"There is a naked man laying on the beach near the water, Luis. I thought he was dead, then I saw his arm move. Felina wants to move in closer so we can see better.

Artega grunted. "Probably a drunken Mexican robbed by his friends last night."

"I don't think so. His skin is dark everywhere except in the middle of his body; there it is very white. Like a Gringo who wears shorts."

Artega digested this information without comment. A naked Gringo laying on a Mexican beach at ten in the morning provided all sorts of interesting possibilities for consideration.

Felina slowed the boat to an idle a hundred yards offshore and squinted at the form on the sand. She glanced back to Ruis and her father as they studied the naked man through the glasses.

"He looks like he has been wounded. Maybe a guest from one of the hotels—beaten and robbed."

He handed the binoculars back to Ruis.

"How deep is the water? Can we run up to the sand?" He motioned his daughter to ease the bow onto the beach and got to his feet, following Ruis to the prow of the fiberglass deck. The keel scraped the sandy bottom about ten yards from shore. Felina switched off the diesel engine.

"Get my bag out of the cabin," he called to her as he jumped off the side into the shallow water behind Ruis, wading ahead of him.

The man was laying on his back, his eyes closed except for the bottom corner of his left eye, which had been dragged open by the loose flesh cut to the bone. It was a vicious looking gash that split the cheek in half. Artega could see the man's bicuspids, white under the pink flesh and coagulated blood. Sand flies and a few ants were crawling in the open wound. He checked the pulse at the throat. It was weak, but steady. He lifted an eyelid, the good eye, and peered at it closely.

"Humph! He has concussion." He felt gingerly about the back of the man's head until his fingers touched the huge bump hidden by black curly hair. He slid his hand expertly over the rest of the inert body and probed the knife wound in his side.

"Superficial." He grunted. Felina waded ashore with his worn black Gladstone bag and handed it to him.

"Is he still alive?"

"He has a concussion and two knife wounds. He'll live. He's young and strong," Artega announced professionally. "Let's try and get him onto the boat where I can work on him."

Felina tried to keep her eyes from the man's crotch and pale thighs which stood out in startling contrast to his deeply tanned body. Except for the huge gash across his face, he was terribly handsome, she decided.

Carefully, they lugged the man through the water to the boat, lifting him over the side from the stern ladder. Felina pulled him aboard under the armpits, using her foot on the low teak railings for leverage. He was very heavy. Artega and Ruis carried him down to the cabin bunk and wrapped him warmly with blankets. The doctor went to work on the man's face at once, swabbing out the congealed crusts of blood, sand and flies around the edges of the wound. When it was clean he scraped it open to overcome the healing process, already begun. As it started bleeding freely, he compressed the two sides of the cheek together evenly and taped them into position.

"Stitches will only make him look worse," he told Ruis. "As long as he keeps his mouth shut as it heals."

"Did you ever meet a Gringo who could keep his mouth shut, Don Luis?"

Artega nodded, remembering the American ambassador to the Republic who had known about the coup to overthrow him weeks before it happened, but, not wishing to interfere with local politics, had said nothing.

"I've known one or two of them, Ruis."

He wrapped the unconscious man's head in ice packs from the refrigerator, then sewed up the gash in his side with seven neat sutures. He wrapped the big body back in the blankets and stood back to survey his handiwork with a critical eye.

"We'll take him back to Tampico. He should be in a hospital until we know how serious the concussion is." He touched the man's carotid again. The pulse was still weak, but steady.

Felina backed the schooner away from the shallow water and swung the nose out to sea, pushing the big throttle handle up to maximum power. The boat thundered away from the shoreline, the bow creaming, then flinging a fine spray back to the afterdeck as it sliced into a steep turn southwards to Tampico.

The man in bed number 112 on the fifth floor of the hospital had healed well over the past weeks. *Everywhere, except in his mind*, the Chief Resident Physician admitted. It was a puzzling case. The man had absolutely no memory of anything except waking up in the hospital four days after he had arrived in an ambulance from the

Marina. They had checked with the police, the hotels, even the Federales in Mexico City. There was nothing to identify the patient in bed 112. Now, the fingerprint report had come back from the U.S. and it too was blank. The Chief Resident shrugged and laid this latest report back on his desk. It was a mystery. The patient spoke English like an American. He spoke Spanish like a Latin. He spoke both languages with the vocabulary of a well educated man. The tests showed he had skills in mathematics, literature, engineering, and seemed to know something about airplanes. Where had he learned about these things? Why wasn't someone looking for him? Someone who loved him—a mother or wife—a sweetheart perhaps? There was a light knock at his office door, and the secretary poked her head inside.

"Dr. Artega is here to see you sir. His daughter is with him."

The Chief Resident nodded. "Show them in."

He stood up, smiling politely as Felina and her father entered the office and sat down on the pale green, antiseptic-looking chairs before his desk.

"Any more news, Doctor?" Felina inquired.

"I'm afraid nothing constructive. I received this report from the American Embassy this morning." He handed over the official sheet for her to examine. "He is unknown in America to the FBI, which means he has never served in their military. Since we have estimated his age to be about twenty-five now, it means he would have been eligible for the draft in the U.S. during the Korean War if he was an American. His fingerprints would be on file."

"Then you don't think he is an American?" Artega inquired.

The Chief Resident shrugged. "Maybe, maybe not, Doctor. Everything points to it. His size, dental work, vocabulary, the colloquial expressions."

"But he has the same sort of colloquial expressions in Spanish," Felina interrupted. She laid the sheet of paper from the embassy back on the metal desk. "Surely that could mean he might be a Latin who also learned both languages simultaneously?"

"Perhaps."

"Well, in any event, Doctor, we will collect him today and keep him with us until his memory recovers, or he decides what he wants to do with himself. At least we know now he is not a criminal with police looking for him." Artega smiled.

"It may be a long time before his memory returns, Doctor Artega. I have known cases personally that have taken as long as five years for full recovery, even when the patient knew his identity."

Artega agreed. "The mind is a strange thing, Doctor. Sometimes the reasons for a blank memory in the amnesiac are because the patient doesn't wish to remember; the psychosomatic defense mechanism within the mind prevents cure. Friedman and Jung wrote an interesting paper on the subject. No doubt you have read it?"

The Chief Resident hadn't, but wouldn't admit it to a colleague, particularly a foreign colleague.

"Yes, Doctor, of course the damage can be psychological long after the physical damage is repaired, but it is rare."

He was annoyed by Artega's soft voice and placating mannerisms. He disapproved thoroughly of any physician becoming involved in politics, regardless of their national origins. Politics should be left to politicians. The Chief Resident disliked all politicians. He glanced at his wristwatch with an air of slight impatience.

Artega and Felina stood up immediately. "You have been very kind to give us so much of your time, Doctor. And, of course, your valuable service." His voice was tinged with slight sarcasm, not sufficient to offend. He shook the Chief Resident's hand as he rose to his feet.

"Just stop off at the discharge desk on the main floor, Doctor, and sign the release. I'll phone to tell them you're coming." He ushered the visitors to the door, bowing slightly as they left the room.

The Chief Resident walked back to his desk, phoned the main floor to insure the discharge would be effected speedily and was told that the patient from bed 112 was already in the lobby waiting to leave. He picked up the file on the man, stuffed the latest letter into the fat manila folder and tossed it into the Out-basket sitting on the corner of his desk. His mind was already occupied with more important matters than a simple amnesia victim.

Artega and his daughter met the tall nameless man in the lobby, after signing his discharge papers. He smiled and stood up when he saw them coming. Over the weeks spent talking to the girl and her father from his hospital bed, he had come to know them as friends interested in his well-being.

"I'm free?" he asked.

"You're free," Artega confirmed. "Come, Ruis is waiting with the car."

The trio left the building into the warm sun, walking across the lawn to the parking lot.

"We must have a name for you, call you something. What do you suggest?" Artega inquired.

The big man walked on for several moments, then stopped, raising his hand to the plaster tape on his face.

"How about 'Chirlo' for the time being?"

Artega nodded. "El Chirlo it is."

3

1961

P.O. Box 463
Freeport, Grand Bahamas.
B.W.I.
November 17, 1961

CONFIDENTIAL
Sir Edward Mangrum, O.B.E.
Managing Director
Underwriters Investigation Services Ltd.
28B Kensington Court
London, W.8
ENGLAND

Sir:

In accordance with your instructions of March 12, 1961, I have this day completed my investigations on the disappearance of Peter James Colley. Policy No. C-15567397, issued August 3, 1959, in the amount of one million dollars (U.S.), with double indemnity rider. I am forwarding the documentation on this investigation to you under separate cover. However, a precis of the facts are as follows.

Peter James Colley entered into partnership (unregistered) with one Charles Race Corbin, sometime during the summer of 1958 in the City of Miami, Florida. The purpose of this partnership was operation of a cargo flying service between Miami and Central America. The business prospered. The following year the partnership was operating five twin-engine aircraft, of which Beechcraft 8 17 Z was one.

The company, SAC (Servicios Aereas Cargas) Limitada, was incorporated in San Salvador C.A. on May 22, 1959, superseding the partnership. (See copy of Escruitura Letters Patent attached to documentation.) Charles Race Corbin became Managing Director and business head of the new company. Peter Colley provided the operational expertise necessary for the flying, maintenance, sales and personnel management. Negotiations were undertaken with three neighboring countries in Central America for landing rights, and were accepted on the basis of Colley's salesmanship as much as anything else. (See attached Ministry of Aviation Directives.) Three more aircraft were then purchased to meet the requirements of this expansion.

Survivor partnership insurance was taken out by both Corbin and Colley on August 3, 1959 for one million dollars. This decision was due to the realization by both men of their dependence upon each other for future business success. I have confirmed that the double indemnity rider was added to the policy after much persuasion by Mr. David Liebe, representing the Underwriters at the time of sale. In point of fact it was Mr. Liebe who sold the rider to the policyholders, not the other way around. Colley and Corbin were not interested in this added expense. I think this is an important consideration.

We now come to the date of Colley's disappearance in Beechcraft 8 17 Z on the night of November 27, 1960. First, it should be understood that SAC Ltd. was at this date, operating eight aircraft, all of them fully paid. The last payment on the three Douglas C-47 machines was made on October 31, 1960 to Banco Nacional de Fomento in Tegucigalpa, Honduras, C.A. (see attached loan discharge agreement in the amount of 300,000 Lempiras). Bank records indicate that at the time of the accident there were combined cash balances in all countries of operation in the amount of $132,567.18 (U.S.). Trade payables, wages and overheads for the end of November, 1960 amounted to less than half this sum and would have been offset fully by accounts receivable. In short, the company was in excellent financial shape.

Colley had a personal attachment to Beechcraft 8 17 Z which

was why he flew it himself. It was the first aircraft the partnership had purchased and was really a bit uneconomical to fly, compared to the type of equipment purchased later. All company aircraft were superbly maintained under contract in Miami with Flight Standards Engineering Inc. (see attached maintenance report of 817 Z). Colley filed a VFR (Visual Flight Rules) Flight Plan with Miami Center at 7:00 p.m. November 27, 1960 for a direct flight to Ilopango airport in Salvador. He had fuel on board sufficient for 1,200 statute miles, fully functioning radio and emergency equipment (F.A.A. Flight Plan copy is attached).

Although the flight plan indicates the aircraft load was within the permissible operating limits, the Beechcraft was in fact probably overloaded. There is no evidence to prove this was the case, however. It is no secret among local aviation circles that much of SAC's success story was due to its ability to fly overloaded aircraft consistently, without getting caught. Colley was stopped once by an F.A.A. (Federal Aviation Agency) inspector who weighted out the same aircraft that disappeared and found that instead of its legal 2,650 pound gross weight, the machine had 3,935 pounds all up weight. This particular incident was dropped when it could not be proved that Colley had known about the overload in advance of his arriving at the airport from the motel where he had spent the night.

At 8:34 p.m. the radio operator from the tanker Sonderstrom picked up Colley's distress message in the Yucatan Channel. The tanker, out of Galveston, Texas, was enroute to Panama. The time of transmission is consistent with the elaspsed time of the aircraft at normal cruising speed after it had departed Miami. The radio operator confirmed that between the first and second transmission, a time lapse of two minutes, there was a marked fading in signal strength. This is also consistent with an aircraft descending towards the water.

The U.S. Coast Guard was notified immediately and arrived over the estimated location of the downed aircraft at dawn, November 28. The vessels, Creasy and Koolby, swept the Yucatan Channel with the aid of two S-58 helicopters. Just before dark, one of the helicopter pilots sighted wreckage and an oil slick approximately halfway between Cape San Antonio, Cuba and the Mexican mainland at Latitude 21 degrees 22 minutes north, Longitude 86 degrees, 15 minutes west. Portions of wreckage were picked up later that evening by the Koolby and a sweep for the pilot continued into the following day. The search was abandoned at midnight, November 30 (see attached U.S. Coast Guard Report USCG 60/4631).

37

The debris recovered included several pieces of Beechcraft component parts, most interesting of which was a complete wingtip, obviously torn from the aircraft with great force. The end is crumpled (see photographs) which would be consistent with the theory that the pilot misjudged his height over the water in the final ditching approach and leveled off too high. The aircraft then stalled, dropping one wing, which struck the water, causing the aircraft to cartwheel and disintegrate. This would also explain the recovery of such unlikely objects as a package of sandwiches, still wrapped in their wax paper and secured with a rubber band, Colley's shaving kit buoyed up by the matching pair of wooden hairbrushes, plus an assorted collection of aeronautical charts.

Both the F.A.A. and Coast Guard reports on the accident coincide with the theory outlined in the previous paragraph, copies of which were forwarded to me by your office at the time my investigations were requested. Officially, the matter is a closed book. However, there are a number of puzzling inconsistencies which bother me and for which there are no logical explanations. Taken individually they mean nothing, but when one combines the list, they begin to take on an entirely different perspective.

1. Colley was an experienced bush pilot who had spent over half his flying experience landing on water. Surely he would have been capable of judging his height more accurately on a clear tropical night.

2. Charles R. Corbin commenced immediate liquidation of all SAC's assets within a week of the accident. These transactions had been completed before I entered this investigation. Knowing the length of time required to formulate any business sale in Latin America, I have a feeling these arrangements were started some months before Colley's disappearance; however, I cannot prove it.

3. No seat cushions, clothing or other types of floatable debris were recovered from the presumed crash site. If the aircraft did indeed disintegrate, where did all this additional buoyant wreckage go?

4. Next there is the question of two engine failures on the same aircraft within ten minutes of each other. I have searched FAA records covering the past thirty years on Pratt and Whitney R-985 AN and SB engines. There has never been a recorded case where two recently overhauled engines on the same aircraft failed within a few minutes of each other on the same flight, except through fuel starvation, when the pilot ran out of gas.

5. *Finally, Colley's girlfriend and fiancé, Peggy Elaine Gibson, is still keeping close company with Corbin. Although their housemaid stated that the relationship is purely platonic and they sleep in separate bedrooms, I find this extremely odd. It is as if she and Corbin are waiting for Colley to reappear.*

I have a gut feeling that Corbin engineered Colley's accident, arranging for him to disappear into some Latin American country, more probably in South rather than Central America. When the policy is paid, I feel certain that he will reappear. I would, therefore, respectfully suggest the Underwriters invoke the seven year law to withhold payment until 1967.
I remain,

> *Your humble and obedient servant*
> *M.R. Matheson.*

MRM:ac
Encl.

Sir Edward Mangrum folded the letter carefully and slipped it back into the tan manila envelope, together with the assorted documents that had accompanied it. He sat up in the high-backed leather swivel, folding his hands across his portly middle, and swung the chair from the desk sideways so he could park his feet on the steam radiator beneath the window ledge. The afternoon sun had started to burn off the heavy fog that had made him take the 8:07 that morning from Bagshot instead of the Rolls. Visibility had improved to such an extent he could see the edges of Round Pond through the tall trees in Kensington Gardens. He watched two elderly model boat enthusiasts just make the light on the corner ahead of the halted traffic on Kensington Road. They lugged their toy steamers up the pathway towards the Round Pond as the line of impatient rumbling traffic started flowing again on the street below his window.

Sir Edward considered the letter he had read. Matheson was a good bloodhound. When Matheson said 'gut-feeling', it meant he was positive, but could not prove it. Sir Edward had the same feeling. The claim was too pat. Too neat and tidy. A normal accident of this type had all sorts of loose ends that dangled enticingly until the investigator unravelled them. There were no threads dangling anywhere on the Corbin claim. Sir Edward reached over to the dictaphone at the corner of his desk and removed the speaker from its cradle.

"Mrs. Beggs, this letter is to be made in four copies—office, one to the Underwriters, one to Mike Matheson in Freeport and one to David Liebe in El Salvador. The original goes to Mr. C.R. Corbin, 3527 Lacanada Drive, Tamiami, Florida. You might check the American region code on that address."

He paused, flicking the switch on the speaker handle while he collected his thoughts.

"Dear Mr. Corbin. As a result of our investigations into the disappearance of your associate, Mr. Peter James Colley, over the Yucatan Channel on the evening of November 26th, 1960, we regret that the Underwriters will be unable to honor the claim made by you on Policy No. C—— Check the number on that Mrs. Beggs. New paragraph. This in no way should be construed as waiver of the liability recognized by the Underwriters, but rather an adherence to requirements of insurance law, wherein evidence of the remains of deceased persons upon whose life insurance had been placed, must be presented. New paragraph. It is unfortunate indeed that no positive proof has been obtained thus far to confirm your associate's demise. All evidence of Mr. Colley's unfortunate demise can, therefore, only be considered as circumstantial, according to insurance law. Mrs. Beggs, change that last demise to read 'unfortunate disappearance'. It will therefore be necessary to wait the seven year period before Mr. Colley can be declared as legally dead, permitting the Underwriters to process your claim. We apologize for this inconvenience and assure you that should any new evidence appear between this date and November 27, 1967 which proves the death of your associate, then the Underwriters will be only too happy to provide payment on your claim. Yours most respectfully, etcetera."

Sir Edward hung the dictaphone speaker back on the machine and stood up. It was well past lunch, his stomach had informed him sometime earlier. Stomachs were very delicate things that required proper attention at scheduled times. Schedules should never be interrupted. He phoned Mrs. Beggs to ring his Club and tell them he would be along in fifteen minutes, then took his private elevator to the main floor and went out into the brightening afternoon to hail a cab.

Corbin picked up the letter on the day he and Peggy had taken the afternoon flight to Mexico City to meet Peter Colley at the Hotel Del Prado. The meeting was scheduled for the evening of November 27, exactly one year after the accident. They had agreed the insurance company would probably stall for the first year until they decided whether or not to use the seven-year ruling. The November

27th meeting had been anticipated as the first date Corbin would know whether Colley would have to remain underground for another six years, or could surface within the immediate future. It looked as if he was going to have to stay submerged for another six years. Peggy had been frantic when he had shown her the letter.

"I'll be an old woman by the time this is all over and we can get married," she had complained bitterly at the airport in Mexico City.

They drank the usual complimentary frozen Daquiries in the lounge while they waited for customs clearance. That had been four days ago and the only problem with their plans now was—where in the hell was Colley?

Corbin stirred the swizzle stick in his empty glass, bouncing the ice cubes around the bottom. He signaled the barman for another. He was slightly drunk. *Might as well,* he decided; *Peter isn't going to turn up, not tonight, not tomorrow night, never.* Like the Coast Guard and the FAA, Corbin was convinced now Colley had cartwheeled the aircraft into the Gulf. He hoped that death had been instantaneous. He sipped at the new frosted glass the barman placed in front of him and felt an assault of conscience over the way everything had worked out.

The whole affair had been Corbin's idea from the first. Sensitive to the winds of political change, he had foreseen the supression of SAC's juicy cargo contracts in favor of National airlines within the countries they had served. Just as Pan Am had been squeezed out in the passenger business after pioneering it in Latin America, so too would SAC be squeezed until the balance sheets forced capitulation.

"Let's take our money and run, Pete, while we've still got something to sell," he had told Colley.

His partner had listened gravely, thought about it for a few weeks, then agreed. The insurance rip-off would be an added bonus. Corbin's Spanish was too poor to deceive anyone into thinking he was anything but Gringo, so it had to be Colley that disappeared. Peter didn't like the idea. It seemed sacriligious to destroy a perfectly good aircraft. It took a lot of talking to convince him.

Then, just as they were getting ready to put the show on the road, Colley turned up with the Vassar do-gooder on one of his trips from Miami. It had been lust at first sight. Inside of two weeks Peggy Elaine Gibson had Peter wrapped around her little finger. The capper came when they had floored Corbin by announcing their nuptials a few days short of the planned ditching and Colley's death.

"Are you out of your tree, you silly sonofabitch?" Corbin had yelled in the humid airport office at Illopango while the rattling air conditioner attempted to cool the moisture-laden air. "You're supposed to be dying at the end of the week, not getting married! What about our plans?"

Their plans were revised and Peggy told the reasons for the wedding postponement. She had accepted the situation with good grace once it was made clear that as Peter's wife, she stood to share the million dollar benefit. She had gotten a little cute just before Peter left for Miami on the last trip and tried to push him into a fast marriage, but Corbin had managed to head it off by telling her that Colley had left a day early. Since then, she had stuck to Corbin like glue.

The company liquidation after the accident had been easy. He had pre-arranged most of it months in advance so that by the first week in January he was back in Miami with Peggy and over a half million dollars in the bank. By then he had realized that Peggy was a pain in the ass. Naturally, he had tried to seduce her while they were still in Salvador. She acted like a Vestal Virgin, so he had given up and assumed that she would go home and live with her parents in Westchester County when they returned to the States, until the Mexico meeting when Peter would re-emerge. Instead, she had moved right into the house he had rented in Tamiami's exclusive Garden Grove district.

For a day or two Corbin thought she might decide to relent on his overtures and had welcomed the arrangement, until she made it clear nothing had changed. Finally, he gave up trying to sleep with her and left her with a Cuban maid to run the household affairs, while he charged about the States looking for investment opportunities against the day when they would all be millionaires. In a way he had admired her faithfulness and began to enjoy her company as a friend, taking her out to dinner or dancing and a show every week or two. Sometimes they played cards in the evenings at home or in a neighbor's house, but always when it came time for bed, both retired to their separate rooms. Corbin had begun to believe her act, when one afternoon he discovered her lover.

He had been up to Lauderdale examining some property and had not expected to return home until the following day. The trip turned out a waste of time so he had arrived back in mid-afternoon and walked into the living room. Peggy and her stallion were thumping away on the sofa. She screamed when she saw him standing in the doorway. The stallion merely nodded affably, and kept on humping. Corbin had taken his overnight bag off to the bedroom, saying nothing. Privately, he had been glad to see her

42

standing on the ground now at eye-level, instead of atop the pedestal he had started building for her. Peggy discussed the affair with him later, explaining defensively that the man was an old friend with whom she had lived before meeting Colley. The situation, however, did not change between herself and Corbin, although she became more open with her paramours during the months that followed. They were all, it seemed, boyfriends she had known before meeting Colley.

He looked at his reflection in the bar mirror, glumly sipping his drink. A pretty high-class hooker nodded invitingly to him through the mirror from several seats away. She looked American. Maybe she wasn't a hooker. He shook his head slightly and watched her feign a pout, then look away. Corbin finished his drink and signed the barbill with his room number, then headed for the elevators.

Peggy was sitting on the couch in the living room of the two-bedroom suite when he opened the door. Her eyes were still red from the crying jag that had forced him to retreat to the bar several hours before. He stood at the center of the room examining her to see if the flood of tears was past, or pausing. It was past. She smiled at him slightly.

"I'm sorry I yelled at you. I didn't mean everything I said."

He shrugged and sat down beside her.

"You meant it and it's all true. If I hadn't got the bright idea in the first place none of this would have happened. You and Peter would probably have your first brat by now and working on the second. I buggered it up. I'm the one that's sorry."

He watched her light a cigarette, then regard him quizically through the ascending smoke.

"What do we do now, Chuck?" she asked him quietly.

"First off, I'd say we get the hell out of this place and back to Miami. Then—I don't know. There isn't going to be any money on the insurance till sixty-seven. I'll have to can some of the deals I've been working on and set my sights a little lower. Ironic isn't it? Now that we know Peter is actually dead we have to wait seven years to collect the insurance. If he had been alive we would probably have got it immediately!"

"What about your situation?"

"Us? Oh, I see what you mean. I'll drop the house and get an apartment I suppose. What are you going to do?"

"I'm going to do whatever you want me to do. Whether you know it or not, you need me and I need you."

"Oh. How do you figure that?"

A whole vista of possibilities was opening. He needed a few minutes to collect his thoughts and plan the assault, or defense, whichever was necessary. The key word was need—not love or affection—need.

Peggy looked at him evenly.

"Several reasons. First, you and I are the only people to share this secret on how you talked Peter into killing himself. Second, in 1967 when the policy is paid off, I want Peter's share. Third, I think I know you better than any man I've ever met, including Peter. After all we have lived together for a year in the same house, darling."

Corbin's mind began to work out plans for defense; assault was out of the question. The bitch was trying to blackmail him. Arguments were on the tip of his tongue.

"Finally, there is the matter of our mutual security. A wife cannot give testimony against her husband, and vice versa."

Peggy leaned over the coffee table and butted her cigarette; she glanced over at him.

"That's a marriage proposal, Chuck, in case you missed it."

She sat back on the cushions, with a faint feline smile.

Corbin's mind reeled under the impact of her words. He held his eyes on hers, steady. After a long pause, he said, "Persuade me."

She stood up slowly, smoothing her dress, then kicked off her shoes and walked seductively over to the light switch to kill the ceiling glare. The glow from the small lamp on the side table bathed the room in a soft film of warmth. Peggy turned the radio cabinet to some soft Mexican music and, swaying with the muted tempo, began to undress. She dropped the dress on the sofa and wriggled out of his reach as her feet stepped out of the half slip that fell to the carpet. Still moving with the music, she reached behind her back and unhooked her bra, then quickly cupped her hands over both breasts to keep the filmy lace in position as she continued the dance. She allowed it to slip gradually until her nipples were bare, then dropped it languidly on his lap and piriouetted across the room, her breasts rocking with the movement. She stopped, then peeled her black lace panties to her knees, pausing to watch them drop to the floor in mock surprise, before stepping over them and continuing her dance. Peggy twisted, leaned, swayed and circled the sofa, cupping her breasts provocatively, then stopped in front of Corbin, as the music ended. She reached between her legs and spread the pink lips on her golden Venus mound with one hand, dragging Corbin's head towards her with the other.

"I'm persuaded," he murmured, just before he buried his face in her liquid flesh.

They were married two days after they returned to Miami. By the end of the fourth month, when Peggy told him she was pregnant, they had all but forgotten Peter Colley. They gave up the house in Tamiami and moved up to Tampa, where Corbin decided to climb aboard the Gulf Coast land boom. He met Don Affleck at a house auction the week after they had moved, while wandering through a large home, examining the last visible earthly remains of an old couple who had been killed in a car accident. The middle aged children were selling off their parents' retirement paradise en tota. Corbin was standing in the huge living room waiting for a beefy florid-faced auctioneer to begin the sale, when Affleck had approached him.

"Are you family?"

Corbin glanced at him and shook his head. "Bidding. You?"

"I'm trying to get the house if I can. Got a buyer for it."

"You in real estate?"

"I'm in anything that makes money. Today it's real estate." He smiled self-assuredly.

Corbin thought his teeth were too perfect to be real.

"I'm after some furniture for my house."

"Just moved to Tampa?"

Corbin nodded as the auctioneer began his countdown. The affair lasted several hours. Everyone idled from room to room digesting the contents as the beefy barker disposed of each lot. Affleck dogged Corbin's footsteps. By the time the contents of the house had acquired new owners, Corbin had managed to furnish most of his own home, and develop a liking for Don Affleck. He waited beside him on the front lawn listening to the auctioneer bidding the house buyers up to forty-two thousand dollars before Affleck dropped out. The bidding continued as they walked away.

"How much did you have it sold for?" Corbin inquired.

"One hundred cash tomorrow morning."

Corbin stopped. "You stopped at forty-two?"

Affleck shrugged. "That's all the money I've got."

"Will you split the profits?"

Affleck's too perfect teeth broke into a wide grin.

"Sure will!"

They went back to the bidding, which had settled at sixty-eight with no takers. Corbin bought it at sixty-nine five and wrote out a check for the autioneer. Later, over supper at the Yacht Club, celebrating their good fortune, Affleck asked him about his personal finances.

"Look, Chuck! I don't mean to pry, but anyone who can write out a marker for seventy G's doesn't usually turn up at an old folks home to buy second-hand furniture, then dive on a deal with a stranger."

"I'm not risking anything, Don. I know the house is worth over eighty. If you don't turn up with your customers, I'll sell it to someone for less."

"Yeah, you're right. I hadn't thought of that. Even so, you buying it was still a little strange as far as I'm concerned. You interested in other properties?"

"I might be." Corbin was guarded. "Why, what have you got?"

"I've got a goddam dream of a deal, but I'm scared to death to ask anyone for money on it, 'cause I know they'll steal the whole thing right from under my nose."

He looked at Corbin hard. "How much money have you got? How much can you afford to put into a real estate deal that will be a goldmine?"

"How much do you need?"

"About a million two, million three, tops."

"I can probably arrange it," Corbin told him non-commitedly. "I'd have to know something about it though, before I'd commit myself."

"You mean you'd have to know everything about it?" he countered.

Corbin chuckled. "I guess that's what I mean."

They finished off their main course in silence. It was *Coq au Vin* and it was good. Corbin finished first and sat back watching the row of boats tied to the lighted marina bobbing on their moorings, waiting for Affleck to decide.

"I'll make a deal with you, Chuck," he said finally, toying with a tall Italian wood pepper mill sitting on the table. "I'll put fifty thousand into the deal. It's all I've got. You put up the balance to a top of a million three. We'll split the profits eighty-twenty." He smiled.

"Agreed. And, if I don't like the deal you have my word that I'll say nothing further about it to anyone else. Let's hear it."

"One of the most difficult things in this State is to get approvals for zoning in new developments," Affleck explained. "I know, I used to work in the State zoning office at Tallahassee. That's where I came across this deal." He scratched his ear for a moment. "Have you ever heard of Coral Islands Development Corporation?"

Corbin nodded; Affleck went on.

"They're one of the biggest in the State. Anyway, last year they were finishing off the approvals on a huge development down the Gulf coast, near Charlotte Harbour. I handled the State approvals on the project. Approvals were requested on thirty-two thousand acres of land in Sarasota, Charlotte and DeSoto counties, where the three counties join each other."

He paused reflectively, watching Corbin's eyes beginning to light with interest.

"So?"

"So, they received their approvals covering the three counties and began their development work last year on Phase One in Charlotte County. But, somebody in their organization goofed and title transfers only turned up for Sarasota and Charlotte. The property in De Soto County was never transferred."

"So?"

"So, when I found out about it, I did a title search on the De Soto land and discovered it was still owned by a man named Pendleton from Chicago, who had given Coral Islands a two-year option on the land. The option had expired. I bought the option for twenty-five thousand and resigned from the State government."

"You mean you now have an option to buy land that Coral Islands has already got approved for development and think they own?" Corbin tried to keep his voice flat, suppressing the excitement he felt rising in his chest.

"Yup! Three thousand acres at four hundred bucks an acre and most of it along the waterfront. They're asking forty thousand an acre for the same sort of property in the Phase One area and it's selling like there's a land shortage. For a million two hundred thousand investment we can clear about a hundred million bucks if we develop it ourselves. Maybe half that if we sell it to Coral Islands. Which way do you want to go on it?"

"To the bank, first thing tomorrow morning and get the money to exercise our option!" Corbin stated emphatically.

It took them three weeks to form Coram Developments, Inc. while the loan approvals from the bank were being processed. Corbin assigned the proceeds from the Colley insurance policy, payable in 1967, as a guarantee for the money, together with the balance of his cash on hand in the bank. The eighty percent shareholder of Coram and his twenty percent partner dropped into the executive offices of

47

Coral Island Development Corporation in Sarasota the first Monday in May to introduce themselves to their unknowing senior partners in the land project. The senior partners were not amused at the turn of events.

"We'll sue!"

Corbin smiled at the bluff company president.

"You said that before, Mr. Weinbolt; you're repeating yourself."

"It's our project. It's our land. It was our idea. We got the approvals"

"You can't tack yourself on the hind end because of an oversight and expect to get away with it."

His florid face was beet red.

Corbin sighed. "I've been very patient with you, Mr. Weinbolt, but now I'm losing my patience. If you don't come to terms with us then we will sell the block to someone else and you can deal with them. The documentation is all in order. We own the land. Either you buy from us, or you buy it from someone else. Which is it going to be?"

"We had no plans on that land until 1968. We can't afford your price at this time without jeopardizing the rest of the project. Be reasonable for Christ's sake, if we pay you millions of dollars before recovering any of our money out of Phase One, there won't be any Phase Two and the land will be worthless."

"Land is never worthless, Mr. Weinbolt," Affleck reminded him.

"What do you propose then?" Corbin offered.

Weinbolt looked around the lovely air-conditioned office helplessly.

"Look fellas, give me a week, will you, one week. I'll come up with a good deal for you, okay?"

They agreed to the one week time period before coming back, allowing the company's legal department to find a loophole through which to wriggle their way out of the mess. There was none. After two days of hard bargaining they settled the matter in the boardroom and left the four lawyers to prepare the paperwork while Weinbolt took Corbin and Affleck out to dinner, his fat face beaming with pleasure at his two new partners. The partners were beaming too. They were to receive ten million cash immediately, plus fifty percent of profits on the Coram land over a five-year period, provided they sold the lots that would be developed by Coral Islands. The package amounted to just under fifty million dollars gross. Everyone was delighted.

4

1962

Galal Jamil was born in 1940 at his parents' home in the port city of Haifa, Palestine. His creation took place twenty-three years earlier at the British Foreign Office in a letter dated November 2, 1917.

Dear Lord Rothschild,

I have pleasure in conveying to you on behalf of His Majesty's Government, the following declaration of sympathy with Jewish Zionist aspirations which has been submitted to and approved by the Cabinet.

"His Majesty's Government view with favour the establishment in Palestine of a national home for the Jewish people and will use their best endeavours to facilitate the achievement of this object, it being clearly understood that nothing shall be done which may prejudice the civil and religious rights of existing non-Jewish communities in Palestine, or the rights and political status enjoyed by Jews in any other country."

I should be grateful if you would bring this declaration to the knowledge of the Zionist Federation.

Yours sincerely,
Arthur James Balfour

At the time this letter was written, there were less than 80,000 Jews in Palestine living peacefully amongst their 550,000 Arab neighbors. During the centuries of rule under the Ottoman Empire, the Jews of Palestine, like the Christians, paid the special head tax levied against all non-Moslems, permitting them to keep their places of worship, laws and properties. The Arabs had always regarded Christians and Jews as misguided brothers, but brothers nonetheless. Abraham, Moses and Christ were Moslem prophets too. The Great Prophet Mohammed had carefully instructed the faithful to observe the religious rights of others when his hordes of tribesmen swept out of the desert thirteen centuries before to create an Empire greater than Rome.

As the last remnants of this mighty Empire collapsed during World War I, the Ottoman carcass was carved up among the victors by the Sykes-Picot Agreement. Lebanon and Syria became French Mandates, Palestine, a British Mandate, the Trans Jordan area, created into a new country called Jordan, with a puppet king of the powerful Hashemite Clan installed on its throne by the British. The British Foreign Office managed the Kingdom of Iraq and tiny principalities along the Persian Gulf from Kuwait to Oman at the mouth of the Red Sea. The warring factions of nomadic tribesmen who had helped the Allies defeat the common Turkish enemy were subjugated now themselves; confined to geographic identities which had existed for nearly a thousand years before the arrival of the Turks.

It was, however, subjugation with a difference. Other than the most cursory supervision by the Protecting Powers in matters of defense and international policy, each country was allowed to pursue its own internal business and commerce with the world at large.

Family squabbles between tribes, or vocal rumblings of Arab nationalism, were settled swiftly when they erupted by the Colonial Offices in London or Paris with the aid of the Sir John Pasha Glubb's Desert Legions from Jordan or the Foreign Legion of France. For three decades an uneasy peace descended upon the torpid Arab countryside.

At first, a trickle of Jewish immigration flowed into Palestine under the British Mandate. By 1929 this trickle became a river and the Palestinian Arabs, alarmed at the militancy of the Zionist movement, rioted to protest this swelling incursion of their homeland. The government of Ramsey MacDonald moved quickly to allay the fears of both Jews and Arabs, promising equal consideration of their interests. In 1936 the Arabs rioted again when the river of immigration had become a flood. Lord Peel was appointed to head a Royal Commission and study the problem. He published his findings in 1937 in which he recommended the partition of Palestine. The Arabs rejected the plan. The Zionist Congress was almost equally divided in its opinion. The population of Jews had now risen to 400,000 within the Mandate. Their immigration was well organized and sponsored financially by international Jewry. The new arrivals were industrious, hardworking and filled with the zeal of religious knowledge that they had, after nearly two thousand years, returned to their homeland. In comparison, the Arabs appeared lazy, incompetent, relying on British promises and their own vocal opposition to stem the flood.

Adli Jamil's family had come to Palestine from Istanbul in 1822, a reward for efforts in fighting the unsuccessful battles of the Ottomans against the Greeks and Balkan countries, who broke away from their Turkish overlords. Hakim Jamil was given the post of customs officer for the port of Haifa, with all the financial perks that accompanied such a position. His son, Aziz, inherited the post from his father in 1845, as did Benbuna, old Hakim's grandson in 1871. However, Benbuna's sons were not interested in their birthright of government service to the Ottoman Empire, so the Jamil family holdings over the shipping commerce within the port of Haifa expired with Benbuna's death in 1903.

Two of the Benbuna sons used their father's position to place themselves in the world of commerce by opening the offices of Jamil & Co., Importers & Exporters, in a small office along the waterfront. Initially, their service provided the uncanny ability to clear any inbound or outgoing cargo swiftly for a reasonable fee. Gradually, they began buying and selling their own cargos from the fat profits which had accumulated through peddling their father's influence along the quays. By the time Benbuna died, they had achieved a stature of respectable Haifa merchants, in a time when corruption was synonomous with respectability. They grew fat and wealthy and lived to see the rotting carcass of their Ottoman patrons expire with the arrival of the British.

Only one of their sons had decided to eschew the world of pleasure and vice available to the very rich. Adli Jamil developed a thirst for knowledge and curiosity about the world in general. Unlike his brothers, he remained in Cairo to finish the four years of courses at the university. His father and uncle were terribly proud of their progeny and when he expressed a desire to continue with his studies in England, they sent him off in style with a retinue of servants. In

1912 no young man should arrive on the shores of the Queen of Empires to study without some visible evidence of his own substance, or so the two Jamil brothers thought. Adli sent the servants home to Haifa a month after he arrived. He discovered he spent more time concerned with their welfare in the foreign country, than studying. He took a flat of rooms in Oxford and disappeared into his books.

The Great War interrupted his education and, unknown to the rest of the family, he volunteered for the British Army as an intelligence officer for Middle Eastern Affairs. The move was prompted more by a sense of Turkish Ottoman injustice, generally, than any obligation to the British crown.

After three dreary years at the Middle Eastern desk at the War Office in London, he was posted to General Allenby's staff. He accompanied the General to Egypt when he assumed command of the British Army there from Sir Archibald Murray, who was making a hash of things. It was Adli's intimate knowledge of the Gaza area that helped Allenby in his campaign plans. Six weeks after Beersheba had been captured, Jerusalem surrendered to the British Army. The intelligence staff spent the next months in Jerusalem planning the final overthrow of the Turkish Army. Later the army swept forward beyond the Jordan Valley to Damascus and Aleppo; the Turks were crushed in the battles that followed at Megiddo during September and October of 1918. Allenby was promoted to Field Marshal, made a Viscount and voted a grant of fifty thousand pounds by the British Government. Adli Jamil was discharged as a Lieutenant Colonel, given a gratuity of 136 pounds and returned home to Haifa with a new passport admitting him as a British subject.

His uncle had died during the war and his father was in poor health. The disruptions of the past decade to the way of life his father had found so secure, had vanished along with the Turks. The new British rules refused to countenance corruption or commercial bargaining and expected everyone to speak English instead of Arabic. Gratefully, his sick parent turned the family's business interests over to his English-speaking son with the shiny new British passport.

The commercial advantages of British citizenship were not lost on Adli Jamil. Swiftly, he reorganized the archaic business methods of Jamil & Sons into an efficiently profitable enterprise according to the prevailing standards of British business ethics. Soon juicy government contracts for military and civil requirements within the new Mandates of Palestine and the Kingdom of Jordan flowed through the Haifa offices of Jamil & Sons. He opened a branch in

London to keep his finger on the pulse of opinion and heartbeat of political influence.

When his father died peacefully in his sleep in 1922, Adli felt that the future of the Jamil family looked very rosy indeed. He had managed to reform two of his errant brothers, sending them off to Jerusalem and Amman to run branches. There was only one dark spot on the horizon. Jews had been flooding into the country since the war at an alarming rate. From a small individualistic minority minding their own business, living in their funny prison farms they called *Kibbutzim*, they were becoming a nuisance, their hysterical vocal and printed Zionist propaganda shrieking for world attention. Adli could not understand it. The problem was not with the old Jewish families that had lived in the area for hundreds of years, but with the new Zionist immigrants who seemed determined to force themselves and their ways into the Ottoman vacuum before the British awakened to the threat. Now, the Zionist immigrants were waving the Balfour Declaration in everyone's faces and the British High Commissioner for Palestine appeared unwilling to take a stand. Allenby had been appointed the High Commissioner in Egypt. But before his recall to England when the Kingdom of Egypt was declared by the British, Adli visited him in Cairo. Jamil, when he had been shown into his former officer's presence, went straight to the point.

"Sir, is the government at Whitehall unaware that at the present rate of Zionist immigration the Arabs will be a minority within a decade?"

"Nonsense, Jamil. There are less then 80,000 Jews in the Mandate and over a half million Moslems," the High Commissioner replied testily.

"One hundred and fourteen thousand Zionists to be exact, according to their own census. General, if this scale of immigration continues there will be grave problems for everyone. No one is objecting to a homeland for the Jewish people, but it is my homeland too, and I say it is getting too crowded. Your Balfour Declaration stated that the rights of the people of Palestine would be protected; that means Moslem rights and Christian rights as well as Jewish rights," he explained patiently.

"Look, Jamil, I didn't participate in the idea of Jewish immigration, but now it is a matter of policy. Have some compassion for the poor blighters, man. They've been kicked from pillar to post for centuries."

He rubbed a hand over his pate absently.

"I disagree, General. They are not poor. They are well

organized. They are militant. At no time in history were the Jews persecuted or kicked, as you say, from pillar to post by any Moslem nation. Why do you now permit them to kick us from pillar to post in our homeland? They buy our lands, then refuse to hire our people to work them. They build businesses and factories, but hire Moslems at lower wages than Jews and always they cry out that we are discriminating against them!"

"What do you want me to do?"

"There is only one thing to do. The immigration must be slowed or the results will be disastrous."

Allenby considered the visitor.

"You're a good sort, Jamil. Tell you what I'll do. Give me your written appreciation of the situation and I'll put it in the right hands at the War Office. Beyond that . . ." his voice trailed off. "I'm a soldier, Jamil, not a politician. I have learned that what is common sense to politicans, often appears ludicrous to soldiers like ourselves."

He stood up, smiling. "That's the best I can do."

Adli never knew whether anyone besides Allenby read his voluminous report on the Palestine situation. If they had, they might have marvelled at his prophetic insight during the twenty-five years that followed. He misguessed the expulsion of the Palestinians from their homeland by five years, but then he had not anticipated World War II slowing events at the time he wrote his report. His house and family were blown up with Irgun hand grenades in April 1948, one week before the Irgun and Stern gang had massacred the two hundred and fifty inhabitants of Deir Yassin. The Jewish Hagana professed official shock at the two events. The Jamil Family was executed as a threat, the people of Deir Yassim, as a lesson. Fortunately, young Galal Jamil was visiting his uncle in Amman, Jordan, at the time.

Galal Jamil met Yasser Arafat in West Germany a few weeks before graduating from the University of Bonn. The civil engineer from Kuwait impressed the young Jamil with his persuasive smiling manner and precise Arabic articulations, acquired from the University of Cairo, from which Arafat had graduated. Although his accent was Egyptian and his employment Kuwaiti, Arafat was still, like Jamil, a Palestinian refugee from the Gaza Strip, dispossessed of his birthplace in Jerusalem by the edict of 1948. The idea of a Palestine Liberation Organization belonged to everyone who had been dispossessed. The concept of how the idea might become reality belonged to Arafat.

He traveled widely, visiting the refugees, searching for the cells with which to form the embryos of the new movement. Students, graduates, idealists, these were the clay waiting to be molded. He was, of course, also interested in the working man, the farmer and shopkeeper, as well as the militant layabout that infested the refugee camps throughout Jordan, Lebanon and Palestine, now Israel. They would be the cannon fodder of the new movement. But, his greatest efforts were directed at the young intelligentsia emerging from the universities, bitter and bewildered at the loss of their birthright.

"Our homeland has been taken from us. Now we must take it back."

The words were said simply by the smiling face, at the conclusion of the coffee meeting held in the basement apartment. There were eleven students who had turned up, half of them out of curiosity more than commitment. Jamil, one of the eleven, listened attentively to the arguments presented during the evening. There were several points over which he disagreed, but he kept his counsel and, unlike the others, asked no questions of the speaker until the meeting was breaking up. Then he approached the short, stocky man in the center of the room as he was discussing travel arrangements for the following day's departure with two aides.

"Do you believe everything you told us?"

Arafat looked up, surprised, the smile still in place.

"Don't you?"

Jamil shook his head. "No, Sir. I do not."

The two aides looked uncomfortable, then backed discreetly away as Arafat nodded at them.

"What is it you do not believe, young Jamil?"

"I do not believe there is a political solution to the problem. History has proved large resettlement programs for masses of people are permanent. There is no going back through political negotiations. The political negotiations cause the migration in the first place."

Arafat's eyes lit up. "Ah, you are a student of history? To which migrations do you refer?"

"The Jews leaving Egypt is one example."

"They were expelled and left willingly. Give me another."

"The Russian Pogroms," Jamil countered.

"Jews again, always Jews. Give me an example of something besides Jews."

"The Acadia expulsion. The British took the French from Canada to New Orleans; few returned. The Americans expelled their

Indians to the reservations; they never returned. The partition of India and Pakistan or of Northern and Southern Ireland. There are dozens of examples where people have been torn from their homeland. They never return, ever. When you tell me that political means will bring us home to Palestine, I do not believe you, Yasser Arafat."

The smile softened as he regarded the hawk-faced intense young man standing before him with the dark eyes.

"I knew your father, young Jamil, when you lived in Haifa. Adli Jamil was a good man, a patriot who used his great wealth to fight the edict of '48. All his life he fought it politically at Whitehall, using logic and appealing to the British sense of justice and fair play."

"The British promised justice and fair play to the Sheriff of Mecca when he persuaded the desert tribes to fight the Turks with Lawrence—a homeland for the Arabs. The British are liars."

Arafat chuckled. "Opportunists is a better word. What would you do if your country was losing a war? I would make a pact with the devil himself if it would serve the interests of my country. The British never believed the Balfour promise would have to be honored. If the second Great War had not come to pass, who knows, perhaps I might still be living in Jerusalem. The British were helpless. Their Empire crumbling. Pressured by American Zionists and, of course, as always, needing money to survive."

Jamil waved his arms angrily. "Politics." He spat the word. "What did it do for my family? Death from Zionist hand grenades. Fire must be fought with fire according to the Prophet. Politics is for weaklings, Yasser Arafat."

"Young Jamil, I trained Egyptian and Palestinian commandos and fought the British and French at Suez in 1956. I worked with demolitions in the Egyptian Army at Port Said and Abu Kabir. I am not a weakling. But, I am a realist and as a realist I know the realities of our limitations. We are poorly financed, poorly organized and, as a political force, we do not exist. All this will change with time, I promise you."

"Can you make rivers run backwards?" He smiled sarcastically.

"No. But I can make eddies along the banks, pools of quiet water where our fish will breed and thrive until the day arrives when we can build our dam across the river and water will cease to flow until the river allows us to flow with it."

He took the young man's arm and led him to the side of the room, out of earshot of the other half dozen people who were feigning disinterest in the conversation, but listening avidly.

"I like you, Jamil. You show great promise for the Movement. I need people like you to help, but we must be cautious. Privately, I agree with your sentiments, but publicly I must abhor violence unless it is advocated by someone stronger than ourselves. I believe that President Gamal Nasser will provide us the opportunities to recover our homeland, once he has consolidated his position in the Arab world. It will take time and to make sure our cause is not overlooked during this game of international politics, we must needle, prick, stab and slice at the Zionists continuously."

Jamil was curious, and honored by the private attention being shown him.

"And if Gamal Nasser fails like the Mahdi. . . ." He let the words trail off.

Arafat shrugged.

"There are other ways. I have not placed all our wines in one jar. In the years ahead our financial strength will grow as our brothers in Saudi, Kuwait, Abu Dahbi, Algeria, and Libya emerge with their own nationalism and independence. Look what is happening in Algeria. Ten years ago who would have thought that the French would leave. But now they go. The days of Colonial Empires are over. Soon the British too will leave the Gulf States and the wealth that lies beneath the sands will be ours to dispose of as we see fit. It will all come to pass, young Jamil, and, one day—one day before we die, you or I will stand at the United Nations in New York as a force with which the world must reckon."

"What can I do to help?"

Arafat laid his hand on Jamil's shoulder and grinned hugely.

"You have learned the arts of science, now it is time for you to learn the arts of war. When you have finished here, go to Beirut to a house on the Corniche Mazraa and seek out Abu Ali Iyad; tell him Abu Ammar has sent you for training. He will tell you what to do. Now I must go."

His hand dropped from Jamil's shoulder and they shook hands.

"Allah be with you, young Jamil."

"And with you, Yasser Arafat."

Driving into Beirut three days after his graduation as a chemical engineer, Jamil was dumbfounded by the activity of the city. As a boy he remembered his elders discussing the plight of poor Lebanon starving financially; pleading with King Farouk's Egyptian government to buy their foodstuffs, apples and wheat to keep the economy from total collapse. Now it was all changed. Nasser had seen to that.

The wealthy Egyptians with their brains and technical abilities had taken what little they had left from Nasser's wild nationalism programs and fled to Beirut. Cairo's star had fallen. Beirut's was still ascending.

Haughty, wealthy oil sheiks from Saudi Arabia and the trucial states along the Persian Gulf had grown tired of Cairo radio broadcasts ridiculing their mufti, their ancient Arabic speech, their way of life. They too forsook the Queen of Cities along the Nile and its vanishing enticements to spend their summer vacations in the harbor city of Beirut with its cool mountain backdrop. They brought their millions from oil revenues with them.

As the Mercedes taxi rolled into the outskirts of the city, Jamil could see signs of construction everywhere. There were new banks, apartments, houses, hotels, shops. Construction boomed with the noise of clanking machines, chipping masonry and rumbling dump trucks. A pall of light white dust filled the city with a crescent moon of promise. It seemed everyone was sharing in the new industrial boom. Everyone except the refugee camps of Dekwaneh and Burj-el-Branjneh. There the good fortune of the city was shared at arm's length. The camps provided much of the labor force to the various construction sites. Illegal labor for the most part. Work permits for Palestinian refugees were hard to come by.

Residents of Lebanon for nearly fifteen years, the refugees were still regarded as nothing more than squatters, without rights to work or travel freely, living under temporary sufferance in a foreign land. One day their final disposition would be decided by the Great Powers that had stripped them of their homeland, leaving them to huddle in these temporary camps. In the meantime, the simmering cauldrons of humanity in Beirut, as well as the rest of Lebanon, Jordan and Syria, were reaching the boiling point. The world powers ignored their plight, but provided a token understanding of the problem through UNRWA—the United Nations Refugee assistance program. It was woefully inadequate.

The taxi pulled up at the address on Corniche Mazraa that Jamil had given the driver at the airport. After the usual ritual Arabic shouting, where each swears the other has robbed him, he paid the driver the normal airport fare, plus a tip, in Lebanese Pounds. The driver conceded defeat and drove off whistling, to look for a malleable Christian.

"What do you want?"

The door had opened to the length of the chain that held it on the inside, after Jamil knocked several times. The speaker's face was indistinct beyond the thin opening.

"I have come to see Abu Ali Iyad."

"There is no one here by that name. Go away."

Swiftly Jamil stuck his foot into the opening. The door locked against his instep.

"Tell him that Abu Ammar has sent me from Germany."

He removed his foot. The door closed and he could hear the chain lock being removed from the door. When it opened again, a huge muscular man barred his way, examining him closely, then motioned him inside. Jamil entered as the big man looked out into the street, glancing to the left and right, then shut the door. He frisked Jamil slowly, methodically, watching him closely as he completed the task.

"Who are you?" he demanded as he straightened up.

"I am the son of Adli Jamil of Haifa. My name is Galal. I have graduated from university in Germany. I am a chemical engineer. Last month Abu Ammar visited the students and spoke to me. I have come to help the Movement."

The man regarded Jamil critically for several moments, then smiled.

"Welcome, son of Adli Jamil; you are expected. Come!"

Jamil followed him into the house and up the stairs to the second floor. They paused in front of one of the doors along the dark hallway. The man knocked lightly, then opened the door.

"Galal Jamil," he said simply, ushering his charge into the room, closing the door after him.

Jamil glanced around the group of men and women seated about the room. His eyes stopped at the oldest face.

"Abu Ali Iyad?" he inquired.

"Is it because I look like a hawk of the desert Galal Jamil, that you single me out?"

"No, Abu Ali Iyad, it is because you look the oldest."

Everyone laughed, the tension was broken.

"But apparently not the wisest," Iyad suggested, as the laughter subsided.

He stood up to shake Jamil's hand.

"Welcome to our group, Galal Jamil. Let me introduce you to the others."

He nodded to each of the young people in the room as introductions were made by his host. He fixed the faces with their names into his brain. Four women. Seven men. Some older, some younger than Jamil. They regarded him with interest as he took the only vacant seat left in the room and sat down beside a girl introduced to him as Leila Kemal, moments before. As he sank into the soft couch he recognized the odor of *Channel* from the female body next to him. The smell was incongruous with the surroundings.

"We were discussing the fine difference between Al Fateh and Al Asifah when you arrived. Do you know the difference?" Iyad asked.

"Al Fateh are the reverse initials of the Palestine National Liberation Movement; Harakat al Tabrir al Watani al Filstini. Al Asifah I have never heard before," Jamil admitted.

Iyad smiled. "With every political force there must, of necessity, be a military force, just in case political force fails. Al Asifah is the military arm of Al Fateh. At the moment we are only a theory in the minds of politicans of Al Fateh. Officially, we do not exist nor will Al Fateh admit to our existence because of what we represent. The ultimate solution to the failure of politics!"

He turned his gaze from Jamil and encompassed the room.

"Until now Al Fateh has concentrated its total effort on political action. The time for political action alone is passed. The time for military action has arrived. Al Asifah will pursue this course until final victory for our cause is secure. However, before there can be military activity, there must be a military force that is trained in its ability to function as an army. Not an army of common foot soldiers, but an army of experts, familiar with every technical innovation created by man for the destruction of an enemy. Al Asifah is not interested in soldiers who can fire rifles, but don't know how to load artillery shells into a field gun, or an artilleryman who doesn't know detonation temperatures between plastique C2 and C4. Our military force must be experts in all forms of destruction. Adaptability to circumstances will be our greatest asset. Adaptability requires knowledge and this knowledge you will receive from Al Asifah when you arrive at our camp in Jordan next week."

Iyad paused, his eyes distracted by Jamil's hand waving at him from the couch.

"You have a question?"

"Yes sir. How do I go about joining Al Asifah?"

"My dear Jamil, no one joins Al Asifah. Al Asifah selects them as members. You were selected in Germany four weeks ago. I thought you knew."

Everyone laughed again.

They sat in a cafe near the waterfront eating *fattet makhdous,* the Arab dish of mixed yogurt, egg-plant and bread.

"Where did you live in Palestine?" Jamil inquired.

"Haifa. We lived on Stanton Street near the Hadar. My father ran a store until we were expelled in 1948. And you?" Leila Kemal asked, dipping into the bowl of fattet.

"Haifa—then Amman after '48—I lived there with my uncle until I went to Germany.

They continued to eat in silence, watching the traffic hurrying along the street in front of the cafe. Leila stopped eating and pushed her bowl away. Jamil glanced at her for an instant for permission, then poured the contents onto his own plate and continued to eat greedily.

"Then you were never in any of the camps?"

"No, thank God. I visited Wahdat camp a few times with my uncle Aziz, delivering supplies. It was terrible. Were you in any of them?"

"I grew up in Dekwaneh camp here in Beirut until I was fourteen, then I got out."

They ordered thick sweet tea and cakes to finish off their supper.

"I worked as a prostitute while I went to school," Leila continued, waiting for a reaction from Jamil.

"Interesting work," he grunted, sipping his tea. "How far did you get in school?"

"That doesn't bother you?"

"No, it's just the right temperature." He sipped noisily again.

"I didn't mean the tea."

"I know you didn't. Everyone has to survive. How far did you get in school?"

"I'm still at the American University, or was until a week ago, after Fathi spoke to our Palestine students."

"Fathi?" Jamil set his cup down on the table.

"Fathi Arafat, Yasser's brother."

"I didn't know he had a brother. What's he like?"

"I joined Al Asifah," she stated simply.

"Where do you live?

"Why?"

"I need a bed until they ship us to Jordan. I'll pay for it."

"It's only a single bed in a small apartment." Leila admired his impudence.

"I'm not fussy. Do you kick?" Jamil signaled for the bill.

"Why don't you stay at a pension?" she countered.

"Why pay them when I can pay you?"

"I'm not for sale anymore," she bristled.

"I'm not buying your body, only renting your bed, woman."

Leila laughed. "But that's not the way it will turn out."

Jamil smiled. "Who knows how anything turns out?"

They walked back to the house on Corniche Mazraa so Jamil could pick up his suitcase, then took a taxi to Leila's apartment near Jewett Hall, the women's residence for the American University. Jamil followed her shapely rump up the three flights of stairs. Inside, he looked around the large room quizzically.

"I thought you said it was an apartment?" He dropped his bag beside the double bed, "with only a single bed."

"It's a single room apartment with a double bed. I lied."

He stripped off his clothing to his shorts and washed himself in the porcelain sink that served the room as bathtub, basin and kitchen sink. As he turned to grope for a towel to dry his face, his hands touched her body standing beside him. She was naked. He forgot the wetness of his face as he kneaded the nipples of her breasts, then pulled her to the bed with him, kicking off his shorts along the way. The ancient coiled springs squeaked in rhythmic protest as they satisfied their lust.

5

Father Francisco Montelegro stood behind the rows of benches in the south transept of the cathedral listening to the bearded man speaking to the group of people gathered before him. From his vantage point in the trancept, he could keep his eye on the front doors of the nave, as well as the entrance into the church from the cloisters. If the soldiers decided to break up the meeting in this House of God, entrance would have to come from either of these two doors. Father Francisco watched, and listened, his dark eyes sweeping across the backs of the assembled heads to the ornate gilt doors to the cloisters and nave. It was hard to decide which he loved more: the beautiful four hundred year old cathedral, built by the Spanish conquistadores and entrusted to him for safe-keeping during his time on earth, or the forty-five souls seated on the hard wooden benches in the trancept, looking for a solution to their grievances under the oppressive dictatorship of Colonel Gaspar Guererro. The country had fallen on hard times since the revolution. Now Father Francisco hardly knew the people who came to pray. The Cathedral of the Blessed Heart provided a bellweather for good and bad times. In good times, attendance filled a small part of the huge nave. In bad times, it filled to capacity and he said five masses on Sunday in order to meet the needs of his parishioners.

Using the church as a meeting place had been his idea after he had attended three earlier abortive meetings, when the soldiers had come and smashed everything. They had led Felina and the big man she called El Chirlo away at gunpoint. They were detained a few days, then released. The Colonel might have shot them if Father Francisco had not intervened. Guererro moved swiftly to silence opposition to his regime, but where the Church was concerned, he moved carefully. The bishop in Panama had approved the action Father Francisco took to spare the lives of the old President's daughter and her companion, when he described the events in a letter to him later, although he wasn't so sure his bishop would approve using the church as a public meeting place for dissidents. He resolved to tell him after the event. Making the Colonel back down from his original stand had been a triumph he relished. Less than an hour after the soldiers had broken up the first meeting, he was standing in Guererro's office regarding the fleshy man with his soft brown eyes.

"What do you want, Father? It is late and I am a busy man." The Colonel had just started undressing for bed with his current mistress when he had been informed of the visit by the priest.

"Your soldiers broke into a peaceful meeting at the Tienda Ramada this evening and destroyed the premises. Several people were beaten badly with rifle butts and two people were taken away. A man and a woman. I want them released."

"Where did you get this information from, Father?"

"I was at the meeting. I saw what happened."

"So! Since when does a priest involve himself with revolutionaries?"

"I heard no talk of revolution at the meeting, Colonel."

"What else would Artega's daughter and her lover talk about?" he growled. His aides stirred uneasily.

"Colonel Guererro, seven years ago you overthrew the constitutionally elected government of this country in a bloody revolution. You promised peace. We have had peace everywhere, except within the country. You promised free elections within five years. We are still waiting for those elections. As a priest, I cannot be a politician. But, I will tell you this much Colonel, as a priest, you push people too far. And the people are the church. I want the man and the woman released, or there will be grave trouble."

"What will you do, priest? Excommunicate me? Ha!"

"No, Colonel, it is not my position to excommunicate anyone. However, I will send a complete report to my bishop who will, no doubt, forward the information on to the Holy Father."

If it had been anyone besides the daughter of the former President of the country, Guererro would have thrown the priest out of the building and executed the prisoners. The church was his one weakness. It had always been his weakness. He was afraid of its power. Guererro understood power. He laced his fingers together under his double chin and contemplated the elderly wizened man standing calmly before him. He noticed the black cassock was threadbare and two of the buttons were missing their cloth domes where the metal crucifix had knocked them in half. It might be dangerous to tempt Providence further. Besides, he could afford to be generous.

"I'll release the girl, but the man remains where he is."

"Both, Colonel," Father Francisco replied evenly, then bowed slightly, and walked from the room, his leather sandals slapping the terrazzo.

The room was silent for several minutes after he left. No one moved. Finally, Guererro swore, "Puta Madre! I'd like to string that priest up by the cojones!"

He stood up from the desk and scratched his belly. "Fucking priests. Always sticking their noses into politics. Keep the man and woman for a week on bread and water, then release them. No rough stuff. I don't want them marked when they get out."

He paused by the door.

"Cadalso. When they get out I want them followed everywhere. I want to know who they see and where they go. If there are any more meetings, break them up. But no arrests or beatings. Perhaps they'll get tired and go back to Mexico, eh!"

"Si, Excelencia. I will see to it personally." Cadalso nodded as the Colonel left the room.

For the first few days after leaving the Tampico hospital Chirlo had wandered the doctor's estate like a man in a busy airport terminal trying to find the right gate for his flight home. Felina and Artega walked with him about the gardens of the beautiful property the exiles had rented four years earlier as their temporary home. Keeping their conversations light and amusing, they probed for some spark to awaken the dormant memory. Chirlo appeared interested outwardly, grateful for their company. Inwardly he was a seething mass of uncertainties and fears, at times bordering on panic.

The house was a relic of the Spaniards who had ruled the land two centuries earlier. A gift from a governor to a favorite mistress in an era when noble men kept their paramours at arms' length for the sake of propriety, but in residence for the sake of convenience. The formal gardens had been overgrown with weeds and swamp grass when the doctor first discovered it, hidden at the end of a cul-de-sac only a few blocks from the center of town. The last resident, a British Consul, had departed in 1940 to attend a war, leaving everything intact. By the time he and his family arrived in Liverpool three weeks later, vandals had stripped the estate of everything that wasn't nailed down. Doctor Artega picked the lease up for a song, then spent a hundred thousand dollars to recapture its former glory. With the help of two full time gardeners, three maids and two kitchen staff, he had managed to create the illusion of transitory permanence in an alien land.

Chirlo was given one of the guest rooms on the second floor. It was a huge airy place with tall windows that looked out over the back lawn and gardens. The adjoining bathroom had been a maid's room before the days of indoor plumbing. It had an enormous tiled tub surrounded by mirrored walls. It amused Chirlo to see his crowded reflections watching him whenever he bathed, like a roomful of Peeping Toms.

Beneath his bedroom, on the main floor, the doctor had a well stocked library. Most of the books were beautifully bound rubbish, bought by the yard to fill the rows of empty spaces along the mahogany paneled walls. There was, however, a small section devoted to Artega's tastes and interests. Medical books and post bound journals, political works of every idealogy, as well as standard library classics and a twenty-four volume collection of encyclopedias. It was the encyclopedias to which Chirlo directed his attentions. They were filled with photographic plates of cities, places, people and events. He spent days poring through the collection. Some of the pictures he recognized from his past, but not the incidents surrounding their familiarity. It was frustrating.

Sometimes he would drive out to the market with Ruis while the major domo renewed the household provisions. They would drive around the city afterwards for an hour or two exploring different areas. Once, as they drove past the airport at the north end of town, Chirlo suddenly ordered Ruis to stop.

"I've been here before!" he exclaimed. "I can feel it. The place is familiar."

They drove into the parking lot of the terminal and sat in silence as Chirlo's eyes swept the area carefully.

"Over there." He pointed to a maintenance hangar near the terminal. "There was a blue and silver Learjet in there the last time I was here. Let's go and see if it's still there."

It was, but no one remembered seeing the tall man before. They visited the terminal and flight office afterwards. Still no recognition. With a defeated sigh, Ruis drove him back to the house and lunch.

That same evening they went to the Bikini Club on the outskirts of the city along the road to Vera Cruz. It was the best bordello in Tampico. Artega prescribed the sexual therapy as an outlet for the frustrations of the airport encounter. He visited the Bikini Club occasionally himself, but had recently acquired a mistress with her own apartment in the city, which rendered his public exposures at the Club unnecessary. Besides, of late, he was becoming concerned over his houseguest's apparent lack of interest in the opposite sex.

For a young man in his twenties it was not natural, despite his illness.

"Perhaps he is a *Reina?*" Ruis suggested with a wry smile.

"Perhaps," Artega shrugged. "We shall see."

They arrived shortly after ten and took a table on the edge of the dance floor next to a group of loud Norwegian sailors ogling the bikini-clad merchandise roaming about the large room in a continuous display for customer approval and selection. They ordered two cold beers and sat back to watch the parade of flesh. Several girls nodded as they passed. Finally, one of them stopped in front of the table, her eyes wide with recognition.

"Peter! You did come back." She threw her arms around his neck and nuzzled his face, then drew back.

"What happened to your face, mi amour?"

Ruis choked on his beer. Stunned, Chirlo said nothing.

"You know this man, Chiquita?" Ruis demanded.

"Sure, it's Peter." She looked perplexed. "You are Peter, aren't you?" Her voice was uncertain. She stood back, examining him. Chirlo recovered his composure and smiled.

"You have a good memory."

The girl laughed. "I remember your smile, but it is a crooked smile now. Where is your Gringo friend?"

"My friend?"

"Your amigo, Chuck. The serious one who kept bargaining with everyone for the best price."

"He is back in the States. Do you remember his last name?"

"No, just Chuck. Do you want me for tonight, Peter?"

"Do you remember my last name?" Chirlo persisted.

The girl shook her head impatiently. "You never told me."

She took him by the hand and led him to her room, in the

courtyard beside the Club.

Later, on the drive home, Ruis inquired, "Did you learn anything else?"

Chirlo shrugged. "I was here last May for three weeks with another man; an American who spoke Spanish badly. We were friends or business partners. The girl was my steady screwing for the three weeks I was here. She didn't know where I lived, but thought I had told her I grew up in Peru. Not much help."

"Oh, I don't know. At least you know your name is Peter and you used to be quite a swordsman—every night for three weeks last May. Phew! I wish I could compete with that."

Chirlo laughed dryly. "That was last May. Tonight I couldn't even get a hardon. Some swordsman!"

"It will come back," Ruis promised.

Chirlo studied the shoreline from the flying bridge with the binoculars as Felina slowed the boat towards the beach. He lowered the glasses.

"You are sure this is the place?"

"Positive. Just in front of those dunes. They are the highest part along the beach for several miles. See that group of palms"—she pointed—"they were just off the bow when we beached the last time. It's only been a few weeks, Pedro, I haven't forgotten."

They had all decided on calling him the Spanish form of Peter, when Ruis related the news of their discovery at the Bikini Club over breakfast the following morning. Felina had lowered her eyes modestly as Ruis related the story. Artega was immensely relieved to hear their guest's disinterest in women was mental, not physical. It confirmed what he had suspected, eliminating any nagging doubts. The boat trip to the scene of his discovery had been Felina's idea. Perhaps the familiarity of the beach would provide a clue.

The keel slid onto the submerged sand. Felina switched off the engine. They waded ashore barefoot and walked a few feet up from the water.

"Look! There's the marks where we dragged you off the beach." She pointed to the twin grooves where Chirlo's buttocks had trenched the sand. He said nothing.

They stood together looking up and down the shoreline, then walked to the top of the dune. Again Chirlo scanned the deserted shore. They walked down the other side of the sand hill and stopped in front of the charred remains of a fire. Something stirred his memory.

"They were sitting by this fire cooking beans."

"Who?" Felina demanded, excited.

"I don't know. There were four or five of them dressed in white. A tall one and a short one. They had machetes and asked me to share their supper."

"Then what happened, Pedro?"

Chirlo paused, his eyes clouding. "Nothing—I don't know. I can't remember."

He looked inland, his eyes picking up a cluster of crude adobe huts.

"There is a village over there." He started towards it, then stopped after a few paces.

"They might recognize me as their victim. Go and find out the name of the village. I'll wait here."

Felina nodded and ran back to the boat to get her shoes. Chirlo sat down by the dead fire and contemplated the village a half mile across the open land from the dunes.

Teniente Hector Ortona brushed a fly off his desk blotter as he examined the pile of clothing, wristwatch and boots sitting on his desk. The watch was a Rolex in a stainless steel case with a silver flexible wrist band. It had a twenty-four hour hand that covered the hours around a moveable bezel, which was divided into days and nights. There were, in addition, the usual twelve hour hands and a full second sweep. Ortona studied the watch. It was a complicated looking timepiece. He had never seen anything like it. Finally he picked up the cloth moneybelt which had contained the thirty-two thousand dollars his men had found with the bandits at the village of San Felipe.

It was a puzzling case. First, the doctor from Tampico had come with his daughter to police headquarters in Altimira asking to have the coastal village of San Felipe checked for any sudden local riches among the inhabitants after November 28. Ortona had been suspicious of the visit until he had checked the doctor's credentials with Colonel Bianca in Tampico. Then it was a different matter. A matter to be taken seriously. It took less than a day to break the mystery of the doctor's request.

Several local troublemakers in the village had blossomed with sudden riches during the last week in November. A short painful beating by Sgt. Romero had produced electrifying results on site in San Felipe. Within an hour Ortona had a full confession from the group, plus the collection of loot now lying on his desk. The money was in the police security vault at the bank. He had called Dr. Artega immediately with the news. This time the foreign doctor arrived with a tall somber man with a huge scar on his cheek. *The victim?*

"Senor. Would you please try these boots?" Ortona stood up and brought the brown quarter-Wellingtons to Chirlo. He watched him critically as he pulled them on. There was no doubt they fitted his feet perfectly. Chirlo stood up and walked to the desk, fingering the watch. He slipped it on his wrist.

"That is an unusual wristwatch, Senor," Ortona commented.

"It's not a watch, Teniente.It's a chronometer adjustable to Greenwich Mean Time, for navigation."

The explanation startled him as he had spoken the words. He turned back to the desk and picked up the empty money belt.

"How much was left?" he asked absently.

"Exactly thirty-two thousand American dollars, Senor. How much is missing?" He watched the scarfaced man's eyes closely.

"There was fifty thousand dollars." Again Chirlo was startled by his own knowledge.

Ortona smiled. "Correct, Senor. They spent the rest of your money foolishly, I am afraid. Televisions, furniture, cockfights, drinking—I am sorry."

"Can I speak to them?"

Ortona was surprised. "Why?"

"Curiosity." He gave him a lopsided grin.

The Teniente shrugged. "If you wish."

"Privately, if that is possible."

Ortona raised his eyebrows.

The doctor interrupted his suspicions. "I think, Teniente, Senor Pedro would like to examine the men out of earshot of the police. He might be able to learn whether there is any more money hidden at the village."

Ortona bristled. "I can assure you, Doctor, if there was any more money my men would have recovered it."

The thought occurred to him suddenly that they felt more money had been found and the police had kept it. He relaxed his attitude.

"However, just as you wish. I'll have them brought up to the visitors room. Follow me please."

The meeting provided no further information except that he had been walking south to Altamira when they had attacked him. They said he had told them of a wife waiting at one of the hotels.

Chirlo signed the receipt for his money and effects as 'Pedro

Artega', thanked the police officer for his efforts and presented him with a thousand dollars as a reward for his integrity. Ortona bowed them all the way out to the parking compound and saluted smartly as they drove off.

"We are getting closer, Pedro Artega," the doctor said, after they had left the outskirts of the city.

Chirlo looked up startled, then smiled apologetically.

"I am sorry, Don Luis. I couldn't sign myself as Chirlo."

"You honor my name, my boy. What is troubling you?"

"I was thinking about this watch. It is something a ship's officer might use. Do you think it is possible I might have fallen overboard from some vessel going into Tampico?"

"Or been thrown overboard, or trying to escape from something; disappear with your fifty thousand dollars. How did you know the amount?"

"I don't know that I did. Maybe it seemed logical that seven peasants would only have time to spend eighteen thousand dollars in two months. A good guess."

"*If* it was a guess," Artega observed. They drove on in silence until they were back into Tampico.

"Now that you have money, my boy, what do you plan to do with yourself?"

"I don't know," Chirlo admitted frankly. "You have been very kind, but I think it is time I left. Perhaps go to Mexico City. I don't want to overstay my visit."

The doctor pulled up for a stoplight. "Nonsense. You are like a breath of fresh air around the house. Felina adores you, but then you know that." He glanced at him sideways, speculatively for a moment. "I think you should stay here with us. This is where your memory left you. Everything we have learned has been discovered here. With patience, who knows, maybe the rest of your mystery can be solved. I'm sure you will find nothing in Mexico City."

He drove through the intersection weaving about the traffic. Chirlo stiffened in the seat beside him as he missed a noisy smoking diesel bus by inches, yet managed to brush the rumps of two clinging passengers, who hurled epithets at the black Mercedes as it passed.

"Jesus. Don Luis! You're a terrible driver!"

The doctor chuckled. "Felina and Ruis have told me the same thing. You are in good company, my boy."

To occupy his time and mind, and preserve his sense of independence, the doctor hired him as private secretary when he discovered Chirlo was a fast, accurate typist, both in Spanish and

English. His quick keen mind often changed the shading of words the doctor dicated in his official correspondence, so the old President's letters began depicting a tough bantam rooster, prepared to fight his way back into the chicken coop, instead of a tired old cock in exile, standing on his Mexican perch. Artega accepted the changes without comment. The results of Chirlo's hardening the doctor's written attitudes in the weekly column of *El Diario*, the Republic's largest newspaper, were swift. The column, sent weekly from Tampico to Cosecha Rica, regularly became lost in the mails. The comments of *El Raposo*, 'the Fox,' the pseudonym Artega used, were no longer welcome by Colonel Guererro's censors. The loss of this weekly platform to his people was a bitter blow and he confronted Chirlo with the responsibility. Chirlo shrugged.

"I disagree, Don Luis. You have lost nothing. Your weekly columns were tolerated in the past because they said nothing. When you started saying something worthwhile, Guererro stopped it."

To make matters worse, Ruis and Felina agreed with their houseguest. The thought that the weekly paragraphs he had been sending from Mexico over the years to his homeland were regarded as rubbish by everyone except himself, cut him deeply and he sulked for several days. Ruis and Chirlo kept up the correspondence with his supporters in Cosecha Rica. The time for promised elections in the country had long passed. It was obvious Guererro had no intention of relinquishing power until he was overthrown or died. The country, meanwhile, was ruled by Presidential decree.

Every evening during dinner, they all played a guessing game the doctor had devised to jog Chirlo's vacant memory. Each would say a word to which their guest was supposed to reply with the first word which came into his head. They had played the game for months, learning all sorts of odd things about the man, but nothing that provided a clue to his identity. The game stopped suddenly one evening while they were drinking their coffee after the meal.

Felina's turn had come again.

"Let me see now. I have a word for you. Airplane!"

"Crashed!" The reply was instantaneous. Then, Chirlo's face had turned grey and he started to shake uncontrollably until he had to leave the table and lie down. Artega followed him to his room, intensely curious about the reaction to his daughter's question. He sat beside the big man on the bed as the shaking subsided.

"It was close to the surface, wasn't it?"

Chirlo nodded.

"Did you remember?"

"Almost, but something blocked it out," he whispered.

"Counter-reaction from your subconscious, my boy. Your mind doesn't want you to remember. Something has happened that your mind thinks is too terrible to remember. We will stop playing the game." He looked at him compassionately, his own feelings over the loss of the weekly column forgotten.

"Sleep now, my boy." He waited until Chirlo had closed his eyes before leaving.

As he started down the stairs, he realized for the first time how much the young man meant to him. *He is the son I never had.*

Felina and Ruis were standing in the hall as he came down.

"Is he all right, Papa?"

"He is sleeping now. He had a shock." He shook his head as they followed him into the library. "I don't think our guest will ever recover his memory. The loss is, I think, permanent."

"What will happen to him now?" Ruis asked.

"He needs a name, an identity." He looked at his daughter, smiling. "Do you think you could stand having him as your brother, if I adopted him?"

"Maybe he doesn't want to be adopted, Luis," Ruis protested.

"Nonsense. He needs an identity to survive—to get a passport."

Felina eyed her father. "You sound as if you have plans for our Pedro."

Artega poured a small Kahlua from the liquor cabinet and sat down in one of the soft leather chairs. With a great deal of ceremony, he lit a cigar and sipped the liqueur.

"I have decided that young Pedro Artega is going to be our emissary to Cosecha Rica. He will be our passport back to power."

He held up his hand imperiously as Ruis started to interrupt.

"Our problem is simple. Neither you nor I can set foot in the country without being arrested. Felina could go—but who would believe a girl in politics? What could she do, Ruis?"

Ruis was silent. Artega puffed at his cigar reflectively.

"I have given this matter a great deal of thought. We need a physical presence in Cosecha Rica to be our eyes and ears—later, our voice. On the other hand, our Chirlo needs an identity, a purpose to his life. My plan fulfills both needs. I propose to give him an intensive study on the history of our nation, then send him into the country as a geologist from Mexico on a field exploration trip for minerals. We can set up a cover company in Mexico City in case Guererro checks him out. I want him to visit all our supporters, but I don't want any of them to know who he is until we discover whether we have supporters, or merely avid political theorists. Fair weather socialists or bad weather capitalists."

"But Father, how do you know he will agree to go?"

"More important, Luis, what are his politics."

Artega smiled at them contentedly. "He will agree to go because he is young, adventurous and has nothing else to do. Most of all he is curious because his memory is blank. Not just curious about himself, but about everything. I have watched him these past months, soaking up knowledge like an Aegean sponge, right here in this room. But unlike our minds, with lifetimes of memories crowding the cranial space, his mind is as open to knowledge as a child, with the same capacity for retention. It is an interesting phenomena. I should write a paper on the subject," he added as the professional medical mind momentarily took over from the trend of political thought.

"Do you know, the other day he not only told me Hobart was the capital of Tasmania, but he knew the principal streets, monuments and industries in the town as well. I tell you he has memorized the Encyclopedia! Amazing. Hobart, Tasmania. I didn't know that."

"Where is Tasmania?" Felina inquired.

"An island off the south coast of Australia, child," the doctor told her reprovingly. He polished off his liqueur.

"As for his politics, I think for the moment he is apolitical. A true pyrrhonist, uncontaminated by any religious or political beliefs. Religion and politics are governed by man's environment. The patterns are established in youth when the developing mind is most influenced by adults. Chirlo is already an adult and now can be influenced only by his own reason or logic—by what he sees as truth, not what some misguided parent has told him when he was a boy. I really should write a paper on this."

He puffed the cigar, his eyes alight at the prospects ahead. After a long silence, Ruis spoke up.

"You might be right, Luis. It could be that he is the only way any of us will be able to go home."

His crash course on the Republic of Cosecha Rica took Chirlo three months to complete. Equipped with a new Mexican passport, legally identifying him as Pedro Artega de Miranda, he flew into Panama on Pan Am direct from Mexico City. He transferred onto a tired C47 for the trip into Cosecha Rica. Four hours later he joined the incoming passengers shuffling through *Sanidad*, *Migracion*, *Aduana*, at the decaying, fly-blown airport terminal in Bahia Blanca, the coastal city of the Republic. His passport was stamped *Entrada* without comment by a bloated quasi-military official and he was waved on to a group of shouting taxi drivers standing outside the building. Chirlo ignored the babbling sales appeals and selected the best looking vehicle among the junks parked along the road and climbed in the back seat. The owner detached himself from the mob of drivers and slid into the front with a grin.

"To San Ramon, Senor?"

"To San Ramon," Chirlo confirmed.

"Welcome to Cosecha Rica," the driver said as he pulled out of the line of parked cars.

The city of San Ramon was typical of most urban centers founded by the conquistadores. Nestled among mountain foothills that formed the first vertebrae of the Andean spine, it funneled the cool air off the slopes behind the city into the urban sprawl that covered the surrounding hills. Originally, it had developed as a silver mine, dedicated to the glory of God, and its patron saint, San Ramon. The Spaniards had looted the riches of the mountains with the unwilling help of the indigenous native population, a mixture of Mayan and Petana Indians. They died like flies under the Spanish overlords, filling the insatiable demands of bullion by the treasure ships that sailed out of Panama each year for Cadiz. At length, the wealth of the mountains had died along with most of the native population, but the city remained peopled by the racial mixture who had fought the mountains for its riches. There were no more Indians now, just as there were no more Spaniards. There was a miscegenation of people calling themselves Cosecha Ricans. When Simon Bolivar, the architect of dissolution for the Spanish Americas, passed through the area and announced to the startled inhabitants they were now an independent nation, without a name, they selected Cosecha Rica. A democratic republic in the early part of the nineteenth century was a very rich harvest indeed. The name had remained, but the tiny undemocratic country had averaged one government every year since Bolivar had ridden off into the pages of history.

The cool hills sloped down to a rich, tropical, fertile coastal plain and the seaport of Bahia Blanca, where the Republic's international airport was located. Once the trip from the coast over the hills to the silver mines above San Ramon took two weeks by pack mule. Now the sixty-mile drive, with its split S-turns over a rough graveled road, took less than four hours. Progress. The million and a half inhabitants had entered the twentieth century.

"Why hasn't someone paved this road?" Chirlo inquired, as the taxi sliced through a cloud of dust, trailed by an antique diesel bus that passed them, swaying down the first hills to the coast. The driver shifted into second gear for the long climb.

"Part of it was paved by our last President. He had promised to pave the rest at twenty-five kilometers a year." He shrugged. "But then we had another revolution."

"The new President likes dusty roads?"

"Quien Sabe, Senor? Who can tell what Colonel Guererro likes?"

They drove the rest of the way in silence.

October 17, 1961

My Dear Don Luis:

I am having this letter mailed in Panama by a friend. I think it is best that all correspondence to you should be done in this fashion. I apologize for the long silence, but until I had something to say, there was little point in putting a lot of irrelevant thought to paper.

The situation here is catastrophic. It is difficult to imagine any place with a worse political climate for the conduct of free speech, assembly or thought. The country is now divided into three distinct ruling cliques comprising less than 5% of the population.

The first clique is the ruling political group headed of course by Guererro and his cutthroats, backed by the military. Next in line are the local and foreign owners of industry, commerce and agriculture, who support the government completely. Finally, there is the middle class intelligentsia, composed of doctors, lawyers and professional men. The faceless 95% of the population, who suffer the brunt of the misery, are the illiterate or barely literate peons that fill the towns and villages with a sense of hopeless despair. The only vocal or visible disagreements to disturb this nightmare of status quo are the students at the University of San Ramon and the Agricultural College at Bahia Blanca. Their demonstrations and occasional melees with police are tolerated because their parents belong to one of the ruling cliques. When the situation gets too far out of hand, as it does occasionally, Guererro selects two or three students whose families are outside the cliques and arrests them as communists. The Tigre Fortress is filled with these young men, some of whom have been there without trial for years.

The U.S. influence is everywhere and it is obvious to the most casual observer that the American government has given full approval to the way the political affairs of the country are conducted. The army is equipped with U.S. weapons and material. Its officers and men are trained at the U.S. Jungle Warfare School in Panama. The air force is equipped with giveaway American aircraft, including seven F80 jet fighters recently arrived from Texas. The pilots and mechanics are trained in San Antonio or Corpus Christi. There are no less than 125 American personnel at the huge new U.S. Embassy in San Ramon.

Towering over this charade of democracy sits fat Guererro, safe and secure. The vigilant fascist sniffing the winds for communism. Terror, rage, pillage, expropriation, assault and murder. Nothing is for greed, fear or revenge—just an endless fight against the communists. One would think the hills were filled with an army of front line Russian troops poised and waiting. So far I haven't met a communist, only a lot of staunch but frightened nationalists, who would welcome a change from this hyprocrisy of the past years, but are powerless to instigate any action necessary for change. These are your faithful supporters. They are neither faithful nor supportive of anything except their own skins. Support must come from the people, not the cliques. The cliques have too much to lose. The people have nothing to lose.

My kindest regards to Felina and Ruis.

Chirlo

January 12, 1962

Dear Don Luis:

I disagree with your viewpoint concerning the advisability of identifying me to your so-called supporters. As I mentioned in my last three letters, the official position of the government is that the Artega faction is communist. You are a communist. By association, that makes me a communist. I know it is difficult to understand, but a subtle brain-washing has taken place over the past five years. American aid to Guererro is related directly to the communist threat. The bigger the threat, the bigger the aid. Communism has now reached proportions of an imminent and continuous threat to the country. Any discontent with government is branded as communist influenced. I know it is hard to understand, but this is a fairyland, where fantasy rules as fact. Please do not blow my cover. I trust no one—particularly your loyal supporters.

Tell Felina my beard is fully grown now. I look like Machiavelli, but the scar has vanished behind the fur.

Regards,
Chirlo

July 8, 1962
Don Luis:

Do not *send Felina down here. It is too dangerous. I have nearly completed my work and should be able to return to Mexico next month. I want you to arrange a trip for me to Cuba. I will explain my plan when I return.*

Chirlo

Felina Artega arrived at Bahia Blanca on July 27, dressed as a nun with a Mexican passport made out in the name of Sister Theresa Tomez from the Mission of Angels near Torreon. Chirlo met her at the airport. He watched as she came out of the terminal with an elderly priest. The mob of taxi drivers parted in front of them with respectful acknowledgement to the cloth. A car drew up to the cassocked couple. Felina caught Chirlo's eye as she ducked into the back seat. He started up the Land Rover, and followed the black Chevrolet out of the terminal onto the main road to San Ramon. After a few miles driving across the flat coastal plain, the Chevy slowed to a stop. Felina climbed out with her suitcase and waved as the car drove off. She was wearing Levis and a white shirt, open at the neck. Chirlo rolled the Land Rover up to where she was standing on the road with her thumb stuck out. He had forgotten how beautiful she was.

"Hello, sister." He gave his crooked smile.

"Hello, brother Pedro." She climbed into the bucket seat beside him with a happy grin. He turned the vehicle around and headed back towards the coast.

"Who was the priest?"

"Father Francisco. We met on the plane. He was visiting his Bishop in Panama. He thought I had taken my vows!" She laughed.

"Will he talk?"

"No. I explained the situation to him. He baptized me. He hates Guererro too."

"But approves of using the Church as a disguise for your intrigues."

Felina looked at him quizzically. "My we are touchy, aren't we? Taking me from the airport was his idea, not mine, Pedro. What's wrong?"

"You shouldn't have come. I told your father not to send you."

They drove in silence a few minutes until the gravel changed to pavement near the airport.

"Did anyone else recognize you?"

"No. No one. Where are we going?"

"Tippitaca. I have a place there."

"Tippitaca? But that's miles away, near the border!"

"It may be miles away, but it's the center of everything I am doing in Cosecha Rica."

"Can we stop in Bahia Blanca? I'm hungry. They gave us dried sandwiches on the plane."

They parked in front of the Hotel D'Oro and went into the dining room. It was mid-afternoon so the tables were deserted. The proprietor appeared.

"Chirlo! It is good to see you again. Any luck yet?"

He handed out menus. Chirlo winked, nodding towards Felina.

"Things are picking up, Gomez." Everyone laughed.

They ordered the special fish dinner and two bottles of Taurus Beer. Gomez bustled away to the kitchen after uncapping the bottles.

"Why did you come?" Chirlo asked quietly.

The ceiling fans made a soft whishing sound as they stirred the leaden air above the tables. The blades turned at different speeds, giving a throbbing sound from the lack of synchronization. It reminded Chirlo of airplane propellors. He didn't know why.

"Father has been worried you are heading in the wrong direction; remember it's his country."

Chirlo said nothing.

"The suggestion that you should go to Cuba upset him. He felt you might be planning on resorting to violence! That would make us no better than Guererro and his butchers!"

"And that would soil his conscience?"

"Something like that. He is a man of high principles."

"So is Guererro. Only his are different. His principles worked. Your father's didn't."

"That's not fair, Pedro."

"Reality seldom is." He swigged the bottle of Taurus.

"What is reality?" she countered archly.

Chirlo looked at her with sympathy. "Reality, Felina," he said softly, "is Guererro's army of 20,000 trained soldiers. Reality is his 38-plane air force. Reality is his control of the radio stations, the newspapers, the airlines, the railway, the shipping and the capital of this country. Reality is that the U.S. government supports him. Finally, my beautiful sister, reality is that your father and Ruis are a pair of dewy-eyed idealists trying to dream their way back into power."

Gomez arrived with two steaming plates of food.

"Fresh caught this morning by my son-in-law," he announced proudly. He did not notice that the beautiful woman's eyes were filled with tears.

"*Boonapetit!*" Gomez's French was terrible. The fish was superb.

It was after dark when they drove into the village of Tippitaca. Chirlo parked in front of a white adobe house near the end of the cobblestone street leading out of the village to the border. Although the frontier lay less than two miles beyond the settlement, there was little traffic on the main road to or from the sister republic. Occasionally a caravan of Airstream trailers towed by new Cadillacs passed through the village; a spillover of elderly American tourists traveling the Pan American Highway on the Pacific Coast who had decided on the adventure of the Atlantic Road to Panama, instead of the beautifully paved Pacific Highway. They never stopped in Tippitaca and never returned after driving the tortuous uneven road. There was a border office shack, where the road crossed the frontier and a swinging barrier pole dividing the two republics. It was seldom manned by either country, and the barrier was perpetually raised so as not to block the road, in case there happened to be some traffic.

"We will spend the night here," he announced, and climbed out of the Land Rover. Felina followed him to the door of the adobe, carrying her suitcase. Inside they were greeted by a teenage smile in the white light of a hissing Coleman lamp hanging in the center of the vestibule.

"Buenos noches, Don Pedro, Senora." She curtsied politely to Felina, then took her case.

"Hello, Anita. This is Senorita Felina. She will be staying with us for a while. Is Paco back yet?"

"No, Senor." She stood uncertainly in the white light.

"Give my room to the Senorita. I'll sleep with Paco, or you." He grinned at her. She giggled, her black eyes sparkling. Felina followed the girl into the small open courtyard outside the room. They walked around the quadrangle to the bedrooms at the rear of the square. A large saumon tree, its branches stretching to the top of the surrounding red tiled roofs, filled the yard with a sound of rustling leaves. Chirlo sat down at the table under a tree and waited for Felina to reappear.

"It's not Tampico—but it's home," he said as she sat down at the table. "The water comes from the pump over there." He jerked his thumb to the corner of the yard. "The shower is that can hanging on the pole beside the pump. When you want to bathe, Anita will connect the pump hose to the can and swing the handle for you. It's not very private, I'm afraid, and the water is lukewarm," he added apologetically. "The toilet is next to your room. I connected it to a septic tank when I first moved in. You have to use a pail of water to make it flush."

"As you said, it's not Tampico." She smiled.

Chirlo sighed. "Sorry I upset you back there. I've become so involved here I suppose I can't see anyone else's point of view but my own. When I came to Cosecha Rica I came with no preconceptions. I traveled the length and breadth of the land. I met the people, the real people and the pretenders. I know now its industrial potential, resources, agriculture and its problems. Now I love this country and its people and I know I can help them. I have no quarrel with your father in ridding ourselves of Guererro. We are both agreed on that point. It's a matter of method. Don Luis' will not work, mine will."

She laid a soft hand on his arm. "You haven't tried my father's method, Pedro. How do you know it won't work?"

Her hand felt cool. Chirlo shook his head. "I haven't tried my method either, but I know it will."

"Tell me your method."

He told her, slowly at first, testing her reactions, then speaking rapidly, he outlined the complete plan for taking over the Republic of Cosecha Rica. It was midnight by the time he had finished. Felina was silent.

"Well?" Chirlo demanded.

"Many people would die. There would be reprisals."

"I know. Nothing worthwhile comes easy." He stared at her.

"I cannot disagree with you, Pedro. I think you are probably right. But father would never approve."

"It can be done without him."

"You would do that?"

"No, I suppose not." He shook his head. "What is the alternative?"

"Let us try it his way first. If that fails, and I'm not sure it will, then we will try your method. Agreed?"

She smiled at him. Chirlo looked into her eyes. He didn't answer. After a few moments she stood up.

"I need a shower after that drive. Will you pump for me?"

She walked over to the corner of the yard and began shedding her clothes. Chirlo followed and connected the hose onto the pump, hanging the other end into the perforated tin on the pole. He began to work the handle. The water rained down from the can. Felina stepped under the stream and began soaping her body slowly. It was the first time Chirlo had seen her naked. Her body was magnificent. As she rubbed the soap on her breasts he felt his manhood rise and an aching in his groin. She rubbed the soap between her legs, then turned her bottom to him and bent over, spreading her cheeks to allow the soap to wash away. He could see the pink lips of her vulva shining in the moonlight. Felina straightened up and stepped from under the can. Chirlo stopped pumping.

"If you like, I'll pump for you."

She stood like a dripping wood nymph under the saumon tree, her eyes glistening with desire.

He undressed quickly and stepped under the stream of water, soaping himself. The flow of water stopped as Felina walked over to him and took the bar from his hands. Slowly she began soaping his crotch, rubbing her fingers around his testes and pulling her soapy hands back and forth along his erection. Chirlo groaned with pleasure as he neared the swelling orgasm. She stopped suddenly and returned to the pump. The water began to flow from the can again.

When the soap was rinsed away he turned to Felina and pulled her into his arms. Their wet bodies compressed in the moonlight.

"Oh, Pedro, I have waited so long," she whispered.

As he carried her across the yard to the bedroom he could hear Anita giggling at them from the shadows.

The Land Rover raised a rooster-tail of white dust as it sped down the narrow road towards the finca.

"I bought the farm last fall from a lawyer in San Ramon," he explained.

They had been driving inland from Tippitaca for nearly an hour, paralleling the border. The country was open land, some of it planted in young cotton. The farms, which appeared periodically on either side, were small and well-tended.

"This lawyer inherited the land years ago and did nothing with it after his farming relation left it to him. It has a decent hacienda, a good road and lots of water. I've put a complete plumbing system into the house," he added, smiling at her.

"I didn't know you were a farmer, Pedro."

"Or a lover, until last night."

They both laughed. "Actually, the Agricultural College in Bahia Blanca provided me with everything I had to know. Dr. Thompson is attached to the College by the United Nations. He's a South African expert in cotton. We have become good friends."

They slowed for a gate at the end of the road. Felina jumped out and opened it as Chirlo drove through, then stopped to wait as she closed the gate. A huge field of young cotton stretched before them to the edge of the foothills into the mountains. In the center of the field a group of farm buildings were visible, their metal-clad siding reflecting a polished silver in the morning sun. In the midst of the building cluster stood the main house of the hacienda, a one-story rectangle sitting atop a group of poles, twenty feet above the ground. They drove up to the house and parked under it between a row of poles. A cluster of smiling peons came over from the sheds to greet them.

"Hola, Paco!" Chirlo called to a thickset man who detached himself from the group.

He nodded to Chirlo, then bowed to Felina. "Welcome to the Finca Esperanza, Senorita Artega."

"Esperanza?" Felina repeated.

Paco shrugged. "We all have hope, Senorita."

They went up the wood steps to the house. Paco followed them inside. The rest of the assembly drifted back to work. Felina gazed out the windows opening on all sides to the land and the dry green mountains beyond the nearby hills.

"The border is just over there where the cotton ends." Chirlo pointed.

"Pedro, it's enormous!"

"Thirty-two hundred hectares altogether. We have only planted cotton in five hundred though. If the rains are kind in September we may be able to double that next year, eh Paco?"

"Con Esperanza, Don Pedro," Paco replied gravely.

A young girl came up the steps with a jug of coffee, set three mugs on the table and left. They sat down.

"How are you coming with the airstrip?" Chirlo asked.

"It goes slowly, but it will be ready in time. We will plant the grass next week. I wish we had a grader. The work takes so long with shovels. The insecticide arrived yesterday. I piled the barrels by the airstrip near the watertower. The gasoline too."

"Good. I spoke to the fumigation company at Bahia Blanca yesterday. They promised the airplane for the first spraying on September 4. I may not be here, so you will have to look after it."

"You will be in Mexico so long?"

"I am not going to Mexico. I am going to San Ramon."

Paco sipped at the mug, his dark eyes studying Chirlo. "The plan has changed?"

"Not changed, postponed."

"My father wants to try his way first, Paco," Felina interrupted. "If that doesn't work, we'll do it Pedro's way."

"I see."

"Assuming we are still alive after the first attempt fails," Chirlo added.

The first political meeting at the Tienda Ramada in San Ramon ended in disaster before it started. Chirlo and Felina were kept imprisoned a week as a lesson to troublemakers. Upon release they learned that freedom had come as a direct result of Father Francisco's efforts in confronting Colonel Guererro. The newspapers and radio blared of Dr. Artega's new communist conspiracy, nipped in the bud by the democratic forces of Guererro's regime. Most annoying were the two bloodhounds they picked up as they left El Tigre prison. The pair of security agents made no attempt to keep in the shadows and followed them everywhere. They waited a month, then tried to hold another meeting at the country club, arranged through the lawyer from whom Chirlo had purchased the finca. It was quite a spread: a buffet supper laid out across the table in the big lounge of the club, together with a visiting band from Mexico City hired for the occasion. Ten minutes before the meal ended, when Chirlo was supposed to speak, a convoy of jeeps from the Securidad Publica swarmed into the parking area outside the rambling building, spilling out blue-helmeted soldiers, who promptly surrounded the place at gunpoint. Again, Chirlo and Felina were led away. This time they were taken back to their hotel and with gentle courtesy dropped at the front door.

During December Holy Week, they tried again at a gathering of industrial workers. The Society of Trabajadores was the closest thing to a labor union permitted by Guererro's government. When moans of discontent became too loud at the society's weekly meetings the leaders would vanish mysteriously the following day. The official explanation for these disappearances was always the same: urgent family or business matters abroad, requiring immediate attention. No one returned from these foreign trips. With the utmost secrecy Chirlo arranged to address the members after their parade in Constitution Park. He actually got to say the first few sentences of his prepared text before gunfire broke up the thousand-odd listeners in the park, sending them fleeing through the night, dispersing into the narrow streets around the square, running for home. No one was injured when the firing stopped. Chirlo and Felina were alone on the raised bandshell in the middle of the park when Captain Ornez drew up again in his blue jeep and offered to drive them back to their hotel across the street.

"Gracias, Captain, but we prefer to walk."

Ornez shook his head as Chirlo and Felina climbed down from the bandstand.

"When will you learn, Chirlo? There aren't going to be any meetings. Why don't you go back to Mexico?" He sounded resigned.

He watched them walk back to the hotel. As he lit a cheroot he noticed they were holding hands. A third figure joined them when they crossed the street. In the glare of the headlights from one of the machine-gun mounted jeeps he could see the black robes of the third figure.

"A priest?" he said aloud. He jumped into his vehicle, signaling the driver. *Major Cadalso will be interested to hear about the priest*, he thought as they drove over the sidewalk leading out of the park.

"I cannot attack the Church, Cadalso! Are you sure they plan a meeting here?" Guererro's brow furrowed with anger.

"Positive, Colonel. January 16 at 8:00 p.m. My informant has never been wrong. He will attend this meeting too."

Guererro drummed his fingers on the table; the stacatto pierced the silence in the large chamber.

"Fucking priests," he muttered. "This Chirlo and his whore are exhausting my patience." He continued drumming on the table top.

"If I might offer a suggestion, Colonel." He paused, uncertain.

"Go on man, don't stand there like a dummy!"

"You could allow this meeting to proceed, then arrest everyone as they come out of the church, including the priest. Then a stern letter to the Bishop of Panama complaining about the church being used for communist revolutionaries and asking if the bishop approves such action."

Guererro smiled, his fat face creasing with pleasure.

"Putting the bishop on the defensive immediately. Good. Go on!"

"You could release the priest, as a gesture of goodwill to the bishop, on the understanding he be reprimanded severely. Later, release those arrested, but keep Chirlo and the girl, pending a full investigation."

"During which they try to escape and are shot by an alert guard who didn't know who they were. I like it, Cadalso. What about your informant? Can he take three weeks in El Tigre?"

"Colonel, he is a patriot!" the thin major confirmed.

"All right, I'll leave everything in your capable hands. Be sure you don't make the opportunity for escape too obvious. Chirlo is no fool."

"I plan on using the priest."

Guererro roared with laughter as Cadalso bowed himself out of the room.

Father Francisco started to relax. The meeting was over and no one had invaded the sancity of his cathedral. Chirlo had held them spellbound for two hours. He had answered their questions frankly, directly, making no concessions to the reality of their situation. He had made a deep impression on his listeners.

Now the meeting had broken into small discussion groups as everyone prepared to leave. They were shaking hands with Chirlo and Felina, a few of the older men patting Chirlo's broad back, the younger ones patting Felina. The first of the groups nodded to Father Francisco as they passed into the nave, heading for the front door. When the door opened a spotlight flooded through the opening, filling the far end of the cathedral with light. A crisp mechanical voice rode the beam from a bullhorn outside in the street.

"Father Francisco! This is Major Cadalso of the Securidad Publica. You and your communist friends are under arrest. Do not attempt to escape. The church is surrounded. Please come out with your hands up. Now!"

The tinny voice went silent. The light remained.

The frightened faces grouped around Father Francisco seeking guidance.

"I think, Father, we should all join Major Cadalso with our hands up," Chirlo said pleasantly, and taking Felina's arm, sauntered down the nave into the light and through the open door. The others followed.

Outside the church the street was filled with trucks and soldiers. They were herded into three canvas-covered army vehicles. Captain Ornez looked up at Chirlo and Felina as the soldiers slammed the tailgate on their truck.

"You'll never learn, Chirlo, will you?" he said sadly from the pavement.

Chirlo smiled. "On the contrary, Captain. I have learned a great deal."

Ornez waved the armed soldiers into the back of the truck and strode back to his jeep. The convoy moved off through the deserted streets to El Tigre Fortress.

Captain Bermudez was a sadist. A thin cadaverous man with a drooping mustache, slightly wall-eyed, he loved the feeling of inflicting pain on others to a point of sexual gratification. Everyone in El Tigre feared Bermudez and his cronies from the prison director to the lowest orderly. Inmates were terrified of the slight man with the wide mad eyes. Major Cadalso loathed him, but knew such men as Bermudez were necessary in any well-run prison.

"The priest and the others are not to be touched. Is that clear?"

Bermudez nodded. "And the Chirlo and his woman?" His eyes glittered.

"They are yours, Captain. But do not cripple or blind them. They must be strong enough to escape, or Colonel Guererro will be very unhappy. Do you understand?"

"Si, Major Cadalso, perfectly." Bermudez felt a stirring in his loins.

"Keep them isolated from the others." The major left Bermudez' small office, his nose wrinkling in disgust at the open lust on the captain's hollow face.

Bermudez lit a cigar and studied the glowing end, his brain running hot with anticipation of the night ahead. He shouted through the closed door.

"Pena!"

The door flew open and Sgt. Pena crashed to attention, his shoulders bulging the material of his uniform jacket.

"Captain."

"Take the girl and the big one to the conference room. Strip them and hang them—the man on the barbecue pole—the girl by the ankles. Use the shackle chain on the woman—I want her legs spread apart." He licked his lips.

"Si, Captain." Pena saluted and left.

Bermudez sat quietly, sucking on his cigar another ten minutes, savoring the anticipation, then stood up and opened the zipper to his breeches. He reached in his desk and removed a condom from the pencil tray and slipped it over his erection. He zipped the fly then paused to adjust his hard member, laying it flat against his belly, patting the barely noticeable swell in his pants to a vertical position. Bermudez was a fastidious officer. He left his office and descended the stone steps to the *conference room.*

Pena stood up as he entered the damp, grey stone room. Four soldiers paused in their work until Bermudez waved to them. Chirlo was hanging by his knees, his wrists tied to his ankles. He glared at the thin captain. The soldiers finished manacling Felina's wrists to the floor chains and stood back. She hung upside down, her legs spread in a wide *V* by the ankle shackles suspended from the ceiling. Bermudez walked over and peered at her black venus mound.

"Too much hair to see properly. Match!"

He snapped his fingers. One of the soldiers produced a book of matches. Bermudez lit one and touched it to the base of the pubic hair. Felina screamed as the flames consumed the hair in an instant, filling the room with an acrid odor. He glanced at Chirlo for a reaction. There was only the same malevolent stare. Bermudez shrugged and lit another match. He touched the flame to Chirlo's groin. There was a flash of flame as the hair on his legs, arms and chest were consumed, in the brief holocaust, Chirlo grunted with pain, but said nothing. Bermudez was disappointed.

"Perhaps you would like to fuck?" He waited for a reply. There was none.

"We have the facilities." He snapped his fingers at Pena who rolled a small steel cabinet across the floor. The top was covered with wires attached to metal dildos and alligator clips. He picked a dildo off the tray and drove it into Chirlo's rectum, then snapped one of the alligator clips onto the head of Chirlo's penis. Chirlo gasped with pain. Bermudez was delighted.

He repeated the operation on Felina, driving one dildo into her rectum, the other deep into her vagina. She whimpered, then screamed in agony as he knelt and clipped the alligators to her nipples.

"Comfy?" Bermudez inquired. He felt his erection swelling. "You're going to love this, I promise you."

He flipped on the current switch beside the cabinet and began turning the dial. Felina screamed as the electrical shocks thudded into her body. Chirlo groaned. Bermudez' eyes danced with pleasure while he watched them writhe in agony. Finally, his breath came in short gasps; the orgasm began flooding into the condom, his knees buckled, his eyes glazed crazily as his sperm pumped into the rubber. He sighed, relaxing, and switched off the machine.

"They're all yours, Pena—no damage now!" Fuck them both till they gurgle." He smiled benevolently at the officers, then went back to his office.

The days floated into weeks, the weeks into months. The visits to the conference room became less frequent as their physical appearance deteriorated. Finally, when the soldiers lost interest in the two human wrecks, they were left alone. Felina lost track of time when she missed her second period and knew she was pregnant by one of the soldiers.

Near the end of the fourth month, shortly after the noon meal of rice and beans, a guard ushered Father Francisco into Chirlo's dark, smelly cell and closed the door. He was sitting on a dirty mattress on the floor.

"Hello, Padre. Are you here for the last rites?" He gave the priest his lopsided grin.

"My son, what have they done to you?" he asked in horror. Chirlo struggled to his feet, adjusting the ragged clothing.

"Sgt. Pena tried to fuck me to death. How is Felina?"

Father Francisco winced, then came forward and put his arms around Chirlo's skinny frame. The body odor was overpowering.

"I have not seen her yet."

He slipped a leather-covered sap into Chirlo's hands from beneath his robes together with a long stiletto, then backed away from the smelly body.

"Your escape has been arranged by one of the guards. Tonight, after the evening meal, your cell door will be left open for a half hour—no more. Felina is directly above you on the next level. Her door will be left open too. Remember, a half hour, no more."

"Who is the guard?"

"His name is Rolando; he is a friend."

"One of Bermudez' men?"

"Yes. But he is not like the others," the priest explained.

"I'll bet. It's a trap, Padre. We are supposed to try and escape so they can shoot us." Chirlo sat down on the mattress, slipping the knife and sap under it.

"How can you know that?"

"Logic. Is Bermudez up in his office now?"

"Yes, with Sgt. Pena."

Chirlo smiled. "Good, then we'll leave now. Call the guard."

Father Francisco looked uncertainly at the door a moment, then nodded. Chirlo moved over beside the door, flattening himself against the wall. Father Francisco called the guard. A pair of eyes peered through the small barred inspection panel.

"Listo, Padre?" He had a young, stupid face.

"Ready to go, my son," the priest acknowledged.

As the key turned in the lock, Chirlo pushed the old man aside and yanked the door open. The guard followed his attached keys into the cell, his eyes wide with surprise. Chirlo clamped his fingers into the man's windpipe and yanked the rifle off his shoulder. It clattered onto the stone floor. He spun the guard against his chest, changed arm positions quickly and broke the man's neck. The snap sounded like someone chewing peanut brittle. He let the body slide to the floor, then closed the door. Swiftly, he stripped the dead man's outergarments and boots. He handed them to the priest along with the rifle and helmet.

"Let's go get Felina."

Chirlo's chest was heaving from the unaccustomed exertion. He picked the cell keys off the floor, removed the sap and knife from under the mattress and looked out into the corridor. It was deserted.

They found Felina's cell on the second level and opened the door. She was lying on her mattress. She looked disgusting.

"Pedro! Padre!"

Chirlo put his finger to his lips.

"Shh. Put these on. Tuck your hair into the helmet."

She stripped her rags quickly and donned the guard's uniform. Father Francisco averted his eyes from her pathetic bony nudity.

"Ready," she announced and followed Chirlo and the priest into the corridor. They crept up the steps to the main floor single file. The door to Sgt. Pena's office was open. A radio was playing a Lucho Gatica love song. Chirlo motioned to Father Francisco, whispering, "Stand in the doorway and ask Pena to come out for a talk about his plan to shoot us."

He followed the priest to the door, crouching beside it, the stiletto between his teeth, the sap in his hand.

"Sgt. Pena! Why are you using me to set up your murders?"

Chirlo heard the big man jump up from his chair and start for the open door.

"Why Padre, what gave you an idea like. . . ." The lead sap hit Pena in the temple, imbedding itself. Chirlo tried to hold the lifeless corpse, but crashed to the floor under its weight.

"Pena!" Bermudez called from the inner office.

Chirlo scrambled from under Pena's body and grabbed the .45 automatic from its holster. Felina joined them at the door.

"Drag him inside and close the door. Then undress him. I'll look after Bermudez," he whispered.

"Pena! Goddamnit!"

Chirlo kicked open the door to Bermudez' office and ran in, the

.45 leveled at the captain's face.

"Keep your hands on the desk!" he hissed.

The eyes behind the desk went wide with fear. "Listen Chirlo, I . . . ."

"Shut up! We're leaving El Tigre and you're coming with us. Now pick up that phone and order your car. If you say anything else, I'll blow your head off."

The thin Captain obeyed, his voice shaking. Felina came into the room, holding the rifle.

"Keep him covered while I dress." He went back to Pena's office and sent the priest to join Felina. They watched the captain in silence. Then the door opened and Chirlo reappeared, dressed in the Sergeant's uniform and carrying a white basket.

"Let's go!" He handed the basket to Bermudez, removing his pistol as he stood up.

"You carry this—it will keep your hands where I can see them. Lead the way, Bermudez, I'm right behind you."

They walked out of the offices into the corridor. Pena's office floor was covered with blood. The dead Sergeant's bare legs stuck out from under his desk. He walked down the hall and passed the reception desk. Bermudez acknowledged salutes from the soldiers at the door with a nod of his head.

The car was waiting at the bottom of the steps. The chauffeur saluted and held the rear door open. Father Francisco climbed into the front seat. Bermudez sat wedged between Felina and Chirlo in the rear. The driver climbed back into the car.

"Captain?" he inquired.

"If you could drop me off at the church, Captain Bermudez," Father Francisco asked politely. Bermudez glanced at Chirlo, who nodded.

"The cathedral first."

"Si, Captain." They drove out through the open gates of El Tigre Fortress and headed into the city.

Three hours later, with the sun sinking to the mountains behind them, Chirlo ordered the driver to stop the car. They were cresting the last of the hills before the flatlands and straight road to Bahia Blanca. Felina sat in the front seat covering the driver with Bermudez' pistol. Chirlo was still in the back with the captain, who held the waste basket between his knees.

"What's your name, boy?" Chirlo asked the frightened driver.

"Private Polo, Senor."

"Well, Private Polo, Captain Bermudez will not be needing your services again so you are free to go. I suggest you go to your village and tell them El Chirlo has escaped, but he will return. Will you do that for me?"

"Si, Senor. Mil gracias."The boy climbed out. Felina slid behind the wheel. Chirlo rolled down the window.

"Captain Bermudez has something he would like to show you."

The lad peered in the opening as Chirlo tipped the basket to him so its contents were visible. He removed the paper covering inside. The boy's face blanched and he reeled back from the car, vomiting. The decapitated head of Sgt. Pena, its mouth stuffed with penis, scrotum and testes, leered at him like some hideous glutton from the bottom of the metal basket. Bermudez began to cry.

"Tell your village what happens to Guererro's monsters," Chirlo called softly, as Private Polo stumbled across the road.

It was dark when Felina stopped the car on a sideroad outside the airport perimeter and switched off the ignition. Chirlo prodded the captain.

"Get out—bring Pena with you."

They left the car and circled around the end of the runway to the far side of the airport, near where the air force hanger was located, and slipped under the fence. Keeping Bermudez in front, they crossed the tall grass to the taxiway leading to the air force ramp. A group of aircraft were parked in a line. Some mechanics stood working on a high tubular stand near the front of an open hanger, replacing the engine cowling on a C46.

Chirlo paused by the twin rudders of a Beechcraft parked in the line. Something stirred his memory. He hissed at Bermudez to stop, motioning him to the aircraft. Chirlo swung the stepdoor open and they climbed inside. He pulled the door closed.

"Keep him covered," he told Felina, then disappeared into the cockpit. He sat down in the left hand seat, holding the control yoke. Everything seemed familiar; the dials, instruments, even the luminous hands on the seven-day clock ticking quietly on the panel. *It's either deja vu, or I've flown this aircraft before*, he reasoned, shaking his head. He flipped the master switch alongside the panel. Soft light illuminated the dials. The electric gyros started to hum. He glanced at the fuel indicators as the needles swept up slowly to 'F' on their gauges. As if in a dream, he unlocked the controls working the elevator and ailerons. He pushed his toes down on the rudder pedals to release the week brakes. *Chocks*, he thought. *There will be wheel chocks*. He climbed back through the cabin and opened the door. Two forked metal chocks were blocking the wheels. He removed them from the front of the tires and climbed back into the airplane, carrying the chocks by their short ropes. He tied Bermudez' ankles and wrists tightly.

"If he so much as moves, kill him," he told Felina as he went back to the cockpit.

He buckled himself into the seat and switched on the magnetos for the left engine, then squirted in four shots of fuel with the primer. He hit the starter, the propellor made three revolutions and the engine burst into life. Quickly he switched to the right engine, repeating the process. As the second engine roared alive, the mechanics started running toward the machine from the hanger, waving their arms.

Chirlo unlocked the tail wheel and spun the aircraft in a semi-circle, using power from the left engine. He taxied swiftly through the grass to the runway, lowering the flaps to 20 degrees. They were halfway down the black asphalt with the tail in the air when the first tracers streaked past the co-pilot's side window. A searchlight flooded the cockpit as he lifted the aircraft towards the sky and retracted his undercarriage. He kept low until the tracers had disappeared, then climbed a few hundred feet, heading south towards Tippitaca. Felina leaned through the narrow opening into the cockpit, smiling.

"I didn't know you were a pilot!" she exclaimed.

"Neither did I," Chirlo admitted.

He swung the Beechcraft out to sea, paralleling the coastline until they were abeam the lighthouse at Punta Rio. Then he turned inland, following the black river past Tippitaca and along the dark straight slash of road to where it ended at the base of the hills. They circled the Finca Esperanza while Chirlo picked out the airstrip. There were lights in the hacienda. They came in over the hills, flaps and wheels extended. Near the ground, Chirlo switched on the landing lights. The twin beams picked up the water tower alongside the strip. They were too high and too far to the right. He cut the power instantly on both engines, side-slipping the craft into line with the short airfield. They touched down in the first third of the grass strip and rolled to a stop at the end. Chirlo taxied back to the water tower and shut off the engines. They lugged Bermudez out of the door and dropped him on the ground. They held their arms around each other in silent relief as the Land Rover drew up, outlining them in its headlights. Paco ran up laughing, with three men carrying machetes.

"Hijo de la grande Punta! Is it really you?" He flung out his arms, embracing them both, then retreated.

"Phew, you smell like goats. Dingo! Get some soap and towels," he ordered one of the men, who scurried back to the hacienda.

Paco's eyes caught Bermudez' inert figure on the grass.

"You brought a friend?"

"Captain Bermudez. The El Tigre tiger." He looked down at the thin captain. "Strip him and stake him out by the arms and legs. I have a job to do before we leave.

Chirlo sat down on the grass with Felina and watched as Paco and the two men worked on Bermudez.

"Did we have a good crop?"

"Excellent, Don Pedro. We doubled our money."

"Use the money on tinned food and equipment for the caches in the mountains."

Paco finished tying Bermudez to the four short stakes, and stood up.

"Then we are going to start your plan?"

"We have already started. Give me your knife." Chirlo stood over Bermudez, looking down at the terrified face sardonically. 'The man returned from the hacienda with the towels and soap. He stopped by the circle of men in front of the headlights, his chest heaving from the efforts of his run.

Chirlo knelt beside Bermudez, gripping his penis and testes.

"It would have been better, Captain, if you had never been born." He sawed off the members with Paco's knife, while the man screamed. Chirlo stuffed the bloody handful into the screaming mouth and stood watching with satisfaction as he strangled on his own organs.

When the struggling ceased and Bermudez lay still, Chirlo took a machete from one of the men and severed the head from the corpse. He picked it up by the hair and handed the machete back to its owner.

"Go and get Sgt. Pena," he said quietly to Felina.

When she returned with the basket, he tossed the captain's head into the can and handed it to Paco.

"Wrap them both in plastic bags and box them. A gift for Guererro. Make sure he gets them."

"It will be done as you say," Paco confirmed.

"Bury him in the middle of the strip. I want to roll over him when I come back."

He took the towels and soap and walked over to the water tower. Felina followed him. As they started to undress, the headlights were turned off in the Land Rover. They danced like lunatics under the clear gushing water, filling the night with laughter.

Later, dressed in clean clothes from Chirlo's wardrobe at the hacienda, they filled their stomachs with beef stew, rice, beans and tortillas freshly made that evening.

"I have enough fuel to make it to Merida on the Yucatan. We can pick up the airline from there," Chirlo explained. "We'll be okay once we reach Mexico."

"You'll come back soon?"

"I'll be back on this airstrip within sixty days with a planeload of weapons and ammunition. Start looking for me anytime after 30 days between midnight and three a.m. I'll need lights next time—flare pots, like the truckers use, will do. Hire some men and add another 500 feet onto the runway—we may need it."

They drove back to the Beechcraft and parked. The others had removed Bermudez' decapitated body and the stakes.

"Vaya con Dios, Don Pedro, Senorita Felina," Paco said solemnly, embracing them.

"Usted tambien, Paco," Chirlo said. He followed Felina into the aircraft and pulled the door closed behind him.

Colonel Guererro finally got over the fright of the two severed heads delivered to his home in hat boxes, addressed to his wife. Then the picture postcard from Cuba arrived in the mail. It was a photograph of El Moro, the bleak prison fortress in Havana Bay. The handwritten message on the back was brief and to the point:

"Do not go away, Gaspar. I am coming back for your head soon. Chirlo."

6

1964

Morris Levy turned off the highway where the AECL sign indicated the paved sideroad leading to the Rolfton facility. He felt like a pioneer when he first moved into the partially completed administration building three years before. After the beauty of the close knit society at Chalk River, Rolphton, on the Ottawa River, was like a wilderness. It *was* the wilderness. Bitterly cold in winter. A torment of black flies in spring and a mind-sapping heat wave for two months during the summer. Except for the annual escapes to Florida, this wilderness area of Canada had been his home since graduating from M.I.T. in 1954.

A Cum Laude in nuclear physics, he had written his doctorate on the theme of heavy water vs. light water reactors. It had rung the right bells with the selection team from Atomic Energy of Canada Ltd. and they had outbid the U.S. Atomic Energy Commission for Levy's services by a sizeable margin. In point of fact there wasn't much difference between Oakridge and Chalk River, so far as the amenities of living were concerned, and money had never been a problem to the Levy family. Morris owned a sizeable slice of the family New York banking fortune. No, it had been the decision on the heavy water by the Canadians that had tipped the scales.

He slowed the car by the main gate, reaching for his I.D. The guard recognized him, waving him through with a smile. He parked in front of the white and black stencilled name plate bearing his name, slid his briefcase across the seat and climbed out.

His breath fogged the chill morning air as he crunched across the carpark to the administration building. A light snow had dusted the hardpacked icy undersurface during the night. It made for careful walking. Inside, Morris slipped off his galoshes and, carrying them by the straps with his free hand, climbed the stairs to his office on the second floor.

"Your wife called, Doctor Levy," Miss Dionne told him as he crossed into his office.

"I just left her!"

"She said it was important," the secretary replied with a shrug.

"Okay, get her back please Miss Dionne."

He went into his office, dressed the single clothes tree with his coat and hat, dropping the overshoes beside its base. He had just sat down when the phone rang.

"Hello, Sarah."

There was a male chuckle in his ear.

"I understand you want to have a chat, Morris." It was Dr. Edgar, the director.

"Oh, sorry. Expecting a call from Sarah. Yes, I'd like a half hour when you can spare it, Derek."

"Problems?"

"I have that copy of the new export policy you circulated. I think the government is nuts."

"Not very loyal words from a newly licensed citizen."

The Levys had taken out Canadian citizenship the previous month.

"Maybe as an American I wouldn't be so concerned," Morris countered.

"Let's say ten o'clock—my office?"

"Thanks, Derek."

Before he lowered the receiver, Miss Dionne switched Sarah from the hold button.

"Morris. It came and it looks beautiful!"

His mind tried to shift gears from professional to domestic analysis.

"What came?"

"All the information we sent for on CorAm Developments in Florida—you remember? The mailman just left."

"Oh sure." The gears meshed. He released his mental clutch.

"How much for the waterfront lots?"

"They vary. It's about a hundred thousand for what we want."

"Steep," he grunted.

"But wait till you see the photographs, Morris. It's beautiful!" Sarah really sounded excited. He smiled into the mouthpiece.

"Photographs always make everything look marvelous, dear. Let's wait till we see it next week before getting carried away. It may be a mangrove swamp filled with malarial mosquitoes," he suggested sceptically.

"All right, Morris," Sarah sighed. "You'll see, it's exactly what we want, betcha?" She laughed and hung up.

Morris cradled the receiver, smiled, then swung his chair around to the thermopane picture window. He leaned back, pyramiding his fingers, elbows resting on the leather-padded arms of the chair. The mental gears shifted again as he watched the wide, deep, cold river flowing beyond the nuclear power building. Sentinels of green pines on the far bank reflected dimly the morning water from the winter morning sun. The concrete of the thermal discharge building on the bank below the power station glittered whitely. He could see where the discharge plume of warm water that cooled the reactor met the colder temperature of the river with a thin fog in a myriad of eddys, merged, then drifted on to meet the St. Lawrence River and the sea. Everything looked so peaceful. So secure.

The 30 Megawatt NPD—Nuclear Power Demonstration—facility at Rolfton had proved the heavy water hypothesis for cheap nuclear electric power. The Rolfton unit was the test bed for the hundreds of stations which would be put into service over the rest of the century in Canada. The Chalk River laboratories had provided the gestation period for the Rolfton NPD by the experiments with its NRX and NRU reactors during the Forties and Fifties. Now, with Rolfton's proven success, Atomic Energy Canada Ltd., the government-owned company that employed Morris Levy, was going to sell, or give away this technology to lesser nations of the world. A spirit of political magnanimity that scared the shit out of Morris Levy.

It was bad enough when the smooth-talking Dr. Homi Bhaba, founder of India's atomic energy program, had managed to sweet talk an NRX reactor out of the Canadian government in 1956. A gift of aid to an impoverished nation. But, to dive now into a world export market with giveaway nuclear reactors, Morris knew, would be courting disaster.

The weakness in the system was the waste production of plutonium, a potential fuel source, like uranium. With a waste reprocessing plant to extract the plutonium, a scientific halfwit could build a nuclear bomb. Any third world mickey mouse nation could become a nuclear power. It was only a matter of time before India would make the big bang.

Somehow, Morris decided, AECL had to be made to realize what an evil genie they were uncorking. He hoped Derek Edgar could see through the logic of his arguments in abandoning the export market. Would he agree to present the cause to the mandarins in Ottawa and push to change the government's new policy? Morris glanced at his watch. It was seven minutes short of 10:00 a.m.

"There's only one way to find out," he said aloud as he swung out of the chair, heading for the door.

Corbin poured himself another cup of coffee and set the fat glass pot back on the burner. Peggy, still in her dressing gown, glared at him from across the table as he folded the newspaper in half again and went back to the ritual morning study of the market indexes.

"Chuck?"

"Hmmm." Most listings were up again. A good bull market. His tax position would be horrendous for the second year running.

"I want to talk to you." Peggy was in the sixth month of her third pregnancy and felt grotesque.

"Mmmm." Airlines were all up, but he knew that wouldn't last. He thought fleetingly of Peter Colley. Flying Tigers was the only airline stock he held. Not an airline in the strict sense of the word.

"Chuck! I said I want to talk to you!" Her voice pierced the AMEX listings. Corbin lowered his paper and looked up quizzically.

"So, start talking. I'm all ears."

"I want out of here."

"Out of where?"

"Here. This house. Tampa. I want to move down to Charlotte Harbour with you. I hate these weekend visitations. Friday night to Monday morning, week after week. This is the third year!"
Marriage and a fifty-fifty split on the insurance in '67—remember?"

"That was then—this is now."

"So, what's changed? Pangs of remorse over your choice in Mexico City?"

"Perhaps. Perhaps I've fallen in love with you since then."

"Oh, for God's sakes, Peggy, let's not go through that crap again. You're in love with yourself, money and the kids. I come a poor fourth," Corbin snorted.

The doorbell rang.

"That'll be Rick. I've got to go." He stood up gulping his coffee, then picked up the newspaper and kissed her cheek perfunctorily. At the door he paused.

"Drive over to the Club for the day. Have a cluck-in with Vera Denning—you'll feel better. See you Friday." He disappeared out the door with a wave.

Peggy lifted herself from the chair. The back pains were starting to bother her again. She pulled the dining room curtain aside, watching her husband striding down the walk to the convertible parked at the curb. Rick Rogers, the CorAm company pilot, followed, carrying the B4 bag and Corbin's briefcase. He waved to her briefly again as the car pulled away. Peggy waved back, hot tears rolling down her cheeks.

"Shall I clear up now, Mrs. Corbin?" She hadn't heard the maid enter the room.

"No, leave it for now, Lila. I think I'll have another cup of coffee," she said, without turning. The swinging door to the kitchen whooshed diminutively as the maid returned to her roost. Peggy sighed and sat down.

What Corbin said was true, she admitted, or at least had been true. But now she had fallen in love with this strange mercurial man whose mind worked with machine-like rapidity every working hour. She had underestimated him. Peggy knew that now. In Mexico City she had thought he was just another greedy schemer like herself. Since then she had learned that Corbin, far from being greedy, regarded money only as a tally sheet for keeping score on his own abilities in business. He gave her everything she wanted: clothes, cars, jewelry, money, the house. Even the children had been her idea. Everything, but love. Now she had everything she had ever wanted, plus another million dollars coming in three years from Peter's insurance. If she could, she knew she would trade it all gladly in a moment to be flying down to Charlotte Harbour with Corbin that morning, because he wanted her with him, because he loved his wife. The mistake, she decided, had been in thinking that Corbin was like Peter. Poor dumb Peter. The big friendly bear without a brain in his head. How she ever could have believed that Peter Colley was the better catch of the two partners she could not imagine. Now, when she had made her choice, it was too late. Salty tears continued to roll off her cheeks as she sipped the coffee.

"Are you holding any Penn Rail, Rick?" Corbin asked. He tossed the newspapers into the back seat of the Piper Aztec. Rogers leveled off at 7,000 feet, heading south. The morning air was smooth and clear along the Gulf coast.

"A little."

"Unload it," Corbin advised. "Pick up some more IBM."

"Thanks. I'll do that."

Rick Rogers had been the company pilot for two and a half years. His wages were $1,500 per month plus expenses. He would have worked for nothing. Since meeting Corbin, he had netted nearly two hundred thousand on business advice and stock market suggestions from his employer. Not bad for an unemployed F86 Korean fighter pilot that had been hanging around the Tampa airport as a part-time instructor, when Corbin met him in the coffee shop.

"You a pilot?" the intense man had asked.

"Yup."

"Any good?"

"The best," Rogers answered.

"We'll see about that." Corbin told him to find a good buy on a light executive twin, made a job offer and left him his card. The next day Rick phoned him on the Aztec he had located at Orlando for forty-five thousand.

"Offer them forty on a five year lease and a side agreement for a buyout of one dollar at the end of the lease. I'll pay twelve percent interest."

Corbin had hung up and Rogers went back to Orlando with the offer. He couldn't figure out why it was accepted with such alacrity. Later, Corbin explained. "Simple. They still own the aircraft for five years. So they can keep deducting the annual depreciation on their capital cost. They are making about twenty thousand interest on their money over five years, plus getting back their capital, on which they have a capital gains tax break. When they sell it for one dollar they can report a huge loss. On the other hand, I get a one hundred percent tax deduction for the cost of the lease, plus your wages and expenses. Never buy an asset if you can lease it. Simple."

Simple. It was on the strength of that brief discussion *Rich Ricks Aircraft Brokers* went into business in a one-room office on the Tampa airport. He had been making money hand over fist since plunging the profits into the stock market as Corbin advised. There was a tax advantage there too, but Rick had never been certain how it worked. He left that to CorAm's accountants when they filed his returns.

He had made some beautiful deals over the past two years. The best was a sale of two C47's the previous summer to a bearded nut with a scar on his face, who he learned later had flown the pair of them to Cuba; at least that's what the FAA investigators had told him when Rogers had been interviewed afterwards on the sale. He told them the exact truth. The nut was one hell of a pilot, he recalled, smooth as silk. Rogers had spent five hours flying with him, practicing short field landings at night. No, he hadn't said anything at all. A real closemouthed cat who had paid the asking price in cash with crisp new thousand dollar bills. The investigators had seemed satisfied with his story.

As they approached the indentation of water at Charlotte Harbour, he eased the throttles back and began his descent for the customary fly around the development before going in to land on the private paved airstrip. Although the huge Venetian canal system and surrounding land was owned by Coral Island Development in Sarasota, all sales were conducted now by CorAm.

Sol Weinbolt discovered early in the association with Corbin and Affleck the difference between order-takers and hustlers. Coral Island's sales staff, commuting daily from Sarasota in the early development stages, were order-takers. The CorAm team of hustlers had moved right in amongst the earth-moving equipment with their trailers, grabbing everyone in sight for eighteen hours a day, seven days a week. After three months of unbelievable sales volumes, Weinbolt had fired his sales force and turned the whole thing over to CorAm to sell. Weinbolt was happy sitting in Sarasota. Corbin was happy sitting on site. They met at their monthly board meetings grinning at each other like Cheshire cats. At the present rate of sales Corbin figured the last lots would be gone in six months, two years ahead of schedule.

CorAm's tax position on profits was staggering. They had ploughed money into gas and oil exploration, movies, two broadway shows and a small growing chain of franchised hamburger places along the Atlantic coast to Delaware. No tax haven seemed to be working. They struck offshore oil and gas first time out. Three of the four movies where hits. One broadway show was still running to packed houses and it seemed everyone from Florida to Delaware was snacking at the *Burger Bunnies*. The attraction was due probably to the bunny-clad waitresses more than the burgers. Corbin had tasted them. They were revolting. He didn't know how many million they were worth. He had lost count. But he knew that whatever it was, Uncle Sam was owed the lion's share.

"Okay, Rick, take it in," he said to Rogers after the second flyaround.

Minutes later the Aztec squeaked onto the runway and rolled to a stop. Corbin's work week was about to begin.

Morris and Sarah Levy were standing by their car looking out over the marina and bay as Corbin drove past from the airstrip. He glanced at the Canadian Ontario plates on their dark red Buick.

"Stop here for a minute, Rick. I want to talk to those two."

Rogers stopped the Jeepster and backed up to the parked Buick. Corbin climbed out.

"Great view, eh?"

Morris looked around, his eyes taking in Corbin's pleasant smile, underneath the peaked red flying cap.

"Are you a salesman?"

"Isn't everyone?"

Morris laughed. "We're just looking around, on holiday." Sarah nodded in confirmation.

Corbin's fine tuned ears picked out the New York accent, his eyes, the slight fine Jewish features of the man's pleasant face.

"What's a nice Jewish couple from New York doing in Florida driving a Canadian car?"

Analytical mind, Levy thought with interest. "You have something restricting Jews from purchasing property?"

Corbin grinned. They were buyers and had the money.

"The only restriction here is the price of the lots. Most people think they're too expensive."

"They are."

"I agree, that's the restriction." They both laughed as common ground for rapport was established.

"I'm Morris Levy, this is my wife Sarah."

"Chuck Corbin."

They all shook hands. Corbin came directly to the point.

"Have you seen the lot you're considering?"

"It's marked on your map as SR61-3. Whatever that means. We got lost." Sarah held up the colored map sheet.

"South Range, lot 61, phase 3. If you follow me, I'll take you over there now," Corbin offered.

The Jeepster led the way to a large point inside one of the buoys and stopped. He told Rogers to go to the office without him. He'd get a lift back with the Levys when he had closed the sale.

They stood in the center of the land looking out at the bay. Corbin explained the building restrictions, utilities, shore line regulations and mooring depths.

104

"The lots are pretty small aren't they?"

"Buy two," Corbin suggested.

"Any discount on volume?"

"Depends on the volume; on two, no!"

"How about the whole point?" Levy waved his pipe to encompass the area.

"Are you speaking academically, or realistically?"

"You have thirty-two lots on this point. At four thousand each that makes them worth one hundred and twenty-eight thousand. If you have one buyer instead of thirty two, your boss should be saving something he can pass on to the purchaser. The question is how much?"

Corbin's mind switched into *calculation* mode. At that volume he knew the man was looking for a 20% discount. Quite reasonable. An even one hundred thousand would be the final price. He needed three compromises to reach it. He flipped back to *sales* mode.

"Oh, I don't know. A hundred and twenty might do it."

"A six percent discount! I was thinking closer to eighty thousand."

"That would never go, Mr. Levy. It's unrealistic. I might try one fifteen and see how that fits. It will be a stretch though."

"Too high, Mr. Corbin. We're not rich New York Jews, just poor Canadian Jews." He smiled.

"Gee, Mr. Levy, you sure drive a hard bargain. Let's be realistic, shall we. You tell me your best price offer and I'll see what I can do."

"Ninety-five tops."

"Stretch another five and I guarantee a deal."

"Agreed. One hundred thousand."

They shook hands again, smiling, the game ended.

"Are you sure the boss will accept it?" Sarah asked.

"I'm sure he will. I'm the boss."

Levy chuckled. "The Cor in CorAm. I should have guessed." They walked back to the car.

During the drive back to the office, Corbin learned two interesting facts: Morris Levy was a nuclear physicist and there were no capital gains taxes in Canada.

By the end of the week Corbin had decided to fly up to Canada for a first hand examination of the business potentials coincident with an American citizen seeking a financial haven. He spent most of the week pumping the Levys for information on their adopted country. Unfortunately, their area of knowledge was limited to the Ottawa River valley, but Corbin enjoyed their company in spite of this parochial outlook of a country larger than the U.S. with only a tenth of the population. The place had to be dripping with opportunities for anyone with money and talent. He knew he had both.

"You might have a crack at the construction business. It's always booming in the major centers. You could even try subcontracting on the nuclear generator plants the government is planning," Morris suggested over dinner one evening near the end of the week, after Corbin told him he had decided to fly up on the Air Canada flight from Tampa into Toronto.

"They are going to build a big 200 megawatt commercial plant at Douglas Point on Lake Huron, starting this year. It's an Ontario Hydro project, so they'll be subcontracting everything.

Morris cut into his filet and popped a rare chunk of superficially singed meat into his mouth, chewing thoughtfully.

"As a matter of fact, Canadian General Electric is just signing a deal now for a turnkey nuclear plant in Pakistan this year—you might get in on that."

"I don't know anything about building nuclear plants, Morris."

"Neither does anyone else, really. It's all new. That's why I thought you might be interested." He swallowed his mouthful of beef. "Good food here, Chuck."

"You know anyone I can talk to?"

"Sure. I've met most of the fellows running the projects." He placed some baked potato and sour cream on the fork. "It's strange how everyone gets overly cautious when the idea of nuclear construction comes up. Like you. People don't seem to understand. All a nuclear plant amounts to is using fission heat instead of coal or oil to turn water to steam, to turn turbines. It's no big deal. Everyone acts like we're making A-bombs with Mr. Magic Chemistry sets and erector kits." He filled his mouth.

"I do wish you two would stop talking business for five minutes so I can find out something about our house," Sarah interjected before Corbin had a chance to comment on Levy's last remark.

"Sorry. Afraid I'm being rude, Sarah. I think the design office will have your plans finished tomorrow. I'll speak to Don Affleck in the morning and call you. Okay?"

He smiled at her winningly.

"When can you start construction?"

"Right away. Soon as you approve the design."

"We have to leave in two weeks," she reminded.

"Everything will be underway by then. Promise."

Sarah appeared satisfied.

"There are one or two problems with nuclear reactors," Morris continued. "Leaks and water storage. But those are engineering problems, not construction. Most of these are solved now. Say, are you interested in this Chuck, or am I boring you?"

"I'm fascinated. Go on."

Levy laid down his knife and fork. "Well to start, you have to understand how a nuclear reactor works. There are different types. Ours is a heavy water type."

"What is heavy water?" Corbin asked.

"An American development, although the Americans don't use heavy water in their reactors. I'm really talking like a Canadian, aren't I? Anyway, the U.S. gave Canada patent permissions to produce heavy water last year. In ordinary fresh water the percentage of heavy water, which is called deuterium, is about 145 parts per million. By using a hydrogen sulphide water exchange process, this 145 parts per million of deuterium is increased to a 99.75 percent concentration. It's an expensive process though, about $500 per gallon. By raising and lowering the temperature of ordinary water while mixing it with hydrogen sulphide gas, extra hydrogen atoms from the gas enters to join the hydrogen in the water, making it heavier than the H_2O tap variety we drink. I'm oversimplifying, but that's basically what heavy water is all about. Understand?"

Corbin nodded. "Why do you use heavy water?"

"First to keep the reactor fission cool, much the same as the water circulation in a car radiator cools the engine. The second use is as a barrier with the moderator. Imagine, if you can, an electric kettle. That is the moderator. Got that? Okay. Now fill the kettle with heavy water. Instead of using an electric coil to heat the water, we use a hollow rod filled with common uranium oxide in pellets. The rod is sealed at both ends and inserted horizontally into the kettle. The nuclear reaction begins when uranium 235 atoms within the sealed rods are bombarded by slow-moving neutrons, causing these atoms to split in two pieces which fly apart, generating heat. At the same time more neutrons are given off, which, when slowed down by the heavy water in our kettle, split other uranium 235 atoms, maintaining a chain reaction of atom-splitting and steady heat generation. If we pipe a tube of heavy water coolant through the kettle, in one side and out the other, the heat from the rod of uranium is transferred to the coolant water in the pipe, which is moved along to a hot water boiler, where it heats up ordinary water into steam. The steam is used to turn the turbines and produce electricity."

"What is a neutron? The thing that splits the uranium atom?" Corbin asked.

"Every atom of any substance is composed of an equal number of positive and negative charges, called protons, the plus charges, and electrons, the minus charges. That is the nucleus of an atom. The greater the mass of protons and electrons, the greater the mass of the nucleus. Neutrons, however, within any given element, can vary. They are like hitch hikers. These variations are called isotopes. For example, in ordinary hydrogen, a mass number of one proton and one electron is given an atomic number of one H-1. When we add that extra neutron of hydrogen from the sulphide gas we make it H-2. These neutron hitch hikers wander. In wandering, they split the uranium atoms, starting the chain reaction."

"Morris stop talking and eat your food before it gets cold," Sarah pleaded, finishing her main course and laying the knife and fork neatly together on the empty plate.

"Yes dear." Morris returned to his food with reluctance. He'd started warming to his subject as the food had cooled. Now the food was cold. He ate another mouthful, then pushed his plate aside.

"It is cold."

"I'm not surprised."

They ordered dessert and coffee. The waitress removed the plates.

"Where are the problems in the system?" Corbin asked.

Levy glanced at his wife before replying. Sarah shrugged, then smiled, shaking her head with exasperation.

"One problem is if a leak occurs from the uranium oxide in the tubes or a leak of heavy water from the kettle. The leaks would be radioactive. All the resulting used material is radioactive, especially the uranium rods when they have been expended. The waste is a combination of highly dangerous products. Plutonium is part of this waste.

"Where did it come from?" Corbin inquired.

"From the nuclear reaction between the uranium atom and hydrogen neutron. Plutonium is one of the waste by-products."

"What happens to the waste?"

Levy reflected a moment.

"At the moment all wastes are stored in water pools twelve feet below the surface. That keeps the radioactivity from escaping." He toyed with his spoon. "Later on, plans are to try and use the wastes, turning them into something else. We may be able to use plutonium itself as reactor fuel, like uranium. Then turn the rest of the radioactive wastes into something more stable, like ceramic or glass. That's still experimental, though."

"How long does it take before the radioactive stuff is safe to handle?"

"You mean how long before it breaks down to where there is no more danger from the radioactivity?"

Corbin nodded.

"Well, plutonium takes 250,000 years, but most waste breaks down to safe levels within about 300 years."

Corbin laughed. "You're kidding! You mean we have to store lethal wastes for a quarter of a million years?"

Levy nodded glumly. "If we could use the little plutonium that is created we could produce as much power as the original uranium 235 which created it."

"But Morris, Jesus! The recorded history of man is only 8,000 years, and you're talking about storing stuff for thirty times that long! You can't be serious?"

"Very serious," Levy said defensively.

"But what about earthquakes or erosion or just natural decay of building materials?" Corbin couldn't believe a positive idea of waste disposal hadn't been formulated.

"We're looking at a variety of methods. Deep sea storage in lead and concrete. Shooting the stuff into the sun. Storage in salt mines; there are salt mines that have been stable for 400 million years."

"But so far nothing definite, eh?"

"No. Nothing definite."

Corbin was appalled. The waitress returned with their desserts and coffee. She smiled at Corbin and handed him the bill. He glanced at the total, his eyes skimming the machine addition on the card, then handed it back with a credit card.

"Isn't plutonium used to make nuclear bombs?" he asked, stirring his coffee.

"Among other things. The waste would have to be reprocessed to extract the plutonium." Levy took a spoonful of pecan ice cream.

"So all you need is a processing plant for the wastes and you have your bomb plutonium. How do you explode it?"

"Two plutonium masses shot towards each other inside a four foot steel tube would do it. It's not that simple to build a waste reprocessing plant for plutonium, though—expensive," Morris said, his mouth full of ice cream.

"But not impossible for a country like Pakistan. Isn't that where you said General Electric was building one?"

Levy nodded. "Or India, which already has one of these reactors. Or any other country they sell these units to. I agree with you Chuck, it's crazy. But that's the government policy—helping low cost nations with low cost power." He shrugged. "What can I do except point out the obvious?"

He set his spoon on the table. "You know what my director told me when I offered an opinion? You and I are scientists, Morris. Let's leave politics to the politicians."

They finished their dinner in silence, each lost in his own thoughts. When they stood up to leave, Corbin asked, "How many of these installations are projected over the next 20 years?"

"By 1985 they will have about 30 operating in Canada. Probably close to the same number sold or donated abroad."

"To backward third world nations which have the capability of building waste processing plants to extract plutonium, and build their own bombs."

Levy stood for an instant, holding the back of his chair, his dark eyes studying Corbin reflectively.

"Yes, Chuck. I'm afraid so. Enough to scare the shit out of you, isn't it?"

Corbin took the Air Canada Viscount to Toronto Saturday morning. Peggy drove him to the airport. He had been unusually quiet after returning from Charlotte Harbour Friday evening. This nuclear reactor construction potential for profits and horrors of proliferation learned from Morris Levy had left him numb. The magnitude of the disasters which could evolve from this program of nuclear giveaway when combined with the disposal of the thousands of tons of lethal waste growing year by year, shocked him to the very core of his being. He felt like a passenger on a roller-coaster, who knows the tracks lead into a cement wall over the next hill and can't figure out how to get off or stop the headlong plunge into eternity. He could only sit in disbelief, watching, listening to the insanity from the other passengers shrieking with delight aboard their doomsday express to disaster. That there would be profits, huge profits in the construction and engineering of domestic and foreign reactors, he had no doubt. Government programs were always profitable moneymakers for any sector of private enterprise that became involved, provided

110

some lunatic didn't bid a job into the ground. In the present situation, Corbin felt, there would be little competition, since the whole idea of nuclear power was so new to the general construction industry. Somehow, he decided as a businessman, there had to be a way of wangling his way into the specialized nuclear field near the top, where decisions were made. As a human being he was interested in positioning himself somewhere along the tracks where he might be able to change the course on the roller-coaster's ride from madness to moderation. It was worth a try.

Politicans spouted idealistic drivel to get elected every four years. Then in order to hold office, sat back on their haunches, allowing private beliefs to be suppressed or swayed by whatever was popular or expedient during their elected term. Like lemmings, they rushed off together on policy, trampling anyone who tried to stop or change direction from the mob of fools scurrying towards their own demise with a righteous certainty of their cause. Corbin knew the only escape lay in being at the side or rear of the column, where one could veer away or stop and let them run off on their own. Few politicans were prepared to accept the risk of political isolation, desertion by the rest of their fellow lemmings, even when they knew their rush was an appointment in Samarra.

Sometimes, a successful businessman was in a better position to alter the course of political actions. Answerable only to his shareholders or himself, he could afford the luxury of logic against the demented mass of popular political policies without fear of voter retribution. In the final analysis it was always the businessman who swayed the people. Not the other way round. Unfortunately, Corbin had discovered, most businessmen ignored politics until their own balliwick was threatened. With the exception of the oil industry and a few international giants, businessmen generally left the foreign policies of their governments to politicians as a playground for posturing. At least that was the way it worked in America. He was certain Canada would be the same. Korea and Vietnam were very good for domestic business. Idiotic foreign policies dictated to idealistic politicians by business, for profits. There was no end to the duplicity of politics and business.

He sat in the paneled study alone until well after midnight exploring possibilities and permutations between politics and business. Peggy was asleep when he climbed into bed, so he had to wait until breakfast before announcing the trip north.

"When will you be back?" she asked listlessly.

"A week, two weeks. Hard to say."

"Are you going to start commuting to Canada now?"

"No. If things work out, we may move there."

She looked at him in surprise. "When did you decide all this?"

Corbin shrugged. "The lots will be gone by the end of summer. There's nothing to keep me at Charlotte Harbour, or Tampa for that matter."

"How definite is this?" Peggy's eyes were alight with interest. "I thought there was more land you could develop in De Soto County?"

"There's always more land to develop everywhere. I want to do something different." He grinned at her. "If we do move, you'll have to buy some winter clothes."

She smiled. "It can't be any colder than New York in January."

"Do you feel like driving me to the airport?" It was the first time he had asked her to do something for him since they had been married.

At the airport she insisted on coming into the terminal while he bought the tickets and checked his bags. They sat in the busy coffee shop killing time before the flight announcement. Peggy was beaming.

"What are you glowing about?" Corbin asked.

She sipped her cup of tea. "I don't know. I just feel happy. Wish I could go with you."

"It's not a pleasure trip."

"I know. It would be dull for me sitting in a hotel room away from the kids, waiting for you to come back. I'd still like to be with you."

Corbin felt slightly uncomfortable. He was silent. Thinking.

"We haven't had much of a marriage, have we?"

"Not much, Chuck. I guess that was my fault, wasn't it?"

"Someone once said my interest is in the future, because that is where I will be spending the rest of my life." He looked at her. "Pax?"

Peggy put down her cup and laid a slim hand over his. "Pax."

Corbin spent two hours driving around Toronto in the cold winter rain with a rented car, before heading out of the city for Ottawa. He reached a swift conclusion on Toronto. Too big a city for fast results and too far away from the seat of federal power to engage in personal political relationships. The rain changed to wet snow as he headed north, away from Lake Ontario along the highway to the capital. As it turned dark the snow became heavier, making driving treacherous. Finally, he pulled into an isolated motel and spent the night. In the morning, when he looked out of the frosty pane of the overheated room, the landscape reminded him of a stereotype Christmas greeting card. He couldn't believe the amount of snow that had fallen during the night. He stepped outside, hugging the thin raincoat to his body. The sky was clear. The trees surrounding the motel in a semicircle from the highway, were motionless in the deafening silence of the still morning air. The snow was too deep to walk over to the coffee shop in low shoes. He threw his gear into the car and started the cold engine, his breath fogging the windows in the freezing interior. He used the wipers to clear a peekhole on the windscreen, then backed up blindly, praying the area behind the snow-covered rear window was still vacant. He drove the few hundred feet over to the coffee shop, pausing before going inside for breakfast, to watch a mammoth snow plow rumble down the highway. The plow spewed a white avalanche along the roadside as it passed. He ducked in the door to avoid the floating drift and sat down on one of the uncomfortable chrome chairs in front of a cracked arborite counter. Another man sitting two chairs further down the row, cut into a stack of pancakes. A fat, middle-aged woman appeared from the kitchen. She rubbed her hands on her apron.

"Morning. What'll it be?" She handed him one of the plastic covered menus.

Corbin studied the typewritten sheet. It was a carbon copy. He noticed *porridge* was spelled wrong. He ordered a breakfast and looked around the room. The fat woman vanished into her kitchen.

"Which way are you going?"

Corbin glanced over at the man. He was wearing a good-looking, warm tweedy suit with a shirt and tie.

"Ottawa."

The man nodded. "Should be okay now. Long as we stay behind the plows. Glad I'm not going south. I heard Smiths Falls are buried." He went back to his toast.

"Do you live in Ottawa?"

"Yup. Well, Rockcliffe."

"A suburb?"

He nodded again, his mouth filled with toast and marmalade.

"That was quite a snowfall."

The man swallowed. "Last of the year, probably—in like a lamb, out like a lion—same thing every year in April. You an American?" He waited until Corbin nodded before going on. "Thought so.

Suntan and accent. Florida?" He waited for another nod. "Nice place Florida. Too hot in the summer, no place to ski in the winter. You ski?"

Corbin shook his head as the fat woman returned with his breakfast.

"Should try it. Lots of fun. Great sport skiing, I mean." He stood up, reaching into his pockets for tip change, then picked a heavy car coat off the rack against the wall and walked to the cash register. The fat woman punched the keys on the old ornate wrought iron National Register, and gave back the change in multi-colored bills.

"See you around." The man waved and went out the door. A ball of chill air poured into the room as he left.

Corbin wrapped his hands around the warm coffee cup as the cold air pressed down the row of chairs, heading for the door marked *Restrooms*. He ate breakfast quickly, paid the bill and left. The place depressed him.

He drove into Ottawa shortly before noon and checked into a stone hotel fortress called the Chateau Laurier, complete with uniformed doormen. After the motel, he felt like the pauper who had become a prince. He picked up a selection of newspapers from a newsstand in the lobby, before following an elderly bellboy over to the elevators.

Corbin had learned the quickest way to discover the mood and tempo of any city or town was to read the local papers. He spent lunchtime and part of the afternoon examining the mood and tempo of Ottawa. His conclusion, by three o'clock that afternoon, was one of puzzlement. It was obviously a staid conservative city, with an undercurrent of French Canadian unrest, which, in some ways, resembled the complaints of the American Negro minorities. Although, unlike the Negroes, Corbin couldn't understand what there was for the Canadian French to complain about. He drove around the empty Sunday city park until dark, noting myriads of construction projects underway, despite seasonal restrictions from weather and temperature. He took the car back to the hotel and went to his room to consider the first practical moves for the following day.

He waited until rush-hour traffic vacated the streets, then drove out to the west end of the city and parked in a space marked *Visitors* alongside a new two-story brick building. The building, one of a half dozen similar types in a small industrial complex, was captioned by a neat block-lettered sign between two raised square

114

poles on what would have been the front lawn, if that hadn't been covered with snow. He went over to the glass door in the center of the building. The black letters on the transparent door were identical to the lawn sign, *Venture Design Engineering Ltd.*

He went inside. The girl behind the reception desk was speaking French into the colored phone attached to a secretarial console. Corbin stood in front of her desk several minutes until she finished.

"Yes?" she asked, challenging him, her eyes wary. They were very pretty eyes.

"Want to fight?" Corbin smiled.

The girl's face relaxed a bit—still no smile, though.

"Not particularly. Who do you want to see?"

"The president, or owner, or whoever is head honcho."

"Honcho? She examined him more closely. "Are you an American?"

"Does it show?"

This time she smiled. "A little. No tie, suntan, light raincoat in winter. It all adds up. The president is Mr. Holmes and he is in. Who shall I say is calling?"

"Charles Corbin, from Tampa, on a personal matter," he added as an afterthought.

She rang through; there was a brief mumbled discussion which Corbin missed.

"He'll see you now. First door on the left through there." She pointed to the double doors at the side of the reception room.

"Keep smiling." Corbin went through into a large open office, filled with deserted desks and covered typewriters. He knocked on the door plaqued *Warren W. Holmes, President* and walked in.

"Mr. Corbin?" Holmes was a tall studious thirty-year old with functional steel rimmed glasses and wearing the iron ring of a professional engineer on his pinky. They shook hands. Corbin took one of the two chairs in front of the uncluttered desk and sat down. He reached into his breast pocket and removed a torn newspaper clipping taken out of the financial section of the *Ottawa Citizen* the previous evening. He placed it on the desk.

"Saturday's paper advertised you were looking for a finanical partner in the engineering field."

Holmes picked up the clipping, studying it as if he had never seen it before.

"Yes, that is our ad," he confirmed at last, his tone indicating the possibility of forgery. Corbin said nothing, studying the man with level eyes. Finally, when the silence became unbearable, Holmes

115

stopped toying with the piece of newsprint and asked, "You have money?"

Straight to the point, Corbin thought. "How much do you need?"

Holmes dropped his eyes. "About a quarter of a million dollars."

"What do I get for it, assuming I had that much?"

"What do you want?"

"The truth."

Holmes sighed. "We're broke and in debt. Not enough cash flow."

"You expanded too fast too soon and now you're too deep to survive."

Holmes nodded. "We have the work to pull ourselves out."

"But not the cash on hand to pay the people required to do the work."

He looked at Corbin with interest, nodding. "You've had some experience in this sort of thing before? I've tried the banks, but. . . ."

"They said they would advance only on work completed or in hand." Corbin finished the sentence for him. "Well, Mr. Holmes, let's see how bad it is, shall we? Then I'll tell you what I might be able to do."

"What do you need to know?"

"Let's start with your last few annual statements, then we can go through the books, daily journal, ledgers and so forth."

"We have only been operating three years. I just have two annual statements," Holmes explained, apologetically.

"Fine. Let's get started, shall we?"

Holmes picked up his desk phone and punched the intercom button. "Elizabeth, would you lock the front doors, put the phone on answering service and come in here please?"

"Do you have other principles?" Corbin asked when he had replaced the receiver.

"Four of us started the company. Jeff Wilson went to work with Montreal Engineering. Bill Dodge and Eric Brunig are down in Toronto looking for financing. It's a four-way partnership. We take turns being president." He looked at Corbin thoughtfully. "Do you really have the money?"

Corbin smiled at the earnest, appealing face. "Better than a hundred times what you say is needed." A stunned look spread slowly over Warren Holmes' features. The secretary came into the room, looking at them both expectantly. Corbin stood up.

116

"Hello Elizabeth, Mr. Holmes would like you to bring in the company statements, books and ledgers. While you're at it, you might get the articles of incorporation, letters, patent and shareholders' register, as well. Will you need help?"

The girl looked at Holmes uncertainly. He nodded.

"Can I use a vacant office?"

Holmes recovered himself and stood up. "Certainly, Mr. Corbin. Use Bill Dodge's office next door. Do you need anything else?"

Corbin thought a moment. "A pad of columnar paper, some pencils and an adding machine."

"Get them, Elizabeth, and anything else Mr. Corbin needs."

"Let's make it Chuck, shall we, Warren? We don't stand on formality too much where I come from; it's a waste of time."

Corbin sat down at the desk in the vacant office and waited for the requested documents. He saw a light button go on at the desk phone and knew Holmes was trying to round up his other partners to tell them about the American mullet that had walked into the office with a bag of money. The light was still on when Elizabeth returned ten minutes later, her arms loaded down with post binder books. She slid them on the desk with a sunny smile and left to get the calculator. Corbin went to work on the books.

He sat back from the desk. Outside it was dark.

"Finished?" the secretary asked, watching as he stretched luxuriously.

Corbin glanced at his watch. "Wow! I didn't know it was that late. I'm sorry to have kept you here till this hour."

"That's all right. I enjoyed it."

"Why don't you go tell Warren we're through and I'll take us all to dinner?"

"He left a couple of hours ago. His wife phoned. He told me to lock up when you were finished."

"Then I'll take you out to dinner, unless you have a husband or a date waiting for you?"

She smiled. "No husband, no date."

"Fine! Let's pack this up and go eat."

They decided on the dining room of the Chateau Laurier. Elizabeth agreed to meet him at nine-thirty after stopping by her apartment for a quick change. Corbin met her in the lobby of the hotel. She appeared radiant in her black evening gown. The small gathered waist accentuated the bust line where two narrow shoulder straps of black material crisscrossed her full breasts. The straps were just wide enough to be decent, but not so wide as to hide the magnificent attributes of curved flesh spilling out from containment. Corbin was still wearing the same suit, although, in deference to his surroundings, had donned a striped tie. It made him feel he was being strangled. He looked at her with open admiration as they met in the center of the huge lobby.

"My God, Elizabeth! You look like a page out of *Vogue*!"

"Like it?"

"The dress or what's in it?"

She laughed self-consciously. They entered the dining room and surveyed the white starched linens topped with sparkling crystal and gleaming silverware.

"It's an illusion," Elizabeth whispered. "The linen has holes in it, the cutlery is stainless steel and the glasses are water goblets from Woolworths."

The maitre d' wafted them to a table for two along one wall. They ordered Brandy Alexanders. Doubles.

"Who are you, Mr. Corbin? Are you really the angel that's going to save Venture Design?" She had a pale oval face framed by jet black hair. The eyes were a Caribbean green and there was a tiny dark mole high on her cheek. Beyond that, the skin was without blemish. She was wearing lipstick, but no makeup. Corbin realized suddenly he had been with her all day and noticed nothing until now. She was a knockout. He felt a stirring.

"I'm just a lovable American boy that struck it rich in real estate and answered a newspaper ad. Simple as that."

"I don't believe you."

"Why not?"

"A multimillionaire flies in from Florida on Sunday to answer an ad in Saturday's newspaper for Monday morning. It doesn't make sense.

"How do you know I got in Sunday?"

Elizabeth smiled. "Checked with the hotel desk from my apartment before I came over." The waiter returned with their Brandy Alexanders and stayed to write down their order. When he had retrieved the gilt tasseled menus and departed, she asked, "Are you married?"

Corbin nodded. "With two kids and another due in a couple of months."

She considered this information. "I was married once for a couple of years. He was a twit," she added.

"A twit?"

118

"Nitwit. Big zero. A teenager in a man's body."

"So when you grew tired of the man's body you couldn't cope with the teenager's mind."

Elizabeth nodded. "Something like that. How old are you?"

"Does it matter?"

"I suppose not. I'm twenty-four."

"You look nineteen and talk like a thirty-year old. I'm thirty five." Corbin sipped at the frothy fat glass.

"I'm Mother Superior for Venture Design. Somebody has to look after that quartet of babies."

"You sound defensive."

"No. Not really. They are all such good, straight-forward honest citizens they can't believe everyone else isn't the same."

"Professional Engineers—not businessmen," Corbin suggested.

"Exactly. We've had a couple of MBA's in over the last two years, supposed to be running things, but they were more interested in lining their own pockets than making a financial success of the company. You know the sort of thing. Kickbacks for underpricing the services, big expense accounts. When I found out about the last one and told Warren, he didn't have the heart to fire him for another five months—can you beat that?"

The waiter arrived with two white-jacketed escorts, carrying the crab salad and consomme openers.

"What did you decide from your examinations?" Elizabeth continued, when the trio had left.

"Good potential. Excellent concepts. Lousy financial management. Terrible industrial management. Bankruptcy in thirty to sixty days." Corbin spooned the clear consomme.

"That bad?"

"Worse. It's a disaster already found it's place to happen." He sipped the soup from the spoon with an imperceptible slurp.

"So you're not interested in investing?"

He finished siphoning the consomme off his spoon. "Would you put money into a disaster?"

She shook her head, making the black hair shimmer. "No, I suppose not, but then I'm not rich, you are."

They ate for several minutes in silence. The service trio timed its return at the exact moment the salad and consomme had been consumed. They swept up the empty plates, returning full ones to the table, and departed. The roast beef was thick and lean, the way Corbin liked it.

"I guess I'd better start looking for another job."

Corbin said nothing. He didn't think Holmes had enough savvy to set him up with the girl for a play, but the way the man had disappeared from the office, leaving him alone with his faithful stacked secretary, smelled of intrigue. Either Warren Holmes was crude as an intriguer or plain dumb as a businessman. The girl was a sharpie. The afternoon working with her in the office had proved that. *Maybe all Canadians are like this*, he considered, *guileless and good.* He remembered Peter Colley had been a Canadian. *Peter didn't have a mean streak in his whole body*, he recalled. *It must be something to do with the climate. They are all too busy shoveling snow and trying to keep warm to screw each other.* He chewed his food thoughtfully.

"Would you like a bottle of wine?"

She nodded. "As long as it's not Canadian. Our stuff is terrible." They ordered a French Bordeaux.

"When are you going home, Mr. Corbin?"

"In a day or two." He resisted telling her the truth. It was a game. "I'll drop in to see Warren before I leave. By the way, my name is Chuck. Let's forget the Mr. Corbin routine."

Elizabeth smiled. "Okay, Chuck." They spent the rest of dinner discussing everything but Venture Design. Elizabeth Avery nee Beauchamp had a French Canadian father and Welsh mother. Her father had been a ship's officer and married her mother in Cardiff two months before World War II started. Lt. Commander Beauchamp went down with his torpedoed vessel in 1943, but not before sending his wife and infant daughter to safety in Canada on a returning troop ship. They settled with his parents in the town of Mont Joli. Elizabeth grew up speaking English to her mother, French to her grandparents and everyone else. When Elizabeth was thirteen her mother married a St. Lawrence River pilot and they moved to Montreal. A bright girl, she finished High School and graduated from the University of Montreal with a B.A., then took a secretarial course in typing, shorthand and bookkeeping before joining Venture Design. She came to Ottawa originally to try and get a government job in External Affairs, but there were no openings. Warren Holmes and his engineering partners seemed the next best thing at the time. She had married Norman Avery in her sophomore year at the university. Avery was a third year engineering student. They were divorced when she graduated. He was still a third year engineering student.

"For all I know he's still trying to pass into fourth year. Unless he drank himself to death."

"He drank?" Corbin asked as they finished their coffee.

"Like a fish."

"Sad." Corbin signaled for the check. The dining room was practically deserted. The wide doors leading out to the foyer had been closed for some time. It was nearly eleven when they were unlocked by the maitre d' to allow them out.

Corbin held her arm while they walked to the check booth to retrieve her coat. He decided it was time for the acid test.

"This is the point in the evening when I normally make my play," he explained with mock seriousness. "I suggest you come up to my room for a nightcap before going home and you are supposed to say 'I'd love to, but just one.' " He handed the coat check to the booth attendant.

"Then what happens?" the green eyes were mischievous.

"Why, we get smashed and wind up in the sack. Then you don't leave until after breakfast-in-bed tomorrow morning."

"If you can change the choreography slightly, for me to leave at six, in time to change into an office dress, it sounds like a good deal, Mr. Corbin."

"Call me Chuck." He took her coat, slinging it over his arm, then guided her to the elevators.

They rode to his floor with a tall, severe, white-haired man wearing a bristle mustache and frown. Elizabeth giggled when they left the elevator. "That man is a Cabinet Minister!"

"I'm a Lutheran myself," Corbin said.

Elizabeth continued giggling down the corridor to his room. They decided on another bottle of wine. She kicked off her shoes while Corbin called room service.

Later, when the bottle was nearly empty, Corbin tried to steer the conversation around to Venture Design again.

"Where will you go when the company folds?" He couldn't believe she was really this easy to seduce under normal circumstances.

"Haven't thought about it. Maybe go back to Montreal." She had hung her dress in the closet and was sitting on the bed in her slip and bra, nursing the last of the red wine. Her face was flushed, solemn.

"Anything between you and Holmes, or the other partners?"

Elizabeth uncurled her legs and stood up, swaying. "Are you kidding?" They're all slide rule straight married men. I'm going to have a bath," she announced and began to wriggle out of her slip.

"So am I." Corbin studied her legs. They were perfect.

"You may be married, but you're no slide rule. More like the arc of a circle."

She unhooked her bra, and draped it over the chair, then sauntered to the bathroom, her breasts swaying with the movement. "Join me?"

Corbin climbed off the bed and began to undress as she disappeared into the big bathroom. He heard the water start hollowly in the tub. *She is for real* he thought, shaking his head finally. He peeled his socks off and strode in to join her.

The tub was enormous. A white porcelain oversized monster, installed when the hotels built everything larger than life in a golden era, now passed. He hopped in at the sloping end, bringing the water level dangerously near the lip. They regarded each other silently across the expanse of hot water.

"I've never tried it in a bathtub," Elizabeth said finally. "Have you?"

Corbin's throat felt dry. He shook his head. "Not in one this size, at any rate."

He reached for her. This time the water did overflow.

Warren Holmes introduced him nervously to the other partners when Corbin arrived at the office shortly after eleven. He had left the hotel with Elizabeth at dawn, following in his car to her apartment. She had changed, then cooked them breakfast. They made a twenty minute detour into her bedroom, before she left for work. He asked her to tell Holmes he would drop by during the morning after clearing up some personal business. Elizabeth promised to say nothing discouraging to the partners until Corbin spoke to them first. There was, of course, no personal business to occupy him for the morning. He wanted to keep Warren and his boys on the cliff as long as possible. He spent the time poking around the apartment finding out as much as he could about the girl. Photo albums, pictures, letters, bank statements, wardrobe, car, financial payments, tastes in books and music. He missed nothing, replacing everything neatly the way he found it. Satisfied at last, he locked the door behind him after propping a note on the dinette table against the flowering cactus centerpiece.

The partners crowded into Holmes' office looking at Corbin like expectant fathers.

"I think Mrs Avery should be here. This does concern her as well."

They looked at each other blankly, then Warren called Elizabeth in from the front desk with the same instructions as the previous day on the front door and answering service. When she had seated herself beside Bill Dodge on the office couch, after looking at Corbin blandly with a professional gaze, he began.

"Yesterday Warren gave me the full treatment on your corporate history, work performances to date, and of course, your present unfortunate financial position."

They stirred uneasily.

"Finally, after going over your books, I am surprised you managed to last this long without going under. Venture Design is one of the best examples of mismanagement and misuse of funds I have seen in a company for some time."

"Misuse of funds?"

Corbin looked at Brunig, the partner who had assumed the role of company treasurer.

"I mean misuse in the practical, not legal sense. For example, this building is a misuse of funds—you don't need it. It's too expensive and too big. Your company cars should be Chevys, not Oldsmobiles and Buicks. Your contract pricing should be based on profits, not public recognition by some government department that doesn't give a damn about your prestige anyway. In short, gentlemen, you have been tried and found wanting."

He regarded each in turn before going on.

"In my opinion you are all highly capable and competent engineers, but completely incapable and incompetent business managers. You have a dead horse on your hands and are waiting for someone to come and tow it away."

Corbin stopped talking. He noticed Elizabeth looking at Warren Holmes sadly. The others had lowered their eyes with embarrassment.

"As you know, I am an American with considerable financial interests south of your border. One of the big disadvantages with making substantial profits in any enterprise is the taxes which have to be paid. You are probably aware there are tax agreements between your country and mine. Were I to buy your company for a tax loss against one of mine, it would clear your personal liabilities in this Venture Design fiasco. At least you could escape with your personal credit intact."

"You are suggesting you would buy the company for its tax loss?" Dodge inquired hopefully.

"I would be prepared to pay off your personal liabilities in exchange for all the outstanding and issued company shares."

"Then you would own everything," Holmes said dully.

"Yes, I'd own everything in a bankrupt company called Venture Design. You make it sound like I'm skinning you alive, Warren." Corbin smiled. "You boys have personal liabilities of one hundred thousand bucks; I doubt if you have ten thousand worth of assets and most of that is in furnishings here that you don't need. I'm giving you a chance of climbing out from under your pile of problems and living to fight another day." Everything was silent for a while.

"I guess there's no alternative really?" Holmes made it sound like a question as he looked at the others. Each of them either nodded or shrugged his acceptance or indifference. "How do we go about it?" he asked Corbin.

"You have company attorneys?"

"Our lawyer is Bud McCrea. He founded the company for us originally. Harding & McCrea. They're on Laurier Avenue. I forget the number."

Corbin jotted down the firm's name. "I'll find it later. Why don't you give McCrea a call and explain what we're doing. He can get all the shares together while I get my attorney in Tampa to call him and arrange the payouts. I'll use the phone in the next office." He stood up and smiled good-naturedly at the somber faces before leaving the room.

He called Don Affleck at Charlotte Harbour and gave him a number on what he wanted.

"Are you sure there isn't a bag of shit in there somewhere, Chuck? It sounds too easy. They should fight a little. For appearance sake, if nothing else."

"Wait till you meet them, then you'll understand. Get our attorneys on it right away," Corbin instructed. "I'll be back tonight sometime if the airlines don't jam me up." They exchanged a few more minutes of gossip, then hung up.

He went back to the other office. Holmes was still on the phone. It sounded complicated the way he was trying to explain it. Corbin leaned over the desk and took the phone gently out of Warren's hand.

"May I?" he asked with a smile.

"Mr. McCrea. This is Charles Corbin of Tampa. My holding company, CorAm Investments, Inc., incorporated as a Delaware company, is buying all the issued and outstanding shares from the principals and treasury of Venture Design for $173,000 Canadian funds, plus disbursements and legals. This represents the personal debt only of the principals. The company debt will be assumed by CorAm. "Is that clear?" He got a *yessir* through the earpiece.

124

"Good. I have made arrangements to transfer $200,000 U.S. to your trust account. You can phone my attorneys in Tampa at three today for the transfer method." He gave the address and phone number, making him repeat it back. "Good. I want this matter cleared by Friday. You will act for both sides under my attorney's direction. Is that clear?" He got another prompt *yessir.* "Nice talking with you, Mr. McCrea."

He hung up, but remained standing in the middle of the room.

"There will be some things for everyone to sign on Friday. Let's hope no one pulls the plug on us before the end of the week."

"Will you stay in town?" Holmes inquired. He felt a little like a third year engineering student again, talking to his professor on arrangements for private tutoring during off hours. He was concerned now the American would disappear, the whole deal fall apart, followed by personal ruin.

"No." Corbin looked at his watch. "I'm not needed. The attorneys can put it all together and do their turkey dance at the registry office Friday. There's a two o'clock flight; I'm going to try and make it if I can. If you run into any problems phone me. You have my card."

Holmes nodded glumly.

"It takes a lot of guts to admit you've made a mistake."

He looked around at them. "And a whole lot more to do something about correcting it. If it's any consolation, you have made the right decision."

No one said anything.

"I'd better scoot. It's been a pleasure meeting you all." He rounded the room, shaking hands, then left. Elizabeth followed him to unlock the front door.

"Will I see you again?"

"Do you want to?" Corbin paused, his hand on the door bar. She nodded with a quick smile.

"Then you will." He walked down the steps to his car. She waved to him as he drove off. He waved back. She relocked the doors and went back to her reception desk. There was no point in going back to join the misery in Warren's office, she decided. She sat down, staring out through the glass doors to the vacant yard and road beyond. Corbin had not been unkind to the partners. He had told them the unvarnished truth, something she had been trying to do for eighteen months. At least they would be left with their reputations intact. There were always jobs available for competent engineers. She sighed, deciding to forego lunch and instead start phoning the agencies about a job for herself. She reached for the yellow pages and flipped to the section entitled "Employment."

Elizabeth saw the handwritten note the moment she walked into the apartment at 5:30. Smiling, she picked it up. There was a $1,000 bill attached to one of the spikes of the cactus plant.

Dear Green Eyes, This will confirm your employment as my bilingual executive secretary starting tomorrow morning. The job pays $300 per week plus expenses and a car. As I have not advertised this position, you are my only applicant. Hope you will accept. I need your help. Will be returning Sunday after next and require you to complete the following for me by that time.

1. Find house in a commercially zoned residential area suitable for renovation to offices. About 4,000 square feet.
2. Find two-bedroom apartment close to house available on one year lease with parking.
3. Get best price on five Chevrolet four-door cars. Two year lease.
4. Advise Warren and the boys of my return *after* all the papers have been completed for the transfer of Venture Design to CorAm. I want to offer them permanent jobs.
5. Locate names and phone numbers of every senior offical in private industry and government connected with the nuclear reactor program covering construction, sales, research, operation and export.
6. See if you can find a place where we can buy one of those Chateau Laurier bathtubs for my apartment— we've got to stay clean.

Chuck

7

1965

Jamil crouched in the shadows, just beyond the floodlit barbed wire fence of the Kibbutz. He could see the others taking up their positions, quietly squirming over the road embankment until they were lost in the darkness. He pulled back the wool wrist band on his leather jacket. It was seven minutes until the hour. He slid the wool back over the glowing timepiece, and stared through the barbed wire into the Kibbutz, an internment camp in the middle of nowhere designed to keep inmates from outside intruders. *Stupid fucking Jews*, he thought, *first they let the Germans lock them up behind barbed wire. Then they come here and steal my homeland so their own people can put them behind barbed wire.* The paradox never ceased to amaze him.

There was a sound of sliding gravel toward the end of the fence. The guards in the watch tower at the corner of the lighted perimeter stopped talking, and peered out into the darkness. Seconds later a searchlight flooded the blackness, probing for the sound. Jamil froze, tilting his blackened face to the ground. The light began a slow traverse of the land outside the fence. The spot paused periodically as it encountered hummocks of earth and bodies, indistinguishable from the rest of the landscape. Finally, the light went out. Jamil let the air slide out of his lungs with relief. There were two new recruits on this raid, replacing the two they had lost during the raid on the Saieykah settlement the previous month. One of them had probably slipped or dropped his grenade bag. He hoped the instant alertness from the guard tower had demonstrated the effectiveness of the Israeli defenses. He tilted his head up from the earth and wiped the sand off his lips and nose, then checked his watch again. It read three minutes to three. He eased the grenade bag off his shoulder and opened it. He took out four of the dull metal fragmentation explosives and laid them on the ground in front of him neatly, then slid the bag down to his side and hooked the ring clips onto his belt. There were six more grenades in the bag. He pulled himself into a crouch, moving the automatic rifle next to his feet, then picked up the first two grenades, and removed the pins, holding their spring handles in position. He could see Mustafa's dim form appear suddenly in a similar crouch thirty yards further along the perimeter. The others would all be in position now, ready for attack. Jamil licked his dry lips and waited. He felt very calm. The clear-headedness was not an illusion. He had trained himself a long time for these precious but infrequent moments of revenge. He prayed Akbar's throwing arm was accurate when he took out the guard tower. It usually was.

There were two simultaneous explosions. The tower top disintegrated in a shower of flames and splintered wood. One of the towermen was still screaming as he landed on the ground twenty feet below. The second tower, beyond the buildings, exploded fifteen seconds after the first. Jamil couldn't see it, but he heard the explosion. He slung his grenades into the fence posts ahead of him, then grabbed his rifle, pausing until all four explosions erupted the wire into a serpentine coil. He had needed only two of the precious explosives. The third and fourth grenades had merely enlarged the opening made by the first two. Running in a crouch, keeping his silhouette low, he charged through the opening and rushed the buildings, spraying the windows with short bursts from his automatic rifle. He stopped at the corner of the first, a low-roofed single-story, multi-windowed dormitory, and lifted one of the grenades from the bag. He jerked the pin, counted, then tossed it through the broken glass. Before the explosion came he had already passed on to the next window with another grenade. He tossed it in, then ran to the end of the building, where he knew those inside would be bunched in a crowd. The third grenade landed among them. He ran around the corner into a half dozen Israelis heading across his path. He dropped to the ground as they fired, his own rifle pouring a stream of lead into their midst. Four of them fell, the other two spun into a crouch and vanished back into the shadows of the next building. They were still firing at him as he rushed over to the next hut. It looked like a storage depot. He slung his last grenades through the single window, and ran on, changing the clip in his rifle. The firing was growing more concentrated as the Israelis, overcoming the initial shock of the attack, grouped rapidly into compact defense teams, covering the area between the buildings with coordinated fire. It was time for the raiders to withdraw. With the fence lights out, retreat was simple, once they cleared the buildings and reached the fence line. Singly and in pairs, they slipped through the blasted opening at the west end of the camp. Akbar was the last one through after Jamil. They raced across the country for a quarter mile, then slowed to a steady trot. Finally, pausing to rest, they made a head count. Everyone was present. There were flashes of white teeth in the darkness while they congratulated each other on the success of the mission.

"Did you hear the stupid bastards still shooting at each other after we left?" someone said. "Hope they have as much luck with their aim as we did," Jamil said.

Everyone laughed. They relieved themselves, letting the tensions of the past quarter hour flow out with the urine. It was sunrise as they crossed the border back into Jordan and paused to kneel on the sand, facing Mecca.

"Allahu Akbar—God is Great. There is but one God and Mohammed is his prophet."

The sun rose golden in the new dawn. Another day for the calendar of eternity.

It had taken three weeks before arrangements were made for Jamil and Leila to leave Beirut for Amman. They spent their days with the rest of the group at the house on Corniche Mazraa, getting to know one another and listening to Abu Ali Iyad. Jamil realized they were being assessed by the old vulture. There were other visitors to the house who spoke of the cause, defining the dedication required from all of them in stark realistic terms.

"Unless you are prepared to die, there is no place for you in Al Asifah. Because you will die. That much I promise. Next year. In five years. Perhaps tomorrow."

Dr. Wadi Hadad was a graduate from the American University in Beirut during the Forties. With Dr. George Habash, Hani El-Hindi and Ahmad El-Khatib, he was the most important figure of the ANM Jamil had met so far. The Arab National Movement had started originally as a Pan Arab ideology for federation of Arab States. Although the AMN professed activism along with its ideology, it was Nasser and other political activists who held the power, paying only lip service to the ANM so long as it suited their own ideologies. ANM had become an impotent cauldron for purple prose. A sop for armchair idealists within the movement. For Jamil, and some of the other listeners, it was a song they had heard before. Impressive but impotent.

"We have had peace with Israel since 1957 when President Nasser in his wisdom banned our guerrilla activities. Like fools, Arabs have been sentinels protecting the Jews. No more!" he thundered. "Now we shall rebuild our shattered dreams alone. If Cairo will not help, then Amman will. If Hussein follows Nasser, then we will move to Lebanon. Our hopes, our faith and our future lies in your hands. You must not fail!"

Later, as they lay naked on the narrow bed in the steamy room, smoking cigarettes, Jamil asked, "Did you believe him?"

Leila looked at him sharply. "He is a great man. He must speak the truth."

"The truth from Hadad? I think he's full of shit. He spends a half an hour telling everyone to get ready to die, then drives back to have supper at the Phonecia Hotel. I'd like to see the sonofabitch at a training camp doing something besides talk. These political yappers are all the same. Big talk. No action. They make me sick." He said it angrily, stubbing his cigarette.

Leila propped herself up on one elbow, her breast spilling onto his chest. "But he helped found the Movement! He has been elected, Galal."

"Who elected him? A bunch of political yappers like himself. He can yap better than anyone else so they elect him. What has he ever done to produce one centimeter of success? Eh? Talk. Talk. Talk. All they do is talk. Where is the one who will lead the fight where everyone uses guns instead of vocal cords?"

"Perhaps Abu Ali Iyad?" Leila suggested, stroking his chest.

"Perhaps."

She worked her hand down to his belly. "Are you prepared to die, Galal?"

"If I thought it would recover one hectare of land I would die tomorrow, gladly. But I know if I did, some fool like Hadad would give it back the next day."

Her fingers reached his manhood and began stroking it. "You don't know that."

"I know." He reached for her.

The camp outside of Amman was a desert. Beyond the wire fence surrounding the low tents and buildings, the land was devoid of vegetation. Daily, the shimmering sun seared the low hills until everything appeared to shrink in size. Reality was measured by the mental absorption rate of dehydrated brains and aching muscles, attempting to ingest the demands of basic training. During the first twelve weeks, under the iron discipline of British trained Palestinian officers of King Husseins's army, the recruits learned the rudiments of military knowledge. Their weapons came from every army in the world. Russian, NATO, American, British and Chinese. They learned each type until they could fieldstrip them blindfolded, repair them when they jammed and conceal them when they traveled. They became marksmen; pistols, machine guns, grenade launchers, bazookas and flame-throwers. They learned to handle them all until they were experts and Abu Ali Yad smiled benevolently at their progress. The physical conditioning was the hardest. There were long aimless route marches across the uneven desert while loaded down with water, food and weapons. By day they parched in the dry blazing sun; by night shivered in the cool air. As the training continued, more young men and women joined them at the camp and on the marches, prodded by the screaming noncoms from the Jordanian Army. Little nut-brown men in checkered ghutras who never seemed to tire as they raced around the marching columns on bandy legs, yelling their incomprehensible Arabic. When it was all over there was no graduation ceremony, only a division of those who finished the course. Most went back to the refugee camps from where they had come with the authority of Al Asifah to teach their skills to others. Jamil, Leila and a select few went on to learn about other things.

One day in November Jamil was summoned to report to the camp's orderly office. Abu Ali Iyad introduced him to his new supervisor, Abd Arheem Jaber. Jaber came to the point immediately.

"You have done well here, Jamil. Top of your class I am told."

Jamil nodded. He had worked very hard to make certain he would be the best.

"I am forming a Special Operations Squad. Are you interested?"

"What sort of Special Operations?"

Jaber shrugged. "They vary." He looked at him closely. "Special Operations require special people. Highly trained and completely dedicated to the cause. I have been looking over your file. I think you are what I am looking for."

"Are there others?"

Jaber ignored the question. "The woman, Leila Kemal?"

"Yes?"

"You are lovers?"

"In off duty hours we are sometimes," Jamil admitted frankly. "Lovers, but not in love with anything but the cause, Abd Arheem Jaber."

"Good. Do you think she would be a good choice for Special Operations?"

"A woman?"

"We already have one woman. Amina Dhahbour. It is not sex that makes a fighter, Jamil, but dedication."

"Then she will make a good choice."

"I think so too. Could you work with her in the field?"

"I will work with anyone I am ordered to work with."

Jaber smiled. The meeting had concluded. "I will advise you later when you will leave. Go tell Leila Kemal to come and see me now, Galal Jamil, and welcome to Special Operations Squad."

He stood up from the battered metal desk and shook hands with Jamil formally.

"Allah Maak."

He nodded to both his superiors. "Allah Maak—God be with you," and left the office.

The first task was a simple one. The execution of two collaborators who had fled to Rome when their duplicity was discovered in Jerusalem. It was a menial job as Jamil discovered later, but a necessary indoctrination required for everyone in Special Operations, enabling Jaber to assess the quality of material he had acquired. Four days after the meeting in camp, two forged Lebanese passports, money and complete instructions were delivered to Leila and Jamil at the orderly room. They left for Rome the same afternoon on Royal Jordanian Airlines, traveling as man and wife. Upon arrival they checked into a tourist hotel near the Coliseum and were taken up in a shaky elevator to a back room on the fourth floor, furnished in Early Mussolini. After three days of waiting for a contact, they were notified at last by the desk clerk as they came in from dinner at one of the sidwalk cafes that a Mr. Pandini had left a message and would call back later. Jamil thanked the clerk and headed for the elevator.

"Someone calling himself Pandini phoned."

Leilia looked at him. "Pandini?"

Jamil shrugged. The contact's name in their instructions had been Doula.

"Maybe that's his cover."

As the doors opened, another man sitting in one of the frayed sofas in the lobby, stood up and lugged his suitcase towards the elevator. Leila held the stop button until he had crammed himself into the small space. The door closed. The man smelled of garlic.

"I am Pandini," be breathed when they started to ascend. His English was accented with Italian. Leila smiled politely. Jamil said nothing. They ushered him into their room.

"You wanted to see us?"

The fat man nodded quickly. "I am working for Mr. Doula. Mr. Doula sends his most compliments he. Mr. Doula she say I give you bag. She say everything are inside for yours." He nodded again, handing over the large suitcase. It was heavy. Jamil laid it on the bed. He looked at it suspiciously for a moment.

"She safe bag. I pack bag for Mr. Doula. Two guns, one rifle, one telephonic sight, plenty bulls soft heads." He smiled widely, baring his bad teeth, then reached past Jamil and began undoing the retaining straps that circled the case. He flipped the locks and opened the top with a flourish.

"See?" He stood back, pleased.

"Do you have anything else for us?"

"Ah, yes Senora! I have envelope too she give I." He pulled it out from inside his crumpled suit and handed it to Leila with a happy smile. She ripped it open and read the Arabic script. Jamil peered over her shoulder.

"The man Pandini may be trusted completely. He is your contact with me. He will take you to your assignment when you are ready. He will take you to the airport when you are finished. Doula."

The message was authentic. Three characters of script in the first sentence were underlined in the correct places.

"Do you have a car?" Jamil asked.

"No car me. Mr. Doula she have car. I drive I."

"Where is it?"

"Next block side street front of bookstore. Fiat. Green. We go we?"

Jamil shook his head.

"Be here after nine-thirty tomorrow morning. We want to see the place in daylight."

The fat man bowed. "I your service I. Nine-thirty o'clock. I wait at front door with taxi sign on car. You tourist you. Tourist for city. No problem.''

He smiled his fangs into view again, and went out the door with surprising agility for his bulk.

The green Fiat was parked at the front door of the hotel the following morning when they walked out into the grey rain. Pandini, dressed in semi-uniform, leaned in the window of another cab, gossiping with its driver. He appeared oblivious to the downpour. They squeezed into the tiny car and shot off down the street. A few minutes later the windows were steamed over and the interior reeked from the wet wool of Pandini's serge jacket. Jamil, in the front seat, rolled down his window.

"Frosters no froster," Pandini explained.

Jamil grunted. They sped towards the outskirts of the city in silence, finally slowing as they came upon a group of highrise apartments where the road turned off to Fumicino Airport. Pandini parked the cab halfway down a side street between a row of the huge pale yellow buildings.

"Apartment 603. No elevator," he nodded. "They there they." He pointed to the second building down the street.

"Leila, you take the front, I'll take the back. Meet us here in thirty minutes," he added to Pandini as Leila climbed out. Jamil waited until she was walking up to the entrance, before stepping out into the drizzle himself. The Fiat roared away as he slammed the door.

An alleyway separated the building from its neighbor. Jamil sauntered through the gap to the rear between the two buildings. There didn't appear to be a back entrance accessible from the alley. A high fence enclosed an open garbage area filled with mounds of wet rubbish. He saw several faces peering at him from the lower windows. A child waved. He waved back, then retraced his steps. He felt hot and sticky inside the transparent plastic raincoat, although the air was cool. He passed across the front of the building to the alley on the other side, and looked up. There were two fire escapes spidering down the sides of the apartments on this side. He climbed slowly up the steel lace steps to the first level and tried the door. It was open. He climbed two more flights, checking the door. It was open. At the third floor, he entered the building. The hallway was dark and humid. The first two doors facing each other were numbered 306 and 307. He walked down the corridor and stopped in front of 303. It would face the rear of the apartment complex, like 603 three floors up. 303 and 304 were divided by a set of wide double stairs leading down to the lobby. He looked up the stairwell to where it disappeared dimly at the roof. Leila looked down the well at the same moment. She smiled, then gave him a thumbs-up sign. Her head disappeared. Jamil went back to the fire escape and descended to the street. He hugged the building and lit a cigarette, watching the rain.

Pandini was waiting as Leila and Jamil joined each other on the sidewalk and climbed back into the car.

"Okay?"

Jamil nodded. "Fire escape door open on the sixth?"

"On the seventh and fifth too," Leila confirmed.

"When is the next evening flight out?"

"Airplanes fly every time. Where you go you?" Pandini inquired. He slipped the car in gear and drove up to the end of the street.

"Back to the hotel. We'll check out this evening. See if you can pick up two tickets to anywhere out of Italy around midnight."

"Egyptair fly Cairo at midnight."

"Fine. We'll go to Cairo."

They returned to the hotel listening to Pandini expound on the glories that once were Rome. Jamil had been to Rome before. Leila wasn't interested. Neither said anything until he pulled up in front of the hotel taxi stand.

"Pick us up at nine. Bring the airline tickets with you," Jamil instructed the fat chauffeur.

"Nine positively."

They climbed out and went back to their room. It was early. Too early for lunch. Leila took the plastic raincoats and shook them dry in the bathroom, then hung them over the towel rack. When she came out Jamil was sitting in the chair looking out of the window at the rain. She came up behind him and put her hands on his shoulders, kneading his neck muscles. He stiffened, then relaxed. Leila saw he was holding the two photographs in his hand. Two smiling young men in their twenties.

"You don't want to kill them, do you?" She continued to massage his neck.

"I don't want to kill anyone if I can avoid it."

"They are traitors!" she exclaimed.

"That's what I don't understand. How could Palestinians be traitors to the cause? If they were Jews or Englishmen I would understand it. But Palestinian . . . ." He held the pictures up and studied them.

Leila stopped working on his shoulders and sat on the bed.

"Perhaps for money—they did it for money?"

Jamil threw the photographs aside. "Whatever the reason, they deserve to die. They should be grateful to die quickly. Such people deserve a slower death." He stood up and stretched, looking at Leila, "Does it bother you?"

"Killing them?"

"Yes. Killing two people you don't know, because someone else passed judgment and made you executioner. Does that bother you?"

"A little."

Jamil smiled sourly. "Me too." He gave a dry laugh. "Jaber says that after you kill the first one, the rest are easy."

"Jaber should know."

"We'll find out tonight."

Pandini parked the car halfway down the street from the building. Jamil slipped the barrel of the silencer into his belt.

"Give us ten minutes, then come back and keep cruising until you see us," he said, as he climbed out. The rain had stopped.

"Good lucky you!"

"Thanks. Remember—ten minutes!"

They walked down the lighted street to the alleyway and climbed the fire escape to the sixth floor. Jamil opened the door, then drew back, letting it close.

"Three people in the hall talking," he muttered to Leila. They waited a few minutes. He tried again. The corridor was clear.

"Keep me covered." He slipped through the door.

Leila wedged her toe in the jam as it closed, keeping her eyes on Jamil. She held her machine pistol ready, the safety off, the snout pointing through the crack in the door.

Softly, Jamil walked down the hallway to the stairwell and checked for traffic above and below the sixth floor landing. There were some people descending below. No one above. Swiftly he went to the door labeled 603 and withdrew his pistol. He signaled Leila to join him. He flattened himself against the wall as Leila knocked on the door.

"Who is it?" a man's voice called from the other side. He spoke in English.

"Sophia, amore," Leila called seductively, putting her mouth close to the varnish-flaked wood.

"Sophia who?"

"Sophia, mi amore!" She made her voice sound exasperated.

For a moment there was a mumbling beyond the door, then the noise of a slide bolt. Jamil swung into the opening as the door opened, driving the two occupants back into the room as he kicked it open. He fired from a crouch at the first man, drilling a small dark red hole in the center of his forehead. The second man tugged for the Baretta hanging from the shoulder holster tied over his shirt. He was dead before the first one hit the floor, with two bullets through his heart. He sagged backwards over the sofa, a surprised look on his face, eyes wide with astonishment. Leila closed the door before the girl screamed. She was dressed in a slip and had come out of the kitchen alcove when her friends hit the floor. Her screams were hysterical, wild, insane shrieking. Jamil stopped, uncertain whether or not to kill her. Swiftly Leila slapped her cheeks with an open hand—once—twice. The screaming stopped. The girl's eyes bugged with horror.

"You have nothing to fear from us. We did not come to kill you. We will not harm you if you keep quiet. Our job was to kill your friends. We will not hurt you." Leila's voice was soft and soothing.

The girl flinched as she was led to the sofa and pushed gently onto the seat. With her back to the bodies, she started to regain her composure. Leila looked at Jamil questioningly. He nodded, stuck the pistol back into his belt and walked around the sofa to face the girl.

"We are Israeli agents sent from Tel Aviv to perform a job on two traitors. We know you are not a part of their crimes." He nodded to the bodies behind her. "And we have no wish to harm a citizen of this country, nor have we any wish to get you mixed up with the police. How long did you know these two?" he asked absently.

"Since three days when Mika picked me up at the Club Strada." The accent was neither Italian nor Arabic. Jamil relaxed. The woman was a whore, probably an illegal alien herself from Turkey or Greece, he decided.

"You have been living here?"

She nodded, her eyes filling with tears.

"Go pack up your things. You are leaving with us now."

The girl got up and went into the bedroom. Leila followed, the machine pistol hanging loosely from her shoulder. Jamil went through the pockets of the dead men and removed every scrap of identification down to the labels on their clothing. Then, systematically made a careful check of the whole apartment, taking anything which might trace the origin of the Palestinians. Leila and the girl were waiting for him in the living room when he came out of the second bedroom carrying a pillowcase filled with bric-a-brac.

"Let's go."

The girl turned towards the stairs as they left.

"Straight ahead to the fire escape door," Leila instructed her.

The girl hesitated. "Quickly now!"

They slipped out onto the metal grating and shut the door. As they started down the steps, Jamil saw the Fiat slowly passing the alleyway and disappear from view. When they reached the ground and safety of darkness in the alley, Jamil took the girl by the shoulders and looked into her face closely.

"You are free now. Go back to your Club. You saw nothing. You know nothing. Do you understand?"

He gripped her shoulders tightly. She nodded several times.

"Go then."

He released her. They watched her walk to the sidewalk, then moved to the corner of the building to view her progress down the street. She did not look back.

"How did you know she spoke English?" Jamil asked.

"They hadn't been here long enough to learn Italian, so she had to speak Arabic or English—I bet on English."

"It was a good bet," Jamil grunted.

"I'm glad we didn't kill her.

"So am I," Jamil said. "She was much too pretty to die."

The Fiat pulled up and stopped as Pandini saw his passengers walk out of the shadows into the street light. They climbed into the car.

"To the airport you?" Pandini inquired anxiously.

"To airport we," Jamil confirmed. For some reason he felt happy.

They passed the girl halfway down the second block of apartments. She looked neither left nor right as they went by. Jamil noticed her head was bent as if in prayer, or thanksgiving. He smiled and settled back to light a cigarette.

They were stuck in Cairo for six weeks at the Shepherd Hotel awaiting word on their next mission. In the heyday of British rule the hotel, situated on the banks of the Nile a few short steps from the Cairo Museum, had been a palace for the wealthy. Rich indolents from the dismal English winter climate spent their weeks ensconced in the luxury of the Shepherd. The orange guilt reading rooms and writing alcoves had faded with the Empire that had produced its patrons. The bellboys and house staff, dressed in their threadbare Arabian Nights costumes, reminded one of a theatrical road company which had overextended its welcome. The Russians had replaced the rich. Somber coarse-featured men who carried black briefcases and dressed alike, rarely speaking to anyone. It was a depressing place to spend six weeks.

For the first days Jamil and Leila had rushed the gamut of sights, expecting to be sent off on their next assignment momentarily. But always, when they returned to the hotel at the end of each day and checked at the desk, there were no messages. The day after they arrived and reported the success of their mission, PLO headquarters in Cairo had told them to wait until they were summoned. The Central Office was courteous enough, but Jamil disliked the patronizing attitude he had received from the Deputy Director, an erudite effete who spoke Arabic with a lisp. Jaber, he could respect. The PLO nonentitites in Cairo he knew he would despise if forced to spend any length of time working with them. He stayed away from the office entirely and spent his time with Leila chasing the sights in and around the city. It was while having supper one night in the hotel dining room the first indication of ending their exile appeared. A messenger arrived at the table, after being directed by their waiter, and handed Jamil an envelope. He tore it open and read the contents.

"No reply," he said.

The messenger departed with a pair of copper coins and a smile. He handed the note to Leila. It said simply: "Room 446 at 2100 hours."

"One assumes the room is in this hotel," Jamil commented.

"Then why didn't the sender use the hotel messenger?"

Jamil shrugged. "Maybe he hasn't checked in yet."

He signaled the waiter and asked him to phone the desk and find who was registered in 446. The man returned a few minutes later to announce the room was unoccupied.

They dawdled over coffee until shortly before nine, then made their way up to 446 and knocked.

"Welcome. I am George Habash. Please come in."

He ushered them into the room. They seated themselves on the chairs sitting stilted against the wall. Dr. Habash smiled good-naturedly.

"I do apologize for keeping you hanging here since your arrival, but many things have been happening which required further clarification before you could be assigned another project."

139

He sat down on the bed. There were no other chairs in the room. After propping two pillows at the headboard to rest against, he swung his feet onto the bedspread and continued.

"I was very pleased to hear of the dispatch with which you finished your mission in Rome. I congratulate you both. I wish there was more I could give you now to help our cause, but there isn't—at least not for the present."

"You mean we took all that training for nothing?" Jamil demanded.

"No. Not for nothing. I am sure it will soon be put to work again, but for the moment there are larger considerations involved." He paused, examining their faces.

"Let me explain some basic politics. Over the past weeks I have been attending meeetings with our Syrian and Iraqi brothers. In the next few weeks the Baathist groups in these countries will seize power, probably in February or March. They will then make formal declaration for Arab Unity with President Nasser for the United Arab Republics. I personally do not believe President Nasser will allow anyone to share the limelight with him, so the whole exercise is pointless. We of the ANM do not have power. We help to create power, but we do not have it yet. Not here, in Syria, Lebanon or Iraq. Using Al Fateh and Al Asifah, we have provided the means for others to obtain power and later hold it, but always power has escaped us. Can you see why?"

"This is January, 1963, Dr. Habash. You have had nearly fifteen years to seize power. I would say you are doing something wrong," Jamil spoke, keeping his voice respectful towards the older man.

Habash laughed. "Or others have been doing something wrong while we have been advocating what is right. But you are correct. ANM have spent too much time theorizing on the concept of overall Arab unity and not enough dealing with specific problems. We intend to change that now."

"How?" Leila asked.

"By devoting our attentions to the Palestine situation exclusively. It is the one cause upon which all Arabs are united in thought."

"I thought that was what we were doing—why we were accepted by Al Asifah," Jamil countered.

"The ANM do not recognize the existence of Al Asifah officially. When we do, it will have to be another name, another identity more acceptable politically. What do you think of the Palestine Liberation Organization?"

"Instead of Al Asifah?"

"As a politically recognized movement. Not only recognized by the ANM but by the rest of the nations of the Arab world. Think of it! Official recognition!"

He paused in his rhetoric, considering the possibilities himself.

"With official recognition there would be no problem with financing, or refuge for our people, in any Arab country. We become a real political force."

"How can we help?" Jamil was curious.

"With patience. We must do nothing to upset the delicate balance I have obtained from our brothers here in Cairo. For a while we must lie dormant. Sleeping until our objectives are achieved. Then we strike."

He swung his feet off the bed and stood up.

"Return to Amman and tell Abu Ali Iyad what I have said. There is a message to take to him."

He opened his briefcase and removed a bulky brown envelope, handing it over to Jamil.

"It may take six months or a year before we are ready. But I promise you that when we are ready you will be called. Keep in touch with Abu Ali Iyad," he told them.

"We work for Abd Arheem Jaber," Jamil said.

"Only when you are in the field on operations. There will be no more operations until I instruct Abu Ali Iyad," he stated emphatically. "We have too much to lose with any irresponsible actions by unthinking eager activists. Remember, first persuasion, then politics, and finally, punishment!" He shook hands with them again as they stood up. "Allah Maak."

They returned to Amman the following day and reported back to camp. During their absence, little had changed. People were still undergoing training and the stacatto of small arms fire could be heard from the firing range.

"We still seem to be in business," Jamil observed.

"Maybe they haven't received the word yet."

They climbed out of the battered Scout car, thanking the driver for the lift from town. They had to wait in the outer office for an hour until Abu Ali Iyad was free. Finally the door opened and the trio of guests departed, Kuwaitis, dressed in their bedsheets. Jamil looked at the bearded men sourly. They nodded to them gravely as they left the waiting room.

"Welcome back. Did you enjoy Cairo?" Abu Ali Iyad stood up, greeting them with a smile.

"The pyramids are still there." He handed the envelope to his superior. "Dr. Habash instructed me to deliver this to you."

Abu Ali Iyad nodded them into chairs and opened the letter with a short model scimitar lying on the desk. "Please, sit down."

Jamil's seat was still warm from its previous occupant. They watched while he scanned the contents of the envelope. There was a series of maps, typewritten sheets and a package of photographs held together with a wide rubber band. On top of the pile was a handwritten letter. Abu Ali Iyad picked it up and started reading. He read through it twice, then tossed it aside with a sigh.

"It appears we are to suspend our operations for awhile until the political situation has stabilized. Jaber will be unhappy to hear this." He riffled through the rest of the papers and pictures quickly, then looked up. "I'm sorry. You did a good job in Rome, but I'm afraid there is nothing more for you now."

"We were told in Cairo," Leila said.

"It is temporary, I am sure."

"Can we be of help here, training?" Jamil suggested.

"Of course. We still need soldiers at the camps. There is work for both of you if you wish to stay. If not, make sure you contact me every month where you can be reached. In a war things have a habit of changing quickly."

"Thank you. We will stay," Jamil told him.

They left the office, closing the door behind them. Outside the clapboard hut, they stood in the yard compound. The air was cold, the sky overcast. It smelled like rain. The wind whipped a dust devil past their feet. It was a depressing day for everything. Leila grabbed his arm.

"I don't want to stay here, Galal. It's like walking backwards."

He paused to light a cigarette. "What do you want to do?"

She shrugged. They started walking slowly across the yard to the women's quarters.

"I don't know. Maybe I'll go back to the American University and finish my degree. I can always get a job teaching."

She tried to make the idea appealing. It wasn't. They continued walking in silence, stopping finally before the entrance to Leila's quarters, uncertain what to say to each other. They shook hands formally, feeling awkward. Jamil walked away without a word. She climbed the three wooden steps into the building. She felt like crying. Not over the parting with Jamil, but because of the frustration of what had started out as a grand adventure, with worthwhile objectives, now crumbled. The adventure was over; the objectives had become obscure. She went to her room and started packing.

As Dr. Habash had predicted in Cairo, the Baathists seized power in Iraq on February 8. In Syria, exactly one month later, to bolster their new regimes, they called immediately for Arab unity. As previously agreed, Cairo acknowledged their requests for a United Arab Republic and a new proclamation was issued to this effect. The formal merger was to take place in the Fall. Although Nasserites within the Baathist Parties of the two countries had been in great part responsible for the success of the takeovers, the central Baathist political control still rested with those who mistrusted Nasser. The Baathist leaders returned from Cairo and began to purge the Nasserites, finally removing them from power completely. In July, Nasser retaliated by releasing the recorded tapes of his talks to Al-Ahram, the newspaper mouthpiece of the Egyptian middle class. The editor, Mohammed Heikal, serialized censored verbatim accounts scathingly critical of the Baathists. The disclosures provided proof that Nasser had no intention of proceeding on the autumn merger with Iraq and Libya. Nothing would be subordinate to the national interest of Egypt. Since Nasser was Egypt, he had no intention of sharing his power with lesser men.

Leila returned to the American University in Beirut and took up her studies towards a degree in teaching. She managed to get a room in Jewett Hall, the women's residence which she shared with an American girl. Her roommate, Prissy Lewis, came from Baton Rouge, Louisiana. She had a whining nasal voice that grated on the ear. Her father, an embassy official, had been transferred to Athens, leaving Priscilla to finish her education in Beirut alone. Although she was three years older than Leila, she seemed much younger. She had an astonishing number of boyfriends with whom she fell in and out of love, almost on a weekly basis. Periodically, she tried to take Leila out on a foursome for a dance, dinner or a movie, but as always, Leila declined politely.

"Honestly, Leila, I don't know what's wrong with you! You just never go anywhere! It's not healthy, honey. You sittin' in here studyin' all the time."

Prissy was busy positioning her strawberry curls in the appropriate framing for her oval face. Her latest beau, as she called them, was a tall marine corporal from the Embassy.

"I'm expecting a call. If I went out I might miss it."

It was a lame excuse. Leila had used it before.

"If he hasn't called by now, honey, he's never gonna call. Charlie has a real cute friend, a sergeant too. How about it?"

She worked the lipstick around the 'O' of her lips, examining it critically. She looked over at Leila curled up on the bed.

"No thanks, Prissy." She watched her roommate finish her boudoir, fling a careless shawl over her shoulders, carefully adjusting it for effect, then disappear out the door with a wave.

"Have fun!" Leila called, but the door had closed already.

She lay back on the bed and lit a cigarette. She felt frustrated. Nothing was happening. Each month she had written faithfully to Abu Ali Iyad reconfirming her address and availability for work. Once she had inquired about Jamil. So far there had been no reply to any of her letters. Now it was November and the *Voice of the Arabs* radio broadcasts from Cairo beamed out across the world were finally speaking in positive terms on the idea of Palestinian identity. The new name would be the Palestine Liberation Organization and it would be backed and funded by the Arab world. How much was fact and how much rhetoric, Leila could not tell. She knew Jamil would know, wherever he was. It was the certain knowledge that great events were occurring of which she was supposed to be a part that frustrated her. She felt stagnant and deserted. Leila sighed, and went back to her textbooks.

At the camp near Amman, Jamil threw himself into the training schedules with dedication, determined to produce the best combat-ready assault teams in the Middle East. He studied advanced training manuals used by the British, American and Israeli armies, poring over their suggested methods of insurgency and counter-insurgency. He spent hours in the camp library during off-duty hours, reading everything he could find on the art of war; tactical treatises from Napoleon through Clausweitz to Mao Tse Tung. By early summer he had absorbed the theory of practical warfare better than any man in camp. He longed to put the new knowledge to more useful purposes than drilling and training the superb combat teams he was turning out in the classrooms, or on the difficult assault course.

One day in June he was stripping his bedding to return it to the clothing department for his weekly issue and heard a knock on the door.

"Come in. It's open," he called in Arabic.

It was the big bearded man with a huge scar on one cheek he had seen earlier that morning watching him with Abu Ali Iyad during a lesson in unarmed combat Jamil was conducting in the yard. "I'm sorry. I don't speak Arabic. Only English and Spanish. Col. Iyad said I would find you here." He looked about the tiny cubicle. "May I sit down?"

Compared to Jamil, he looked like a giant. The single wooden chair beside the bed was the only seat in the room. The man lifted it by the back and swung it around, draping his elbows over the upright rear as he sat down. Jamil stood, his arms filled with bedclothes, waiting for the stranger to speak.

"My name is Pedro Artega de Miranda. I am called El Chirlo—because of this," he indicated his scar with a lopsided smile. "It means Scarface in Spanish."

Jamil said nothing. He dumped the sheets and blankets on the thin mattress and sat down.

"I come from the Republic of Cosecha Rica where I am engaged in guerilla war to overthrow an American imperialist dictatorship." He paused, studying the effect of his words.

"Col. Iyad informs me that you have been trained as a guerilla fighter and that you have had experience in the field."

Jamil thought Abu Ali Iyad was overstating the experience. Assassination of two traitors hardly constituted formal field experience, however, one might stretch his imagination. But, he reasoned, if the bearded man had been told this by his superior, there was probably a good reason for it. He waited for Chirlo to continue.

"I am told also that you could be permitted a leave of absence for a few months, maybe as long as a year. The same thing applies to your co-workers." He stopped to extract a long thin cigar from a case in his shirt pocket. He offered one to Jamil who shook his head. He lit it carefully, his eyes still on Jamil.

"It is suggested by Col. Iyad that you and some of your friends might be interested in joining me in Cosecha Rica for the final phase of my operations there."

"I am a Palestinian who is prepared to fight for his homeland. Not a mercenary for hire to your banana republic."

"I see. However, I don't remember offering you any money."

Jamil laughed. "You expect me to go halfway around the world to fight with you for nothing? You must think we are all simple-minded here!"

Chirlo continued puffing the slim brown cigar.

"You must make up your mind, Jamil. First you say you are not a mercenary. Then you are outraged that I will not pay you for being a mercenary. Which is it?" He flicked the ash onto the uneven wooden floor. Jamil said nothing.

"Neither Dr. Castro or Guevara were Cubans, but they liberated Cuba. I am not a Cosecha Rican, but I intend to liberate it."

"Are you a communist?"

"I am whatever I have to be in order to achieve victory," Chirlo replied evenly.

"And after victory?"

"Then I can afford the luxury of nationalism."

"Why should I help?"

"Because more than anyone you understand what it means to be victimized by others. The oppressed must fight the oppressor, regardless who is the oppressor or who the oppressed. The cause is international. Your cause is here. Mine is an ocean away. But they are the same cause. Help me with mine and perhaps someday I can help you with yours."

Jamil stood up. The man made sense. "But why come to the Middle East? Why not use Cubans—at least they speak the language?"

"Precisely why I don't want to use them. The revolution would be labeled as communist inspired. The Americans might invoke the Monroe Doctrine and then I would be fighting the Americans as well as their Cosecha Rican puppets. With people like yourself I know when the work is finished, you will leave to fight your own cause, leaving me to build mine."

"And what do I get out of it all?"

"Something more valuable than money, Jamil. Experience and the satisfaction of knowing you helped right an injustice for two million people."

Jamil stood, considering the offer. It made a lot of sense. The bearded Chirlo spoke with a quiet common sense which affected him. That he was a born leader of men, there was no doubt. In some ways he reminded him of Jaber. They were the same types. Born with the mantle of authority. Resolute and determined.

"How many of us do you need?"

"A dozen."

"So few?" Jamil was surprised.

"Doctor Castro landed in Oriente Province with eighty one. A month later he was down to a dozen men. Two years later he had conquered Cuba. It is not the numbers that are important, Jamil, only the quality of the numbers."

"You think I have that quality?"

"I know you do." Chirlo butted his cigar and stood up, crushing the smoking ember with his heel. He looked at Jamil questioningly.

"I accept—on one condition."

"Which is?"

"That you never ask me to smoke one of those goddamn cigars."

Chirlo chuckled. "I promise."

Jamil heard him still chuckling to himself as he walked down the corridor. Jamil kicked the door to his cubicle closed and began to remake the bed. At best, he decided it would take the Spaniard a few days to round up the rest of his crew of volunteers. He tried to visualize a map of the Americas, attempting to position Cosecha Rica geographically in his mind. Suddenly he laughed aloud. He realized he had volunteered to fight a war in a country where he couldn't speak the language and didn't know where it was.

"Chirlo. You are one smooth talking bastard!"

The PLO was set up formally by the Arab League States in January, 1964, as the kings and presidents of the Arab nations met in Cairo. Although privately the leaders agreed there would be no confrontation with Israel, their people were led to believe they were preparing for war. In launching the PLO, Arab States felt they could contain the Palestinians, supposedly giving them an instrument for their liberation. But the PLO was born crippled. The Arab States would not permit Palestinians to act independently of their supervision, or act themselves with any apparent desire to safeguard their interests. The PLO became a skeleton put on display. By June the realization of this fraud came home to those who had been swindled in their beliefs. Ahmed Shukairy was appointed Chairman of the new PLO—not by the Palestinians—but the kings and presidents of the Arab States. Dear old Shukairy could be relied upon to make the important necessary pronouncements in purple prose without precipitating a political crisis or allowing the Palestinians to organize themselves into a fighting force.

Early in May, Jamil returned to Beirut from Cosecha Rica after an absence of eleven months. He dragged Leila out of her class in the middle of the afternoon, and they went back to the same restaurant to eat fattet where they had gone the first day they met. Jamil had changed. He seemed surer of himself than when they had parted in Amman the year before.

"We are being betrayed by fools," he announced as soon as they had seated themselves at a table. "Have they contacted you at all?"

Leila shook her head. "Nothing."

"Nor I."

They ordered their meal from a garrulous waiter who wanted to offer them anything but fattet. In the end he admitted they were out.

"Then why didn't you say so in the first place. Fool!" Jamil snarled at him.

They settled for lamb stew.

"I have no patience with fools. You have heard news of the Congress?"

The Palestinian National Congress was scheduled to be opened in Jerusalem by King Hussein on May 28. Three hundred and fifty delegates, representing a cross-section of the Palestinian people in exile, were scheduled to attend.

"I hear they plan on keeping Shukairy as Chairman," Leila observed.

"Idiots! They must be stopped. The whole thing is an exercise in futility."

"How can they be stopped?"

"I don't know yet, but I am going to Jerusalem to find out. Have you heard where Jaber or Abu Ali Iyad are?"

"No, I have heard nothing."

"They will be in Jerusalem. That much I know. We have wasted enough time playing political games with fools."

The waiter brought their plates of stew, running to the table with the overloaded dishes. He served them swiftly and rushed off for the bread and cheese that accompanied their meal. Jamil stared after him angrily.

"What was it like in South America?" She decided it was time to change the subject. A further discussion on the PLO would only anger him further.

Jamil smiled grimly. "The best training ground in the world." He paused. "Central America, not South America. Too bad you couldn't have been there, Leila. I wish Chirlo was here now. He would know exactly what we should do." He took a mouthful of food, chewing thoughtfully.

"What was he like?"

Jamil swallowed. "A giant among pygmies. A Hercules. If we had a few like him in the Movement, even one would do it," he sighed. "What do we have? We have Ahmed Shukairy. Lucky us," he added ironically.

"Do you want me to go with you to Jerusalem?"

Jamil considered the idea a moment. "No, I'll go alone. Stay and finish off your courses. You're too close to graduation to throw it all away."

He pushed the rest of the stew aside and looked at her. "Leila, I am going to Jerusalem to do one thing; only one thing. Either those idiots will make the PLO a vehicle for the liberation of Palestine, or I'll create my own vehicle. Whichever way it works out you will be part of it, that I promise." He looked around for the waiter. "Let's get the hell out of here and go to my hotel." He glanced at her as the waiter rushed the table. "Unless you have something else to do right now?"

Leila laughed. "I thought you'd never ask."

Two days later Jamil arrived in Jerusalem. It took another two days before he located Dr. Habash at the St. Georges, where he had registered under another name. By pure accident they passed each other in the lobby. The hotel was filled with delegates to the Congress. It appeared everyone had registered under assumed names. The purpose of the Congress was brotherly love, but it was also an excellent opportunity for settling old scores for those that were so inclined. Jamil elbowed his way through a swarm of coat-tailers surrounding the doctor.

"Doctor, I would like to speak with you when it is conveneint." He blocked the group's progress to the front door. Habash looked startled, then his eyes relaxed as he recognized the young Palestinian.

"Jamil, isn't it?"

"You have a good memory sir." Jamil bowed slightly. A few of the swarm craned their necks, seeing to whom their queen bee was speaking. The buzzing voices drowned any chance of hearing their conversation. Jamil lowered his voice. "I must speak to you privately."

Habash looked at the intense dark eyes and nodded, his smile still fixed in place.

"Tomorrow morning at eight. Join me for breakfast. Room 501." He said the words quietly without moving his lips. Jamil stepped back. The procession moved on through the lobby and out the door to the waiting cavalcade of cars.

"Do you know George Habash?"

He hadn't noticed the American before in the crush of people. Jamil looked at the man standing beside him. His breath smelled of whiskey.

"Slightly."

"I'm Max Bruner, Consolidated Press." He stuck out his hand. Jamil ignored it. "Are you Jewish?"

"Jewish?" He lowered his hand, looking perplexed. "Oh, I see what y'mean. Bruner is German, not Jewish."

"In that case, I'll shake your hand." They concluded the ceremony.

"Can I buy you a drink?"

Jamil nodded, following him into the lounge bar. Bruner ordered Bourbon. They didn't have any. He settled on *Teacher's Highland Cream*. Jamil ordered orange juice.

"You don't drink?" Bruner raised his eyebrows.

Jamil smiled. "Not when I'm drinking with a newspaper reporter, Mr. Bruner."

"Call me Max."

"You are covering the Congress?"

"Not so much the Congress as the people attending it. How about you? Are you a delegate?"

Jamil shook his head. "Not yet."

The waiter brought their drinks. Bruner downed half the contents of his glass thirstily, then sighed with satisfaction. He regarded Jamil over the rim of his drink.

"Attending but uninvited, eh? You known Dr. Habash long?"

"Who?"

"The man you stopped in the lobby with that crew of parasites. Did you make an appointment to see him?"

Jamil sipped at his orange juice. "What is your interest?"

"Look pal, I don't even know your name, but I've been sitting in the lobby of this hotel for the past few days watching all these birds float in and out. Besides Arafat and Habash, who won't see me at all, you're the first interesting guy to turn up I could talk to since I got here."

"Interesting?" Jamil asked, disbelief in his voice.

"To me. Who are you?"

He shrugged. "I am Galal Jamil, a Palestinian from Haifa and I want to go home."

"Say—I like that. Can I use it?" Without waiting for a reply he whipped out his notebook and pencil and began scribbling. "Do you people think anything will come out of this Congress?"

As if in reply, there was a burst of loud laughter from another table.

"I don't know. But if nothing happens after this Congress there will be no further meetings. The Palestinians are tired of hearing how other people will settle their problems."

"This meeting is supposed to be different, I hear," Bruner persisted.

Jamil gave him a thin smile. "We shall see." He finished off his glass of juice.

"I'll tell you the story, Max, an exclusive story when the Congress is over, whichever way it turns out. Now, if you will excuse me I have an appointment to keep. A friend, you understand?" He slid out of the seat as Bruner winked in understanding.

"Sure Galal, see y'later." He downed the rest of his whiskey and signaled for another. Jamil left the lounge.

There was no appointment to keep, but he didn't feel in the mood for a three-hour examination by a progressively-drunken news reporter. He took a cab back to his hotel and went into the dining room for supper.

"Jamil!"

"Akbar!"

They embraced, slapping each other on the back. Khala Akbar had been the second highest graduate from weapons training in Amman at the refugee camp. He was a rolly-polly, bandy-legged comic with a beatific smile. He was the only man Jamil had ever met who could make him laugh.

"Are you hiding or can't you afford the prices at the Intercontinental?"

Jamil laughed. "Are you staying here too?"

"It's all I can afford." He held Jamil by an elbow and steered him toward his table.

"Join me, I have ordered the American steak. The waiter recommended it. It's probably Jewish lamb." There was stony silence from the rest of the dozen or more patrons in the dining room as they watched and listened.

"You look older, Jamil."

"You look the same, Akbar." He smiled. "You will always look the same." He ordered the American steak from a soiled, white jacketed cadaver. It was a tourist hotel.

"Have you been here long?"

"Checked in this morning from Kuwait. I have a job there on the new television center. You?"

"I've been overseas doing some work in Latin America. Even learned to speak a bit of the language. Are you here for the Congress?"

Akbar nodded vigorously. "Wouldn't miss it for the world. I want to be on hand when they sell us down the Jordan again. Do you know those goddamn Jews have most of the river bypassed into irrigation projects now. I hear there is only a trickle left for us."

"So much for the big Jordanian dam project," Jamil said wryly.

"Last year it was a big dam project for 13 million dollars. This year it's the Palestine Liberation Organization. I wonder what they have in mind for 1965?"

Jamil laughed at his solemn face. The waiter brought the American steaks.

"Do you think they're serious this time?"

"Aren't they always; until the meetings end and everyone goes home. I tell you, Jamil, someone has got to do something. Something drastic. Even if it means going back to the type of thing the fayadeen were doing in the Fifties. At least we were fighting and killing Jews instead of talking about it."

"Someone is going to do something."

"Who?"

"Me."

Akbar's eyes lighted up with interest. "I hear the mob in the streets. Run quickly and find out where they're headed. I am supposed to be their leader."

Jamil laughed. "Exactly, my friend. We are a mob seeking a leader."

"You have a plan?"

"Better than a plan. I have an alternative." Between mouthfuls, he explained his idea to Akbar. It had been simmering formlessly in the back of his mind since his return to the Middle East. Meeting Akbar had solidified the shapes into definite form. The words spilled out. They were drinking coffee by the time Jamil had finished and sat back, stirring the bitter dark liquid. Akbar said nothing for several minutes. Jamil sipped his coffee. "Well?"

"A terrorist organization within the PLO. Sort of popular front; an arm of the PLO which refuses to recognize the PLO as its own body. Aren't you merely creating a new Al Asifah within El Fatah?"

"No. Al Asifah was created by El Fatah to serve it. We will create this popular front to serve no one. Nothing but our interests. Don't you see, Akbar? We advertise our philosophy of terror and use the PLO as the vehicle to obtain our political aims. It is as if Al Asifah controlled El Fatah, not the other way around."

"Shukairy and the rest of them will never approve."

"Fuck them! Who cares what they approve? We will tell them what we are going to do, then do it. Let them figure out what to do with our successes in the political arena. That's their job."

"As Churchill observed, we give them the tools and they finish the job."

Jamil laughed. "That's it, my friend. What do you think?"

Akbar grinned hugely. "I think it is the most traitorous and scandalous suggestion I've ever heard. When do we start?"

"Right now. I have an appointment with George Habash for breakfast tomorrow morning. Come with me and see how the idea affects his digestion."

There were three other men in the suite of rooms when Jamil and Akbar arrived for breakfast promptly at eight. Two were obviously bodyguards and were not introduced. The other man was presented as Colonel Fawzi of Egyptian Army Intelligence. Everyone, except the two bodyguards, seated themselves about the table of gleaming crystal and silverware. Three carefully sliced fat grapefruit with red maraschino cherry centers were laid out. An order for a fourth setting was filled quickly by room service.

"I apologize, Dr. Habash, but Khala Akbar arrived yesterday and I did not have an opportunity to speak to him until last night."

Habash waved a hand nonchalantly, indicating the inconvenience of an uninvited guest was of no particular importance.

"Well now, Jamil, tell me what I can do to help you and your friend."

The grapefruit spoons were pointed, fitting the slices perfectly. He popped one section into his mouth and contemplated his guests.

"We did not come for your help, Dr. Habash. We came to tell you what we are going to do, so when we are successful, you may use our successes for the Movement."

Dr. Habash was Secretary General of the Arab National Movement. He swallowed the slice of grapefruit.

"You are speaking of independent action?" His voice was severe.

"Yes."

"I see." He slipped another slice into this mouth and chewed thoughtfully. There was an uncomfortable silence in the room. "You are both with Al Asifah?" He glanced at Akbar, who nodded with a smile.

"For whatever good that is, sir."

"Then you are both under military orders," Col. Fawzi observed.

"When there is someone around capable of giving us orders, Colonel. Are you accepting this responsibility?" Jamil inquired evenly.

Habash waved his pointed spoon. "Let's not deal in semantics. Get to the point. What are you proposing?"

"I propose nothing, Sir. I am telling you I intend to form an organization made up of Palestinians like myself who are tired of rhetoric. Since there doesn't seem to be anyone capable of taking decisive action or making a positive decision on anything, we shall relieve them of the responsibility. Our results will be swift and sure. As a courtesy I tell you of the plan, so that when it happens it will not come as a surprise, and you are free to use it on whatever political harvest you feel inclined."

"Impossible!" Col. Fawzi said loudly. "The Egyptian government forbids any sort of independent action outside the political control of recognized authority."

Jamil swung his gaze slowly to Fawzi, fixing him with calm dark eyes.

"Colonel, I don't give a shit what the Egyptian government forbids."

The Colonel jumped to his feet. "This is an insult."

"It was supposed to be," Jamil replied calmly.

"Gentlemen, gentlemen, there is no need to quarrel. We are all brothers. Colonel Fawzi, perhaps you would be kind enough to leave me alone for a few minutes with these young men while I try and straighten this matter out?" It was an order, not a suggestion.

Fawzi bowed and left the room. The bodyguards followed him. Even in mufti, they all walked like soldiers. Habash sighed.

"I'm afraid President Nasser has turned Egypt into a Colonel's paradise."

He pushed the empty grapefruit aside and wiped his mouth with a starched napkin.

"I understand now why you wanted to speak to me privately, Jamil."

"I apologize if I have embarrassed you."

"You have, and I accept the apology. How old are you, Jamil?"

"Twenty-five."

"When I was twenty-five I felt the same way. As one grows older it is necessary to compromise idealism for reality; zeal for common sense. Don't misunderstand me. I am just as much an idealist now as I was before, probably more so. I think I told you last year—January wasn't it?—I said to have patience. Wait and let us try the political action first before we attempt the violent. Now we are at the crossroads. You think the PLO will be one more sop. You may be right, but at least we have an identity recognized by everyone when this Congress ends. We have achieved the fine balance between all factions of the ANM at last. For some, it is too much. For you and I, not nearly enough. But it is a start. Tell me what you plan. If I cannot help, at least I can offer advice."

"We want to build a popular front. A popular front for the liberation of Palestine. Its purpose will be armed aggression against the Jews or anyone else who supports them. Part guerilla, part terrorist, like the IRA. A few highly trained people to provide incidents which will draw attention to our plight. International attention. We will wage a war of the flea. Attack, then vanish. Each incident may be nothing in itself. But, as incident after incident occurs, world publicity will focus on our actions. People will begin to ask each other, 'Who are these madmen and why are they doing such terrible things?' The resulting political advantages I leave to you. Yasser Arafat told me once that one day we would stand in the United Nations as representatives of our country. I believe this. But it will never happen unless we make it happen."

"Do you feel this way too?" Habash looked at Akbar.

"Everyone in Al Asifah feels the same, Dr. Habash. We have been trained for nothing. Working as engineers in television stations or managing money for illiterate Kuwaitis and other Emirates."

"Have you spoken to others of this plan?"

"Only to you," Jamil confirmed.

"Of course, I cannot condone your actions in an official sense, but I agree with the approach as long as you don't start dictating to the PLO or the ANM."

"How can we? Publicly we would expect the PLO to disown us. State their dismay at our actions."

"While at the same time use the benefits," Habash laughed. "Clever, Jamil, clever."

They were silent for several minutes, each deep in thought.

"All right. I approve. However, I agreed with President Nasser last month to work towards an Arab unity for the liberation of Palestine. He impressed me as sincerely interested in our cause, so long as it does not conflict with his own ideas of Arab socialism. At the moment our paths are identical. However, sooner or later they are bound to diverge. Gamal Nasser is far too ambitious for his own good. The Yemen adventure is a good example. That war is costing Egypt a fortune in wasted men and materials. A war Nasser can never win. A Phyrric victory if he succeeds. A loss of Karamah* if he fails. Can you wait three months before starting anything?"

*Karamah—Arab loss of 'face.'

"It will take three months to organize ourselves, Dr. Habash," Jamil confirmed.

"You will let me know what you are doing?"

"No problem. You will be able to read it in the newspapers."

Habash laughed. "Good. Well, that's settled. Let's eat our breakfast. I'm starved."

The Congress opened as scheduled the following week with its majority of Palestinian traditionalists. Radical elements were barred from attending. An Executive Committee of seven was elected, which in turn, reconfirmed Ahmed Shukairy as its Chairman. A ponderous proposal, in stylized prose, was issued from the Congress, electing all sorts of heady state committees to operate the apparatus of the forthcoming revolution. This National Charter embodied the ideology of every armchair tactician in the Congress. The PLO was given a Palestinian seat at Arab League Headquarters in Cairo. After a few more days of mutual admiration and self-congratulation, everyone went home satisfied. Jamil and Akbar went to find Max Bruner at the St. Georges hotel. He was in the bar.

"Ah, friend Jamil, join me in a libation. Share my sorrow. Bartender! Who's your friend?" Bruner noticed Jamil was not alone.

"Max Bruner—Khala Akbar."

"Akbar? Means 'great' in Arabic. Are you great, Mr. Akbar?" Max was drunk.

"The greatest!"

Jamil laughed. "Can we tear you away from your sorrows for a talk?"

"Ah hah! I am going to tell my story after all." He shrugged sadly. "Too late, pilgrim. I have been dismissed by the authorities in New York as unworthy of my salary." He hauled a rumpled telex out of his shirt pocket and handed it over. Jamil glanced at it.

"A reporter incapable of containing his censors and liquor is useless. You're fired.

B.J. Bronstein."

"Who is Bronstein?" Jamil inquired.

"B.J. is my editor-in-chief. A heartless tyrant."

"What does the B.J. stand for, Mr. Bruner? Big Jew?" Akbar smiled widely.

"Benny Jordon—Big Jew—I like it, Mr. Akbar, may I use it?" He grappled about for a notebook and pencil, dropping both on the floor by the bar. " 'Fraid I'm a little under the weather, boys."

"You're drunk. Come with us." Jamil grabbed his arm, hauling him off the stool. "What room are you in?"

Bruner told him.

They lugged him off to the elevators, propped him against the wall until the doors opened at the fourth floor, then hauled him out and searched his pockets for the room key. When they finally slipped him onto the bed, in a comatose state, Jamil phoned room service for a pot of black coffee.

"This is a newspaper reporter?"

Jamil shrugged, "He's all we've got for the moment. He does talk sense when he's sober."

"Galal, you weren't even born the last time this man was sober," Akbar observed, looking at the flabby bulk of the middle-aged man laying on the bed, snoring lightly.

Jamil laughed. "It's an occupational hazard for news reporters."

"Is it contagious?"

"Let's hope not."

They poured six cups of coffee into Bruner, and helped him into the bathroom where he heaved out his stomach into the toilet, then passed out cold back on the bed. Jamil phoned the desk clerk, room service and the assistant hotel manager, giving instructions that under no circumstances was Mr. Bruner to be given any liquor during the next twenty-four hours. The assistant manager asked if he required a visit from the house physician. Jamil informed him blandly that he was a graduate from the University of Edinburgh, internal medicine department.

"What do we do now?" Akbar demanded.

"We pack our things and leave as soon as friend Max is sober enough to travel."

June 23, 1964
Amman, Jordan

Dear B.J.:

I am writing this on a canvas foldaway table inside my tent at our new base camp in the Ghor mountains. We have been here under a week, but already things are beginning to hum. I haven't had a drink since leaving Jerusalem and have been told that if I do, I will be shot. Can't decide whether they are serious or not, but have decided not to press my luck. As you already know the particulars of the Congress Manifesto concluded at the Jerusalem meetings, I shall refrain from belaboring the contents other than mentioning a key resolution concerning the immediate opening of camps for military training of all Palestinians. Palestinians will also be attending the

157

various military academies in the Arab countries. I apologize for not getting the complete Manifesto to you on the wire, but truthfully, the censorship was very tight. I'm afraid the U.P.I. men got the inside track through their previous associations with King Hussein. (I should be so lucky!) In any event, I understand the reason for your firing me and accept the dismissal with, I hope, good grace. However, as an independent writer and former employee, I do feel certain loyalty to the firm and felt you should have first crack at the attached material. If it is of no interest maybe you'd be good enough to send it over to UP or AP and let their boys have a look at it. May amount to nothing, but at least I'm johnny-on-the-spot.

Regards, Max.

MAX BRUNER, GPO, AMMAN, JORDAN.
LISTEN WISEGUY AND LISTEN GOOD. STOP. NO DISPUTE ON YOUR SALARY FIVE HUNDRED PER WEEK PLUS STOP WIRE ALL MATERIAL TO ME DIRECT YOUR BYLINE STOP DEPOSIT FOR YOUR EXPENSES AMERICAN EXPRESS AMMAN STOP PLAN ON INDEFINITE STAY STOP STAY OFF THE BOOZE STOP IF THEY DONT SHOOT YOU I WILL STOP REGARDS B.J.

Amman, Jordan. C.P. Correspondent Max Bruner has been attending the September Palestinian conference in the Middle East. The Conference representatives were all Palestinian members of the Arab National Movement or ANM. The conference adopted three basic principles:
1. Armed struggle is the only way to liberate Palestine.
2. All secondary conflicts should be subordinated to the conflict with imperialism and Zionism.
3. The different revolutionary groups should be unified.

This is the first time Palestinian militarists have spoken officially on their position. When asked to comment on the results of the Conference, a young Palestinian spokesmen, who did not wish to be identified, stated that first incursions into occupied territory had already taken place for the purpose of laying down supplies of food and arms for the sorties which are to follow during the next few months.

Bruner's breath came in short dry gasps as he lugged the pack of ammunition across the open field to the marshalling point. He cursed his stupidity for asking Jamil to let him take part in the operation from the moment he started down the mountain with the pack. Although he had completed the hard physical training with the rest

158

of the group, he was twenty years older than the youngest. Age had taken its toll on his stamina. He had not had a drink in months. Now he ruefully resolved he would have to stop smoking as well. "The goddam fanatics will kill me from overwork before I ever see any combat," he cursed and stumbled into a furrow of newly ploughed earth. He lay still, his chest heaving while he recovered his breath and let the perspiration dry in the cool night air.

Twenty-two of them had started out from the camp in the early afternoon. Each carried an 80 pound backpack of canned foods, ammunition, weapons or medical supplies for the new marshalling area. Over the past six weeks Max had watched enviously as the group had waved goodbye to the rest of the camp and made the trek down the mountain to each of the caches Jamil was setting up throughout the occupied parts of the country. Always, they returned the next day without incident. By taking individual circuitous routes, they had managed to avoid Israeli patrols completely. Tonight would be the last sortie. Max wanted desperately to go on one for a first hand account.

"I'll even carry something if you want me to, Jamil."

"You're goddam right you will, if you go," he had told him yesterday morning.

Now Bruner wished he had kept his mouth shut. He knew he would be the last to the rendevous. The thought moved him from his prone position in the furrow, back to his feet. He stumbled on towards the road and cluster of date palms, now less than a mile away. His eyes scorched from the sweat that had been running down from the webbed headband across his forehead. The headband took some of the weight from the pack, exchanging aches in his back for one in his neck. He cursed Jamil again as he slogged on towards the palms.

Sergeant Lev Asher watched the progress of the solitary figure with its backpack as it stumbled across the furrows. He lowered the night glasses, glancing at the rest of his patrol crouched among the trees.

"What do you make of him?" Corporal Zabin whispered.

Asher shrugged. "Hard to say. A smuggler? Maybe a baker with a load of bagels making his evening delivery to the neighborhood."

Corporal Zabin chuckled. One thing he loved about Sgt. Asher ᴿwas his sense of humor. Everything was funny to Sgt. Asher.

"Move two men over there behind the knoll; two more over on the other side to cover us. Tell them not to kill each other with their own crossfire." He added as an afterthought, "Or us."

Zabin moved away into the shadows to give instructions to the squad. Asher squatted on his haunches to await the arrival of the solitary figure in the field.

Bruner was so close to Sgt. Asher before he saw him that he nearly bumped into him.

"Good evening! Bit late for a cross-country hike, isn't it neighbor?" Asher said pleasantly in Yiddish, his Uzi leveled at Bruner's stomach.

Bruner froze in his tracks. "Sorry, I don't speak Hebrew." Something had gone seriously wrong with the plan. Furiously he began thinking of a plausible reason for his presence on Israeli soil.

"Yiddish actually, not Hebrew," Asher said in his perfect English accent. "And you are an American, judging from your pronunciation. The question is what would an American be doing tramping across an Israeli field at two-thirty in the morning. Would you care to discuss it?"

He motioned to Cpt. Zabin to search the pack. His eyes never left Max's frightened face.

"Ammo packs. Seven millimeter it looks like." Zabin handed one of the cardboard boxes to the Sergeant.

"You planning on doing some hunting?" Asher's voice suddenly turned cold. Bruner shivered.

"No I.D., Sergeant." Zabin finished going through their captive's pockets.

"What's your name?"

"I demand to see the U.S. Ambassador."

"Place the backpack on the ground very slowly, then raise your hands and clasp them over top of your head. Do you understand?"

Max nodded, doing as he was told. The big Israeli didn't seem very friendly or very British any longer. There was a sinking feeling in the pit of his stomach. He cursed himself for getting involved in such a hairbrained scheme in the first place.

"Now we will move down the road to our patrol cars." He motioned Max with the Uzi. "Try not to walk too quickly. We are all tired and I can promise we won't bother chasing you if you decide to run. Do you understand?"

Max nodded. He thought he heard the other soldier chuckling, but he couldn't be sure.

There were nine of them in the patrol. Four of them spaced themselves out on either side of the narrow paved road while the man with the Uzi walked down the middle behind Max, the pack of ammo dangling from one shoulder. When the gunfire erupted from alongside the road, Max dropped to the pavement. He could hear bullets whistling over his head and screwed his eyes closed in an attempt to shut out the sounds. It seemed to go on for hours. Then, quite suddenly, all was quiet. He heard footsteps beside him and opened his eyes for a peek.

"You all right, Max?" It was Jamil.

"Sure, fine, top of the morning to you." He felt slightly hysterical as he scrambled to his feet.

"Where the hell did you get to? We waited for over an hour until the patrol came."

"I got lost," Bruner admitted, sheepishly.

"Fuckup."

"Galal! Khalid is dead." Akbar came trotting over to the center of the road. "Got a slug right between the eyes, lucky shot from one of the Jews on the point. Bastards! They won't be shooting anyone else."

Bruner looked around at the array of bodies for the first time. "You mean you killed them all?"

"Khala. Drag them into a pile on the side of the road. Strip Khalid. We'll have to leave him here."

Akbar nodded and trotted over to the corpse of Sgt. Asher. He removed the pack, then dragged him by the wrists to the ditch and rolled him in. Lev Asher was quite conscious at the time. He had managed to count at least twenty of the guerillas and memorized the names he heard—Max—Galal—Khalid—Khala. They would tell him more before they left, he reasoned calmly. Palestinians were always a gabby bunch of bastards. He let the weight of his body roll him down to the bottom of the ditch. He wondered how many of the others were playing possum.

Amman, Jordan. November 2, C.P.: Correspondent Max Bruner reports that in a brief clash with elements of the Israeli army one Palestinian was killed today. The Arab National Movement has released the name of Khalid al-Hajj as the victim of the Israeli encounter during a peaceful reconnaissance by elements of the Palestinian Liberation Group into occupied Palestine. The Israelis suffered heavy casualties during the brief encounter. The remainder of the Palestinians involved returned safely.

"Sister Leila! As principal I must insist you stop these political activities at once. The Shaab School is apolitical and will remain so." The gimlet-eyed woman drummed her fingers on the table, studying the effect her words were having. "I am told you have been into Kuwait City recently, campaigning for funds to support the PLO. This must stop too. Karam Salem has also advised me your short sleeves are an affront to Arab dignity. It is quite enough refusing to wear black, but white short-sleeved dresses cannot be tolerated by this school."

Leila listened while the stubby woman droned on, her fingers beating their nervous stacatto in time with her complaints. Originally, Leila had felt herself fortunate to have won the teaching job at Al Jahrah. Out of the dozens of applications received, only hers had been accepted by the directors. Later, she learned it was because she was Palestinian. Since the Jerusalem Congress, Kuwait government policy had been one of support for the exiles. Al Jahrah, a small dormitory town thirty-five miles from Kuwait City, provided schools and accommodations for many foreign workers in the country.

The tiny nation, sitting on top of twenty percent of the world's known oil reserves, was a land of paradoxes. Austere, conservative, authoritarian and fantastically wealthy. Its 360,000 citizens were provided free services on everything from the day they were born until the day they died. Few worked at anything more strenuous than designing mini-palaces or foreign holiday visits to enjoy the forbidden pleasure of wine, liquor and women—commodities unknown in their own country, by directive from the Seif Palace where the Emir ruled supreme.

A generation earlier they had been illiterate fishermen, smugglers, desert nomads, clinging to a humid strip of sand along the shores of the Gulf. Now they earned six million dollars every hour, day and night, as the B.P. pumps sucked the black blood for the industrial world from the porous earth beneath their sandaled feet. Rolls Royces, Mercedes Benz, Learjets, trick watches, cameras, televisions, a desalination plant and whole new world of air conditioning; nothing was too expensive so long as the oil kept flowing. There was even talk from the palace of nationalizing the whole industry—as soon as they could figure out who would run it for them when B.P. and the other oil companies left.

Yet, for all their wealth, the Kuwaitis still clung to their tribal ways. Women were to be seen veiled and covered—preferably in black, never alone. Girls practiced anal coitus to protect their virginity before marriage and female circumcision had only recently been abondoned. It was hot and humid but most of all rich, which was why Jamil had suggested Leila go to Kuwait in the first place.

Al Jahrah proved to be a polyglot of Arab dialects and people.

Syrians, Iranians, Egyptians, Palestinians. These were the technicians who came with their families to do the work while the Kuwaitis stood back and watched the proceedings with a peculiar detachment. There were no movies, dances, night-clubs, boyfriends or visits permitted off the school campus during the week. Weekend visits were allowed by special permission. It took Leila three months before she arranged a visit to her cousin in Kuwait City.

The imaginary cousin turned into reality on her third visit to the city when she bumped into Torval Kemal, a first cousin of her father's from Nabulus. He was working as a technician at the desalination plant. They spent the rest of that weekend planning the *Kuwait Fund for the Liberation of Palestine.* In mid-December Leila transferred a deposit of $736,000 American into the Bank Mizr at Beirut for Jamil with a promise of much more to follow. They were ecstatic until the Ministry of Education heard about the efforts by their grade school teacher from Al Jahrah and ordered the funding activites to cease forthwith.

"Sister Leila! Are you listening to anything I'm saying?"

Leila came back to earth with a start.

"Yes, Madame Souad. I'm listening." She looked at her tormentor with disgust. A petty tyrant dressed in black linen.

"You have nothing to say?" Again, the stubby fingers started drumming the desk.

"A great deal." Leila took a deep breath. "First, my politics are nobody's business but my own. I am a Palestinian. I was born a Palestinian and I will die a Palestinian. As for long sleeves in this heat, the Director must be insane if he thinks he can dictate dress fashions to me or anyone else." She looked pointedly at the long black sleeves of Madame Souad's dress. "I will dress comfortably, within the bounds of what is generally accepted as female decency anywhere else in the world. If that is unacceptable, too bad. I have no intention of changing. Finally, I am a political activist for my country and its cause. Politics cost money. The Western Powers give this country billions of dollars for oil they discovered under the sand. I see no reason why I shouldn't be permitted to continue trying to obtain some of this money in donations to our Arab Cause. It's your Cause too, Madame."

Leila sat back. She hadn't intended to make a speech, but the old woman was a fool and deserved to be told the truth; something none of the other teachers on staff had the courage to do. The fingers drummed at a furious rate, then abruptly stopped.

"That is your answer?"

"It is."

"Very well. You are excused. I shall take your case up with the Director at once. I am sure he will be most displeased. I will advise him to relieve you of any further details with this school. This is no place for revolutionaries.

Leila stood up. "Just as you wish, Madame Souad. Good afternoon." She paused by the door of the white office. "The word is guerilla, not revolutionary." She smiled sweetly. "There is a difference."

She went back to her quarters across the quad to begin packing her bags. There was no point in staying around to await the outcome of the Director's decision. She knew the answer already. She could continue her work with cousin Torval in Kuwait City.

Jamil and the rest of the commando group returned to camp shortly after noon. The foray against the Kibbutz filled their spirits with new hope.

"One of these attacks every week, Galal, and they should start to notice us in a few months, eh?" Akbar grinned as they piled out of the truck.

Jamil nodded. "It could take longer. Those Kibbutz Jews are pretty dumb."

The truck moved off down the dusty road to the camouflaged motor pool. The tired group of men started up the pathway to the mountain camp. A few hundred feet above them, where the path led through the narrow defile into camp, Max Bruner breathed a sigh of relief, then lowered his binoculars. He jogged back to the command post.

"They're all back, no one missing. Notify Amman."

The radio operator smiled. "At once." He signaled his partner in the corner of the tent, munching on an apple, to start cranking the hand generator. He flipped the radio over to the command frequency of Camp Wahdat a few miles south of Amman. Bruner left the tent to join the others running out to meet the patrol as the first members appeared walking single file through the slice in the hills on the other side of the plateau. There was much back slapping and excited conversations between the greeters and those being greeted. Jamil stopped in front of Bruner and smiled tiredly.

"How did it go?"

He raised his Russian-made Seminov aloft. "With this sword I will wash my shame away. Let God's doom bring on me what it may! You can quote me on that, Max."

They both laughed happily.

164

8

President Artega mounted the podium of the Congress to a thunderous applause from the assembled members. The visitors gallery was filled to capacity with officials of the diplomatic corps, news reporters from the major international wire services, plus an assorted group of foreign businessmen who enjoyed the rewards of Dr. Artega's victory at the polls by receiving special business concessions within the Republic. Everyone's faces were flushed with the heady wine of success. The crescendo of desk top thumping from the members on the floor of the Congress rose and fell to the cheers from the gallery. Dr. Artega raised his arms aloft, smiling. He looked above his head to a small gallery enclosure where the television cameras pointed down, sweeping the room with penetrating eyes, imprinting ecstatic faces on video tape for posterity. Sitting beside the camera crews, Chirlo and Felina peered over the railing. Artega pointed his finger at them and motioned for them to stand. As they stood, the roar of applause reached a fever pitch. Those who were seated rose to their feet in homage to the man that had made it all happen.

"Chirlo—Chirlo—Chirlo—Chirlo." They howled their approval.

Beside him the cameramen backed away to fill their scopes with a striking bearded profile shot, which later the press would use when-

165

ever the Strongman of Cosecha Rica's portrait was needed in a newscast. Chirlo held Felina's hand up, smiling and bowed briefly to Dr. Artega, then sat down. The huge chamber fell silent as if his seating himself was a sign.

"Mr. Speaker. Distinguished guests. Your excellencies. Members of the Congress. Ladies and gentlemen." Dr. Artega paused, his gaze sweeping the room. The acoustics were perfect. His quiet voice soared to the domed roof and penetrated every crevice of the Corinthian pillars lining the white stucco walls. Morning sunlight splashed through the glass windows in the dome and splayed a chorus of colors across one wall.

"Let us all welcome each other home."

There was a brief roar of applause.

"I welcome you back to the House of representative government. Welcome me back to my homeland. Our prayers have been answered by Almighty God. The Beast has been consumed. Let us pray that this great meeting place never again will be closed to the ideas and opinions of free men in our great Republic."

There was another outburst of prolonged cheering.

"It has been stated by some that this government is communist. I wish to correct that error. This government is neither communist, capitalist, socialist or idealist. The Peoples Democratic National Liberation Party is exactly what the name implies. A National Party democratically elected by the people of this country to represent them. We hold the right to free speech as a sacred trust. We boast our prisons now hold criminals—not political detainees who disagree with our beliefs. As long as I am President, this will remain the foundation of our government."

He paused to let the applause subside.

"We welcome dissention from those who oppose our political views. We support the right of every citizen to dissent with his government within the bounds of free speech, decency, verbal exchange on the floor of this house, without fear of reprisal, or recrimination. We expect constructive criticism from our learned members of the Opposition Parties. And, if the day should come five years from now, that the citizens of this country decide in a free election that one of these Opposition Parties is more qualified to direct the destiny of this land than the PDNLP, then we will step down and obey the wishes of the people without bloodshed, without passion, without hindrance. That I promise."

Chirlo watched the desk slapping as it continued for several minutes. He nodded to himself with satisfaction, squeezing Felina's hand. The speech sounded just right. A proper balance between logical common sense and political eyewash. It was going down well with the diplomatic corps. He glanced over at the U.S. Ambassador. Mr. Harding Russell met his eyes and winked; his mouth remained expressionless. Harding worried him. He could never figure him out. Pro Artega or pro Guerrero? The man was a chameleon. He nodded to the ambassador and swung his eyes back to the podium. Artega was starting the part on cooperation between nations. Chirlo had sweated over this part of the speech for several days. The country was bankrupt, seriously in need of foreign aid. A policy statement begging for help was out of the question politically. The urgent request had to be couched in diplomatically acceptable linguistics, satisfying honor and need. He listened as the doctor put the request across the hall in his quiet sincere voice. Chirlo relaxed. It sounded perfect. It was by far the best speech he had ever written for his patron.

The relationship was working well now that guidelines had been established after the disaster of 1963 when he and Felina barely escaped the country with their lives. He kept his eyes on the grey head, bobbing in tune with its words, at the podium, while his mind drifted back to Tampico.

"From now on, Doctor, I'll do the thinking, you do the talking. We should all live longer."

"I don't think that remark is necessary," Ruis muttered defensively.

"Don't be a goddamn fool, Ruis. We are talking about facts, not some idealistic claptrap. I told you not to send Felina, you did. I told you it would not work your way, it didn't. Now I am telling you we are going to do it my way, or I wash my hands of the whole affair here and now. Which is it going to be?"

He stood in the middle of the library, his hands over his hips, his eyes burning with resolution. Ruis turned his head to Artega sitting in the other chair. Artega looked very old and tired. The shock of his daughter's reappearance had been nearly as great as the news of her loss in the dungeons of El Tigre Fortress. He admitted to himself Chirlo had been right. He had been wrong. Terribly wrong. Were it not for the tall emaciated man standing in front of him now, he might have lost everything he loved in life—his daughter, his country and his adopted son. The doctor sighed and looked up at the glowering eyes.

"You're quite right, my boy. I've been out of touch with the situation for too long. I should have listened to you in the first place."

He stood up, placing a hand on Chirlo's shoulder. "I turn the problem over to you. I'll agree to abide by your decisions from now on. I'm sorry I put you through so much, my boy. It was the vanity of an old man. Will you forgive me?"

Chirlo lowered his head. "There is nothing to forgive. We are both wiser men for the experience."

Artega shook his head. "No, you are wiser. I—I am just older. Now if you will excuse me, I feel a little tired. I'll just look in on Felina, then go to bed. Goodnight."

Ruis stood up. "Goodnight, Don Luis."

"Goodnight, Papa," Chirlo said.

Artega paused at the door, smiling. "Ah, Chirlo. Always the diplomat. How much more I must learn about you."

"You have just seen the destruction of a great man," Ruis said bitterly a few moments after the door had closed. "I hope you are satisfied."

Chirlo looked at him sadly. "Ruis. You poor loyal fool. That was not destruction. That was the first step in the creation of the new President of Cosheca Rica." He winked at him. "Wait and see."

"It was still a cruel thing to say. You know he worships you."

Chirlo folded himself into the chair Artega had vacated and studied Ruis for a moment. "How much money do we have in our war chest?"

"That is something you should take up with Don Luis."

Chirlo sighed. "Sometimes I wonder about you, Ruis. Maybe you've spent too much of your time looking at the birds." He pulled his beard reflectively. "I have about fifteen thousand dollars left in my account here. If I am going back to the Republic with a force of men and sufficient equipment to maintain them, I don't think fifteen thousand dollars is going to be enough, do you?"

Ruis smiled. "How much do you need?"

Chirlo shrugged. "I don't know until we've worked it out. But I'd like to know if we start looking for money first, or men and equipment if we already have the money."

"Would a million dollars be enough?"

"More than enough."

"Then we have enough money. Where will you go for the equipment?"

"Cuba."

"Cuba?"

"It's communist!"

168

"Is it now. How did you arrive at that conclusion?"

"Jesus, Mary and Joseph, Chirlo! Don't you ever read a newspaper? Cuba is supported by Russia!"

"So that makes it communist?"

"What else would you call it?" Ruis demanded, exasperated.

"I don't know. Why don't we go over to Havana and find out?"

Ruis examined him carefully. "You're serious, aren't you?"

"Completely."

"It would be difficult to arrange."

"Why? Don Louis should have no trouble talking to the Cuban Ambassador in Mexico City. An exile interested in returning to his homeland; seeking assistance from the foremost revolutionary government in the Western world."

"But will he do it?"

"How do we know until we ask him?"

"He will object. I know him."

"Possibly. He doesn't have to go himself. I want permission only for you and I to travel," Chirlo explained.

"But Cuban soliders in Cosecha Rica!"

"Who said anything about Cuban soldiers? I want their equipment, not their soldiers. I'll get the soldiers somewhere else."

"Mercenaries?"

"Mercenaries are too expensive. Idealists perhaps, from some foreign country, helping us for the sake of brotherhood, but leave when the job is done."

"You think such people exist?" Ruis was intrigued by the idea.

"Everything exists—the problem is finding it."

"Don Luis might agree to that sort of an approach," he mused.

"I'm sure he will, Ruis."

"Are you always so sure of everything, Chirlo?" Ruis laughed. "How do you manage it?"

He shook his head. "Not everything, Ruis. I still haven't the slightest idea who in the hell I am." He stood up and stretched.

"I hope your are right, my friend. Goodnight."

The following morning Chirlo looked in on Felina. She was propped up with several enormous pillows eating breakfast. The dark circles under her eyes had faded. She looked much better. The chattering maid left discreetly as he sat down on the edge of the bed. Felina regarded him quizzically, noting the neatly trimmed beard and pressed suit he was wearing. It was the first time she had seen him without rumpled khaki fatigues since they met at the airport in

Bahia Blanca.

"New worlds to conquer, Gallant Knight?
More maidens saved distressing plight?"

He laughed. "You're feeling better! Good! Looking better too. I was worried."

"I don't believe you. You never worry about anything." She bit into a piece of trimmed toast, catching its dripping butter with her hand.

"I worry about you." He said the words slowly.

Felina munched the toast thoughtfully, then swallowed. "Why?"

"Because I love you, Little Kitten."

She slid the tray away from between them and pulled him towards her, burying her face in his chest.

"That's the first time you ever said it."

He stroked her hair.

"I was beginning to wonder if it was my deodorant."

"It was, but now that you've bathed I've decided to let myself go, live a little."

She looked up at him, her dark eyes enormous. "Oh Chirlo! I love you so much."

She held him tightly, first seeking his lips, then pulling his head to her breast, shrugging off the shoulder strap of the thin nightie. His beard tickled her breast, then the nipple swelled as he rolled it with his lips and tongue. He felt the wetness starting between her legs. He stood up and moved the breakfast tray to the floor, then laid his clothes neatly over the stuffed chair. Felina slithered out of the nightie and held her arms out to him. Her heart was pounding. He knelt beside the bed, kneading her Vee lightly with his fingers and tongue. She lay back, moaning with pleasure.

Later, when they lay exhausted and apart, Felina turned her head, looking at him.

"I didn't think it would be the same again after . . ."

"Nothing is ever the same again." Chirlo placed a finger on her lips, interrupting the words and thoughts. The doctor had been terribly worried by the continuous rapings at El Tigre from Bermudez and his men, which, when combined with the swift abortion he had performed on his daughter upon their return, might permanently have affected her mental outlook on life. Chirlo picked up her thoughts, but changed their direction.

"I'm afraid I upset your father last night."

"He told me. He understands."

"I hope so." He brushed his lips across her mouth, then swung off the bed to dress. "I'm going to Miami for a few days. I told Ruis where he can reach me if there's anything you need."

She propped herself up on one elbow. "Just remember to come home when you're finished."

Chirlo stared at her with mock lust eyes. "That, Little Kitten, I will always do. Count on it." He gave her a lopsided grin as he left the room.

Ruis drove him to the airport to catch the Miami flight. They drove in silence most of the way, each lost in thought. A half mile from the entrance they stopped behind a line of vehicles on the highway. Ruis climbed out, then came back laughing.

"Some idiot let his cow loose. It's wrapped around a bus. They're cleaning up the mess now." He glanced at his watch and got back inside. "Lots of time."

Another car joined the line behind them and began blowing its horn. Ruis stuck a cocked finger out the window in the universal sign of displeasure. The blaring stopped.

"You spoke to him this morning?"

Ruis nodded, lighting a cigarette. "And last night for an hour."

They were silent a few moments. A blue police car roared past in the other lane, its siren whooping, light flashing.

"He will transfer one hundred and fifty thousand to the Airport Bank of Miami in your name today. He agreed to phone the Cuban Ambassador this morning for an appointment to discuss our visit. I told him our interest is in their equipment." He glanced at Chirlo. "He didn't like it, but he agreed."

A pickup truck with two policemen clinging to either door drove past going in the opposite direction, its box filled with bloody pieces of heifer. The traffic in front began to move. Ruis started the motor and followed the line as it picked up speed. They passed the bus, still parked alongside the road. There was a scattering of glass and some broken chrome molding lying on the pavement. A policeman was picking up the pieces carefully and tossing them into the ditch. The passengers from the bus were climbing aboard. The show was over.

"Tell the airport manager I'll want parking space for two cargo aircraft later in the week."

"For how long?"

"A couple of weeks—maybe a month."

Ruis swung into the airport roadway. "Who will you get to bring the second one?"

"I'll bring them both—one at a time."

They pulled up in front of the terminal building and stopped. The duty policeman started to walk towards the car, removing his summons pad, then glanced at the Diplomatic CD license plate on the Mercedes and changed his mind. He saluted as he sauntered by.

"Anything else?"

"Nope. See you within the week." Chirlo gripped him by the shoulder affectionately, then slid out of the car and slammed the door. He stuck his head in through the open window with an afterthought.

"Look after Felina, will you. She's been through Hell. Keep her mind occupied with other things. Maybe start working on those maps and plans. She means a lot to me, Ruis."

Ruis shook his head in wonder. "Chirlo, I would never have guessed. Don't be so goddamn stupid—I'm her Godfather!"

He smiled. "That's right, Ruis. I forgot. You are one of the family too, aren't you?"

He waved, then disappeared into the terminal building, carrying nothing except the ill-fitting suit that clung to his gangling frame.

"There goes a man con heuvos y corazon tambien! *(with balls as well as heart!)*." He said the words aloud to no one in particular. For some reason it made him feel better to confirm his sentiments aloud.

Chirlo spent the next day wandering around Miami International Airport examining the inventory of used aircraft, followed by a swarm of brokerage sharks who had detected blood the minute he arrived to ask directions. He passed over the rows of four engined aircraft as being impractical for his purposes. Finally, he was presented with a pair of clean looking twin-engined C47 aircraft, recently taken in on trade from a mining company which had switched to turbo-props. They were well maintained, few oil leaks from the low time engines and had long range fuel tanks installed inside the cargo bays. The school of sharks dispersed as he was informed the broker handling the C47's maintained his office in Tampa. He extracted a phone number from one of the reluctant departing maneaters and phoned Rich Rick Rogers Aircraft Brokers.

They met next morning outside Butler Aviation after Rogers had parked the Piper Aztec he had flown down.

"Mr. Artega? Rick Rogers—Rich Rick's." He flashed a sales smile along with his hand.

"And are you rich?" Chirlo asked seriously.

"Wish I were." Rogers laughed. The big customer made him feel uneasy, slightly uncomfortable.

"Understand you're interested in that pair of forty-sevens. Real beauties, aren't they?"

"Are they?"

"The best. Wait till you fly them."

"Whenever you're ready, Mr. Rogers."

"Call me Rick." They walked over to the taxi ramp and drove out to the aircraft. Chirlo spent an hour examining the log books, maintenance schedules and AD's, then checked the engines, propellors, instrumentation and radios. They were indeed clean, well maintained aircraft with no corrosion or apparent problem. He started the engines and called the tower for taxi clearance to make a test flight. To Chirlo it was *deja vu* all over again. Everything he examined brought a flooding of memories from his subconscious. As they taxied out to the runup point, he knew instinctively he had flown this type of aircraft before. Even stranger, he was positive he had flown a C-47 from Miami International. After fifteen minutes Roger's gushing sales pitch dried up when he realized he could evoke no response from his silent customer on anything unrelated to the operation of the aircraft. They flew around for an hour, then landed.

"I want five hours of fuel with you tonight at some short field grass strip. Do you know one in the area?" Chirlo parked the aircraft and locked the brakes. The propellors windmilled to a stop as the engines died.

"Sure do. Know of several. What time do you want to go?"

"I'll meet you here at nine. How much for both aircraft?"

Rogers looked over from the co-pilot's seat speculatively. He had bought the pair of them on a consignment basis for seventy thousand.

"Well, I'd like to get an even hundred and twenty grand—that's sixty apiece."

"I can add, Mr. Rogers. I'll give you one hundred thousand cash tonight. I want full tanks on both, including the long range reserves, two drums of oil in each machine and that company name and emblem removed from the tails."

Chirlo didn't wait for a reply as he slid out of the seat and went back to the cabin door. Rogers followed him down the aisle and picked up the boarding ladder. When they were both standing on the tarmac he asked, "I guess there's no point in my dickering with you a little on that price, is there?"

"That's up to you. If it makes you feel any better, go ahead.

But that's my offer. My only offer."

Rogers stuck out his hand. "Okay, Mr. Artega. I guess you've got yourself a couple of C47's. I'll see you tonight. Should have everything finished by then. I'll speak to the boys at the office now on the gas and oil. It may take a day or two on that logo removal, though."

The following day as Rogers was heading back to Tampa in the Aztec with a bag of thousand dollar bills, Chirlo was clearing the Key West VOR radio outbound at 8,000 feet across the Gulf for Tampico with the first aircraft.

There had been no difficulty for Dr. Artega to obtain an audience with the Cuban Ambassador to discuss permission for two emissaries to visit Havana. He outlined the delicate reasons for the visit over a delicious dinner at the Rio El Choco in Mexico City. The Ambassador had already heard of Chirlo's escape from El Tigre through, as he termed them, 'private sources.' He thought the hat boxes mailed to Madame Guerrero most amusing. He wiped his mustache politely with the white linen table napkin.

"Such originality of thought, my dear Doctor. I must meet your son. I do so enjoy a sense of humor."

It took another week before the visas were granted. Chirlo delivered the second aircraft to Tampico, then spent the remaining days working with Ruis and Felina on the bundle of plans and maps while the Doctor remained in the background. He listened to their arguments with half an ear, but was never invited to participate, or advised on the outcome of the various plots they were hatching. Chirlo presented the completed neatly packaged bundle to him as they were leaving for the airport.

"Something for you to consider while we're gone, Papa."

He said it offhandedly. Artega accepted the challenge in the same manner. "If I have time, my boy. If I have time," then dropped the whole package carelessly on the hall table while he bid them goodbye, his eyes dancing with anticipation. Felina had no sooner cleared the driveway before he was immersed in the documentation. It was the plan to return home to Cosecha Rica as president.

The Ambassador kept them waiting for an hour before phoning down to tell the secretary to bring them up to his office.

"Terribly sorry, gentlemen. A matter of trade with the Deputy Minister." He apologized, rubbing his hands together as he nodded them to the chairs circling the coffee table at one end of the office. "Coffee? No? Something to drink, then? Cuban Rum? Ah! I thought so! Rum and Coca Cola—the only thing we see eye to eye on with the Americans. Ricardo!" He called at the wall lined with bookcases.

A tough looking waiter appeared in a tight-fitting red jacket with a bulge under one armpit.

"Rum and Coca Cola."

The bookcase door swung shut as the waiter bowed, then opened a bibliographic bar hidden behind the shelves. The Ambassador beamed and sat down to join his guests.

"So you are Chirlo?"

"In the flesh, your Excellency," Chirlo replied soberly.

The Ambassador chuckled. "Quite so. Quite so. I have heard of you. Your father and I spent such a pleasant evening together last week. I am happy to say his request for permission for you to visit Havana has been granted by the Prime Minister himself. Quite an honor, I think. Dr. Castro doesn't see every visitor who comes to Cuba."

"Dr. Castro is most generous with his time, your Excellency," Ruis agreed.

The waiter served the three frosted glasses of amber iced rum, setting them on the table. He bowed again and disappeared behind the bookcase. The door shut soundlessly after him.

"To a successful trip, gentlemen!" They held the glasses out formally, then relaxed to sip the contents.

"Your father discussed few of the details on the purpose of your visit. Merely that you were seeking help for a return to Cosecha Rica." He paused, waiting for either of them to pick up the thread. There was an uncomfortable silence.

"Naturally, I don't expect you to tell me the details of what you have in mind; some idea perhaps. I might be of help."

"Actually Excellency, it all started a couple of weeks ago when Ruis told me that Cuba was communist. I said it wasn't so. We decided to go and find out for ourselves to settle the argument."

The Ambassador looked at Chirlo in disbelief, then burst into gales of laughter. The wall panel slid open and the waiter appeared suddenly, his eyes alert for trouble. He relaxed when he saw his employer was laughing, and slipped back behind the door.

"That Ricardo is a real Peeping Tom, Excellency," Chirlo observed.

The Ambassador's laughter developed to a further crescendo till he was gasping for breath and wiping his eyes with a huge silk handkerchief.

"Please, no more. My heart." He held his hand over the trouble spot while his laughter subsided, then went to his desk and picked up the two passports.

The Cubanair flight from Mexico City landed at the Joes Marti International Airport with a vicious bounce that rocked the Ilyushin turboprop violently. For a moment Chirlo thought the pilot had lost control as they swung towards the grass, then the reverse thrust of the paddle bladed propellors bit into the air. With some fast footwork on the rudder pedals, the aircraft slowed to a stop in the middle of the runway. Ruis crossed himself and looked at Chirlo for a comment.

"Interesting landing technique," he observed as they trundled over to the terminal building.

"Senor Ruis? Senor Artega?" A bearded man in green fatigues met them at the bottom of the stairs. He had a revolver strapped to his waist and was holding two passport photographs in one hand. "Welcome to Cuba. I am Captain Bianco, your escort." He shook hands. "Good trip?"

Other passengers passed at the bottom of the stairs and looked curiously at the trio.

"Excellent flight, Captain, thank you," Chirlo said with a smile. Ruis said nothing.

"Splendid. Your bags will be delivered to the hotel. I have a car waiting. Please, this way." He ushered them across the tarmac to a parked Hillman Minx. They squeezed into the tiny vehicle, Captain Bianco in the front seat. The chauffeur ground the gears, and with a lurch from the engine timing, they jerked out of the parking area. Chirlo's knees were locked into the front seat.

"How far to Havana, Captain?"

"Twenty minutes. No more. You have visited Cuba before?"

"No."

"Ah, then there is much to see." He began a long speech on the history of the island, turning his head occasionally to make sure his passengers were listening. Chirlo's legs were numb by the time they pulled up with a backfire at the front door of the Internacional and crawled out of the car. The engine was still firing periodic protests from its carboned pistons as they went into the lobby. Their rooms were first class accommodations by any standard, although some of the fixtures were cracked.

"We have a shortage of American produced replacement parts," Bianco explained apologetically. "Your bags will be delivered after dinner. I will be back to see you this evening. Please remain in the hotel until I return."

He saluted and left the room.

"I take it we are being examined?" Ruis suggested.

"Our bags are, for a certainty."

"Will we see the great man?"

Chirlo shrugged. "When they are satisfied we won't try to kill him."

"After that plane ride I need a rest. Call me if anything exciting happens." Ruis wandered through the door to the adjoining bedroom. Chirlo went over to the window and looked out across the rooftops of the city. For some reason the scene was familiar. He was certain he had seen the view before, but from a different angle. He rubbed his eyes and sat down in the frayed armchair to study the buildings, while his mind sorted out the list of priorities for discussion with the Cuban Prime Minister, if and when they were granted audience. He has promised Paco he would return after 60 days. There were 37 left in which to complete his work and fulfill that promise. There was a knock at the door. He swung out of the chair to answer it.

"Good afternoon, Chirlo."

"Good afternoon, Dr. Castro." Behind the Premier a group of fatigue uniformed men with rifles crowded the corridor, most mimicking the beard of their leader.

"May I come in?"

Chirlo stood aside, bowing his head slightly as the idol of the Revolution strode into the room. The others remained outside in the hallway. One of the officers smiled briefly and closed the door. They were alone. Castro took the chair by the window that Chirlo had vacated to answer the door. He parked his feet on the sill and lit a cigar.

"I've always enjoyed the view from this particular room. Gromyko never liked it. He said it depressed him so we had to move him to the other side. I wonder why Russians never like a view of the sea?" He dropped the match into the ashtray stand.

"Possibly it's the idea of being on an island that worried them." Chirlo pulled the chair away from the writing desk and joined the Premier by the window.

"Everyone is on an island."

"But not everyone thinks their island is going to sink, Doctor."

Castro laughed. He had a pleasant laugh, almost girlish. For some reason it reminded Chirlo of Johnny Weismuller acting out a Tarzan movie he had seen as a boy somewhere. A conflicting tenor voice in the body of a giant man. Crazy thoughts.

"I am told you need some help. What can I do?"

"I need rifles, machine pistols, mortars, explosives, bazookas, rockets and ammunition. I also need radio equipment, medicines, bandages and your permission to bring two C47 aircraft here with U.S. Registry to transport everything to Cosecha Rica. I'll need one good pilot to captain the second aircraft and three co-pilots. After delivery I'll be staying behind. You keep the aircraft. Your pilots can bring them back to Cuba."

"Only one trip?"

"One trip. I figure with 6,000 pounds in each machine we'll have enough to start. After that I can take everything else I need from Guerrero."

"The War of the Flea. Did you know Richard Taber lived with us here in Oriente when we started? A great newspaper man."

"Yes, Doctor, I read his book."

"Too bad the rest of the Yankees didn't read it too. What will you do for cadre?"

"I do not want Cuban soldiers in Cosecha Rica."

"You want my equipment, but not my men. Why?" He rolled the cigar in his fingers.

"You might decide they should remain afterwards."

"And that would be bad?"

"It might cause Washington to wave the Monroe Doctrine. Guerrero I can handle."

"Supposing Washington decides to help Gaspar; he's their man."

"They won't as long as it remains a national revolution undertaken by Cosecha Ricans. They will regard it as an internal matter. There will be claims of Cuban soldiers and Russian help anyway, but that will be for the newspapers. As long as it cannot be proved, Washington will not act."

The Premier eyed him speculatively. "You're sure of yourself, aren't you, Chirlo?"

"Positive, Doctor."

"You still need a cadre of trained officers. If only Che . . ." his voice trailed off.

"I know where I can get the cadre." He scratched his head absently. "They are trained, available and speak neither Spanish or Russian."

Castro looked at him with interest. "So?"

"Palestinian guerillas from Jordan. They have had years of combat experience. I'll enlist their aid."

178

"As mercenaries?"

"If necessary. But I think I can persuade them in other ways to join our cause until it is completed." He shrugged. "At any rate it is worth a try."

"Do you speak English?"

"Fluently."

"I have had some dealings with Arafat. I could arrange a meeting. Cairo perhaps, or Beirut."

"It would be appreciated, Doctor."

"When would you bring the aircraft here?"

"As soon as I return to Mexico."

"Very well. I will instruct Bianco to assign you space at one of the military airfields. Give him your shopping list of equipment. It will be loaded and waiting when you want to take it out. The pilots too. Give the Ambassador your flight time arrivals and aircraft registrations the day before you leave Tampico so we don't shoot you down." He smiled and stood up. "In the meantime, I'll see what I can arrange through Moscow for a meeting with Arafat. You'd have to fly through Russia to get there; we have two flights a week to Moscow. Have you ever been to Russia, Chirlo?"

"I don't think so, Doctor."

Castro looked puzzled. "Well, if you had, surely you would have remembered?"

"Not necessarily."

The Premier shook his head, seeking a deeper meaning, then shrugged. "There is space for you and your friend back to Mexico on tomorrow's flight, unless of course you wish to spend a few days sightseeing?"

"Thank you. Perhaps some other time when the Revolution is over."

"Ah, Chirlo. The Revolution is never over, for you or for me. Good luck." They shook hands. He accompanied the Premier to the door. Castro held his hand on the handle a moment.

"If you should get into trouble, I'll keep the aircraft ready to lift you out of the country."

"Thank you, Doctor, but that will not be necessary." Chirlo smiled. "We will succeed."

"I hope you are right." He slapped him on the back. "Welcome to the Club!"

Besides Jamil, there were ten others from the Jordanian camp on board the VC 10 as it lifted off the runway at Heathrow, circled the traffic roaring down the M4 into Hounslow and vanished through the leaden grey overcast. The Palestinians were scattered throughout the tourist class cabin, careful to have selected their seats well apart from each other. Jamil glanced across the empty seat at Chirlo. Their eyes met blankly in non-recognition, then returned to reading their magazines. The flight to Nassau would take nearly seven hours. Chirlo sat back in the seat, letting the magazine slip from his lap as he closed his eyes. So far everything had run according to plan. It appeared now he would beat his deadline by a comfortable margin. Both cargo aircraft were sitting in Cuba at the military airport near Cienfuegos. He had met his Cuban pilots and checked them out in the machines. They had been superbly trained by their Russian instructors. The Cairo meeting with Yasser Arafat, arranged through Moscow, resulted in a letter of instruction to Abu Ali Iyad, introducing Chirlo to whichever men in Al Asifah he thought qualified to accept a temporary leave of absence for training purposes. Jamil turned out to be his first recruit after he had talked to him briefly at his quarters in the camp. After explaining details of the venture to the Palestinian, he decided to make him his aide and turned over to him the responsibility of finding others to enlist in the group of cadres he needed. Jamil's selection was excellent. Out of seventeen prospective applicants, Chirlo narrowed the field down to ten. They left at once for England under a variety of identities and passports provided from the Al Asifah documentation branch in Beirut. All killers who had proven their worth in the field, Chirlo was delighted at the standard of training and discipline they showed in following orders without question. Unlike the Latins with whom he was familiar, the Palestinians asked few questions, drank little or no alcohol and appeared unmoved by the thought of personal dangers. He was glad he had come to the Middle East. He realized that someday, after the revolution was over, he would be called to repay his debt to the intense young man. It was a debt he intended to honor. The aircraft broke through the overcast into brilliant sunshine skies at twenty-three thousand feet. The sun's rays hit his closed eyelids and he pulled down the shade. Across the aisle, Jamil glanced at his movement, then settled back to sleep.

They landed at Nassau in late afternoon. The airport was swarming with vacationing tourists milling about the terminal, sorting out bags and hotel reservations. After the quiet efficiency of Heathrow, Nassau airport was black bedlam. The Palestinians were swallowed by the crowds as they cleared customs and immigration with their multi-national passports. Two made connections to Caracas;

four others into Miami on the evening flight; while Jamil and the rest of the team were scheduled to spend a night on the Island taking flights out the next morning. By the weekend all would make their separate ways into Cosecha Rica. Chirlo booked himself on the first Mackay Airlines flight to Miami and was back in Tampico the following afternoon. They were all at the airport to meet him. Felina flung her arms around him as he came through the gate. Ruis and Artega nodded happily, their eyes filled with anticipation.

"Well?" Artega demanded, when Chirlo had finally extricated himself from Felina.

"Well Papa, when would everyone like to go home?" he replied, laughing.

The old man hugged his adopted son.

"Everything is ready?" Ruis asked incredulously.

"They expect us early Sunday morning," he confirmed.

Ruis slapped him across the shoulders. Artega stood back. "Then we shall leave tomorrow. Come, we have much to do."

They marched out of the building, following the doctor. The airport policeman saluted as they climbed into the Mercedes. Chirlo returned the salute. The man was startled, then smiled broadly as they drove off.

Paco read the letter the strange man brought with him to Tippitaca. He had come on Thursday afternoon by bus from Bahia Blanca and knocked on the door of the house in town. Jamil was his name. He walked into the house, handed Paco the envelope with a nod, then proceeded to examine the rooms carefully, while Paco trailed him about the courtyard reading the long letter from his employer. There was no doubt about the signature or the handwriting. It was from Chirlo. He studied the instructions carefully, then called Anita out from the kitchen and told her to go and find her mother. With eleven more mouths to feed, he was going to need another cook. The girl looked at Jamil with interest, removed her apron and slipped out the front door. Paco's English was slight. Jamil's Spanish nonexistent. Between them, with smiles, gestures and many 'ah's,' they managed to organize sleeping quarters for the expected arrivals. Three more turned up on the 9:00 p.m. bus in time for supper under the saumon tree. After the meal, they grouped around the table in conference while Jamil studied the road map he had picked up from an Esso dealer in Bahia Blanca. Paco traced the road into the hacienda with his finger and marked an 'x' for the airstrip. Jamil appeared satisfied, thankful the word 'map,' 'airport,' 'bus' and wrist watch numerals were the same in both languages. They went to bed shortly before midnight. The rest of the group arrived the following day.

Saturday morning Paco drove them out to the Finca Esperanza in the Land Rover. It took two trips. On the first run he showed Jamil where the flare pots, fuel barrels, pumps and other equipment were stored. The farm workers stood about in smiling curiosity, while he toured the buildings and sheds with the six swarthy guests. He told the workers they were to help the Palestinians and that the Patron was coming home that very night. There was an excited buzzing of conversation. Jamil stopped talking to one of his men, looking over at Paco.

"What did he tell them?"

"How th'hell would I know, Galal? I don't speak Spanish."

Jamil glared at Malmalli. "Either he told them Chirlo is coming in tonight, or that we are here to take the country. Either way, it's a breach of security. See that none of these workers leave the place. Make a head count now; families too; their shacks are over there. Post a guard at the gate."

When Paco drove back to the main road he could see the activity he was leaving in the rear view mirror. The slim young leader of the Palestinians was organizing the work groups swiftly. He could see Dingo starting the diesel tractor while two others pulled the tow bar of a flatbed wagon up to the hitch. He sighed, feeling a little jealous. They were, after all, his workers. He should be directing them, not the dark young man from across the ocean. Still, Chirlo had said in the letter that they would all go home when the revolution was over. Paco hoped it was true. He shifted gears and pressed the accelerator towards Tippitaca.

They finished work in mid afternoon. The gas barrels were all upended on the wagons, their bungs loosened. The seven wagons parked in a neat line alongside the grass runway. The flare pots were in position and Jamil had posted two men on the hills behind the finca with binoculars to watch for air or ground intruders. The rest of the afternoon he spent scouting the area on horseback, starting at the border of the farm where it joined its sister republic, then following a path into the hills. It was dark before he joined the two sentinels, and dismounted. He walked with them back to the hacienda.

"Do you think he will be in tonight?"

"If he said he would be here, then he will, Iradis." They had to pick their way carefully over the stones. The horse seemed more surefooted.

182

"Can horses see in the dark?"

"I don't know. Why?"

"I just thought he might be a better guide through this country than you, Jamil, why not let him go first and give it a try?"

The women had supper ready when they reached the hacienda. Rice, beans and tortillas. The group of Palestinians ate sparingly and with little conversation.

"Well, at least they know how to make rice!" Malmalli murmured, sliding back from the table. "Now, if we could just teach them to make Pilaf."

"You'd better learn to live without it." Jamil sucked at his teeth thoughtfully. "Beans and tortillas are their national dish."

"It's no fucking wonder they're having a revolution!"

Paco couldn't understand what they were talking about, but everyone seemed happy after the meal. He joined their laughter.

The first aircraft arrived overhead at exactly 2:27 a.m.; an unlighted black shadow against the silky, starlit sky. It circled back over the hills, waiting for the lights. Jamil lit the yellow flare atop the water tower, signaling the men waiting by the flare pots. Within a minute all pots were burning. As the aircraft's black form dropped below the horizon of hills, swinging onto its final approach, he saw the outline of the second machine passing overhead. He couldn't hear the sound of the first one land, but knew it was on the ground when its shape blocked the flares on the far side of the runway intermittently as it rolled past. It stopped, and swung around to taxi back to the unloading area. Jamil extinguished his flare. The runway lights went out. He watched the C47 swing onto the apron below the tower, propellors raising clouds of dust as it castered its tailwheel and stopped, nose facing the side of the runway. He relit the flare. The runway lights winked back for the second aircraft. By the time it was parked alongside the first and the runway lights were out, Dingo already had pulled the refuelling wagon alongside the wing and was handing a fuel hose to the man standing on the catwalk. The loading pump motor started barking. Jamil clambered down from the tower. Chirlo stood in the doorway of the first aircraft, a broad smile on his face.

"Anyone for a Revolution?" he inquired, then clambered down the ladder. Felina, Artega and Ruis followed. Chirlo introduced them to Jamil. The men from the flare pots drifted into the group, smiling and bowing to Dr. Artega. They seemed shy, self-conscious, standing back in the darkness. Paco charged among them.

"Quickly now, Hombres! It will be light in four hours. Start unloading. Vamos!"

The knots of men broke up and formed unloading lines from the doors of the aircraft, passing the cargo from hand to hand into the empty wagons. As the fuelling wagons emptied, their drums were piled against the tower and the men pushed the empty flatbeds in line by the aircraft doors for the weapons and ammunition spewing from the interior along the human chain. Felina took her father and Ruis up to the hacienda. Dr. Artega had refused pointedly to talk to the Cuban pilots. Chirlo stood with the four young air force officers by the tower watching the progress of the ground crew. The pilots were munching sandwiches out of the carton of food packed for them at the Officers' Mess that evening. Chirlo shared the sandwiches and thermos of coffee.

"The Doctor doesn't like the Cubans?" Captain Alseino inquired, watching the retreating figures walking towards the hacienda. He was senior officer of the group and had captained the second aircraft into the strip behind Chirlo.

Chirlo shrugged and swallowed some lukewarm coffee. "I think it is pilots he dislikes, not Cubans. He thinks we're all crazy."

The Cuban smiled in the darkness. "You are a diplomat as well as a revolutionary, Colonel Chirlo."

Chirlo chuckled at the compliment of his imaginary rank. "And you, Captain, are a diplomat as well as a pilot."

Jamil appeared from the shadows, nodding to the Cubans. "We should be through within fifteen minutes. The fuelling is completed. You'd better check the gas and oil caps and make sure they put them back properly."

He waited for Chirlo to translate this information to the Cubans, then stood watching them disperse to the aircraft.

"Did you locate the caves in the hills for the caches?"

"This afternoon on horseback. I think they are too close to the farm. They should be moved further into the mountains."

"We'll move everything inland later when we sort it out. Right now get it into the caves after you give everyone a weapon and some ammo issue. Make sure each of your men get a walkie-talkie. I don't want them losing themselves in the mountains."

"How many men does Paco have available for training?"

Chirlo flipped his cheroot into the water barrel. It extinguished with a hiss.

"If he is using all the workers there should be about sixty-five good men."

"I'll break them into five or six man squads. How many speak

184

English?"

"A few. There should be enough of the University boys to act as translators. We'll have more after our first strike. They'll come flocking down to this end of the country."

Jamil smiled wryly. "I know they'll come flocking down, Chirlo, but will it be to join us or kill us?"

"Wait and see." He walked over and said goodbye to the Cubans, handing the boarding ladder up into the doorway of Capt. Alseino's aircraft.

"Drive carefully!" he called.

The Captain waved. "Buena suerte, Colonel!" He reached out and pulled the big cargo door shut.

Moments later the big engines coughed and fired into life. Chirlo covered his face from the enveloping dust cloud as the aircraft moved off to the runway. The second machine followed the first, disappearing in the darkness. The dust settled. He waited several minutes, then saw the quick flash of landing lights, signaling for the flare pots. The men were still lighting the last few when Alseino's aircraft, roared past, lifting into the night. The second machine followed almost in its wake. The noise faded as they hugged the land, heading towards the coast and their island home. The runway lights went out. Except for the chugging of the diesel farm tractors lugging the loaded wagons off to the foothills, the night was still. Chirlo walked up to the hacienda to join the others. He felt tired.

"Colonel!" He stopped by the shed. It was Jamil, sitting astride the horse. "Get some rest. I'll handle everything."

"Thanks." He watched the horse move off, then called, "Oh, Jamil! It's Coronel, not Colonel."

"Not until I improve my Spanish, it isn't."

He laughed as horse and rider were swallowed in the night.

The radio made a clicking sound. Chirlo pushed the button on the walkie-talkie.

"Bandit Six is in position."

The voice was a metallic whisper. He placed the unit speaker next to his lips.

"Check Bandit Six." He spoke the words quietly, then glanced at his watch.

Everyone was in position now. The airport was ringed with the assault teams. The row of T33 and F86 Sabre aircraft glowed a dull silver in the moonlight. The two painted camouflaged Hercules Transports and eight A26 attack bombers directly in front of him were less distinct. The plan was simple. While the mortar teams stationed back by the perimeter pounded the hangers and buildings, the demolition groups took out the aircraft under fire support from the machine gunners stationed at either end of the long tarmac. Anyone trying to run across the tarmac to the aircraft would be knocked out before they reached the concrete apron. The roadblock at Curtaba, where the highway into the mountain narrowed, would stop any chance of reinforcements coming down to the coast from the army barracks at San Ramon. Jamil and his group were to hold the roadblock until nine o'clock the following morning, by which time the airport demolition teams would be dispersed back into the hills and able to cover his withdrawal from Curtaba.

"Ready?"

Paco nodded, handing the Very pistol to Chirlo. He turned to whisper to the rest of the men crouched behind him. They picked up their knapsacks of explosives and hunched, ready to charge the aircraft. The green flare arced into the night with a 'thunk' and burst into light over the hangers. The mortar barrage erupted as they rushed the aircraft. They worked quickly, clamping explosive packages onto the fuel tanks, twisting the timers, then rushing off to the next. There was still no sound from the machine gunners, although a few spasmodic shots could be heard beyond the hangers. Chirlo and his group were working on the third A26 bomber when the first explosions came from a fighter aircraft at the end of the line. The other demolition assault teams were moving quickly through the fighters. He glanced down the tarmac at the white magnesium light as the aircraft settled to the cement in a molten fireball. The one next to it erupted, then the next. Suddenly the machine guns opened up as a swarm of assorted airmen and soldiers came plunging through an opening between the hangers. The leaders, carrying rifles and machine pistols, slumped to the ground. The others turned quickly and ran back to the safety of the burning buildings. A mortar dropped among them. The machine guns stopped chattering. At the far end of the field a huge explosion rocked the ground, lighting the whole airport. The Bandit Six team had blown the main fuel storage tanks. Chirlo could feel the heat on his face and hoped the group had managed to clear the area before the explosion. He went back to work on the charges for the remaining bombers. The fighters continued exploding with metronomic consistency. While they finished the last bomber, the first and second Hercules blew into a pair of fireballs. He could see the figures of the other groups racing towards the machine gun position, running behind the row of burning aircraft. The mortars continued thumping the hangers and buildings, which were now a raging sea of fire. Chirlo triggered the yellow Very light. The mortars stopped. He waited until the machine gunners from the far end of the tarmac came trotting by, lugging their equipment, before signaling with the red flare for withdrawal. The assault teams disappeared into the daylight of burning darkness to their rendezvous points. Chirlo waited with the second machine gun crew until he was certain the airport was cleared. He smacked the gunner on the head with an open hand.

"Okay, Deadeye. Let's get out of here—fast!"

They disassembled the weapon from its tripod, picked up the ammunition boxes and ran to the road. There was still no sign of troops from the inferno that once had been the headquarters and main air base for Cosecha Rica. *They're probably trying to put out the fire,* he thought as he jogged up to the open fence at the airport perimeter. *Not much point to it,* he considered. *They don't need it now. They have no aircraft.*

He climbed into the bus with the rest of the men and drove back down the road to the highway and Bahia Blanca. The men were joking, congratulating themselves on the effects of their fifteen minute expedition. The driver pulled up at the checkpoint on the edge of town. Chirlo dropped off, and waved the driver on through. "Any problems?"

Mahout, the man Jamil had selected to isolate the town, grinned.

"We wiped out the police station and had a few minutes arguing with some air force mechanics on a 24-hour pass, but other than that the place is locked up tighter than a drum. That's quite a display, Colonel!" He nodded towards the glowing sky. Chirlo turned to look at it. He had to admit the man was right. It was one hell of a display.

"Round up your men. Jamil probably needs some help at Curtaba."

Mahout yanked out his radio and called his men to their assembly point.

Colonel Gaspar Guerrero was sweating profusely, although the morning air of the mountains was cool.

"What do you mean you can't get through?"

He was sitting on a camp chair outside the open back doors of his armored car parked in the middle of the highway. Inside the command vehicle, a radio operator tried frantically to raise the command post of the forward elements sent in to punch their way through the Curtaba roadblock. The last message had come a few minutes earlier when the Captain in command had stated he was commencing his assault. Since then there had been no further communication. The two artillery helicopters had been shot down shortly after dawn when they first appeared over the town on a reconnaissance flight to determine how strong a force they were up against. Now the eyes of Guerrero's army were blind. He had no more helicopters. Judging from the lack of success in raising the forward elements of his army on the radio, he was also deaf as to what was going on down below at the town.

"The problem, Colonel, is that they have mortar positions in the mountains covering the highway. They only fire three or four times, then move to another location. We have lost three hundred men, maybe more, and twice that number wounded. We need tanks, artillery to blow our way through."

Cadalso was starting to sweat too. The damn tanks had been out of service for so long they all needed major repairs. He had told Guerrero the situation repeatedly. The Dictator had ignored the problem, trying to wheedle more modern tank units out of the Americans, using the unserviceability of his present equipment as the lever. Guerrero glared at him from the camp stool.

" Major Cadalso, I am not interested in excuses, just results. If we can't have the tanks, where is the artillery?"

As if in reply to the question, a slow convoy of three-quarter ton trucks appeared around the bend in the highway, towing the field guns. The lead truck drew to a stop a few yards short of where the command vehicle was blocking the road.

"The artillery, Colonel." Cadalso announced.

"Well. What are you waiting for? A medal?"

"Your staff truck, Sir. It's blocking the highway."

"Then move it, Major," Guerrero said calmly. He stood up and folded his canvas seat.

Lying a few hundred feed above the road, the lookout Jamil had posted wriggled back from the outcropping of rock ledge where he had been covering the highway since dawn. When certain no one would see him, he stood up, slinging the Russian made Kalachnikov over his shoulder, and slipped the binoculars into their pack. He yanked the walkie-talkie out of the leather case on his belt.

"This is Periscope One. Do you Read?"

Jamil's voice came back at once. "Command here. What is it?"

"Six field artillery pieces and ammo trucks are moving down. They look like four inchers. You should have them in sight within five minutes."

"Roger. I'll check that. Pull out now to Hill Seven and cover the Point for withdrawal."

"You sure you don't want me to snap Lardass? He's right below me. It would be an easy shot."

The voice came back sternly. "Negative. Repeat, negative. Chirlo wants him for himself. Pull out now. Confirm."

Abdum Allam sighed as he pushed the Comm button. "Yessir. Leaving now for Hill Seven. Out."

He glanced back at the ledge for a moment, shook his head, then disappeared into the trees. He disliked leaving such easy shots.

Guerrero nodded grimly to the last driver as the artillery convoy rolled past him down the hill. He walked back to his command vehicle, now parked on a cant at the side of the road. He could hear birds chirping above the sound of the receding trucks. Guerrero stopped, realizing suddenly the mortar bombardment had ceased the thumping he had been hearing all morning.

"The bastards! They saw us coming!" he yelled, running to the command truck. The radio operator stuck his head out the back doors.

"Colonel! The bombardment has stopped." He sounded excited.

Guerrero smacked him across the face. "Idiot!" He whirled on Cadalso. "Into the jeep, Major. Let's get down to Curtaba and see just how badly they've fucked everything up."

The radio man stood on the pavement holding his stinging face, watching the two officers roar off around the curve. When they had disappeared, he spat after them, then went into the command truck and proceeded to smash the radio equipment with his M1 rifle. Suddenly he stopped. A new idea came to him. He dropped out the rear and went round to the driver's door. Quickly he aligned the steering wheel, slipped the gear shift to neutral and released the emergency brake. The heavy vehicle started to roll, gradually picking up speed until it plunged over the embankment and disappeared from sight. He stood fascinated, listening to the crash of metal against rock echoing its destruction from the chasm below the highway.

"Fuck you, Colonel!"

He walked across the road and started climbing towards the ledge that Periscope One had vacated a few minutes before. He didn't know where Chirlo could be found, but somewhere in the mountains he would find him. When he did he had no doubt the scarfaced one could use the services of an experienced radio operator.

Warden Berryman did not like Gaspar Guerrero. But, as CIA agent-in-charge at the San Ramon U.S. Embassy, his personal preferences were immaterial. Guerrero was State Department's man and the orders were to do everything possible to keep him in power, short of bringing in the Marines. He had no doubt the bandit Chirlo was a communist plant from Cuba, trained and armed by Fidel Castro. The report he had read earlier that morning left no question as to the political dangers inherent in the neighboring Republics of Central America, should Chirlo and his Cuban supporters win control of Cosecha Rica. Like a pebble tossed into a quiet pond, the ripples could spread throughout the Latin American World. A terrible thought. So far the CIA had nipped the problem in Guatamala during the Fifties—Bolivia would be under control shortly. The situation in Cosecha Rica was getting progressively worse. During the past year Guerrero had managed to lose control of most of the country through military incompetence, tactical stupidity and mistaken belief he was dealing from a position of power. The power was with the people and the people were with Chirlo. Guerrero might control the cities of San Ramon and Bahia Blanca, a few towns, plus some deserted lakes and mountains at the north end of the Republic, but Chirlo ruled elsewhere. It was due only to Chirlo's desire to keep the highway bridge open between the coast and the capital that San Ramon itself was not under siege. Armed escort vehicles running to and from the airport and docks at Bahia Blanca fooled no one. The highway would remain open so long as Chirlo allowed it to remain open. Time was running out on Gaspar Guerrero, which was why Washington had ordered Berryman to propose the final solution to this nagging problem. It was a rotten way of doing things, but then most of the things that Berryman did for Washington were rotten. It was a rotten business to be in.

"Colonel Guerrero will see you now, Mr. Berryman." Major Cadalso had lost a lot of weight over the past twelve months and developed a tic in his right eye, which created the illusion of a conspiratorial wink with everything he said.

"Thank you, Major."

He picked up his briefcase and followed Cadalso down the hall into the Dictator's office. A staff meeting of field officers had just finished. Guerrero was sitting at the low coffee table, poring over a collection of army field maps covered with red and green crayon markings. He pushed the pile of papers aside as Berryman came into the room.

"Ah. Mr. Berryman. Such a pleasure to see you again. Please sit down."

He rang the bell for a tray of coffee. Cadalso started folding away the pile of maps that had been pushed onto the floor.

"And what is the news from Washington, Mr. Berryman? Do I get those new fighter aircraft?"

He ignored the question. Guerrero seemed to think aircraft were the solution to his problems. So far he had managed to lose two complete air forces while they sat on the ground. The first, a year before. The second, a few months later, the day after the machines had landed at the partially reconstructed air base in Bahia Blanca.

"I have been instructed to advise you that it is our belief the situation can be stablilized only with the assassination of Chirlo and Doctor Artega."

Guerrero stared in disbelief, then burst out laughing.

"Forgive me, Mr. Berryman, but what do you think we have been trying to do for the past year? Invite the hijos de las Puntas to a fiesta?"

Berryman continued without regard to the interruption.

"To this end it is suggested you agree to meet with Dr. Artega and Chirlo for the purposes of discussing details of holding free elections within the country and the transfer of power to whoever is elected by the people."

He paused, waiting for Guerrero to interrupt again. He didn't. His pig-eyes narrowed, assessing the possibilities relative to this approach.

"You will invite them to a meeting here or at some neutral ground that is mutually satisfactory, where both sides may be protected by their own troops."

"And then?"

"And then, Colonel Guerrero, we will kill them, since you are apparently incapable of doing it yourself."

He stared at the Dictator with ice blue eyes. Cadalso coughed, covering his mouth politely, injecting himself into the conversation.

"What guarantee would the Colonel have that you would succeed at such a meeting? You did say both sides would be protected by their own men."

"He has a point, Mr. Berryman." Guerrero looked at Cadalso's lean frame standing by the table with approval.

"What guarantee is there that you will have the opportunity?"

"Colonel, we are not amateurs in this business. You may have several meetings. There may be only one. In any event, an

191

opportunity will present itself at the appropriate time and we will act. What I am looking for now is your agreement permitting us to pursue this course."

Guerrero considered the suggestion for several minutes, slurping his coffee. He looked at Berryman speculatively.

"Does Mr. Russell know of this plan?"

"The Ambassador will be told when it is necessary for him to know. He is a diplomat—a politician—not an intelligence officer."

"There is also a question of blame, Sir." Cadalso spoke up quietly. "Mr. Berryman should perhaps explain who he intends to blame for the assassinations."

Berryman replied without shifting his gaze from Guerrero.

"A communist betrayal from within by Cuban radicals unhappy with Chirlo's popular appeal, eclipsing Castro on the eve of success. His weakness in accepting a compromise of free elections, instead of absolute personal control."

"Do you have bodies to produce for the newspapers when my police shoot these assassins?"

Berryman raised his brows slightly.

"Colonel Gurerrero, I am sure you can produce a half dozen dissidents from inside El Tigre only too happy for a chance to shoot you. Arm them with weapons—faulty firing pins—place them in the crowd covered by your police. When our assassins kill Chirlo, you kill the armed plants. Surely you have enough resources to arrange something as simple as that?"

Guerrero glanced at Major Cadalso with inquiring eyes. The Major nodded and winked.

"Do I get my air force back?" Gaspar loved his air force. He missed it.

"When Chirlo is dead."

"Then, Mr. Berryman, it will be done as you say. I will give the order to the newspapers and radio stations for a Press Conference."

He beamed a fat smile. The CIA Chief stood up.

"Do it quickly, Colonel Guerrero. There is not much time left for posturing."

He inclined his lean frame, nodded to Cadalso and left the room, leaving the door open. The Dictator glared at the retreating figure.

"Pendecho!" He murmured, then sat back in the chair, clasping his fat hands pensively.

"How many communists do we actually have in El Tigre, Cadalso?"

"They are all communists, Colonel."

"I know they're all communists, Major, but how many of them are real communists?"

"I'm not sure sir."

"Then find out. There must be four or five communists in the country somewhere. We need them."

He contemplated his fingers, checking the manicured cuticles carefully.

"Set the press conference up for tomorrow morning at ten—television cameras—radio stations—I want everything ready."

He looked up at Cadalso's nervous wink. "Now get out. I have to write my speech.

They had finished the noon meal at the trestle table under the camouflage netting. It was February. The rainy season was over and the mountain air cool. Dr. Artega read the handwritten copy of the radio broadcast for the tenth time. The radioman had taken it down in shorthand two hours before, when Guerrero broadcast his pleas for negotiation. Chirlo had said nothing during lunch, listening to the discussion as it ranged the table between Felina, Ruis, the Doctor and others in the Headquarters Staff. For weeks they had been planning the final assault to topple Guerrero so that by Holy Week it would be all over. This appeal for negotiation made everyone pause.

"Abdul?" Chirlo looked at the Palestinian for comment. He was the only one of Jamil's group who had chosen to remain when the rest of them returned home the previous May. His Spanish was excellent now and he had developed an attachment for the country. Chirlo knew Abdul Allam would never return to the Middle East.

"My opinion is biased, Colonel." He smiled self-consciously. He was planning to marry the sister of the Headquarters Staff radio operator as soon as hostilities ended. "But Jamil used to say that Conferences always turns out a waste of time."

Felina laughed. "Is that why he ran back to Jerusalem for the May Conference last year? To waste his time?"

Abdul smiled at her gravely. He liked Chirlo's woman. "He went because he is an Arab. I am in favor of ignoring negotiations and continuing with the assault plan to cut the main highway."

"Well, I think it's worth exploring further. It would save a lot of bloodshed. We will have our hands full now in rebuilding the country when this is over."

Artega held the paper in his hand.

"Provided, of course, the offer is real, Don Luis," Ruis suggested.

"Colonel Chirlo! It is a trap!" Surprised, everyone looked at Paulo Benez sitting beside Abdul. The two young men had been inseparable friends ever since Abdul had captured the young radio man a few hours after he had wrecked Guerrero's command truck. As Headquarters radio operator he was permitted to share their table. He spoke rarely to anyone except Abdul Allam. Abdul was engaged to marry Paulo's sister.

"I worked for Colonel Guerrero three years. I know him. When I heard his voice this morning as I wrote down that speech, I knew it was a trap to kill you. I could tell it in his voice. He is a liar and a murderer."

Chirlo nodded his head. "I agree with you, Paulo. It is a trap. But, perhaps there is a way the quarry can become the hunter, eh?" He glanced around the table at the rest of them. "The whole purpose for the meeting will be our assassination—make no mistake about it. Guerrero is not stupid. He knows the revolution will collapse without us. This is his last chance. The question now is how can we use his offer for our assassination to assassinate him? Think about it. We need a plan.

The Ambassador's black limousine drew up softly in front of the Cathedral and stopped. Dorothy Russell waited until the young Marine Corporal chauffeur had run around to the rear door and opened it, before she stepped out. Corporal Radiksz loved the ceremony of his job and became irritated when the formalities of protocol were not observed. Dorothy would just as soon open the door for herself, but she was fond of Corporal Radiksz.

"I'll be fifteen minutes, George."

"Yes, Mrs. Russell," he said politely, shutting the door, then turned to watch her shapely rear disappear into the church, heels beating a swift stacatto on the granite slabs. For the life of him, Corporal Radiksz couldn't understand why she had ever got mixed up with the Ambassador. He was thirty years her senior; dull as hell for a sexpot like Dorothy. But every time he broached the subject during their lovemaking, she always shifted the conversation away to something else.

"Hell, he can't even get it up any more, Dodo; where's his action?"

Earlier in the day they had been lying naked in the private balcony outside her bedroom on the second floor of the house, soaking up the winter sunshine. After copulating steadily for two hours, Radiksz had paused for what he termed 'recharge time.'

Dorothy sat up on the long cushion taken from the patio lounge chair. The effort produced a wet stain on the cloth between her legs.

"Be a darling and get my kleenex off the bedside table."

He had obeyed. Corporal Radiksz had been trained to obey from the time he joined a Polish street gang in Chicago at the age of thirteen, skipping classes to be eligible for membership. Now he was twenty-two. He walked into the bedroom to get the box of kleenex, his limp but still swollen manhood swinging in time with his marching bare feet. Dorothy laughed at him when he returned, grabbing his soft penis.

"He's not the only one who can't get it up anymore!"

That was one of the things that pissed Corporal Radiksz off about the Ambassador's wife; she would never answer his questions. *But, Oh God!* he thought, *is she ever a good screw!*

He climbed back in the front seat of the limo, and turned on the radio. Lucho Gatica was wailing a love song. It made Corporal Radiksz feel sad.

Inside the Cathedral, Dorothy Russell made her way to the confessional, and slipped behind the curtain. She knelt down on the velvet cushion and bowed her head. "Father, forgive me for I have sinned."

Inside the box Father Francisco slid back the wood screen.

"The words are 'Bless me Father,' not 'Forgive me' my child. Only God can forgive. I am only permitted to bless. Has it been long since your last confession?"

"Sixteen years, Father."

The priest was silent. Shocked. There had been rumors about the Ambassador's wife. Perhaps they were true after all. He peered at her closely through the lattice.

"I am making this confession because I have heard you are a friend of the one they call El Chirlo. What I will tell you can save his life. Will you get the information to him, Father?"

"I am not permitted to divulge anything given to me inside the confessional."

"Oh for God's sakes, Father, let's cut out the crap, shall we! I'm not here to confess to anything—we'd be here all night. I came to give you information for El Chirlo. If you are his friend you will pass it on. If you are not then he will be killed next Monday by the CIA when he arrives for the Conference."

She had switched into English, spitting out the words. The priest replied in the same language.

"I'm sorry, Mrs. Russell. I didn't understand. When you phoned earlier asking for a confession I thought . . . ." He left the words hanging, drifting in the musty cubicle.

"Four CIA assassins arrived today from Panama. They have been sent to Mr. Berryman by Washington to kill El Chirlo. I have their photographs."

She slipped the small pieces of paper through the screen. "I'm afraid they're not very good. They are photocopies from their Embassy files. My husband told me of the plan last night. It has been agreed between Colonel Guerrero and Mr. Berryman." She outlined the details quickly and finished by saying, "My husband is a decent man. He was shocked and completely disapproves. But he is a diplomat. He takes his orders from Washington and Washington wants Guerrero, not Chirlo and Dr. Artega."

"Why do you tell me this, Mrs. Russell?"

"I have already explained, Father."

"Not really. Why are you betraying your husband's confidence, your country?"

"Father Francisco, I have lived in this country for three years. I have watched what has happened. I know Guerrero. I know the people of Cosecha Rica and I know just how the Washington schemers operate when they think they might lose some influence in Latin America. I don't know if El Chirlo is a communist, but I do know what Guerrero is. Chirlo has got to be an improvement. Let's just say that for the first time in sixteen years, Father, I have decided to do something decent for a change. Goodnight."

Corporal Radiksz hopped out of the car as soon as he saw her leaving the church. He was waiting by the rear door as she came up. She stopped in front of him.

"George, let's go somewhere and park. I'm feeling sinful again."

Corporal Radiksz smiled politely. "Certainly, Mrs. Russell, I know just the place."

The long convoy of trucks filled with Chirlo's well disciplined and heavily armed soldiers reached the outskirts of San Ramon. The highway up from the coast had been devoid of traffic, but now they could see the first indication of their anticipated arrival by Guerrero's men. Two military Jeeps, parked beside a road sign, moved out to block the lead truck. Chirlo, dressed like the rest of the soldiers seated in the back of the third truck in the column, leaned out to watch the discussion between the young Lieutenant of Guerrero's army and Ruis, the driver in the first vehicle. He could see the young officer climb on the running board and thrust his head in through the open window, then jump down, salute, and return to his Jeep. Ruis' voice crackled through the walkie-talkie Chirlo held.

"He is to provide lead escort into the city. He asked where you were. I told him you were arriving later. Out."

Dr. Artega, sitting on the steel bench across from him, nodded he'd heard the message. The motion caused his steel helmet to wobble. The brim slid over his eyes. He pushed it back on his head with a grimace. Felina, beside him, laughed silently. The rest of the soldiers smiled sympathetically. The company began moving slowly past the road sign; a girl drinking coke.

"Let's hope we're all in shape to 'Buvez Coca Cola' by this evening!" Chirlo muttered.

The Jeeps held their speed to a cautious 20 miles per hour as they rolled through the narrow streets of the city. By the time they swung into the open square of the Palacio Central, it appeared the whole city turned out to greet the revolutionaires. It was a strange greeting. The crowds, packed in behind the rows of blue helmeted soldiers lining the curbs, were silent. Watchful. Waiting for some sign. They parked the trucks about the square. The engine noises died; replaced by sounds of booted feet as the soldiers piled off the vehicles with their weapons and took up the assigned positions. Machine guns, bazookas, mortars, flame-throwers and anti-tank guns were assembled swiftly. There was a dull murmur of anxiety from the crowd. They shrank back, watching the methodical efficiency of Chirlo's army. The delicious anticipation of disaster. Animal curiosity. The body wants to run and hide but the mind wants to stay and see what will happen. The mob in the streets. Chirlo had picked the Conference site well. Although Guerrero's soldiers outnumbered his own by ten to one, the mob outnumbered them both a hundred to one and today the mob was armed. An eerie silence fell across the square in the brittle morning sunlight. A group of pigeons clustered about the Simon Bolivar statue in the center of the square sent a sound of soft cooing and busy wings vibrating through the air with acoustical perfection. Time paused. The silence passed.

"Colonel Guerrero! I am here." A mechanical replica of Chirlo's voice boomed out across the square. The pigeons lifted from the pavement in a flutter of surprise, then settled on the high ground of Bolivar's horse and outstretched sword arm. The crowd stirred in mumble. On the rooftop of the Grand Hotel, Agent Mike Spanik scanned the area about the sound truck through his sniperscope, searching for the owner of the voice. Nothing. Everyone looked the same. Beards, khaki fatigues and machine pistols. He reached along the side of the scope to flip the lever to 300 power magnification.

"Freeze or die!"

Mike Spanik decided to freeze. He had heard that type of voice before. It came from a professional.

"Slide the rifle backwards—butt first—one hand behind your head—move!"

Agent Spanik obeyed, slowly, but with no sign of hesitation. The rifle disappeared as someone picked it away from his side.

"Both hands over your head, now—duck-walk back to the door. Move!"

Now he could see the man with the pistol covering him. *Short, muscular, half Indian, broken nose, alert eyes—too alert.* Spanik decided to forget about the Walther pistol under his armpit. If his hands ever left their clasp over his head he knew he would be dead. *Mr. Berryman is not going to be pleased,* he thought idly, as the half-Indian with the muscles and alert eyes chopped him into unconsciousness with a sharp blow on the back of Spanik's neck.

"Hunter three is out."

"Roger, Hunter three. I check that."

Down in the square, Paulo passed the information to Chirlo. The vanguard covering the CIA assassins had slipped into the city during the night and taken up their positions before dawn. Chirlo nodded.

"One more to go. Keep me advised, Paulo."

"Come, come, Gaspar. I'm waiting!" The loudspeaker echoed again. There were a few nervous giggles from the crowd, then the big doors of the Presidential Palace swung open and the smartly uniformed armed military escort marched down the steps to the first landing and lined the bannisters on either side, their weapons at the ready. The crowd was breathless, watching the dark behind the open doors. Suddenly Guerrero appeared in the full dress uniform of President. He was chest bejewelled and sashed. A ceremonial sword hanging from the blue cummerbund wrapped around his girth. A few steps behind him, Major Cadalso and three other senior officers shifted nervously, their eyes sweeping the square.

"Hunter Four is down."

Paulo was standing beside Chirlo when the walkie talkie confirmed the last CIA man had been neutralized.

"Roger, Hunter four. Well done. Out."

Chirlo smiled at Paulo. "Why don't you take a hand microphone over to Colonel Guerrero so we can start our Conference."

The radio operator picked up the roll of wire beside the loudspeaker truck and jogged up to the steps of the Presidential Palace. The cable snaked out beneath the hand grip from the spool. He paused at the foot of the steps to connect the microphone, then walked up to Colonel Guerrero and saluted.

"Good morning, Sir. Colonel Chirlo asked me to deliver this to you."

Stunned by the recognition of his former radio man, Guerrero grasped the microphone. He glared at Paulo.

"You fucking weasel!" His words boomed out across the square from the loudspeakers.

Smiling, Paulo trotted back down the steps to join the soldiers, moving in with a mortar company well away from where Chirlo was standing.

"Now, Gaspar, is that any way to start off our conference?"

The crowd signaled its approval with laughter. It was to be a duel of mechanical voices; an open air discussion in which everyone could hear the player's lines. Chirlo was in control, heard but unseen. Guerrero had already exposed himself, so it was too late to retreat. Flustered, he stood his ground, rising to the bait.

"My apologies, Colonel Chirlo. I did not know the traitor Corporal Benez had joined your group of communists. I had thought he had died honorably in battle. I see now I was mistaken. He was only a traitor."

"Life is full of little disappointments, Gaspar. You should learn to live with them."

More laughter from the crowd. A few hundred people standing on the curbs, sat down. It appeared the Conference might take some time to conclude.

"Colonel Chirlo, why can we not sit down like gentlemen and discuss our differences in the privacy of my office?" There was an edge of pleading in the voice.

"Because Gaspar, neither you nor I are gentlemen and your office is not private."

The crowd roared in delight at the riposte. A few hundred more sat down around the square. The blue-helmeted soldiers started to relax as the threat of mob violence receded. Paco and his team paused in their slow journey through the crowd until those seated on the curbs had finished arranging themselves. He hoped he could locate the young communists within the mob, before everyone sat down. His group had worked its way completely around the square and was now positioned directly across the street from the

Presidential Palace, watching Guerrero and his group from the end of the building. The crowds were thickest at either corner, where the Avienda Grande swept by the front portals of the Palace steps. Then Paco saw them—not the communists, but the plainclothesmen of Guerrero's secret police. He recognized two, and followed their gaze into the crowd. There appeared to be six of them. They were the only ones not looking towards the Palace steps. Paco motioned to his team. They fanned out around the group, nudging the crowd aside until they had the six men encircled tightly. At fourteen to six it was no contest. The plainclothes policemen were disarmed without struggle, handcuffed and quietly shunted out of the crowd to the Avienda Grande. Paco slipped through the front of the crowd by the Palace and touched the bearded whitefaced young man holding a raincoat draped over one arm. The youth turned his head quickly, his eyes opening with surprise.

"The firing pins have been removed from your weapons by Guerrero's police."

The man jerked his head back from the whispered words and glanced down at his raincoat.

"Who are you?" His voice was hoarse from lack of use.

"A friend of Chirlo's. Your weapons are at four locations about the square waiting for you." He nodded to the tops of the hotels and the Central Bank building. "On the roofs. Our men are there to cover your escape. Round up the rest of your people. Good luck."

Paco melted back into the crowd, then paused to watch the youth move quickly down the curb to talk to another man holding a raincoat. They both glanced at their raincoats, then towards the roof tops, before splitting up to merge into the sea of packed humanity.

"We have been wasting time, Gaspar. Let us get down to cases. What is it that you are proposing to settle our differences?" The harsh metallic words caused the crowd to pause. The jokes were over. The square was silent again.

"I am prepared to offer free elections within one year and a general amnesty for all political prisoners." It was weak, but Guerrero could think of nothing else to say while he stalled for time. *Where the hell were the CIA marksman?* There was an ugly boo from the mob below the steps.

"Maybe within six months," he added lamely. His armpits felt wet. His forehead glistened.

"That's a pretty thin offer for a defeated dictator, Gaspar. Suppose I tell you what we want. First, your immediate resignation." There was a yell of approval from the crowd. "Second, release of all

200

political prisoners today from El Tigre Fortress." Another roar. "Third, reappointment of the man whose government you overthrew, as President pro tem until an elected government can be constituted within the next thirty days. And finally, you will place yourself under arrest for murder and treason."

The mob howled with delight, swarming though the barriers of armed soldiers who stood aside, helplessly at first, then joined them to embrace the group of revolutionaries in the square. Suddenly a shot rang out. Everyone stopped in their tracks, uncertain. Guerrero clutched the jewelled insignia at his breast. His knees buckled as he toppled forward, flopping down the wide stone steps. The ostrich plumed helmet clanged to the sidewalk down another flight from where his body lay. Three more shots reverberated about the square The fat body twitched from the impact of the bullets. A woman screamed. For a moment there was silence, then with a roar of rage, the mob surged towards the gaudy fat carcass lying on the palace steps.

"Stop!" Chirlo's voice rang out imperiously. The swarms of people turned to face the loudspeaker truck and watch Chirlo climbing onto the roof the cab. He surveyed the square slowly, his eyes seemingly covering everyone.

"The destruction is over. It is the time to rebuild our lives. Our hopes. Our country. Please go home and start. There is much to be done. The time for warriors is past. Now is the time for men of reason to decide how they must govern themselves. Vaya Con Dios."

He climbed down from the truck and vanished back to the anonymity of his men. Somewhere in the crowd a beautiful tenor voice began to sing the country's national anthem. A few picked up the refrain, until by the end of the first verse, thousands of voices filled the square as they dispersed slowly into the side streets back to their homes. Simon Bolivar and his pigeons watched in silence.

Felina and Chirlo were married a month later in the cathedral by Father Francisco Montelegro. It was a gala social occasion. Although news of her desecration at the hands of Bermudez and his men was public knowledge, no one seemed to mind a wedding dress of virginal white. "Virginity is a matter of attitude, not hymens," was how the social columnist of El Diario indelicately phrased it. They left the church covered with confetti, rose petals and good wishes from the crowds, to be driven with police escort down to the airport at Bahia Blanca and catch the Pan Am flight to Panama, with connections to Europe. The honeymoon, scheduled to last six

201

months, was cut short in Zurich during late October when Ruiz flew in to see them. They were eating a late breakfast in the dining room of the Baur Au Lac Hotel, reading the Paris edition of the *Herald Tribune*, when he joined them at the table. Ruis looked bushed.

"I'm getting too old for these sort of trips," he admitted, after they had embraced and settled their surprise at seeing him. "Jet travel is for younger men."

His red-rimmed eyes smiled tiredly. He examined Felina.

"You've put on a little weight, child. You'll have to watch your diet!"

"It's the free Swiss air."

"And about the only thing here that is free, apparently. Your charge accounts have been astronomical. Don Luis couldn't believe the purchases. By the way, what is a Zarf?"

"A what?"

"A Zarf. There was a bill from Sotheby's in London for two thousand pounds for one Zarf."

"Oh, that Zarf. It belonged to the Duke of Argyle. Bonnie Prince Charlie gave it to him as a present in 1748. It's priceless," Felina explained.

"It certainly is, but what is it?" He looked at Chirlo.

"A container for liquor. She fell in love with it." He laughed.

"Really Ruiz, we had to buy something for the new house while we were over here." She said it defensively, then clasped her hands. "How is Papa? His letters are always so vague."

"Busy. Very busy with the elections. He is on the road every day. By January I swear he's going to know everyone in the country on a first-name basis."

"But he is having problems?" Chirlo folded the newspaper onto the table.

"Several. Not with the election. He'll win that of course by a landslide. The Americans are being difficult. The AID program has been stalled in Washington, and he can't seem to get anywhere with World Bank on these development programs. He tells me it's a temporary situation until his re-election is confirmed, but I know him. He is worried. The Americans don't like the idea of our pulling the country out of the Organization of American States."

Chirlo shrugged. "That is a debt I promised to pay Castro. We all agreed. We must honor our commitments, Luis, however distasteful they might appear now."

"I know. I'm not arguing the point, only stating the problem it has created. Though one unexpected ally turned up as a result of the

OAS decision—Canada. They have agreed to set up an embassy in San Ramon. Apparently the Canadians are sympathetic to our leaving OAS. They refused to join the organization at the beginning."

"Any chance of aid from them?"

"Perhaps. We'll know more after the election. I thought maybe Dr. Castro could help us there—with the Canadians, I mean. After all, Canada has been dealing with Cuba for years and ignoring Washington's disapproval."

"I don't know how close Fidel is to the Canadian government. In any case, Ruis, I think it would be unwise. The man has done one favor already. I don't want to make a habit of running into Havana every time we have a political or economic problem we can't solve for ourselves. He might get the idea of providing a permanent arrangement with us."

The immaculate Swiss waiter paused by the table to inquire if the new guest would require any breakfast. He ordered black coffee.

"You want us to come home." Chirlo looked at Ruis. "That's why you came, isn't it?"

Ruis shook his head. "You misunderstand me. I came to bring you the news, first hand. Spend a few days soaking up the rain. Nothing more."

The waiter returned with a silver-plated coffee pot, multi-colored sugar briquettes and thick yellow cream in adjoining silver containers. Ruis examined the array.

"I only wanted a cup of black coffee."

The waiter bowed. "In case you change your mind, Sir."

Ruis smiled. "So this is how they manage to make a cup of coffee cost twenty francs!"

"Clever Swiss. Did Papa send you?" Felina asked.

"No. I told him why I was coming." He sipped at the Dresden china cup.

"He needs you both home. He needs help, Chirlo, an organizer to get things done. Don Luis is too kind-hearted to be a politician. Too hard-hearted to be a diplomat. He has a problem."

He eyed them both speculatively for a moment, then returned to the coffee cup.

"We were going to Amman next week to see if we could find Jamil," Felina said.

"We can cancel it. He's probably not there anymore." He looked at Ruis closely.

"I wouldn't drink any more of that coffee if I were you. It will keep you awake. If we're flying back tomorrow, you're going to need all the sleep you can get."

Ruis set down the cup. "Thank you. Sorry to be such a nuisance."

". . . . we are a nation of independent people capable of governing ourselves. We will always be prepared to listen to advice from sister nations; that does not mean we will follow their advice. We will always be prepared to accept the offers of help from our sister countries; that does not mean that we will relinquish the control over how the help is used . . . ." There were prolonged cheers from the floor of the Congress, a thumping of desk tops. Chirlo's mind snapped back to the present. Felina nudged him into clapping at Dr. Artega's words.

"Don't you approve of the speech, Pedro?" she whispered. Chirlo started clapping.

"I should approve, after all, I wrote it."

The applause died. President Artega concluded. "We walk forward together into the sunlight of a new season for our land. The rainy season has ended. The storm clouds have gone. Let us plant our seeds of peace and reason so that we may, in time, harvest the fruit of contentment. God bless you all."

To a man, the Congress was on its feet, shouting 'Bravo' when the small doctor left the podium wreathed in smiles, and vanished through a side exit with his entourage. Chirlo glanced at his watch. The speech has lasted exactly one hour.

"Let's go. I have an appointment with the Canadian Commercial Secretary."

They nodded to the TV men and joined the rest of the crowd leaving the visitors gallery. Chirlo guided Felina down the steps to the west wing of corridors. Although she was only two months pregnant and perfectly capable of managing for herself, he had become intensively protective of the mother and what he hoped would be his first son. He kissed her goodbye at the private exit from the west wing, then walked to his office in the Foreign Affairs Department at the end of the corridor. The Commercial Secretary was sitting in the outer office waiting for him.

"Mr. Price." The young man adjusted his hornrimmed glasses and stood up. He was much taller standing that he had appeared on the chair.

"Colonel Chirlo." They shook hands.

"Please come in. I hope I didn't keep you waiting." Chirlo knew he was five minutes early for the appointment. He ushered him into the private office and sat down behind his desk.

"You said you had some news, Mr. Price?"

"Good news, Colonel. May we speak in English?" He paused, the slim briefcase poised on his knees.

"By all means, Mr. Price. I seldom have a chance to practice the language these days."

Price opened his case and drew out two-ribbon-bound folders. He handed them across the glass table top.

"The top one is the Canadian International Development Agency Proposal for the assistance we discussed. The other is the power project for Atomic Energy of Canada. They are of course only rough drafts of what my government is prepared to offer and will not be put into final form until you have approved the contents."

Chirlo opened the neatly tied ribbon on the top file and flipped through the pages swiftly. It was all there. The two hospitals, dairy station, airport improvements, highway equipment, schools; everything he had discussed with the serious young man when he first arrived in San Ramon as the Commercial Secretary for the new Embassy. He opened the second folder. It covered pages of power requirements, estimated for a ten year period, by the Canadian group of experts. There was a three-dimensional drawing of the proposed nuclear power plant to be built down the coast from Bahia Blanca. He folded them back into the file.

"I will study these later, Mr. Price. Assuming we are in agreement with everything, what is the next step?"

Price cleared his throat. "I will have the final draft completed and returned to you for signature by the President. The President would then submit the formal request to your Ambassador in Ottawa, for presentation to the Canadian government. Since the approvals have already been agreed upon 'in camera,' so to speak, official approval will be forthcoming immediately, say a month at the latest. Will that be satisfactory, Colonel?"

Chirlo nodded.

"Are there any other questions I can answer for you, Sir?"

"No, Mr. Price. That about covers it, I think. I appreciate your help."

He stood up to usher his guest to the door.

"I'll phone you as soon as I've studied the proposals—shall we say tomorrow for dinner at Richi's? I hear he's done wonders with the place."

"Thank you, Colonel. By the way, I have taken the liberty of advising one of the contractors who will be building the reactor, of this project. He advised they will be sending a man down here within the week. A Mr. Donald Affleck of CORCAN Engineering Ltd. I'll bring him over when he arrives."

"I'll look forward to meeting him, Mr. Price."

They paused by the door. "Excuse me Colonel, but are you sure you have never been to Canada?"

Chirlo smiled at the tortoise shelled frames. "Why do you ask?"

"Your accent, Sir. You say 'house' and 'about' like a Canadian—quite distinctive speech traits. I studied language at the university. Off-hand I'd say your accent was from the Ottawa Valley, around Carlton County. Course I could be wrong."

"Perhaps I should apply to your Ambassador for a Canadian passport."

They both laughed as Price left. Chirlo went back to his desk and lit a thin cigar. His hands were shaking. For a moment, one fleeting moment, in his mind's eye he had seen a young man skiing with a blonde girl on a mountain slope in Canada. The mountains were the Laurentians and the young man was himself.

9

1967

The March snow was still well packed, the trails fast. Corbin figured that with any luck they would get another two or three weekends at the lodge before packing it in for the year. Learning to ski had been Elizabeth's idea. Two years before they had gone up to St. Jovite and stayed at Gray Rocks Inn. After his first lesson, the sport became a passion. He bought a small cabin in the Laurentians less than two hours driving from Ottawa, and had run away every weekend unless business travel kept him abroad.

He parked the black Porsche under the eaves of the carport. The carport, like the cabin, resembled a huge inverted V, the roofs of both buildings sloping sharply to the ground. It was a common enough design in Switzerland, but in the Canadian Laurentians the highly varnished fir planking nestled among the conventional log cabins scattered through the valley appeared misplaced. Corbin loved it. It was Utopia. He untied the skis and poles from the tubular trunk rack on the Porsche, handing Elizabeth the poles. A wisp of light snow was starting to fall from the leaden skies. The early wetness from the morning sun had frozen in the colder air of the overcast afternoon, leaving a thin crust above the softer snow to collapse with a crunch at each footstep. Corbin followed up the steps to the door and waited while she unlocked it. The cold key stuck to her mittens.

She dropped the poles.

"Damn!"

"Still got the key?"

Elizabeth held it aloft with a smile, and unlocked the door. Corbin followed her in, picking up the poles on his way. He stacked the equipment against the wall, and shucked off his boots and outer clothing. There were a few low embers still glowing in the huge stone fireplace. Elizabeth poked at them, separating the black ashes, then piled some kindling sticks on the embers, waiting for them to catch. Corbin slipped up behind her and wrapped his arms around her waist, pulling her rump towards his body. She wriggled her bottom seductively for a few moments until she could feel his erection through the tight ski pants, then stopped and turned around.

"We're nearly out of wood."

Corbin groaned. "Where's your sense of romance, woman?"

She laughed. "Where's your sense of timing? Here!" She handed him the poker. "Don't let the fire die—I'll get the wood."

He watched the yellow ski pants and trim rump crossing the room. It was ridiculous. He felt horny just looking at her. She paused to stick out her tongue before going outside to the wood pile.

Corbin sighed and began poking the fire. Over the last two years he knew he had discovered his own personal Nirvana. Its creation had been by accident. Its discovery by design.

Like the old Ealing Studio movie he had seen on the late show starring Alec Guinness: "Captain's Paradise;" a bigamist ship's captain sailing the straits of Gibraltar on a ferry boat with a sexpot in Algiers, a homebody in Gibraltar and the stimulation of male companionship aboard the vessel in between.

Nirvana. He stabbed the kindling. It ignited. He had Peggy and the children comfortably installed at the house in Rockcliffe Park where he stayed during the week. The attentive husband and father. He had Elizabeth every weekend, sometimes more if they were traveling, and in between, the stimulation of his many business interests. Nirvana. The door burst open and Elizabeth staggered inside, her arms laden with short logs. He crossed the room to help. She kicked the door shut with a ski boot.

"It's really coming down now—too bad we have to leave in the morning."

"We could always come back late."

They dumped the logs into the metal rack beside the fireplace.

"Forsaking business for pleasure? Ha! That would be the day. Don's due back tomorrow, or had you forgotten?"

Affleck had been away supervising the construction of a new nuclear reactor in Central America. It was supposed to be finished and ready for operation April first.

"No, I haven't forgotten, sweetheart, but we could get a morning's skiing in before going back. He won't turn up until noon anyway."

"See how you feel in the morning."

She knew that by morning he would be anxious to return to the city. There was no point in discussing the subject further. Corbin arranged the logs in the middle of the flaming kindling. The wet wood hissed and spluttered, pushing tendrils of steam up the flue, then the bark caught and the fire took hold. He sat back on his haunches to watch the dancing flames. Myriads of weaving light, rising and falling. Uncoordinated heat. Nothing like a nuclear reactor.

Idly, he remembered the first time he had seen a nuclear pile raising the steam pressures at the Rolphton Plant and Morris Levy explaining what was happening as the diamond-headed needles started to climb on the control room panel.

"The fuel bundle is reacting within the calandria heating the water for the condensers. They in turn, heat more water, changing it into steam. The steam drives the turbines. Now watch this!"

Levy changed the flow rate of the heavy water into the calandria; the needles slowed, they stopped their temperature climb.

"The chain reaction between the Uranium 235 in the fuel bundles and its slow neutrons is now constant—steady nuclear fission."

Corbin stared at the dials, transfixed. He could hear a faint hum from the turbines in the power room beyond the concrete walls. Levy smiled.

"Now we'll reduce the heat."

He turned the flow of heavy water from the moderator into the calandria again. At once the needles started sliding down their scale.

"The fission process is slowed now by the neutrons bouncing off the heavy water, instead of splitting the uranium atoms—the nuclear pile is cooling down. Simple process, eh?"

"What happens if a pipe bursts?"

"We have a fast shutdown procedure using shutoff rods, or liquid poison injection into the moderator. It takes less than five minutes to Max. Safe status. So far we've never had a pipe burst. They shouldn't burst. They're stress tested to better than fifty times any temperature or pressure requirements we use before they're installed. The only problem to date has been with the zircaloy fuel sheaths where the uranium pellets are inserted to make up the fuel bundles. We had a few cracks show up, but we've got that licked now."

They went back outside and across the yard to the storage pool building where the spent fuel bundles were left to cool before transfer to permanent storage. The water emitted an eerie blue-green phosphorescent glow. Beautiful and deadly.

"The depth of the water above the bundles contains the radio-activity. It's quite safe," Morris explained.

Corbin nodded. "Yeah, like the elephant trainer."

"The elephant trainer?"

"He spent years training the animal from the time it was a baby. Treated it like a child. Taught it every trick in the book, then went to the circus manager and said 'look.' He lay down on the ground and let the elephant put its foot on his chest."

They walked back into the yard towards Levy's office.

"So what happened?"

"The elephant crushed him to death."

Levy hadn't smiled. That was two years ago. Now CORCAN Engineering had finished work on the first phase of the KANUPP reactor in Pakistan and the CANDU CR1 was scheduled to go on stream in two weeks at Punta Delgado, Cosecha Rica. He didn't understand really how they worked, except in the most simplistic terms, but the contracts to build them had made CORCAN and the old Venture Design Engineering Ltd. into very fat cats indeed.

Corbin backed away from the fire as the intensity of the heat began to grow. He stood up and undressed, feeling the warmth glowing on his body. Then he lay down on the huge white Polar Bear rug, propping himself up on one elbow to watch the fire. Except for the thick ski socks, he was naked.

Elizabeth came back into the room from the kitchen with two champagne glasses and the bottle of Mumms. It was a weekend ritual. She set the glasses down, working their bases into the white fur of the rug, then popped the cork on the bottle and filled them.

"To the great unwashed!" The words were said simultaneously, solemnly, "wherever they may be."

They sipped the chilled wine. Elizabeth stood and started undressing.

"I do wish you'd take your socks off, Chuck." She pulled the wool sweater over her head and reappeared with tousselled hair, smiling. "It always makes me feel you're getting ready to run out on me."

She unhooked her bra and wriggled out of her ski pants, then sat down, straddling his thighs, her labia opening with the movement, glistening, honey-coated. She fondled him until his swelling was full, then slid forward to meet it.

Don Affleck hadn't been at all keen on moving up to Canada when Corbin had returned home three years before and announced the purchase of Venture Design Engineering. He liked living in Florida. He liked the sunshine, the holiday atmosphere and easy leisure of life. He had formulated a set of arguments for remaining in Tampa when the CORAM lots were sold. He would hold the fort of American interests for their corporation while Corbin spread his wings and flew north. Fat chance! He looked out the window from the seventh floor of the Lord Elgin Hotel at the snow swirling behind one of the city's buses on its way up the hill to the War Memorial.

"Shit!" he said aloud and phoned room service to send his breakfast. He hated the cold, the snow, the winter, Ottawa, Canada, the whole scene. He wandered into the bathroom to shower and shave, remembering the sales job Corbin did on him the day after he had returned home.

"It's unbelievable, Don! They're at least twenty years behind us in everything. Talk about opportunities to expand—and no competition! Do you know you can walk right in on the government officials without an appointment and start talking turkey? Try that in Washington—or Tallahassee, for that matter."

"What's the weather like?" Affleck had been sceptical.

"Colder'n Toby's arse right now, but they say it warms up in May."

"May? When does winter start, June?"

"November, I think, but everything's heated."

"Big deal."

Corbin ignored the remark. "I figure we can set up headquarters in Ottawa, then run everything down here as a sub. The boys can handle it on a monthly basis, and you or I can run down for the board meetings. But the kicker is this nuclear business. It's going to be the energy of the future, Don. Stands to reason oil isn't going to last forever. We'll be in on the ground floor."

"Chuck, there is no shortage of oil."

"Not now maybe, but what about in ten years? Think of it! We'll be in a position to take first crack at everything that comes in the field—we'll be experts!"

He had gone on to explain how he was going to buy a house for

Peggy and the kids, had already hired a secretary and arranged for an apartment; then went into a long explanation about the possibilities for fast-food outlets, lumbering, heavy construction and agricultural farm land. Affleck could see there was no point arguing with him. His mind was already made up, and despite the reservations he had to admit it did sound like a hell of a place for a corporate headquarters. It was a hell of a place, all right! The only time he had spent in Canada during the past years was during infrequent winter visits.

He didn't believe Canadian trees produced leaves. He had never seen any. He was toweling himself when room service knocked at the door with his breakfast.

"Bonjour, Monsieur!" The waiter pushed the linen covered dolly into the room. He had a blue chin and bad front teeth.

"Bonjour," Afleck agreed, although judging from the snow whipping past the window, he couldn't for the life of him see anything to 'bonjour' about. That was another thing he missed. At least in Florida everyone spoke English, once you got out of Miami.

"Voila!" Bluebeard uncovered the eggs with a flourish as if indicating he had entered the room with an empty plate and the whole thing was magic. Affleck felt foolish.

"Bravo!" He signed the check and fumbled in the pockets of his pants for a coin to tip the man, then dropped the trousers back on the chair.

"Merci, bon appetit!"

Yesterday it had been "Gracias," today it was "Merci," in Pakistan it had been—what? Affleck had forgotten his Urdu. Naked, he sat down to eat breakfast, watching the snow.

By the time he had finished off the lot sales in Charlotte Harbour, then straightened out his own business affairs, it was November when he had arrived in Ottawa to join Corbin. The city was in the midst of its first heavy snowfall of the season; everybody bundled in long parka-coats, ear muffs and thick gloves, their feet encased in ankle-length zipper boots, pant cuffs tucked into the tops. Faces pinched red with cold, runny noses with perpetual dew drops at the tips. Fortunately, Corbin had met him with an overcoat to insulate the thin linen suit he had worn up from Florida, as he walked through the Customs and Immigration barrier. Corbin was wearing a thick hip-length coat sweater, covered with dull red maple leaves knitted into the weave. It looked warm.

"I see you've gone native already!" Affleck said, slipping into the overcoat.

"When in Rome . . . ." They walked out to the parking lot,

dodging splashing snow puddles where the heavily salted road had melted the silent white downpour on contact. Affleck's shoes were soaked by the time he climbed into the car. He removed them and stuck his wet socks and feet against the blast of hot air from the car heater as they drove into the city.

"We got the contract in Rajastan," Corbin announced.

"I thought it was Pakistan?"

"It is, Rajastan is in Pakistan. You'll be leaving next week as soon as Warren finishes putting the rest of the group together. We've got to keep an 80% Canadian personnel ratio on the project to keep the government happy."

They pulled up behind a truck. The wipers smeared a dirt-snow-salt scum across the windshield, blinding them. Corbin hit the spray button and the wipers slicked out a semi-circle of visibility as they passed the truck. Affleck relaxed, seeing the road ahead was clear.

"You'll be in charge over Warren—watch him carefully on the cost overrruns. Holmes is a good engineer, but a lousy businessman. He'll bust us if you're not careful. You read the specs?"

"Uh huh, they're in my case. It's a straightforward construction job, except for the nuclear part of the program."

"That's not our concern, we're just hired to build and equip. A turnkey factory with all the right plumbing according to the specs. Canadian General Electric and Atomic Energy of Canada Limited handle the operational responsibilities. Morris Levy is supposed to be number one Taco on that job, but it's not definite yet. There's a bit of a power play going on internally. You know the sort of thing; Levy is an American, G.E. is American, I'm an American, now you turn up, another American. Their nationalistic pride is outraged. They may opt for a Canadian."

"I thought Levy said he became a citizen."

"He did," Corbin laughed, "but that still makes him an American. Up here, unless your ancestors fled north after the Battle of Yorktown or immigrated from Britain a hundred years ago, you're a foreigner. Except of course, for the French, and everybody thinks they're foreigners and they think everyone else is the same."

Affleck fell silent, considering the information, finally giving up and changing the subject.

"How did we do on those Expo '67 bids at Montreal?"

The World's Fair was scheduled to open in Montreal in 1967 and CORCAN had been bidding on a variety of jobs for the project.

"No luck on the highway contracts; the French Canadians have got them all tied up in the Province of Quebec, but I think we have a good shot at two of the pavillions, plus the work we're doing there now. These Canadian unions are a bunch of bastards to deal with, particularly the ones in Quebec."

That had been two and a half years ago. The pavilions were finished and Expo '67 was completed. Canada's birthday party for the world. KANUPP in Rajastan should be on stream producing nuclear power by 1971, now that they had straightened out the disorganized mess from the product suppliers; Punta Delgado should have its power flowing sometime in the next couple of weeks. It was ironic to think India and Pakistan had provided the test bed for mistakes so the reactor in Cosecha Rica could be constructed without a flaw, ready for power long before the prototypes upon which it was founded, were completed.

"We learn from our mistakes," was the way the Canadian General Electric spokesman had explained away their construction delays to a group of newsmen visiting the KANUPP site.

"Some suppliers evidently thought our specification criteria permitted substandard equipment." He smiled good-naturedly. "They were wrong."

"Does that mean the equipment was shipped under fraudulent circumstances?"

Affleck remembered thinking at the time, *You're goddamn right, buster, and that's why we're going to be screwed up here for another two years rebuilding the whole fucking plant,* but he had, as sub-contractor, said nothing and marveled at C.V. O'Brien's smooth reply to the reporter.

"Not at all. It means merely that some suppliers were under the impression we would permit, and accept, variations on the specifications for certain valves, plumbing and piping that they agreed to supply. It is understandable. Variations on specs are an accepted practice in the heavy construction industry. However, nuclear power generating plants cannot permit such luxury of deviation. To do so would be to court disaster."

That was the reason C.V. O'Brien was the only one permitted to speak to visiting firemen in Rajastan. General Electric had to rebuild most of the plant after removing truck loads of inferior parts of backup equipment. It had been one scandal that had never reached the newspapers during a period of Canadian history filled with political pork-barrelling and governmental incompetency. C.V. O'Brien had been a wise selection. It was due to C.V.'s report to Ottawa on CORCAN, and in particular on Don Affleck, that the

Cosecha Rican project had been handed to them on a silver platter, in a manner of speaking. Corbin had telexed him to leave the mess in Pakistan for General Electric to straighten out. It was their problem as prime contractor anyway. In Cosecha Rica CORCAN would be prime contractor, and Affleck, the C.V. O'Brien for that area. Pakistan had been the training ground. Cosecha Rica would be the finishing school.

The telephone rang at the beside table. Affleck swallowed a mouthful of coffee, wiped his mouth with the napkin, then rose to answer it.

"Don Affleck here."

"Welcome back to the snow. How was your trip?" It was Peggy Corbin.

"Hello Peg! Isn't this weather something else?" He laughed. "Christ, I swear it does nothing but snow up here. Chuck there?"

"No, that's why I'm calling. He phoned in from some gas station on his way down from the cabin—he goes off every weekend skiing—said he'd be in before noon. I guess the roads are bad."

Affleck looked at his watch. It was half past eight. Three hours to kill.

"Want some company?"

"Mmmm. Love some. Wait 'till I get dressed and I'll come over and get you. 'Bout nine-thirty all right?"

"Fine, Peg. I'll be at the front door waiting." They exchanged a few more pleasantries and hung up. Affleck went into the bathroom to shave. The image of his tanned face startled him. He had been looking at white-faced Canadians since the previous evening and looked like an East Indian by comparison. The white midriff gave him away. He smiled at his reflection and began lathering the original. He had tried to grow a beard once years ago, but gave up when it started to itch in the humid Florida weather. He had decided he didn't like beards. Well, not all beards. Colonel Chirlo had a beard that looked like a Rembrandt portrait. In this case it was just as well. The beard hid the monster scar on the side of his face. He remembered their first meeting with that nerd, Harry Price of the Canadian Embassy.

"Colonel, may I present Mr. Donald Affleck, Vice-President and General Manager of CORCAN."

The big man had crushed his hand, growling a welcome, his eyes gauging Affleck. He ushered them into chairs, then sat on the edge of the desk in front of them.

"How can I help you to help us, Mr. Affleck?" The direct

approach.

He remembered thinking how well the Colonel would get along with Chuck Corbin. Never mind the bullshit. Straight to the point. Affleck had explained exactly what he wanted to do and how he intended to do it. Straight to the point.

The big man had reached for the SWEDA upright phone on the desk behind him and given someone the necessary instructions. He had then written a short note that Harry Price later had translated.

"This man is a friend from Canada. Help him and you help me. Help me and you help yourself. Chirlo."

The letter became his passport through the tiny Republic. Never before had he worked with such a group of cooperative people. Months later, when the construction work was well underway, Chirlo appeared suddenly at the Punta Delgado site. He drove up alone in a Land Rover and climbed out. Affleck saw him arrive from the window of his office in the new administration building. Chirlo stood holding his hand to his forehead, a low statuette, shielding his eyes from the glare of the white concrete reactor building at the end of the point and the bright ocean beyond. Affleck went outside to greet him.

"Colonel Chirlo! I was hoping you would find time to drop in and see what we were doing here." They shook hands.

"I have been reading your progress reports with interest, Mr. Affleck."

He gave a lopsided smile.

"I should have come earlier, but I have been occupied."

They started walking towards the white domed building.

"Congratulations on the birth of your twin boys. You must be very pleased—I mean, getting two for the price of one so to speak."

Chirlo chuckled. "Two for the price of one. I like that. I must tell my wife. Are you married, Mr. Affleck?"

"No Sir. Haven't found the right girl yet. Maybe I've been too busy to look."

"You don't have to look, Mr. Affleck. She will find you, no matter how busy you are."

They walked in silence. Several trucks passed on their way to the main gate and docks at Bahia Blanca for another load of supplies. The drivers waved carelessly as they passed, then stared bug-eyed when they recognized El Chirlo on foot. A roll of dust passed them, drifting off the point to the water.

"Are you going to pave this?"

"Yes Sir, but not until all construction work is finished. Paved roads are the last step before our part of the job is over and the Atomic Energy Canada people take over with their bag of tricks. If we paved it now, the trucks would wreck it by the time we were ready to leave."

Chirlo said nothing when they arrived at the reactor building. Affleck led the way through the main entrance, opening offices as they went down the corridor to the control room. Console panels covered the center of the floor in two semi circles. They were devoid of instrumentation. The people from IBM weren't due in for another 60 days. Affleck explained the gaps on the panel, then moved down to the turbine room.

"There are four 75 megawatt steam turbines in here, giving us a 300 megawatt capacity."

Chirlo placed his hand on one of the curved pipes rising from the floor to thrust into the turbine cover. "And these pipes come from the nuclear pile beneath the floor." It was more a statement than a question.

"Not exactly. The nuclear pile heat is inside a calandria—like a kettle—which in turn heats the heavy water passing through it, which in turn heats ordinary water in a condenser, which in turn produces the steam that passes through that pipe under pressure, turning the turbines."

Chirlo removed his hand suddenly, as if the pipe were hot. Affleck took him down to the calandria and explained the webbing of pipes and valves bundling off in various directions.

"What happens if everything blows up?" Chirlo asked with the strange smile.

"It can't blow up, Colonel, but if everything failed everywhere and we couldn't cool the pile, then it would simply melt the building, steel, concrete, the works, and settle into the ground, giving off one hell of a dose of radiation."

"Would it keep sinking as it melted the ground?" Chirlo seemed curious.

Affleck shrugged. "No one really knows. It's never happened. Presumably it would stop at the earth's core. I can't see it going straight through to China! Chairman Mao would never permit it." They had both laughed.

Affleck was standing between the weather barrier doors when Peggy drew up in the white Imperial. He waved, picked up his briefcase and went outside. The hotel doorman opened the car with a nod. Affleck slid across the seat and planted a kiss on Peggy's proffered cheek, before they drove off into the traffic stream to Laurier Avenue.

"God, but you're brown, Don!"

"God, but you're white, Peg!" She giggled at the retort, glancing at her face in the rear view mirror.

"We did have a lovely summer and the fall was just beautiful. I have never seen such color anywhere, except in Vermont when I was a little girl. My tan has gone now. I did have one."

"Glad it's got some redeeming features." He looked at her quizzically. "You happy?"

"Is anyone happy?"

"I am. As long as I have something to bitch about, of course." He smiled.

"How's Chuck? How are the kids?"

The kids are great. Usual colds, of course, but that's normal this time of year."

They angled past the Russian Embassy with its three stories of shaded windows and swung north for Rockcliffe Park.

"You forgot to mention, Chuck." Affleck prompted.

She lifted a shoulder, her eyes intent on the slippery road ahead.

"I don't know, Don. I guess he's all right. He still has that affair going with his Limey secretary. They go up north every weekend skiing. I get him the rest of the week."

"You make it sound like he's beating you. How do you know about the secretary?"

"I know—but it doesn't make any difference, really. He is a good father. A good husband too, I suppose. I have everything I need—except love—Elizabeth has that."

"Elizabeth?"

"The secretary. You mean you didn't know?" She took her eyes from the road to look at him, disbelievingly.

"I've been away for a while, remember?"

"You were here last November." She said the words accusingly.

"For two weeks. As a matter of fact, I went out a few times with Elizabeth."

"But forgot her name."

"I meet a lot of Elizabeths in my travels, Peg. None of them worth remembering."

They drove on in silence. It wasn't exactly true. He remembered the first time he had met Elizabeth Avery in his wet shoes and socks after Corbin had picked him up at the airport and taken him to the

218

apartment. She was an absolute knockout; a Playboy figure and green eyes set off by long black hair. They shook hands awkwardly. Two conspirators playing their part in the Corbin scheme of things. Corbin moved him into the spare bedroom. When he had changed into some dry clothes, they went out for supper. Corbin left them mid-evening to go home to Peggy and the children in Rockcliffe Park. Affleck went back with Elizabeth to the apartment. They had slept in separate bedrooms, of course, but that didn't alter the fact he was sleeping in an apartment with Corbin's girl. Later he had come to know Elizabeth much better.

Peggy swung the car up the double driveway and stopped in front of the garage doors. It was a beautiful stone house, unlike anything Affleck had seen anywhere else in the world. He never ceased to marvel at the uniqueness of French Canadian architecture. It never occurred to him the house, like most of the others in the area, was modeled after the country houses of French nobility two hundred years earlier. Affleck had never been to France. The rough slabbed grey granite gave both house and observer a sense of permanence. The Mansard roof, with its graceful curved eaves, presented an illusion the second floor had been added as an afterthought to the attic, with its bedroom windows punching through the slate shingles high above the low eavestroughing. Spiderwebs of bare ivy clung in desperation to the granite sides of the house, waiting for spring to cover their naked entrails. The sidewalk across the front door, like the driveway, was clean. Corbin had installed a hot wire system under the concrete to save himself the burden of shoveling snow or chipping ice. He followed Peggy up the walk past the leaded French window panes of the study to the front door, waiting while she unlocked its brass ornamental handle. Affleck noticed it was no longer snowing, although the wind still blew loose surface particles across the covered lawn in a weaving helter-skelter motion. They went inside.

"Mommy! Hugo say Daddy stuck!" The little girl hung back when she spied Affleck.

"Hello, Alice—remember me?"

Alice shook her head solemnly.

"Well, I remember you. How are you?"

"Very well, thank you very much." She curtsied briefly with a wobble. She looked like Corbin.

Hughette, the French Canadian maid, appeared behind the tiny figure.

"Mr. Corbin phoned and said he slid off the road near

Kingsmere and would be a little late arriving." She spoke with a slight accent, dropping her aitches. "He's in a snowbank," she added, with disapproval.

"Thank you, Hughette. Would you bring some toast and coffee, please?"

The maid nodded and left. They went into the living room, Alice trailing inquisitively. Affleck settled into one of the comfortable sofas. Alice joined him, working herself in closely beside him.

"Who are you? Are you a friend of Daddy's?"

"And Mommy's and yours too, I hope. I'm an old, old friend. My name is Donald."

"Mine's Alice Marguerite Corbin." They shook hands. Alice sat back, satisfied.

"Where are the other two?"

"School."

"In this weather!" Affleck had thought everything would be shut. He imagined frozen little bodies peppering the snowbanks through the area, as they failed on their trek to school.

"We've become a hardy people. Actually the kids love it—the snow, I mean. It's just a matter of dressing them warmly and scooting them out the door. They always seem to get back for meals." They laughed. Alice laughed too, although she missed the point of the joke.

"Run along, Alice, and help Hughette with the toast. Uncle Donald and I have things to talk about."

Obediently she slipped off the sofa and skipped out of the room.

"She's beautiful, Peg."

"They're all beautiful—everything is beautiful—this house, the snow, you, me—everything."

She said it bitterly, with a bright smile. "Tell me about Central America."

"Nothing to tell. The construction work will be finished in a couple of weeks and the new plant will be on stream. Another year or two and they should have it producing power for the country. I got us another contract for the KV transmission towers to San Ramon, so I'll have to go back again in a month, in order to miss the good weather again," he added wryly.

The maid appeared with a silver tray. Toast, marmalade and coffee. She set it on the coffee table in front of the fireplace, served them and departed, dragging Alice out with her by a tiny hand.

"Course I won't have to stay down for months again. Just the odd visit to check on things. It will take the Atomic Energy Canada people another 24 months before there's any power, so there is no rush on the lines." He sipped his coffee.

"Meet any interesting people?"

"One. The President's son-in-law. He's called Chirlo. He runs the country."

"Oh. I remember seeing him on television. The man with the beard that everyone thought was another Castro. You know him?" Peggy was interested.

"Not well. I guess we've spoken together four or five times. He invited me out to his ranch once, but I couldn't go. We had a problem on the site. He's one hell of a guy, though, Runs the whole country like a one-man board of directors. They love him down there."

"They do? I would have thought the opposite."

"You'd be wrong. He's the idol of the masses, despite what anyone says about him."

"Is he communist?"

"Are you republican?"

"He overthrew the government, didn't he?" Peggy persisted.

Affleck munched some toast. He would have preferred some good American jelly instead of the thick Seville orange jam.

"Yeah, I guess he did. But everyone I spoke to down there says he's one hell of an improvement over the sonofabitch they had before. Anyway, I try and keep my nose out of local politics. I still think he's one hell of a guy."

"I remember seeing him on TV—last year, I think it was. He reminded me of someone," her eyes went vacant for a moment, "a long time ago. Does he speak English?"

"Perfectly. Do you think he's the same man you knew?"

"No. He died in a plane crash. More toast?"

"No, thanks, I ate a big breakfast."

Peggy set down her cup. "Well now, if you are going to be here for a while, I'll have to arrange a few parties so you can meet some girls; unless you've already found someone?"

"Not yet, Peg. I'm still the perennial bachelor. Probably will be as long as that husband of yours keeps me running around the world."

"Good, then that's settled. I'll arrange the first one for Wednesday evening. Cocktails at six-thirty. Suit you?"

"Fine. Isn't that a bit early?"

"With a six-thirty invitation, no one comes before seven forty-five. This is Ottawa. No one wants to appear anxious to do anything during the week. Where are you staying?"

Affleck had been wondering about that himself. A month at the hotel would be ridiculous. A house like Corbin's pretentious. A small apartment like Elizabeth's might be the right answer.

"Oh, I don't know, Peg. Maybe I'll look around here for an apartment. It's time I started thinking about settling down in one place for a while."

Corbin was ushered into the Chairman's office at ten o'clock Wednesday morning. Morris Levy and Derek Edgar were grouped around the planning table at the side of the room.

"Ah, Mr. Corbin, you know Derek and Morris, of course." Everyone nodded with polite smiles.

"Well, I have some good news for you. We've decided to go ahead with the enlarged storage facility program at Punta Delgado. It makes more sense than flying the waste back here every few months. This way we can let it accumulate a few years, then bring back a shipload. A hell of a lot safer, too. Cheaper all round. It was a good idea."

"I'm glad you liked the approach, Sir. Actually it was my associate, Mr. Affleck, that suggested the idea. Those are his drawings."

"Quite so. Too bad we have to make the storage pools so far away from the main plant, but I guess that's our fault for not giving you a bigger site to work with in the first place, eh?" The Chairman of Atomic Energy Canada Ltd. chuckled good-naturedly as if the extra three million dollars' worth of self-propelled gantry cranes and track bed required to move the nuclear waste an extra three and a half miles was a typographical error in the original report his team of experts had submitted in their study. Corbin would have fired them if they had been working for him. Morris Levy looked unhappy with the decision. Corbin knew he'd hear more about it that evening when the Levy's arrived at the cocktail party. "Will it be a bid job, or an amendment to the original contract, Sir?"

The Chairman winked. "Tell him, Derek."

"It will be an amendment to the original contract specs, Mr. Corbin. The Chairman feels CORCAN has earned the right."

The Chairman beamed. "How's that suit you?"

"Just great—I'm very pleased. We'll do you a first class job."

"Quite so. Quite so. Now there are a few minor alterations my chaps have suggested to your drawings. Perhaps if you have time we

222

could go over them now."

He went back to the table without waiting for a reply. Corbin and the other two followed, grouping themselves on either side of the paper rolls.

"Like the man who traveled the whole world looking for a four leaf clover . . . and found one in his own backyard wheh he came home." They both laughed.

The building superintendent looked at them mystified.

"I'll take it," Affleck told the wizened French Canadian.

"Eh Bon!" The gnome looked pleased and rubbed his hands.

Elizabeth leaned against the wall while the financial arrangements were discussed in broken English with the new tenant. Elizabeth glanced about the room. It was a two bedroom layout, exactly the same as her own three floors below, except the floor plan was reversed. The kitchen color scheme was olive drab. She preferred her own brighter yellow, although Affleck's bathroom was a better color combination than her own. She wondered idly how he would furnish it. *American chrome and glass. Modern art. Pseudo Dali*, she decided, glancing over at his tall tanned figure. The new wool suit he'd bought off the rack at Tip Top Tailors the previous day fitted perfectly. Not like Corbin's figure, which required everything tailor made. Corbin's shoulders were too heavy for rack suits. She had covered most of the city with Don Affleck, buying clothes and helping him look for an apartment. She had the feeling that nothing was going to satisfy him unless it was close to her own. She had been right. The moving and occupancy arrangements completed, she followed them out the door. They left the super at the fifteenth floor and went down the hall to her apartment.

"You don't mind my being in the same building?" He sounded genuinely worried. Elizabeth knew that was not what he meant.

"It's a free country, Don, and as far as Chuck is concerned, I don't think he gives a damn where anybody lives as long as they're available when he needs them. Want a drink?"

She went over to the glass bar table. Affleck looked at his watch.

"A small one. Remember, we have that cocktail party at six thirty."

"A small one." She poured out some more of the Bourbon from the new bottle he had purchased the day before. Since coming to Canada, Corbin had switched to Rye. Elizabeth liked neither, preferring the blandness of Vodka. They sat down, contemplating each other in silence. It was not uncomfortable. They understood. Finally:

"Will you help me with the furniture?"

"Are you sure you want me to?"

He swept his hand about the room. "I'm sure. Something like this—maybe not quite so feminine. More heavy woods, darker. Teak always reminds me of those decks I used to scrub on the pleasure boats weekends in Miami when I was a kid."

"I would have thought you'd prefer chrome furniture. Functional and bright."

"Ugh. I hate it." The phone rang. Elizabeth got up to answer it.

"It's for you, Don—Chuck!" she called from the kitchen.

Affleck picked up the extension in the spare bedroom.

"Hi, Chuck! What's new?"

Elizabeth hung up the kitchen receiver and went back to the couch. Through the open door she could hear the audible half of the conversation.

"Glad to hear you liked it—what changed?" Pause. "I see." Pause. "No, that shouldn't be any problem, but I don't see how it will improve security, hiding it from the road." Pause. "Fine. We'll see you later. Bye."

He came back into the living room smiling with his too-perfect teeth.

"We got another three million bucks worth of work out of AEC at Punta Delgado. They want to go ahead on the expanded waste storage site I picked." He sat down looking pleased and gulped his bourbon.

"Does that mean you'll have to go back early?"

"No. There won't be any wastes until they start generating power. Another couple of years. I'll have lots of time to work on it."

She watched his eyes cut her out of focus and could almost see the gears behind the iris' start turning as his mind studied the various complexities of the new construction contract CORCAN had been awarded. *You poor fool, Donald Affleck,* she thought, *you're nothing but a robot!*

Morris Levy scooped another shrimp croquette off the platter as Hughette threaded her way through the masses of guests. He popped it into his mouth and glanced around the room looking for his wife. He had last seen her talking to two women by the open double doors leading to the library. Now they were gone. He turned back to the discussion with Corbin and Affleck.

"I still think it's a mistake to let that waste supply build up down there before removing it. Why leave temptation around when it's unnecessary?"

He sipped his cocktail.

"You make it sound as if Chirlo will rush straight in, grab everything and start extracting plutonium for his arsenal. My God, Morris, they haven't got more than ten decent paved roads in the whole country! How in hell could they build bombs?"

Affleck couldn't see the logic in Levy's caution. He looked at Corbin for agreement.

"What about the written safeguards, Morris? They look pretty tight to me."

"Bullshit! All bullshit and you know it. What right do we have to enforce any agreement in a foreign country? The age of gunboat diplomacy is passed, Chuck."

A shriek of laughter soared over the conversation level. It was after eight. The murmured polite discussions of the first and second drinks had been replaced with loosened ties, vocal chords and inhibitions while they downed their third and fourth. Levy paused.

"Let me tell you two something. That 300 megawatt nuclear generator at Punta Delgado produces about 2800 waste bundles every 18 months. That's around seventy tons of radioactive garbage. Process that garbage and you extract enough plutonium to keep the most unimaginative anarchist happy. I'd still feel better seeing that garbage up here where we can keep our eye on it. But, as Derek Edgar keeps telling me—it's a political decision, not a practical one."

"Don, for heaven sakes, mingle. It's supposed to be your party!"

Peggy Corbin came up on them smiling, clutched Affleck by the elbow and led him away. Corbin and Levy watched him vanish into a crowd of females.

"Funny he never married."

Corbin laughed. "Tragic that we did."

Morris smiled. "Oh I don't know, Chuck. No man can remain an island for long without sinking."

"Don is still detached and afloat."

"So I notice. He's a good man. Conscientious as hell. You're lucky to have him. He's made a big hit with Colonel Chirlo, according to the reports I've read. Someday we may need an intermediary down there."

"You mean for the next revolution? Jesus, Morris, you're a pessimist."

"I have to be. That's my job." They split apart as a chubby

woman reached between them for a handful of peanuts from the dish on the table nest.

"Oh, Mr. Corbin, I do like coming to your parties!" She swallowed a handful and reached for more. Levy backed away discreetly to find his wife. Corbin was trapped between the peanuts and the woman. Mrs. Maude Daggerson's husband was a member of Parliament for one of the socialist ridings in the prairie provinces. Corbin loathed the pair.

"My parties are always good, Mrs. Daggerson, but I'm starting to worry about the quality of peanuts." Maude laughed uproariously, failing to see the joke. Corbin left her to the shrinking nut dish with a bow. He worked his way out of the library into the living room, a plastic smile encasing his face, nodding with false interest to various greetings along the way. He spied Elizabeth by the fireplace talking to a tall good looking army officer with a bristle mustache.

"Hello, Mr. Corbin. Do you know Colonel Martin?" The army officer whirled, spilling his drink across his sleeve. He ignored it.

"Don't believe I do; how do you do." They shook hands with bright tinny smiles.

"Who are you with, Colonel, or shouldn't I ask?" He looked at Elizabeth, his eyes alight, waiting to see if the man would catch the double entendre. Elizabeth had, and her eyes frowned.

"Mobile Command, Mr. Corbin."

"Splendid, Colonel. We've got to keep the Army mobile, haven't we? I'd hate to see them run out of gas." He patted the man on the arm and moved away from Elizabeth's glare. He was beginning to enjoy himself.

He crossed the hall to the dining room and joined a quartet of older men telling dirty stories. They were all slightly drunk.

"Hi Chuck!" A fat one waved, and went back to the story.

Corbin picked out a slice of pastrami from the meat tray, lathered it liberally with hot mustard and slipped it between two slices of rye bread.

"Hsst! Dad! Can I have a piece?" He looked down at the small hand clasping his pant leg from beneath the table cloth. Peter's face appeared; head hooded by the linen. His eyes were wide with the guilt of youthful innocence. Corbin squatted down so they were at eye level.

"What are you doing down here?"

"Hiding till I could get something to eat. Don't tell Mum," he cautioned in a hoarse whisper.

"I won't. You hungry?"

"Uh huh."

Corbin scanned the room from his crouch. The four were still engrossed in their story. Swiftly, he pulled the cheese and meat plate off the table and slipped under the cloth to join his son.

"Move over." Peter giggled with excitement. They gorged themselves in silence, rocking with silent laughter, watching the various leg movements around them from their mahogany roofed fort. When they had finished, Corbin whispered, "Don't you tell Mum either—promise?"

Peter crossed his heart and grinned. "Promise."

"Okay, now git." He held up the table cloth as the pajama clad figure scurried out to the kitchen to rejoin Hughette for his bedtime story. Corbin sat back, leaning against one of the central pedestals, his feet stretched out in front of him. He watched the procession of marching feet storm the table, pause and retreat. One pair he recognized from the ankles; they belonged to Elizabeth. He was on the verge of grabbing one when a second pair of female feet joined her. When he heard Peggy's voice about him he marveled that he hadn't recognized them in the first place.

"Hello, Elizabeth. Are you enjoying yourself?"

"Oh hello, Mrs. Corbin—yes. It's a super party. How's Don making out—anyone interesting?"

"Seems to find all the ladies interesting—even you!" There was a bite to the words.

Elizabeth laughed. "Even me?" Both pairs of feet remained motionless.

"How did you enjoy your skiing weekend with my husband?" Corbin could visualize acid dripping onto the maroon carpet. When Elizabeth replied her mouth was full.

"The skiing was great, but he drove us into a snowbank on the way home. I thought he phoned you?"

Peggy's feet pivoted quickly and marched away. Another pair of shoes, highly polished, joined Elizabeth's.

Corbin recognized the Colonel's sotto voice. "May I take you home, Mrs. Avery?"

"I have my own car, but thanks anyway."

"Perhaps we could stop by my place for a drink. You could follow me in your car." The authoritative voice of Mobile Command. Corbin was surprised when she replied:

"Why not? I'll get my coat."

He watched her ankles recede from view and noticed from the rustling of the tablecloth above his eyes the young Colonel was

227

either scratching his groin or adjusting his machinery. Mobile Command.

Later, when he and Peggy lay in bed watching the eleven o'clock news he turned to her and said, "You put on one hell of a party when you get started, don't you?"

She smiled, pleased at the compliment. "Don seemed to like the Chalmers girl, didn't he?"

"Who?"

"The Chalmers girl—the one he went home with."

"I didn't notice. I thought he came with Elizabeth Avery."

"He did, but she left with Colonel Martin." Peggy couldn't resist the dig. She watched his face. He seemed unperturbed by the news. She had a twinge of disappointment.

"Colonel Martin, eh! Well I hope he knows how to ski." They went back to watching the news.

"Speak up, Dobey, for God's sakes! You're starting to mumble again."

The CORCAN general auditor looked at Corbin, flustered, then tipped his eyes back to the scimitar-shaped half lenses perched on his nose and plunged on with the report. His voice was much louder. Corbin leaned back, satisfied. Morton Dobey was a brilliant accountant and financial analyst but needed a course in corrective reading.

". . . . the initial surveys indicate there are eighty-four inactive gold mines which can be purchased at nominal sums. However," he raised his eyes above the lenses and looked directly at Corbin, "governmental regulations will require considerable expenditure annually for equipment and labor in order to maintain the mineral rights. The question is whether the drain on reserves is worth the investment, since the price of gold has remained constant for the past two decades." He paused significantly, looking around the room.

"Well, come on, Dobey—get on with it!" Corbin said testily.

"Initial reaction suggests that investment in producing copper mines would be a wiser and more prudent selection." He sat down, folding the report neatly into his file folder.

"Whose initial reaction are you speaking about, Morton?" Corbin inquired.

"Mine."

"Ah! I thought so. Any comments from the directors?"

The seven others grouped about the boardroom table considered his question. These quarterly board meetings for the executive directors of the CORCAN companies were the only times Corbin got to meet his senior employees face to face at the corporation's Ottawa headquarters. The purpose, in addition to keeping everyone posted on what everyone else was doing, served also as a sounding board for new ideas. The purchase of unproductive gold mines in Canada and the States was one of Corbin's pets at the moment. He had a sneaking feeling gold was going to take off sometime soon from the $35.00 per ounce fixed price. All the signs were right. Few of the major world currencies were tied to their bullion reserves. Since World War One, everyone had been slicing and hacking away at the percentage of gold backing their paper money, till now the whole thing was a joke. If everyone tried redeeming their American dollars they might get a penny in gold for each one—if that. Governments were talking now about the real wealth of their nations being in their people and ability to produce higher GNP figures. When governments started talking that sort of nonsense it was only a matter of time before they bit the bullet and shrugged off the gold standard to an open market, doubling or trebling the value of their own worthless paper in the process. Abandoned mines, profitless at $35.00 per ounce, would become priceless treasures at $70.00 per ounce. Corbin had the feeling it was going to happen. For some months he had been pushing Dobey to buy gold on the Zurich and London markets with any spare liquidity CORCAN held.

"Don, what about you? Agree or disagree?" As 20% shareholder in the company and president of the American subsidiary, CORAM, Affleck had the right of speaking first.

"I'm not in touch with the situation, so anything I say would be personal. The acquisition figures are reasonable enough, but the cost of maintenance for mineral rights appears excessive, particularly if we have to wind up replacing a lot of antiquated equipment to get the mines into operation again."

"That secondary expense will not arise unless the price of gold is freed from $35.00. At that time the additional costs are academic. However, you're right. I think we should hit the government for an adjustment on maintenance rights. I'll make a note of that."

He scribbled briefly on the yellow pad in front of him.

"Warren—anything to add?"

As president of Venture Design and CORCAN Engineering, Warren Holmes would have the responsibility of engineering studies for the new mines if they were purchased.

"Yes, Chuck. I'd like a look at the existing site drawings from each of the locations, if they're available. We could make up the amended design and equipment lists on them now, so if and when they go into production we're ready to go to work immediately."

"Good point, Warren. That will save us a hell of a lot of lead time going into production. Keep those equipment lists up to date—semi-annual updates. Try for uniformity on our purchases with the heavy machinery so it's all interchangeable.

Corbin wrote again on his pad. He glanced up the table as one of the others raised his pencil aloft. Corbin nodded.

"It might be an idea also, Warren, if we could arrange 'bounce back' orders on all equipment and machinery requiring more than a thirty day lead time for delivery. Otherwise we could wind up with six month delays on a back order."

Ben Roman handled the chain of CORAM's 'Burger Bunnies' fast food restaurants. They were expanding through the American Southwest. He was familiar with problems of equipment delivery delays. The 'bounce back' ordering system, loathed by equipment manufacturers, was one sure way of providing hard to get items without waiting for production lines. The corporation would send in a purchase order on the equipment for a future delivery date. If, by that date, the purchases were not required, the original order would be bounced back for a minor amendment and everything re-ordered for another future delivery date. The manufacturer never had any problem selling the original order to someone else, and the corporation could always keep itself at the head of the delivery line without spending money. The danger was if the equipment was never required, or an improved type was developed by one of the manufacturer's competitors. A manufacturer might sue on the original order.

"I disagree with that approach." Morton Dobey spoke up without raising his pencil, as courtesy dictated. "It's unethical." Everyone laughed. Corbin nodded.

"I agree, Morton. It is unethical. I'm surprised at you for suggesting such a thing, Ben."

He looked back at Warren Holmes with a smile. "Just make sure you do all your 'bounce back' ordering from German manufacturers, Warren. That way we can keep any lawsuits on the other side of the Atlantic."

"I'll make a note of it." Warren returned the smile.

"How about you, Dix—anything you want to say?"

Dix Fowler was the oldest man at the table. A Texas wildcatter from the old school. He had spent his entire life in the oil and gas business. A rough, tough, outspoken, leather-faced, lantern-jawed opportunist, who had made and lost several fortunes in the gas and oil game. He had come to Corbin five years before at the bottom end of one of his cyclical swings from riches to rags, begging for backing on a group of drilling rights off the coast of Louisiana. He had wandered into the office, brushing aside the secretary's protests, and cornered his quarry. He didn't even take off his sweat-stained Stetson.

"Howdy, young feller! The name's Dix—Fowler. People tell me you're a hoop artist with some money to burn—that right?" He leaned over the desk. Whipcord encased in bluejeans.

"What's your deal, old man?" Corbin demanded.

"Got me a slew of producers offshore in the Gulf. Need a few bucks to start drilling."

"How much?"

"Two million, sonny—you got it?"

"What's the split?"

"Sixty-forty. That's sixty me, forty you."

"No, it's not—it's sixty me, forty you."

"Don't have time to argue—y'got yourself a deal. Shake!" They shook and he walked out of the office, his high heeled Tyler Texas boots pitting the carpet.

The actual cost had run closer to three and a half million before the first wells came in pumping the black blood and intestinal gas from the bowels of the Gulf. CORAM Gas & Oil Exploration Inc. had made nothing but money ever since.

Fowler rubbed his jaw, squinting down the table at Corbin.

"Y'know sonny, y'all gave me an idea talking 'bout them gold mines. First off, I think yer right about gold futures—stands to reason. Any lame brain can see it comin'. Now the thought jest hit me there's a gob of unproductive oil wells scattered all over Pennyslvania, Oklahoma and Texas that fellers have had capped. We could pick 'em up fer a song and hang on until it was time to start pumpin'."

"And when do you think that is going to be, Mr. Fowler?" Morton Dobey asked tartly. The whole idea of buying futures was getting out of hand, as far as he was concerned. Dobey liked to deal with reality. Not pie in the sky.

"Been talking to some of the boys. Tell me the Middle East is gonna blow up one day. Them petropoliticans are starting to make noises 'bout nationalizing everything for 'emselves. Figure when they do they're gonna raise the price. Form a club or somethin'. Be the end of three dollar a barrel oil."

"That's ridiculous!" Dobey was exasperated by the if's and when's.

"Yup. Sure is. Ever hear of PEMEX, sonny?" PEMEX was the nationalistic creation of the Mexican government when they took over foreign oil holdings before World War II. Fowler had wildcatted in Mexico and lost one of his fortunes there.

"I like it, Dix. How long do you think we'd have to hold?" Corbin was interested.

The Texan shrugged. "Three years, mebbe—five at the outside. I figger oil's gonna to go ten bucks a barrel. You see the consumption curves for North America lately? 'Nuff to scare the shit outa gila monster. Your nuclear power plants ain't gonna handle it, sonny."

"Makes sense to me, Chuck," Affleck spoke up.

"Good. Let's dig it out then. Dix—see what you can put together for the next quarter."

The Texan nodded and went back to scratching his chin.

"Anyone else with comments. Pat? Ed? Rolly?"

The three shook their heads. They were junior members of the corporation's Canadian acquisitions. Pat Mulligan handled farming interests, Ed LeBlanc ran the construction company and Rolly Parrish headed up cutting and production operations for CORCAN Forest Products Ltd. Corbin looked at his watch. It was after six. They had started at one.

"Okay, there being no other business to discuss, I declare this meeting adjourned."

"I second the motion." Affleck concluded the ritual. Everyone slid their chairs back from the table and headed for the door. A couple stopped to banter outside the boardroom with Elizabeth, who had been taking notes of the session in shorthand. Corbin waited until they had all gone before leaving his chair. He lit a cigarette and wandered down the length of the table, looking at the yellow pads scattered about the gleaming mahogany surface. Elizabeth came in to pick them up.

"Ever notice how they all doodle?"

She paused. "Doodle?"

"On the pads." He picked up one, tearing off the top sheet. "Look at this! Ed LeBlanc does square doodles all joined into each other. Then over here." He tore another sheet off, reaching across the table. "Old man Fowler doodles arrows with skinny tips. I wonder what they all mean? Tell you what, sweetheart, write down everyone's name on their doodles and send them off to Doctor whatshisname at Personality Research and see what he comes up with." He chuckled. "I'll give everyone his doodle profile at our next board meeting."

"What about your own?"

"I don't doodle—I just write. See!" He held up his pad. "I just doodle with people—never with pads."

It was a gorgeous sunshine day. The weather was still nippy, but now, snow was melting faster at midday. The grey colored mounds piling the boulevards had shrunk to a porous facade of their former clean white hills as passing traffic splashed gobs of watery slush against them. It was spring. Elizabeth drove Don Affleck to the airport to catch his Toronto flight with connections on to Cosecha Rica.

"This is the closest I've come to date. Real progress."

She looked at him quizzically. He laughed. "The snow is melting—I actually stayed here long enough to see the goddamn stuff melt. I tell you, I'm gaining on it every visit!"

"This time you'll be back to see the summer," Chuck promised. "I'm a witness, Don."

"I may need one, because come hell or high water, this time I'm coming back in ninety days."

They joined the traffic stream into the airport terminal building and were waved onto the parking lot by a harassed young Mountie in slush-spattered boots. Elizabeth rolled down the window, giving him her brightest smile.

"Can't we stop for a minute, officer, this gentleman is catching a flight?"

The Mountie was unmoved. "So's everyone else, Miss, the parking lot is straight ahead." He walked on past the car to argue with someone else.

Elizabeth said "Shit!" quietly and drove on. They hoofed it through the slush to the teriminal. Affleck handed over his coat, rubber ankle boots and scarf.

"Hold them till next winter."

"Take care, Don." She kissed him goodbye and stood watching as he walked down the long concourse to the ticket desk. *The perfect robot*, she thought, and yet there was more to him than mechanical obedience to Corbin's wishes. He enjoyed his work; that was obvious. Yet there was much more to him than met the eye. She had slipped under his superficiality only once on a Sunday evening after returning from a dull weekend at St. Jerome skiing with Colonel Martin. He had been a lousy skier, an even worse lover. Affleck phoned her the moment she arrived home, asking if he could drop down for a minute. She thought for a minute he must have a bug in the apartment to know the moment of her return so precisely, then reasoned he must have been phoning at regular intervals since suppertime. He knocked a few minutes later and came in with his usual cheerful smile.

"Hi, how about a smash of Bourbon?" She poured him one on the rocks and sat down to hear what he had to say.

"Why did you do it, Elizabeth?" he asked pleasantly.

"Why did I do what?"

"Take off with the soldier boy for the weekend shackup."

"I think you'd better leave." She stood up angrily.

"Sit down, Elizabeth." He was no longer smiling. His eyes were ice. Not wanting to, she obeyed, lowering herself back to the couch slowly, fascinated at the sudden transformation.

"That's better." He sipped the Bourbon. "You may not like what I'm going to say. In fact, I know you won't. The truth is never pleasant." His eyes bored into her face. "Whether you like it or not, you belong to Charles Corbin—the same way I do. When you run off with someone to spite Chuck, you are biting the hand that feeds you—the same way if I refused to do the things he asks me to do for him. Understand me, I don't deny your right to run off with anyone you want—screw every man in Ottawa if you feel like it, but you make your break with Chuck first, clean and final. That is the least I'd expect from you—he would do as much for you. You know that.

"He couldn't care less about me—or you for that matter." She had never seen him so intense.

"If you believe that, Elizabeth, you're a goddamn fool. Let me tell you something you don't know about this guy. First of all, he's a genius—I know, because I'm one too. But beside him, I'm small potatoes. My genius is in business—his is in recognizing the opportunities for business, an entrepreneur. I've never met his equal. He picked me up in Flordia flat on my ass and turned me into a multi-millionaire, so now I'm making more money every year than some banks have on deposit. A dozen times he could have aced me out of the whole thing. He never did. I used to wonder why. Then it dawned on me. He needed me—the same way he needs you—or Dobey or Dix or anybody else he has around him. Each of us provide him with a fulfillment to a part of his life—we are his life."

"And his wife and kids?"

"A part too. We all have a part, and when anyone of us start trying to grab more than their share, then we all suffer. Never worry about his eight-balling us out of anything Elizabeth, worry about ourselves eight-balling him, because it is the easiest thing in the world to do. You've been eight-balling—I want it stopped!"

Elizabeth considered what he said carefully. She had never looked at her relationship with Corbin in quite that light. She didn't know whether she believed it anyway. Corbin never struck her as needing anyone. To him, everyone was a convenience to be used according to whim. Maybe there was some truth to what Affleck told her.

"I'll think on it, Don." She said the words simply.

"You do that." He polished off his drink, thanked her and left.

She had sat alone a long time thinking afterwards. The problem was her relationship didn't lead anywhere. But then, she reasoned, neither did his relationship with his wife, his business associates or anyone else. Where was it supposed to lead? She wondered why Affleck had never discussed the subject again, and the following day at the office he was his usual cheerful self. Soft veneer covering cold steel. In a way, he frightened her. She walked back to the car, tossed his boots and clothing into the rear seat, and drove back to the office.

In the weekends that followed she went with Corbin to the cabin, helping him with repairs to the dock where melting ice jams from the small lake had knocked away some of the planking. One weekend they slid the boat out of the lockup under the cabin and dragged it down to the water. They spent the afternoon fishing but caught nothing. It was not until mid June when Elizabeth realized suddenly and understood what Affleck had told her was true. A letter, addressed to Corbin, marked personal and confidential, arrived on her desk. All personal mail was sent up from the mail room unopened for her attention. Few of them were really personal or confidential, and she managed to save Corbin a great deal of time by sorting out those letters she considered important enough for his attention. Generally, they were requests for money, membership offerings to country clubs or Board of Trade luncheons, which she answered herself. However, this letter was different. It was registered and it was from England. She opened it and read it through. It was from an insurance company dated June 12, 1967.

Dear Mr. Corbin:

The Underwriters take great pleasure in advising you that they are prepared to waive the remaining months under their payment withholding rights contained in sub-paragraph (d) on page 6 of your policy on the life of

Peter James Colley, Policy No. C-15567397.

Please find attached Underwriter's cheque in the amount of two million United States dollars ($2,000,000.00 U.S.) as payment in full. The Underwriters regret the necessity of invoking the provisions of sub-paragraph (d) and trust that this delay in payment has not resulted in undue hardship to yourself.

We remain your humble obedient servants . . .

The letter was signed with an indistinguishable scrawl under which was neatly typed *"on behalf of the Underwriters."*

Elizabeth was flabbergasted. She had never seen a check of such size in her life, much less one sent through the mails to an individual. There were two release forms enclosed requiring Corbin's signature, relinquishing any further claims. She flipped the intercom switch on her desk.

"Mr. Corbin, may I see you a minute?" She maintained a frigid formality during office hours in case of eavesdroppers, unless she was alone with him inside his office.

"Sure. Come on in."

She closed the door and walked across the thick carpet, laying the letter, forms and check in front of him. "This just arrived." She watched him pick it up and saw the color drain from his face. He appeared transfixed by the letter, ignoring the mauve check. When he looked up, she saw his eyes were clouded with tears. The first crack in the armor.

"Who was Peter James Colley, Chuck?" she inquired softly.

He shook his head, clearing a memory, smiling sadly.

"Once, a long time ago, he was my best friend, and the only real mistake I ever made."

Elizabeth hadn't understood then. It was many weeks before he told her the story of Peter Colley. He picked up the letter and check.

"Cancel my appointments for the rest of the day. I'm going home."

"Chuck, if there's anything I can do—if anything's wrong."

She had never seen him this way. Suddenly his smile returned. Brittle. Iron.

"Wrong? How could anything be wrong. I've just been given two million dollars, Green Eyes."

Corbin parked the car alongside Peggy's red station wagon and wandered around the house to the back yard. At the rear, the broad lawn, punctuated with gardens, sloped down to the banks of the

236

Ottawa River. The river was less than a mile wide at this point, swelling by a steady ten knots to meet the mighty St. Lawrence at Montreal for its final thrust to the sea. There was a majesty in the river. A dark power from its black waters. Steady resolute motion. In winter, ice crept towards the center, clutching the icy flow, then stopped, defeated and yielded, overpowered by the cold black waters. Both of them had been concerned by the nearness of the river when they had taken the house. With three small children it presented a continual threat to their safety. But, as time passed, the river became an object of admiration instead of consternation. The children were taught to stay away from its banks. Corbin had installed an indoor-outdoor pool their second year. Now all three were skillful swimmers. He paused to watch and smile at the assortment of small children splashing about the pool. Alice already had obtained her 'Shark' badge from the YWCA and would be trying for the 'Porpoise' rating later in the summer. He could see the bright Shark badge against the chest of her black bathing suit, where Peggy had sewn it on her chest. Three mothers were grouped about the patio by the pool, sunning themselves in monokinis. They were drinking coffee and talking. Corbin noticed Peggy's figure showed much better than the other two. One of the mothers spied him and scrambled for her halter. The other eyed him coldly from across the expanse of grass, deciding to ignore her mammary nakedness, knowing her breasts had not sagged to the grotesque porportions of her neighbor. Peggy, stretched out on the lounge chair, waved. He waved back, and went down to join them, taking off his jacket and tie along the way.

"Hi, Darling! You know Sue and Debbie?"

Corbin nodded. "Good afternoon, ladies."

Sue Langley leaned forward, tipping her bosom towards him with a seductive smile to shake his hand.

"Don't lose your balance on my account, Mrs. Langley." He ignored the hand and dropped into a chair beside Peggy. They all laughed, relaxing.

"You're home early. What's the time?"

He glanced at his watch. "One forty. Felt like taking the day off. How's the water?"

"Peter says it's holding at 80 degrees. Going for a swim?"

"Maybe later." He looked beyond the pool to the river and the scattered houses on the Quebec side. A tug, trailing a heavy log boom, forced it way upstream; an absurd thrashing of propellors and bow wave for the speed it was making against the current. Everything looked so peaceful.

"Are you coming to the Shafton's party tomorrow night, Mr. Corbin?" Sue began putting on her halter, adjusting her orbs carefully in the process. One last try.

"I didn't know they were having a party." He turned to Peggy. "Are we going?"

"Up to you, Chuck—I'm easy."

"We'll see." A sudden tearful howl from one of the children and the women rushed poolside to investigate. It was nothing. A skinned elbow from horseplay. Harsh words from Debbie Cadeiux in volatile French to the offending member of the brood. Corbin gave Peggy their high sign. She followed him into the house.

"Something wrong, Darling?" She looked concerned. They stood together in the kitchen. Hughette ignored them, she was listening to a French Canadian soap opera on the radio by the sink, scrubbing the supper potatoes. Corbin handed the letter and check over without speaking. He waited until Peggy had read it and examined the check, then left her, going upstairs to change into his bathing suit. He could hear her padding along behind on bare feet. She stopped in the middle of the bedroom, staring at him as he undressed.

"I don't want it, Chuck. It would make me feel dirty." He watched her walk across and lay the check and papers on his dresser. "Funny isn't it! There was a time I thought that one million of mine was the most important thing in the world. Now it's just—just a piece of paper."

Corbin chuckled mirthlessly as he sat down on the bed to peel off his socks.

"Not quite, Peggy. The knowledge that the money was coming gave me the credit to build everything we have today. The land— CORAM—CORCAN—everything. Without that credit then. . . ." He shrugged and tossed his socks onto a chair. "Who knows what might have happened?" He looked at her searchingly. "For one thing, I would never have married you. I guess you know that."

She looked very appealing suddenly, standing framed by the window and the river beyond. Peggy nodded. "There would have been no Peter, no Emily, no Alice, no love."

"Has there been love?" he asked idly.

She could see the erection rising between his legs, and slipped out of her bikini brief, tossing it over his socks on the chair. She came toward him and kneeled by his legs, laying her head against them. She began stroking him.

"From me there has been love. From you . . . ." Her voice trailed

238

off as she watched the glans coloring swell into a rich hue. She glanced up at him. "Love or lust, what's the difference?"

"Three letters." She laughed, her lips parted to take him into her mouth wetly. Corbin groaned, holding her head gently to the steady motion.

Later, while still coupled, lying on the bed, he examined her eyes, inches away from his nose. "You're starting to get crow's feet."

"And you're starting to lose your hair." They both laughed, embracing in a long, slow kiss of satisfaction.

"What will we do with the money?" She sat up. Corbin rolled on his back, clasping his hands behind his head on the pillow.

"I don't know, sweetheart—how about a trust fund for the kids? In the meantime we could put it into government bonds." He considered the idea a moment while she got up and went to the bathroom. He could hear Peter and his sisters talking and laughing in their bedrooms while they changed out of their wet suits. He thought Colley would approve of the trust fund for them; he had, after all, named his son after him. He glanced at the dresser, looking at the reflection of the green check from the mirror above the leather jewelry box. He knew with certainty that if he could bring Peter Colley back to life at that moment he would give him half of everything he possessed, gladly. It belonged to him. For some reason the thought made him feel much better than he had all day. He swung his legs off the bed and reached for his bathing trunks, calling into the bathroom. "How about joining me for a dip?"

Peggy's face appeared around the corner. "You afraid you'll drown without me?"

"Who knows? Perhaps I might," he said slowly, sadly.

10

1968

The El Al Boeing 707 lifted off the long runway at Athens Airport smoothly, flashing past the Olympic Airline hangars as it rotated. There was a slight vibration when the landing gear retracted, then takeoff power was reduced. It swung out across the harbor of Pireas to begin its long climb to cruising altitude over the sky blue waters of the Gulf of Corinth. Captain Elik Shavan watched his co-pilot's performance carefully. Dov Goldman had switched to the left-hand seat for the second leg of their trip from Lod airport. Most captains held the left-hand seat when they turned the aircraft flight log over to their co-pilots. Shavan believed differently. If a co-pilot was going to act as Captain, then he should be sitting in the proper seat for the job. It was a small point, but one that was appreciated by every junior officer that flew with him, though frowned on by the airline's chief pilot. Goldman was doing an excellent job. He signaled full flap retract at exactly the proper moment on the climb out. Shavan flicked off the smoking sign, paused, then doused the seat belt indicator as well. There was no turbulence to speak of, so there was no need to imprison his passengers any longer than necessary. He picked up his mike to call the Air Traffic Control Center, now his job as co-pilot.

"Center. El Al niner zero two passing through seven for ten."

"Roger niner zero two, check that. You are now cleared to flight level thirty-seven. Call passing through twenty." The controller's English was accented by his Greek heritage. Shavan reconfirmed the reporting height and hung the mike. He swept his eyes across the panel and looked at Goldman, nodding briefly. He glanced out the side window, staring at the ridge of bare rocky yellow hills parading down to the blue waters far below. The laconic drawl of a TWA flight inbound, interrupted his gaze. The voice was pure Texas, unhurried, precise. He heard the Athens Controller give descent clearance. The only Controllers Shavan had trouble with were the French. He hated talking to the French. Most of them spoke indecipherable English; some refused to speak anything but French. It was one of the five languages Captain Shavan didn't speak. He would be co-pilot on the Zurich-Paris leg that afternoon and wondered idly if he would be forced into another French lesson at Orly. He hoped not. The weather reports for Orly did not look good. He watched the altimeter wind towards the twenty thousand foot level and picked up the mike. "Athens Center. El Al niner zero two passing level twenty for three seven."

"Check that El Al. Report reaching cruising altitude."

"I've got a little heat on number three engine, skipper." Manny Richler tapped him on the shoulder from the flight engineer's position behind the co-pilot's seat. Shavan swung his head around.

"So why are you telling me? Tell the captain. It's his problem, not mine."

Goldman grinned, pleased with the compliment. "I'll back off on number three—it should drop. Keep your eye on it, Manny."

Goldman adjusted the engine throttle. Richler swung back to his console to monitor the pipe temperatures.

In the first class section, directly behind the cockpit, Jamil nodded pleasantly to a sloe-eyed stewardess and lifted two finger-sized canapes from the proffered platter. He was sitting in seat 1D, exactly seventeen feet behind Captain Shavan. He looked out the window at the yellow hills of the Hellenes, watching them amble off into the horizon from the gulf to the borders of Albania and Yugoslavia. *So far so good*, he thought. Security check at Athens where they boarded had been a joke. He could have lugged a fifty calibre machine gun through the gate if he had wanted, instead of the grenades. He had four taped to his body. One under each armpit; one behind each leg at the knees. The metal felt cold when he had first taped them on in the Terminal washrooms. Now they were body temperature. Part of him.

In the last row of first class seats, Khala Akbar sat in 10A, massaging his tummy. *It had to be the fish,* he decided. *I was the only one that ate the fish. Fucking Greeks and their fresh fish! Fresh, my ass!* He had been up since three that morning heaving his stomach into the toilet bowl at the sleazy hotel in Piraeus. Jamil and Leila asleep in the next room, heard nothing; they had eaten lamb. He should have listened to Jamil. He knew that now.

"In England, roast beef. In America, steaks. In Italy, veal, and in Greece—lamb. Stay with the national dishes and you'll never go wrong," Jamil had told him wisely. Akbar had ordered the fish. Now he was paying for it. The stewardess held out the canape tray. His stomach flipped and he shook his head, trying to crease a smile for her. His face wouldn't work. She looked puzzled an instant, then went back to the front of the cabin through the blue curtain separating the galley.

"Touch of the golliwobble, old man?"

Akbar glanced across the aisle at the white haired occupant in 10C. The man looked like an ad for Rolex watches. 'When it's time to travel for the Business of Nations—it's the Rolex time for business.' Akbar saw the man was wearing a gold Pate Phillipe. "Something I ate in Athens. It's passing now."

"Frightful food in Athens, what? About the only thing that's safe is the lamb. Always trust the lamb—it wasn't lamb, was it?" he asked as an afterthought.

"No. Fish."

"Ah! Thought so. Well, there you are, then. Pity really, when you stop and think about it."

"Yes." Akbar thought he was referring to his stomach agonies.

"I mean to say they have all that fish out there floating around and none of the blighters have the slightest idea how to cook it properly. Bad show, what?"

Akbar agreed. "Bad show."

"By the way, my name's Harcourt—Aubrey Harcourt." He extended a manicured hand over the aisle. Akbar accepted it gingerly, reaching across the empty seat, his stomach wincing at the movement. "Mohammed Ali," he said solemnly.

"Like the boxer! Good show. Going far?"

"Algiers."

"From Rome?"

"From here." Akbar couldn't resist. He felt better already.

"I'm sorry, old man, but I think you must be on the wrong plane. This one's going to Rome."

"Really? I must have been misinformed." He was enjoying himself hugely now.

"I think your booking agent gave you a bummer, if you don't mind my saying so. Bad show, that."

Akbar agreed. "Bad show."

In the 707 cockpit First Officer Goldman slipped the nose trim forward slightly, his eye on the winding altimeter. The needle slowed, then stopped at 37,200 feet. He tipped the nose slowly, building up speed and pulled back the throttles to cruising rpm. Slowly the altimeter unwound, settling at exactly 37,000 feet. He centered the autopilot and sat back with a smile. Shavan picked up the mike.

"Athens Center. El A1 niner zero two is level at three seven."

At the sound of engine power being reduced, Jamil removed the two grenades from under his armpits. The tapes ripped off mats of hair in the process, making him gasp. He lay the grenades on the seat between his legs and rolled his pants up to remove the other two. He laid the other two on the seat beside him and stood up, looking back to Akbar.

Conversation with the Englishman was terminated, as the Palestinian slid out of his seat and patted the Saville Row shoulder. "I'm afraid I don't have time to go to Rome. I'll just pop up front and see if I can persuade the Captain to go to Algiers. Good show?" His tummy ache was gone. He moved swiftly to the front of the cabin and took two grenades from Jamil. They removed the pins from all four. Akbar stood aside, letting Jamil slip behind the galley curtain before turning to face the nine first class passengers. He held his grenades aloft with a smile watching their faces closely. By the time he was satisfied there would be no problems with his fellow travelers, Jamil was standing in the open door of the flight deck, behind the frightened stewardess. She held a wobbly coffee tray. "I'm sorry, Captain Shavan, he ordered me to do it."

Shavan turned back to the instrument panel. "That's all right, Miss Weber, we could all do with some coffee anyway." Jamil watched while she served the cups around the flight deck. "May I go?"

Jamil nodded. "Go to the galley curtain and remove it, then take a seat in first class."

The stewardess looked around uncertainly, her eyes resting finally on Shavan. He glanced at her. "Do as he says, Miss Weber."

The stewardess left to remove the curtains.

"Now Captain Shavan, you will set course for Algiers."

"Algiers? You must be joking. We don't have fuel to make Algeria."

"Captain, I know how much fuel you took on board at Athens. I can see how much is left." He waved a grenade at the engineer's instrument console. "And I know you never take on fuel at Leonardo Da Vinci Airport because of the price—Jews are very price conscious. Your next refuelling stop is Zurich. So let's dispense with the excuses shall we? Turn this aircraft to Algiers and do it now. I won't ask you again."

Shavan regarded the dark hooded eyes standing in the doorway. They were calm, sincere eyes. No sign of fear or panic at the edges. He knew the man was a killer; had killed before and if needed, would kill again, personal safety notwithstanding. An intelligent maniac. He sighed and turned to Goldman. "Dov, I have control." Goldman raised both hands off his armrest, signifying the relinquishment of command. "You have control, Captain Shavan."

Lieutenant Lev Asher had just come on duty when the call came in from the Airport Control Center. As a paramilitary airline, El Al's security was handled by the Intelligence Section of the Israeli Army from Lod Airport. Asher picked up the phone.

"We have a red alert on flight nine oh two out of Athens for Rome. No contact after reaching cruising altitude at thirty-seven thousand. Captain is Elik Shavan, first officer Dov Goldman, flight engineer Emmanuel Richler. I don't have the names of the eight stewardesses or the passengers yet."

In the background Asher could hear excited conversation of other controllers talking with each other; telephones ringing.

"How many passengers?"

"One hundred and seventeen. The Athens agent is telexing the names out now."

"Patch it through to CIF soon as it comes on the wire. Keep me informed."

"Roger—so long." The background noise and ringing phones vanished with a click. Asher replaced the phone to its cradle. He considered the information. It could be radio failure, a hijacking, or a crash at sea; the severity, in that order. Radio failure was unlikely, although possible. A complete electrical failure on board the aircraft caused by—what? Sabotage? This brought up the next possibility of a crash at sea. He wished he knew more about Boeing 707's. Rocket launchers, tanks, personnel carriers he knew about. Unarmed four-engined civil aircraft were a complete mystery. His wounds from

245

the Six Day War had taken him out of active military service. A combat Sergeant with a limp, and half his thigh missing could hardly be exepcted to instill confidence in front line soldiers. So the Army had promoted him to the officer corps and transferred him to its intelligence branch when he was released from hospital. He had started at the bottom of the ladder in the new branch, tracking down AWOL's and drunks. Asher had begun to think the whole Israeli Army were alcoholic AWOL's by the time he had been moved up the next rung to the post of airport liaison intelligence officer. The job called for Captain's rank, but so far the promised promotion had not appeared from Army headquarters in the weekly promotion sheets.

He lifted the phone again as it started to ring. "Lieutenant Asher here."

"Asher? Colonel Borodam. Can you handle it?" Borodam was senior intelligence officer for Asher's section, reporting to the Chief of Staff. A man of few words.

"Yes, Sir. I can," he told the gruff voice calling from downtown Tel Aviv.

"Good. Keep me posted." He hung up.

Asher rubbed his thigh thoughtfully, forming an attack in his mind, then called the U.S. Embassy liaison officer. "Sammy? Lev Asher. I need a favor. How fast can you get through to your Mediterranean Fleet Command in Athens?"

Sammy Bernstein was a New York Jew and a Major in the U.S. Army, but first of all he was a Jew.

"Got a problem?"

"Possible crash at sea or a hijacking out of Athens for Rome—report just came in. The last word we had, the Captain reached his cruising altitude at 37,000 feet. Can you work out a flight path from Athens for a 707 climb to 37,000 feet starting at about ten oh five this morning and see if there's anything directly below that area? Probably be down at the mouth of the Gulf of Corinth if it's a crash."

"The fuckers are still at it, eh? Give me five minutes and I'll get back to you."

Asher called through the glass door of his office, "Sergeant Kronig!"

A noncom rushed in and saluted. "Yessir."

"There's a list of names of passengers coming in on the teletype from Athens. I want you to run down the identity of everyone on that list, including women and children. Get some help if you need it. It's a red alert priority. Got it?"

246

"Yessir. I'm on my way." He started to turn when Asher added, "And for God sakes do your tunic buttons up, you're starting to look like an Egyptian general staff officer."

Another thought struck him and he reached for the phone. "Get me Sol Borman at United Press." He sucked his teeth, waiting for the connection. Borman had been a friend he met at the military hospital. Lying next to each other for those long weeks after the Six Day War in sterilized surroundings, they had learned much about each other. Borman had nearly died from his stomach wounds. A reporter, who had suddenly thought he was a soldier and answered the call to arms. Somehow, he'd wrangled his way into the leading tank columns as they rolled through the fleeing army of Egypt. The armor piercing shell that stopped the tank had spattered everyone. Borman still couldn't remember climbing out of the flaming wreck; nor could he recall a jolting ambulance ride back to the field hospital with a young nurse who held his entrails as they spilled off the stretcher. A field station doctor clamped him back together for the helicopter flight to Tel Aviv. When finally he was released from the hospital, he married the nurse; Ruth Borman had become one of Asher's favorite people.

"Hello, Lev. We just got it on the wire here. What is it?" Borman's voice sounded concerned. A newspaperman with a conscience. Unusual.

"Hello, Sol. It's either a crash or hijacking. I'm betting on hijacking. We're trying a sea trace through the Sixth Fleet in Athens. I'll let you know soon as I hear anything. In the meantime could use your contact with that chap in Amman—what's his name?"

"You mean Bruner—Max Bruner." Borman knew Asher hadn't forgotten the name. He hated him.

"That's the one. He's living with the bastards; maybe he knows something."

"Unofficially?"

"Of course unofficially. Are they doing anything exciting across the Suez which might account for something like this—mutual admiration meeting—anything you know about?"

"By God. That's right! There is a Summit going on at the Nile Hilton between the PLO and Fateh. Arafat is there with his goons, Habash—all of them. We had it down as another of their meetings to disagree. Maybe there's a connection. I'll check it out and call you back."

"Thanks Sol. I'd appreciate it." He hung up. There was an excellent chance Borman would come up with something. He had come up with a photograph of Max Bruner for the intelligence files as soon as he had been released from Hospital. Asher was taking his daily therapy treatment, learning to walk, when a smiling Borman dropped in and handed him the eight by ten glossy. Asher recognized the face as the man he and Corporal Zabin had stopped and searched one dark morning in 1964. Now Corporal Zabin was dead, along with most of the other men on that patrol. Only Asher and three others who had played possum, survived. He never got a good look at any of the faces of the ambushers, but Max Bruner's face he never forgot. He also remembered the names. Galal and Khala. Galal had been the leader, of that Asher was sure. But who was Galal? Intelligence files showed nothing specific. There were lots of Palestinians named Galal, and Khala, for that matter. The phone rang. He snapped it to his ear. "Lt. Asher here."

"We've found your airplane, Lev. They're tracking it now. It's heading out into the Med westbound. Naval command says if it maintains present course it will hit the Algerian coast in another two hours. How's that for service?"

"Thanks, Sammy. I appreciate it."

"What are you going to do?"

"That's not my decision. I'll call Colonel Borodam. If there's any change in that course call me back, will you? Tell them not to lose it."

"They won't. The Captain still has his transponder on—the Navy say they can track him right out into the Atlantic. Good luck!"

Leila picked up the intercom phone in the rear galley and called the cockpit. Jamil answered. She could see him turn around, looking at her down the long tubular fuselage. "What is it?"

"Some of the passengers want to use the washrooms."

"Stay at the rear with the doors open. I'll make the announcement."

Leila hung the phone back on the wall and waited. No *trouble so far*, she thought, *everyone is cooperating, just like Jamil said they would*. She'd had misgivings about the audacity of the scheme when he had first proposed it.

"Supposing they have armed guards on board, Galal?"

"I don't give a shit if they have a whole company of commandos. One look at those grenades without their pins and everyone will be lambs. It's human nature to protect your fellow man from danger. Just pray we have some passengers. If we only have the crew to threaten we might be in trouble."

He had been right—practically everyone fell over themselves to cooperate. Jamil's voice came through the loudspeaker suddenly. Calm, authoritative.

"May I have your attention, Ladies and Gentlemen." It was a command, not a question. "You have all been very patient during the last thirty minutes. As I told you earlier, patience and cooperation are the best safeguards for your protection. We regret this inconvenience to your travel plans, however, after we have landed at Algiers, arrangements will be made, no doubt, to speed you on your way. We will be serving dinner shortly. In the meantime we ask you kindly to remain in your seats. For those of you that wish to use the washroom facilities in the first class or at the rear of the tourist class cabins, my two associates will take you, one at a time, in order, starting from the rear of the aircraft, moving forward. Please signify your desire to leave your seat by raising your hand. Only one person will be permitted to stand up at a time in either cabin. Women with small children excepted.

He repeated the instructions in German and French in the same calm, quiet voice. He concluded by giving them apologies for the necessity of leaving the washroom doors open while they were inside, but promised his associates wouldn't peek. It managed to raise a few nervous chuckles. Akbar and Leila began answering the scattering of raised hands. Jamil watched their progress for another moment, then turned back to the flight deck.

"You haven't told me your name yet?" Captain Shavan said. Jamil said nothing.

"Or what you hope to gain by all this?" Shavan tried again. Still no answer. Jamil's face was impassive, but his mind replied. *It's like this, Jewboy; there's a meeting of people going on this minute in Cairo between my people and a bunch of gutless bastards who have promised to help kick you out of Palestine. So far it's all been talk. Maybe—just maybe, when they hear about this little diversion of ours, everyone will get the idea we are serious. Serious enough to make a habit of grabbing airliners, only instead of letting everyone go afterwards, we'll blow them up, the passengers with them.* He looked at his watch. Forty-four minutes had elapsed since they had taken over the aircraft. By now he knew the radar picket ships of the U.S. Sixth Fleet had found the El Al 902 phosphorescent bleep on their screens from the steady transponder signal on board the aircraft. They would be tracking it carefully. He wanted to make certain they didn't lose it.

"Turn your transponder to emergency hijack code, Captain."

Shavan was startled. He too knew they were being tracked by radar and had been concerned as well with a contact loss, once their dot merged with the hundreds of other aircraft flying the busy Eastern Mediterranean flight routes. He had thought the slim young Palestinian knew nothing about the transponder. He had underestimated him. He looked at Jamil strangely.

"You want them to track us?"

"The emergency hijack code, Captain. Just do as you're told."

Shavan reached out to the radio console and twisted the code selector to 3200. He felt much better, satisfied the whole exercise was to be a demonstration of potential, rather than actual destruction.

Asher yanked the phone again. His ear was getting sore from pressing against the receiver. "Lt. Asher here."

"Lev! Your Captain has just changed his transponder to the hijack emergency I.D. They'll have no tracking problem now." Major Bernstein sounded pleased.

"I didn't know there was a problem, Sammy."

"Apparently there was a chance they might have lost him in the traffic shuffle along the Straits of Messina. There's no guess work now."

Asher paused to consider this information. "I wonder why he waited so long to go to the frequency?"

"Maybe he didn't have a chance before?"

"Or maybe someone let him, knowing the traffic flow near Messina. Thanks again, Sammy."

"Anytime, pal."

He was still holding the phone when Sergeant Kronig rushed into the office. He looked like a cat with all the cream. "I think we have the hijackers, Leiutenant!"

Asher dropped the receiver. "Good work."

First, we checked everyone out of Lod who continued on from Athens. They all checked out. At Athens, there were another twenty-six boarded for Rome and beyond. Out of those twenty-six, three came up red. Their tickets were only as far as Rome. Two men and a woman. The names are Michael Archero, Gabriela and Elijah Angelo. All Italian passports." Sergeant Kronig stopped, thinking. "Say I never noticed, but . . ."

"The archangel Michael, with the angels Gabriel and Elijah." Asher interrupted dryly. "Very original. See if anyone at Athens remembers enough to give us a description for composites. I'm particularly interested in the Archangel Michael. The sonofabitch!"

Jamil watched the city of Reggio di Calabria coming up out front of the cockpit windows. Beyond the toe of Italy, the northern coast of Sicily stretched westward from the Messina passage. The waters were dotted with shipping, the clear sky, with vapor trails. They had reached the first third of their journey. To the north, he could see a triangle where water, sky and land met in a roll of clouds. He turned to the wall phone and signaled Leila. "Are they all watered?"

"Just finishing now."

"Good. Use the two stewardesses to serve the meals. Tourist cabin first. You stay where you are. Pick the two weakest-looking stewardesses. Give them a pep talk before they start."

"Start now?"

"Start now." He flicked over to the cabin intercom. "Ladies and Gentlemen, we will serve your meal now. Tourist class first. I am afraid it will take a bit longer than usual because we will have only two ladies serving, instead of the usual six. Please be patient. There will be another washroom sortie after all the trays have been cleared." Again he repeated the announcement in the other two languages.

"Do you gentlemen wish to eat?" he inquired politely of the flight crew. They all nodded.

"So do I. We'll eat with the first class passengers." He glanced back to the rear. Leila had two stewardesses backed against the wall by the galley, laying down the law; the ground rules for serving operations. He smiled inwardly, remembering how insistent she had been at being permitted to participate in the hijacking. He had played with her, knowing full well she had earned the right, but tantalizing her with the thought that, as a woman, she might not be up to it.

"Galal, you bastard, I can do anything a man can do!"

"Except piss standing up!"

"That too. I'm going with you, that's all there is to it."

Jamil had stared at her thoughtfully. "We'll see."

Leila had joined him at the camp periodically over the past three years. She went on every patrol, lugging equipment with the rest of the men. She arrived first in early June, 1966, a week after President Nasser had announced to the second Palestinian National Congress that he had no plan for the liberation of Palestine. Leila had left cousin Torval in Kuwait and rushed to the mountains near

Amman to find Jamil. "We have been betrayed! What are we going to do?"

Jamil laughed at her; an intense brown spitfire outraged at the duplicity of her hero. To make matters worse King Hussein, alarmed by the growing power of El Fateh in Jordan, was beginning to clamp down on their activities. It was clear Hussein wanted the Palestinian training camps removed from his kingdom. So far, Jamil had ignored the pressures to decamp and move elsewhere. When he heard Nasser's speech over the radio it was obvious an Arab conspiracy was afoot; an attempt to contain the volatile Palestinians from bringing down the wrath of the major powers upon the heads of offending nations within the Arab League, nations that tolerated Palestinian presence and activities. It was a dicey game of deceit.

"Is that anyway to greet a lover, Leila?" he inquired, smiling at her tormented face when they met at the clearing in front of the command post. Bruner had brought her up from Amman in his little Citroen, bombarded by invective during the entire two hour drive. He stood back, waiting to hear how Jamil was going to handle the situation. Leila, he knew, was too valuable as a fund raiser in Kuwait to be wasting time in the mountains discussing politics.

Leila relaxed, running her fingers through her hair self-consciously. "Hello, Galal."

Jamil walked up to her and held her by the arms, then pulled her to him, kissing her fiercely. "That's better." He stood back. "Hungry?"

"She should be, after all that raving from Amman," Bruner observed. "I got hungry just listening to her."

They laughed and walked down to the mess tent.

Later he took her with him alone to his favorite spot on the summit of one of the hills enclosing the camp. They sat down to watch the fires of sunset die on the horizon, turning the rolling desert plains to purple, ochre shadows. The air was silent except for an occasional drift of light laughter floating from the camp below.

"You'll notice it always sets over Palestine—never rises."

Leila nodded. "I noticed."

"Perhaps one day we can change that, God willing."

"Perhaps?" She was surprised at the word. It was so unlike him to deal in possibilities.

He sighed tiredly. "It will never happen this way—the way we are going at it now. Without the support of all Arabs there will be no victory with El Fateh. It seems everything we try—the Arab National Movement—Palestine Liberation Front—Al Asifah—the PLO—the

Popular Front—all pawns in the game. I used to play a lot of chess with Chirlo. He taught me the rules. In the end, we were evenly matched. He used to tell me 'Jamil, mask your intentions with your pawns. They are expendable.' " He looked at Leila. "He was right. We are expendable."

"Now Hussein is joining Nasser." They had been discussing the Jordanian pressures during supper with Max Bruner. From his office/apartment in Amman, he kept his ear close to the rustling leaves of opinion. Not the opinions of press or radio, nor even politicans, but the drift of truth coming directly from the palace of the little Hashemite king.

"We are becoming a source of embarrassment for everyone. Political pariahs."

"What can we do?"

He shrugged. "Go on. What else? Keep doing what we are doing. Try to find other ways of hitting where it hurts most. Where the enemy is most vulnerable."

"Where's that?"

"I don't know yet. I'm still thinking on the problem. We must find things to do that will rock them to their boots."

"The Arabs or the Jews?" Leila wasn't sure who they were talking about.

"Everyone. Arabs, Jews, Americans, everyone. Something that will scare the shit out of them all. Something that can be done with limited resources by small groups. Do you know what I mean? Shooting the shit out of a bunch of Kibbutz' is old hat. It's been going on now since the Fifties and where has it got us? The Jews are still there!" He pointed to the horizon's glow. "And we're still here. Nothing has changed."

"Except we have less support now than we did when it all started," Leila added.

With the disappearance of the sun the air took on a chill. They wriggled closer to each other, searching heat. Jamil put his arm around her shoulders, the hand resting on her breast. He kneaded the nipple through the shirt. After a few moments she reached down feeling his groin, rubbing her fingers over the swelling bulge. "There's something else that has never changed." He chuckled and drew her to him.

Jamil plucked the phone from the wall in answer to the rear galley buzz. Leila had finished serving the tourist passengers and the trays were cleared. "Do you want the pee parade now or after the first class eats?"

"After." He was hungry. "What is it?"

"The meal? Lamb Shishkabob—skewers and all. A real Arab dish!"

He could visualize her smile. She was doing fine. "But you can bet it's been Kosher killed. Bring me two of them." He hung up the phone. They were out over the Mediterranean now. The land and vapor trails were far behind. They were alone.

Lt. J.G. Harper watched the tracking plot on the big screen in the dimly lit operations room. There was no doubt now on the hijackers destination. Straight for Algiers. The course had varied less than two degrees in the past half hour. He pushed the relay button at his desk and punched out the estimated time of arrival for Algiers, paused to watch the figures flash on his own flourescent desk screen, then picked up his phone. "MEDCOM Priority One." The main switchboard on the picket ship transferred the call to Naval Command Headquarters in Athens. It took seven seconds before he heard Commander Byson's crisp "This is MEDCOM, Go!"

"Lt. Harper, Sir. That El Al 707 will arrive overhead Algiers at ten fifty-two Greenwich. Steady on course. Steady airspeed."

"Thank you, Lieutenant." There was snap of static on the disconnect. Lt. J.G. Harper replaced his phone and leaned back to watch the blip of El Al nine zero two making its way slowly across the big screen at the end of the operations room. Four minutes later Lev Asher had received the information from the U.S. Embassy in Tel Aviv. He called Col. Borodam at once and reported the news.

"Anything else?"

"We're trying a composite I.D. in Athens. We have four people who remembered them."

"How soon?"

"Later today. They promised a telex photograph by four o'clock, Sir."

"Good work, Asher. I'll take over from here. You stay on the composites." He rang off before Asher could thank him for the compliment. He considered the composites. They would show the facial characteristics of the hijackers so far as four people could remember them. By the time he received them the plane would have been on the ground three hours in Algiers. Composites were a waste of time. He needed photographs. Close descriptions from people who had talked with the hijackers. He needed to be in Algiers to talk to the passengers. The damn phone rang again. He picked it up, holding it slightly away from his sore ear. "Lt. Asher here."

"Lev, I got the information you wanted from Max Bruner's office. His secretary said that Mr. Bruner will be away for a couple of days. Went to Algiers last night. How does that grab you?" Sol Borman demanded.

"The rotten sonofabitch. He knew about it all the time!"

"Now wait a minute! Lev, this is all strictly off the record."

"Okay, Okay, Sol. I haven't forgotten. Strictly off the record. Thanks."

"Anything more I can do?"

"Yeah. Get me into Algeria to meet El Al nine zero two when it lands."

"'Fraid I can't help you there, but I've notified our Algerian office to get someone out to the airport and try for a few photographs of these screwballs. That do?"

"Oh God, Sol, I hope they manage to get through security. Let me know, will you?" It was too much to hope for, Asher knew.

Jamil watched the slight stewardess running the first two trays to the flight deck. She stopped by the door, uncertain. "Captain and Flight Engineer first." He stood aside to let her through the passage. She thrust the trays out for Richler and Shavan, then left abruptly without looking at Jamil. She passed her counterpart rushing forward with the next two trays. Jamil took them and placed them on the jump seat behind the flight engineer. "One more," he told the girl. She nodded, her eyes wide. The desire to obey. He noticed she was beautiful, with sloping almond-shaped eyes; beautiful considering she was a Jewess. He picked the hot skewered lamb from the first tray and began gnawing at it, still holding the two grenades while balancing the hot skewer on this thumbs. The first girl returned with the single tray for the co-pilot. He nodded her through to the cockpit. As Goldman took the food he said something to the girl. Jamil saw her freeze momentarily then lean forward to listen. She nodded.

"Silence!" The girl straightened, stiffening as if she had been struck, then turned her head slowly.

"Come here!" She walked to him fearfully. He pushed her outside the cabin door. "What did he say?" he asked softly.

"Nothing—only if he could have another tray."

"Get it!" Jamil went back into the flight deck. "What did you say to the stewardess?"

Goldman had been watching. The co-pilot's face relaxed.

"I asked for a second helping; I'm hungry."

Satisfied, Jamil returned to the skewered chunks of meat on his second tray. "She's bringing it." The second batch of lamb pieces were considerably cooler than the first. He remembered the shishkabob he and Leila had eaten one night in Beirut after he had left Jordan with his men. It had been expensive and tough. He had sent the whole mess back to the kitchen and ordered Fattet Makhdous instead. That was in 1966 and great events were building in the Arab world.

Hussein had banned all troops of the Palestinian Liberation Army from Jordan. The American Government had banned all further wheat sales to the United Arab Republic. The Arab leaders had abandoned their summit pledges and began falling out among themselves, blaming each other for not carrying forward their earlier resolutions. Nasser now supported Fateh, but only when Hussein made it clear there would be no complicity with the PLO, not because Nasser supported Fateh's objectives, but because his policy of the moment suited such an alliance. According to Nasser, the Arab world was divided clearly now into two factions. Progressives and Reactionaries. He proclaimed himself leader of the Progressives. The year of promises had passed. The year of reaction was about to begin.

After a few weeks in Jordan, Jamil sent Leila back to Kuwait to continue her fund raising. She made several more visits to the Jordanian camp in the hills of Ghor until political pressures reached a point finally where it became wiser to decamp and move to more hospitable surroundings. For several weeks Jamil toured Syria and Lebanon. In the end he chose Lebanon because the Lebanese Army was weak and the country's borders with Israel ideally suited for swift incursions of retribution. Moving out of Jordan had been simple. They had motored up the highway to the Syrian border past the Golan Heights and into Lebanon to set up their new camp in the lush hills rising towards Mount Hermon. The country was quite different from the parched Jordanian desert. Scattered forests, scenic landscape rolling off toward the Jewish border. They made camp near the refugee settlement at Bint Jbail under watchful eyes of the other Palestinian guerilla commanders scattered about the hills. For the first months, Jamil's Jordanian intruders were regarded with deep mistrust; deserters from the common cause of fighting Hussein's edicts.

"I came to Lebanon to fight Jews. Why should I stay in Jordan and fight Arabs?" he had growled at the beefy commandant from one of the nearby camps. "If you are so anxious to fight Hussein's

Legions, my friend, there is the road to Amman! Go!" The logic was irrefutable, yet the suspicions remained until they saw how superbly Jamil's highly trained compact little force operated during their sorties across the Palestinian border. The turning point in their scepticism of Jamil and his forces came with the raid on the village of Bar Kava. It was one of several villages dotting the road between Baniyad and Metulla where the boundaries of the three countries joined. The area was heavily patrolled by Israeli troops working in flying columns along the ten miles of border. They could assemble rapidly to concentrate in one area if a serious problem developed at any point along the sector. Bar Keva lay in the middle.

For months, the Palestinian methods of infiltration for terror had remained consistent: small ten-man patrols would sneak through small gaps in the Israeli lines of defense, move a few miles inland then strike swiftly, and disappear. By the time the flying columns arrived, the attackers would have fled back across to Lebanon, or, if too far inland for retreat north, slip eastwards across the Syrian border. Local Palestinian commanders kept close contact with one another when arranging these raids so there would be no chance of two or more groups running into each other in the same area simultaneously. Jamil had placed himself on this roster for notification. For several weeks he waited for the right opportunity to present itself in the planned sorties from the other guerilla camps, before embarking on the Bar Kava attack. Finally, a weekly action forecast arrived which appeared ideal. Five individual penetrations had been planned between ten at night and two the following morning, covering a wide area between Baniyas and the ancient ruins near Qirat Shemona. Two of the groups were to provide feint attacks east and west of Bar Sheva. While the Israeli columns rushed to the feints, the main attack would hit the real target areas. Jamil decided to take the whole plan a step further.

Without discussing his idea with the other commanders, he mobilized his three hundred man force into three units. Loading down two wing units of fifty men with claymore mines and bazookas, he sent them off behind the two main attack groups from the other camps with careful instructions to keep well clear of Palestinian as well as Israeli troops. The fifty men split into their two twenty-five man units and disappeared into the quiet night. Jamil took the rest of his force and descended the hills along the border until they were directly opposite the village of Bar Kava. They flattened themselves against the ground and waited for the feinting actions to begin to the east and west of the settlement. From their vantage point a few hundred yards from the barbed coil defining the border, they watched the small Israeli vehicles passing back and forth along the road below the wire.

"How many do you think are down there?"

Jamil looked at Mahout's blackened face beside him and adjusted himself onto one elbow. "Soldiers, or in the village?" he asked quietly. Whispers carried further than soft-toned speech.

"I mean after the soldiers leave."

"Two, maybe three hundred in all. Why?"

"Nothing. Just hoping we'll have time to kill them all. It's a lot of people."

"There will be time. We'll make time," he said grimly. He felt elated at the prospect ahead. He loved the kill; savoring these moments before the actual attack when his throat went dry and saliva glands refused to function. His bladder filled within minutes after emptying it for the tenth time in less than an hour. He wondered if Mahout experienced the same sensations. He didn't ask in case the question be misunderstood as something more than idle curiosity. He unzipped his fatigue pants and relieved himself onto the ground, pressuring the stream downhill, away from where they were laying.

"Again? I always knew you where full of shit, but piss?" They chuckled softly, nervously in the night. He did up his pants and lay back, waiting.

The explosions startled him when they erupted, lighting the landscape. The action to the east was less than half a mile away. The fireworks on the west started a few seconds later. These were farther away, beyond the rise in the next depression of land. An Israeli halftrack troop carrier passing on the road in front of them, stopped suddenly to reverse direction, until the second explosions started beyond the rise. Then the vehicle clattered off, its engine racing. Jamil waved to the group around him. The force slithered forward on their bellies, stopping a few feet short of the barbed wire. At several points along their front, men slid up to the wire and cut a path; two men at each opening, bundled in heavy clothes, rolled against the wire tangles either side, holding the narrow pathway clear for the rest to slither through. In less then five minutes everyone was through the wire and regrouping across the road. The wire holders disentangled themselves, rewired their slices together and joined the others. They split into two groups and ran crouching through the darkness to circle the village in a pincer movement from the south. Chattering weaponry still filled the air from both directions. Suspecting a ruse, an Israeli command vehicle with search lights roared down the road from the east, its beam playing across the high barbed coil to the slopes rising beyond. It passed the temporary bindings where the Palestinians had cut their way through and disappeared over the rise toward the gunfire in the west. When they had gained the southern end of the village and rejoined forces, they paused again to wait.

"The west end of the road is mined—we put down six." Jamil nodded to the young sapper who appeared suddenly at his side. A few minutes later, the sapper from the east reported the same information from his end. "Good work. Go back now and cover the withdrawal. We'll use the bangalore torpedo on the wire going out." They nodded and moved off.

Suddenly, the distant firing stopped like a break in the film of an old war movie when the crowd boos.

"The other action has started. We'll give them ten minutes to clear out."

Mahout nodded, squatting on the ground, his automatic rifle resting on its butt between his open knees. They could hear occasional spats of rifle fire as the withdrawal proceeded. The noise thinned, then stopped altogether as the other commando units scurried back through their wire openings onto the safety of Lebanon. Far away Jamil could hear the dim sound of the main attack in progress. He glanced at his watch, staring at the second sweep circling to the top of the dial. He waited till it was exactly on twelve.

"Let's go!" The whole force stood up and began walking slowly towards the village. As they neared the first houses, he could see some of the villagers outside, standing in their yards discussing the gunfire beyond the low hills. The first group never knew what hit them as Jamil and those beside him opened fire, spraying them from the hip, still moving forward at a leisurely pace. The firing blinded the night along the quarter mile front as they moved into the first houses slaughtering the screaming, pleading occupants, then setting fire to the buildings.

Jamil, in the center of the advancing crescent of men, shattered the hinges on the door of the first house in his path. He kicked in the splintered wood, and leaped into the room, Mahout directly behind him. Two small children were huddled protectively in the arms of their mother at one corner. The woman's eyes were terrified, pleading. In front of her, an old man stood glaring haughtily at the intruders. He pulped the haughtiness into a red mush with a short burst, knocking the old man against the wall, then swung the barrel onto the Jewess and her brood. The children went limp without a sound as the bullets thumped through them. Mahout flung an incendiary grenade at the quartet of bodies. They rushed outside to the next house across the lane. About them the roaring village flamed. There was no one in the next house. Another fire grenade and they moved onto the next building, joining another four Palestinians running out of a burning house next door. Someone shouted at them in Arabic that it was a home for orphans.

"Bullshit!" one of the guerillas screamed back, spraying his fire in the direction of the voice. It gurgled hoarsely and stopped. They crashed into the building. It was a huge single room filled with low homemade cots. From the firelight through the row of windows behind the line of beds, Jamil could see the faces of the girls and boys; some curious, some frightened, all of them sleepy. One little girl in the first bed was crying, keening softly. Her friend in the next bed joined her with a wet sob. The Palestinians opened fire, covering the tiny cots with a tattering violence. Jamil noticed absently the terrified children died in silence, or with barely a whimper as they bumped about the floor to the cadence of bullets, turning them quickly to dark, wet, disjointed bundles. It was over in ten seconds. Someone tossed another incendiary into the middle of the lifeless room and they rushed outside into the smoky air as the phosphorus began to ignite the small wrecked bundles closest to the flame.

People had fled the rest of the houses and buildings they smashed through. Quickly, they fired them and moved on, finally reaching the road. He could see villagers running up into the fields towards the wire and down the road in both directions; some were carrying babies. The Palestinians spun them into bloody eerie gargoyles with a concentrated fire. Jamil paused to look back at the village. Every structure was in flames. His eyes swept the area for a sign of life. Nothing was left. He blew his shrill whistle. The firing stopped, then the bangalore torpedoes whooshed through the barbed wire ahead of them, blowing a wide laneway into the safety of the Lebanese country beyond. He stood in the middle of the road watching his men stream though the opening. He waited until the sappers came jogging up before starting for the opening himself.

"Come on, you two, get a move on!" They speeded up and passed him grinning. "What's the rush, Galal? There isn't a live Jew around for miles."

"I know, but I prefer to piss in Lebanon. So move!" Laughing, they trotted through the opening in the wire together and rejoined the others for the hike back to Bint Jbail.

The success of their attack in which a complete village of three hundred and forty-one people had been killed, and the village itself razed without a single casualty, made the accomplishments of the other five commanders pale in comparison. The road mining with the claymores by Jamil's two rearguard parties sent in behind the main forces to stop Israeli traffic, had been responsible for a terrible destruction of troops and vehicles. Thereafter, the Jordanian deserters were held in awe by all the camps scattered along the slopes of Mt. Hebron and into Syria.

"Bullshit!" was Jamil's comment when Mahout told him of their newly won fame. Secretly he was pleased.

Leila kept the flow of money coming from their Kuwaiti sponsors. Between the fat account at Bank Mizr in Beirut and the fat haul of weapons and equipment from Palestine during the weekly raids deep into Israel, their small force became the envy of less fortunate commando groups in the area.

"We've reached a stalemate. We go neither forward nor backward." Jamil studied Leila across the table in the restaurant. He had come to Beirut to meet the MEA flight from Kuwait, bringing her back to him. "In fact, we are immobile." He dipped the fattet and began chewing throughtfully.

"A new approach, then?" she offered.

Jamil nodded, swallowing. "Exactly. A new approach. That is why I asked you to come back. I've decided to expand our activities." He smiled wolfishly. "We're going into the skyjacking business!"

"To what purpose?"

Jamil was disappointed with her reaction. "I should think that would be obvious."

"Not to me. Where are we going to take the airplanes? Cuba? What do we gain besides getting our names and pictures in the paper and exposing ourselves?"

"Exactly." He went back to his food.

"This is your new approach?" Jamil nodded. "It's not very original, Galal."

"It's the first step. I'm not seeking originality. I'm seeking world attention." He looked at her face, searching the dark brown eyes. "Can't you see what is happening, Leila? We are a forgotten people. No one gives a shit anymore—Nasser, Hussein, even Arafat is playing politics now. It's cuddle time in Cairo. Everyone supports Fateh so long as it can be controlled. No one supports our group unless we agree to take orders from Fateh. Maybe the others believe that garbage coming out of Cairo, but I've heard it all before. The

261

activists are swallowed by the pacifists as soon as they become too active."

"I suppose Karameh was a defeat," she countered. The month before Fateh had engaged the Israelis in the Battle of Karameh, a Palestinian city on the east side of the Jordan River. The Israelis had tried to obliterate it and failed. It was a Phyrric victory for Fateh and caused a sensation throughout the Arab world. Even Hussein claimed to be a Fateh commando in the afterglow of action. It had been the only solid Arab confrontation against the Jews which everyone could relate to.

"That was in March—this is April," Jamil said sourly.

"Support money is still pouring in from everywhere to help Fateh, Galal. I know. I've seen it happening in Kuwait. Six months ago they gave me money for us—now they give it to me for Fateh."

"My point exactly. We are the orphans again. Nasser will use Karameh as a focal point to rally political support for his needs. Nothing to do with our interests."

"He may wind up fighting a war."

"Then he will lose."

Leila shook her head. "I disagree. The Egyptian Army outnumbers the Jewish Army by four to one."

Jamil smiled sadly. "Ah! Leila, my hawk, have you learned nothing in these past years? The Jews outnumber us too, by thousands to one, but we survive because we must. If Egypt goes to war with the Jews, they will lose. Egypt will fight for politics. The Jews will fight for survival. The Jews will win."

They were silent, watching the noisy traffic; smoking Mercedes diesel taxis thunking through the street, the acrid odor of their exhausts, trapped along the narrow airless sidewalk. Suddenly, two Lebanese jumped up excitedly from one of the other tables and yelled with delight. One of them held a small portable radio aloft.

"He has agreed! Nasser has agreed to help Syria! Listen! He turned the volume full, distorting the excited Arabic coming from the small speaker. A few patrons stood up from their tables; some came forward smiling, others sat back; everyone listened.

". . .information from army intelligence has now confirmed the Syrian claims of massive troop buildups along the Israeli border during the past seventy-two hours. Premier Levi Eshkol repeated his early warnings to the Syrian government of their continuous bombardment of Israeli territory from the Golan Heights. 'We are reaching the end of our patience with Syria,' he said. President Nasser reaffirmed his pledges to Syria today from Cairo, and said the United

Arab Republic will not stand idle in the face of flagrant threats of violations to Syrian neutrality . . . ."

"Galal. Did you hear that?" Leila's eyes glowed in excitement. Jamil pushed his plate aside and looked at her sadly.

"Bullshit—it's all bullshit!" He signaled for the check and stood up. "But just in case that idiot is serious, I'm going back to camp and get our people out of the line of fire until this is over."

"You're going to desert?" She was incredulous.

"No, my hawk, I'm going to depart—there's a difference."

"What will be our official reaction, Mr. President?"

President Houari Boumedienne considered the question carefully. "That will depend on what happens after they land at Dar El Beida, General. I have heard nothing to indicate who they are or what they intend to do. Obviously they are coming to Algeria for sanctuary. It is therefore logical to assume they will do nothing to disgrace themselves or us on Algerian soil. I would expect something." He glanced at his watch. "Say, within the next half hour, they will be contacting us on their intentions." He smiled benignly. "Therefore we shall wait. All things come to him who waits, General Madanoux."

"They are Palestinians. I'm sure. No one else would take an El Al flight."

"You have the advantage of prophecy, General? I am sure of nothing until we hear otherwise. Keep me informed." He nodded his dismissal to the general and his gold shoulder tasselled young aide then picked up his phone. He waited until his guests had left before speaking. "Contact airport security. If and when that Israeli flight lands, I want it completely cordoned off from the rest of the field. No photographers or newspapermen, unless they are cleared by Intelligence in writing. The people responsible for the hijacking are to be treated courteously until I find out who they are. Do it." He hung the phone back on its cradle slowly.

A thought occurred to him. If they were Palestinians, he decided he would like to meet them. Houari Boumedienne always appreciated revolutionary discussions with guerilla activists. He had been one himself, taking on the might and power of De Gaulle's Fourth Republic. That was in 1962. He had won.

"We are thirty minutes out now." Captain Shavan turned in his seat, looking to Jamil for instructions. They had been flying parallel to the North African coastline for some time. Algiers was now two hundred and fifty miles ahead. The food trays had been returned to the galley, the post meal parade to the washrooms completed. Leila and Akbar had joined Jamil in the flight deck, locking the cabin door behind them. The stage was set for the last act.

"Contact Algiers approach control for a 'straight in' then advise them you want to be patched into the national radio network with a Cairo monitor."

Shavan turned back to the console and switched to the Algiers frequency. He received an immediate clearance for descent and request to stand by five minutes for the radio patch. Jamil nodded, satisfied with the report as he listened to the conversation through the flight engineer's headphones. He noted with satisfaction Shavan had said nothing in reply to the stream of questions from the traffic controller.

"Switch me onto the cabin loudspeaker, Captain. You may reduce power." Shavan adjusted the radio switches to pipe Jamil's voice back to the passengers, then reached for the throttles to reduce the engines for their descent into Algeria.

"We are now starting our descent into Dar El Beida airport at Algiers. Everyone will remain seated until the aircraft has been parked and the engines stopped. There is no cause for alarm or panic. Arrangements will be made for your orderly departure from the aircraft. Thank you for your cooperation." He repeated the message in the other languages and switched off the microphone.

The nose of the 707 slanted slightly. The altimeter began to unwind. Akbar winked at him from the jump seat and jerked his thumb up. His eyes were laughing, although his face, like Leila's, was grave. The crowded flight deck was silent, except for a sound of rushing air outside the fuselage, more an awareness than a feeling of sound.

Jamil remembered the same sort of awareness, the imminence of disaster, as he had driven Leila back over the Lebanese hills to the camp hear Bint Jbail. Swiftly they had decamped the next day, moving their columns of men, trucks and equipment north to the fertile plains near Baalbek. They pitched their tents and huts and waited. They did not wait long.

Nasser called upon the United Nations for the immediate withdrawal of troops along the Israeli Egyptian border, then closed the strait of Tiran, shutting the gulf of Aqaba and the Israeli port of Elat to shipping. Swiftly the noose of commercial strangulation tightened on the Jews. Under popular pressure, Premier Eshkol appointed Major General Moshe Dayan, the hero of the Suez crisis, as

Defense Minister; Nasser collected his promises of support from Iraq, Saudi Arabia, Algeria and Jordan. The powerful voice of Cairo Radio screamed its defiance at the Jewish nation. Befuddled by the rapidity of events, the superpowers watched uneasily, voicing half-hearted threats between themselves as their junior antagonists squared off without benefit of a referee. The bell sounded on the morning of June 6 when the Israeli air force swept in across the Egyptian dunes to flatten their Russian air force in a preemptive strike. Cairo radio, by noon, was spouting the fantasy of huge Israeli losses and stunning Egyptian military victories in the field. Jamil was sitting in his tent with Leila, listening to the broadcast intently, when Akbar poked his head around the flap.

"Do you have a moment, Galal?"

"What is it?" The Cairo announcer boasted of staggering tank losses the Jews were suffering in the Sinai as their mobile steel met the impregnable fortress of Arab soldiery.

"Some of the men would like to speak to you about returning south."

Jamil had been afraid this would happen. "How many want to go?"

"All of them."

"You too?"

"Yes."

"I see." He couldn't blame them. It was their war too. He stood up from the camp stool.

"I'll come out." Akbar smiled guiltily. His head disappeared. Jamil looked at Leila. "What about you, Hawk Eyes?"

"I'll wait until I hear what you have to say." It wasn't what she wanted to tell him. What she wanted to say was her heart ached for him. He had given so much to these men. Security, a sense of purpose, pride in themselves and in what they were doing. Now they were going to desert him because they believed him to be wrong. Perhaps he was wrong, but that did not excuse their actions. Leila hated them for it. She wanted to tell him to go with them. To continue to lead them as he had before. To order them to stay. To kill them if they refused to obey. Instead, she smiled, holding her upturned palm toward the tent flap.

"Galal Jamil, your public is waiting." She followed him outside into the searing noonday sun. They were all waiting. Three hundred and twenty-seven members of the Palestinian Liberation Youth Brigade grouped in a semi-circle to await the compromising words of their commander so they could desert him to fight their Jews with clear consciences. Jamil gazed about the sea of brown faces, meeting their eyes. The murmuring died. There was a pause in the shuffling motion of the group. The sound of a heavy truck's engine revving as it shifted gears to climb the incline on the road to Maqnah drifted down from the highway above the camp, then faded as it crested the hill.

"The siege of Leningrad lasted 1000 days. Almost completely surrounded, and outnumbered by a superior German army by ten to one, the Russians held. They held with soldiers, factory workers, shopkeepers, farmers and women. They starved as they fought and they died. But they held. One soldier, Ivan Kadakov, a sniper from Rostov, killed three hundred and seventy-two German soldiers. He was successful because he worked alone, moving from place to place around the perimeter, never firing twice from the same position, blending always with the landscape; picking off groups of three or four Germans at a time, never tempting their strength to discover his weakness. When the siege ended, although tens of thousands of soldiers and civilians lay dead, Ivan Kadakov was still alive. If the Russians had only had a single division of Ivan Kadakov's there would have been no siege. Ivan Kadakov was a guerilla in an army of soldiers. You are an army of guerillas who wish now to become soldiers. I wish you luck in your new careers. Allah Maak."

He turned abruptly and went back to his tent. The group of men stood in silence a few moments, then broke slowly into conversational cliques. Leila watched them arguing quietly, then went to join Jamil. She stood in the canvas doorway. He was laying on his cot, hands folded behind his head, smoking.

"Well, Hawk Eyes?"

"I'm staying."

"Good. Get me some coffee."

President Boumedienne leaned back in his chair looking about the faces in his office.

"Have you notified the Conference delegates in Cairo to listen to the broadcast?"

"Yes, Sir. They are at the Nile Hilton. Members of Fateh and the PLO. Dr. Habash, Arafat and Heikal. I spoke to Mohammed Heikal personally." Colonel Ismar's communication center had reacted swiftly to the radio patching request. He had got through to Cairo on the short wave band in three minutes flat.

It took another five to explain the situation to Heikal when the editor of *Al Ahram* had been tracked down at the conference room inside the hotel.

"Good. Then I think we're ready." He looked at General Mandanoux's aide. "If you will notify the air traffic controller, Major, we can hear what they have to say."

The young major called the airport while a junior captain from Colonel Ismar's branch adjusted the radio controls on the conference table. A sound of suppressed static filled the room. As the major replaced the telephone, the radio erupted loudly. The captain turned the volume down quickly.

"El Al niner zero two, this is Algiers approach control." There was a pause. The reply came back distinct, laconic at slightly lower volume.

"Roger Algiers, niner zero two."

"Niner zero two, we have your radio patch in operation now through to Cairo monitor. Over."

"Thank you, Algiers. Stand by, one."

All eyes in Boumedienne's office were staring at the speaker on the table, waiting for Shavan's voice to return. The pause was interminable to the listeners. Then to a startled five million listeners came a soft female voice.

"Brothers and sisters of the revolution! This is the Voice of Free Palestine. Today while those that call themselves our leaders sit and talk and do nothing in the luxury of expensive hotels deciding on the next excuse to explain their lack of courage and unkept promises to the enslaved people of Palestine, we have acted. We have taken our cause to the people of the world by seizing an El Al airliner of the paramilitary air force of the Zionists as an example of what can be done by a few dedicated orphans seeking the legitimacy of their parenthood from the nations of the world. Today we will bring this airliner and its passengers to Algiers safely and with no harm to anyone. It is hoped this demonstration of our ability will be sufficient to make our voice heard; our hopes for justice realized. We know this is doubtful; yet we ask for nothing that is not rightfully ours. Our homeland. Nothing more. Nothing less. We want to go home. Is that so difficult to understand? You will call us guerillas, terrorists, savages and animals. You will call us heartless bloodthirsty fascists, or communists, with no respect for human life or property. We are none of these and yet we are all of them. We seek justice for our cause. In 1920 Palestine lived in peace. In 1930 the Zionists brought us misery. In 1940 England brought us war. In 1950 over half our country had been stolen from us, approved by the United Nations, that platform of world opinion for which you are all to blame. In 1960 our leaders told us to wait, saying they would correct this wrong. Last year, without warning, the Zionists struck again, gobbling up the Sinai, the Golan Heights from Syria and the rest of Palestine they missed in 1948. All this while the world stood by! Poor Jews. So oppressed, so threatened, so willing to live in peace with their neighbors. Now our leaders sit in Cairo and plan new lies to give us hope. Our hopes died on the battlefields of Sinai and Jordan a year ago. Now we will take command of our own destiny with our own solutions, and woe to those of you who do not listen. You have the power, the might, the wealth and the means to save yourselves by giving back what you have taken. We have nothing, except our lives, to offer in return, and these we give, gladly. Your weakness lies in your strength. You have much to lose. Our strength lies in our weakness. We have nothing to lose. Hear my voice, oh people of Israel, in Europe, in America, in England, the United Nations and in Tel Aviv. Hear my voice and tremble. It is the voice of truth. The Voice of Free Palestine."

The radio speaker returned to the soft static burr. Two of the desk phones started ringing. The President picked up the black phone as the Major answered the white one. Both conversations were muted. The Major's, out of deference to the surroundings; Boumedienne's out of the common sense. The Major finished speaking, replaced the receiver and whispered into General Mandanoux's ear briefly. The General nodded and the Major left the room. The President continued with his conversation. It was the editor of the official government newspaper, the mouthpiece of the PLN Party, inquiring how he should handle the broadcast. He outlined the various approaches possible. Boumedienne disliked Gamal Nasser, but respected him as a clever politician. The Palestinians were always the bone that stuck in his throat at any of their meetings. He blew hot and cold on Egyptian involvement, depending upon the political expediencies of the moment. As a military leader, he had been a disaster. As a politician, Boumedienne considered him purely an opportunist.

"Give it front page verbatim reporting on the message, but no sentiments. Leave the airport arrival until we see what happens." He hung up, smiling at the others in the room. "That is what I call a revolutionary edict! I want to meet that woman and her friends as soon as they land."

Leila was trembling when she handed the microphone back to Jamil; she searched his face, seeking some sign her delivery of his

268

message had been satisfactory. His face was impassive, the hooded eyes alert but devoid of emotion. She sat down on the jumpseat and fastened her seatbelt. Akbar, leaning against the flight engineer's console, smiled happily at her as she looked up. He shook his head slowly in wonder. Leila felt better. It had been a strange feeling speaking to the world from inside a stolen airplane. She had felt the same way when news of the disaster had reached them at Baalbek on June 15 the previous year. Then it had been Jamil that had provided the comfort to her shattered emotions. After his short announcement to the men, he and Leila had been drinking coffee in the tent when Akbar reappeared. He had stood nervously inside, silent, embarrassed; searching for words. Jamil had raised his eyebrows speculatively.

"Back so soon, my friend? How was the battle?"

"I'm not going—a few others will stay, as well."

"A few others? Let me guess who they are." He sipped the harsh black coffee.

"Malmalli, Mahout, Hassad, Aziz and the rest of those who were with me in Cosecha Rica—but no one else. Am I right?" He knew he was. Akbar nodded.

Jamil sighed. "It is the difference between those who have participated in success and those who have known only disaster."

"Salim would like to know what equipment he can take with him?"

"So, Salim is to be the new Prophet?" His voice was not bitter, merely curious at the choice of leadership. Salim Salaak was more of a politician than a soldier. Perhaps that was the reason for his election.

"Give them anything they want to take. Leave us two vehicles and supplies for three weeks."

"The weapons?"

"Give them everything except some small arms for ourselves."

"Everything else, Galal?" Akbar couldn't believe his ears.

"Everything, man! They will need it. We are going to continue battle at a time and place of our own choosing. They have no choice. They are going to war!"

By late afternoon the camp was deserted except for six tents, one transport truck and Jamil's little Fiat. The following morning Israeli tank columns were slicing through the fleeing armies of Egypt and Salim Sallak while the rest of the men were locked in combat beside King Hussein's Desert Legions on the west bank of the Jordan. On the fourth day they were surrounded by the Israeli army and wiped out to the last man.

The dust of discourse settled. Israel occupied the Golan Heights, the Gaza Strip and the whole of the Sinai Penninsula. The Gulf of Aqaba was reopened to shipping for the Port of Elat, but by that time everyone had forgotten it had been the reason war had been started in the first place. The following week they heard what had happened in Jordan from one of the Fateh convoys returning from the south. The men in the trucks looked beaten, disillusioned, dejected. Leila had wept with frustruation, cursing hysterically. He said nothing at first, but led her away from the side of the highway and helped her back into the Fiat. For a while he drove in silence listening to Leila's sobs, waiting until they subsided. A mile short of Baalbek, he turned off the highway, drove a few hundred yards and parked.

"Come. There is something I want to show you!" She allowed him to lead her from the car and across the gravel road, into a field. "Look at it!" He pointed to the stone monolith. "Solid granite eighty feet long, twenty feet high and twenty feet wide. Perfectly cut and dressed over at that quarry." He pointed at the hills over a mile away. "Think of the weight!" When the Romans came, they found these stones forming the base of an abandoned temple in the town. They built their temple to Baal on the same foundation."

"Now that temple is in ruins, too." Leila was familiar with the history of the temple at Baalbek.

"That's not the point." He looked back at the grey monolith before them. One end had sunk into the earth over eons of time, giving the other end an impression of a huge square cannon rising from the ground. "The point is that someone made a mistake in calculation. Look at it! There is nothing built today that can lift it. Yet thousands of years ago someone gave orders to make these stones to form the foundation of a temple. When the foundation was finished they found they had one stone too many. The orders went out to leave this one where it was. All that work, cutting, dressing, moving, for nothing. Now, here it sits, useless. What a waste!"

"But the temple was completed without it."

"Exactly! In the end, the temple is always completed by men who do the work and build. It is those who plan foundations that make mistakes, wasting human lives and effort."

Then she understood. For some reason it made her feel better knowing the past was prologue. They went back to the car and returned to camp to begin packing their equipment for the move to Beirut which would become their permanent headquarters for the years ahead.

Andre Beauchamp took the last Galloise from the paper package and hung the tip on his lower lip as he studied the roadblock into the airport. He tossed the crumpled pack out the side window of the Peugot and considered the situation. "Maybe they'll park it over by the military."

Beauchamp looked at the U.P. man sitting beside him in the battered car.

"Norman, ami. They will park near the terminal but away from the rest of the airlines." He lit the Galloise absently.

"How can you be sure, Andre?"

A Gallic shrug followed the two live streams of smoke from the photographer's nose. "The airliner is filled with Jews. Papa Bouddy would never permit them near the military installations. Nor by the storage tanks over there—just in case." He was talking to himself now. "So, that leaves the far apron as the only alternative." He nodded. "And that is where it will be parked. Allons!"

He put the car in gear and backed into a semi-circle, reversing their direction and drove off, skirting the fence along the airport taxiway. "Just beyond the end of the fence there is a gate. They still use it for construction trucks." The Galloise bounced on his lip, dropping ash on his lap. "We can park nearby and walk back."

"The gate? Is it locked?"

"It's possible." Another shrug. "If it is we'll climb over. They will not be looking at this end of the airport after the plane lands."

"Are you certain the telephoto will pick up everything from this distance?"

The U.P. man squinted back anxiously at the receding terminal buildings. Beauchamp slowed the car as the fence ended suddenly to run a right angle toward the sea. He stopped and switched off the ignition. Then yanked the two bags of photographic gear from the back seat and slammed the door, smiling. "The flea on a rat's ass at one mile, mon ami, if we use the tripod." He spat the wet cigarette onto the ground, then stamped it with a toe.

"Here!" He handed one of the bags to the U.P. man. Let's see if that gate is locked. How good are you at climbing barbed wire fences?"

Max Bruner stood apart in the control tower, scanning the eastern sky with field glasses. He glanced at his watch. El Al nine zero two was due any moment. Air traffic in and out of the field had been suspended pending the arrival of Athens flight. The tower was strangely quiet, after the bustle of communication clearances that had snapped back and forth fifteen minutes earlier. Bruner had heard Leila's voice over the tower loudspeaker. He'd felt a surge of pride when she finished speaking and everyone had cheered the words. Even the sour-faced intelligence captain had nodded with approval.

"They're on the scope!"

Bruner joined the others in the tower examining the twenty-five mile radar sweep. A single dot from the east, clearly defined, moved slowly towards the center of the screen. The tower operator picked up his mike. "El Al niner zero two, this is El Beida tower. You are twenty-five east of the airport. Say your altitude."

Shavan's voice came back quickly. "Passing through three for the outer marker."

"Roger, El Al, you are cleared for straight in approach on two-seven call by the outer marker."

Now Bruner could see the growing dot low in the sky where the Sahel hills sloped into the Mediterranean. He watched it expand through the distance, then saw the wheels lowering.

"Niner zero two is cleared to land, check gear down and locked."

Jamil positioned himself between the two pilots as the gear rumbled into position. From the front window the city looked like a white amphitheater in the bright sun. The stage was the blue waters of the Bay of Algiers; the bleachers, the sloping Sahel hills rising in a vast semi-circle from the sparkling white buildings in the orchestra pit.

"Full flap!" Shavan ordered. Goldman extended the pedestal lever to the end of its travel. The huge machine, suspended between heaven and earth, sank forward onto the runway.

There was a squeal as the tires hit. The wing spoilers popped up and Shavan pushed the reversers. The aircraft trembled and slowed quickly.

"Niner zero two is cleared straight to the first taxiway. Contact ground 119.7 when clear. Good luck."

Shavan acknowledged the instructions as they trundled down the pavement and swung off to the taxiway. Two small French-built armored cars took up position at either wingtip, their turrets trained on the 707. Shavan was alarmed.

"El Beida Ground. Niner zero two. I hope those gunners have

their safeties engaged."

"Proceed straight ahead past the terminal building to the parking runup apron at the end. Do you need passenger assistance with injuries?"

"Negative. We're all just fine."

"What are your intentions?"

Shavan looked at Jamil standing between the seats with earphones, monitoring the conversation. "Tell him you want the stairs to disembark three passengers, plus fuel to continue on to Rome. That you will be leaving as soon as you are refueled."

Shavan repeated the instructions exactly.

"Roger El Al. I check that. Park the aircraft and wait. Do not leave this frequency."

Shavan turned to the flight engineer. "Manny, work out our fuel to Rome."

He swung the aircraft in a slow semi-circle at the edge of the concrete apron and shut down three of the engines, leaving the fourth to run the on-board electrical systems. The armored cars parked beneath the wings, turrets still trained on the Boeing. "Well, Mr. Voice of Free Palestine, what happens now?"

Jamil straightened. "We leave. You continue on to Rome."

A convoy of vehicles drew up around the aircraft; two white Citroens, several Jeeps filled with soldiers and a tandem fuel truck. One of the jeeps towed portable stairs. The soldiers unhooked it swiftly and pushed in up to the fuselage door behind the flight deck.

"Open the door!" Shavan released the safety switch on the cockpit panel. Jamil jerked his head at Leila and Akbar to leave the flight deck. Still holding his two grenades, he backed to the open cabin doorway. After a moment, he heard the fuselage door open.

Akbar called from around the corner. "It's clear!"

Jamil smiled at the faces of the crew. It was the first facial expression he had allowed himself since boarding the plane. "Captain, gentlemen. It's been a pleasure working with you. Perhaps someday we can work again—who knows?"

He turned to leave, then paused halfway through the door. "You might like to keep these as souvenirs." He tossed the grenades to them. One to Shavan, the other to Goldman. The spring detonating clips separated in mid air, dropping to the floor. He didn't wait to see if they managed to catch the explosives, as, still smiling, he vanished through the opening to join Leila and Akbar. The three walked slowly down the steep steps to the group of people waiting expectantly on the white concrete below.

Shavan watched the meeting on the tarmac from the cockpit; saw the three terrorists being greeted courteously then ushered deferentially into one of the Citroens. It drove off with its large red dome light flashing. He sighed and slumped back in his chair, smiling to himself. He held his grenade up, examining it. It was a child's plastic toy. The only metal it contained was the spring clip, now laying on the floor. They had all been had. He looked at Goldman sourly. The co-pilot was studying his own grenade in wonder.

"I'll be a sonofabitch! Plastic! We were never in danger at anytime. We could have told them to go fuck themselves!"

Shavan considered this hindsight observation. "True Dov, but the point is we didn't, did we?"

Andre Beauchamp packed the last piece of his equipment back in the leather bag.

"You have a cigarette?" He searched his pockets, knowing he had none himself.

"You asked me that before—I don't smoke. Are you sure you got them?" The U.P. man had nearly knocked the tripod and camera over in his excitement when the three figures emerged from the 707. The Frenchman had pushed him aside, cursing, his eyes never leaving the telescopic sighting for the camera. The automatic shutter had zipped through eighteen frames while the three figures descended the steps. After that he had taken pot luck with the group on the ground as they enveloped the trio. He knew there were at least two good three-quarter facial shots of each of them. He was satisfied. Now if he could just find a cigarette. "You used to smoke. I remember when you smoked." He said the words accusingly, still groping through his pockets uselessly.

"I quit—the pictures, Andre!"

Beauchamp hated reformed drunks and smokers. They were such a sanctimonious bunch of bastards.

"Can't tell until I've developed them. Let's go." If he had to squirm for a cigarette, he'd make the U.P. man squirm too—well, at least until they got into town and he could buy a packet of Galloises. They walked back through the unlocked gate to the car, lugging the two equipment cases.

"Lev. We got the photographs! I've just heard from our man in Algiers!"

Asher's knuckles whitened as he tightened the phone against his sore ear. "Did he say how good they were, Sol?"

"Several facial shots of each coming out of the aircraft. The photographer is a guy we use from *Paris Match*. He's good."

"How quickly can I get them?"

"The fastest connection is to Paris on Air Algerie tonight. Gets in around midnight. I told him to get them to New York on the photoprinter from our Paris office. We'll have their faces spread around the world tomorrow morning."

"Good work, Sol. I'm trying to play down the toy grenades—if you . . ."

Borman cut in " . . . The wire service boys are all keeping it out by changing it to plastic grenades—get it? Plastique—plastic." He chuckled. "So someone on the teletype can't spell! The Arab newspapers will carry it banner line. You can bet on that."

Asher knew. "I'm not interested in the Arab newspapers. It's the Mrs. Goldblooms in New York, London and Paris reading the story over morning breakfast that worry me. I don't want them getting the wrong idea."

"The passengers okay?"

"Far as we know. They spent forty-five minutes on the ground, then left for Rome. They should be getting in within the next hour. Our people have a VIP departure lounge laid on for interrogations."

"Well, it should be brief now that we have the photos."

"Brief?" Asher's mind had begun to consider the problem of the delayed irate passengers asked to delay longer for interviews.

"You don't need composites any more."

"Unless somebody hijacks Air Algerie tonight," Asher observed humorlessly. They hung up.

Asher reported the news to Colonel Borodam immediately.

"Do the Algerians know about the photographs?"

"I don't know, Sir. I doubt it."

"Find out. Call me back."

The recall to Sol Borman provided no information either. The U.P. man in Algiers only had said he had pictures, not how he had obtained them. Asher took the massive international airline schedule from his desk drawer. The Algerian flight left at 10:00 p.m. local time. He phoned Borodam, giving him the new information. The Colonel was silent for a few moments. Asher could visualize him at the other end of the line, frowning.

"More than four hours to departure time. I'd better get a cover on the photographer. What's his name?"

Asher wasn't aware Israeli Intelligence had any underground liaison 'covers' in Algiers. "There are two men involved, Sir. The photographer and the U.P. newsman. I don't know their names."

"You're supposed to be an intelligence officer, Asher. All officers are intelligent. Very few have intelligence. You were picked because someone thought you had. Obviously they were wrong. Hereafter, do not call me unless you have all the intelligence information required to make an intelligent decision. Do you understand, Asher?" It was the longest speech he had ever heard the Colonel make.

"Yes, Sir."

"Splendid. Then call your friend back and get me the information." The line clicked dead.

He redialed Borman's number, feeling like a fool.

The white Citroen took them into the city, along the Boulevard Zirout Youssef to the Prefecture, where they swung in a narrow laneway beside the building and disappeared through an opening into a large garage. The doors slammed shut behind them. After the initial Arabic greetings at the bottom of the mobile stairs from the 707, they had made the ride from the airport in silence. The driver and his companion were both officers, Jamil was sure of that, but as the shoulder insignias were unfamiliar, he could not determine their ranks or who outranked whom. Relaxed, he had settled back into the plush seat of the executive Citroen and smoked a cigarette, watching the sights along the way into the city. At one point Leila, sitting in the middle of the back seat, reached over to squeeze his hand. Akbar appeared to be sleeping, his face angelic.

The rear doors were opened courteously by the two officers. "Would you please accompany us?" Other police and plainclothes-men in the garage looked at them curiously as the close group walked past rows of cars and through the heavy doors marked *Private* in Arabic and French. The elevator was small and noisy. It lurched into motion. It had not been designed for five occupants, and the air was stifling inside its tiny compartment. Everyone studiously avoided looking at anyone else, all eyes concentrating on the flashing panel digits. At '6' the door opened and a rush of cool air enveloped them from the high wide hallway. They squeezed out of the vertical coffin and marched to the end of the hall, where one of the officers knocked lightly at a door, paused for a moment, then opened it and motioned the three Palestinians inside. They entered. Jamil stood between the other two surveying the surroundings. He heard the door close and knew their escort had left.

The room was magnificent in its decadent opulence. A

combination of French Provincial and Arabian functional design; a perfect blending of two factions; tacit acknowledgement of the best from two cultures. Two men sitting on plush red velvet chairs in front of a huge ornate desk stood up, smiling. They recognized President Boumedienne from newspaper pictures. He seemed to be shorter than his photographs, but the face was unmistakable. He came forward.

"Welcome to Algeria!" He clasped them, indivdually, French-Arab fashion, then turned to his companion.

"My friend, Commissioner Fibray of the Securite." The Commissioner repeated the President's greeting in the same fashion. Boumedienne pulled in two chairs from the side of the room, and grouped them around the other three in front of the desk. Everyone sat down, arranging themselves pleasantly. The Commissioner clapped his hands loudly. A police officer appeared with a silver tray to offer sweet tea or coffee.

"You are the Voice of Free Palestine?" The President looked at Leila kindly.

"One of them." Her look was defiant

"And your friends?" His eyes remained fixed on Leila.

"My brothers, Comrade Boumedienne," she corrected.

"What is your name?" He waited, then realized she was not going to answer. "Come now, you are among friends. What is your name?" He saw Leila look at Jamil questioningly. "Ah! So you are the leader of this army?" Boumedienne regarded Jamil with interest.

"I am Galal Jamil of Haifa. The woman is Leila Kemal, also from Haifa; and my friend, Khala Akbar from Nabulus."

"Well, Galal Jamil from Haifa, what do you have to say for yourself?"

"We seek asylum from the government of Algeria."

"Granted. What else?"

"No disclosure of our identities to the press or other governments in the ANM."

"Are you afraid of reprisals, my friend?" Boumedienne was curious.

"No. Capitalization on our efforts—everyone claiming to have had a share in the deed."

"Is that so bad? Think of the support," Commissioner Fibray suggested.

Jamil looked at the handsome officer and shook his head. "The support would last only until the next deed. Then everyone will disown us."

"Next time we will blow up the airplane," Leila stated flatly.

"But without the passengers." Akbar smiled. "That is planned for the third deed."

"I see." Boumedienne rubbed his chin reflectively. "I hope you do not plan on coming here to do that. I might be obliged to execute you."

"We'll bear that in mind, Mr. President," Jamil said wryly.

Boumedienne chuckled. "Do you think it will do any good?"

"For our cause, perhaps not. But for theirs it will do a lot of damage. Consider the feelings of passengers traveling on major airlines about the world, Sir. They will be wondering every time they climb aboard whether that will be the aircraft we will blow up. In time, maybe they will look behind the threat to examine the reasons for the threat. If we can accomplish that much, I will be content."

Boumedienne shook his head slowly. "You are in too big a rush, my friend. Matters such as these take time to find solutions. Remember, it took the Zionists fifty years to capture all of Palestine. You are starting only now to try and take it back." He waved his hand as Jamil started to speak. "I know. I know, you are impatient, but that does not change the circumstances. The battles of revolutions are won from within the country, never from without. The Jews won theirs because they worked from within after 1917, while your people sat by and let it happen. When you woke up, it was too late to stop. Now you think you can influence world opinion by hijacking airliners? I think you will be disappointed by the results, my friend. You will be hunted down like a dog and exterminated; and the one or two airliners you manage to wreck, or the few hundred passengers you manage to kill, will be as nothing in the overall scheme of things. The airlines will impose massive security checks. Airports will bristle with inspection stations; tens of millions will be spent, all because of you. They will never spend money to help your cause, but they will spend it to protect themselves against you, that I can promise."

The room was silent, except for the overhead fans high on the ceiling, slowly turning, stirring the damp sea air.

"You have a better suggestion, Mr. President?" Jamil asked evenly.

"I have a word—patience. More patience, and still more patience." He smiled at the disgust registering on the Palestinians' faces. "Let me tell you a story, my young friends." He paused, collecting his thoughts, looking at the ornate walls where they met the vaulted ceiling.

"In the late seventeen hundreds, two Algerian grain merchants complained to the Turkish Dey about payment shortages for some grain they had shipped to France in good faith. They wanted their money. A perfectly reasonable request." Boumedienne lowered his eyes to his guests. "Fifty years later the problem still had not been resolved. The merchants died. A new Dey assumed governorship of Algeria from the Ottomans. This new Dey, Husayn, took up the matter with the French government, again on behalf of the descendants of the two merchants. On April 30, 1827, Dey Husayn had a violent argument with the French Consul on the subject of these wheat payments, and during the course of the argument struck the Frenchman across the face with his fly whisk. That simple act was treated as an insult to the dignity of France and led to the conquest of Algeria in 1830. It took us one hundred and thirty-two years to get rid of them! Now, you tell me you are not impatient when you say you intend to dislodge the Jews a year after they have seized all your country—and you aren't even inside the country to begin the fight!"

"You suggest we give up? Go back to our refugee camps?" Leila spat the words bitterly. "Is that it? Forget about our homeland. Wait a hundred years—leave it for our grandchildren to take back?" Her fists were clenched; two brown knuckle balls. Boumedienne shrugged, then looked at the Commissioner. Fibray opened his palms, French style; resignation to inevitability. "How long do you wish to stay?"

"A few days. No more. We have passports," Jamil said.

Fibray's lips puckered. "I'm sure you have. Money?"

Jamil nodded.

"Might I suggest the Aletti Hotel?" It was an order phrased as a question. The Commissioner had the city's three deluxe hotels covered fully by his intelligence service. He was not so concerned with the trio's activities, as he was with repercussions from the actions by dissenting Palestinian factions who might arrive on the scene seeking revenge. The Cairo radio patch had embarrassed a lot of people. The implication was not lost on Jamil.

"As you wish."

Boumedienne stood up, signaling the end of the meeting. "Have any of you been to Algeria before?"

They shook their heads, as they walked towards the door. "We have a number of interesting sights to see. The Maliki Mosque dates from the eleventh century. An excellent example of early Moorish architecture, I think." He opened the door. "Then of course, there is the Fortress of the Kasbah, from where the Ottomans ruled this part of their Empire." Boumedienne smiled. "I'm sure you'll find lots to keep you amused—and out of trouble. If there is anything you need, please feel free to call on the Commissioner."

They thanked him for his hospitality and rejoined their two escorts in the hall outside. The President and his Commissioner listened to the sound of retreating footsteps.

"Around the clock surveillance, Fibray, until they leave. I want no incidents. You understand?

"Yes, Sir."

"We have sufficient idealistic fools in the city already." He shook his head sympathetically. "Poor naive children! Starting out to fight a battle when the war has ended."

"But dangerous, General."

"Yes, Fibray—very, very dangerous."

Bruner met them in the hotel dining room when they came in for supper. He had been sitting as usual, in the bar talking to an associate. Bruner had checked into the Hotel Suisse when he arrived the day before, until he located Jamil's whereabouts from Commissioner Fibray. He had told Fibray about the planned hijacking early in the morning when he was certain the Palestinians had seized the El Al flight. The information gave him access to the airport control tower, first class security treatment and permission to use the government wire service to send his unedited story scoop to New York minutes after the plane landed. He had switched rooms from the Suisse to the Aletti after another phone call to the Commissioner. He was the fair haired boy.

"Well, you did it!" Max beamed his approval. "A beautiful job."

They greeted him affectionately, noting he was a bit drunk on more than the reflected aura of their own success. They arranged themselves about one of the linen covered tables in the huge dining room, chatting animatedly. It had been several weeks since they had spoken to Bruner. During his last visit to Beirut they had given him a planned outline of their proposal for the Israeli flight from Athens. Bruner had been shocked, until he'd learned the operation was to be a demonstration of capability, rather than an example of ruthless extermination.

"You got the story out?"

"Every word—just the way we wrote it in Beirut—course I added a little of my own prose for a happy ending to clean up the loose ends. It's Pulitzer Prize stuff, Galal! B.J. will wig out when he reads it. I scooped everyone. It'll be on the streets in the States just about now—evening editions. Too bad I got scooped on the photographs."

Startled, Jamil looked up from the gilt menu. "Which photographs?"

"The three of you coming off the plane." He reached inside his jacket pocket. "Here, I've got copies." He fanned a set of four by five inch glossies across the table. They were curled slightly. Jamil dropped his menu and picked them up, examining them closely. He passed them to Akbar.

"Where did you get these, Max?"

"From a U.P. man I know. Just had a drink with him in the lobby bar. He thought I could use them on a followup story for the weekly inserts. Good stuff, huh?"

Akbar passed the packet of photos to Leila. He was not smiling. "Did you ask who took them, Max?" He clutched at Bruner's wrist. Max's eyes widened.

"Andre Beauchamp of *Match*. He's a resident photographer here. Everyone uses him. What's the problem?"

"I told you no pictures," Jamil reminded.

"I didn't take any. I can't control what U.P. decides to do, now can I?" His voice took on a slight whine.

"Where does this Beauchamp live?"

"He has a studio apartment off the Zirov; it's in his name. Second floor."

Akbar glanced at Jamil, then stood up quickly and left the table, heading for the foyer.

"The U.P. man, Max. Where can we find him?"

Bruner's eyes looked frightened. "In the bar, I guess, unless he's gone to the airport. He's on the night flight to Paris."

"Point him out to me?" Jamil stood up, Leila followed. Bruner looked at them both, started to say something, then changed his mind and got up, leading the way to the lobby bar. He scanned the dimly lit room slowly, soberly, from the doorway. "He's gone."

"Try the desk," Jamil ordered. They walked quickly across the thick carpeting to the reception desk. Bruner stopped suddenly, midstep, looking at a group of men standing in line at the cashier's window.

"Which one? Don't point, Max!"

"The one with the raincoat over his arm," Bruner said in a stage whisper.

"Take Leila back to the dining room and order dinner. I'll see you later." He walked off through the front doors and stood at the curb. A taxi from the lineup pulled towards him. He waved it away. It stopped abruptly before losing its place in line. A moment later, two men came out and signaled the cab. It pulled up to the entrance. The driver reached across the front seat to open the side door for their suitcases. As the two passengers were loading their bags, the U.P. man strolled out of the hotel to signal the next cab in line. He carried a small attache´case and overnight bag. When the second cab pulled up and stopped, Jamil opened the door, keeping his head low. The Frenchman slid into the back seat. Jamil slid in beside him.

"To the airport, driver."

The cab pulled around the first and nosed out into the street. Jamil picked up the attache´case. It was locked. He looked at the U.P. man. "Key!"

"Who are you with, if you don't mind my asking?"

"I do. The key!" The man glared at Jamil, then his eyes widened in recognition. He produced the key quickly from his trouser pocket. "I only have the prints."

Jamil popped the case and rummaged through the vertical folders. "I know." He found three sets of four by fives and a set of eight by tens. He pocketed them and snapped the case shut.

"Empty your pockets and roll up your pant legs." The man obeyed. There was another set of four by fives in his suit jacket. "Now the suitcase." The man emptied the contents. There was a set of pornographic color photos, held together with a thick rubber band. Jamil rifled through quickly, then replaced the band and handed them back. "Thank you. I am now going to get out of the cab. You will continue straight to the airport for your flight to Paris. My colleague is waiting for you. Do not attempt to phone anyone at the airport, or along the way." He jerked his thumb over his shoulder. "You are being followed." The statement was in fact true, although Jamil did not know it at the time. Two of Commissioner Fibray's bloodhounds had picked him up as he left the hotel and now were loafing along three car lengths back from the taxi. Jamil switched back to Arabic for the driver. "Pull over. I'm getting out." The man obeyed. He opened the door. "Have a nice trip to Paris."

He stood on the sidewalk watching the taxi and security tail pull back into the traffic. It was then he knew he was being followed. The man who had dropped off from the black Peugeot stood a half block away, watching him disinterestedly. Too disinterestedly to be real. Jamil began walking towards him. As he approached, the man turned his back and started to saunter slowly in the same direction.

A block later they were abreast.

"Do you have a light?" he asked the man in Arabic. The man turned. He looked like a policeman.

"No, I don't smoke. Perhaps the Kiosk on the next corner," he suggested.

"Would Commissioner Fibray object to your sharing a cab with me back to the hotel?" The man smiled.

"It was that obvious?"

Jamil hailed a taxi to curbside. The man waited until Jamil had climbed inside before joining him.

"Hotel Aletti!" The driver nodded, snapping the electric meter as he pulled away.

"Who was your friend?" the man asked.

"A newspaper reporter. I hadn't seen him for years. He's on his way to Paris tonight. I offered to accompany him part way to the airport."

The man nodded. He didn't believe a word. It made no difference; his partner would follow the cab to wherever the rendezvous had been arranged. They drove back to the hotel in silence.

Jamil rejoined Leila and Max in the dining room. Akbar had not returned. He ordered his dinner.

"Any trouble?" Leila inquired.

Jamil passed the bundle of photographs across the table to Bruner. "Nothing to speak of. I was followed. Fibray is keeping close surveillance on each of us. Max, I want you to destroy these with the ones you have." Bruner clutched them furtively and stuffed them into his jacket. "Depend on it. And the negatives?"

Jamil smiled. "Akbar will look after them." On cue, the smiling Palestinian appeared at the entrance to the dining room, paused, then joined them.

"Am I late?"

"No. I just arrived myself."

Akbar sat down and picked up the menu. Jamil saw his knuckles were skinned and bleeding lightly. "You've had an accident," he murmured.

"Yes. I bumped into one of Fibray's men near the Zirov plaza. We had a bit of a tiff. He was resting comfortably when I left."

"The pictures?"

"The Frenchman was very cooperative. I paid him one hundred U.S. dollars for all the prints and negatives. Then took the money back after. How is the lamb?"

"After what?" Bruner demanded.

"After he tried to kill me. Yes, I think I'll have the lamb." He closed the menu and signaled the waiter.

"I'm afraid I broke his neck—poor fellow. Frenchmen tend to be very emotional, don't they?"

Jamil and Akbar ordered their dinner.

"I think we should plan on leaving in the morning," Leila suggested.

"There's no rush, Leila. They won't find the body until it starts to smell. I stuffed him into the attic through the trap door in the clothes closet. It will be a few days before he starts to percolate." He grinned at Jamil. "In the meantime, let's eat. I'm famished!"

He passed the photographs and negatives to Jamil, who pushed them across the table to Bruner.

"Same thing with these, Max."

Bruner's forehead glistened with beads of perspiration. "You can depend on me, Galal!"

Akbar laughed as the waiter returned with the hors d'oeuvres. "I certainly hope so, Max." They all began eating.

11

The Cosecha Rica Consulate's office in Caracas was located on the sixth floor of the FINDEVEN S.A. building downtown. The door, across the hall from the elevators, was affixed with a brass formality, covered with fingerprints and tarnish. *Consulado de la Republica de Cosecha Rica*, it announced in bold Gothic. Underneath, someone had taped an inked message written on the back of an envelope, using the gummed flap to hold it in place: *Con cita solamente! Tel. 77-65-39.* It took Leila and Jamil three days to track down the owner of the telephone number and make their appointment for visas. The Consul turned out to be a Cosecha Rican businessman, but long time resident of Venezuela who fulfilled the consular function in honorarium. He had made his fortune in the Maricaibo district, so the periodic issuance of visas to his homeland was merely a necessary annoyance in exchange for the police immunity and C.D. license plates he enjoyed on his vehicles as a member of the local diplomatic corps. He looked at neither picture when he searched their Syrian passports for a blank page on which to stamp the visa. The charge had been ten Bolivars each.

"Have a good trip!" It had been his only comment as he ushered them out of the cubicle office and shut the door in their faces. They went back to the hotel to pack, then caught the next

285

Viasa flight to Panama, and spent the humid evening walking the streets, sightseeing until after two. A pseudo-husband-and-wife enjoying their honeymoon like normal people.

"What is that?" Leila pointed out the window of the 737 as they approached the airport at Bahia Blanca. The aircraft was paralleling the coast, crabbing slightly inland towards the runway. Jamil leaned across the seat to look at the white domed building passing under them on the point of land below.

He sat back, stunned. "It's a nuclear power plant generator!"

"I thought it was an observatory."

"No. Same sort of dome, but that dome is filled with water to provide a radiation barrier." His mind raced back to his studies at the University chemical engineering course in Germany. There had been three hours of lectures on nuclear power physics. He visualized the young square-faced lecturer extolling the class on the virtues of this unlimited power source. He had used the words deuterium, uranium, 235, or was it 237? Problems with waste products which took forever to break down. Recycling the waste to produce more fuel. Plutonium! That was the other fuel that could be produced from the uranium waste. "You can make atomic bombs from plutonium."

"What?" Leila looked at him strangely.

"Nothing. Just thinking." The aircraft flared, paused for an instant, then kissed the runway smoothly and began the ritual of engine reversers. When they slowed to turn off at the taxiway, he looked across at the familiar sights of the military hangars and barracks, newly repaired and gleaming in the morning sunlight. There was a row of De Havilland Caribou twin-engined transports and a couple of Douglas DC4's with their tail-tip rods dangling obscenely to the concrete below their fuselages. He noticed F101 fighter aircraft scattered in separate sandbagged islands about the field. The oil storage tanks were gone. *Underground?* Jamil wondered, smiling inwardly. Chirlo obviously corrected the defensive weaknesses he had exploited so successfully during Guerrero's regime. The plane stopped in front of the new terminal building. It was an expansion and further extension of the one he remembered when he had first arrived in the country six years before. Progress.

They were cleared through customs and immigration quickly, and courteously. Out front, in the reception concourse, they pushed their way through the usual mob of friends, relatives and sightseers that crowd any international airport. Jamil waved at one of the policemen for a cab. The taxis were kept back from the main entrance by police order, and left their designated area only when waved in for a fare.

"The correct fare to Bahia Blanca is four dollars. Twenty-five dollars to San Ramon—each person," the policeman informed them politely.

Jamil was surprised. "Thank you."

They climbed into the air conditioned Chrysler, and headed out of the congestion of waiting cars and waving policemen.

"How much do you charge by the hour?" Jamil used his rusty, imperfect Spanish on the driver.

"It depends."

"On what?"

"On how long you want to hire me."

"A few days."

"Very expensive."

"I'll pay the gas and give you fifty dollars each day and a full tank when I no longer need you."

"Make it sixty dollars."

"Make it forty," Jamil replied.

The driver glanced through the rear-view mirror, his eyes perplexed.

"You are supposed to say fifty-five." He saw Leila laughing. He smiled back through the mirror.

"Okay, mister, fifty dollars. Where do you want to go?"

"Tippitaca."

"It is very far."

"I'm paying the gas—remember?"

The driver grinned. "Okay, we go to Tippitaca."

"What is Tippitaca?" Leila asked curiously as they swung out onto the main highway.

"A house and a farm. The place where my formal education first started.

The cotton harvest was well underway. Another picking and it would be over for the year. The fall rains had been kind and the green bursting bolls with their long white threads were full and heavy. Chirlo loved the finca at Esperanza. It was his escape from the rigors of politics, intrigue and family life. He dropped the cheroot from the balcony railing to the ground, watching it smoke for a moment until the wind scudded it beyond his gaze. The warm breeze whipped dust devils about the workers and beyond in the vast acreage that stretched now all the way to the border of the next country where it met the cotton fields of Don Pandro Berganna. He had a mutually satisfactory arrangement for sharing equipment and labor costs with the displaced Cuban who had moved in next door. Between them they had nine thousand acres of cotton under cultivation. That Berganna was an opportunist there was no doubt, but Chirlo's Intelligence Section had given him a clean bill of health, so now he allowed himself to trust the outrageous Cuban, in addition to socializing with him.

Although Don Pandro's farming interests were in the sister Republic, he kept his house in San Ramon, preferring the cooler climate of the Cosecha Rican mountains to the sea level heat in the capital of the other Republic. The bouncy Cuban had suggested the sharing arrangements two years before when he had run out of money clearing his own land. Chirlo had financed him for the crop and labor the first year, to get him started. He had been glad to do it. Now it was paying him dividends. During the periods when work held him in San Ramon or abroad on official business, Don Pandro kept an iron grip on the Esperanza farming operation. The arbitrary way he was being treated by the Cuban had brought faithful Paco to the Presidential Palace in tears. Chirlo had soothed him and suggested he join the office staff as his personal aide. Paco turned out a much better aide than he was a cotton farmer, and peace returned to Esperanza.

From the corner of his eye he caught the movement of the horses coming down from the hills. He swung the field glasses to his eyes. Paco was explaining something to Don Affleck. The Canadian was laughing uproariously. Chirlo smiled and lowered the glasses. He should have gone with them, he decided. He enjoyed Affleck's company. He was going to miss him when he went home in the next week or two. Affleck had become one of his closest friends. If only the Americans were as cooperative with him as the Canadians! He sighed and sat down in his stuffed worn rocker, parking his boots on the railing.

"The trouble with the Americans is they're too goddamn suspicious of everyone—including themselves." He said the words aloud for emphasis.

Try as he might, he had never been able to convince them he was neither communist nor socialist, merely a dedicated nationalist trying to rebuild a looted economy which the Americans had supported while it was being looted. He could not for the life of him figure their motives. The Canadian Aid had infuriated them more. Finally, he had given up bothering to talk to either the Charge d'Affairs or the Ambassador. It was pointless wasting his time in animated discussions that led nowhere. At least Doctor Artega's application to the World Development Bank had given the country credit on a new road program for the interior. But that was as far as they would go. Everything else was cash on the barrel, although he had managed to have the antiquated telephone system replaced by the Japanese on a twenty-year financing program. *God they were efficient!* he remembered. It took exactly one hundred and twenty days from the time their two ships anchored off Bahia Blanca and the little brown men swarmed ashore in their vehicles and helicopters, to change over the country's complete phone system. They had worked three shifts around the clock, crashing into every telephone location in the country with their yellow safety hats, bowing and hissing as they yanked out the offending antiques and installed their bright new Mitsubishi replacements, then vanished as swiftly as they had come. He had been holding a conference with some village alcaldes when two of the yellow-helmeted workers had burst into the room spouting their incomprehensible idiom, ignoring security officers, while they went about their business in rewiring the Presidential office. Chirlo had laughed and waved the guards away. After watching them work, Chirlo had become convinced the whole world one day would be controlled and efficiently operated by these little brown men with their thick glasses and bulging briefcases. Best of all, after they left, the automatic telephone system worked to perfection. There had been one minor flaw at one micro-wave relay tower in the mountains where the cement based had cracked, yet even this was not the fault of the Japanese, but that of a subcontractor, who had shortchanged them on cement. It was an efficiency completely foreign to Cosecha Rica—grudgingly admired, but basically resented.

A rooster tail of dust billowed along the road toward the finca, its brown swath enveloping the field as the wind whipped it to the south. Chirlo raised his binoculars to study the vehicle. It was a black Chrysler. It stopped by the closed gate and he watched the driver climb out and open the barrier. He brought the license into focus carefully, then lowered the glasses. The license was green. A taxi plate. Curious, he got out of the rocker and went down the steps to meet the visitor. The car pulled up. The man and woman in the back seat stepped out either side of the car. Chirlo was thunderstruck.

"Jamil!" He ran to him and wrapped him in a bear hug, lifting him off his feet.

"The name is Shabiri this trip—Akmed Shabiri."

Chirlo laughed and set him back on his feet. "Why not—what's in a name?" He looked at Leila. "And this of course is Mrs. Shabiri?"

Leila came forward smiling. "Colonel Chirlo, Galal has told me about you. My name is Leila. She held out her hand. He took it, turned it gently, palm down, and kissed her fingers gallantly. Leila looked at Jamil with embarrassment.

"Where did you two come from?"

"Caracas. We're on our way home. I thought we would pass through Cosecha Rica. Leila has never been out of the Middle East, and I—well, I wanted to see what happened after I left."

He looked across the fields of cotton. "You've expanded! Even the airstrip is paved."

"The advantages of power in a land of prejudice. Come, both of you, join me in a toast! Paco will be along in a minute—he's out riding with one of our Canadian visitors. Carla!"

He called the housekeeper as he started up the stairs. Leila and Jamil followed. The taxi driver stood alongside his car dumbfounded. His passengers were friends of El Chirlo! Good friends too! What a story he would have for his wife and children! He stood in awe watching their retreating rumps disappear through the wide doorway of the hacienda.

Later, after Paco and Affleck returned, they sat down on the balcony and watched the sun sink beyond the mountains, while Carla prepared their supper. The wind had died with dusk and for a while they rekindled memories of the frantic times they'd shared in what now seemed another age. Affleck and Leila were quiet, listening to their voices.

During supper, conversation shifted to the present. Chirlo outlined the Canadian generosity for their new air force and nuclear power plant at Punta Delgado; the lack of assistance from anyone else. He shook his head.

"I don't understand it. What did fat Gaspar have that we don't?"

"Malleability?" Leila suggested. "Corruption is always malleable."

"You might be right. The Americans seem to prefer corruption in their satellites. Maybe it gives them security at home knowing there are governments more corrupt than their own."

"I think you're being too hard on our American friends. I was born in the States. We're not all that bad, really." Affleck said the words lightly.

Jamil snorted. "Oh, I agree, Mr. Affleck, you come from the most generous country in the world. It gave Eastern Europe away to the Russians. It gave Palestine away to the Jews and now it gives billions of dollars away to support the corruption in Southeast Asia and Latin America. I tell you, Colonel, when dealing with America there are only two choices—become a tyrant for them, or start a war against them; either way you can't lose."

Chirlo laughed. "I'll give it some thought, Galal. How is your battle coming against them?"

"We're not fighting Americans, just Jews."

"Isn't it the same thing? Bonds for Israel come from American Jews—Canadian Jews, too, for that matter." Affleck couldn't follow the intense dark man's logic.

"And America supports Israel," Chirlo added, spooning a mouthful of fish fillet. "Ergo—you are fighting America."

Jamil was silent.

"Exactly what do you do, Mr. Jamil?" Affleck inquired reasonably.

"I am a Palestinian terrorist!" He spat the words, his eyes challenging the polite smile with the too perfect teeth.

"How interesting—the politics of despair—as the IRA describes it. Are you achieving anything as a terrorist?"

"We have killed a lot of Jews!" Leila defended.

"Is that the object of the exercise?" Affleck asked, his fork poised. He found the fierce Palestinian and his sloe-eyed wife amusing caricatures of political cartoons which appeared from time to time in the weekend papers at home. Idealistic lunatics lunging toward destruction; either their own or everyone else's—it didn't make any difference. He could not take them seriously.

Jamil laid down his knife and fork on the table carefully. His eyes glittered like coals. "Mr. Affleck, I'm glad you find us amusing. Let me ask you a funny question. Supposing some foreign country decided to take over your homeland and everyone ordered you not to fight this invasion. Let us suppose you were told to leave your land, house, possessions—everything that was dear to you, and go away to live in another country which didn't want you—wouldn't give you a job, passport, money—nothing. So you had to starve; live in a flea-ridden hut in the middle of other flea-ridden huts with nothing to look forward to, and nothing to remember, except how you were destroyed. You have a curtain of burlap sacking separating you from your neighbor in the hut. If you're lucky—very lucky—you might have a bed. Tell me, Mr. Affleck with your beautiful smile, what would you do? Tell me! I'm interested in your advice. Your wisdom; your vast experience in righting society's international wrongs!"

Affleck's smile vanished. "I'm sorry. I didn't realize . . . ."

"Ah!" Jamil said softly, "then you are in good company. Very few people do."

He picked up his cutlery and went back to his supper. An uncomfortable silence followed the outburst. Affleck reconsidered the Palestinian in a different light. Now he was curious to learn more.

"But surely there are better ways to achieve your aims than killing Jews. Killing anyone for that matter. It seems so pointless."

"Not at all." Chirlo spoke up. "Sometimes it is the only message anyone can understand. Our case here, for example. Without a revolution, there would have been no democratic government. The legislative method was tried and failed. First, by my father-in-law, later, by me. Fat Gaspar's absolute power had corrupted him—absolutely. Violence was the only way to dislodge him. Unfortunately, many innocent people died in the process. To an outsider, looking at the situation out of context on the basis of individual incidents, the deaths would appear—as you say, Don—pointless. Acts of terror without rhyme or reason. Yet, when one stands back from these cameos of terror and examines the whole mural, it becomes obvious the cameos are an integral part of the painting." He lowered his eyes. "Forgive the artistic definition. All the same, the parallel is identical in the case of the Palestinians."

"But where does it end?" Affleck persisted.

"It ends with justice," Leila said.

"Justice for whom?"

"For whoever wins," Jamil said flatly.

"By whatever means," Chirlo added.

"But supposing, in your case, Colonel, you had lost and Guerrero had won?" Affleck argued.

"Then I would be dead."

"And that would be justice?"

"Absolutely. I would lose and die because I did not deserve to win and live. Those are the stakes in the game when you start to play."

"Then the stakes are too high."

Jamil smiled. "Then Mr. Affleck, one does not play."

Chirlo met his eyes across the table and held them for a moment in complete understanding; the teacher and the student—the successful revolutionary and the successful terrorist. They knew how the game was played. Later, after the others had gone to bed and Paco had driven off in the taxi to visit his relations in Tippitaca,

Jamil and Chirlo sat alone on the balcony with their feet up, talking and smoking. The warm air was still; the night cloudless with a velvet sky reaching to a billion winking stars. "I like your wife. She reminds me of mine. Same intensity. Children?"

"No," Jamil said.

"I have three. Twin boys and a girl."

"I envy you, Colonel."

"No you don't. You'd have children too if you wanted them."

"Not because you have children, but because your fight is over and you are able to have them.

"Ah!"

"How is Felina?"

"She is a lady in the drawing room. A maestro in the kitchen. A tyrant in the nursery and a wanton in bed." They chuckled, then fell silent for a few minutes, studying the night.

"The Doctor?"

"He has become a statesman presiding over Utopia. Just and wise. He leaves the dirty work necessary to keep the illusion constant, for me to handle. King Solomon in a den of thieves. A great man. A good man. I love him dearly."

"I always thought him to be naïve, Colonel."

"He is. But then so was God when he created man in his own image." He relit his cigar. The smoke compacted about his face, then drifted slowly across the balcony out over the yard.

"And you? Why did you come?"

Jamil considered the question. "I don't know really. An impulse perhaps. Cosecha Rica was the only success I've had so far in life. A return to the scene of triumph? Do you keep abreast of Middle East politics?"

"I know what is going on, but I'm not sure I understand it," Chirlo admitted.

Jamil gave a dry laugh. "Neither do I—or anyone else. It shifts like the sands. I have a group of good people. We work out of Beirut. But lately, for every step we take forward in victory, we wind up two steps back in defeat. I needed to get away and think."

"You the man responsible for the skyjackings?"

"Most of them. Leila and I did the first one last summer into Algeria."

"I remember reading about it. I read the Manifesto you broadcast. Impressive."

"For all the good it did, we might as well have stayed at home."

"There are many inches in a mile." He glanced across at the

Palestinian. "Is there anything I can do to help?"

He shrugged. "Within your sphere there is nothing I need—except some advice. How would you tackle the problem? Palestine, I mean."

"Does it matter?"

"I'd like to hear your opinions, as an outsider, an observer. Maybe we're too close to the situation to be objective anymore—Leila, myself and the others. No shortage of courage or dedication—only ideas on method." There was a faint arpeggio of female laughter in the high octaves drifting across the night from the workers' camp by the road. They both looked towards the blackness of the sound. The strobe lights from the TACA late flight to Panama joined the stars above the black horizon line in the distance. The noise from its jet engines floated down to them some time after the strobes had vanished among the stars.

"Text book procedures are all I can offer, Galal. Step one; use legal political methods. Step two; use terrorist incidents to gain recognition for the cause. Step three; use armed revolution when the time is ripe to overthrow the enemy on your own terms. Step four; consolidate your position after victory. Step five; relinquish your control to the Moderates to govern your successes. You're still in the middle of Step Two and there are many miles to travel.

"And even more inches!"

Chirlo chuckled. "Touché! Our problems here with Fat Gaspar were microscopic compared to what you are facing. In the larger picture, who really gave a damn about Cosecha Rica? But Israel, or Palestine; much different. Everyone is involved. Every Jew in every country in the world. Every Arab everywhere is involved; the Big Powers as well. It's a huge spider web. Palestine, in the center and all the strands spinning out to various interests, real or imagined. Pluck one thread and they all begin to vibrate. You are looking for a method of cutting all the strands simultaneously and running off with the prize. The only way it can be done, my friend, is by making those that hold the strands drop them of their own choice, either through desire or fear. But, as each of them have different reasons for wanting to keep their thread intact, you will have to find a reason acceptable to all. One that each can understand because it is to his own best interests. That brings it down to one of two factors; economics, or fear of destruction."

"Or both," Jamil mused.

"And you're not going to do it by hijacking airliners."

"Agreed."

Chirlo stood up. "Let me think on the alternatives." He flipped his cigar over the balcony. "I have agreed to fly Affleck back to Punta Delgado in the morning for a meeting. Why don't you come with us. It should only take a couple of hours, then we can continue on to San Ramon. Besides, you might like to see our new nuclear generating plant."

"I'll send the taxi off in the morning. Thank you."

"Goodnight, Colonel."

The air force light twin Aztec landed for them at La Esperanza next morning during breakfast. The five of them climbed into the blue and white machine and took off towards Bahia Blanca. Chirlo, sitting in the front seat with the young pilot, had an arm draped across the Captain's seat. He spent the whole trip across the country listening and talking to the young officer in low tones. Jamil noticed the Colonel still had the golden touch when dealing with his subalterns.

They bypassed the international airport, swinging out to sea, then curved back towards the land and began a slow approach to the short paved airstrip beside the nuclear plant. The pilot had the small craft stopped in less than three hundred yards. They taxied to the end and parked along the side of the runway. The small propellors jerked to a stop. Chirlo opened the door, clambered out on the wing and jumped to the ground. The others joined him. It was a short walk to the administration building. A group of seven men came out of the doors of the white concrete stucco headquarters. One of them waved. Chirlo waved back.

"Don, why don't you find someone to show Galal and Leila around the place for a couple of hours while we have our meeting," Chirlo suggested.

"Sure thing, Colonel. I'll get one of the boys from Methods. Full VIP treatment."

Paco, Leila and Jamil hung back as Affleck and Chirlo greeted the five men who had come out to meet them. Everyone was speaking English. Jamil turned to Paco, the faithful shadow, who had never learned the language. Out of courtesy to Affleck and Leila, Chirlo had been conducting all conversations in English, leaving Paco to guess what was being said. Jamil addressed him in his broken Spanish.

"You must get tired of listening to that idiom, Paco!"

"No, Senor Jamil, it is much like background noise with a radio. No one listens to it unless it is speaking to them." He smiled, but his eyes remained fixed on the movements of his Colonel. The group began to move into the building. Paco bowed slightly. "Con permiso," he said and left to follow them, in case he was needed. Another two hours of background noise from the English radio. Leila and Jamil strolled towards the domed plant.

"How does it work? What does it do, Galal?"

"Produces electricity by heating steam with an atomic pile. Nuclear fission."

"Like an atomic bomb?"

"Almost—more like a slow burning atomic bomb. The fission is controlled."

"Do you know how it works?"

"I know the principle of how it works, but not the mechanics." They both turned as a voice called out behind them. A man in a white pharmacist's jacket waved. Jamil returned it and waited until the man had jogged up to join them.

"You Mr. and Mrs. Shabiri?"

They nodded.

"Thought so. I'm Norm Pinder, your tour guide. Hi!"

"How do you do, Mr. Pinder." They shook hands. The man's face was sunburned, his nose peeling slightly. He had a row of pencils clipped to a plastic sheath on his breast pocket.

"Ever been through a Nuke before?" he inquired.

The Shabiris shook their heads in unison. The man nodded. The information appeared to satisfy him. His blue eyes, surrounded by their sun squint, sized up the two visitors. He disliked VIP tours with people who professed technical knowledge and invariably turned out to know nothing on the subject. The Shabiris would be a change from the normal gawkers who had infested the place since the plant went into operation the previous year.

"Fine, then I'll give you the full treatment. Mr. Affleck said we have two hours, so we'd better get started. There's quite a bit to see."

They walked towards the building while Pinder started on the basics of nuclear fission. Jamil's heart was racing with anticipation, but his face remained masked with the normal curiosity of the uniformed. Leila listened attentively. After an hour and a half they had covered the control rooms, reactor, calandria, turbines and the generators whining smoothly in the center of their concrete beds. Pinder led them through a safety door into a glass-walled corridor and stopped.

"This is the primary cooling pool for our waste. Pretty, isn't it?"

They looked through the thick glass to the big olympic sized pool glowing an eerie green beneath its still water.

"The waste rods—you remember these bundles of fuel rods that were put into the face of the reactor?"

"The thing that looked like a honeycomb?" Leila asked.

"That's it! Well, there's an automatic unloading device on the other side of that honeycomb for removing the used fuel bundles. They are transferred through a shielded pipe to this pool. The bundles are hot, but the water and concrete sides in the pool contain the radiation and heat until the bundles have cooled enough to remove them to permanent storage or for recycling." They walked along the corridor to the middle of the pool and stopped, peering into the depths. "How long does it take them to cool before you can move them again?"

"Not long. A few years," Pinder told them.

"Ten?" Jamil persisted.

"Oh no. Not that long. Two or three years and we should be ready to move the first bundles over to the long term storage facility."

"How many bundles do you use each year?" Leila asked.

"Five bundles per day—one hundred and fifty each month."

"That's a lot of waste!" Jamil exclaimed.

Pinder disagreed. "Not really. You have to compare it to fossil fuel for a realistic comparison. For example, back home in Canada it takes two tons of coal to produce enough electricity for the average house each year. The waste ash after burning the coal amounts to 200 pounds. One hundred and forty one grams of uranium oxide pellets in those fuel bundles will do the same thing with less than two grams of radioactive waste. That's not so bad, is it?" He regarded them questioningly.

"How much of that waste is plutonium?" Jamil asked off-handedly.

"Oh, you know about plutonium! Interesting stuff. Discovered by an American in 1940—he won the Nobel Prize for it—it's heavier than uranium. Very lethal. There's some thought to using it as a fuel in the future, after it's extracted from the waste. We get about a half gram of the stuff in the waste from that one hundred and forty one grams of uranium pellets. Not much."

They moved on down the corridor and back outside through a rear door. From the second story balcony Pinder pointed out the thermal discharge building on the shore a few hundred yards away. In the sun, his eyes receded once more behind his squint.

297

"We use ordinary seawater for cooling. We suck water in on this side of the point, pipe it through the cooling system, then discharge it over on the other side—there!" He pointed. "You can see the eddies out a way. The intake and outlet pipes are a thousand feet offshore. The water temperature is twenty degrees higher after being cycled through the plant. Doesn't appear to bother the fish, though—at least the local fishermen haven't complained."

They went back inside and returned to the main reception area to turn in their white coats, radiation badges and plastic safety helmets. On the way to the administration building, Jamil pointed to a set of narrow tracks leading from the back of the plant. "You have a railway, Mr. Pinder?"

"A small one—three and a half miles of track is all. It hasn't been used yet. It runs from the cooling pools out to the permanent storage area further up the coast. When our first bundles are cool enough next year, we'll be moving them in their containers out to the new storage area."

They continued walking, passing the edge of the runway. The air force captain was sitting on the wing of the Aztec smoking a cigarette. He gave them a casual wave.

"What will happen to them after that?"

Pinder shrugged. "Hard to say. Originally the plan was to fly all waste back to Canada for intermediate and long term storage. Now they've decided to leave the intermediate storage down here. I guess the reason is because no one knows what the best method for long-term storage will be. Then, if a decision is made to extract the plutonium for fuel, the waste would all have to be reprocessed anyway. They might even set up a reprocessing plant down here to do it."

"Is that practical?" Jamil inquired.

"Sure. Why not? Not much sense lugging the stuff back to Canada if you could clean the whole thing up here."

They climbed the two broad steps into the building and went through the glass doors.

"No," Jamil said, "not much sense at all, Mr. Pinder."

They sat down in the green vinyl chairs in the waiting room while Pinder went off to find out if the meeting had ended.

Chirlo's home was at the top of a winding private road which snaked up from the cluster of elegant Spanish style residences in the hills that edged the city. Originally built by a demented millionaire after his escape from political retribution in one of the neighboring republics during the middle thirties, the house had an unusual style of architecture. It was constructed in three separate, interconnecting buildings, perched on different levels. The outside walls were solid mahogany logs, which, at the six thousand foot altitude, blended admirably with the tall statuesque pines scattering the hillsides. The place had been abandoned, then looted after the death of its former resident. The oiled gravel road had been rutted by horizontal rain washes over the years, so that eventually even the curious had ignored the strange dwelling. In the end, the government had taken ownership of the property through tax default when the owner's descendants, now living in Uruguay, had shown a singular lack of interest in paying anything towards the maintenance of their own property rights.

The Colonia Bolivar development, seventeen hundred feet below the abandoned triumverant of mahogany, started in the early Fifties to accommodate the country's newly-emerging middle class merchants and professional men who desired something better than the four hundred year old city architecture in which to live. Although a part of San Ramon from a taxation standpoint, residents in the Colonia provided their own services for hydro, water and sewage through private subscription. Modern comforts bordering the discomforts of antiquity. The diplomatic corps, senior government officials and the well-to-do shared this modern paradise. Doctor Artega and Ruiz moved in to Guerrero's palatial estate in the Colonia after paying the Colonel's widow a fair market price. He had suggested Chirlo and his daughter move into the Cadalso house directly across the street, after the major and his associates had been executed for treason. Chirlo examined the property and vetoed the idea. For a few months he had lived with is father-in-law, until one afternoon, while out testing a new helicopter the Bell people were trying to sell him for executive transport, he noticed the development on the hills above the Colonia. He had asked the pilot to land on the overgrown grass yard between the trio of low buildings. It was a tight fit, but the Jet Ranger had settled into the front of the littered yard like a feather, flattening the tall grass in waves and flinging paper litter down the slopes to Colonia Bolivar.

The Texan pilot toured the log home with its broken windows, following Chirlo as he explored the place. Afterwards they stood to their knees in the grass, looking out over the city to the mountains beyond, which slid hazily towards the sea.

"The Eagle's Lair!" The pilot exclaimed at the panoramic view below.

"It looks like the house was moved in here by Skycrane from Oregon."

"Or from Canada," Chirlo thought aloud deciding then and there it would be his home.

Workmen started on it the next day so that by the time he and Felina had returned from their honeymoon with the furnishings, it was finished, complete with a newly-paved private road beginning at the Colonia Bolivar and ending at the wide driveway in front of the four-car garage. At first, Doctor Artega had thought the pair of them insane, but later, after visiting the completed work, changed his mind and agreed it suited them. When the twins arrived, the old man had visions of his two grandsons rolling down the hill to the Colonia while playing outdoors, and bothered everyone daily with emergency phone calls to check on the toddlers' whereabouts until Chirlo hired two young men from the military police to provide surveillance on the children. The President of Cosecha Rica relaxed. The anxious phone calls ceased.

Felina was sitting on the front lawn watching the children tumble about the manicured grass when they drove up to the parking lot. Jamil spied her when they got out of the car. He waved and she waved back. She stood up as they climbed the stone steps to the lawn and gardens. The three children paused in their games to watch the new arrivals, then rushed to Chirlo, shrieking with delight. He caught them at the top of the steps and hugged them to him, laughing joyfully. Everyone was smothered with kisses and introduced to Leila and Jamil. The children clung to Chirlo's pantlegs, uncertain in their shyness. The nursemaid came and took them back to their games, clucking mild admonishments at their shyness. The game resumed with a whoop as Felina held out her arms to Jamil and hugged him tightly.

"Oh Galal! It's so good to see you again. We tried to find you when we were in Europe, but they said you had moved from Amman."

Jamil kissed her Latin fashion, on both cheeks, and stood back, smiling. "This is Leila," he said.

The two of them measured each other, deciding in that moment of female intuition that neither was a threat to the other. The ice melted as Felina hugged her. "Welcome to Cosecha Rica, Leila."

"Paco!" Chirlo switched to Spanish. "See if you can reach Don Pedro and Senor Ruis. Ask them to join us for dinner."

"The President is having dinner tonight with the Mexican Ambassador and his wife, Colonel," Paco reminded. "You and Dona

Felina are supposed to attend."

Chirlo struck his forehead with his palm. "Of course. I forgot." He thought a moment. "Then ask them all to join us here. We haven't used the big dining room in ages. If they agree, call the Officers Mess at El Tigre. Have them send up the necessary men and food. Wines too."

Paco nodded, and headed off for the lower of the three houses which served as a patio, study, reception area and living room for the other two log buildings step-terraced above them.

Felina linked arms with Jamil and Leila, walking them back to the lawn chairs. "We thought you had forgotten us. Where have you been hiding?"

Everyone arranged themselves in a semi-circle facing the view. The mid-afternoon sun had started its dance of shadow tones among the orange and green across the valley to the purple mountains.

"Forget you?" Jamil said. "How could I forget? They were exciting times."

"Have you eaten?"

"At the Officers Club on the way home," Chirlo told her. He signaled the childrens' nurse. "Ask Anita to bring some coffee. I'll watch the children."

The nurse departed for the house.

"Is Anita still with you?" Jamil asked.

"And married to our gardener. You wouldn't recognize her now."

"I remember the night we all arrived for the first time at the house in Tippitaca; Paco and Anita trying to understand our English—we trying to understand their Spanish."

"I thought I gave you a letter of instructions for them," Chirlo recalled.

"You did, but I couldn't read the letter to know what you'd told them." Leila smiled. They all laughed. "Cunning revolutionaries. Everyone so secret no one knows what is going on! It sounds like a meeting of the Arab League."

"It wasn't quite as bad as that," Jamil said.

"Well, never mind the memories, what are you doing now, or should I ask?" Felina demanded.

"Officially, we are on our honeymoon. Unofficially, we went to Venezuela to visit some friends to the Cause in Caracas," Jamil explained.

"The Cause?"

"The World Revolutionary Cause. They have been doing some

interesting things in this part of the world."

"I didn't know there was an underground movement in Venezuela," Chirlo said. "There is an underground movement everywhere; probably one here in San Ramon, too, if you look deep enough," Leila suggested.

Chirlo smiled. He knew she was quite right. There was always a lunatic fringe from the university howling about the lack of freedoms under the new government. President Artega had been hissed and booed at graduation exercises the month before for being too soft on fascists within the government. A few years before, students had booed Guerrero for being too soft on communism. He found the paradox amusing, although to the doctor the whole affair had been unnerving and beyond comprehension.

"Those responsible should be arrested, my boy. Rabble! That's all they are. Rabble!"

Chirlo had already received a full report from the security men who had attended the graduation and knew there had been no violence or missiles flung at the little doctor.

"What about your promises on freedom of speech, Papa?" he inquired.

"What about them? I've kept them! There is freedom of speech, but I don't think it should be that free!" But the point had been made.

The doctor regarded Leila in amusement. "You're quite right. Yet, that is the price of power in a democratic society, or any society for that matter. There is always a small hardcore group of idealists who are satisfied with nothing less than anarchy. In enlightened societies, they are placed in mental hospitals, where their Napoleon complexes can be treated. If they become violent, they are arrested, tried, convicted and sent to prison to cool off for a while."

"What happens to them here?" Leila demanded.

"At present, nothing."

"You are very tolerant."

"Not at all, they haven't done anything yet except talk and write hate literature, which no one takes seriously anyway. If they become violent, then that is something else."

"Would you arrest them?" Jamil inquired.

"If they had committed a crime, yes. Criticism is not a crime here anymore. Violence still is." Chirlo could see where the conversation was leading.

Jamil smiled. "Like attempting to overthrow the government by force." Everyone laughed. The Palestinian shook his head. "Colonel, you have crossed the river to meet the enemy and found the enemy is you."

"Fidel Castro said the same thing to me once in Havana when I asked him for help, only he used different words. He said, 'You will learn the Revolution is never over.'" Chirlo observed soberly, then smiled. "I didn't know what he meant then. I do now."

Anita arrived with a tray of coffee cups. They rattled on their saucers as she set them on the table. She smiled shyly at Jamil. "Que tal, Anita?"

Jamil noticed she had filled out into a beautiful woman. The white uniform with the ruffled balloon sleeves accentuated her bust, full ripe melons. Married life appeared to be agreeing with her.

"Donde esta los ninos?" he inquired.

Anita blushed. "Una dia, Senor Jamil."

He knew when the ninos came her figure would turn as all other Latin women; thick and gross. Female beauty had a cut-off point somewhere between twenty-five and thirty. Felina was the exception. She had grown thinner. Jamil introduced the girl to his wife. An older man in a green jacket arrived with another tray, carrying the coffee. Anita arranged the cups and left with the older man.

"This, by the way, is grown here in Cosecha Rica—grown back in the mountains," Felina announced as she poured.

Jamil sipped it tentatively. It was of poor quality, slightly bitter in after taste. "It has a bite," he announced.

"Which means?" Chirlo asked.

"Which means he doesn't like it," Leila confirmed. "Galal, surely you drank it when you were here before?"

"Never," he said emphatically. "We got all our coffee supplied from Guerrero's stores, didn't we Colonel? It was either Colombian or Salvadorian grown."

"Nothing but the best for the revolution." Felina laughed. "How times have changed. Now our austerity programs have taxes so high on imports we all have to drink our own stuff."

"Why the austerity program?" Jamil was curious. Everything looked prosperous in the city.

"It's a matter of economics," Chirlo explained. "Our money was pegged to the American dollar during Guerrero's regime. Free exchange. In actual fact we were running horrible deficits, but the Americans covered them for us. Now, we are on our own.

"Our currency is as good as our reserve, and we have no reserves. What Guerrero didn't steal, the Americans held back in payment of what was owing them. Now the value of our money has shrunk two hundred percent. Many businessmen will not accept the Bolivar at all, only American dollars. So we have put the cost of imports so high on luxury items and non-essentials, people will keep the foreign exchange here. In this way, we will rebuild our reserves gradually to a point where the currency will stabilize and we can balance our foreign exchange between imports and exports. It's starting to work, but it takes time." He grinned lopsidedly at the Palestinian. "You will learn that after the victory the real battle has just begun."

Paco returned to join them on the lawn. "The President and Senor Ruiz will serve cocktails to the Ambassador and his wife first, then continue here at 8:00 p.m. I have made the arrangements with Major Utero at the Officers Mess. His men will be here at 6:30."

"Thank you, Paco. Make sure the cars are parked in the garage and the Major sends the truck back before the guests arrive." Parking on the hillside was always a problem in the confined area available for visitors.

"Si, Colonel." Paco sat down, accepting a cup of coffee from Felina.

They fell silent, watching the shadows deepening in the city below them. It was very peaceful sitting on the cool lawn listening to the busy birds in the pines and watching the children playing.

The meeting had gone off well, Affleck decided, as he said goodbye to the others and left for home. Chirlo had signed the amended safeguard agreements without a murmur after reading them through. The addition of the intermediate storage site required an additional safeguard agreement, but, Affleck thought, it should have been done at the beginning of the project—not the end. "Typical bureaucratic forgetfulness!" Chirlo had smiled his peculiar smile after reading the lengthy, legal-sized package of paper.

"I see this is dated from when you started work in 1967, Don. Are the Canadian mails that slow?"

The Atomic Energy of Canada Limited officials had laughed uncomfortably. "What will you do if I don't sign, tear everything out?"

The laughter had stopped abruptly. Only Affleck knew he had been joking.

He turned on to the new highway past the gatehouse, and pressed the gas pedal for Bahia Blanca. He knew he would be leaving in a matter of days now that the safeguard agreements were completed. His job was over. Still mid-summer, and he was going home! There was only the problem of Rina to settle before he left.

Thus far, his little spitfire mistress was unaware of his approaching departure for Canada. It was an awkward situation, much the same as the Pakistani girl he had left behind in Rajastan. She had accepted the termination of their affair with typical Eastern stoicism. Rina, on the other hand, had never embraced the stoic philosophy on anything. He swung past the work bus from the plant, filled with laborers returning home. It had left a few minutes before his meetings had ended. They waved at him as he passed. The driver sounded his big claxon. Affleck beeped back weakly on the horn of the British built Ford.

He stopped at the post office to check his box. There was a letter from Elizabeth. He kicked the box shut with his toe and stuffed the letter into his hip pocket. He could read it later, he decided, when the confrontation with Rina had been settled. He nodded affably to a couple of local shopkeepers standing in the line at the timbres wicket on his way out to the street. Over the two years he had been living in town, he had come to know everyone on a nodding basis, from the fat pompous Alcalde to the street urchins, with their bundles of rags, prepared to shine anything from shoes to a car windshield for ten centavos. He liked them all and they liked him.

"Hey! Meester Affleck, how abouta shine?" There was a group of five ragamuffins in tattered pants with dirty T-shirts standing in front of his car. They were all smiling with anticipation.

"Whose turn is it today?" he demanded, searching his pockets for coins. The ragged cherubs looked at each other, deciding.

"Miguel—it's Miguel's, Meester Affleck!" the rest agreed. He flipped the urchin a coin. The boy caught it expertly and with a grin went to work on the car's glasswork; headlights first, then side windows—finally the windshield. The rest watched critically, offering comments when he missed a dried bug squashed on the passenger side, and overlooked the rear window completely. When the child had finished, Affleck thanked him and waved them all goodbye.

Rina was waiting for him at the front gate when he arrived home. She flung herself into his arms, then grabbed his briefcase and pulled him into the screened veranda, chattering like a magpie. He removed his jacket and handed it to her, then swung onto the string hammock that stretched from the door post to the corner of the house behind the enclosed screen. She had bought the hammock in Salvador when they had gone to La Libertad for a holiday. He strung it up on the veranda for a joke, then, encased in the white string cocoon, sipping an ice cold beer shandy, discovered he enjoyed its relaxing motion at the end of his workday. Rina, still chattering, disappeared into the house to get his drink, and hang up his jacket. He began a slow swing, wiggling his butt, pushing the floor with the leg he had left draped out the side for locomotion. The problem with Rina careened through his mind. He started forming plausible, reasonable explanations why it would be impossible for her to return with him to Ottawa.

Affleck had met Rina de Felipe the day he arrived in the country. She was handling the Hertz reservations desk at the airport and, bubbling with enthusiasm, told him the four available cars were already out, but might be back the following week. She looked like a Hertz magazine advertisement, standing behind the counter in her spiffy yellow uniform.

"But I have reservations!" he protested to the pair of wide brown eyes.

"You did?" She examined his face with polite concern. Her English had a musical lilt. She searched the pile of papers in the cubbyhole behind the counter, then straightened up brightly. "Is your name Richards?"

"No, Affleck, Donald Affleck. I already told you. Donald Affleck from Canada."

"I've never been to Canada. Is it nice?"

"Just great—do I get a car?"

"Where are you staying?" she countered.

"I don't know yet—why?"

"In Bahia Blanca?"

"San Ramon first, Bahia Blanca later."

"Oh good! No one ever wants to stay in Bahia Blanca. Personally, I like living here. You'd like it too. When are you moving in? If you need any help with a house I have a friend who knows a man who has moved to the States and his house is for rent. Nice house. Would you like me to talk to my friend, Mr. Richards?"

Affleck noticed her for the first time as a person instead of an object behind the counter. He smiled at her earnestness, momentarily forgetting the car.

"Perhaps later. I don't know when I'll be moving down here 'till I've spoken to some people in San Ramon." He gave her his name and the address where he could be reached through the Canadian Embassy, then took a taxi to the Capital.

She tracked him down next day at the hotel after his meetings with Chirlo and the pompous young Commercial Secretary from the Embassy. With the telephone connection from the airport, her voice was barely audible.

"Mr. Affleck, this is Rina de Felipe from Hertz. Hello!"

"Oh yes, Miss Felipe—did you find me a car?" He had to pause a moment while some furious static subsided.

"A car?" Pause. "Oh! No, I still have no cars, but I did talk to my friend about the house, if you're still interested."

"I don't remember saying that I was, Miss Felipe." More line crackling.

"Good! I'm off for two days so I'll take the bus up tonight. See you later, Mr. Affleck."

Mystified, he dropped the squawking receiver in its cradle and stared at the instrument with disbelief.

She bounced into the dining room while he was eating supper and sat down, announcing she was famished. He ordered another meal, then noticed she had brought a small airline overnight bag with her, which she plunked unceremoniously on the floor beside the chair. She had changed into mufti and the light cotton dress fitted snugly—too snugly in places, he thought.

"Did anyone tell you that you have a pretty smile, Mr. Affleck?" Without waiting for him to reply, she continued, "I told my friend about your smile. She said she was sure you could rent the house."

"Because of my smile?" he laughed. The girl was incredible. She looked at him seriously. "It's true!" Affleck was sure it was.

"Do you have relatives in San Ramon?"

"Oh, many relatives—friends too. How did you enjoy your meetings? Were they important people. Were they nice?"

Affleck considered the contrast between Chirlo and the Commercial Secretary. "They were certainly different." The waiter brought her food. Affleck ordered a second cup of coffee and sat back watching her devour her meal.

"Don't you put on weight?"

"Never." Her mouth was full. She swallowed. "When I was a little girl I was fat. Now I'm thin. I think I'll stay thin." She forked in another mouthful, her eyes dancing.

"You're not that thin, Miss Felipe; just thin in the right places."

She swallowed again. "But fat in the breasts, right?" She inhaled deeply, thrusting her chest out, straining the thin cotton dress. "I have nice breasts, don't you think? Big nipples too—I'll show you later. Do you like big nipples?" Her eyes were guileless.

Affleck felt himself blushing and glancing around to see who else was listening to their extraordinary conversation. The other occupied tables were out of earshot.

"Oh sure. Doesn't everyone?"

She considered the question, her fork poised above the flattening mound of food on her plate. "I don't think so. I had a friend—Charlie—a pilot on TACA—he lived in New Orleans—he said they were too long." She filled her mouth again.

"Too long?" He had to await another swallow for the reply.

"When he kissed them or sucked them, they grew even longer. You'll see!" She smiled at him mischievously. "Do you think I'm terrible?"

"No, not terrible; perhaps a bit unusual. Do you always follow your customers up to San Ramon and join them for dinner?"

"Never!" she said emphatically. "Only once before when I first started work at the airport. He was a Colombian coffee broker with beautiful eyes, like a sleepy dog."

"Bedroom eyes."

"No, like a sleepy dog."

"What happened?"

"Nothing. We had dinner, then I changed my mind about him. He had dirty fingernails. I hate men with dirty fingernails, don't you?"

Affleck glanced at his fingernails automatically. They were clean and well-manicured. She watched his quick examination with amusement. "You have clean fingernails, Mr. Affleck. I checked them at the airport."

She giggled and slipped another mouthful between her lips. She finished off the main course, a side order of fruit salad and an ice cream compote, before announcing she was filled, all the while keeping up a light, provocative, but mindless conversation on every subject that happened to occur to her. Affleck sat watching, certain the whole thing was a put-on; that at some appropriate moment she would jump to her feet, yell "Sucker" to the dining room at large, and race back to the airport. She plucked the napkin from her lap and wiped it daintily across her full lips, then proceeded to fold it carefully and lay it alongside the supper debris littering the table.

"I am finished, Mr. Affleck. It was very good. Thank you. Now we must both walk to settle our food before going to bed. It is not good to go to bed with a full stomach." She stood up and signaled for the bill.

"Why?"

"Gas," she replied mysteriously.

He signed the check with his room number and followed her

308

out of the dining room. She dropped her shoulder bag off at the desk with tart instructions for its safekeeping.

After they returned from their walk around the square, she had shed her clothing the moment Affleck closed the door to the hotel room. She stood smiling at him invitingly, arms outstretched, tawny skin glowing in the soft light, then threw herself at him, biting and chewing in a fury of passion. She had torn his jacket and ripped the seam of his pants at the crotch, yanking off his clothes, then pushed him to the floor and mounted him in a frenzy, thumping his buttocks into the coarse weave of the carpet. She screamed with delighted anguish during her multiple orgasms which seemed to last forever, then collapsed on top of him, exhausted. The whole affair had taken less than five minutes, Affleck remembered, and he had just begun to get into the spirit of the thing himself, when it was over. It was a switch. However, she had been quite right, he decided; she did have lovely long nipples.

Afterwards, Rina became his official mistress—unofficially. In due course, they set up housekeeping at the rented casa in Bahia Blanca. From time-to-time he had toyed with the idea of making it a permanent arrangement, taking her back with him as a wife when he returned, but always, before making the vocal commitment, backed away for one reason or another. Now the time had come to decide.

She returned from the kitchen and handed him his Shandy, still chattering away like the background noise in a penny arcade. "Rina, I want to talk to you seriously."

He took the tall cold glass from her outstretched hand and looked at her severely. She paused in mid-sentence, leaving her mouth open with surprise, waiting. Affleck sipped the drink, dribbling a little on his chin from his supine position in the hammock.

"I'm going back to Canada next Wednesday," he announced. "For good. I won't be coming back."

She leaped at him with a squeal of delight, spilling the glass across his shirt, smothering him with kisses. "Oh Donee! How wonderful!" The glass smashed to the floor. She swung herself onto him, arching her body backwards to accommodate the hammock's curve, and began squirming against him, rubbing his groin with her pelvis.

"We'll have to get married right away, won't we?" He felt his erection rising to meet the squirming flesh, as her fingers slipped between them to find his zipper.

Oh what th'hell, Affleck thought, then aloud, turning his face from her hungry lips a moment, said, "See if you can get Father Gomez to marry us on Saturday." He turned his attentions to the awkward work at hand.

Paco slipped into the office, nodded politely to the four men seated in front of the massive desk, and walked around to whisper to Chirlo.

"The President would like to see you as soon as possible, Colonel. The Americans are being difficult again."

Chirlo nodded. "I'm afraid I'll have to terminate our meeting now, gentlemen. The President wishes to speak to me." He stood up. The four men rose from their chairs together.

"But you do agree in principle to our demands." They were union leaders, representing the plantation workers. The spokesman was a young lawyer who had taken his labor training at the University of Chicago. Chirlo smiled. "I make it a policy never to agree to demands from anyone except my wife or father-in-law. Requests, I am always ready to consider on their merit. Now, if you will excuse me."

He left them looking at each other perplexed. Paco followed him out the door, then stood outside waiting for the union quartet to vacate the premises. He disliked all of them, particularly the lawyer, Munoz, who had never done a day's work in his entire life and now had the gall to set himself up as the savior for the country's banana workers. He watched them leave, his face impassive, listening to Munoz telling the other three semi-literate unionists in a smooth voice how no government could stand in the way of social progress for the workers. The comments, Paco knew, were for his ears and to be passed on to Chirlo. He shut the door, and went across the hall to the President's office, knocked lightly and entered. The argument had already started when he walked in.

Theodore Ranklin, president of Consolidated Fruit Company, was stating his company's position, sarcastically.

"In case everyone has forgotten, Consolidated produces sixty-two percent of your entire foreign exchange. Anything that hurts Consolidated is going to hurt you. So let's stop talking about the rights of these goddamn bandits and get down to cases, shall we?"

He was a grey, angry man with steel rimmed glasses holding square panes in much the same fashion the white suit encased his own stocky frame. Chirlo sat relaxed, his chair swivelled slightly towards the antagonists. Ranklin was flanked by the U.S. Ambassador and his secretary on one side, the Vice-President of Consolidated's field operations and his under-assistant on the other. Dr. Artega sat alone behind the presidential desk. It was obvious they had come to intimidate the old man.

"You don't think the workers have any rights, is that it, Mr. Ranklin?"

"Listen Colonel, we have operations in Panama, Honduras and Ecuador with less problems in a whole year than we have here in a week, and this is our smallest banana acreage!"

"It sounds as if your operations here are creating huge economic losses to the company."

"You're goddamn right they are, Colonel!"

"Then I would suggest you close down and move elsewhere. I would hate to see good corporate citizens such as Consolidated Fruit being victimized through their own generosity."

Artega coughed uncomfortably. It wasn't what he had in mind at all. Everyone looked at Chirlo with surprise. "Are you serious, Colonel?"

"Quite serious, Mr. Ranklin."

"But we've been here for a hundred years—we put this country on the map—hell, we built it!"

"All good things must end one day, Mr. Ranklin," Chirlo said quietly.

"I think what Mr. Ranklin means, Colonel, is there's a distinct danger the company will be unable to compete in world markets if it is forced to bow to the workers' demands, which seems perfectly understandable," the Ambassador cut in smoothly. His voice had a calming affect on Ranklin.

"That's it! Exactly. Costs go up, markets fall to adjust to the upward spiral and the competition moves in to fill the gap."

Everyone nodded in harmony.

"What competition?" Chirlo countered. "I understood from your last annual report Consolidated Fruit controls seventy-two percent of the market—that sounds like a monopoly to me."

"Only the North American market, Colonel, only the North American market. In Europe we are under twenty percent."

"You have my sympathy." He looked at them all with disbelief. The frail Cosecha Rican economy depended on their banana exports, and huge profits Consolidated Fruit reaped from their vast plantation along the coast. He knew their profits were staggering and the workers of the tiny Republic the only group in the company's chain of plantations throughout Latin America which had thus far failed to unionize. They were the lowest paid; the poorest of the lot.

"What are you proposing, Mr. Ranklin?"

"I want this union business stopped—stopped once and for all. If these birds want a union the company will organize one for them—hell, we have a Society of Banana workers now. They are already represented. We listen to their grievances every meeting, don't we, Bill?"

Bill nodded hurriedly and confirmed, "Every week, Mr. Ranklin."

"So you see, Colonel, it's already being taken care of. Consolidated always takes care of its own—has for a hundred years." He bared his capped bullet teeth in a smile.

Chirlo was unimpressed. "This is a free country, Mr. Ranklin. If your workers want to have a union, there is nothing to prevent them from doing so as long as they do not break the law in the process. The difference between your Society and their Union should be obvious. The Society is yours—the union would be theirs. I cannot sympathize with your position on production costs, but you are quite correct on the country's need for your taxes and foreign exchange. However, although I do not profess to be a businessman, it seems your best course of action under the circumstances would be to try and operate your local company responsibilities on a more efficient basis in order to save costs, to pay the extra wages you will need for the workers in order to avert a strike. Failing this, I'd suggest considering cost equalization accounting for banana production between here and your other countries of operation—sort of bookkeeping equalization for costing purposes. If this is too impractical, then you have only one alternative—pull out. We will be sorry to see you go, of course, but I'm sure we will survive."

The room was silent for a long minute.

Finally, the Ambassador spoke up. "I see. That is your final word, Colonel?"

Chirlo looked at Artega for the reply. Final authority lay with the President. "Yes, Mr. Collins. I think that is the last word on the subject," Artega said.

Ranklin jumped up. "This may mean the end of Consolidated Fruit in Cosecha Rica, Mr. President. You know what that could mean?"

"That the government would be going into the banana export business?" he asked blandly. "I understand there are several openings in the European market not being covered at present." He bowed his head slightly as the rest of them stood to leave. Paco opened the door. Ranklin left at the head of the procession.

"Was that wise, my boy? Don't misunderstand—I agree with you, but couldn't you have phrased it a little more kindly?"

Chirlo shrugged and thrust his hands deep in his pockets. "The subject who is truly loyal to the Chief Magistrate will neither advise nor submit to arbitrary measures."

His father-in-law looked at him closely, thinking. "Cicero? No—wait, don't tell me. I've got it. Plutarch!"

Chirlo shook his head. "Sorry Papa. It was Junius. It's as true today as it was in ancient Rome."

"What did Munoz and his workers tell you?"

"The reverse of what Ranklin told you." Chirlo paced slowly back and forth across the front of Artega's desk.

"And the truth of each position lies somewhere in between—as it usually does. One wants too much, the other willing to give too little. What do we do?"

"For the time being, nothing. Let both sides flex their muscles through the newspapers, then you step in and arbitrate a negotiated settlement, which will be satisfactory to neither of them," Chirlo suggested.

"Then why would they agree?"

"Because neither of them will be getting what he wants and both will know the other to be dissatisfied. Misery loves company. It will all work out in the end, but we must give them a few weeks to strut and threaten for appearances sake." He stopped in front of the desk. "By the way, Don Affleck is getting married to that girl of his. Felina and I will be going to the wedding. It's this Saturday in Bahia Blanca. It would be nice if you could attend—he's leaving on Wednesday. It will make good newspaper copy in Canada with the announcement and pictures. Can't do us any harm."

"Good idea, my boy. Ruis and I will be there. Full pomp and ceremony? Trappings of power? You'll notify the papers?"

Chirlo laughed. "Papa, you're a ham. Leave it to me, I'll make the necessary arrangements. Now do I have your permission to leave—I have work to do?" He headed for the door.

"Certainly. By the way, how are Jamil and Leila? I did enjoy that dinner tremendously." *Never knew the man was so deep. Nice girl. Pity they're both a bit insane.* He looked at Chirlo. "Were we that intense during our struggle with Guerrero?"

"Worse, Papa. Much worse." He paused at the door beside Paco. "They'll be at the wedding too. They're going back to the Middle East the day after. Waving casually, he left the room. Paco followed him down the hall back to his own office.

"I think it is time to reconsider your security, Colonel." For two years Paco had been insisting on arranging bodyguards to protect him from mishap, either planned or accidental. Chirlo always dismissed the idea with a laugh. Paco followed him over to his desk.

"For example, Colonel, an assassin could slip into the garden behind these windows and shoot you in the back—or in the front—some visitor with a complaint, perhaps." He looked out the tall French windows onto the back lawns of the building. "It would be very easy."

Chirlo gazed out the windows, considering the suggestion anew. He disliked the idea of putting a wall of bodily insulation around himself. It was the first step in isolation from the very people he wanted to meet. Still, there were always one or two madmen who would take the law into their own hands to prove a point. He had certainly made no friends today, either with young Munoz and his workers or Theodore Ranklin and the American Ambassador. He wished that Harding could have stayed in the post. He disliked Collins, who was much too smooth to be anything more than an opportunist. His under-secretary, Chirlo knew, was the CIA agent-in-charge, or so army intelligence had informed him. They were usually right. He remembered the CIA plan for his assassination on the day Guerrero died.

"Yes Paco, you may be right. Look after it for me, will you please. Nothing too obvious now. I don't want to appear a fool."

"That would be very hard for you to do, Colonel. I will attend to it at once."

Chirlo sat down and reached for the mass of paperwork on his desk. Paco slipped out to visit Major Martinez of military intelligence at El Tigre Fortress. He knew the major would be pleased with Chirlo's decision. All senior military officers at various times had commented on Chirlo's lack of concern for personal safety. Now everything would change, Paco thought happily, as he backed the big limousine out of the Presidential parking area and headed for El Tigre Fortress with the news.

The Church of the Virgin of Bahia was older than the Cathedral in San Ramon. Built by the Spaniards when they first arrived along the Atlantic seaboard looking for plunder, the church had been named in honor of a valiant virgin who had held off a band of Moorish marauders by organizing townsfolk to repel invading Arabs. The particular bay which had been defended, and led to the cannonization of the Virgin, unfortunately was located in Spain, a few miles down the coast from Cadiz. Never one to quibble with geographic detail, the Spanish decided nonetheless to honor their brave Virgin Saint of the old world in the new. There was even purported to be a relic of the Virgin encased in gold beneath the altar, although no one had ever seen it, as it would have required destruction of the beautifully carved mahogany table to God. The legend therefore, was safe.

It seemed the whole countryside around town turned out for the wedding. It was planned to start at siesta hour so everyone who could not gain entrance into the church could at least fill the street outside and gawk at the proceedings. Locally, everyone knew Affleck and Rina de Felipe; some of the younger air force officers knew her much better than he. The main thing was everyone appeared happy. Chirlo, Felina, Ruis and Dr. Artega arrived in a cavalcade of cars with a screaming motorcycle escort and were ushered majestically inside to the applause of the crowds and whirring of news cameras covering the event. The President shook hands with Don Arnaldo de Felipe and his enormous wife, congratulating them on their lovely daughter, who, at the moment, was trying to keep her bosom from falling out of her wedding dress in one of the rooms off the cloisters. The stitching of her mother's dress had ripped at the front. The dress had been designed for a much thinner woman than Rina, as her mother had once been. Two bridesmaids with needles and cotton thread worked frantically, racing against time, to repair the damaged seams.

"Don't breathe so deeply, Rina. Take small breaths," the dark elfin girl ordered as she worked a small needle through the straining material.

Chirlo joined Affleck as best man and chatted amiably to ease his forboding. "Nervous?"

"Scared to death," Affleck confirmed. They were standing at the back of the church, surrounded by eyes from the open door to the street and stares from the curious guests, who swivelled in their seats to examine them from inside the nave. At the front of the church the organist climbed into his loft across from the choir and flexed his hands. The congregation quieted to coughs and sneezes. Behind, the organ men pumped the manual bellows and a sound of leaking leather hissed through the building. Finally, satisfied he had enough head pressure, the organist opened the reeds with an air blast, erupting into a Bach Prelude. He played loudly and badly. Everyone was delighted.

Jamil and Leila watched the proceedings with interest. They

had come early, slipping into a pew beside one of the eight mottled pillars that marched down either side of the nave, supporting the roof. It was a good spot to see, without being seen by news reporters or photographers. The Bach Prelude came to its crashing conclusion. The organist sat back, watching the entrance for the first signs of the bride's assembling cortege. Chirlo and Affleck walked down to the front row of pews and took seats next to the aisle. Everyone waited expectantly.

Fifteen minutes later they were still waiting. Finally, there was a flurry of activity at the back door as Rina assembled her bridesmaids, grabbed her father's arm and waved to the organist. The bellows hissed a few moments, the Wagner Wedding March boomed out across the guests, and the ceremony began. Rina, bound tightly, taking short breaths, walked slowly down the aisle, hanging onto her father. Twelve bridesmaids in yellow dresses smiled self-consciously, bringing up the rear.

Affleck arose to join Rina at the altar. Don Arnaldo relinquished his daughter's arm and backed away with much aplomb, smiling happily. Father Gomez descended to meet his nuptial task at the wooden communion railing, then paused while the organist rushed through the last few bars of Wagner to end the musical heraldry.

Twenty minutes later it was all over. The ring, the promises, the kiss, the tears from Donna de Felipe and the triumphal organ dismissal from the church back into the sunshine, and applause from the crowd outside. Chirlo kissed the bride several times from various angles for the benefit of photographers, then passed her over to Doctor Artega once he was certain all cameras were properly focused. At that point her dress split, spilling her two orbs. Unaware of what had occurred, Artega began struggling from Rina's embrace when he felt the congratulatory kiss had exceeded a normal time limit set by propriety. Rina held him tightly, whsipering fiercely in his ear.

"Good God, girl!" He glanced down to see both bare breasts pressing against his dark suit.

"What will we do?" Rina asked.

"Faint!" Artega suggested.

"What?"

"Damnit, girl—faint!" She clung to him trying to make up her mind. The crowd was beginning to snicker. "If you do not faint immediately I will have you arrested for treason—now faint. That's an order!"

Rina fainted. Deftly, he scooped her into his arms, keeping his back to the cameras, and carried her into the church, where he draped his coat over the bare shoulders. Chirlo and Affleck joined them inside.

"We'll leave through the side entrance," Affleck offered, taking her hand. "I'll get the coat back to you at the reception."

Chirlo and Artega nodded numbly, watching the laughing bride and groom fleeing to the side door behind the confessionals.

"Extraordinary! Did you see that, my boy. Simply extraordinary." The President looked at his son-in-law with awe. "That girl has the longest nipples I've ever seen!"

They held the reception at the Hotel D'Oro in Bahia Blanca. The proprietor, Senor Gomez, younger brother of the priest, had renovated the establishment several times over the years. The first expansion took place after the fall of Guerrero; the second, when the nuclear power plant went into operation at Punta Delgado, when he discovered the visiting Canadians preferred to stay at a modern motel, rather than rent houses locally. Now the D'Oro boasted a private reception hall and open air dance floor, complete with artificial fountains and colored lights enclosed behind the original stone walls of the whorehouse it had replaced. Madame Stephano and her girls had moved to more spacious premises on the edge of town, though she still held the first mortgage on the Hotel D'Oro.

Jamil and Chirlo sat alone at one of the tables near the fountain and watched the laughing dancers attempting the latest new American wiggle. Leila and Felina were on the floor; Affleck dancing with Felina; one of the young army officers with Leila. After retrieving his coat, the President danced with Rina several times during the evening.

Ruis sat apart at the table, watching Chirlo, listening to the conversations with the Palestinian; listening, but not a part. He mistrusted Jamil. There was something evil about the man, yet he had served them well against Guerrero. Ruis cast his mind back to the months of camp life in the mountains when together they shared dangers and hardships as hunted men; trying to remember how he had felt about Jamil in those days. He decided he had mistrusted him even then. Now he spoke to Chirlo like some rich banker discussing loan arrangements with a prospective client. How Jamil would have 50 million dollars in cash available to lend to Cosheca Rica was beyond Ruis' comprehension.

"You have that much?" Chirlo was looking at the Palestinian

closely in the subdued light.

"I have more, but fifty million is all I can afford to send you."

"In bullion?"

"In bullion," Jamil confirmed.

Chirlo glanced back to the dance, which was on the verge of ending to a round of mutual applause by both dancers and orchestra. Faces were flushed from exertion; eyes too bright for sobriety. Soberly, Chirlo considered the possibilities for using the bullion. To begin, he could lever a tenfold credit line through any foreign bank. At a ten-to-one ratio, the fifty would become five hundred million in purchasing power. It would open a whole vista of opportunities for the Central Bank in agricultural and business development loans, in which the government could participate on profits—his mind raced ahead to a dozen different projects he could develop in joint ventures with foreign investors once they knew the local government would put its own money into the project, as well. He turned back to Jamil. "What sort of interest do you want?"

The Palestinian shrugged. "Usury is forbidden by the Prophet, Colonel. Let us say I am giving it to you to store for me, and while it is in storage you may use it as you see fit."

"You are being very generous," Chirlo said softly.

Jamil chuckled grimly. "It is only pretty yellow metal which will sit idle wherever it is stored. The greed of man may give it value, but it is the accomplishments of man that give it worth."

The others came back to the table, laughing uproariously. Affleck slid his new wife away smoothly, winking at Chirlo as he led her off to the far side of the patio tables. The officer who had been dancing with Leila held out her chair, bowed politely to the group and left to join his friends across the room. They all began talking at the same time, then stopped and laughed again. Ruis leaned over to speak to Artega in low tones, The President's eyes widened and he swung his gaze to Jamil with new interest.

"So you are going to help us once again!" he said warmly. "Always, at the eleventh hour, Galal Jamil arrives on the scene to succor our nation. We are very grateful—to you both." He clasped the Palestinian by the shoulders emotionally, then kissed Leila on the cheek affectionately.

"You must forgive me, Galal, but I am by nature a suspicious man. What exactly do you want us to do for you? Surely you expect something in return for your generoisty?" Ruis made his voice as polite as he dared, without appearing sarcastic.

Jamil regarded the President's friend for a moment, thinking.

Artega interrupted, "Now Ruiz, isn't that being presumptuous on our part?"

Jamil raised his hands. "No, I think it is a fair question. I'll answer it." He rested his elbow on the table and pulled at his ear lobe. "You're quite right, Ruis. I do want something from you, but for the present I haven't the slightest idea what it is. Helping our cause would be the only basis on which I would ask for payment—but Colonel Chirlo promised that to me the day I met him in Amman."

He glanced at Chirlo, who nodded in agreement. "So now I can help you again—this time with gold instead of men. Fine. Gold or men, what's the difference. The debt is still the same. But, what you can do to help at the moment I can't say. It may be that there will never be anything you can do to help our Cause—and then again. . . ." He left the words hanging in the surrounding laughter from the other tables, looking at each of them in turn.

Artega picked up his wineglass. "Then I will drink to your Cause, and to the day we may be able to help you in it, as you have helped us!" They all drank to that. "You are leaving tomorrow?"

Jamil nodded. "PAN AM at nine in the morning. We're spending the night here in the hotel."

The orchestra started again. This time, in view of the hour, the tempo was slower, softer. Older couples came from the tables to enjoy the less energetic requirements of the music.

Artega glanced at his watch. "Ruis, time we left. It's a long drive back." He stood up, looking about the tables . . . "Where are the newlyweds? I'll get them." Ruis moved away to look for Affleck and Rina.

Artega extended his hand to Jamil and Leila. "Thank you for coming to see us and honoring us with your presence—and of course, helping us with your purse." He smiled warmly. "Our best thoughts go with you, always. Goodnight!" He shook their hands, and embraced them. "Come back and see us soon."

Ruis appeared with Affleck and Rina. "Ah! Mr. Affleck, I thought for a moment the lovebirds had flown. My best wishes to both of you for a long and happy life—health, wealth and an abundance of heirs."

The doctor embraced them. Rina giggled. Smiling and waving to the tables, Artega, Ruis and Chirlo, made their way through the guests to the front of the hotel. Paco trailed them watchfully. As they appeared at the front door, the escort motorcycles started with a throaty roar.

Artega looked annoyed. "Ruis, I thought I told you to let those boys go home after they brought us here?"

"I did!" He looked perplexed.

Paco slid into speaking range from his hover in the rear. "The fault is mine, Mr. President. I countermanded the order. Until the present union matters are settled I felt it wise you should have armed escort in case of incidents.

"Quite right too!" Chirlo chimed in before the Doctor could argue the point. He linked arms with his father-in-law and Ruis and walked with them down the steps, then stood by while the chauffeur saluted and opened the door to the seven passenger limousine. They moved off behind the cyclists. A military escort car took up the rear. Chirlo and Paco walked back into the hotel.

"Don't you think you're taking this security business too far?" he asked Paco severely.

"No Colonel, I don't; neither does Major Martinez."

"First you're worried about me; now Don Luis. Who is next? At this rate we'll have half the country swarming with bodyguards to protect the other half."

"I have assigned four men to protect the President and yourself on eight hour shifts, day and night. They are all officers and volunteers with the best qualifications, Colonel."

They passed through the side room into the open air addition to rejoin the wedding party, nodding their way back to the table. The slow dance music was still playing. Chirlo looked at Paco. "When do these nursemaids start work?"

"They started two days ago."

Chirlo opened his eyes in surprise. "I haven't noticed them."

"You weren't supposed to, Colonel. One of them is the waiter at our table, the other has been sitting at the table behind you all evening."

"I see . . . ." For the first time he did. They sat down. Affleck was telling Jamil something about nuclear safeguards when he was interrupted. Leila and Rina were off dancing with two air force officers. Felina was listening intently to the conversation between the Palestinian and Canadian.

"I am getting an education on nuclear treaties, Pedro."

Chirlo chuckled. "Only one, I hope. I signed only one, didn't I, or did you deceive me with all that paper, Don?"

"No, Colonel, it was all the same treaty; merely a matter of form. Everyone signs it."

"Mr. Affleck tells me you may not use your new electric plant at Punta Delgado to make atomic bombs," Jamil told him. Everyone laughed.

In his new office atop the Mirbella Tower, Licenciada Rodolfo Munoz could look across the whole city of San Ramon and beyond its girdle of mountains to other mountains, invisible to anyone not privileged to the dizzy heights of the 25th floor. It gave him a feeling of superiority and comfort knowing he was one of those privileged few. His only regret was his father would never see the success he had made for himself out of the banana business.

In a land where illegitimacy and illiteracy captured sixty percent of the population at birth, the Munoz family had been the exception. The Elder Munoz had taught himself to read and write at the age of twenty, tortuously struggling through grade school books until he could understand their words. During days, he worked as a stem cutter on the banana plantations twelve hours, six days a week. In the evenings, and on Sundays, he buried himself in the primer knowledge of the world, first from the viewpoint written for a seven year old, later for a high school student, until finally, shortly before his thirtieth birthday, he was studying the classics. He was a shy man; serious, introverted, hoarding to himself the knowledge he had acquired out of fear of offending his co-workers. He married late, so that by the time he was thirty he had produced only three children; two girls and young Rodolfo, Jr. The girls, he ignored for the most part, but upon Rodolfo he lavished affection and the knowledge he had struggled so hard to find for himself. He took the boy with him to the plantations as soon as he was old enough to understand what it was all about. They would walk out in the dawn, a skinny stooped Mayan Indian, carrying a long machete in one hand, clutching the tiny fingers of a four year old with the other. He would sit the boy on one of the wagons that followed the stem cutters. Pausing between trees, he talked to him, priming his curiosity for the journey of life ahead. In the evenings and on Sundays, he taught him to read and write. Young Rudolfo learned the rudiments of mathematics by counting bananas; five to seven in a hand measure; sixty hands to a stem. By the time he was eight he could add, subtract and multiply bananas into any combination of fractions or abstracts and was laughing at the characters in Don Quixote as the elder Munoz carefully explained the allegory of these comedy situations. It was time the youngster went to school, but there were no schools available, unless one had money. Stem-cutters made barely enough to feed and clothe their families. The Fruit Company provided an

American school for management and clerical employees, the white collar workers who ran Consolidated's administration offices. But, for the poor ragged illiterate workers, there was nothing. One day Providence intervened. Roldofo Munoz Senior cut off his hand.

The Barbe Amarillo snake which inhabited the banana trees was an endless source of concern to the stem-cutter. It was a rare week without two or three bites reported from this small vicious reptile. Normally, it occurred when the cutter pulled a stem from the tree with his left hand, swinging the machete in his right to cut away the green banana clusters. Death from the poison was swift and horrible. Young Rodolfo heard his father cry out atop the twenty-foot ladder, first in surprise, then moments later in agony, as he held his arm on top of the ladder platform and sliced it off at the middle of the forearm. The boy watched in horror as the severed limb fell to the ground beside the ladder and his father staggered down the steps above him, holding the arterial gusher from his stump, the evil machete still dangling from his wrist. His father collapsed into the arms of the other workers as young Rodolfo screamed his anguish, kicking and punching everyone, then running away through the trees, blindly seeking solace for himself, screaming, "Papa! Papa! Papa!" They found him later in the afternoon, asleep, curled on the grass near one of the watering depots. They carried him back to the company hospital to see his Papa, who, although very weak, was alive and well. The doctor kept the patient in bed five days, until he was certain the flap and the stitching would not turn septic, then released him to his family. A report to the company offices stating young Munoz should be entered into the American school at once, and his father assigned to clerical duties, was sent in by the doctor the day after his patient's release. He had watched and listened to father and son during their daily visits; the son, reading to his father, pausing to question him on items of interest or needing further explanation. Patiently, the older man would enlarge the subject until his son understood.

"I didn't know you could read and write, Rodolfo," the doctor said slyly after the first visit. "Where did you go to school?"

"I didn't, Doctor. I taught myself. Now I teach my son."

"Your son reads very well; understands too."

"He is a bright boy," the elder Munoz agreed.

"You will send him to school?"

"I am—was—a stem-cutter, Doctor. Stem-cutters do not have money for such things as schools." He lay back in bed, ignoring the doctor and gazed out the window to the columns of banana trees stretching to infinity. Then he slept.

The report to the company was read. Its suggestion was approved and the maimed employee rehired as a stem-checker at twice the wages he had been earning; young Rodolfo, the Mayan Indian from the mud adobe hut on the outskirts of San Raphael, went to the American school to get an education. In two years he was fluent in English and at the top of his class; an interloper to the company's elite, part of them, smarter than any of them, and yet never really a part of anything except the desire to excel.

Licenciado Munoz swung his gaze back from the window on the 25th floor and grinned optimistically at the visitors. They looked misplaced in the rich surroundings. It took every bit of effort he could muster not to appear patronizing.

"I did not expect a solution to our problems overnight." He leveled his gaze at each in turn, noticing they averted their eyes from his direct stare. It annoyed him." The threat of strike is more powerful than the strike itself."

"But, Licenciado, you promised that if our demands were not met, we would strike. I have told my members we will strike. How can I go back and say to them, 'Don't Strike!' I will look like a fool. I will lose face."

The six other union leaders nodded in agreement, looking at each other for support. Zapa Sanchez represented the stevedore membership who loaded the banana boxes from the warehouse to the company's refrigerated ships. Physically, he was the biggest. Intellectually, the weakest. Munoz would have preferred dealing with Sandoval, the Timekeepers Union representative, letting him settle the others later. It was too dangerous. Besides having the smallest membership among the 20,000 workers, Sandoval was too timid when dealing with his associate union bosses. In many ways he reminded Munoz of his own father, carefully hiding his intelligence and abilities from the other workers.

"Gentlemen, gentlemen, let us remember what we are trying to do. Are we trying to protect our own images, or are we trying to get our members more benefits from the company?"

Everyone made the appropriate reply.

"Fine. Now as I explained to you before, the use of strike action is the final act—the last step to show we mean business. Therefore, when we begin asking for our rights we must promise the company we will strike if we do not get them. We ask for much more than we know they are willing to give. They give a little. We give a little. In the end, we end up with what we wanted in the first place!"

"But Licenciado, you said we were going to strike!" Zapa Sanchez had a one-track mind.

"And so we will, Zapa, but only—and I repeat—only if we do not get what we want from the company. Can you afford to be out of work for many weeks? Can any of you?"

They shook their heads.

"Then let's not rush out and strike until we learn there is no other course open to us."

"When will that be?" Sandoval asked quietly.

"It may take several weeks or it may be settled the day after tomorrow. It all depends on how far we get with our negotiations. So far, from a position of outright refusal to talk about anything, their representatives have agreed to meet and argue over our demands. I call that progress."

"I call it a waste of time," Zapa growled.

Sandoval looked at the square man. "You would."

Zapa whirled at him. "Listen, stupid! If you got a better idea let's hear it. I say fuck the company, fuck their bananas, we should all go out on strike for a month and let them come begging us on their knees to go back to work."

"And if they don't come begging, what then?" Munoz interjected between the two.

"Then we'll burn the warehouses and administration buildings. They'll come!" He laughed mirthlessly. "Punta Madre, will they come begging then!"

"They'll come, all right, Zapa, only it won't be the company, it will be the army and we will be right back where we started—working for nothing, with no union, no benefits—nothing." Sandoval looked at the big man blandly. "And after we've burned everything down and a few hundred of us have been killed and the company decides to leave Cosecha Rica, will you promise to feed everybody in the union who's out of work?" There was no reply.

Munoz adjusted his tortoise-shell glasses against the bridge of his nose with his fingers. "Well, that's all settled then! The next meeting will be tomorrow morning at ten. Bring your notebooks and pencils with you this time. I'll see you all at the residency in the morning."

They stood up and shuffled out. He could hear Zapa in the outer office growling about too much talking and no action. Sandoval held back.

"Are you sure they will capitulate, Licenciado?"

"Aren't you?"

"Not really," the senior timekeeper admitted.

Munoz smiled. "Neither am I, Sandoval."

"I know."

"But we must keep trying," Munoz said earnestly. "And try and keep that dummy from doing anything to ruin our position. I need time."

The timekeeper smiled sadly. "As the Gringos say, Licenciado, 'My voice would be like a fart in a windstorm'."

"Then you must keep farting, Sandoval—keep farting for all of us."

Paco ushered Don Affleck into Chirlo's office. He was alone, behind the usual pile of papers.

"I've come to say goodbye, Colonel."

Chirlo stood and came round to the front of the desk. "How was the honeymoon?"

Affleck laughed. "I'm still on it. That party was quite a do. Thanks for coming." He held out his hand. Chirlo took it warmly.

"I shall miss you, Don. You have been a good friend." He put an arm over his shoulders, walking him back towards the door. "I hope you can find time to come back and visit us again."

"My wife is from Cosecha Rica, Colonel. I think it is inevitable don't you?" Chirlo laughed.

"Oh, by the way, I had a telex from Jamil this morning. He is in Germany visiting his old alma mater. It seems he has talked some German chemical industrialist into examining Cosecha Rica for a factory and wanted to know if there would be any objection to setting it up near Punta Delgado to save on power transfer. I didn't remember if there was any restriction in our agreements on that—can you recall?"

"Hell no! Park it right next door to our property if you want. Then you'll be able to blame the Germans for half the pollution in the area. What sort of a factory?"

Chirlo shrugged. "He didn't say exactly. A chemical factory— whatever that means. It may amount to nothing; these inquiries seldom do. We'll see." He opened the door and patted Affleck on the shoulder. "Have a safe trip home, Don, and my best regards to your wife. Goodbye."

He watched him walk down the corridor, then paused to wave once more before disappearing around the corner to the front doors. Chirlo went back to work.

12

"O GOD OUR HELP IN AGES PAST. . . ." The choir opened the service with Peggy's favorite hymn. The sad music from the beautiful reflective prayer soared out across St. Paul's Anglican Church to meet and join the voices of the congregation. Corbin, standing in the front row with the children ranged on either side, was silent. His throat felt constricted. The words would not come. He fought back the tears that kept filling his eyes and breathed deeply to relax the tightening bands of anguish in his breast. Peter, standing beside him, tall and straight in his new dark suit, lifted his soprano voice with innocence and clarity. For him, the pain had already passed. The wonderful resilence of youth. Knowing, feeling and accepting loss without prolonging memory of sorrow, Peter's tears had ended the morning after his mother had died. Corbin's were just beginning.

" . . . OUR HOPE FOR YEARS TO COME. . . ." The girls had wept because their brother was weeping and it seemed the proper thing to do. It had been several weeks since either of them had visited the hospital to see the ravaged form lying quietly, lost among the white sheets on the high bed, surrounded by hanging tubes and bottles. The girls had been more interested in the elevator ride to the cancer ward on the seventh floor and the array of mysterious looking paraphernalia surrounding their mother's bed, than in the occupant. Finally, when Peter had explained to them that Mommy had gone to heaven and was never coming back, they had both stopped crying. For the two girls, Mommy had been gone a long time before the day she actually made her final trip to heaven.

"Will they have a big elevator in heaven so we can go and visit, Peter?" Alice had asked, her liquid eyes wide with anticipation. She had learned heaven was a happy place from the Sunday school teacher at St. Paul's and had longed to visit.

Peter shook his head, sobbing. "They don't allow visits."

Corbin, his forehead resting against the cool wall outside their door, heard Emily state, "Well, I think that's really mean of God!"

Up until that point he had managed to control his own feelings, but the simplicity of his daughter's statement broke the thin dam holding back his emotions and he walked quickly to the bedroom so the children would not know their father was capable of tears.

"... OUR SHELTER FROM THE STORMY BLAST...." There had been so much he wanted to tell her; explain why he was not the cold, calculating, machine-like image he projected. It was all an act. An act which, over the years, had finally become so comfortable a part to play, that in the end it had devoured him. Yet, underneath his granite surface the soft core had never changed its texture for love, compassion and understanding. He wondered if Peggy had known all along; if the reason she had tolerated his pecadillos had been because she knew he would always belong to her. He studied the flower-covered coffin through swimming eyes. *Perhaps she knew*, he thought. He felt Emily tugging on his sleeve, and bent his head to listen.

"Is Mommy inside there now?" She pointed at the mount of flowers atop the mobile bier.

Corbin shook his head. "No darling, she is in heaven." His voice broke on the last word and he straightened up, clutching her small hand tightly "... AND OUR ETERNAL HOME...."

Affleck had read the news about Peggy's diagnosis the previous summer on the airline into Miami. An hour after leaving Bahia Blanca, Rina found the letter from Elizabeth in her purse when she opened one of the zippered compartments looking for a hand mirror. The bag was new. A wedding present from one of her bridesmaids. She handed the letter to Affleck, apologizing for the delay.

"I put it in my old purse when I packed your suits. I found it in one of the pockets. Then I transferred everything to this one and forgot where I'd put it. I thought I'd lost it. Are you mad?" She looked at him with concern. Affleck laughed, studying the familar handwritten address and Canadian stamp.

"Not unless you read it—it's from a girl-friend."

Rina snatched it back and for a few moments they struggled, laughing until she had opened it. He wanted her to read it, proving the relationship with Elizabeth was purely one of friendship, until he saw her stop and hand it back with a startled look. He took it from her slowly and began to read. It was dated three weeks earlier.

"*Dear Don: I have just learned Peggy Corbin has cancer and had a breast removed a few days ago. Apparently it has already spread so the doctors will be removing the other one too. How horrible. It is something every woman dreads. Chuck is stunned of course, and walking around in a complete fog. I can't seem to get through to him at all. He comes to work and sits in his office all day doing nothing—talks to no one—then leaves. If there is any possibility of your getting back here early I'd suggest you try and arrange it. Perhaps you can bring him back to earth. No one else seems to be able to do it so far. I'm too upset to write anything else so will end this quickly. Affectionately, Elizabeth.*"

He folded the letter carefully and slipped it back into the rumpled envelope. He had a terrible foreboding the cancer was terminal; that she had waited too long before visiting the doctor. The vanity of women. When they landed in Miami he phoned Elizabeth from the airport.

"Don! Where are you?"

"Miami. How's Chuck?"

"Terrible. What time do you arrive here?"

"We're supposed to get in to Ottawa at 8:15 tonight."

"We?"

"I have someone with me—my wife, actually."

"Oh Don, how wonderful! I'll meet you at the airport—eight fifteen." She paused. "I'm glad you're coming home—we really need you."

"See you later, Elizabeth." He hung up.

"... A THOUSAND AGES IN THY SIGHT. ..." He remembered the bravely cheerful look she had given him when he had come home after the July holiday weekend at the cottage with Elizabeth. There was no pretense any longer where Elizabeth was concerned. She knew. He knew she knew. And she knew that he knew that she knew; so what the hell. Why bother playing games? They were both too adult for that.

"I had a visit with George Bailey on Saturday."

"Oh. How is George these days?" He was leafing through the Friday morning mail on the table in the downstairs hall. Elizabeth had gone up to the cottage with him from the office Friday afternoon, so he had missed the delivery. Corbin wasn't much interested in how George Bailey was at any time. He thought the doctor dull and unimaginative.

"George is fine, but I have to go into the hospital for some tests."

He glanced at her sharply, noticing for the first time the dark rings under her eyes and drawn look of concern. He put down the mail. "What sort of test?"

"It's called a biopsy," she replied.

"A biopsy of what?"

"My right breast. There's a lump in it. Right here!" She pointed an index finger to the curved dress. "He said it is probably a benign tumor, but it will have to be removed to check. Here! You can feel it!" She directed his hand under the bra, past the nipple. It felt like a small hard pea.

"Does it hurt?" Corbin asked.

She shook her head. "No, it's just there."

He withdrew his hand and stood staring.

"When did you find it?"

"Last week. I made an appointment next day. I'm sure it's nothing to worry about. George said it would only take a day in the hospital." She smiled tightly, then rushed into his extended arms, sobbing. He held her close, stroking her head, feeling like an absolute heel. ". . . ARE LIKE AN EVENING GONE. . . ."

When he had gotten her settled down in bed, he drove straight over to see George Bailey. The doctor was at the hospital delivering a baby, according to the babysitter, and Mrs. Bailey was out to her regular bridge club. Corbin tracked his quarry down at the hospital and caught him in the locker room changing into his street clothes.

"George! I want to talk to you about Peggy." Bailey looked up from his chair. He was lacing his shoes.

"Why hello, Chuck! What brings you into this neck of the woods?"

"Peggy says you are putting her in the hospital for some tests on that lump in her breast. How serious is it? Now don't bullshit me, George. I want the straight story."

Bailey stood up, adjusting his suitcoat, then closed his locker.

"Well Chuck, old man, I can't answer you with a straight story until I've seen the biopsy. Why don't you give me a call around three tomorrow afternoon. Should have something by then."

Corbin grabbed him by the shirt front and slammed him against the row of lockers. "Listen Bailey, don't try patronizing me! You made a diagnosis of my wife Saturday. I want to hear about it—all about it! Do you understand?" He glared into his face menacingly.

"Really, Chuck! There's no need to lose your head!" He removed Corbin's hand very gently from his crumpled suit front and smoothed the creases.

"Sit down," he said quietly. Corbin obeyed. "All right, I'll give you my exact diagnosis. Your wife has a pea-sized tumor on her right breast. Under normal circumstances I would assume it to be benign. However, she also has numerous lymph nodes in the right armpit area and one or two in the left, which have to be the prime barrier between the nodule and the body in general. Whether these are neoplastic or inflammatory, I can't say at this point. My diagnosis is they are neoplastic because of the incipiency, lack of tenderness, fixed position without mobility and a slight follicular dimpling of the overlying skin—but that is only my diagnosis. I could be wrong."

"And if you are wrong?" Corbin demanded.

"Then your wife will have a hairline scar near the right nipple from where the benign tumor has been removed—she should be able to live with that."

"And if your diagnosis is correct?" Corbin asked dumbly.

"Then Chuck, I'm afraid Peggy has a particularly high grade form of malignant cancer which eventually will kill her. I'm sorry—but you asked."

He put his hand on Corbin's shoulder. Corbin's eyes never wavered in their stare at Bailey.

"How long would she have?"

The doctor reflected a moment. He lowered his hand. "If I have to perform a radical mastectomy on both breasts—and I am assuming the worst—she would have six months to a year. Now, why don't you go home and get some sleep. There is nothing you can do about it now. Whatever damage is done, is done already." He stood waiting.

Corbin stood up slowly and started for the door, walking like a man in a trance. He stopped under the red exit sign and looked back, his eyes hungry for a lie. "You still could be wrong—about the diagnosis I mean."

"Yes, Chuck, I could be." But George Bailey's eyes refused to lie.

Corbin gave him a quick tight smile. "Sorry I bruised your suit, George. G'night."

He vanished into the green hallway. The pneumatic door hissed closed behind him. " . . . SHORT AS THE WATCH THAT ENDS THE NIGHT. . . ."

Rina couldn't believe her eyes. It was after eight and the sun, although low, was still shining when they landed in Ottawa. In Cosecha Rica the seasonal variations were measured in minutes. Affleck laughed. "We make up for it during the winter."

"What happens then?"

"It's dark from four-thirty in the afternoon until seven next morning."

The aircraft stopped smoothly in front of the tanned concrete terminal as the engines died. Elizabeth was waiting for them in the lobby. She shook hands formally with Affleck, pumping his arm artificially until he laughed and threw his arms around her and kissed her on the cheek with a bear hug. She still looked as beautiful as he had remembered.

"This is Rina—Mrs. Affleck." They measured one another defensively and shook hands. There was the usual uncomfortable strained conversation between friends who have been separated for a long period and suddenly meet in the presence of disaster and a stranger. For a few minutes they stood talking nonsense in the center of the reception area while swarms of busy people warped by them.

"Let's get our bags and get th'hell out of here!" Affleck suggested.

The charade of conversation was over.

"I was beginning to think you had brought nothing more than a new purse and your briefcase."

Later, during the drive from the airport, Elizabeth brought him up to date on the medical developments. "The doctor has removed both breasts. It's terminal cancer. She has less than a year to live."

"Is she out of the hospital?" Affleck inquired

"They only kept her a week. She's home now."

The northwestern afterglow settled burnished gold on the horizon's edge, paused, then slipped beneath the darkness. Yesterday had vanished.

"How is Chuck handling it?"

She drove a few blocks before replying. "He's withdrawn into himself—yes, that's the word. Withdrawn. He's still the same, but there's a barrier now against everyone who tries to get too close—even me." She glanced at him. "I haven't seen him anywhere except at the office for the past three weeks. It's as if I had suddenly become his secretary."

"Aren't you his secretary?" Rina asked.

Affleck had told her Elizabeth's position in the company. Elizabeth considered the question, then nodded.

"Yes, when everything is said and done, I guess that's all I really am—or ever will be. Yes, I'm his secretary."

"What about the business?" Affleck changed the subject quickly, speaking as a twenty percent shareholder.

"So far, no problem. What Chuck has set aside, I've handled, waiting for you to get back. There are several important items coming up in the next few weeks which require commitment decisions. I can brief you on them later. I've prepared a complete outline on each company's status—financial—budgets—work in progress—and problem areas for you to look over. You'll have them in the morning."

"Good work. Will he be in tomorrow?"

"I'm sure he will—same as usual. You're not going over to see him tonight?"

"No." He smiled at her in the dark interior of the car. "You know Elizabeth, you're quite a gal."

She laughed dryly. "I sure am, Don. Good old reliable Elizabeth; always on the job; in the sack or in the office. Business comes first."

They drove the rest of the way to the apartment in silence. There wasn't anything to say.

"... BEFORE THE RISING SUN. ..." Outside the church summer rain clouds had parted. Now the sun streamed in through the stained glass windows on the west side. One shaft hit the flowered coffin full, illuminating the various colored petals in a kaleidoscope of beauty. Corbin's eyes traveled up the shaft of sunlight to the colored window. It was a seated Savior surrounded by children. One was sitting on his lap. His tiny index finger was pointing at Christ's beard. Beneath the glass transparency were the gothic letters, 'SUFFER THE LITTLE CHILDREN.' He swung his face back to the altar. *And what about the little men that suffer too?* he thought. *Would Christ have suffered a suffering Charles Corbin to come unto him?* He doubted it. He doubted there had been a Christ. Some sandalled nomad wandering about the hills of Galilee spouting eternal platitudes to a bunch of ignorant Jews; followed by twelve opportunists looking for a soft touch in the reflected glory of their super salesman leader. For two thousand years it had been one hell of a scam, he decided. As far as fairy tales went, it was one of the best. It had to be. It kept European man submerged in the dark ages for a thousand years, while a few elite worked everyone else to death based on the promises of a rosy afterlife. *I know this life is the shits boys. Can't be helped though. That's the way it is. But, and check this—if you work your asses off for us I'll guaran-goddamn-tee you'll go straight to heaven. Now what do you say to that for a deal?* How long had it taken to build the cathedrals at Chartres, Cologne or Salisbury? He remembered someone telling him Cologne took over 800 years to complete; whole generations of families passing the responsibility on to the next as the work continued—and for what? For a mound of stone, like the church he was standing in, to the greater glory of what? Man? God? Or the ripoff artists who milked the system, taking their piece on the way through. *Just sign your mark here on the dotted line brother Gustav. I know we've shortchanged you on the stone, but everyone has to make a living don't they?* There was life, and there was death, then there was nothing. For Peggy there was nothing. " . . . BEFORE THE HILLS IN ORDER STOOD. . . ."

He remembered the morning he had come into work and found Affleck waiting in his office, feet up on the desk, scratching an armpit.

"Hello stranger! Looks like you've collected yourself a dose of crabs."

Affleck stopped scratching and laughed. "Yeah, pesky little devils, aren't they? How are you, Chuck? You look like hell."

It was Corbin's turn to chuckle and he remembered it had been the first smile his face had held since the day Peggy told him about her visit to the doctor. "You finished down below?" he asked, dropping into the other chair beside Affleck, at the front of his desk.

"Yup—all through. Sweetheart job. What do you want me to do next? Any other nukes in the mill?"

"They're talking to everyone now—Koreans, Argentinians, Indonesians—you name the country. If it's broke and radical, ACEL has had a team out to sell them on a CANDU."

"Anything firming up yet?" Affleck knew there was nothing. He had spent two hours going over Elizabeth's reports that morning before breakfast. Corbin looked terrible. He had lost weight and his eyes were red-rimmed, deep black circles beneath them from lack of sleep. He wanted to keep him on familiar ground a few minutes before broaching personal problems. Corbin shrugged non-commitedly.

"I hear a lot of stories, but no, there is nothing for us to get excited about yet; we're at the head of the line, though, if anything breaks." He looked at Affleck's tanned relaxed face. "How do you manage to stay so young, Don? What's your secret?"

"You promise not to say anything?"

Corbin raised his hand in mock seriousness. "Promise."

"I masturbate." They both roared with laughter, then Corbin stopped abruptly, his eyes filled with anguish.

"Peggy's dying, Don."

"I know, Chuck."

"She's dying and there isn't a goddamn thing I can do about it! It's the shits, isn't it?"

Affleck agreed it was. He watched Corbin looking out beyond the window, beyond the city. "You know, Don, it's a funny thing, but I never really knew how much she meant to me until I discovered I was going to lose her. We all take so much for granted in life—our health, or wealth, or happiness, our kids. Things like music, the ballet, or a good movie or play; it's all there, and all ours to have or use and enjoy. Take away any of them and, Oh God, how we miss them! We never expect our families to be affected. Oh sure, everyone gets sick, measles, the flu, whatever, that's not what I mean. Cancer is something you read about in news reports; how close they are to solving it, or it's what happened to the guy you used to meet in the bar at the golf club, or some well-known public figure, but it never happens to you." He was silent a moment. "And then one day—phsst!" He snapped his fingers in emphasis, dragging his gaze back into focus with the office and Affleck. "You know what I mean, Don?".

"Yeah, Chuck. I know what you mean. How are the kids taking it?" He was curious what method his partner had used telling the children.

"They don't know yet, only that their mother is very sick. I'm trying to get myself adjusted first, before inflicting it on them," Corbin explained lamely.

"Hughette still with you?"

"Uh huh—thank Christ for small blessings! I hired a full-time nurse too. A Mrs. Wheable. Matronly widow. Good sort, with her head screwed on tight. She has a calming effect on poor old Peg. Hughette handles the kids."

"Sounds like you've got everything organized."

"Always the organizer."

"Who's organizing you?"

"What?" Corbin looked at him as if he hadn't heard the question, his mind searching a reply.

"You heard me."

"Well, no one. What th'hell, Don. I don't need to be organized. I can look after myself."

"Can you?" He looked calmly at the red-rimmed eyes. "I wonder."

". . . OR EARTH RECEIVED ITS FRAME. . . ."

Of course Affleck had been quite right, Corbin remembered; that was his whole problem. He had never needed anyone before in his life. Now, suddenly, when he did, who was he to turn to for help. Everyone he knew and trusted were employees. He was the boss. How could a boss ask an employee for personal help and yet maintain the employer-employee relationship? It couldn't be done. Affleck was different. He was a partner. It had been Affleck who had provided the keystone to build the empire they had started at the crazy house auction in Tampa so many, many years ago. Affleck was the only man who he would hear as an equal. He had never seen Don assert himself before.

"I don't know who to feel more sorry for, Chuck—Peggy or you."

"Me?" He was incredulous.

"You. I'll bet you're in worse shape than she is. I agree you don't need anyone, Chuck, but what about Peggy, doesn't she need you? Don't the kids need you?"

"You don't understand, Don."

"Bullshit! I understand perfectly. You figure by hiring a middle-aged matron with glasses and a uniform Peggy is getting the best money can buy. I'll bet you even gave Hughette a raise to look after the children full time, didn't you?"

Corbin nodded he had.

"So what do you do with yourself? You come in here and mope around the office like a hermit until it's time to go home and check if the employees have been doing their jobs."

"So what do you want me to do? Stay home all day?"

"For starters, yes. Instead of buying or paying for everything you give, why don't you try giving something that costs nothing?"

"Like what?"

"Yourself. Don't you think Peggy and the kids are worth it?"

336

"You're talking nonsense, Don. What can I possibly give her? Life? She's dying. There is nothing I have to give. I wish there were," he said bitterly.

"*Things.* It always comes down to *things* with you. I'm not talking about things. I'm talking about yourself—you. Your time. Time spent with her, with the kids. She knows she's dying, for Christ's sakes! It's no secret anymore, so why don't you spend what little time she has left, with her, instead of sitting about this fucking office like a turd on a plate. Go home! Talk to her. Play gin rummy. Listen to music. Have some movies sent in for that layout in the library you never use. Hold hands. Do I have to draw diagrams?"

Corbin looked at him oddly. "But what about the business?"

"You've got a group of the most expensive managers money can buy, every one of them a greedy, grasping sonofabitch in his own right who would screw his grandmother if he could do it legally. They built this corporation for us. Sure, it was your brains, but they made it work. For Christ's sake, go home, Chuck, and stay there. I'll take over things at this end. If it's on the verge of falling into chaos and we're being petitioned into bankruptcy I promise to phone and give you enough time to blow town."

Corbin smiled at the absurdity of the suggestion. He stood up, looking down at his partner sprawled on the chair, his feet on the desk in exactly the same position they had been when Corbin arrived.

"You know, Affleck, I always knew you were full of shit, but full of shit or not, you're still one hell of a salesman. Thanks." He paused by the door. "Drop over and see us now and again, y'hear?"

"Sure will Chuck. See y'around." He waved him out the door and heard him saying to Elizabeth, "I'm going to stay home for a while. If anything important turns up, give it to Don. He's number one Taco." ". . . FROM EVERLASTING THOU ART GOD. . . ."

For the first weeks, Affleck worked long grinding hours in Corbin's office, siphoning every piece of information of their far-flung and still growing commercial interests. He postponed the September quarterly board meeting until October first. He wanted to be certain he was familiar with every aspect of what the other corporate heads were doing before facing them as arbitrator and chairman. Elizabeth helped him, staying late to give him the background information he needed on the myriads of commercial webbing into which the holding company was entangled. Corbin's methods of reaching success fascinated him.

"He always seems to know what's going to happen months before anyone else, doesn't he?"

Elizabeth laughed. "Always."

"And the thing that gets me is that he's always right! How does the sonofabitch do it?"

"Maybe he's psychic?"

"Is he ever wrong?"

Elizabeth thought for a moment. "On the important things— never. But he's pulled some terrible boners on a number of small decisions. One was the big lodge in Northern Ontario the railway was unloading for a song. He jumped in on that and nearly drowned."

Affleck was interested. "I never heard about that one. What happened?"

"It was a beautiful place. Completely inaccessible except by rail. Huge main lodge, all done in cedar logs with a group of outlying private cottages, nearly thirty of them, as I recall. Fully furnished and equipped. Terrific fishing! The place had everything. The price was a fraction of true value. He heard about it through some promoter in the Federal Econimic Expansion office here, who was touting the place for the railway." She got up and went over to the bookcase and poured herself another cup of coffee. "You want one?"

Affleck nodded. She brought two mugs back from the bar and sat down.

"The promoter turned up here loaded down with material; maps, diagrams, building photographs, everything. Chuck was ecstatic. Within a week he had a private airstrip planned, a new road into the place from the trans-Canada highway, a marina. You name it, he had it planned. The price tag was going to be close to five million by the time it was ready for operations." She sipped her coffee, reflecting.

"So what happened?"

"Fortunately, before he had a chance to sign the transfer papers some officious little man turned up from the Ontario Government at Queen's Park in Toronto and announced the lake had been banned for fishing because of mercury poisoning. It seems all the Indians in the area who fished the lake for food had been coming down with some symptoms of mercury poisoning. The little man told him he could operate a fishing lodge as long as there was no fishing. Great deal, eh?"

Affleck shook his head. "And he always kept telling me to look before I leap!"

Elizabeth laughed. "He always does, unless it happens to be a pet project that grabs his interest. That was the biggest. The others were much smaller. The funniest one was the cinnamon story." She began to laugh, thinking about it. "He'd read in some farm magazine where a corn grower from Iowa had noticed that blackbirds shied away from cinnamon—the smell or something. Chuck was off and running. He was going to solve the problems of bird ingestion by jet aircraft at all major airports in the country. He contacted the Ministry of Transport here, the FAA in the States, and the British Ministry of Aviation, with his plan; spraying cinnamon particles in water every week around their airports. We ordered ten tons of cinnamon from some broker in New York and contacted a local crop-dusting company to spray the stuff. He told me all about it one weekend up at the cottage. I said I didn't believe a word of it. We drove to the local store and bought some cinnamon and sprinkled it over a few slices of bread, then laid them out in the yard for blackbirds."

"What happened?"

"They loved it!" They both fell into paroxysms of laughter. "The worst part of all was we had only put the cinnamon on half the bread slices—the rest were set out plain. The birds ate the cinnamon ones first!" There was more laughter.

"It sounds like I got back just in the nick of time."

"Speaking of time, it's after nine, Don. Rina will be wondering."

Affleck glanced at his watch. "I'll phone her, then we'll go."

He called home to say he'd be along in a few minutes. They turned out the lights and left the building to the night watchman.

When he came into the apartment he could feel the chill. He tried to ignore Rina's brief pointed sequence of icy stares until he'd removed his jacket and tie and picked up the front section of the newspaper.

"How was your day, Darling?" He called the ritual from the sofa. She remained in the kitchen alcove, refusing the bait. Affleck scanned the front page. There had been a revolution in Libya. King Idris had been overthrown by a group of young army officers, led by twenty-eight year old Muammar al Qaddafi. He studied the news photograph of the square-faced young man. The black eyes looked a little too close together. The article went on to question whether the revolution was communist inspired. The writer suggested the whole thing might have been arranged by the Russians. Affleck remembered Chirlo telling him once how his revolution had been reported as being communist inspired and, according to the Americans, still was. The major American and British oil companies expressed their concern about the Libyan takeover. *I'll bet they're concerned!* Affleck thought and went on to read the number of barrels of Libyan crude shipped daily into the Esso, Texaco, Shell and B.P. tankers at Tripoli. He wished the thin-lipped young man in the picture good luck, and tossed the paper aside as Rina came into the room to glare at him.

"You look mad. Something on your mind, Sweetheart?"

She clenched her fists into tight balls, scorching the ceiling with upturned eyes. "Ooooooh you! Where have you been?" She directed her firebeams to the couch.

"At the office working." He forced a smile.

"It's after ten! You promised to be home at six tonight! No more late nights you said this morning. Huh!" She spat the last word, then paused, her expression changing to one of concern.

"Donee, you are having an affair with Elizabeth—she is very beautiful—you knew her before me—a long time before me—now you are home and you have become lovers again. I knew it. How could you do this to me?" She burst into tears, and fell into his arms sobbing. Perplexed, Affleck rested his chin on top of the head buried in his chest and stroked the hair soothingly.

"Rina, will you stop talking nonsense."

She continued to sob, pausing to mutter indeciferable comments between the heaving sorrow, when she could spare the extra breath. Affleck waited until the heaves began to subside, then tilted her face around.

"Rina," he said softly, "there is nothing between Elizabeth and me. She is Chuck's secretary and mistress. I thought you understood the reasons I have to spend so much time at the office?"

"I do, Donee, but why is she always there when you are there? You are there all alone with her, and I am all alone here, and it's not fair." She began to sob again, making another head dive for his chest.

He held her face. "She is there because she is the only one that can explain what Chuck has been doing with the company. I've got to know everything we are doing before I can run it properly. It will be over shortly, I promise. The board meeting is next week. After that I'll be able to keep normal office hours." He looked at her tenderly. "Rina, I love you. You're my wife. There isn't anyone else. I don't need anyone else. I have you."

He kissed the parted wet lips and felt her tongue probing into his mouth hungrily. She reached her hand down between his legs and began working her fingers skillfully on the swift swelling.

"Oh Lord! he thought, and on an empty stomach!

"... TO ENDLESS YEARS THE SAME ...." Corbin remembered the first time Affleck came to visit Peggy. It was the day after the quarterly directors' meeting. He brought his new wife, who swept into the house bursting with beauty and enthusiasm, kissed Peggy resoundingly on both cheeks, and dragged her away for a tour of the house, chattering happily. He saw the stunned look in Affleck's eyes when he had greeted Peggy. She looked like a wraith. Corbin had been with her constantly during those past weeks, doing all the things Affleck had suggested.

At first is had been a terrible ordeal for both of them. Then, gradually the realization of their mutual needs crumbled the barriers of artificial restraint and they made love again. The terrible mutilations from her operations hadn't made any difference to either of them. After that they were simply two human beings in love; one at the zenith of life, the other at the twilight. It was fact. They accepted it.

"You're looking a hell of a lot better than the last time I saw you."

Corbin nodded. "Feeling a lot better too, Doctor Affleck. Drink?"

"Sure, why not? Let's live a little!" He tried to bite his tongue before the words went out. "I'm sorry Chuck, I didn't mean ...."

"Now who's being defensive?" he laughed. They went into the library.

Affleck settled into one of the comfortable leather chairs and watched the bar performance. "Easy on the soda, just a splash."

"How did your Board meeting go?" He handed one of the fat tumblers to Affleck and sat down.

"I told you last night."

Corbin waved his hand. "Telephones! I want the story in vista-vision and living color. How's the old man?"

"Dix Fowler? As irascible as ever."

"Did he call you sonny?"

"No, as a matter of fact, he didn't. He called me D.A. I still haven't decided whether it meant Don Affleck or District Attorney." They laughed.

"You'll never know either. So what happened?"

"You want it blow-by-blow?"

"Blow-by-blow." Corbin settled back, his eyes alight with

interest.

"Well, the chairman assumed the chair at nine fifteen and brought the meeting to order. . . ." He went on, giving Corbin complete details, spicing the high points with wry humor and personal comments. They were both laughing when Peggy and Rina came back from their tour to join them. Corbin saw Peggy was relaxed and happy. The chattering Latin girl had been good therapy. They settled themselves into the deep red leather couch.

"How 'bout a drink, you two?" Corbin stood up.

"Mister Corbin, you have a lovely home. Much nicer than ours."

"We don't have a house, Rina," Affleck reminded.

"No, that's right. We don't have a house." She turned to Peggy. "We should have a house, though, shouldn't we? Who wants to live in an apartment?"

Peggy agreed. "A house would be nice, although I've never lived in an apartment. A house is a lot of work, Rina."

"I'd hire a maid."

Corbin, at the bar mixing the new order, looked over at Affleck. "Keep your eyes on those two. They're starting to plot. Ice, Rina?"

"Yes please. Not a huge house like this one; smaller but the same sort of design, you know what I mean, Donee?" She took the drink from Corbin.

"Yes Rina, I know what you mean."

"Good. Well that's settled, then." She turned back to Peggy. "I'll come over tomorrow and pick you up and you can show me some of the houses around here. We'll see if there are any for sale. What time do you get up?"

"I'll be ready by ten."

"Now wait a minute, Rina, maybe Peggy doesn't want to go house-hunting with you," Affleck cut in, before things got completely out of hand.

"Oh no, I'm free all day. I'd love to go. That is, if you have no objection, Chuck?"

Corbin shook his head. He thought it was a splendid idea. He didn't know whether Rina had been primed by his partner to babysit his sick wife, or whether the whole idea had been as spontaneous as it had appeared, and Rina was simply that sort of demented scatterbrain who did things on impulse. A thought struck him.

"Do you know how to drive?"

She looked at him aghast. "Mr. Corbin, I'll have you know I used to work for Hertz!"

He knew then she was real and his heart warmed to her.

Rina turned up the next day promptly at ten. Corbin met her at the door. It was a raw, blustery day. The piles of colored maple and oak leaves that the children had harvested so carefully, had been whipped away. The wind was working now on removing the few bright stragglers left on the branches around the house.

Rina blew in through the door, her skirt lifting. "The windy season!" She laughed with delight.

"We call it Fall." Corbin shut the door. "Peggy's ready. Where are you going?"

Rina turned her palms up. "I shall place myself in her hands."

"Did Don set a price limit on you?"

"I'm very expensive."

Peggy came down the stairs. "That's the spirit, Rina, grab everything you can! Don't ever give them time to think 'till it's too late." She kissed Corbin, patted his cheek and followed Rina to the car. Corbin waved as they drove off.

"This is the nicest area in the city, I think. Why don't we cruise around here for a while and see what is available. I have a few addresses I picked out of the paper last night." She searched her purse for the clipping.

"Here it is."

She read off the first name. "First turn ahead on your left. Should be a block or two, then a right."

Rina nodded, concentrating on her driving. They slowed in front of the house, stopping by the curb.

"Oh no, Peggy. That's much too big!" It was. Enormous. "Okay, let's try the next one." She read off another address.

"How long did you know Don before you married him?"

"I met him when he arrived in Cosecha Rica—a few minutes after he got off the airplane. Romantic, isn't it?" She swung right down a treed boulevard. The bare branches from the dual rows of tall maples beckoned them in the wind. "I became his mistress the next day," she added once she had the car heading down the street.

"His mistress?"

Rina glanced at her. "For nearly three years. Now I suppose he will find another mistress."

Peggy considered the possibility a moment. "Yes, I suppose you're right. Men are such bastards sometimes."

"Oh no! I want him to have a mistress! But I'd never tell him that."

"You don't mind?" Peggy was intrigued with the Latin viewpoint.

"Oh, I'd mind if she was better than me—as a wife or lover, I mean. I'd want to know who she was first before I accepted." She giggled. "Maybe someone like Elizabeth would be fine for Donee."

"I think you'll find Elizabeth is already spoken for, Rina. Slow down, this is the place."

Rina stopped the car and looked at the real estate offering. It had possibilities, but she didn't like its looks. "It reminds me of a square cookie tin."

Peggy agreed. They drove on to the next on her list.

"I don't think Elizabeth is spoken for at all. But I don't think Donee is insterested in her, anyway. She is too cold. Donee likes his women warm—I know."

"Elizabeth is my husband's mistress, Rina. She has been for nearly seven years, maybe longer," she said bitterly.

"Oh Peggy, how lucky for you that he has such a good mistress. You must be pleased!"

"Pleased? You're joking! I've hated every minute I knew he was with her."

"Buy why?" she asked, perplexed.

"Because he belongs to me, not her. He's my husband."

"But, Peggy, she never stole him away from you. You still have your husband and now when you need him with you all the time he is there. I think that is very beautiful. Very few men have mistresses that understand wives must always come first—wives and children. I hope Donee's mistress will be as good to me as Elizabeth has been to you. I would never worry."

Peggy regarded her with open admiration. "You're serious, aren't you? I'll be damned! I never looked at it quite that way before—I still don't agree with it, mind you!" She laughed.

They drove around Rockwood until noon without finding anything suitable. By the time Rina aimed the car back to Peggy's house for lunch, they were completely entranced with each other. Rina had given of herself, selflessly, because it was her nature; Peggy had seized it all, because she needed it. When they turned in the driveway to meet the children for lunch, she felt lightheaded. She hugged her brood to her shattered breast.

"Look at what you have, Peggy—not at what you didn't have," Rina had told her at one point during their drive. "No one can have everything. It isn't decent."

She had laughed at the wisdom of the statement. "How old are you, Rina?"

"Twenty-four going on twenty-five, why?"

Peggy sighed. "I'm thirty-five going on to my grave." The sobering thought cast a chilled pall inside the warm car.

Rina was silent, then told her, "You're very lucky to know how and when you will die. Very few people do, so when it happens, they are never prepared. We must all die, Peggy. You—me—Donee—everybody dies. It is part of life—the last part. Think of how you would feel if you had no children—no husband—no beautiful home—no one to love you—no memories to leave behind. How terrible that would be! How terrible to die then! I hope I can live as long as you and have as much."

Peggy smiled wistfully. "That is the nicest thing anyone has said to me since all this started.

"I wasn't trying to be nice—just tell you how I feel."

"I know, Rina, I know." She patted her hand on the steering wheel. "And I wouldn't worry about making it to my age if I were you. You'll live to be a great-grandmother."

"It's a nice thought, but you don't know that, do you? I could drop dead today or tomorrow. That is what is so terrible. You know—I don't."

For Peggy, the whole thing suddenly became crystal-clear in her mind. She shifted her thinking from the self-pity in which she had been wallowing for weeks and faced the issue squarely on her own terms. For her, the game was nearly over. She had been out-bid, doubled, and trebled by the Master Bridge player with the Grand Slam, but it didn't matter anymore; her thirty-five years of winnings had been invested wisely already.

Corbin watched her from the window, astonished at the sudden transformation. He saw the two women and three children run hand in hand across the front lawn, their faces alive with happiness, as they chased October's golden harvest blowing from the trees.

After the New Year's party at the Corbin's, Affleck had been expecting a phone call from Morris Levy. His only wish was that Morris could have saved calling for another day. His head hurt like hell. He glared at the receiver on the desk. "Morris, couldn't you have called later?"

He heard Levy chuckling at the end of the line. "Exactly why I didn't want to talk to you last night—you were flying too high."

"It was New Year's. What do you expect, for Christ's sakes?"

"How do you feel?"

"Terrible. My eyes look like two piss holes in the snow. What do you want?"

"I feel fine, myself; four is my limit anytime. You should try it yourself."

"Listen, Morris, I don't care how you feel. I can't stand people like you and I don't envy your moderation. I feel sorry for you. I know when you wake up in the morning that's as good as you're going to feel all day. We alcoholics have it made. What do you want? I'm busy with my headache."

He could hear Levy chuckling again, quietly, over the sour remarks. Affleck seldom drank to the state he had the previous evening.

"Do you know Doctor Heinz Kastenburg?"

"Morris, I don't need a doctor, just peace and quiet."

"No Don, seriously. We have had a request from Blucher Chemicals of Frankfurt asking for our soil samples and core drillings covering the area you did at Punta Delgado. It's signed Doctor Heinz Kastenburg. Do you know anything about it?"

Affleck leaned back in the swivel chair and pulled at his uncovered ear lobe. He took his aching thoughts to the brief conversation with Chirlo the day he said goodbye.

"Yeah, Morris, I think I know what it's all about. When I left there, Chirlo was negotiating with some German chemical interests to set up a factory. Sounds like they were serious about it."

"What sort of factory?"

"I can't remember offhand. Some sort of chemical processing, I think. Probably for fertilizers or agricultural chemicals. They import all that stuff at the moment. It would be a great boon to the country to have it made locally."

"But why are they picking Punta Delgado? Why not Bahia Blanca, where there's a seaport?" Levy sounded puzzled.

"Probably the same reason we didn't go into the town. Pollution. Public relations. Accident safety through isolation. It's a pretty little town, Morris; I'd hate to see it wrecked with industry. If they stick their chemical smells down the point from the reactor, they'll have less problems. There's an excellent road into Punta Delgado and they're right next door to electrical power. Imagine they're going to need some pretty heavy KV lines strung into the facility. No, it makes a lot of sense when you stop and think about it."

"But soil and core samples for the entire area?"

"Sure. I can see that. The factory might use only ten acres, but

346

if they have any spillage it would be nice to know where the water table runs so they don't wind up killing people through the well water at the airport. That whole district uses wells, you know.

"No I didn't. Okay, I'll send it off to them. You might drop Colonel Chirlo a line, unofficially, and find out exactly what it is they are planning down there. Let me know."

"Sure thing. You sound suspicious. Know something I don't?"

"No, no, not at all. The Director asked me to look into it when the request from Germany came over his desk. I'll give him a report on our conversations and send in the reply you get from Chirlo. That should keep him happy. By the way, when are you moving into that new house?"

"On the weekend. In case I forget, you're both invited to the housewarming. The party is the following Friday."

"Too bad. We're heading down to Florida for our annual, on the tenth. We'll miss it. I'll tell Sarah we were invited."

"How's the place looking down there?" Affleck was curious on the Charlotte Harbour development, cira 1970. Morris and Sarah had made it their second home between his assignments abroad and working in Ottawa.

"You wouldn't remember the place, Don. It has ripened into middle-age. Comfortable, neat and, what shall I call it, secure. It's secure. We're both very happy."

"That's what I like to hear; a satisfied customer. S'long, Morris." He replaced the telephone carefully, then folded his head gently into the crook of his arm as he lay across the desk. He felt horrible.

Why is it? he thought, *why is it champagne gives everyone a headache—even good champagne.* It had been good champagne.

"Are you all right?" It was Elizabeth. He hadn't heard the office door opening.

He looked up. "I'm fine. Give me another fifteen minutes, then call the mortuary. What do you want?"

She smiled sympathetically. "I have aspirin and Alka-Seltzer. Which do you want?"

"Both—and bless you my child for the thought." He sat up as she went over to the little bar sink to get him a glass of water. "How's Rina?"

"She passed out when we got home. She was still asleep when I left. Happy New Year, Elizabeth—in case I forgot last night."

She handed him the bubbling glass of water. "You did. Happy New Year!"

He drank the bubbles and belched loudly. "Ah! That's better.

Did anyone ever tell you, my lovely lady, you'd make someone a hell of a wife?"

She took away the empty glass and rinsed it out, then stopped by the door on her way out. "Many times—but I'm still waiting for an offer."

". . . BEARS ALL ITS SONS AWAY . . . ." By Easter Peggy was slipping quickly. The light was still in her eyes, but her face was hollow and lined by the etchings of pain the drugs failed to suppress. She slept for long periods and seldom went out anymore. The last vigil began a few weeks later when she announced quietly to him one morning she no longer had the strength to get out of bed.

On weekends he carried her, feather light, to the bedroom window and propped her up with cushions on the settee so she could watch the children at play in the back yard; see their Batman kites lifting to the sun in the warm Spring breezes and hear their anger and childish frustrations when the strings tangled in the budding green branches of the trees.

"You must marry again, Chuck. I mean after a suitable period." She smiled weakly.

Mrs. Wheable, sitting across the room with her knitting, but seldom out of earshot, stood up. "I'll just run down and have Hughette fix me a cup of tea." She left her knitting on the chair. Corbin watched her go.

"That woman is a jewel!" He looked back at Peggy. "Who did you have in mind for my next wife, anyone I know?" He kept the question light.

"The children will need a mother."

"You don't like the idea of a bachelor father?"

"Not with you away as much as you are."

"How 'bout Mrs. Wheable, she's available," he chuckled.

"No, I was thinking more along the lines of Elizabeth Avery."

He looked at her in disbelief. "You're kidding?" But he knew she wasn't.

"She's good enough to be your mistress and secretary, but not good enough to be your wife? Is that it?"

"Don't be ghoulish, Peggy." It was a lame remark, but the only thing he could think to say. They were silent for a long time, watching the children playing on the lawn below. When Corbin looked over finally, her eyes were closed in sleep. He got up quietly and adjusted the blanket around her tenderly and started for the door.

She stopped him halfway across the room. "Chuck!"

"Yes, darling?"

She smiled at him tiredly. "Think about it."

Outside the window the string on Peter's kite parted. There was an angry soprano yell as the triangular black plastic disappeared over the trees and away towards the river. " . . . THEY FLY FORGOTTEN AS A DREAM . . . ."

Heinz Kastenburg graduated with his doctorate in chemical engineering from the University of Leipzig in 1940. The Juggernaut of the German Wermacht was rolling through Western Europe to engulf the world in flames. Heinz was twenty-four and a genius of Teutonic genre. The genius had been recognized early by the Bayer Chemical Company in Cologne when a young teenager had written a letter of inquiry from Dortmund requesting an explanation of one of their chemical processes using coal tar. Intrigued, the company agent in Dortmund was asked to check on the background of the writer by Bayer's customer relations department.

It was discovered that the seventeen year old author of the request was engaged in a project to develop fibers from coal tar and had almost succeeded. His main occupation, however, was making soap, which he sold to support himself and his widowed mother. Captain Felix Kastenburg had fallen at the Somme. The Bayer company persuaded Heinz to return to school and later to the university on a scholarship—all at their expense. He was given an allowance sufficient for his mother, his books, tuition and himself.

During summer recesses from the University he worked at the Bayer factories in Cologne; first at menial tasks, while his capabilities were observed carefully, then later in the research department, where Bayer brains developed their products for the world and profits for the company. Heinz Kastenburg had found his home. It was an exciting time in the Fatherland. While the Fuhrer's legions went out to conquer the world and save it from the conspiracy of international Jewry, Heinz Kastenburg went to Norway to conquer the atom. The research team for the heavy water plant was drawn from the best brains available in Germany. It was to be a crash program.

The crash came in 1945 when the Reich, supposed to last a thousand years, expired at less than twelve in an orgy of senseless self-destruction. Kastenburg marveled it had lasted at all as he watched the repeated bombings to the deuterium project on which he and his associates had labored so long. The whole exercise had been completely pointless. That international Jewry was responsible for the German defeat, he had no doubt, but was wise enough to keep the opinion to himself.

The U.S. Marshall Plan started to rebuild the German economy. The Bayer Chemical Research Department started rebuilding product lines for their profits and Doctor Heinz Kastenburg went back to work in Cologne. In 1956 he was offered a chair at the university of Bonn as director of the Chemical Engineering Department. He was forty, unmarried, with no loyalties to anyone since his mother had died the previous year. He accepted the university post and arranged to have himself continue employment with Bayer as a research consultant. The village in which he lived near the airport was the same driving distance to Bonn as it was to the Bayer offices in Cologne. He had the best of both worlds; summer, working on the various research projects; winters, teaching his students.

He met Jamil for the first time in the University library during the winter of 1959. He had noticed the dark features of the Palestinian in his classes when the young man had switched from his Bachelor of Science course to Kastenburg's chemical engineering studies. A look in his files convinced him Galal Jamil was going to be an interesting student; first, because he was of above-average intelligence, and secondly, because, like himself, he had been defeated by interntional Jewry.

"You are Galal Jamil from Haifa?" he asked quietly of the young man studying at one of the large polished oak tables.

"Yes, Doctor Kastenburg, formerly from Haifa, now from Amman."

"Ah yes, the Jews took your homeland."

"Stole it."

"Yes, stole it." He looked at the angry young eyes. "Then I don't suppose you care much for Jews, do you?"

"I despise them!" The Palestinian had raised his voice, causing students at nearby tables to look up inquiringly.

Heinz Kastenburg nodded approval. "What a coincidence, Herr Jamil, so do I."

After that, he always had a moment or a word for the young Palestinian whenever they met. They shared a secret hate.

In 1962 when Jamil graduated he came to bid Kastenburg goodbye; to thank him for his help in making him a qualified chemical engineer. "Ach so! You will return to the Middle East. To Amman?"

"To Beirut. I have been promised a job with my people." He did not elaborate on the discussion with Yasser Arafat.

"As a chemical engineer?" Kastenburg asked.

"No, doctor, as a Palestinian, who is a chemical engineer."

"Quite so!"They looked at one another with complete understanding. He shook Jamil's hand and wished him success, then stopped him at the door. "By the way, if there is anything I can ever do to help—one never knows how things work out. . . ." He smiled through his blond mustache.

"Thank you, Doctor Kastenburg. I'll keep that in mind. One never knows."

Seven years later Jamil phoned him from the Frankfurt Airport fifteen minutes after he and Leila arrived from Cosecha Rica.

One could never tell how things would work out.

Doctor Kastenburg's blond hair had turned completely white during the intervening years. His carefully trimmed mustache gave him the appearance of a younger Hindenburg, complete with slight paunch.

"So, you feel your friend will give you the permission to build such a factory." He swirled the brandy snifter beneath his nose, inhaling the fragrant bouquet. It was an excellent brandy; smooth and silky to the palate.

"Yes, Doctor, he will agree, provided the place does in fact produce some commercial chemical products. It must be two factories in one, within the same building. One producing the commercial chemicals, the other refining the plutonium."

"And building the bombs," Kastenburg added.

"Yes, and building the bombs," Jamil agreed.

They had arranged to meet him at the airport serving the twin cities of Cologne and Bonn, then booked on the next Lufthansa domestic flight out of Frankfurt. The doctor had been very formal in his greeting, bowing to Leila courteously.

"Frau Jamil, welcome to Germany!"

He had driven to his comfortable cottage nearby, where the housekeeper had prepared a massive supper to honor them. He had refused to discuss anything until the meal was finished and the wooden cheese board served.

"Now, Herr Jamil, how can I help you?"

"We want to build an atomic bomb."

Doctor Kastenburg didn't even raise his eyebrows. "Ach so!" He peered at them through the steel rimmed pince nez, fiddling with the black ribbon trailing down the sides of his cheek, his blue eyes unblinking. He removed the glasses and began massaging the bridge

351

indentation of his nose thoughtfully, then replaced them. "To build a nuclear bomb you will need money."

"We have the money."

"You will need a safe place to work, away from the curious."

"We have that too," Jamil confirmed.

"And you will need heavy water to process the uranium."

"We have that now."

"Finally, you will need plutonium to make the bomb."

"That too is available. It needs only to be processed."

Doctor Kastenburg was silent for several minutes. Then he stood up from the table. "I think I'll have a drink. Would you care to join me in a brandy?"

Leila and Jamil shook their heads.

"Ah yes, the Prophet forbids you alcohol. I had forgotten. Pardon my suggesting temptation." He went to the sideboard and picked out a brandy glass.

"It has nothing to do with temptation or the Prophet, Doctor. Neither of us like brandy," Leila explained. "Do you have any beer?"

Kastenburg raised his eyebrows, then went to the kitchen and returned with two steins of foaming Pilsner. They retired to the front room and sat down.

Jamil told him the story of Chirlo, Cosecha Rica, and the Canadian CANDU reactor they had visited the week before; the apparent open access to nuclear waste, and finally his plan on how he intended to steal it from under the noses of the staff at Punta Delgado—with or without Chirlo's permission.

"The question now is what sort of chemical processing plant can we install which is compatible in appearance to the manufacturing of plutonium from those waste uranium rod bundles?"

Kastenburg considered the possibilities through a few sniffs of brandy fumes. "Ja, an interesting problem. We must be producing products requiring extreme safety precautions—isolation areas—lead safety paneling within the walls—pressure piping—mechanical hands —hydraulics." He was thinking aloud now. "There is the matter of engineering staff—security checks—those in the know and those who are not—stainless steel linings—power supplies. Hmmmm."

They waited as his thought process continued in silence. The ornate grandfather clock at the side of the room paired the seconds ponderously. Finally, Kastenburg smiled beneath the mustache.

"Ja, I think that would work nicely. It would explain everything for everyone. Of course you understand there is no guarantee we would be able to complete the work before we are discovered?

"There is no guarantee that we wouldn't either," Jamil argued.

"True, but it is unlikely. Secrets are strange things. Everybody wants to find out about them. Have you noticed?"

"What is your plan, Doctor Kastenburg?" Leila asked.

"Ah, Frau Jamil, I might ask you the same question?"

He was looking at Jamil for the answer. "Why do you want to build a nuclear bomb?"

"Because we think it will be a more effective method of persuasion than a pistol."

Kastenburg chuckled, sloshing the brandy inside the snifter. "True. However, sometimes a pistol can be just as effective."

"We've tried using pistols, Doctor. Now we need a lever."

"A lever?"

"To pry the Jews out of Palestine."

"Ah, I see, give you a fulcrum with a long enough lever and you will raise the world!" He looked at Jamil to see if he had caught the allegory. The Palestinian's face was blank.

"Archimedes," Kastenburg suggested kindly.

"I know Doctor. He said also that truth is the sum total of all the facts of the matter." Irritated, Jamil felt Kastenburg was being coy. "Supposing we dispense with allegories and attack the problem head-on. The truth is we intend to build one or more atomic bombs to use as a lever and force Zionism to meet our demands—with or without you."

"Your bombs—when you have them—what will you do with them, Herr Jamil?"

Jamil looked at Leila, then back at Kastenburg. "I don't think that is relevant at the moment."

"So. You have no plan, beyond acquiring the bombs?"

"I didn't say that."

"You didn't have to." He drained the brandy glass and set it carefully on the table at his elbow, then leaned forward. "Let me make myself perfectly clear. If you want to build nuclear bombs to threaten men and nations with your power, I am not interested in helping waste your time and money. Nor am I interested in wasting my own. However ..." He removed the pince nez carefully and massaged the bridge of his nose with two fingers once again, then replaced them " ... if you are building the bombs to destroy men and nations, as an example of power to force persuasion, then I am prepared to help. In fact, I'll do more than help! I'll resign my post

353

with the University and the company and devote my full time to your project. In short, I will build your bombs. Which is it to be?"

The grandfather clock paused through eleven double-spaced seconds in time, then chimed the hour with melodious magnificence.

"I'm not sure I know how we could use them, Doctor. There is the matter of a delivery system."

"The delivery system is not a matter of concern. I am interested only at this point whether you agree in principle with their detonation upon completion."

"If I am satisfied it will achieve our aims, yes."

"Ah! You have reservations then? Tell me, what certainty do you have of achieving your aims in either case, using the threat of explosion, or using the explosion as a threat? One could assume, with a reasonable degree of certainty, the latter will create considerably more interest in your demands than the former."

Jamil was silent. Doctor Kastenburg had a point, he decided. Leila nodded beside him, thinking on the logic also. The doctor fiddled the black ribbon from his glasses idly. "I put two situations to you: in the first, I plant a bomb in the basement of the Bundestag in Bonn, then demand a hundred million marks from the government, or I will blow up the city; in the second case, I blow up the city, then ask for a hundred million marks or I will blow up Cologne the same way." He smiled. "Naturally, I would move westward from the Rhine to escape any fallout before I exploded the bombs."

Jamil and Leila nodded.

"Now I ask you, in which of these two cases am I likely to achieve the swiftest results to my demands?" The logic was irrefutable to the Palestinians.

"Very well, Doctor, we agree, but the truth of what we intend to do must never be discussed again, until we are ready to detonate. There are those who are willing to help us for the threat, but few who would assist us in any way if they knew our threats would *follow* the explosions. It must remain our secret."

"Naturally." Kastenburg stood up. "I think I'll have another brandy. Would you care for another Pilsner?"

"... DIES AT THE OPENING DAY ...." He took her to the hospital on the twenty-first of May. It was nearly over. George Bailey put her in a big, airy, private room and moved the bed close to the window so she could look out over the city to the Tower on Parliament Hill. Corbin filled the room with flowers. Peggy loved flowers. He spent long hours with her, holding her thin hand in the warmth of his own. Sometimes they chatted, mostly about the children, but more often than not, Peggy dozed and the room was silent. He found himself sleeping in the afternoon, sitting in the comfortable chair alongside her bed and would awaken with a start when the duty nurse whished in through the door to the accompaniment of the hydraulic door arrester.

"How are we feeling today, Mrs. Corbin?"

Such an inane question. If she were not asleep, Peggy would smile weakly, offering a feeble, "Fine," to complete the charade.

He brought the children up to see her for the last time early in June. They didn't know they had come to say goodbye. They talked about school, their friends, their enemies, and the series of birthday parties that were stretching off into the horizons of the summer holidays. There was a new boy in the neighborhood from Ireland.

"He talks funny," Peter announced. "But he sure knows how to fight. He knocked Brian Fitzgibbon *flat* with one punch! Wow—you should have seen it, Mom! Straight to the breadbasket, like this!" He demonstrated on his nearest sister, pulling the punch before it landed. "I'm glad he's my friend. 'Course I could beat Brian too if I really tried," he added modestly. The Fitzgibbon bully had been the terror of the neighborhood's younger set. Corbin had spoken to his father on several occasions, persuading him to take the boy in hand, and learned the son terrorized the father as well. They had him on tranquillizers in an attempt to curb some of the Irish exuberance. Peggy knew Meighan Fitzgibbon slightly; a thin doormouse of a woman with flaming red hair. "I hope he wasn't hurt!" she whispered from the bed.

"Naw! He just cried a little and ran home."

"What do you mean, *Naw*?" Corbin interjected severely.

"I mean *no*," Peter corrected.

After another twenty minutes, Peggy started to doze. He lined them up so she could kiss them each goodbye. He couldn't bear to watch and turned his back to gaze out at a red maple leaf flag fluttering atop a Federal building a few blocks from the hospital. He could hear her whispered talk to each child, and the final farewell.

As they walked out of the hospital into the lushness of the new summer, the girls were chatting about the shoes Hughette had bought them that morning. Emily was of the opinion that Alice had made the better selection. Peter stopped and turned around to look back at the wide front doors. He had not spoken since they left the room. His face was ashen. "We won't be coming back here anymore, will we,

Dad?"

"No son, you won't," Corbin had answered him honestly. Looking into the young brown liquid eyes, he knew Peter finally had understood he would never see his mother again. " . . . O GOD OUR HELP IN AGES PAST . . . ."

Three weeks after their meeting with Doctor Kastenburg, Blucher Chemicals International opened its spacious offices on the Kaiser Wilhelm Strasse in downtown Frankfurt. A trilingual secretary named Heidi Zuber was selected from the dozens of applicants to run the office. Although the company was owned and operated by Heinz Kastenburg, the twenty million marks transferred to the company's credit from the Union Bank of Switzerland came from Jamil's numbered account. The doctor obtained licensing agreements from his employers to produce any agricultural chemical product of which Bayer was a basic producer or held patent rights. To an outsider checking into the Blucher organization, it would appear the company had been functioning successfully since 1911.

The Blucher family had in fact kept the company intact throughout the whole period. It had been absorbed into the Hoest organization in Frankfurt before the Great War of 1914; Hugo Blucher had sold the assets, but not the name. He kept the company as a depository for the family fortune, until his death, then passed it to his heirs intact. Gustav Blucher inherited the company and one seventh of his father's money, which amounted to less than two hundred marks during the rampant inflation of the Weimar Republic. With the emergence of Adolf Hitler and his plans for rebuilding Germany, Gustav Blucher reactivated the company. The sales agreement to Hoest forbade entering the chemical business for fifty years, so Gustav opted for construction equipment, and wound up building a sizable fortune from the new autobahn system being built throughout the country. He died on the autobahn in one of those horrible accidents that occur almost daily on any super highway with no speed limit.

Hugo's grandson, also named Hugo, inherited the business a few days after graduating from the Luftwaffe Flight Training School in Baden. A merciful British Hurricane pilot spared his life during the Battle of Britain, so the younger Hugo Blucher survived the horrors of Germany's collapse in a prison camp at Nun's Island on the St. Lawrence River next door to Montreal. He returned to his shattered homeland in 1946 and took part in the reconstruction program. He used the Blucher Chemical name, with its long history of service to the country, as the door opener to the rich contracts being awarded by the new government in Bonn. As an ex-POW he was a natural, and retired in 1965 to his family estates on the other side of the Swiss border after banking sixty million marks in gold to the safety of the underground vaults of the Bank Gesellshaft in downtown Zurich.

The company, although inactive, retained its formidable reputation and balance sheet in Frankfurt, against the day Hugo might decide to come out of retirement. He never had, and as Jamil learned when he met Herr Blucher in a private conference room at the Union Bank, never would return to the world of construction—or any other business, for that matter.

"Consequently, Herr Jamil, I would be delighted to accept your worthwhile offer—provided of course it solves my little problem."

His *little problem* involved a lawsuit by the German government against Hugo Blucher on suspicion that his private books did not match the set he had been showing the tax department between 1951 and 1965. The tax authorities had been made all the more suspicious by his sudden decamping for the neutrality of Switzerland and the peace of Shaffhausen, the border town at the head of the Rhine. Blucher Chemicals still showed a balance of nine million marks on deposit in Frankfurt. However, as far as Hugo was concerned, it was 'dead' money. The German government would not permit him to transfer it to Zurich, nor to use it for anything other than company operations, until they had examined his other set of books. Hugo Blucher had ignored the whole thing with Teutonic indifference until he received a letter from Doctor Kastenburg, suggesting he might be interested in acquiring the German interests of Blucher Chemicals while at the same time solving the financial annoyance created by unfeeling taxation authorities in Bonn. While not overly optimistic on the feasibility of such arrangements, Hugo Blucher was, nonetheless, intrigued. He agreed by phone to meet Dr. Kastenburg's representative in Zurich to discuss the matter in depth.

"The proposal is very simple, Herr Blucher. 1 will pay you from my account here whatever amount you have in your account in Frankfurt, plus one mark for the company."

"No strings attached?" Blucher puffed on his elegant cigar.

"None, except the bank will act as escrow agents for the company shares and the money here."

"One mark appears to be an outrageous price for a company with nine million marks in its account, Herr Jamil!" Blucher thought he might as well try the ploy.

Jamil was unmoved. "Not as outrageous as nine million marks

for a company which has been inactive for five years and has no office, no employees and no business.

"True, Herr Jamil," Blucher observed politely. He had tried and failed, so he accepted the offer.

The bank had another monetary arrangement to complete for Jamil; fifty million in bullion to be shipped to the Republic of Cosecha Rica.

"Would it not be simpler to keep the bullion here and mail the certificate to the government, Herr Jamil?" Director Grubin asked his customer.

"Simpler, but not as effective. Certificates are paper—bullion is reality."

"But surely, Herr Jamil, our paper representing the bullion transfer to the Republic is sufficient. It is guaranteed by our reputation."

Jamil smiled. "Paper guaranteeing gold, to be given to a government to issue more paper on the guarantee of your paper to guarantee gold. Where does the paperchase end?" He shrugged at the porcine Director. "Who knows? I know where it begins, Herr Grubin. It begins with the bullion. Do as I ask. Ship the bullion to San Ramon."

The Director bowed to him as he left the gilt office on the second floor mezzanine.

The grey soot-stained building with its eleven stories looked lost among the towering neighbors in downtown Manhattan. At the end of the block, sightseers stopped to view the rococo splendor of the Woolworth Building or the gigantic twin black monoliths of the World Trade Center, a few blocks further down on the Hudson River's east bank. Chirlo paused before the small building at 99 Church Street to read the huge bronze inscription above the door: "Commercial Credit is the creation of modern times and belongs in its highest perfection only to the most enlightened and best governed nations. Credit is the vital air of the system of modern commerce. It has done more, a thousand times more, to enrich nations than all the mines of the world. Daniel Webster, Senator, March 18, 1834."

Chirlo went through the glass doors into Moody's Investors Service Inc. Bryce Kelvin, vice president in charge of the Latin American desk, met him cordially.

"I appreciate your taking time to see me on such short notice, Mr. Kelvin," said Chirlo.

"How was your trip, Colonel?" The tall, thin, immaculately

dressed vice president ushered him into his office, politely gesturing him to a plush chair.

"The trip was swift. The taxi drive from JFK is what took the time." Chirlo sat down. Kelvin laughed.

"July and August are the worst times for traveling in New York—humid, hot and horrible. Cigar?" He offered him the humidor. Chirlo shook his head.

Kelvin sat down. "Well, Colonel Chirlo—or is it Artega?"

"Whichever you prefer."

"Yes, well, what can I do to help you?"

"An explanation as to why you gave Cosecha Rica a C rating on our bond issue."

"Ah! I see you believe in getting straight to the point. You disagree with the rating?"

"I do."

"So you stated in the letter our President received which your Ambassador was kind enough to deliver to Mr. Moncreif. Let me reiterate our position. At the onset I must state Moody's does not profess infallibility. We do make mistakes. However, our subscribers have never found fault with our assessments on individual offerings."

"Mr. Kelvin, my country has fifty million in bullion in the vault at the Banco Central in San Ramon. Our deficit is shrinking each quarter and we are putting our financial house in order—no thanks to your government's freeze on our reserves in this country. We have increased agricultural productivity twenty seven per cent in the last year through land reclamation programs sponsored by the Canadian government, and Blucher Chemicals from Frankfurt is building an agricultural chemical factory to serve the Central American region in basic formulations. Surely that counts for something?"

"Indeed it does, Colonel, and you are to be congratulated on the efforts by you and your people since the revolution."

"It is only a revolution if you lose, Mr. Kelvin. When you win, it is called a War of Independence." He disliked the smooth cultured nasal tone of the vice president.

"Quite so. However, Colonel, there are a number of other considerations Moody's must examine when awarding its rating. For example, how many governments have been overthrown in your country during the course of its history?"

Chirlo was silent.

"If my memory serves me, it comes to seventy-one—yours being the seventy-first. Not exactly a record of stability to instill investor confidence. Seventy-one revolutions since 1827! In fact, democratically elected goverments in Cosecha Rica appear to be the exception rather than the rule, wouldn't you agree?"

"Your government saw nothing wrong with my predecessor's regime," Chirlo reminded.

"True, but in that case the financial support came from government aid approved by Congress. The private investment sector operates on something more practical than political considerations, Colonel. Money is the greatest coward in the world. With the first smell of trouble, it flees."

"We have no trouble."

"We are informed you have a great deal of trouble. A young rabble rouser by the name of Munoz has organized the Consolidated Fruit Company's plantation workers into a union to the jeopardy of that company's operations within the Republic. If CFC were to pull out, your financial future would become very bleak indeed, we are told. You would be in a deficit position within eight weeks. How could you meet the long-term obligations of a 250 million bond issue?"

"It is only a five to one ratio on our reserves."

"That's not the point, Colonel. If it was, America would be bankrupt. Our own federal bullion reserves are less than one cent on the dollar, but our credit rating is Triple-A, because no one can doubt this nation's ability to pay its debts."

"But everyone doubts my government can?"

"No, Colonel, I don't doubt your government's integrity in the least. However, the proposed offering will not come due until 1996. Do you know what your government will be in 1996? I can tell you with certainty what ours will be—either Republican or Democratic." He smiled, not unkindly. "We would be happy to give you an A rating, or even a B rating, but unfortunately, the evidence does not warrant anything other than a C. I'm sorry. Truly sorry." He was silent a moment. "There are, of course, money markets to which you could submit your offering. Have you given any thought to Hong Kong? They have a very active bond market; growing all the time."

"Do their investors subscribe to Moody's?" Chirlo asked wryly.

"I'm sure some of them do, Colonel, but that is immaterial. In America our principal bond investors are mutual funds, pension funds, insurance companies—corporate bodies who must be extremely cautious in the handling of other people's trust money. In Hong Kong, the wealth, while not as great as here, is divided more among family consortiums and individuals than corporations. It can make a great difference. At any rate, Colonel, it is something to think about." It was a polite, sincere method of ending the conversation.

Both Chirlo and Kelvin knew offering Cosecha Rican bonds on the Hong Kong market was a waste of time. Every high flier in the world had worked the market to death, and to a point where the Far Eastern investor had become more cautious than his American corporate counterpart. Chirlo stood up.

"Thank you for your time, Mr. Kelvin."

"Not at all, Colonel, my pleasure." They shook hands. "I shall look forward with a good deal of interest to your progress in the years ahead. Your country needs a period of good stable democratic government. Who knows, in fifteen or twenty years you may be able to collect a triple-A rating from Moody's."

He ushered him back to the lobby.

"Where to, Bud?" The cabbie swiveled his head against the plastic bullet-proof screen protecting the front seat from any lunatic passengers that might sit in his cab.

"JFK."

"This is rush hour, Bud. I hope you got lotsa time."

"At least fifteen years, Bud, maybe twenty!"

". . . OUR HOPE FOR YEARS TO COME . . . ." Peggy Corbin died in her sleep on July 12 without regaining consciousness. Corbin was with her until the very end. He had asked her during the last days if she wanted him to contact her parents in Westchester. She shook her head. They had done nothing for her in her life, so why bother them with her death. He had phoned anyway and listened to the whining voice of her mother in New York complaining of her arthritis and Ralph's heart condition.

"Fine, Mrs. Gibson, you and Ralph stay where you are. I'll call you when she dies." He had hung up angrily. Peggy had been right.

She was delirious the last evenings of consciousness, guilty memories crowding her fading reason, and she muttered whispered fears in compromise while they collided with each other in her mind. A slight, real or imagined, against a school chum—which school? Westchester High? Vassar? She never clarified the point. As the sun set deep golden across the rooftops in the summer warmth, she looked at him lucidly for a moment, clutching his hand. "Tell Peter I'm sorry. I didn't mean it—really I didn't." It was ironic the last words of conscious memory were of Peter Colley before she slipped into her final coma. She died during the middle of the afternoon five days later.

He had been dozing in the chair, his usual position during these

361

vigils, when he awoke with a certain knowledge her spirit had flown. He rang the nurse, who came in, checked the skeletal form on the bed, then began disconnecting the tubes without looking at him. He watched her wheel the mobile holding rack of pipes and bottles to the door.

"She is at peace now, Mr. Corbin."

He nodded numbly as she wheeled the rack into the hall.

He didn't know how long he had been sitting in the chair, but the room was dark when Elizabeth came in and turned on the light. She glanced at the bed quickly and then looked at Corbin.

"It's time to go home, Chuck, the children will be waiting."

"Yes. What's the time?"

"It's after ten."

He stood up and looked down at Peggy's face. It was very thin, the skin translucent, but he noticed the face was relaxed and peaceful. He bent over and kissed the cool lips, then walked past Elizabeth through the open door. She followed him outside and down the corridor to the elevators at the nursing station. They passed two men in white who were sitting on a gurney talking. They stopped talking as he went by and slid off the gurney, then began pushing it down the corridor toward Peggy's room. He stopped to watch as they rolled through the door.

"I should tell them . . ."

"It's all been taken care of, Chuck." Elizabeth pushed for the elevator.

Corbin looked at her gratefully. "I'm sorry."

"For what?" The doors opened, then closed them inside. Elizabeth pushed the lobby button. "Sorry for what?"

"For this! For me! For you! For Peggy! For everything!"

They walked out of the lobby into the shelter of the warm air and followed the walkway into the parking lot. Her car was beside his; the only two left in the visitors' area. She stopped him at the side of his Porsche, touching his arm. "When I was a very little girl, my grandmother told me God made each of us to be three people. The person we think we are, the person other people think we are, and the person we really are. And only God and a few others ever get to know the real person. I didn't know what she meant then, until I watched you during these past months. Things may never be the same between us, but I want you to know, Charles Corbin, I think you are one of God's noble creatures."

She kissed his cheek and walked quickly around to her car, then drove off with a wave.

He climbed into his car feeling a sad fool and went home.

The congregation in the church started slipping hymnals back in the pew racks during the last line of William Croft's beautiful hymn. He looked at Don Affleck, standing between Rina and Elizabeth. Both women were crying. Affleck nodded at him in sympathy. He looked back quickly as his eyes uncontrollably filled with tears and his shoulders heaved with stifled sobs. ". . . OUR SHELTER FROM THE STORMY BLAST AND OUR ETERNAL HOME . . . AMEN"

13

1971

The February sun burned down across the city of Tripoli, swaddling the narrow streets with a suffocating heat. Angrily, Jamil looked at his watch for the tenth time and glared out the eighth floor window of the Uaddan Hotel to the harbor.

"Well, we've wasted another day. It's after three, the government offices will be closing."

"Patience, Galal, they'll call." She was reading a newspaper on the bed, her shoes off. She didn't look up. He whirled away from the window and pushed her feet aside to sit down. Leila laid the newspaper down, folding it carefully. They had been waiting a week to see Colonel Muammar al-Qaddafi. Arrangements for the meeting had been confirmed in Beirut weeks before by the Libyan Ambassador to Lebanon. Shakir el Numeiri had been warmly cordial when they visited his residence in late November.

He had embraced them affectionately and led them into his reception room, clapping his hands for sweet tea, which was delivered swiftly by a sandalled servant with no teeth. His Excellency was a dark rotund man with a happy face and piercing black eyes. They sipped the tea thoughtfully and wiggled the tea bowls for a refill before embarking on the reason for their visit. When the second sweetened cups were finished and the toothless servant had cleared

365

the room, Jamil broached the subject.

"Excellency, my friend indicated that your Premier, Colonel al-Qaddafi, agreed to hear me in private audience as soon as his duties permitted such a meeting. I don't mean to rush you, but the particular subject I wish to discuss with the Premier is of a delicate nature—an opportunity for your government to seize the iniative in a certain area, an opportunity which may well pass if we delay action too long."

"Your friend was quite correct. I have been notified by Tripoli this week officially to invite you both to visit our country sometime in February, if that is convenient?" He smiled.

"February? But Excellency, that's three months away! Surely we could plan our visit before February?"

"Visit to be sure, but to see his Excellency, Colonel al-Qaddafi, you will have to wait till February. I'm sorry, but his Excellency is a very busy man as you will doubtless appreciate. There are great events planned on the merging of Arab nations in which his Excellency is, as you are aware, much concerned in bringing to fruition for all our sakes."

"You mean you are actually going ahead with that idea of joining Libya with Egypt!" Jamil knew it was a pipe dream. Since Nasser's death from a heart attack in September, the new Egyptian President, Anwar Sadat, had been wooed by Qaddafi on an Arab Federation. The economics of the idea appealed to Sadat, and to the young Libyan Colonel, anxious to make his mark in the Arab limelight. Jamil knew it was impractical when he had heard the first rumors of such an association. The tubby ambassador looked hurt for a moment.

"You disapprove of such action, Mr. Jamil?"

"My approval or disapproval is hardly a matter of concern to either government, your Excellency. The United Arab Republic was unworkable in Nasser's time and I think an Arab Federation in Sadat's time is equally unworkable—however . . ." He smiled apologetically . . . "I do not profess to be a politician and therefore I bow to the wisdom of his Excellency, Colonel al-Qaddafi."

He lowered his eyes modestly. He had nearly put his foot in it that time. His Excellency appeared satisfied with the explanations.

"If you have your passports with you, I can give you the visas now and a letter of introduction which might be useful when you arrive in Tripoli."

He heaved himself out of the ornate chair and they followed him into his office. Later, on the road back to the camp, they laughed over the pretentious little Ambassador with the harsh Libyan accent, but the ten week delay on the visit to Tripoli was no laughing matter.

Finally, in February, when they had arrived at Idris Airport and taken the drive into the city, they were sure everything had been arranged for an immediate meeting—if not the next day or the day after. Captain Tarbu Zitlan returned the following morning to the hotel and informed them there had been a small delay in the meeting.

"How small?" Jamil inquired.

The Captain shrugged his shoulders. "In the meantime, permit me to show you more of the sights of Libya. We have a rich history."

They collected their things and followed Zitlan to the car. They left the city with the Libyan Captain driving like the wind.

"Where are we going?"

"Leptis Magna." He skirted a mule wagon loaded with bundles and children, and rocketed on by. Jamil and Leila clung to the safety straps.

"Is that a name or a disease?"

The Libyan laughed brightly. "A very good joke. I must remember that one."

Leptis Magna had been a Phoenician trading station in 193 A.D.; restoration and excavation to the surrounding area was still underway, though in a haphazard manner. They poked around the crumbling stone piles for an hour, then raced back to the hotel. The Libyan dropped them off at the front door, saluted and burned rubber as he squealed out the driveway. He was back next day with another apology for the delay in meeting the Premier and suggested they go visit more ruins.

"This is ridiculous, Captain. We didn't come here to see ruins. We're wasting time," Jamil told him angrily. Zitlan looked hurt. It was a repeat performance of the previous day; a thunderball trip through the countryside to Sabratha. Jamil spent the entire tour grumbling, while the Captain tried his charm on Leila, explaining the Vandals' destruction of the premises during the first and second centuries. Jamil was unimpressed. They made the return trip to Tripoli in silence.

The next day when Zitlan arrived at breakfast with the usual apology and another suggestion for a sightseeing trip, Jamil lost his temper.

"Listen, Captain! We're all through with bloody sightseeing trips to piles of rubble. Will you please go find your Major, tell him to find his Colonel and see if you can manage to get the audience with the Premier we were promised? We will be waiting in our room for your call. Good morning!"

The Captain saluted and left without a word. Five days later they hadn't seen or heard a thing from anyone.

"Of course yesterday was the Sabbath, Galal, and you couldn't expect anything on the Sabbath," Leila said reasonably from the bed.

He turned, glaring at her. "That was yesterday. What about today?"

The phone rang and he sprang to his feet to answer it.

"Hello, Mr. Jamil! Colonel Qaddafi here. I'm sorry I kept you waiting. Tell me, are you free to see me now?"

Jamil was dumbfounded. "Yes Sir. At once. Where shall we come?"

"I'll send a car—for you, Mr. Jamil—there is no place for women in the scheme of things. They should stay home and raise their children," he said severely.

"Yes Sir. I'll be down in the front lobby waiting for the car. Thank you." He hung up and looked at Leila. "The Man himself! He's sending a car—for me—no women allowed, he said." He sat down on the bed smiling. "Women are supposed to stay home and raise babies in Libya. What do you say to that?"

"I say 'fuck him!' " Leila glared.

The collision foreseen by Jamil between the Jordanian Palestinians and King Hussein had occurred the previous year. On February 10, 1970, while Doctor Kastenburg pored over the package of maps and reports on terrain features at Punta Delgado, King Hussein unleashed a massive attack against the refugee camps. Amman came under fire from all directions and the battle raged throughout the day.

Hussein was forced to back down and later explained the whole thing had been a simple misunderstanding. The *London Observer* in mid-February suggested his "statemanship" was responsible for averting civil war, heading off the bloodbath because he did not want to be "a hated prisoner in his own palace. It does not seem in Hussein's character, nor to be in his concept of kingship, to contemplate such a state of affairs," the newspaper stated.

Jamil read the article in Beirut. "Bullshit!" was his only comment when Akbar handed him the overseas edition of the newspaper.

"What are we going to do, Galal?" Akbar and the others were growing restless in the security of the Lebanese capital. Well-fed, well-paid, they felt indolent living in the lap of luxury while their countrymen fought and died.

"We already did it—we moved out." He looked at his friend quizzically. "You're not thinking of running back now to throw your life away with the others?"

"No one wants to throw away his life, Galal. But every morning when I shave, I have to face myself. It's becoming more difficult to look me in the eye." He smiled.

"You would rather die a hero like Abu Talaat than live to tell your grandchildren how you expelled the Jews from Palestine—is that it?" Abu Talaat had been one of the courageous commanders who had fallen in Jordan. Akbar was silent. Jamil stood up and looked down at the sunny harbor filled with anchored ships awaiting berths along the crowded waterfront. The dirty windows hazed the view. He decided to tell him the plan—at least part of it.

"What would you say if I told you we are building some atomic bombs?"

Akbar laughed. "Are you speaking rhetorically or academically?"

Jamil turned back from the second floor window. He was not smiling. "They will be built for us in Cosecha Rica under the guise of an agricultural chemical factory. The factory will be built less than a mile away from a nuclear reactor power station on the Atlantic coast."

Akbar stopped grinning.

Jamil took an hour to outline the details of the plan with Blucher Chemicals, then ended by saying, "When everything is finished we will have our atomic bombs. We will make music, my friend! A symphony everyone will hear!"

"How long will all this take?"

"The Doctor thinks three to five years. It is complicated. First we must steal the waste before we can start extracting plutonium. The only problem now is the lack of waste. The plant at Punta Delgado hasn't been in operation long enough to give us everything we need yet." He paused, smiling at Akbar. "Do you like it?"

"Where will we place the bombs for our demands?"

"I haven't decided. The first explosion should be in the Negev desert to illustrate our sincerity—but we may not have to go that far, once we announce we have the bombs. Remember, it is the threat of the bombs we want to use, not the bombs themselves!" He lied smoothly.

"Hell! Forget the Negev, tell the Americans we've got one in New York and the British we've got one in London. Ha! Can you imagine how fast they'd want to make a deal then? God! We don't even have to have the bombs as long as everyone thinks we have them. It's sheer genius." He chortled happily at the thought, his eyes dancing in delight.

"It's also expensive. We are going to need more money. I've sent Leila back to Kuwait to see if our friends are still willing to support the Cause."

"And are they?"

"I don't know. They were when we had an army. Now—well, we'll find out when she returns." He looked back at the harbor. A fast speed boat towing two waterskiers crossed the filthy window panes; he watched the skiers criss-cross the speedboat's wake, jumping the ridge of water, then ducking to clear each other's tow ropes. It was hard to see whether they were male or female. He rubbed the pane absently, uselessly. The dirt was on the outside.

"In the meantime, my friend, we are going to keep pressure on the Jews, where it will do the most damage and gain us the most attention." He turned back to Akbar. "When Leila and I were in Caracas we met an interesting young lad—Pico Ramos—his father is a doctor; one of the best families in Venezuela. He is a revolutionary fanatic, but with no organization behind him. He lacks experience—like we did when we started. I invited him to join us for field training"—he laughed—"returning the favor Chirlo did for me, I suppose."

"Does he speak English?"

"Fluently—French too." He opened his desk. "I got this yesterday. Read it. You'll see what I mean. Ignore the flowery language."

He tossed the envelope to Akbar and returned to the window. The skiers were still swapping places, but going in the opposite direction now, back to the hotel wharf. Akbar removed the flimsy tissue letter and read the contents.

My Very Dear Friends: I have missed seeing you and the buffet discussions on the terrace at the Tamanco. I believe you were both right in your most wise advice to me and I am now making arrangements to come and visit you this next month. The Imperialistic forces of the world must be destroyed and the evolution of the proletrariat established on the carcass of their remains. It can only be achieved by the dedication of all men working together towards the common cause of world revolution, sharing in their experiences, hardships and victories between themselves and between nations. There are no boundaries to world revolution, just as there are no boundaries between nations of men with a uniformity of ideals. It is the imperialistic aggressors that erect the boundaries to contain and control the proletariat to rule, rape and repress the more easily with thievery and corruption. They must all die and it is up to us to ensure they do. I offer and pledge myself to your cause in the certain belief it will benefit my own. Your most sincere friend, Raymondo Ramos."

"I have one question."

Jamil turned to him. "Well?"

"How do we control him? He sounds like a lunatic."

"Not we—you. You control him—murder, rape, arson, destruction, pillage—whatever you want him for, use him. Put him in the front line. If he succeeds, we claim the credit. If he fails—then we know nothing about this—as you say—lunatic from Venezuela."

"He is our sacrificial lamb?" The idea appealed to Akbar.

"Sacrificial only if he fails," Jamil stated. "Let him bring others from his world revolutionary group: from Argentina, Paraguay, Brazil, even Japan. Bring them here, Khala, bring them all here; train them at the camp and send them off in the name of world revolution, but don't expose our own group to any danger. I need every one of us for that final assault when we have our bombs—credit for that we share with no one!"

Joseph Sisco, American Assistant Secretary for Middle Eastern Affairs arrived in Jordan during mid-April to offer a U.S. peace proposal to the leaders of Fateh. The Palestinians refused the plan, but neither Sisco nor Hussein were prepared to relent. Acting under orders from the King, Special Security squads roamed the streets of Jordan's major cities provoking resistance, flouting Jordanian laws, causing chaos and trying to provoke a civil war between Palestinians and Jordanians. The Popular Front grew and the fractured Fateh membership assembled quickly under one banner and fought back, capturing the strategic areas of Amman and seizing the First Secretary of the American Embassy hostage. The Popular Front then moved in to occupy the Intercontinental and Philadelphia Hotels, taking all foreigners captive.

Hussein savagely shelled the camps of his Palestinian charges on the pretext that an assassination attempt had been made on his life. The fighting raged on for a week until the Jordanian king became alarmed and promptly arranged for a cease-fire. Joint committees were set up between the guerrillas and Hussein to supervise the truce. The Americans and the King put their heads together to find a plausible excuse for their underestimating the ferocity of the Palestinians, and in the best American tradition of explaining away any conspiracy, the problem was settled by blaming everything on a single individual General Zeid Bin Shaker. The General's sister was alleged to have been killed by a guerrilla prior to the fighting and he had lost his head over the incident. Both he and General Sharif Nassir, Hussein's uncle, resigned their posts and the king assumed command of the armed forces.

The whole thing was made to sound perfectly plausible to the international press, but Max Bruner made the mistake of sending the true story back to New York and was ordered to leave the country the following day by the American Embassy. He refiled the story when he landed in Beirut and phoned his New York office for instructions. The night man on the desk told him B.J. would phone him when he got in at nine. Bruner checked into the Phoenicia and went to bed. The New York call came in from B.J. at three in the morning.

"Wake up, goddamnit!" Bruner could picture the florid face six thousand miles away. "Can you hear me, fer Chrissakes?" B.J. roared in his ear.

"Yes, B.J., I can hear you fine. What's the problem?"

"Problem? What are you talking about. I'm answering your call. What's all this shit about being thrown out of Jordan?"

"It's not shit. They did it. You got my copy."

"Yeah," he growled. "Fuckers!"

"What do you want me to do now?"

"How about that nut you were with before, isn't he in Beirut?"

"I think so. I'll have to check."

"If you can find him, hang with him for a few weeks and see what you can pick up. If he's out of town, run him down somewhere. Call me back when you find him. Oh yeah, I'll make a switch on your money to American Express Beirut today. Is that bullshit in Jordan over now?" he asked as an afterthought.

"No, there still has to be a final showdown, B.J., but it won't happen until Hussein purges all the Palestinians in high places out of his government and army—late summer—early Fall—is my guess for the final explosion."

"Think you can get back in to cover it?"

"I can try sneaking across the border."

"Now, I'm not asking you to do anything that's gonna get your ass shot off, Max, but I'd like to have the story first hand, if you know what I mean."

"Yes, B.J., I know what you mean. Goodbye." Bruner lit a cigarette. The problem with B.J. Bronstein, Bruner decided, was he would never be satisfied until the news came into the C.P.I. office that Max Bruner had gotten his ass shot off trying to get a story.

Bruner hadn't seen Jamil or Leila for ages, not since the Algerian meeting after the El Al hijacking. They had told him they were going abroad for a honeymoon the last time he had spoken to them, but that was nearly six months ago. He climbed out of bed and rummaged through his suitcase to look for his special address book, then switched on the bedside lamp and leafed through to G. He kept private phone listings indexed by the first letter of the first name. He dialed the number and waited. There was no answer. After ten rings, he hung up, turned out the lamp, and after butting his cigarette, went back to sleep.

Doctor Kastenburg relaxed when he saw the affectionate greeting between the two men. It had been a nagging worry ever since he had agreed to join Jamil; did the young Palestinian in fact have as close a working relationship with the dictator as he assured him he had? He saw Chirlo release Jamil from the bearhug and turned to face the formal introductions.

"Welcome to Cosecha Rica, Doctor. A great pleasure to have you visit us."

Kastenburg noted the eyes and handshake were sincere and firm.

"Thank you, Colonel," he said gravely.

"And my good friend and father-in-law, President Artega." Chirlo presented the beaming doctor of medicine to the doctor of chemistry.

"Doctor Kastenburg—a great pleasure!"

"Doctor Artega, con mucho gusto!" They both laughed and everyone grouped themselves about the table in the reception room. Jamil passed the tubular map case to Kastenburg and sat back to hear the German's sales pitch as they had rehearsed it on the flight from Madrid.

"Gentlemen, my Board of Directors has approved our plans to build the factory!" It was a perfect opening for the withdrawal of the blueprints and their flourished unrolling across the table.

"Blucher Chemicals has long considered the Central Americas as a prime location for agricultural chemical production. From here we can expand both north and south as market requirements dictate." He smiled engagingly. "And frankly, I'm optimistic on our future growth." The others nodded in agreement. "You will see the property we are interested in acquiring lies adjacent to the nuclear waste storage site. This location was picked specifically for several reasons. First, it is as close as we can position ourselves to the power supply from Punta Delgado and still remain far enough away from Bahia Blanca to avoid sending any malodorous scents in their direction—although I cannot say the nuclear plant will not wish we had chosen another location after we have started producing our smells." On cue, everyone chuckled. Jamil was satisfied the pitch was going extremely well.

"Next, is the case of warehousing storage; we wanted our site close to a good, heavy-duty road, but isolated enough to keep out the curious. Since the nuclear plant road ends at the waste disposal pools three miles beyond Punta Delgado, we know any unauthorized visitors will be stopped at the end of the road by a security fence we intend to build around our site. We will simply extend the existing road for another quarter mile—if that is satisfactory?" Again, on cue, everyone nodded in agreement.

"I am bringing twelve heavy diesel trucks in with our first shipment of materials during the construction phase which will provide the necessary nucleus for tanker deliveries about the country and beyond. Initially, we will use them for transporting equipment from the docks out to the site. Later, stainless steel tanks will be attached to the truck frames. The final reason for our selection of this land area"—he waved his hand across the blueprints—"is because we believe that in time the area will become the site for other industrial development along the coast, in which case there will be no alternative but to create new port facilities to accommodate this development. In other words, I look upon using the docks at Bahia Blanca as a temporary situation." Jamil watched the reaction as the curtain descended on Act One.

"That may be a few years in the future, Doctor," Chirlo cautioned. "Seaports are expensive construction projects even for wealthy nations. Ours is a poor country."

"True, Colonel. Time is relative. By a few years—I mean ten or fifteen—who can say what additional facilities will be built along the coast once we have established Blucher Chemicals? A sulphuric acid factory with its industrial byproducts? A cement plant? Perhaps an oil refinery? Nothing is impossible to imagine. It requires that first step and Blucher's is prepared to take that first step."

"Second step, Doctor. I think the Canadian nuclear generator was the first."

Kastenburg shook his head. "I disagree, Colonel. Power to drive the wheels of industry is useless without the industry."

"Yes, well, in any event, Doctor Kastenburg, we are very grateful to both you and Senor Jamil for selecting our country to build your factory." Dr. Artega rubbed his hands together. Kastenburg began the closing pitch. "I must caution you that the work we will be doing is a type of production requiring extreme caution. It may appear we are being over-zealous in our demands on security, safety and employment, but we recognize our responsibilities to the community and will be satisfied with nothing less than maximum safety standards."

Chirlo looked at him blankly. "I'm afraid I don't follow you, Doctor."

Jamil tensed in his seat. This was the final act, the last hurdle necessary to give Kastenburg the total uninterrupted secrecy they required for the whole project. The German smiled good-naturedly.

"Yes, perhaps I should explain what we are doing, exactly." He paused significantly, as if collecting his thoughts, attempting to translate the technical information into lay terms. "Agricultural chemicals are divided into four basic classifications: organic phosphates, chlorinated hydrocarbons, carbonates and elemental. The intensity of toxicity varies with each type and within sub-classifications of the four basic types themselves. The most lethal to humans and animals are the first two and it is these two we will be producing here. Parathion, for example, in its unadulterated form, is so lethal that two drops on the back of a dog's neck, and it will die of horrible convulsions within a few minutes."

"My God! It sounds more dangerous than the nuclear plant!" Artega exclaimed.

"Nothing is dangerous if it is handled properly, Doctor, but there are many things that become lethal when safety precautions are ignored. You can kill yourself by eating two tubes of toothpaste as easily as poisoning yourself with farm chemicals. The point I am trying to make is that any industrial product must be handled sensibly if accidents are to be avoided. Our products must be handled carefully and securely and we intend to see this is done. Our security precautions may appear excessive to an outsider, but I can assure you there is no substitute for safety, nor will I permit it." He looked at the President and his son-in-law for a moment. "Do I have your permission to implement any type of security or safety measures I feel necessary?"

"Without question, Doctor Kastenburg, without question," Artega stated emphatically.

"Thank you." Kastenburg smiled at everyone. He had closed the sale. Jamil smiled back. He dropped the curtain for Act Two in his mind and lit a cigarette, relaxed and satisfied.

"Now if you will permit, I'll go over the blueprints with you in detail and give you a capsulized outline of what we will be doing down on the coast over the next twelve months, assuming of course there are no delays on shipments from Hamburg." He looked apologetic. "We have been having a series of unfortunate labor problems with the stevedores union lately."

"We've been having a few union problems ourselves. I know what you mean," Chirlo admitted, thinking sourly of Rodolfo Munoz and the outrageous settlement he had been forced to cajole the fruit company into accepting. It was a two-year agreement and he knew the clever little lawyer would be back in a few months to begin subliminal bargaining for the next contract, forcing another crisis on the precarious economy.

Max Bruner found Leila in Kuwait after three days of pestering a lonely office girl who had been left to handle the phone and mail that arrived in Jamil's Beirut offices. His first visit had been met with a curious disinterest.

"Who did you say you were?" Her face was American, snub-nosed and freckled, but the accent was French.

"Max Bruner of C.P.I. I'm an old friend"—he paused at her skepticism—"of Leila, Galal, Akbar, all of them. Who are you?"

"I'm the secretary."

"Where are they?"

"Who?"

"Listen lady, I don't know if you're for real or not, but this is important. Supposing you think about it for the rest of the morning and I'll check back later." He left, exasperated, walking down the narrow staircase to the main floor and past a fight between two elderly Turks in the doorway. They paused in their shouting match to watch him hail a taxi, then returned to their gutteral argument.

When he called in mid-afternoon, the girl was gone. He walked back to the hotel, stopping by the American Express office to pick up the money B.J. had wired in from New York. The following day he phoned again and was told to call back in the afternoon after

376

three. When he turned up at the office instead of phoning, the girl appeared angry. "I told you to phone, Mr. Bruner."

"Call me Max."

"I have passed your request on to someone who might be interested in contacting you. You will have to wait for them to phone you tomorrow," she explained severely.

"I see. Can I ask who the mysterious caller will be, or are you going to keep me in suspense until tomorrow?"

"Mr. Bruner—"

"Call me Max," he interrupted.

"Mister Max, this office is a security pipeline to our people and it is my function to insure security is maintained—that's why I'm here."

He reached over the desk and brushed a strand of blonde hair aside, then carefully straightened her large, steel rimmed owl glasses. She blushed.

"I've heard of security, ma petite, but this is ridiculous. If you've spoken to Jamil you know I'm a friend, so why the big mystery?"

"I didn't speak to Mr. Jamil. Parlez vous français?" she asked with interest.

"Un peu." He explained his fractured French. He had lived in Paris for several years working with the wire services's French Bureau. She laughed at him.

"Your accent is terrible! I think we will stay with English."

"What are you doing tonight?"

She looked surprised. "Why?"

"Because I am waiting for a phone call for someone, somewhere, sometime tomorrow and I have a few hours to kill. How about joining me for dinner, dancing, drinks and discussions as to why a French girl is sitting in a Beirut office answering a phone all day—unless you have other plans?"

"No other plans, but I refuse to discuss the cause of world revolution with anyone outside the group for security reasons," she said firmly.

"Then you'll join me?"

"Perhaps. I'll have to think about it. You're much older than I am. I'm not sure I should be seen with an older man." He could see she was examining him critically.

"Why not?"

She shrugged. "People might talk."

"About your having dinner with me at the hotel?" Bruner was

perplexed.

"There are spies everywhere," she said seriously.

"True. I'll make sure they put us in a dark corner of the dining room where we can watch the room and still have our backs to the wall in case someone creeps up on us."

"Now you're making fun of me." She pursed her lips angrily.

"Well, maybe just a little." He regarded her for a moment, seeing her for the first time as a woman instead of a female object. "How old are you?"

"Twenty-four. How old are you?"

"Ah, ma petite, I have reached that age in life when one remembers a great many things, some of which actually happened."

"What's that supposed to mean?" Now she was curious.

"It means I am forty-two and prefer the polite hypocricy of adults to the vulgar sincerity of the young, but for you I will make an exception. What time shall I pick you up and where?"

"I'll meet you in the lobby of the Phoenicia at seven."

Bruner bowed low, sweeping his hand in the Arab form of submission . . . "until seven then," . . . and backed out the door. She giggled.

He was on the street before he remembered he had forgotten to ask her name.

"Bernadette—Bernadette Boivin."

She was dressed in a severe, high-collared black dress with obscure red velvet piping that wandered around the front like a trail of dried ketchup that had been squirted from a plastic serving squeezer some weeks before. He took her arm and marched towards the bar.

"I'll bet they call you Bernie?"

"No, they call me Bernadette." They slid into one of the dark tables.

"Well, never mind, I'll call you Bernie." The waiter came over.

"What is your pleasure?"

"Cognac," she informed him.

"On an empty stomach?" Bruner was aghast. "Bring me a Pimms with a twist."

The waiter scribbled and left.

"Will you be staying in Beirut long?"

"Until I get my phone call, then we'll see. How about you?"

"I will stay as long as I'm needed. I serve the Cause and wherever the Cause requires me to be . . ."

"Then that's where you'll be." He finished for her. She nodded uncertainly. The waiter returned with coaster discs and drinks.

"I keep feeling you are laughing at me, Max Bruner. Are you laughing at me?" She sipped the cognac without blinking.

"Let's say I find your point of view interesting." He held his Pimms aloft. "To the Cause!" She repeated the toast and they both drank to the absurd, seriously.

"When did you first become interested in the Cause?"

"Oh, I've always been a revolutionary—since I was at school. Most revolutionaries are pacifists, but I'm an activist."

"There's a difference?"

"Of course there is. A pacifist believes in the Cause but refuses to do anything about it except talk revolutionary principles and philosophies, but an activist talks very little and instead goes out and makes the revolution happen—it's a big difference."

"Yes, I can see where it would be." Bruner sipped his drink thoughtfully. "So how did you meet Jamil, or was it Leila?"

"Neither; it was Andre; that's his code name. I don't know his real name. Well, actually I do, but I'm not going to tell you."

"Who is Andre?"

She went on as if she hadn't heard his question. "When Pico came to Paris to see Andre, Andre phoned me in Nice to join them with the others. Then we all came to Lebanon—on separate flights, of course."

"Of course." He watched her polish off the rest of the cognac. "I'd like to eat now."

Bruner dusted off his Pimms and stood up. "Fine, let's go find that secluded table, Bernie."

The wall tables were occupied, so the maitre d' seated them at one in the middle of the room. He followed her face as she surveyed the room uncomfortably, then took the menu's unpriced version from the maitre d'.

"Are we safe?" he asked in a stage whisper.

She ignored the question as she scanned the impressive food and wine list. "The deputy commissioner of police is sitting two tables away from us," she informed him.

Bruner resisted his impulse to look. "How do you know?"

"I know. I think I'll have the seafood platter and a bottle of Chablis." She set the menu on the table and smiled at him invitingly. "I spent a night with the commissioner three weeks ago. He is a terrible lover—too fat. I had to sit on top of him." She giggled.

Bruner ordered the seafood platter too when the waiter appeared. He waited until a wine steward had poured the glasses, turning them light amber, then asked her, "If you don't mind my asking, Bernie, what were you doing in bed with the police commissioner?"

"Fucking."

"I see. Do you normally fuck police commissioners?"

"He sent two men to see me at the office. Not me really, they were looking for Andre and the others, I think. They took me downtown and I met the commissioner. She shrugged and sipped her wine. "One thing led to another and the next thing I knew we were in bed—in this hotel, as a matter of fact. You disapprove?"

"No."

"I looked at it as an assignment for information." She smiled wisely. "I got a lot more information out of him than he got out of me."

"Such as?"

"They aren't certain Andre and the others actually arrived in Beirut. The Deuxieme Bureau made the inquiry when their surveillance teams in Paris reported he was no longer at his home. They don't know he left France, they just think he might have gone, so we're all safe for the time being. They'll never get close enough to the camp to see anyone there; so as long as everyone stays away from Beirut, there won't be any problems," she said smugly.

"The camp at Bint Jbail?"

Bernadette nodded. "You've been there?"

"A few times. You?"

She shook her head. "No, Pico decided I should stay here and run the office because I speak all the languages. It's an important job."

"How many languages?"

"English, French, Arabic, German, Italian, Spanish, Portuguese. I know a little Turkish too, but it's a hard language to work."

"I'm impressed!" Bruner *was* impressed. "How did you learn so many?"

"I don't know. I find learning languages easy. It's not really that impressive because Italian, Portuguese, Spanish and French are very similar, you know. English and German are the hard ones."

"And Arabic?"

"My father was born in Algeria. I grew up learning Arabic and French. Are you a good lover, Mr. Bruner?"

"Call me Max." The waiter appeared with the first serving on a heated dolly. Bruner waited until he had left before replying, "I've never had any complaints, Bernie. Why?"

"That's what every man says. We'll see." She picked up her knife and fork, holding them European-style, and looked at him. "I want you to know I dislike anal intercourse, but do enjoy oral clitoral massage, if it's done properly."

Bruner blinked. "I'll bear that in mind." They began to eat dinner.

He could hear her voice dragging him back to consciousness from the deep gorge of sleep. He held her hand when she tried to slap his face for the third time. The phone was ringing. He lugged an arm to the instrument on the side table, knocking everything to the floor, then scrambled naked on his knees to find the receiver.

"Uh hello, hello?" It was Leila calling from Kuwait City.

"Max! How are you?" The connection was clear, but he knew they were being monitored at one end of the line or the other.

"Fine, fine Leila. Sorry if I sound vague. Just woke up." He glanced at his watch. It was after ten.

"Late night?" She laughed.

"Early morning—where's your husband?" He squatted on his haunches like an Indian fakir as Bernadette peered over the edge of the bed smiling. Without the glasses her eyes looked myopic in the morning light.

"He's abroad on a fishing expedition with a friend."

"Big fish?"

"The biggest. Are you staying long?"

"When are you coming back?" he countered.

"I can leave anytime, there's nothing to keep me here any longer. Why aren't you in Amman?"

"I was asked to leave by the U.S. Embassy for my eye-witness account of Hashemite justice."

"Is it permanent?"

"Is anything?"

Leila laughed. "Stay put. I'll be in by the weekend and we can talk."

"Great. I'll go back to bed."

Oh, by the way, Max, stay away from the secretary at the office."

"What?"

"The secretary at the office—Bernadette—I'm told she's a nymphomaniac."

Bruner groaned. "I can verify it—you're about twelve hours too late with that advice."

He could hear her laughter floating up from the Persian Gulf as he replaced the receiver. He crawled back into bed and flopped on his back, exhausted from the effort, closing his eyes.

He felt her tongue and lips working wetly on his inert staff and opened his eyes with a snap to see her lithe tawny figure kneeling over him, her face obscured by the flowing yellow hair.

"For God's sake, Bernie! Can't you wait until after we've had our breakfast?"

On July 23, 1970, President Nasser announced his acceptance of the American peace plan for the Middle East. Not only did he agree to peace with Israel as a long term objective, but also cessation of the war, an arms freeze and agreement to Israel's remaining in the occupied territories prior to negotiations. Even Al Ahram's editor, Mohammed Heikal, was hard pressed to make the announcement plausible to the Arab world as he applauded the "brilliant diplomatic tactic" undertaken by the Egyptian president. Nasser's faithful poured into the streets of Amman, occupied Jerusalem and major cities on the west bank of the Jordan, shouting, "Nasser is a traitor! Nasser is a coward!" Their golden idol had become tarnished.

Swiftly, the Egyptian government closed down the El Fateh broadcasting station in Cairo and expelled the Palestinian students from the University. Nasser called on his allies to assist in stamping out the menace of the Popular Front. A world-wide propoganda campaign began against the Palestinians, accusing them of plotting to upset the uneasy peace. Movement of resistance groups across the various Arab frontiers was monitored carefully.

It was a signal for Hussein to begin systematic liquidation against every terrorist in Jordan. According to the little king, any Palestinian voicing support for Fateh's Popular Front or condemning Hussein or Nasser was a terrorist. Worst of all, the popular financial support so necessary for the survival of the guerrilla groups dried up, as one after another, the Arab leaders, with much hand wringing on the injustice of the policy reversal, opted for peace. After eighteen years, Gamal Nasser, idol of the Arab Revolution, had smashed himself like clay at the feet of the people who had trusted and believed in him for so long. It was a bitter pill for the Palestinians to swallow, and they lashed back in the only way they knew, with the meager funds left to them.

The new camp was set up on the other side of Bint Jbail, northwest towards the higher slopes of Mount Hermon and well away from the Israeli border. Bruner and Leila joined the others at the camp in mid-July to await Jamil's return.

Bruner watched the guerrilla training program without comment. At first, the foreigners regarded him with suspicion, but the Palestinians vouched for his integrity and after a week or two, he was accepted, although reluctantly. They had taken over the village of Balnus, a small cluster of abandoned farm buildings and former headquarters of one of the largest Fateh groups in the area prior to the Six Day War; like Jamil's tiny army, they too had expended themselves on the Golan Heights. It was a cool, quiet location with a sufficiently peaceful surrounding countryside to practice the art of malice, mayhem and murder without interruption. Bruner settled in with Akbar at the headquarters building in the comfort of his own room.

The single-story dwelling had originally housed a dairyman and his family. The open fireplace in the central area was useful in the winter, when brief snow squalls fell among the hills, and in summer it provided perfect ventilation for sucking the body heat out of the crowded room during afternoon lectures. Sometimes Bruner joined them, sitting at the back of the makeshift classroom, listening either to Leila, Akbar, Abu Doud or one of the other Palestinians explaining the intracacies of weapons, bombs or explosives to the rest of the group.

Besides Pico, the Venezuelan, there was Andre, and three other crazed Frenchmen; two Irishmen from the I.R.A.; four Argentinians; and a Bolivian cutthroat who had worked with Che. In early August two Germans turned up from Munich to complete the cast of misfits. The purpose of their existence was destruction. Wide-eyed mystics with no ties, loyalties or beliefs, except to the Cause, which each, in his own way, defined as the complete destruction of order through chaos for the triumph of the proletariat. For Leila, Akbar and the Palestinians, destruction of order meant anything preventing return to their homeland. For Pico and the Latin Americans, order meant the rich landowners and priviledged elite who had stripped their countries for so long, giving nothing, taking everything. For Callahan and Mulroon, order was the British presence in Northern Ireland; for Andre, and the Frenchman, it was the corruption of the Republic.

Bruner never learned why the Germans had turned up to participate. Both were wanted by the Bonn government on charges of kidnapping the son of an industrialist from whom they had extracted five hundred thousand marks—after killing the twelve-year old heir to an electrical appliance fortune. They said little, and kept to themselves. Bruner listened to the lectures with the fascination of a bird hypnotically frozen by the viper as it prepares to strike.

"Of course destroying something like Battersea Power Station in mid-summer is pointless. In summer it would be an inconvenience, but in mid-winter, during a cold snap, ah, well, that's a different thing!"

Everyone chuckled as Akbar continued. "So action must be dictated by the circumstances which will achieve the greatest return. Poisoned water in the Hounslow reservoir system would be a better idea for a summer project. Everyone gets thirsty in summer."

Bruner got up and went outside. He felt thirsty and cold. The past weeks had been like an enormous jesters convention. Absurd. Unreal. But horribly true. He knew they were all serious—deadly serious! He began to walk, passing the few houses to the end of the dusty road. Beyond the village, he climbed the bank through the tall grass until he gained the top of the hill. He sat down and looked out over the broad valley, thinking back to the day before Leila had flown in from Kuwait.

He had been sitting in the office playing scrabble with Bernadette when the phone rang. She had spent fifteen minutes talking in Arabic while he wandered about the room, pausing finally before the shabby wooden bookcase and flicking through the titles. One of them hit his eye and he withdrew the volume. It opened at a worn page. There were underlinings on a paragraph, with heavy notations in the margin. It was the preface to the PLO handbook of aims and resolutions, written in English. He read it slowly. "The revolutionary is a lost man; he has no feelings of his own, no feelings, no habits, no belongings and not even a name . . . he has broken every tie with civil order . . . and with the ethics of this world. He will be an implacable enemy of this world, and if he continues to live in it, it must only be in order to destroy it . . . all the tender feelings of family life, of friendship, love, gratitude and even honor, must be stilled in him by a single passion; day and night he must have one single thought, one single purpose: merciless destruction. He must always be prepared to die and kill with his own hands. The Revolution Catechism, by Sergei Gennadavich Nechayev, 1870." He had read it through a second time, then put it back on the shelf, feeling ill.

When Bernadette had finished her call he assumed his chair at the end of the desk and asked offhandedly, "Who was Sergei Gennadavich Nechayev?"

"A great man. A great revolutionary," she said fervently.

"What happened to him?"

"The Russian Okhrana—the Czarist police—jailed him in Peter Paul prison, where he died. A terrible loss to the world."

"I can imagine it must have been." He had not felt flippant when he added an O K H R from his letter counter to the A N A already on the board.

Down in the valley he could see the roll of dust sweeping out behind a small car as it raced the road towards the village. It slowed as it neared the cluster of houses and then stopped, slewing a reddish-brown powder over the other Volkswagens in front of the headquarters building. He saw a man climb out. He jumped to his feet and ran down the hill.

"Max!" He shouted at him, breaking away from the rest of the group who had surrounded him in the big room.

"Hello, Galal. Back from the wars?" They shook hands warmly.

"From Frankfurt. The war is in Jordan with the midget king. Don't you wish you were still there for the finale?"

"Not really. I am finding this far more interesting than an isolated war." He waved to the assembly in a generalization. "I mean, who needs to go and watch some mickey mouse war when right here in downtown River City we're planning on going to war with the whole fucking civilized world!"

There was an uncomfortable silence until Galal smiled grimly. "But there is a difference, Max. In Jordan we will lose, but only in Jordan!" He looked around the group for a sign of disagreement, but there was none. They clapped him on the back, nodding and muttering their accord.

Later, when they were alone, Bruner asked him suddenly, "Do you know what is going on here?"

Keila and Akbar were working on a radio at the far end of the table. They exchanged glances and waited.

Jamil lit a cigarette. "Suppose you tell me, Max?"

"You're training a bunch of lunatics to create havoc. These people aren't fighting for Palestine or Ireland or Argentina, they're fighting for some fuzzy ideal they don't even understand because they think it's chic to be revolutionaries. You're creating a monster, Galal! They're not idealists, they're common criminals. Look at those two Krauts—Heinman and whatshisname—"

Akbar interrupted. "Schuler, his name is Franz Schuler."

"—Schuler, you call them revolutionaries? I call them a pair of goddamn bandits!"

"Then I take it you disapprove?"

"Of anyone who pretends to be fighting for a cause that simply provides an excuse to enrich themselves or satisfy an urge for thrills. That secretary in Beirut—Bernadette. She's as mad as a hatter!"

"In more ways than one, I understand." Jamil blew a perfect smoke ring towards the ceiling beam above the table and watched it float.

"You know what I mean. Look, Galal, I'm on your side, remember? I'm the guy that walked with the backpack into Israel."

"Palestine," he corrected, narrowing his eyes.

"I'm the guy that met you in Algiers. I sympathize with the shafting you're getting. I understand your aims and reasons for the methods to obtain those aims, however unpleasant they might be. It is a war. But a war for honorable ideals, between honorable men, not a bunch of lunatics!" He realized he had been talking too loud and lowered his voice. "You know what I mean, anyway."

Jamil looked at Akbar. "Do you know what he means?"

The Palestinian smiled and nodded, "I know what he means," then returned to the radio. Its metal cover had been removed and pieces were scattered across the table. Leila was sorting out the wiring leads, using a small screwdriver, checking each color-coded wire against the sheet of diagrams at her elbow. She didn't look up.

"I went over this with Max before you arrived. I think he is beginning to have second thoughts about all of us."

"No! I believe in your cause, and while I many not approve of your actions, I understand them. But this, this new group of—of—of whatever they are!—they don't belong with you." Leila shrugged. "I'm sorry, but I disagree."

"We appreciate your honesty." Jamil butted his cigarette. "Have you told anyone what we are doing here?"

"You mean sent out any news copy?"

"Anyone?" Jamil repeated.

"No Galal, I haven't and I can't. Glowing news reports on how a couple of dozen lunatics plan on wrecking the world from a secret base in Lebanon would get us all arrested for psychiatric examinations by the closest certifiable M.D. We'd be committed to the nearest funny-farm, all of us." He shook his head slowly from side to side, then got up. "I'm going to bed. See you all in the morning."

When he had closed his door, Jamil moved up to the end of the table and joined Leila and Akbar. "What in the hell is going on here?" he asked Akbar quietly.

"Now wait a minute, Galal, it was your idea to keep Pico and everyone occupied until you had the other program ready. I just obeyed orders." He set down a circuit board. "I'll grant you, they're

386

all a bit strange—especially the two Germans, but they're all good men; loyal and dedicated, and when the time comes, they'll perform for us. As far as their World Revolution is concerned, we've made no commitments to any of them. We've just trained them, and believe me, they need training!"

"Then what's wrong with Max? I've never seen him so upset."

"Maybe someone should have a talk with him and explain what we're really doing with our new recruits—using them for cannon fodder to save ourselves."

Jamil shook his head. "No!"

Leila looked up. "You don't trust him?"

"I don't trust anybody on the program except ourselves."

"But Galal, Max is one of us!" she protested.

"He's not a Palestinian, he's a newspaper reporter. His loyalty is his paycheck from B.J." He looked at them. "If you doubt it, ask him sometime. We're just an assignment and don't ever forget it."

He softened his features. "Now tell me, what have you planned for our cannon fodder?"

Akbar stood up. "Let's take a walk." He jerked his thumb at the closed door and Bruner's room, then touched his own ear. Jamil nodded and took Leila's hand.

The night air was surprisingly cool and still. Most of the lamps in the other houses were still alight as they sauntered down the road. They met two of the Argentinians and Jamil greeted them in Spanish. Surprised, they replied courteously, and turned into their lodgings.

"The plan is to hijack three airplanes, bring them all into the Libyan desert and blow them up with their passengers." Akbar put it succinctly, without emotion.

"You have it arranged?"

"Yes. It's scheduled for September twentieth. El Al out of Schipol airport in Amsterdam, BEA out of Heathrow and a Swissair out of Rome or Zurich—we haven't decided on that one yet. Swiss security is very tight these days. I'll have more information on that later in the week. I sent Mahout and Aziz along the routes to check them out."

"Will the Libyans play?"

"I'm betting they will."

"I hope you're right." They walked on in silence past the last dark house in the quarter moonlight. Jamil stopped. "I don't like the idea of killing all the passengers—unless of course they are all Jews."

"They won't be," Leila asserted.

"As a matter of fact, I don't like killing anyone unless they're Jews. Tell Pico the passengers are to be released in Libya as soon as they land."

"He won't like that—he was planning on killing them."

"Screw him! He can hold them for a day or two and see if we can extract any concessions for release of prisoners or amnesty agreements, but nothing more. If he kills them, I'll kill him. Tell him I said so. No, I'll tell him myself." He turned and started walking back to the village. The other two fell in on either side.

Leila held his arm. "How is Doctor Kastenburg?"

"Expensive," Jamil said. "I've never seen a man go through money as fast as our doctor. We're going to have real problems if we don't find a money source," he admitted. He glanced at her. "Nothing from Kuwait?"

"Not a thing. It's dried up."

"We need about fifty million to carry us through."

Akbar whistled softly in the darkness. "Are you sure the doctor isn't playing games?"

"Positive," Jamil said. "I've checked every item requested from the manufacturers myself. By the time Blucher Chemicals of Cosecha Rica is operational we'll have close to forty million sunk into the place."

"How much are we short?"

"I don't want to talk about it. We have six months to find the money before everything comes due," Jamil said bitterly.

"Is there a good market for the chemicals?" Leila asked.

"Certainly, it's a good business investment. As a commercial enterprise it will make us all rich in time—but that doesn't help us now."

"So what are you going to do?"

"I don't know, Khala. That's why I came back here to think. There has to be a way." They paused in front of headquarters. "And to spend a few nights in bed with my woman."

He smiled in the dark at the squat Palestinian. "Goodnight!"

Akbar nodded and watched them drift down the road to Leila's quarters. He saw them stop by the door to kiss, then he went inside to put the pieces of radio away and get to bed himself.

By September, events in Jordan had reached a crescendo of disaster for the Palestinians, as Hussein purged the country of the terrorist infection. Some said the multiple-hijackings of September had caused the reprisals to the Popular Front in Jordan. American

Secretary of State William Rogers, President Nixon's soft-spoken, underrated, arch-imperialist, used the coincidental multiple-hijackings to good effect, but the real decision for Hussein to finish off the Palestinians had been arranged much earlier.

When Hussein had first been pressured into his war of annihilation by the American and Israeli governments, Secretary Rogers had guaranteed the Jordanian success with a backup plan of his own. During the first days of battle when Hussein appeared to be failing, a story of Syrian and Iraqi intervention on the side of the Palestinians was concocted. The idea sprung from the PLO's thrust into Jordan from the Syrian border on the North, during which it nearly wiped out the Fortieth Brigade, Hussein's pride and joy. Israeli Premier Golda Meir rushed off to Washington on the 17th of September for what the *Chicago Sun Times* described as "an unexpected visit." The following day, the *Sun Times* reported on a long editorial meeting its board had held with President Nixon in which Nixon had stated America was prepared to intervene directly should Syria and Iraq enter the conflict and tip the military balance against the government forces loyal to King Hussein. The Chicago paper had let the cat out of the bag only two days before the Syrian intervention took place.

To cover the error and provide credence to world opinion, Secretary Rogers pointedly asked the Soviet Union on September 20th to use its good offices and urge the Syrians to pull back. The Soviet government was mystified by the request. Rogers made it quite clear he felt American intervention was both permissible and logical; Syrian or Iraqi intervention was not. To back up this logic, Operation Brass Strike was set in motion with the 82nd Airborne at Fort Bragg placed on full alert the same day. President Nixon's orders directed the 14,000 paratroopers to be ready for possible use in Jordan; to descend into Amman and rescue 54 hijacked hostages, including 38 Americans and 400 other U.S. citizens living in the guerrilla-besieged Jordanian capital. At the same time, 2,000 troops were alerted in West Germany and ships of the Sixth Fleet cruising the Mediterranean were ordered towards the battle area with 1,500 U.S. Marines. The propaganda campaign intimated that while the 82nd Airborne concentrated on a lightening strike to rescue American citizens, the others would be sent in if Hussein could not hold off the might of the combined forces of Iraq and Syria. It was all nonsense, of course, but that made great breakfast reading in the Western World.

The Palestinians were ruthlessly crushed and by late September it was all over. On October 5th, Arnaud de Borchgrave of *Newsweek Magazine* wrote, "In almost a quarter of a century of foreign reporting, I cannot recall anything remotely similar to what I have seen in Jordan. I have witnessed inter-tribal massacres in Africa and the slow steady blood-letting in Vietnam. But there has been nothing like the urban devastation—both of life and property—that Amman has suffered."

In the wilderness of Arva, north of Elat, King Hussein of Jordan met Ygail Allon, Deputy Prime Minister of Israel, to assure him the Hashemite throne was now secure and Palestinian terrorism from within Jordan suppressed for all time. This November meeting was the tenth such meeting since 1968, between the King and members of the Israeli government.

Captain Lev Asher tended to the security measures for this desert discussion at the edge of the Negev. He was sitting in the little command car when Hussein's private jet flashed over the single paved airstrip, executed a fighter break approach to the airport, and slid smoothly through the wavy heat onto the pavement with a screech of rubber. Asher climbed out of the car and straightened his tunic, then limped over to join the others at the reception point.

The aircraft swung to a stop and the king, sitting in the pilot's seat, gave a wave to the group on the ground. Ygail waved back.

It was the first time Asher had seen Hussein at close quarters. "Cocky little bugger, that!" he commented to Sgt. Kronig as they watched the official group disappear inside the camouflaged officer's mess.

"Yes Sir, very cocky."

The Jordanian security officer came over to him and saluted. "Captain Asher?"

Asher returned his salute. "Captain Armiturk, Jordanian Intelligence. How do you do."

They shook hands stiffly. Asher noticed the Jordanian's gloved left hand was a prosthesis, the encased fingers partially curled.

"One of ours?" he asked.

Armitruk shook his head. "One of theirs." He held it up. "A Palestinian grenade in '66; I missed the war. You?" He lowered his head.

"I never miss anything, Captain."

"A most happy facility for an intelligence officer, Captain," the Jordanian said in mock seriousness. Asher smiled. He decided he liked the man.

"Shall we make the rounds?"

The Jordanian made an imperceptible bow and joined him on the walk around the officers' mess to check the guard posts. Sgt. Kronig trailed behind, a giant shadow waiting to materialize on request.

"I hear you have been having some excitement in Amman, Captain."

"The outcome was never in doubt, Captain Asher!" They turned the corner of the building, nodding to the salutes of recognition from two sentinels. Their young faces looked guilty at the sudden appearance of the officers.

"You're supposed to be guarding, not talking. Leave the triumphs of the bedroom until you're off duty!" Asher told them curtly.

The soldiers parted in opposite directions, their Uzi weapons at the ready for intruders. The officers watched them absently, then continued along the pathway behind the building. The air was hot, the temperature well above 100 degrees, but the negligible humidity kept away the uncomfortable wetness.

They stopped under an awning leading into the back door of the mess. It was a few degrees cooler. Sgt. Kronig remained in the sun.

On an impulse, Asher asked, "Ever hear of a newspaper chap named Bruner—Max Bruner?"

The Jordanian's eyes were hidden behind his dark glasses; the lenses had an outside reflective mirror coating. Asher couldn't tell whether he was looking at him or the red fire hydrant at the end of the sidewalk.

"Is he a friend of yours?"

"Never met the man—I'd like to."

"Socially or professionally?" The lenses were still pointed at the hydrant.

"He knew about the first El Al hijacking before it happened. He met the plane in Algeria."

"Ah! Then professionally." The Jordanian smiled. They started walking again, Kronig following. "Max Bruner was the resident correspondent for C.P.I. in Amman until he was expelled in July by the American Embassy."

"At your request?"

"At our request, Captain. He sent out a news item which was a gross distortion of fact."

"He lied?"

"No, he told the truth—that was the distortion of fact." He

391

chuckled and looked at Asher. They both laughed their mutual understanding.

"Do you know where he went, by any chance?"

"Yes, he took an MEA flight to Beirut—after that, who knows." He stopped and swung the dual mirrors into Asher's face. "Is there something you want me to do, Captain?"

"Reinstate his residence in Amman, then help me meet him privately."

"You mean kidnap him?"

"His wire service in New York had the flight numbers of those three airliners the PLO blew up seven hours before they were airborne out of Heathrow, Schipol and Rome; CPI even predicted the landing location and the release of passengers. Makes you wonder, doesn't it, Captain Armiturk?"

"I wasn't aware the man had those kind of connections with the guerrillas. Interesting."

He removed the mirrors and began polishing them with a clean folded linen handkerchief. It was the first time Asher had seen his eyes. They were warm and friendly, faintly amused, not at all satisfactory for an intelligence officer. Asher decided the mirrored glasses were a good idea after all.

"You have a theory?" He replaced the glasses. They started to walk again, saluting two more guards at the end of the building.

"Not a theory, more of a hunch. I think the hijackings were arranged and planned by one group of terrorists who have disassociated themselves from the main Palestinian organizations. I believe their base is somewhere in Lebanon or Syria. They are a small compact group, well-trained and well-disciplined, and Max Bruner knows them all intimately. I believe they have used him as their pipeline to the world press."

"It's an interesting hunch, Captain Asher."

"Yes, isn't it, Captain Armiturk?"

They continued around the building and back to the front door, then went inside. The chilly air conditioning hit them like a cold shower.

Asher shivered involuntarily. "I'm sure his Majesty's government would be willing to assist the government of Israel in getting to the bottom of this mystery, Captain Armiturk," Asher said hopefully.

The Jordanian smiled. "I couldn't have expressed it better myself, Captain Asher."

Bruner took the telegram from Jamil and read it again. It was from the U.S. Embassy in Amman and had been delivered to Bruner's postal box in Beirut. He had brought it back with him to camp. *"His Majesty's Government has been pleased to advise our Embassy that Maxamillian Gustav Bruner, U.S. Citizen, passport number 4530697 CFW, is no longer considered as persona non grata within the Kingdom of Jordan. Signed. Leo G. Archibald."*

He tossed it down on the table. "I still don't understand it."

Jamil shrugged. "Who knows. A change of heart maybe; change of policy; after all, you are an accredited newspaperman. Things change."

"In five months!" Andre laughed. "Even in France things do not change that fast, mon ami! I smell fish, strong fish, eh?"

Andre, Pico and the other Latins had returned the week before from their successful air piracy adventures. The two Germans had flown out to Munich on some personal business.

"What do you want me to do, Galal?" Bruner knew, in the final analysis, the decision for his return would have to be made by Jamil.

Leila interrupted. "I think you should go back to Amman, especially since they have given you an apology with the invitation."

"Hardly an invitation or an apology, Leila; they said nothing about being sorry and other than I am allowed back, I don't read it as an invitation. A polite notification perhaps."

"But they do say 'they are pleased to advise'—in Royal Jordanian Doubletalk it means the same thing." Leila stuck to her guns. "If you don't go back or don't reply, it might be taken as an official slight, then you'd never be welcome again. I say you should go!" She looked around the table for further approval. Jamil was silent, thinking.

"I still smell bad fish," chimed Andre.

Pico looked thoughtfully at Andre. "I think Andre is right. It's too neat to be the truth. I suspect either the American imperialists or their Jordanian lackeys have arranged a special welcome for our friend Max as soon as he arrives in Amman."

"Why Pico, that's silly! They could have picked him up in Beirut today when he filed his story, if they wanted him badly. Why go through all the trouble of getting him to fly to Amman? What's wrong with Lebanon?" Leila asked.

No one replied.

"Khala?" Jamil looked at Akbar.

The Palestinian smiled, and raised his eyebrows. "I'm a simple soul, I trust everyone's motives. I believe there is good in all men—even in King Hussein." Everyone chuckled. "You are a newspaper reporter who was thrown out of the country for telling the truth during a time when truth was an uncomfortable reality. Now everything has changed. The Hashemite has won his war. Nasser is dead. Sadat is smiling, and Nixon wants to make everything perfectly clear. We are entering one of those strange periods in Arab politics called peace. What could be more natural than the desire of a peaceful government to make amends for the slight caused to a dedicated news reporter. I ask you now?"

Bruner looked at Jamil for confirmation. The Palestinian nodded. "Go back to Amman." He smiled. "If you have any problems, call the U.S. Embassy, if they can't help, call us. I think you are quite safe, but if you are not—if they have something planned—think of the story you'll be able to send to B.J.!"

"I'll leave in the morning," Bruner told them.

The conference was over and everyone slid back from the table and began to wander outside, heading for their quarters.

Leila paused by the door with Jamil and called back. "Max, don't forget to say goodbye to Bernadette before you go, or she'll be heartbroken."

Bruner made a face. He had spent three hours with the secretary that morning when he went in to file his weekly story. They had rolled around on the carpeted office floor behind the locked door, between phone calls, until Jamil returned from his visit to the bank and rescued him from her clutches.

"Do you want me to miss my plane?" He waved at her.

"Goodnight, Leila."

Doctor Kastenburg raised the long pointer to the large display board.

"Now, gentlemen, over here the fence swings back towards the sea. The actual distance from the waste storage pools to that fence-line is two hundred and fifty meters."

The fence-line was defined clearly on the mosaic of low level aerial photographs covering the board, depicting the complete coastal area from the nuclear power plant at Punta Delgado to the far side of the Blucher Chemical property. The busy construction work at the Blucher site was clearly apparent from the concrete forms outlining the building pads and earth moving equipment. A large completed warehouse stood out whitely at the lower edge of the photographs.

The seven men sitting around the room in the comfortable chairs wrote the figures down on their notepads.

"The tunnel," Kastenburg continued, "will start from the pool holding tank here!" He swung the stick back to the Blucher property, pointing to a square uncovered excavation. It looked quite deep despite the lack of perspective in the flat photographs. "The pool will serve as our storage tank for the waste until we can start our processing operation. The tunnel will travel 1.2 kilometers underground in a straight line, beneath their fence—" the pointer moved as he spoke—"to here!" He leaned forward to examine the spot, then looked back at the group. "Ten meters short of the edge of their storage pool." He surveyed the room. "Questions?"

A thin balding man raised his pencil.

"Doctor Suave?"

"Yes, Herr Doktor, I have a question." His accent was from Alsace. "Your blueprints showed the tunnel sloping to within one meter of the surface of their storage pool from a depth of twenty meters at the starting point from our pool. I have two questions. First, since the surface opening at their end is less than three meters in diameter, how do you propose to lift the fuel bundles out of their pool from this access point? It is still ten meters to the edge of their pool, plus whatever distance beyond necessary to retrieve the bundles. The leverage problems are enormous. Secondly, I notice a roadway on the photograph which runs around the site—almost on top of our access. A heavy vehicle might create problems driving over the access port. Would it not be wiser to move it further in toward the pool, or, conversely, further away from the road?

Kastenburg smiled. "Good questions. I'll answer the last one first." He rested the pointer against his shoulder. "The access port or opening was chosen under the middle of the road because we need the road to disguise the movement of the dolly we'll be using to transport the bundles from the pool to the shaft. If we surfaced in a grassy area, vegetation disturbances would be noticed quickly with reconnaissance photographs, but what possible disturbance would be noticed on a dirt road?"

He waited until Sauve had nodded before continuing. "As to your first question, we are not planning on using any leverage mechanism at the access port. It will take four of you in radiation suits to move the hoist assembly in the electric dolly over the edge of the pool and set it up at whichever point we intend to make the exchange of material. The hoist will then be disassembled, packed back on the dolly and driven into the tunnel. The dolly has six wide, low-pressure tires. There will be no evidence left on the grass—as long as you don't keep returning to the same place each night."

"At one load a night, Doktor, it will take a long time."

"I expect it will, Doctor, but we're in no rush." The others nodded. "With luck we should be ready for extraction operations in three years. The beauty of the program is we know which is the hot waste, and which is safe enough to handle." He turned back to the mosaic. "As you can see by this photograph, they have been piling the bundles systematically, starting at the far end and moving down the pool in this bay." He tapped the wallboard. "So that is where we start. Any other questions?" He looked around expectantly. There were none. "Fine, I hope you all have a pleasant Christmas and New Year and we'll meet back here on January 5 for the traveling arrangements. I should have your visas back from the embassy in Bonn by then. At least they have promised them by that date." He swung his head sadly. "I'm afraid they're not very efficient."

He shook hands with each man as they left. One remained behind, still sitting in his chair; he waited until Kastenburg had closed the door, then lit a cigarette.

"You want an opinion, Heinz?" The man sucked the cigarette, waving the match into the ashstand at his elbow.

Kastenburg waited.

"It's not going to work. The whole thing is too goddamn involved, too many people, too many loose ends, too long to complete. It's another Aida with a cast of thousands."

"I've never seen the complete Aida, Kurt." He went over to the wallboard and began taking down the photographs.

"Neither have I and you know why they never do the whole opera? It's too big to get everyone on stage at the same time."

Kastenburg turned around with a handful of the pictures. "You want out?"

"No, I gave you my word when we started. I'll stay through to the bitter end, and believe me, my friend, the end will be very bitter. I can feel it in my bones."

He stood up and went to the window. It was snowing lightly again and the Christmas shoppers that filled the streets were picking their way carefully along the slippery sidewalk.

"I have always disliked Frankfurt, you know. In winter it reminds me of Norway," he said absently. "Remember Norway, Heinz?" He turned back.

"Vividly."

"Wartime security, SS, Gestapo, soldiers. The tightest security net the Reich had ever developed, and for what?" He threw up his hands. The goddamned Norwegians knew what we were up to a week after we moved in." He went back to the chair and sat down.

Kastenburg continued working on the photographs. In a few minutes the board was blank. He piled the pictures into a square cardboard box and folded the flaps carefully, closing it, then placed it on the floor near his desk.

"For instance, how do you know the secret isn't already out? Sauve for example; maybe his stupid wife doesn't want to go and live in the sun."

"No, not Sauve," Kastenbrug stated. "In fact, none of them will fail us, Kurt. I know them much better than you think. They may not believe in the project, but they all believe in the money."

"How I retired with a million tax free American dollars by making atomic bombs—it should be a best seller!"

Kastenburg looked at him. "You don't think we can do it?"

"Oh, we can do it, all right. Technically and mechanically it's simple. The real question is will we be able to do it without discovery. We have eight men who know the secret already, including you and I."

"Actually it's ten, but go on."

"Ten?" Hauser butted his cigarette, scrunching it into the ashtray furiously.

"You're forgetting the Palestinians," Kastenburg reminded him.

"Ah yes, the founders of the feast! Of course, of course. So other than you and me and the Palestinians, of course, we have eight possible security leaks before we start—that is, until they tell their wives, and then we have sixteen."

"Berger and Kraus aren't married."

"Berger has a mistress."

"Have it your way, Kurt, I won't argue, there's always the chance, but I'm betting that million dollar pot of gold for everyone at the end of the rainbow is the best insurance we have for secrecy—better than the SS, Gestapo or the might of the Reich. Wait and see."

Kurt Hauser stood up and put his hand on Kastenburg's shoulder. "Heinz, old friend, I hope to God you're right, for all our sakes. I'm getting too old to go to prison."

"Aren't we all?" They went out to get their overcoats.

When Bruner awoke he reached under the lumpy mattress and removed the curved wire retained from the bed spring and carefully scratched another mark on the steel angled bed frame. There were thirty-four marks now in a neat row. He had decided when he reached fifty he would turn the single strokes into crosses to save space, assuming he was still in the room another fifty days.

They had picked him up in his apartment on December 7th. Five of them crowding into the room with a thin officer. The officer had been very polite and very firm.

"So sorry to trouble you, Mr. Bruner, but I'm afraid I'll have to ask you to accompany me to Army headquarters—probably nothing more than a misunderstanding, but I've been informed you are harboring a fugitive."

The four non-coms gave the premises a half-hearted search while the officer spoke. Bruner laughed at him. "A fugitive from what?"

The officer shrugged, waving a gloved hand. "Who knows, Mr. Bruner, I simply obey orders.I'm sure you can explain everything satisfactorily to the Major."

There was, of course, no Major and no fugitive, as Max learned later when they ushered him into the small room at the Battalion camp outside of Amman. The officer apologized for the slight delay, and said he would try and find the Major. That had been thirty-four days before.He replaced the retaining wire, hooking it back into the springs and climbed out of bed to use the honey-bucket. The soldiers gave him two galvanized pails twice a day, one filled with clean water for washing and drinking, the other partially filled with a mixture of Lysol and water into which he performed his bodily functions. He washed his face and hands, then went back and sat on the bed. He had given up shouting complaints after the first week when the constant yelling had made him hoarse, deciding that eventually, when they were ready, someone would come to see him and explain the purpose of the kidnapping. Andre had been right, the whole thing did smell fishy. He had satisfied himself they did not intend to kill or torture the information out of him—whatever the information was—so he began to relax.

The worst part of the experience so far had been a complete lack of communication; the two soldiers who fed him twice a day and replaced the pails, never spoke. Obviously, they had been instructed carefully. The other annoying part of imprisonment was the boredom. He had absolutely nothing to do. There were no books, paper, writing materials, games, not even a chair. He had a wash basin, towel, one bar of strong soap, two galvanized pails and his bed in the eight-by-ten room. His meals were brought in on a heavy plastic mess tray with a metal spoon; once when he tried to hide the spoon, the soldiers had spent a full twenty minutes searching, until they located it inside the mattress stuffing, where he had worked it through the seam. They didn't seem in the least perturbed or curious and simply nodded when they found it and left.

Bruner stood up and went through his morning calisthenics, finishing off with twenty-five pushups, then jogging in one spot for what he estimated to be a mile. There was one good thing about being locked up—he knew he was going to be in much better physical shape when he got out than when he arrived. It was small consolation. He heard the key in the door and went back to sit on the bed. The soldiers would not enter the room until he was sitting on the bed. They had made that clear the first few days when he had tried to greet them at the door and was met with a gentle push by a rifle butt back into the room. He nodded to them amiably and scratched his beard, and, as usual, they ignored him, going about their food delivery and bucket replacements, and removing the supper tray and spoon from the previous evening's meal. Then they left, locking the door.

Max picked up the tray and sat back on the bed. Scrambled eggs, three sausages, two pieces of bread and honey. The breakfast never varied. He downed the meager portion hungrily, then went over to the water bucket and ladled out a drink with the tin cup. The cup was bent in several places, mementos of the early days when he had hurled it at the soldiers with frustration. They had ducked the missle easily, doing their work while ignoring his rage. He lay down with his hands behind his head to begin working on the sixth chapter of his book. Carefully, he went over the first five chapters, rechecking the story content mentally. He didn't want to lose any of the parts he had conjured up in his mind's eye over the past weeks. It was to be his first attempt at serious literature borne out of the frustrations every newspaperman harbored in reporting the news instead of inventing it with the vehicle of literature. A few had made the transition; Hemingway, Runyon, Forsythe; now Bruner was certain he too could make the leap. He erased the last paragraph of chapter four; the sentences were too bulky for the smooth entrance he had planned for chapter five. Mentally, he began reworking word structures. The doorkey turning in the lock yanked him into reality. He sat up on his elbows as a pair of men came into the room. It was the Jordanian officer with the friendly eyes and another man, much taller, dressed in civilian clothes. He looked vaguely familiar and Bruner flipped through the facial index in his memory, trying to place the features. He smiled at the officer.

"You're late, my friend! And this, I presume, is the elusive Major. Where did you track him down finally? Upper Volta?" He swung his legs off the bed and waited for an introduction. There were butterflies in his stomach. The soldiers brought in two chairs for the visitors, and left, locking the door behind them.

"I do apologize for the delay, Mr. Bruner, but, as you say, the Major was tied up."

"Don't give it a thought, I needed the rest. The main thing is, the Major managed to slip his bonds and is, I see, none the worse for his experience. Do sit down, both of you. I'd offer you a drink, but it's a bit early."

They both smiled at the jest and sat down.

"My friend the Major has some questions he would like to ask you, Mr. Bruner," the officer continued.

"So you said, thirty-four days ago. I've been breathless with anticipation."

"I hope you will forgive the unorthodox manner in which this meeting was arranged, Mr. Bruner, but I was anxious to meet you; have been anxious to meet you for several years now, but you are damned hard to track down for an interview."

The flip file in Bruner's mind stopped when he heard the cultured British accented speech from the tall man in the civilian suit. Icy needles prickled the back of his neck and scalp. Suddenly he was very frightened. He lowered his eyes to the man's feet, thinking furiously.

Bravado, he thought, *bluff them with bravado.* He looked up. "Well I am of course sorry we couldn't finish our discussion on that road back in 1964, but as I recall we were interrupted by an ambush. I'm glad to see you survived, Major. It is Major?"

"You have a good memory, Mr. Bruner, an excellent memory, as a matter of fact. Yes, I survived that ambush—one of the few who did, I might add," he said softly. "While I was laying there I seem to recall you talking to some other people; someone named Galal, then there was Khala, and of course poor Khalid, who didn't make it back from the raid." He looked into Bruner's face calmly. The room was very quiet. "I thought perhaps you might tell me who Galal and Khala were, or, more important, who they are now, and where?"

"Wish I could help, Major, but it's been years since I've seen any of the old group. You know how it is, people move away from the homestead and forget to write." The blow from the officer with the curved, gloved hand knocked him off the bed, blinding him for a minute. He felt the blood running down his cheek. A little higher on the temple and the steel hand would have killed him. Bruner crawled up to the side of the bed and hung on, his knees on the floor. He felt sick.

"In 1968 an El Al airliner was seized out of Athens for Rome and taken to Algiers with one hundred and seventeen passengers. Coincidentally, you happened to be in Algiers to meet the plane—in the control tower, as I understand."

Bruner climbed back on the bed and lay down, closing his eyes.

"In September last year three more airliners were hijacked and once again—coincidentally—you were on hand to meet them; in fact you filed a story on the hijacking with your New York office several hours before the aircraft had left the ground. What would you call that, Mr. Bruner, *deja vu?* Or do you have the gift of prophecy in addition to an excellent memory?" The beautifully tailored voice was tinged with light sarcasm. Bruner groaned from the bed. His face was numb and his head hurt like hell.

He couldn't figure it out. Israelis working with Jordanians, or was it the other way around? Did the American Embassy know about all this? Did they care?

"Look, I'm a newspaper reporter—I collect news for my employer—he pays me for my work." It was hard to talk.

"Of course you are, Mr. Bruner, and a very good newspaper reporter. I am sure Mr. Bronstein would have no objection in sharing your peculiar prophetic abilities with me."

"What do you mean?"

"I'd like to hire you too, Mr. Bruner, for the same wages Mr. Bronstein pays you. I wouldn't expect a prophet to work for nothing and I'm sure Mr. Bronstein would have no objection to sharing you on an equal-time basis."

So that was it, Max thought. Jordanian Intelligence—or was it Israeli intelligence—was prepared to hire him as a double agent, couching the palatability of betrayal with monthly wages. He knew he would have to play along until he could talk to Jamil, appear to cooperate, but not with too much enthusiasm or the tall thin major would not believe him. "What do you want me to do?"

"Ah, that's better, Mr. Bruner. May I call you Max, now that we're entering a less formal relationship?" He waited for a reply.

"Yeah, sure Major, call me anything you want."

"Thank you, Max. I can see we're going to get on splendidly. As to what I want you to do, in a word, nothing. You are a news reporter. You will continue to be a news reporter. However, each time you have a story to file, I want you to deliver a copy of that story to Captain Armiturk twenty-four hours before you send it out to New York. Is that clear?"

401

"Every story?" Max sat up on the bed.

"Every story, Max."

"B.J. will be mad if he's scooped."

"He won't be, I promise."

"I wasn't thinking of you, Major, I was thinking of the competition scooping me with a twenty-four hour lead time," Bruner explained.

"Then you will have to use your extraordinary powers of prophecy to best advantage, won't you." The tall man smiled. "Now perhaps you could bring me up to date on a few points I seem to have missed since we last met." He leaned back in the chair, tipping it comfortably. "Who is Galal?"

"Even B.J. doesn't know that, Major."

"Possibly he is not as interested as I am, Max. Who is Galal?"

"If I tell you, Major, what will you do to him?"

"Do? Why nothing—unless he sets foot in Israel, or Jordan." He glanced at Captain Armiturk. "My curiosity is purely academic, Max; the deeds are done; they cannot be undone. I would like to know the type of man I am up against. In a war it is always helpful to know your adversary."

"He would kill me if he knew I had betrayed him," Bruner protested.

"But why should he know you've told me anything? Unless of course, you plan on telling him yourself, because I have no intention of speaking to him or indeed anyone else about our little meeting here." He rocked the chair dangerously past the center of gravity. "Then there is the matter of that woman who spoke to the Arab world aboard the El Al airliner. I don't suppose you know who she is, do you?"

Bruner shook his head. "I only met her once. She called herself Zena, but I'm sure it was phony. I never saw her again."

"What a pity. We don't seem to be getting very far in our new employer-employee relationship, do we Max? I'm beginning to have second thoughts about hiring you after all. I ask one simple question—just bring me up to date—and what have I got?" The chair tilted forward on its four legs. He stood up, shaking his head. "Nothing. I think we may have to renegotiate our working relationship." He nodded to Armiturk, then turned his back, intent on the door hinges.

The Jordanian officer came out of his chair like a cat, his steel hand raised.

"Wait!" Bruner screamed, throwing his arms aloft defensively.

The gloved hand stopped in mid-air. "Wait, I'll tell you what you want to know."

The officer sat down and the Major returned to his chair. "That's what I like to hear, Max, a man who knows his own mind." He paused significantly. "Now, who is Galal?"

"Galal Awazi. He is a Palestinian from Syria," Bruner lied.

"Formerly from Jordan?"

"Formerly from Jordan. I met him in Jerusalem in 1964. He hired me as a mouthpiece for news on Fateh propaganda he wanted given to the international press."

"Who is Khala?"

"He was one of Awazi's lieutenants. He was killed during the '67 war. His name was Khala Mursam, another Palestinian. All the information on the hijackings and raids I received were from Galal." He rubbed his head, feeling the coagulated blood hardening on the whiskers.

"Where is Awazi now, Max?"

"In Syria, I think. He was in Jordan, then moved to Lebanon, then moved into Syria."

"I see." He stood up smiling. "Thank you, Max . . . I hope our relationship blossoms into a long and fruitful one—I hope so for your sake."

The Jordanian Captain stood up and rapped on the door twice, then turned to Bruner.

"You will be released within the hour, Mr. Bruner. I'll have you taken to the infirmary and let the doctor look at that face. You seem to have a nasty cut there."

The soldiers opened the door and stood aside to let the interrogators pass. The tall one paused. "By the way, Max, I'm not a Major, at least not yet. I'm a Captain."

"Captain what?" Bruner asked from the bed.

"Just Captain. It's been a pleasure meeting you again." He pulled the door closed. Bruner could hear the lock being turned.

As they walked down the corridor Armiturk inquired, "Do you believe him, Lev?"

Asher laughed. "Not one fucking word, but if we play our cards properly he'll lead us straight to Galal whatever-his-name-is—and it's not Awazi! Just hope we don't lose him."

"I've wired his apartment like a telephone switchboard. The obvious ones he'll find in two days. That bug of yours he'll never find. I put it inside the roller of his typewriter. When he goes to visit the Palestinians, his typewriter goes with him—the trackers will be right behind." He opened the door into his office. "Drink?"

Asher shook his head and went in. "As our friend Max observed, it is a bit too early. By the way, Hakim, remind me never to get in an argument with you when you're wearing your hand."

Jamil was standing in the doorway of the Uaddam Hotel when Tarbu Zitlan brought the Fiat sedan to a screech in front and leaned out the window.

"No more waiting, Mr. Jamil—no more waiting!" He grinned broadly.

Jamil walked around the front and slid onto the seat beside him. "Tell me, Captain Zitlan, you ever have an accident?"

The car shot out the hotel driveway with a squeal of tires and cut across the traffic flow into the street. "Never have an accident, Mr. Jamil. You know why?" They veered around a bus and barreled through an intersection against all odds and a red light.

Jamil locked his knees to the dash, cramming his arm out the open window to keep his body wedged in position. "No, tell me."

"I have a theory, Mr. Jamil. Accidents are caused by drivers who stay on the road too long, creating exposure to accidents. When I drive very fast I am not on the road for very long, so, less chance of accidents. It's a good theory?" Zitlan laughed loudly.

Jamil said nothing. The traffic thinned as they neared the outskirts of the city. They turned down the wide boulevard leading to the military base at the end of the street. The guard on the gate recognized the approaching white cannonball in plenty of time and had the checkered barrier raised when they shot beneath it and skidded into the parking lot.

"Straight through that door." Zitlan pointed as he opened the car leaning across the front seat. "You are expected. I will wait to drive you back to your hotel. The Colonel doesn't like swearing or cigarette smoke. Colonel Qadaffi is a very meticulous man."

"Thank you, Captain, I'll bear that in mind." He walked in the direction he had been ordered, climbed the steps and entered the building.

The Colonel was sitting on top of the broad reception desk talking to another officer seated in an office chair. The junior officer listened respectfully. Qadaffi swung his eyes to the door.

"Mr. Jamil, what a pleasure!" He pumped his hand vigorously, then turned suddenly. "Come with me, there's something I want to show you."

Without waiting for an acknowledgement, he strode off down

the hall, talking in his fast strange desert dialect. "Discipline, Mr. Jamil, the whole world has to run on discipline. Discipline and law. No discipline, no law. No law, chaos—it's inevitable. Self-discipline is the first requirement in my officers. Fasting during Ramadam is the duty of every Moslem. Periodic fasting the rest of the year for self-discipline. There's too much indolence—luxury—people get lazy."

He burst through one of the doors. Jamil followed him at a half-run. Inside the big room in the dim light of late afternoon he saw the Colonel leaning over a huge sandbox. He came up to the sides and peered at it.

"Well, what do you think?"

Jamil didn't know what he was supposed to say. The sandbox was divided into ribboned squares, the ribbons thumbtacked to the edges of the box above the sand. In each square there was a number stuck into the sand with a little colored flag. There were miniature villages, railway lines, oil derricks and roads scattered about the squares.

"Very interesting, Colonel. What is it?"

"What is it?" He looked surprised. "It's a Mahafazat. I've divided the country into ten Muhafazat—this one is al Bayda—next door is Gharyan—the ribbons divide the Muhafazat into thirty Baladiyats—the Baladiyats are broken into mahallats headed by an imman or mayor. I'm reorganizing the whole country. The Italians and British left it in a mess. Tripolitania, Cyrenaica, the Surt, foolish imperialistic divisions with nothing binding the people together. The new system works—I have great plans for the country—new schools, roads, hospitals, farming; we need farming; a huge underwater freshwater lake—under the desert—billions of gallons of fresh water to make the desert bloom. No one told us it was there when I was a boy. The Berber's used to die of thirst. Now it will change—discipline and organization, Mr. Jamil, that's all it takes. What do you want?" he demanded abruptly, resting both his hands on the edge of the sandbox.

In the shadowed light he looked slightly mad.

"Fifty million dollars to build a plutonium extraction plant in Cosecha Rica. I've started it already."

"Where is Cosecha Rica?"

"Central America, near Honduras, north of the Panama Canal."

Qadaffi straightened up, clasping his hands behind his back. "Ah yes, you want to make atomic bombs?"

"Yes, Colonel."

"They're not for sale, you know. I asked the Chinese Ambassador to sell me one. Just one mind you—he refused. But then you know the Chinese." He paced the room nervously, short fast steps. "Where will you get the plutonium?"

"From the waste pools of the nuclear reactor in the country— we'll process the uranium oxide waste—extract the plutonium." Jamil caught himself. He was starting to speak in the same jerky style as the Colonel. Qadaffi hadn't noticed.

"You will buy the waste?"

"Steal it. Our chemical factory is next door to the property where the storage pools are located. It's a simple operation—but expensive."

"The theft or the process?"

"Both."

"I see." He continued walking about his miniature Mahafazat. "What do I get for my money, Mr. Jamil?"

"A plutonium extraction plant capable of building atomic bombs, Colonel."

"For whose use—yours?"

"I would prefer to think of it as a mutual acquisition, Colonel. I have my requirements, as I'm sure you have yours," Jamil said smoothly.

"You are planning a war?"

"Not necessarily. I'd say it was more of demanding a position then attacking a defense," Jamil explained.

"The threat of action instead of the action itself. It will require great self-discipline to succeed, Mr. Jamil." He stopped pacing in front of the Palestinian. "If you succeed, I want to buy bombs."

"If I succeed, Colonel, I will sell you bombs."

Quadaffi laid his hand on Jamil's shoulder. "I like you, Mr. Jamil. You have courage." His eyes burned into the Palestinian's. "You shall have your money. I will make the necessary arrangements. Where do you want it transferred?"

Jamil's knees felt weak; everything he had hoped for, prayed for, was coming true.

"To the account of Blucher Chemicals, Union Bank of Switzerland, Zurich."

Qadaffi nodded quickly and removed his hand. "It shall be done, Mr. Jamil. I will give the order tomorrow. Thank you for coming to see me. Please give my respects to Mr. Andre and his friends."

He turned suddenly and strode from the room and down the hall, his boots stamping the rhythm of his rush. Jamil sighed and lit a cigarette.

406

14

1972

Licenciado Rodolfo Munoz always enjoyed eating at *Los Gauchos*. The fashionable restaurant on the mountain road, west of San Ramon, had been built by two Argentinians three years before. The Brothers Vaquero from the Pampas had won the National Lottery on a joint ticket some years before and set out on a world cruise to enjoy the luxuries of life thus far denied them. Why they had chosen Cosecha Rica as their Garden of Eden remained a mystery to everyone who visited their premises on the Cantella Mountain road to San Theresa.

The location had, at one time, been a stopping place for mule caravans making their arduous journey from the interior towns down to the Capital and the coast beyond. Later, when this caravan business vanished, some enterprising tienda owner turned the place into a brothel stop, in an attempt to persuade the vehicular traffic to pause for more than food or gasoline on their hair-raising trips through the mountains on the snaking gravel road. For a while, the place blossomed again. However, although the quality of the road improved over the ensuing years, the quality of women in the brothel failed to keep pace with the progress and, once again, the place sank into a mire of neglect.

Then the Alvarado brothers arrived and for a bargain, bought the decayed houses and countryside. A year later Los Gauchos opened for business. It's patrons had been the wealthy, loyal and hungry ever since. The dining room filled a huge vacant space between three crumbling adobe houses. The lot had been graded carefully, then an interlocking patchwork of mahogany log slices set into the wet cement as it was poured. Similar horizontal slices were also used for tables, their surfaces polished to a high gloss. The walls were tall thick bamboo, woven with crude jute, lending a slightly South Sea aspect to the surroundings; the bamboo poles supported a quarter roof, partially enclosing the dining room on three sides, but leaving the center and front open. This open front gave guests a spectacular view of the mountains and lights of San Ramon, while the open center provided dining by starlight.

In rainy weather, the big uneven circular tables were moved beneath the quarter roof and diners could eat in dry comfort, still enjoy the view, and watch the rain pummel into the center of the room, soaking the small palm, date and banana trees planted around the center.

The brothers had sent to Argentina for their wall decorations: steer horns, ornate gaucho saddles, fancy hats and, of course, several bolas—the three balls tied to thin ropes with which the Pampa's Vaqueros could bring down any steer while riding at full gallop. Periodically the retired Vaquero owners would demonstrate their own proficiency of the bolas for delighted guests. Rodolfo Munoz had seen them demonstrate several times on the large palm tree in the center of the dining room. Finally, after months of repeated lassoings, the trunk had been bound with sacking to avoid destruction of the tree from the pounding of the bola's steel balls.

The place was crowded when Rodolfo Munoz and his wife arrived. Benito Alvarado, dressed in fancy silver spurs, tight black pants and a silver-embroidered waistcoat, met them at the door.

"Good Evening, Licenciado, Donna Ralna!" He bowed courteously and led them to the reserved table near the center of the room beside the bandaged palm.

Salivating smells from the open-faced charcoal grills beyond the bamboo walls drifted over the tables, making Munoz' stomach churn with anticipation over the meaty churasco delights sizzling in the adobe kitchen. Munoz and his wife sat down to wait. There were no menus at Los Gauchos. The fare was always standard. Red wine from Spain, a light mixed salad and the main course. There was no dessert. No one had any room for dessert after the main course, anyway. The Alvarado brothers could do things with beef components that would make a Cordon Blue chef envious—but that was all they could do. Realizing their own limitations, they stuck with what they knew they could do best. The results were a series of gastronomic miracles.

Munoz studied the other tables, waving and nodding to those he knew, and some he didn't know, who nodded at him respectfully. With a strike deadline approaching the following Monday, Rodolfo Munoz found himself one of the most important men in the Republic. People who had been stiffly polite previously, or ignored him altogether, now courted his attention, nodding amicably. The little Liceniado had become a dangerous man to ignore. He carried his newly-won power well. There was no attempt to Lord it over anyone. He knew exactly where he stood and for what he stood. That was the beauty of uncontested power, when one stood at the summit of support from rank and file.

The amalgamation of the beer workers, soft drink bottlers and chauffeurs unions with his banana workers, had been a coup of which he was justifiably proud. Any why not? In the last contract with the company he had brought the standards of the fruit workers out of the dark ages, an eight hour day, time-and-a-half, overtime, free medical care, one week paid vacation, plus two new schools for the workers' children at company expense. The weaker smaller unions were envious. They wanted a piece of the pie and who was better qualified to get it for them than Licenciado Munoz? There had even been a delegation from the new Blucher Chemical company in to see him a few days before, asking if he would consider representing their two hundred and fifty workers at the bargaining table. Munoz leaned back, inhaling the meaty aromas floating from the kitchen, and licked his lips.

"Licenciado! I wonder if I could speak with you a moment?"

He had not seen the man approach. The accent was pure Gringo American; the harsh Spanish pronunciations clanged against his ears. He hated Americans who ruptured his language. He answered the man in English. "Is it business or pleasure?"

"Neither, it is of a private nature." The American spoke quietly. He had a deep voice, full and resonant in the lower octaves.

Munoz was interested. "Are you with the fruit company?"

"No, I'm a visitor, may I sit down?" He waited for permission.

"By all means, if it is that important." He nodded across the table. "My wife, Mr.—?"

"Rimson, Lyle Rimson. "Howdoyoudo, Mrs. Munoz!" He bowed slightly, then sat down between them.

"My wife doesn't speak English, Mr. Rimson, unfortunately."

409

"Ah, my apologies, Donna Munoz." He switched into his horrible precise Spanish and re-introduced himself.

Two waiters appeared, one carrying two plates of salad, the other with two litres of red wine. The wine waiter looked at Rimson inquiringly.

He waved his hand. "I'm not eating, just visiting for a moment."

The waiter uprighted the table goblets and half-filled both from each bottle, then stepped aside with a flourish to allow the salad waiter to serve the wooden salad bowls. Rimson waited until they had left before continuing.

"I work for a progressive organization in the field of labor relations back in the States, Licenciado. It has been suggested you might be interested in joining our group?"

"By whom?"

"I'm not at liberty to answer that at the moment. Our organization operates on a confidential basis in many parts of the world where labor situations require our services."

"You mean clandestine?"

"That's a pretty strong word, Licenciado, but yes, clandestine, if you prefer it."

"I prefer it." Munoz sipped his wine absently, trying to restrain his curiosity.

"Our service provides a complete program for emerging nations requiring specialized help in solving their internal labor difficulties to everyone's satisfaction, if you know what I mean."

The grey eyes looked clear of guile; intelligent eyes, spaced widely, innocently-set in a handsome face.

Munoz forked a mouthful of salad. "I'm not sure I do, Mr. Rimson, but go on anyway; perhaps it will become clearer." He had switched back into English, noticing his wife was beginning to take an interest in the conversation too.

"Our speciality is solving labor problems."

"You already said that, Mr. Rimson. It's my speciality too." Munoz was becoming irritated with the hedging. "Why don't you get to the point?" He ate some salad, while the grey eyes examined him cooly.

"The unfortunate part of labor unrest in third world countries is that the people who are hurt the most are the workers themselves, irrespective of the outcome of the settlement or concessions obtained," Rimson continued. "That is not to say benefits are not obtained—far from it—but often as not, those who are most responsible for these additional benefits do not share in them."

Munoz was lost completely, and chewed his salad thoughtfully, wondering if he had missed something.

"On the other hand," Rimson went on, "there are many ways labor difficulties can be settled to achieve the highest rewards for those who have been entrusted with the responsibility of settlement." Munoz swallowed his salad and dipped the wooden fork for another load of the delicious greens. The general drift of the American's conversation was beginning to take shape.

"You are suggesting a bribe?" he inquired.

"Good Heavens no, Licenciado! What I am suggesting could in no way be construed as a bribe. It is the reward of power, the power to shape the destiny of events. It is the power that creates the wealth, which in turn provides the power to retain power. You have power—but unfortunately, no wealth, therefore, your power will be short-lived. It has no base on which to build its security. What I offer is that security."

"I see." Munoz did see it, quite clearly. The man represented everything he despised. He decided to play along. "An interesting premise, Mr. Rimson. Supposing you tell me how I can join this organization of yours, or how it wishes to join me—and what exactly we are going to do in securing this power base?" He laid the fork in the bowl.

The American seemed more relaxed as he replied, "I thought you would appreciate an opportunity when it was presented to you properly. However, before going into details I will have to report back to my employers that you are interested in discussing the program further."

"How long will that take?"

"Oh, I will have that information later tonight. In any case"—he looked around the crowded dining room—"this is not the place to discuss business arrangements." He stood up. "Supposing I telephone you tomorrow at your office, shall we say ten?"

Munoz slid back from the table and stood up. "I'll look forward to it, Mr. Rimson."

They shook hands. Rimson delivered a tight phony smile to Ralna and departed for the door. He walked with the precise step of a man who had been trained to standards of high discipline and Munoz was certain the training had not been obtained from the Fruit Company's U.S. head offices in New Orleans. He sat down and went back to his salad.

"Who was that man, Rodolfo?" Ralna had finished the first course and was waiting for her husband to finish his salad.

"A Gringo. A Gringo intriguer by the sounds of things—I'll know better tomorrow."

"He is very handsome, isn't he? I mean handsome in a rugged sort of Gringo way—very tall too—did you notice?—and polite."

"I noticed," Munoz said with his mouth full.

"What did he want?"

Rodolfo swallowed and smiled at her. "My ass."

"Did he say he wanted to see you, my boy?" Artega looked up from his coffee and newspapers. He had been reading a horror story about a string of grisly murders in the *Miami Herald*. The President rarely came to the office before noon. Ruis came in and sat down at the breakfast table in his dressing gown and picked up the morning copy of *El Diario*, the country's main daily, scanning the headlines.

"Hello Chirlo!"

Chirlo smiled at him. "Morning Ruis, how's your classification coming?" Ruis had passed the fifteen hundred mark on his classification of birds. The recent goodwill tour made with Artega to South America had helped the private project enormously. Lately he had started showing an interest in plant species, as well, and the house was beginning to fill with their more exotic forms.

"Flora or fauna?" Ruis poured himself a cup of coffee.

"Is there any difference?" Chirlo laughed.

"Don't waste your sarcasm on me until I've had my coffee, Chirlo, then I'll give as good as I get."

"It seems we have a mystery on our hands, Ruis," Artega said. "Licenciado Munoz has requested a private interview with our Pedro—very urgent." He glanced at Chirlo.

Ruis sipped his coffee. "That rabble-rouser! Did he notify the newspapers? 'Last minute attempt to save country from labor chaos by Rodolfo Munoz'—I can almost see tomorrow's headlines in *El Diario*."

"I don't think so, Ruis, he's not the type. It's something else; he sounded concerned," Chirlo said.

"You handle it, m'boy—if it's a revolution, arrest everyone concerned—if it's a strike settlement, tell Munoz I'll make him a Companion of the Republic." He went back to his *Miami Herald;* Ruis picked up *El Diario;* two elderly men in their twilight years at morning breakfast reading about history because they were no longer interested in making it. Chirlo left them and went back to the car. Paco looked at him inquiringly over the front seat.

"To the office," Chirlo ordered.

Paco eased the big limousine out the drive and turned down the Colonia toward the center of the city.

The situation with his father-in-law was becoming more difficult every year. He had stumped the country during the last election and, as predicted, had won by a landslide, but since then rarely involved himself with the day-to-day business of running the country. It was always "you handle it, my boy," whenever Chirlo asked for his advice. Whatever the outcome, Artega appeared to be satisfied. It annoyed Chirlo to see the firey little doctor lose interest. As the President's first minister he held no political mandate, except through Presidential appointment.

It was understood by everyone that Chirlo ran the country. But how long could it continue? Already there were grumblings in Congress about their absentee head of state. When Artega took Ruis and Felina on the two month tour of South American republics, the opposition parties howled their protests both in the Congress and newspapers. Always the criticism was directed to Artega, never at Chirlo, and this worried him too. Was it because of fear, respect, or because he was inviolate with no political affiliations, which made him attractive to all parties? Chirlo didn't know. If the doctor ever dropped dead, what would be his position?

Vice President Stephano Lacayo would become President, an economic theorist from the University, whose absurd theories had led to constant clashes with Chirlo in cabinet meetings. He knew Lacayo would replace him at once with someone more amenable to his pet ideas on the economic miracle for the country. Stephano Lacayo was a fool. He would ruin years of progress within six months, applying his idealistic notions to the slowly building economy.

Chirlo knew he needed another five years at least, without setbacks, to bring them into the black. Already he had released some of the austerity pressures to give the people more room to breathe the freer air, with lower taxes and import duties.

"You know, Paco, I think I'll run for office next election as vice presidential candidate."

He saw the dark eyes in the mirror looking at him. He could see they disapproved.

"You don't agree?" Chirlo was puzzled by the reaction.

"No, Colonel." He swung the car into the private parking lot behind the Presidential Palace.

"Why?"

"How can a maker of kings become a king himself without

losing the confidence of the people, Colonel?"

The little electric car with the big balloon tires whined to a stop at the end of the long tunnel. The air inside the large room was cooler than in the tunnel and felt slightly clammy.

"You have a circulation problem at this end," Kastenburg announced, then climbed out of the open-decked vehicle.

The other four men joined in the center of the room and looked towards the domed ceiling to the large circular steel door implanted at its apex.

"We have a ventilation problem on the last hundred meters, Doktor." Pierre Sauve adjusted his spectacles. "A negative pressure sucking air from in here to the ventilation shaft by our fence line. I'm going to change the bypass system entirely. That should correct it."

"We changed the access port from three meters down to one and a half, Heinz." Kastenburg swung his gaze from the ceiling to Hauser's face.

"So I see, Kurt. I'm not sure I approve."

The original specifications called for a full three meters to enable a dolly and equipment to move through the exit hatch with ample room. Hauser shrugged.

"It was either that or rework the complete hydraulics for the door to carry the soil weight on top." He raised his eyes significantly. "Three cubic meters of sandy loam was too much for the original system, I'm afraid."

The bigger door had been Kastenburg's design, the smaller door, supposed to fit inside the main port, was now the only opening.

"We tested the dolly and tray bundles before we installed it. Everything will fit—just."

"Have you punched through to the surface?"

"Two weeks back when we set the hydraulic rams. The soil is shored-in by the cylinder for the port—up to twelve centimeters from the surface. We finished it off in one night and dusted the soil back. It's invisible."

"How did you get the last man out?" Kastenburg was curious.

Kraus laughed. "They lifted me out with the cherry picker after I finished my artwork on the road."

"We'll use that method when we start the operation—it's the simplest. The other way wouldn't work, Heinz. We've got to know the road looks undisturbed and it can't be done from down here," Hauser told him.

414

"And your excuse for having the cherry picker sitting alongside their fenceline?"

"I'm starting a barrel storage area in that section of the perimeter. We'll need the machine to move the barrels to the height I'm going to pile them."

Kastenburg was satisfied. They all climbed back in the dolly, made a circuit around the underground room, then headed down the sloping tunnel back to the radiation parking area by the storage pool. Hauser drove the downhill road quickly, following the sunken row of safety lights set in the concrete floor every three meters along their journey back to the plant. In the dimly-lit tubular subway, the guidelights flashing beneath the whining dolly gave an illusion of speed; in reality, top speed on the little car was only fifteen miles per hour.

"You've done a good job, Kurt."

Hauser glanced at him from his steering position. "You're wrong, Heinz, this is all just construction work, the real job hasn't started yet."

Kastenburg didn't reply; he knew his friend was right.

Chirlo regarded Munoz warily when Paco ushered him into the Presidential office.

"Good morning, Licenciado!" He noticed the short lawyer appeared worried as they shook hands. Chirlo ushered him into a chair then sat down behind his desk, elbows on the table, fingers pyramided in anticipation. "Well, what is your urgent problem and how can I help?"

"I believe there is a conspiracy afoot within the American Embassy to overthrow your government. I have been offered a part in the plot plus a great deal of money to assist in the plan." Munoz paused, examining the reaction. There was none. Chirlo's scarred bearded face was impassive, his fingers still pyramided. He decided on a different tack.

"Colonel, we may have our differences in the field of labor relations, however, I have come to you as a citizen this time, not as a—as you have often stated—a 'rabble-rouser'." He smiled bitterly, then related the events of Los Gauchos when Lyle Rimson had visited his table, keeping his voice devoid of any inflection or spurious comments which might distort what had transpired. When he finished, he paused, waiting for some acknowledgement.

"And did he phone you at ten o'clock yesterday morning, Licenciado?"

"Ten exactly, asking to meet me in room 714 at the Mirabella Hotel at twelve noon. I agreed. Colonel Chirlo, Lyle Rimson is an officer with the CIA who has been sent to San Ramon to bankrupt this county with a prolonged strike. This way, American-backed interests will be in a position formally to ask Washington for military intervention to protect American lives and property and then set up a puppet government."

Chirlo stood up and sighed. "Coffee?"

"Yes, thank you, Colonel."

He rang the bell and ordered Paco to bring them a tray, then, as an afterthought, added, "See if you can track down Major Martinez and ask him to drop over for a chat." Paco nodded.

"Major Martinez is our chief of intelligence, Licenciado. I think he should sit in on this discussion—if you don't mind?" He waited until Munoz had nodded. "Let's move over by the coffee table, its more comfortable—more in keeping for citizen-to-citizen discussions." He gave Munoz his awkward smile.

The lawyer laughed as he moved into the comfortable stuffed chair. "Oh no you don't, Colonel. I'm impervious to your famous charm. We are still bitter enemies in my fight for the workers of this country."

"Splendid, Rodolfo. I would hate to think your sense of patriotism had got the best of you."

Chirlo dropped into the chair beside him. "You have never intended to strike at any time, have you?"

"How can you say that?"

Chirlo waved nonchalantly. "I didn't get to this office by being a fool, Rodolfo. You had no intention of calling the last strike and you have no intention of calling one this time for the simple reason both you and I know it would destroy the country. In five years—maybe seven, you could pull one off for a few weeks—months maybe—but not now."

Munoz looked at him closely, disbelieving. "You knew all the time?"

"I knew you—the others, that's a different story. I wouldn't trust any of them. But you, you Rodolfo, in spite of your bombastic oratory and rabble-rousing, are still a practical man, and practical men do not set out willfully to destroy what they are trying to create."

Chirlo looked at him kindly. "Don't feel deflated, no one knows the truth and it is not my policy to make a wise man look a fool. You'll get most of what you are asking from the companies. I suppose you know that?"

Munoz said nothing for a minute. Paco returned with the coffee tray and three cups.

"Major Martinez is on his way over, Colonel." He served the tray.

"Do you have a tape recorder?" the lawyer asked suddenly.

"Yes, there is one in the records office, why?"

"I taped my conversations with the American; only thirty minutes of it, though; the tape ran out part way through the meeting," he apologized, producing the thin Phillips Cassette from his pocket, handing it to Chirlo.

"Paco! Would you be good enough to go get that tape recorder and bring it down here so we can all listen to the Licenciado's home recordings?" Chirlo laid the cassette on the table.

The American undersecretary to the commercial attaché finished reading the list of demands the fruit company had agreed to meet. He handed the paper back to Theodore Ranklin, the President of Consolidated Fruit.

"It appears overly-generous, Mr. Ranklin."

The undersecretary was a commonplace man of average stature and features, which was why the CIA had appointed him as agent-in-charge of the Cosecha Rican desk.

"We're not being generous, Matson, we're being practical."

"So am I, and I'm suggesting you refuse to give any concessions on those demands."

Ranklin looked at him scornfully.

"You know the trouble with you guys, Matson? You're all living in a dream world of cops and robbers. You've listened to so much bullshit out of the State Department, you've wound up believing it's true."

"Now wait a minute, Mr. Ranklin," the agent-in-charge bristled.

Ranklin cut him off. "No, Matson, you listen! What the hell do you think we're going to do down here, play Washington politics because some half-baked political theorist comes up with a policy statement on how this country should jump? That may be your idea of logic, but I'm down here to grow bananas, not fertilize asinine pet projects put together by a pack of fools on the Latin American desk, whose closest contact with Latins was a couple of suck and fuck weekends in Acapulco at the Princess Hotel. I work for the company and the company works for the share-holders, and the shareholders—some of them at least, put your Washington idiots into office. Now if

417

I were to ask them which they prefer—settlement of an impending strike to insure a continuous flow of dividends or, no dividends for a couple of years so you idiots can starve the country into submission for a takeover—which do you think they'd buy?"

Matson jumped out of his chair. "Who said anything about a takeover?"

"Who do you think you're dealing with, Matson, some asshole out of the State Department? Jesus Christ! Give me credit for some intelligence. Do you really believe no one knows what you guys have been up to since Chirlo climbed into the driver's seat down here? No AID funds, no bank loans, no development assistance, no military hardware, no nothing! Every time I turn up at one of those idiotic cocktail parties to meet the latest asshole from Washington, all I hear is the 'communist threat.' I've got a flash for you, Matson, there is no communist threat, the threat is from Washington, so why don't you pack up your toys and suicide pills and go play somewhere else, preferably in an area where the company doesn't grow bananas."

He lowered his voice as Matson sat down. The agent-in-charge had a red mottled look about his cheeks. "Look, Monty, you've got your job—I've got mine. Consolidated Fruit has been around a long time. The company has gone through seventy-one revolutions and seventy-eight governments; we have survived three world wars and a whole series of minor ones. We were in business when your grandfather was a little boy and we'll still be in business when your grandchildren are old men—y'know why?" Matson didn't answer. "I'll tell you," he said, not unkindly, "because we've learned to become a part of the landscape—sure, things are a lot different than they were ten years ago; but ten years ago they were a lot different than twenty years before that. That attorney, Munoz, I hate his guts, but I've got to admire him, and I do. Y'know why, Monty? Because he knows just how much to ask for, he knows just how much is right, and that's why there will be no strike. I'll shout like hell about having to give in and go along with the new demands, but that's all eye-wash for the shareholders' report. Head Office knows the score as well as I do. The world is growing up, Monty, and so are the people in it. You can't soft-soap them with promises anymore. They want a piece of the action."

He paused, his granite face cracking into a smile. "You might pass that information on to the Washington assholes, Monty. I'm sure they'd be astounded."

When Kastenburg finished his tour of the plant, it was time for lunch in the executive dining room. He noted the decoration of the small comfortable room was pure Germanic. He approved the effort. The only non-Germanic aspect was the view of the sandy beach and ocean beyond the palms from the wide windows on the third floor. He rubbed his hands together and sat down, then picked up the menu for the day, adjusting his glasses.

The menu provided a selection of good substantial German cooking. He ordered the sauerbratten and a bottle of beer. He decided he was going to enjoy living here after all, surrounded by good German food, German friends and a project worthy of his considerable talents.

"Now, let us turn to the matter of agricultural chemical sales. Are we making headway?"

Hauser shrugged. "We're selling, although there's no profit yet. We have a good competitive advantage, but the majors have the distribution organization and they're fighting like hell. It will pick up in time."

"We've been fortunate to get a good marketing manager out of Shell, a Salvadorian who represented them for years in the area. He has an amazing number of contacts. I believe he started out originally in the insurance business, working with Lloyds." Doctor Sauve paused. "His name is David Liebe. He is a Jew."

Kastenburg shook with laughter. Everyone at the table except Sauve joined in the merriment. "Oh ho, Kurt, you have not lost your sense of humor!"

Hauser smacked his lips and set the beer stein on the table. "It seemed appropriate, Heinz. Besides, he was the best man for the job. He's over in Nicaragua now; you'll meet him later in the week. It's going to take a couple of years to build our dealer organization, but Liebe thinks he can do it. I've turned the whole thing over to him."

Two uniformed waiters arrived to begin serving the food. Kastenburg recognized one of them from the Bayer dining room in Cologne; he nodded to him.

"You're a long way from home, Karl!" The waiter, flattered by the recognition, bowed. He was an elderly man.

"This will be my home now, Herr Doktor."

Berger called from down the table. "I thought we'd hire German experts in every field, Doktor. You know Karl and Gustav were both S.S. mess officers?"

"Why Karl, you never told me."

The waiter shrugged modestly. "You never asked, Herr Doktor."

After the two returned to the kitchen, Hauser confided, "Berger's idea—keep everything in the family, so to speak. What do you think?"

"I like it," Kastenburg agreed as he attacked the sauerbratten with obvious relish. He was feeling in top form. His associates had out-performed his expectations; he had only been in the country twenty-four hours and already he was positive the plan would succeed. He held his stein aloft.

"Gentlemen! To German efficiency—I drink to you all!"

The tape flicked its tail end noisily around the spool. Leaning across the coffee table, Major Martinez switched the machine off. It was the second time they had played it through. The first time, Chirlo and Martinez had listened attentively for general content. However, on the second run, the Major scribbled a series of notes in his fast shorthand. Now he sat back and looked at Munoz.

"Well, Licenciado, what happened after that?"

"The talk went on for another hour, mostly reconfirming the earlier discussions you heard there." He nodded to the tape recorder. "The money is to be deposited into a numbered account in Switzerland when the strike starts, then a thousand dollars a day for every day it continues thereafter."

"No limit?" Chirlo asked sharply.

"No limit."

"What is supposed to happen in the end?"

After the Marines are called in, you mean?"

"Yes." The Major looked at Chirlo.

"He didn't tell me that, but I'm sure they have plans for a new puppet government. My job at that point is to call the workers back to the job and accept the post of economic advisor with the new government—a cabinet appointment."

"Will you work with us?"

Munoz looked at the Major owlishly. "I'm here, aren't I?"

Chirlo leaned forward. "You mustn't believe everything you read in the papers, Major; despite outward appearances, the Licenciado and myself are very close friends."

"Yes sir," Martinez agreed, tongue in cheek.

Chirlo stood up smiling. "Thank you, Rodolfo. I needn't tell you how much we all appreciate you coming to us with this information. Before deciding on a course of action, Major Martinez and I would like to give your report some thought. In the meantime, if Rimson contacts you again, play along." He put his hand on

Munoz' shoulder, escorting him to the door. "As far as the other matter is concerned—I don't think you have anything to worry about."

"Thank you, Colonel."

Chirlo shook hands with him. "And I thank you, Rodolfo. We'll be in touch." He ushered him out the door and then went back to his chair at the coffee table.

"Well, Major, let's hear your thoughts." It was an order.

"Without a further investigation to verify a few points that still bother me, I believe it's CIA sponsored and headed by Charles Matson—our local undersecretary for commercial affairs at the U.S. Embassy. That being the case, it means they have laid their groundwork carefully—probably as far back as the Revolution when the President requested Berryman to leave the country after that abortive assassination attempt. It means the whole thing is being directed from Washington, and somewhere among our loyal citizens are a group of shadow politicians, locally acceptable, who are ready to seize power when the Marines have landed. You, of course, will be executed along with the President, and your family allowed to flee into exile."

He spoke evenly, surely, with a certainty of subject matter.

"To put a stop to this particular matter is simple. Now we know the plan, but what concerns me, Colonel, is what about the next time? Will we have another Licenciado Munoz coming forward to help us, or will we be at war with ourselves before we know what has happened?" He smiled grimly. "Because Colonel, I assure you, they will try again!"

Chirlo was silent, thinking, his eyes staring blankly at the small Japanese tape recorder. A series of possibilities went careening through his head. It was obvious to him now why there had never been anything but token help from the Americans after their continual generosity during Guerrero's regime; it was no wonder Moody's would not underwrite the bond issue and why now their best foreign export markets were Europe and Mexico. Quietly, slowly, and with ruthless political efficiency, Cosecha Rica had been eliminated from the Friends of America sphere in an unofficial embargo. The Major was right of course; they would try again, and next time he might not be so lucky.

"You're a good man, Martinez. A bit of a pompous ass at times with your trick pistol." He glanced at the Major's sidearm, prominently displayed in its gunslinger holster with the holster strings tied to his thigh. It was reported Martinez could quick-draw the silver-plated .45 and hit a bullseye at ten feet in less than a second. Chirlo had wanted to see a demonstration, but had refrained from asking the Major in case the performance swelled the Major's head to greater proportions than were already apparent. However, despite the bravado and showmanship, Chirlo admitted he was a damn fine officer. " . . . and your one second bullseyes, which seem to impress everyone in the officers' mess . . . including me, I might add—but don't let it go to your head!" He grinned at his subordinate.

"Thank you, Colonel." Martinez seldom smiled at anything. He was all business. "Until you decide the course of action, might I make a few suggestions?"

"Go on."

"First!" He laid one finger into view. "Around the clock surveillance on everyone going in and out of the American Embassy. Two!" He flipped out a second finger. "Ditto on Licenciado Munoz, without his knowledge. Three!" He snapped out a third digit. "Telephone intercepts on all calls for Munoz and the American Embassy."

"They have a scrambler," Chirlo said.

"Only at their end. We can pick up incoming calls from abroad or locally before they reach the Embassy, and monitor the un-scrambled ones going outside. They'll have to call the Licenciado on an open line, Colonel, he doesn't have a scrambler, and who knows what else we might be able to pick up?"

"It's a lot of work. Do you have the manpower? Manpower you can trust to keep their mouths shut and who speak fluent English?"

"Yes, Colonel, I have the manpower." He waited for permission to proceed. The two men were silent. Outside the French windows, one of the duty guards peered inside, spied Major Martinez, and hastily withdrew to his post. The Major glared at the guard; he would speak to him later.

Chirlo stood up, scratching his beard absently. "There should be some way we can turn this business to our own advantage."

He was speaking more to himself than the Major. He began pacing the room. "We've caught them red-handed and can prove it with the tape, but who else is involved besides the American Embassy? Is Ranklin a part of it? And who are the local supporters?" He stopped in the middle of the room and looked at Martinez. "You've heard nothing?"

"Nothing Colonel, other than the usual loud mouths at the University, but they're harmless. No, they have had this planned for some time, which means well established local people—"

422

"—Who may not even be involved in politics at present."

"Exactly."

"Foreigners?"

"Possibly, but unlikely. Whoever takes over would have to be a citizen or it would look too contrived for the public to swallow."

"Was Castro a citizen of Cuba when he took power?" Chirlo asked.

"Were you?" The Major didn't smile. "My records show you are still a Mexican citizen."

Chirlo laughed at him. "What else do your records show, Major?"

"I'll bring you your file if you wish, Colonel."

Chirlo waved away the offer. "Some other time." He came to his decision.

"You may begin your telephone taps and close surveillance on the embassy staff. I am particularly interested in any of our local citizens who might be having an unusual amount of contact with Embassy staff. Keep me informed." He went back to his deck as Martinez stood up, saluted and walked towards the door. As Chirlo sat down, he called, "Major!" Martinez stopped, his hand on the brass latch. "Does your file on me indicate any peculiar medical problems I might have?"

"Yes, Sir. You have been an amnesiac since 1960."

"Anything else?"

"Of a medical nature—no, Colonel."

"You're a good intelligence officer, Major, but I still think you're a martinet."

"Yes, Sir. Thank you, Sir." Martinez saluted, his face, as always, serious, and left the room.

The noon-time conversation over luncheon had been light and jovial. To a casual observer, the eight men sitting around the table could have been members of any group of German businessmen meeting in the comfort of one of the private clubs in Frankfurt's exclusive banking district. Kastenburg sat back from the table expansively and wiped his face with a napkin.

"Delicious! Delicious! My exile will not be without its compensations. Now to business."

He stood up and started for the elevator. Kurt Hauser joined him, leaving the others standing by the table. "I have the figures in the safe in my office."

Kastenburg waved jovially to the others, then stepped into the elevator with Hauser and descended to the second floor executive offices. Hauser's room had been positioned next door to the plush corner office Kastenburg was destined to occupy. Slightly smaller and less elaborate than that of the director's premises, it was made to appear larger by clever use of wall mirrors. The handsome, laconic Hauser suffered from narcissism. He swung one of the mirrors aside and opened the safe hidden behind the pivoted glass, then joined Kastenburg with an armload of file folders.

"Do you want to look at them, Heinz?"

"Later, give me a summary, how much we have on hand, and when can we start?"

Hauser dropped into the chair behind the desk and tilted himself back in the swivel, placing his highly-polished heels on the blotter carefully. He laid the papers on his lap for reference and put on his glasses.

"Punta Delgado went into operation with test power in 1967, purely a series of system checkouts. Continuous power generation started in early 1969. The first waste bundles were removed at the rate of between five and six a day from August 13, 1971—last year. Allowing for a three-year cooling period in their storage pool at the reactor, the earliest we can expect them to start deliveries into the outside pool beside our fence line is June or July 1974. From that point on, we should be able to collect enough waste to produce 10 pounds of plutonium a month."

He paused to riffle through his papers, and withdrew one of the pages.

"The ratio we can expect is about one pound of plutonium from every three hundred pounds of uranium oxide pellets. Fifteen spent fuel bundles will give us one pound of plutonium. Right now they are piling six bundles in each of the shielded containers for pool storage. Total weight is about 300 pounds—including the container—"

"—How do you know they are storing six in each box?" Kastenburg interrupted.

"I visited the plant two months ago—complete tour. I asked a lot of questions and got a lot of answers," Hauser explained airily.

"Splendid."

"No problem duplicating the containers, they're simple. I figured we would use the original frame and zirconium tubes in the replacement bundles we leave behind—makes things much simpler. We'll only have to build up the first ten bundles; after that we can use theirs every time we make an exchange."

"Kastenburg removed his pince nez and rubbed the bridge of his nose thoughtfully, then replaced the rimless eyepieces. "So, we have two years to wait?"

"Almost to the day."

"Good! That should give me the time I need for the laboratory work and installation of equipment in the hot room. I think we should practice a few dry runs to make certain the removal equipment will function."

"I planned on it—just waiting for you to arrive before giving the green light. I want a practice session every month until our fellows can do the job with their eyes closed." Hauser folded the papers back into their file and slid his heels from the blotter, tilting himself back to a sitting position. He pushed the file over the desk to Kastenburg.

"Read it, Heinz; it's all there, including the practice runs with the hydraulic hoist—that, by the way, is the only copy."

Kastenburg pulled the file off the desk and stuck it under his arm as he stood up. "You must concentrate on those chemical sales, Kurt. Keep after your Jewboy; I want this operation to look logical, and that means operating at a profit. No excuses, now. Everyone is being well-paid for this project and the chemicals are just as important a part as the plutonium. Remember that!"

"Give me another six months and we'll be turning a profit, I promise."

He stood up and walked with Kastenburg to the door leading into the director's office. "By the way, Heinz, now that we're operational, I've had a number of requests from newspapers and television stations to do a story on us; personal visit by the President for an official opening. I've stalled it until you arrived."

Kastenburg opened the door. "Let me think about it. We don't want to appear rude, but I don't want any snooping either. Perhaps a restricted tour of the safe areas would be in order—a first and only tour of the premises. I'll give it some thought."

He went into his office and nodded to Willi Hendricks. The accountant had his bundles of columnar sheets arranged neatly along the edge of the conference table in the middle of the room.

"Well now, Willi, let's see how you can manage to explain where thirty-two million dollars went to—and it better be good!" Smiling, he went over to his desk and locked the file folder in one of the drawers.

"Thirty two million, seven hundred and ninety-four thousand two hundred and seven dollars and sixty-three cents, to be exact, Doctor!" Willi said with a broad smile.

"Ach so, Willi. My main concern is what did you do with that seven dollars and sixty-three cents?" They both laughed and sat down at the far end of the table. Hendricks began to explain where the money Jamil had received from Muamman Al Qaddafi had been spent during the last twelve months.

"Paco!" The door opened instantly and the aide appeared.

"Colonel?"

"Come in and close the door, I want to talk to you. Do you know the American Ambassador's chauffeur?"

"Yes, Colonel, his name is Sgt. Anderson; he is a marine—he speaks Spanish. I met him at the inaugural ball. He comes from Texas."

"How well do you know him?"

"Not very well, Colonel—he is not a friend."

"Do you know him well enough to meet him for a chat?"

"Yes, Colonel."

"Does he live at the Embassy?"

"Yes, Colonel, he lives in the barracks over the garages."

Chirlo looked at Paco; he had not realized it before, but his aide was growing old; the dark hair was nearly silver-grey at the sides and temples, the pleasant open face wrinkled at the eyes and mouth. He came to with a start, knowing he was staring.

"We've been together a long time, my friend." He said the words softly.

"Ten years, Colonel."

"A long time, Paco. We've grown old and maybe a little tired, eh?" Paco said nothing. "Tell me—honestly now—have I changed?"

"Changed?"

"Changed from the man who came to Tippitaca and hired you as the administrator for La Esperanza." He sighed. "It seems a century ago."

"We have all changed, Colonel. We are older and wiser—much wiser—especially you. You are the wisest man I know." He said it so sincerely it made Chirlo laugh.

"Paco, I'll tell you something—a secret between the two of us: I'm not wise at all, just lucky, but don't ever let anyone else know that or they'll run me out of here tomorrow!"

"No, Colonel, the only way you'll leave here will be because you want to leave—no one will ever try to run you out."

"You think not?" he asked seriously.

"I am certain."

"Well, my friend, I'm afraid you're wrong. Let me tell you who wants to run me out of here and why, then I'll explain why I want you to phone your friend Sgt. Anderson from Texas."

———————————————————

Women's luncheons were one of the major forms of purgatory Felina had to endure as First Lady of the Republic. Two or three times each week she was scheduled for speaking engagements around the country. It had started during the last election campaign, when, as daughter of the incumbent and wife of the country's chief administrator, as well as mother of three, she was looked upon as the epitome of Cosecha Rican womanhood and as such, asked to present her views to the electorate. She was a good speaker with a clear pleasant voice and the ability to adjust her words to meet the vernacular of her audience. Up country, she could drop into the local idiom while addressing a group of poor farm wives with the same ease with which she spoke to a group of female university graduates. For the most part, the newly-enfranchised females of the country were the main reason Doctor Artega had received such an overwhelming majority in the last election. It was said—but only among women—that Felina Artega did in fact run the country, giving daily orders to both her husband and father on how business should be conducted. The fact that they, and not she, held the offices, was merely a sop to the male ego. It was a good story and went down well with the female electorate, who, believing their own fantasy, had been bombarding Felina for personal appearances ever since.

She stood now at the speaker's table, accepting the applause from the room full of women and a thin scattering of men. The thirty minute speech had covered the relationship of women in business. It was a rehash of the same talk she had given at the Continental Hotel to another group four months earlier. She sat down on cue, as the applause diminished and the chairwoman took the podium.

"Senora Artega, on behalf of our members and their guests, I thank you for speaking to us this afternoon. Your comments and criticisms are timely and true. I'm sure we shall all leave this room much wiser than when we sat down to eat our lunch. Thank you."

There was another round of applause. The chairwoman, a short stout matron with bullet teeth and an M.A. in home economics from the University of Mexico, acknowledged the audience's enthusiasm with a gummy smile and returned to her seat. The members of the Ladies League of Liberalism began reaching for their purses and compacts for last-minute touchups before returning to their less

427

liberal occupations as housewives.

"Senora Artega!" A man's voice called her from the floor below the platform of the speaker's table.

He was a young man, very young, Felina noted quickly; bright blue eyes, straight blond hair and slim hips. She eyed him speculatively. "Yes?"

"May I speak with you for a moment?" He gave her a boyish smile, exposing a lovely set of teeth. When he smiled, his eyes crinkled at the corners. She turned to the Chairwoman and excused herself, shaking the stout woman's hand for the sixth time since arriving for the luncheon. The young man was shorter than she had expected and met her at eye-level.

"I'm Rolf Hauser with National Television." They shook hands. His Spanish was nearly flawless and beautifully modulated.

"Hauser? German?" Leila inquired.

"From Innsburk—Austria, actually."

"You speak perfect Spanish—I'm impressed."

"Thank you. Look, do you have a few minutes? There's something I'd like to discuss with you? Perhaps coffee?"

While they spoke, several women barged between them to congratulate Felina on her speech, then returned to the crowd of milling matrons drifting for the exits.

"Lead the way, Mr. Hauser." She followed him while he threaded his way through the room to one of the side doors, then stepped aside to hold it open for her. She noticed he had a nice manly smell about him as she passed into the corridor.

They found a small sidewalk cafe a few blocks from the hotel and sat down.

"Have you been in San Ramon long, Mr. Hauser?"

"Please Senora, call me Rolf."

"Very well, Rolf—but only if you call me Felina." She felt a bit lightheaded. The boy was a complete stranger, and yet . . .

"Not long, Felina. I came in March to visit my father—he's one of the directors of Blucher Chemicals. I liked the country, so I stayed. I got a job with National Television, which is why I wanted to talk to you. I'd like to do a one hour news special on you and your family—you know the sort of thing?" He paused, looking at her. "No, maybe you don't. In Europe and America they have one hour programs—news specials—on important people."

"I know what you mean. I've seen them. I didn't live my whole life in this country, Mr. Hauser." She didn't want him to think she was too parochial.

"Rolf," he said shortly. "I'm sorry, I didn't mean to offend you Felina." He hung his eyes regretfully.

She reached out and held his hand, squeezing it. "Go on, tell me your idea!"

He left his hand on the table. Felina held onto it. Her breath felt tight. It suddenly dawned on her that she wanted to go to bed with Rolf Hauser very badly, right then and there. He began to tell her what he had planned for the television special. She watched his mouth working and heard the sounds, but understood nothing except she was getting wet between her legs and would soon have a visible stain on her dress if she did not move soon.

"It sounds interesting, Rolf," she interrupted him, standing up. "Why don't we go over to your place and discuss it? I feel more like a quiet drink than coffee."

She felt shameless. Young Hauser stopped in mid-sentence and stood up slowly.

"Well, sure if you'd prefer it." He paid the bewildered waiter, who had arrived with the steaming cafe con leches, and took Felina's arm, leading her away from under the awning of the restaurant.

"My car is around the corner," she announced. They walked through the noisy afternoon traffic in silence.

"You drive." She gave him the keys. She felt too nervous to trust herself at the wheel. As he pulled away from the curb, Felina moved close to him and put her hand on his thigh, squeezing him lightly. "I find you very attractive, Rolf." She laughed shortly. "I hope you are not offended."

He didn't take his eyes from the road. "How could I be offended—I'm flattered." He winced as her fingers reached his groin and began to massage. His erection was swift and awesome.

"God, you are enormous!" Her hand moved down the inside of his thigh, tracing the swollen outline to the enlarged glans hidden beneath the grey slacks.

"Look, do you think we could wait until we get to my apartment—I don't want to wreck your car." He glanced at her, smiling with understanding. Felina nodded, but left her hand encasing the swelling.

She restrained herself with difficulty until they were inside the apartment, then threw herself into his arms, hungrily devouring him with her lips and tongue. She reached down as he held her, and slipped the catch on his belt, then lowered the zipper, sinking to the floor, taking his pants and shorts to his ankles. She clutched him greedily with her lips, felt him swell dangerously, then stood up quickly and hurriedly removed her clothes. He carried her to the sofa and squeezed himself into her glistening crevice. She screamed as he pounded against her, tearing at him in agony of delight until their worlds exploded.

Later, still inserted in her softly, he sat up between her thighs and looked down with wonder. "Do you know what time it is?"

She felt warm, relaxed, satisfied. She reached up and brushed his blond hair aside at the temples. "No, my gorgeous Viking, tell me."

"It's two fifteen." He crooked his arm so she could verify the timepiece.

"So?"

"So we've known each other for exactly fifty-two minutes and half that time was spent driving over here." He laughed. "I've heard of world records, but this—this is ricidulous!"

"Are you complaining?" she asked dreamily.

"Hell no!"

"Good. If it's only two-fifteen, it means I still have another hour and a half before the children get back from school." She pulled his head down to her breast and began working her thighs sensuously. She heard him sigh, then felt him shudder and once more he began to grow within her.

The cafe of the Dolphins was primarily a meeting place for truck drivers who traveled the road in an endless series of trips between San Ramon and Bahia Blanca, bringing their ocean cargos into the city. Paco knew some of the chauffeurs who frequented the place, most of whom came to deal in the illicit market of stolen merchandise handled by the Dolphin's owner. Jorge Guzman kept a warehouse at the back of his establishment where he stored the various articles which were forever disappearing along the route from the seaport to the capital. Guzman was the trucker's fence, the intermediary in a thriving business enterprise. It was said that Guzman's warehouse held varieties of merchandise duplicated only by *Carabello's*, San Ramon's main department store, but at half their prices. Since Guzman had a monopoly on the business, the police allowed him to operate without interference. It made matters much simpler for them when something of real value was stolen along the route to drop into one location for the recovery, than to waste valuable time searching alternative locations. Jorge Guzman had an understanding with Captain Orchello of the Guardia Civil—Guzman never stole too much of real value, and Orchello received a flat ten percent on all goods sold, for the so-called Guardia Pension Fund.

However, it had been informally agreed if a hue and cry developed over the theft of any particular item, Guzman would surrender it immediately without complaint, regardless of his investment. It was an admirable arrangement. Orchello had made similar agreements with the local car thieves, house burglars and pickpockets in each of their respective territories. The arrangements were so successful that the incidence of crime had actually declined over the past five years, while at the same time the Guardia's pension fund had reached proportions which could be described only as grotesque. Paco, ever conscientious, had reported the matter to Chirlo when he had first discovered what was going on behind the Dolphins, but to date his employer had done nothing.

"There is a bit of larceny in every man, Paco," he had told him, laughing. "As long as it doesn't get out of hand, there's nothing to worry about. If I sack Orchello, his replacement will be just as venal, and if I tell Orchello to arrest Guzman, who will the drivers sell their merchandise to?"

"Ah! Senor Paco, welcome to the Dolphins!" Guzman beamed over him at the table.

"Hello, Jorge, how's business?"

"Terrible, and getting worse!" He slapped him on the back and laughed uproariously. Then yelled at the bartender. "Hey Miguel! Bring my friend Paco whatever he wants—on the house!"

"I have money to pay for what I buy," Paco protested. Guzman winked at him. "When you come here it is my treat; humor me Paco, humor me!" He clutched his shoulder a moment, then wandered away to greet another arrival. Paco saw Sgt. Anderson park his car through the wide front windows and pause outside, examining the place intensely before coming in.

He spied Paco sitting alone at the table in the middle of the room. He looked very American with his short clipped hair and sunglasses. He glanced round the room—"Interesting place"—then swung his head back—"You wanted to talk to me?"

Paco launched into his carefully rehearsed speech. "I am frightened for your safety, Sgt. Anderson. I think you should go on leave, go back to Texas right away, until the revolution is over, because if you stay you will be killed—your name is on the list too!"

The Marine's jaw went slack in amazement as the waiter came over and asked for their order. Paco ordered a pair of beers.

"What the hell are you talking about, buddy—what revolution?"

"The one your Mr. Matson of the CIA is planning with Mr.

Rimson to take over the country. Colonel Chirlo has known about it for a long time. As soon as the labor movement strikes, he is going to send the army in to force the workers back to their jobs. It is at that time the communists—well, not really communists—they are the Colonel's secret police—they will storm the American Embassy and kill everyone, then broadcast how the CIA tried to overthrow the country and ask the Cubans to help prevent American takeover. It's all been planned for months now"—he waved his hands airily—"but I didn't want to see anything happen to you."

"Jesus Christ, Paco! When is all this supposed to happen?" The Marine's face was pale beneath his suntan; he licked his lips, waiting for Paco to finish sipping the bottle of beer.

"Next Monday. The strike is set for next Monday; the assault on the Embassy will be on Monday afternoon, and the broadcast to Cuba, Monday evening. Do you think you can get out of here in time?"

"Are you sure about all this—I mean, how did you find out?"

"Sergeant Anderson," Paco said haughtily, "I am Colonel Chirlo's personal chauffeur and aide. I hear everything that goes on in the Presidential Palace."

"What else did you hear?" His Quantico intelligence training started to assert itself.

"You're not drinking your beer, Sergeant."

"Can't drink when I'm on duty—how do you know all this is true? I mean, it might just be gossip." He watched Paco swallow another quarter litre from the open beer bottle.

"No gossip, Sergeant Anderson. Your Embassy telephones have been tapped on all local calls and everyone under surveillance for months—there is a Licenciado Munoz, a labor leader—they even know of his secret meetings with your agent, Mr. Rimson, at the hotel—they know everything. Colonel Chirlo is not stupid. Of course, Munoz will be shot for treason." He shrugged his shoulders. "But then I can't disagree with that. The man is a traitor."

"Who else have you told this to, Paco?"

"No one—only you."

"No other Americans?"

"No one. I'm not interested in other Americans. I don't know them, but you helped me once—I'm repaying the favor. Now we are even."

"I did?" Anderson couldn't remember.

"The bulb—the courtesy light bulb in the back seat of the Colonel's car. You gave me your spare—remember?"

Anderson nodded. He remembered—such a small thing. He stood up. "Thanks Amigo, I appreciate your telling me. I'll go and see what I can do about getting a compassionate leave."

"A what?"

"Compassionate leave—when someone dies in the family, they'll let us fly home for the funeral." He shook hands with Paco, and patted him on the shoulder.

"Don't leave it too long, as there will be many compassionate leaves coming from the other direction after Monday, Sergeant." He sat down again to finish his beer.

He felt pleased with himself. His speech had been perfect. He didn't know what was supposed to happen next, but that was none of his affair. Chirlo knew what he was doing; of that, Paco was supremely confident.

"Well?" Major Martinez looked up from his desk of paperwork. Lieutenant Rialto appeared uncertain, shuffling first on one foot, then the other.

"For God's sakes, man, stand at attention! You look like a negro musician—what is it?"

"Sir, I was relieved of my surveillance of Senora Artega at 1600 hours by Lieutenant Vescama, and I thought I should report directly to you." He stopped talking.

Martinez waited, his eyes puzzled. "You had a disagreement with Vescama?"

"No sir, I have something to report on the senora which happened during my surveillance shift—something of-ah-well-er, ah-delicate nature—I thought you should know."

"Sit down, Rialto." The young plainclothes officer pulled up one of the straight-backed chairs and sat down gingerly on its edge, his hands folded correctly on his lap.

"Suppose you tell me the story."

"At 0800 hours I relieved—"

"—Never mind the formal report, just give me the substance— what is it?—she has taken a lover? Is that it?" Martinez suspected it was. Felina Artega was about the right age.

Rialto nodded, saying nothing.

"Who, where and when?"

"Rolf Hauser—Doctor Hauser's son. He works at the television station. They met at her speaking engagement this afternoon and then drove in her car to his apartment, where they remained until 1545 hours, at which time they returned to Hauser's car, and she drove home. Lieutenant Vescama intercepted me while approaching the Colonia and continued the surveillance.

"You have spoken to no one about this, Lieutenant?"

"No, Sir."

"Good. Keep it that way. I want a full written report—*my eyes only*—no copies. Do you understand?"

He waited until Rialto nodded. "How do you know they were actually engaged in the—ah—act?"

"We have Hauser's apartment tapped—his phone too. I listened to the recording."

"Where is it now?" Martinez remembered he had ordered wire taps on all employees of the news media when the first labor troubles started two years before.

"I replaced the spool; it wasn't finished."

"Get it, and bring it to me, then remove all surveillance equipment from the Hauser apartment," Martinez ordered.

"Including the telephone taps?"

"Everything. Do it now. I'll expect you back here by six with the recording and your report. You may go, Lieutenant."

He nodded in return to the young man's salute, then sat back to consider the implications of what he had heard.

Chirlo would have to be told. Major Martinez' first loyalty lay with his superior officer. Would the bearded Colonel thank him for the information? He doubted it. He would probably make some comment about his being a prissy martinet—maybe have him replaced because of the knowledge? He toyed with the plastic ruler on his desk, permitting his mind to wander in different directions, exploring alternative solutions to his dilemma. He was a career officer and did not want to jeopardize his career. He was also a gentleman and fully realized the weaknesses and failings of his fellow creatures. The red phone rang at his elbow; the hot line from the Presidential Palace. He picked it up.

"Major Martinez, Sir."

"Major! Paco has reported back. The plan seems to be working. By now Sergeant Anderson should be at the Embassy. I want a full surveillance at my house tonight and continuous monitor." He chuckled through the line into the Major's ear. "It should be fascinating to hear how they plan on worming their way out of this one!"

"Yes, Sir. Fascinating. I'll attend to your instructions at once, Colonel." He replaced the red phone slowly and bit his lip; he had been on the verge of reporting on Senora Felina Artega's infidelity.

434

The infraction of military discipline was hard to treat even when one knew the diagnosis and the curative.

Shortly after six, Paco pulled into the driveway and stopped the car. Chirlo stepped out and paused to look out across the city. It was a ritual that seldom varied. In the setting sun the hills appeared deep ochre, a rolling softness caressing the fading horizon. The city lights were ablaze, anticipating the darkness.

"I won't need the car tonight, Paco, thanks." He started up the steps to the lawn.

"Good luck, Colonel!"

Chirlo turned. "Good luck?"

"With your plan." Paco grinned up at him and was rewarded by a thumbs-up sign.

"I'll tell you how successful you were tomorrow morning at seven-thirty, my friend. Good night!"

"Good night, Colonel."

He stopped on the front patio and slid into his favorite chair to watch the miracle of night unfold. Felina joined him with a glass of sherry, and sat beside him beaming. He looked at her puzzled. "You look radiant! What's the occasion?" He sipped the small glass without looking at it.

"I don't know. I just feel great. One of those *good days.* Don't you ever have *good days?* Maybe it was the speech. I did it well."

"The ladies were pleased?" he inquired, not really caring.

"I destroyed forever the myth of male superiority in the country."

"That's treason, my darling. Be very careful or I'll have to speak to Major Martinez."

"Pooh on Major Martinez, what's he know about the Ladies of Liberalism." She made a face. He laughed at her affectionately, and took her hand.

"Major Martinez is one man who knows everything that goes on in this country—believe me!"

Her expression, as he said it, puzzled him, but he made no comment and continued sipping the sherry. "How are the children?"

"Eating supper. The twins are both complaining about those front teeth again—"

"My offer still stands," he laughed.

"That's how I finally stopped them from any more complaining at the table. Told them I'd send you in to yank both teeth out and settle the grumbling once and for all."

He heard the telephone inside and waited for the houseboy to call him. The living room glass door slid open and the boy appeared, carrying the open receiver to him, trailing wire.

"The American Ambassador, Mr. Collins, for you, Sir." He handed the receiver over and set the other half of the unit on the glass-topped table, then departed, closing the sliding doors.

Chirlo winked at Felina, covering the mouthpiece with his hand. "Stick around and listen to this one—it's going to be good. I'll lay you odds he says he would like to drop up tonight for a chat."

"How much?" she said quickly.

"Name it?"

"A week in Miami."

He nodded and removed his hand. "Good evening, Ambassador." He switched into English.

"Good evening, Colonel, I know this is a bit irregular—protocol and that sort of thing—but something has come up which I thought I'd like to discuss with you—if you have a moment this evening?"

"Certainly, I have nothing on at the moment. What is it? You sound as if you have a problem—nothing serious I hope?"

"Well, I don't know whether it's serious or not—not yet. That's why I wanted to have a talk." His tone had a strange sense of pleading.

"Go ahead then, I'm listening." There was a ten-second pause.

"Frankly Colonel, it isn't the type of thing I care to discuss over the telephone. I'd prefer to sit with you in person."

"Oh, I see! It's that type of meeting. I don't know whether I can get the President or any of my staff at this late hour, Mr. Collins. Couldn't we put it off until tomorrow?" He was playing with him now and enjoying every minute.

"Oh no, Colonel! This—I mean—I want this to be a private meeting. You know—one to one. Just the two of us and a couple of glasses." He tried to make it sound cozy. "It isn't necessary to bother Doctor Artega or any of your staff—I'll be coming alone myself with my driver—just my driver."

"Well, if you think it's all that important, Mr. Collins, that it can't wait until morning, I suppose you'd better come up and see me. Try and make it before nine—I like to read the children their bedtime stories."

He saw Felina smirking, putting a hand to her mouth. Chirlo seldom read the children's bedtime stories because he found it impossible to control the pre-selection arguments as to which story would be read, and accordingly, left the chore to his wife. He had

436

made his voice sound frosty to the Ambassador.

"I'll leave here at once, Colonel. Shouldn't take any more than a half hour. Thank you so much." He hung up quickly before further discussions could be attempted in modifying the time structure for his visit.

Chirlo laughed. "I win!" He replaced the receiver.

"What on earth was all that about and why is the Ambassador calling on us at this hour?"

He leaned over and kissed her, then swallowed the rest of his sherry. He laid the glass on the table beside the phone and stood up, pulling her up beside him.

"It's called charades. An old-fashioned game for little boys to play when they've been caught in their deceit. Let's eat—I'm hungry and I've a feeling it's going to be a long night."

The German Compound—that is what it was called by the non-German workers at Blucher—had been built along the hillside of a sandy cove two miles up the beach from the company's industrial complex. It had a private road that wound along the low hills for the distance beyond the guarded back gate of the factory. The low modern bungalows—fifteen of them—were grouped on either side of a central clubhouse, which had been built to resemble a Bavarian chalet, complete with swimming pool and tennis courts. Hauser had spent a small fortune in company funds transporting the clubhouse furnishings from an old hotel which he had stumbled across on the road to Innsbruck during a visit the previous year.

The Director's residence, a comfortable three bedroom affair, afforded the best view of the cove in the most secluded area of the compound—the far end. Built closer to the shoreline than its neighbors, it had the additional advantage of a private beach and wharf, well sheltered from the prevailing winds and ocean swells, which, during the rainy season, reached sizable proportions.

"I shall dine each evening precisely at eight, Fraulein Hoffer. I dislike this American habit of eating early." Kastenburg had met the young woman briefly the night before when he arrived, but had been too tired to contemplate discussing more than his pleasure in meeting a buxom young German lady so far from home, and bidding her "Guten nacht."

She had breakfast ready for him when he awoke at six, but he had refrained from speaking to her at all until the car arrived to take him to the office. He had informed her briefly they would talk when he returned.

"I quite understand, Herr Doktor." She was standing in front of him, blocking the view of the ocean's moonlit phosphorescence, a pleasant well-rounded woman, with soft eyes and a single braid of ash blonde hair pulled back severely from the temples. She was not at all unpleasant to look at, Kastenburg noticed. In fact, she was quite charming.

"If for any reason I find I cannot return here for dinner, I will notify you before six, if that is satisfactory?"

"Perfectly," she agreed.

"When are your days off, Fraulein?"

"Doktor Hauser told me I would receive thirty days annual leave and a return ticket to Germany, plus two days off each week, however, if I wished, he said I could work on those days off and credit them to extending my annual leave."

"An admirable arrangement." He removed his pince nez and massaged his nose, then looked up. "And what have you decided to do?"

"Oh, I will work seven days a week for the time being, Herr Doktor, until I decide I need a rest or a visit to the city—the San Ramon city, I mean."

"Splendid." He replaced his glasses. "Now, as to sleeping arrangements—I shall not require you to sleep with me more than once every two weeks—one of life's tragedies for older men, Fraulein; as we gain in wisdom and years, we must sacrifice our potency."

"I quite understand, Herr Doktor. I shall not be demanding, I promise." Her face was open with the genuine concern of her responsibilities.

"Good! Well that's settled! Now, if you would be kind enough to bring me a brandy—perhaps one for yourself, as well—we can toast our association in this tropical paradise."

"Courvoisier?"

"Courvoisier will be satisfactory." He watched her return to the house; she had a spring to her step that made her rump joggle with each movement. He reminded himself to congratulate Kurt Hauser in the morning on his selection, then leaned back in the soft wicker armchair to contemplate the beauty of the night, listening to the water lapping softly over the white sand on the beach.

It had been a successful first day's introduction to his new little kingdom. Absently, he reached into his pocket for the letter that had been awaiting him at the office when he arrived that morning. It was postmarked Munich. He opened it carefully and began reading. It was from Jamil. He had written it in English. *"Dear Doctor, Welcome back to paradise and the land of milk and honey! Our supporter has requested an interim report from me on the projected date for discussing the purchase of certain chemical compounds. He considers —quite justifiably, I think—he has the right of first refusal on your initial production run. I advised his embassy I would write to you at once, explaining I would provide a full report the moment I heard back from you. Two of our German friends have persuaded me to visit Munich this month to watch the competition among nations for the Olympic golds. My competitive instincts were naturally aroused, and so I am here. Do take time to follow the competitions in the newspapers, as I understand there are a number of special events being planned for the Israeli contingent, which should prove interesting.*

Leila sends her best wishes. As ever, Jamil."

He folded the letter back into the envelope and smiled as Fraulein Hoffer returned with the brandy snifters, handing him one. He patted the chair beside him and, with a nod, she sat down. He held his glass aloft.

"Let us drink to paradise and this land of milk and honey—and to the Olympic Gold."

She didn't understand, but drank a toast to it anyway.

He made the Ambassador wait in the study for ten minutes after the big Cadillac with the CD license plates and tiny American flag attached to its fender had parked in the drive. The American was pacing the room when Chirlo came in.

"Sorry to keep you waiting, Mr. Collins; I was on the phone to Doctor Artega; something to drink or eat?"

"No, no thank you, Colonel. I've had supper." He looked agitated.

"You're sure now?"

"Yes, yes, quite sure—nothing, thank you."

Chirlo shut the door, then turned and looked at him quizzically. "Are you feeling all right, Mr. Collins? You look a bit under the weather. A cold?"

"No Colonel, I'm fine—just fine, I assure you."

"Good." He watched for another moment, considering, then raised his hands to signify his resignation. "Well, in that case, let's sit down and you can tell me what it is that makes you refuse my hospitality in offering you a drink when you are feeling fine, but look like hell, Mr. Collins." He dropped his frame into one of the chairs abruptly.

Stunned, the ambassador stood staring at him, then slowly sat down. The room filled with an oppressive silence.

"Well, Mr. Collins?"

The ambassador looked up with a start. "I'm sorry, Colonel, I was collecting my thoughts. There is a matter which I want to discuss with you—informally, of course—which concerns certain information which has been brought to my attention regarding the safety of American lives and property in your country." He waited for Chirlo to say something.

Instead of speaking, his host removed a leather case of thin cigars from his tunic pocket and lit one of the foul-smelling sticks. The wooden match made a loud click as he tossed it into the humidor at his elbow.

"I have been informed by reliable sources there is every likelihood of serious labor problems developing this coming Monday and a possibility that counter-revolutionary groups may attempt to use the event to settle old scores—against yourself, and of course, American influences in the country." He rushed on. "In fact, I have been advised your life may be in danger!"

"Really, Ambassador? I'm astounded! You mean there is a plot to overthrow the country?"

"Well, er, yes, I suppose you could call it that. I felt you should know," he added lamely.

There was another pregnant pause, requiring an immediate conversational caesarian. Chirlo let the blue smoke drift towards the broad lampshade over his head.

"Anything else?" he prompted.

The Ambassador appeared to be considering the question.

"Do you have a recommendation—some game plan that I should follow, Mr. Collins?"

"You don't seem particularly concerned, Colonel Chirlo, if I may say so?"

"You may—and I'm not." He took another mouthful of smoke from the cheroot and watched it drift. There was another long silence.

"Tell me, Mr. Collins, as a matter of personal interest, because I am curious, do you really think I'm as stupid as you are trying to make me believe?"

"I'm afraid I don't follow you," the Ambassador said uncertainly.

"Oh come now, of course you do. You know exactly what I'm saying, so why don't you stop playing games with me and tell me the truth, or does your sense of protocol under the present Republican administration prohibit truth as a matter of policy?"

"I resent that, Colonel."

There was the sound of high-pitched children's laughter drifting by the closed door; it rose and fell several times before being silenced by an older severe adult voice.

Chirlo smiled at him sadly. "How old are you, Tommy?" It was the first and only time he had called the Ambassador by his Christian name. There was no reply as Collins lowered his eyes with embarrassment.

"My information tells me you are fifty-nine, a Republican millionaire from the Midwest that made his money on the Chicago Market during those halcyon years in the Fifties and Sixties when people would buy anything with a decent story. You're not a professional diplomat, are you Tommy?" He waited for a reply. There was none. "You paid for your post here with political contributions during the last three elections, didn't you, and it was Costa Rica you wanted, wasn't it? Not Cosecha Rica? Someone made a mistake on the patronage list and that numbskull Andrews was awarded your post in error, so you wound up with the mess here." He blew a dark smoke ring towards the shaded lamp. "You're basically a decent man, Tommy—that's your weakness. I'm surprised the State Department hasn't realized it by now, but never mind, there's still time. It's a sad day when politics plucks a happy millionaire out of his environment and after a crash course on international affairs, turns him into a diplomat, sending him out to a sensitive area with only the vaguest notion of what he is supposed to be doing when he arrives at the new post to present his credentials. I'll bet they spent more time grooming you in proper protocol for presenting your appointment to our President than they did on politics."

Collins looked at him with surprise. Chirlo was absolutely correct. The Ambassador had learned about the country from a State Department folder borrowed from the Congressional Library four years out of date. He had studied it on his way down in the aircraft.

"So when you arrived what did you learn? You found the place a hotbed of intrigue under the steady control of Charles Montague Matson, Central Intelligence Agency, agent-in-charge, who rushes around the country pretending he is a commercial undersecretary, looking out for American businessmen and opportunities for commercial investment." Chirlo shrugged. "I knew about Charles Montague Matson seventy-two hours after he arrived and began his little charade—but if it makes him happy, who am I to complain? That was seven years ago. The man he replaced, by the way—Mr. Berryman—was the one who arranged for my assassination and wound up killing Colonel Guerrero—the man he was trying to protect." He chuckled. "You know, I've always wondered what happened to that Berryman—poor man—you don't happen to know by any chance?"

The Ambassador shook his head. "It was before my time," he mumbled.

"Hmm, well no matter. In any case, since then I have kept a close eye on Mr. Matson, on the reasonable assumption that lightning—at least where the CIA is concerned—always strikes twice. You'd be fascinated at what I have learned over the years—his agents, sub-agents, sympathizers, plots and counter-plots. When he retires from the service he really should take time out to write a book, provided he can remember it all. My Major Martinez can flush out any lapses of memory from our files if Matson needs help. I don't know how well you know Matson, Tommy, but he is the only secret agent I've ever run into who managed to double-cross himself on at least five separate occasions—an extraordinary fellow, one of the few people I know who can create intrigue where none exists, simply by inventing it at an appropriate moment to keep himself busy." He chuckled.

The Ambassador looked at him, his face imploring. "Colonel, I knew nothing about their plans. They work under the supervision of the State Department."

"And you don't, Tommy, is that it?"

"The CIA is a law unto itself, Colonel. I am told to cooperate. They are accountable to no one—they don't even have to explain how they spend their money. Half the time I only hear of Matson's escapades when they're over."

"What about the other half?" He scrunched the cheroot into the ashtray.

Collins sighed. "Then my information is correct—you do know everything?"

Chirlo smiled. "Try me, Tommy."

"The Munoz affair?"

"Everything— your man Rimson was followed to Los Gaucho's and we observed the meeting."

"Then you know the two Argentinians are our agents?"

Chirlo was thunderstruck. He had eaten often at Los Gaucho's with Felina. There never had been a financial windfall from the

442

national lottery of Argentina; it had all been financed by the CIA! Clever.

"I knew about them a few days after they arrived—I am told they are neither Argentinians nor brothers." It was a guess, purely a shot in the dark.

"They are Americans from South Texas—we call them Tex-Mex —and you're correct, they're not brothers, not even related." The Ambassador shrugged his shoulders, deciding he might as well clean up his whole act.

"Officially, Colonel, Washington thinks you pose a threat to the peace and security of the Central Americas. Unofficially, I am supposed to do everything in my power to ensure any attempted overthrow of your government will succeed. It is a distasteful job, and one which, I might add, I have done very little towards assisting. As a man, I admire and respect you. You are neither a communist nor a fascist; to Washington, you are, therefore, an enigma. Our government's policy is to fight communism and ally ourselves with fascism. We are not equipped to deal with enigmas. If you were a Tachito Somosa and this was Nicaragua, or an Oswaldo Lopez and this was Honduras, then we would know how to react towards your politics. As you know, we have an excellent track record for supporting successful dictatorships."

"With the exception of Colonel Guerrero," Chirlo interjected.

"With the exception of Colonel Guerrero," the Ambassador agreed, smiling, "but you must forgive us for that blunder—after all, we didn't know you, did we?"

"You do now, but would still prefer Guerrero, is that it?"

Collins raised his hands. "Please, Colonel, if it was up to me— well what's the point in discussing it? It's not up to me. My concern now is what you are planning this Monday."

"Is that a question, Tommy, or a statement?"

"I am told you are planning a swift retaliation."

Chirlo smiled, the crooked grin. "That will of course depend upon what events transpire which require retaliation. I shall wait and see on Monday, then act accordingly."

"Let me put it to you another way, if I may? What would you like to see happen to set your mind at rest insofar as my Embassy is concerned?"

"Ah! You mean if wishes were horses and beggars could ride?" He considered the offer, stroking his chin. "It would be a pleasant surprise to learn the Messrs. Matson and Rimson and the other four CIA agents on the Embassy staff were on the early morning

PANAM flight to Miami—recalled for consultations. Then, perhaps a letter from you outlining your regret over the fact they exceeded the guidelines set down by you for conduct while guests of this country—for my personal files, you understand—there would be no publicity. Then, I suppose, it would be only fair for you to have a talk with Licenciado Munoz yourself; explain to the poor man that the financial offer made by Mr. Rimson was done without your knowledge and authority. He will be disappointed, of course—I'm sure he was planning on the funds for his early retirement."

"What about the brothers at Los Gauchos?"

"The Alvarado boys?" Chirlo laughed. "Leave them in peace, they're harmless—besides, if you order them to leave, who will run your restaurant? It's a popular place and I enjoy a night out occasionally with my wife."

"Washington will send someone else to replace the others; you know that?"

"Naturally."

"That doesn't concern you, Colonel?"

Chirlo laughed again. "Balzac once observed a person should begin each day by swallowing a toad; after that, nothing can faze you."

The Ambassador chuckled and stood up. "I will see what I can do about making horses out of wishes and turning your beggars into equestrians." They shook hands.

"Do that, Tommy." He escorted him into the hall and out the front door.

Chirlo stopped at the top of the steps as the Ambassador began the descent to the car. On the third step, he paused and turned. "As a matter of interest, were you really going to launch a major assault on our Embassy?"

"As a matter of interest, Mr. Ambassador, that is the one thing you will never know. Goodnight."

"Goodnight, Colonel Chirlo."

He saw the uniformed Marine Sergeant standing stiffly at the open back door, saw him salute, a tall toy soldier under the garage floodlights manipulated by the strings of discipline. The Ambassador nodded at him and crawled inside. The slamming door reverberated between the stone casings. He waited until the tail lights had disappeared around the turn at the top of the long grade down to the city, then turned towards the trees.

"Who's in charge out there?" he called.

There was a movement among the bushes on the other side of

the lawn and Major Martinez emerged with two junior officers. Chirlo waited until Martinez had saluted him.

"Well?"

"Everything is on tape, Colonel, including his departing comments on the steps."

"Good work, Major!"

"What shall I do with the tape?"

"Take it down to the archives and lock it up under a C-heading."

"For Conspiracy?" the young Lieutenant asked, knowingly.

"No, Lieutenant—C for Common Sense. I'll see you in the morning. Goodnight, and thank you."

He started back to the house. Martinez watched him, then called.

"Colonel, could I speak with you for a minute?" The junior officers went back to the trees to round up their men and surveillance gear. From a side access road around the house the sound of a heavy truck's engine backfired, then toned into smoothness.

"I have something to report to you of a private nature." Martinez looked at him in the dimness of the starry night. It was now or never.

"Can't it wait till morning?" Chirlo said testily.

"I'd prefer to tell you now, Sir." It had to be done. It was his duty as an officer.

"Well?"

"As you know, I have had Donna Felina under protective surveillance for security reasons. He stopped speaking as the front door opened, flooding the two men with light. Felina called out.

"When you're through, darling, I'm taking you up on that offer to read the children's bedtime story—oh hello Major, I didn't know it was you—how's the intelligence business?"

She smiled at him as she came up, putting her arm around Chirlo's waist. Martinez bowed.

"Good evening, Donna Felina. I was reporting to the Colonel that after today, I am withdrawing the protective surveillance on you for reasons of ah, er, economy."

He stared into her eyes and saw the sudden alarm kindled by his words. She gave him a tight smile.

"Why Major Martinez, have you been following me?" She knew he had, never realizing how close the surveillance had been until this moment.

"Yes, Donna Felina, you have been followed—everywhere." He left a light pause before continuing. "However since there has never been anything to report, or any apparent danger to your person from radical elements, I have decided to withdraw the men involved. I feel they can be better employed at other duties—with the Colonel's permission, of course."

"Whatever you think best, Major. Personally I think this whole surveillance thing of yours has gotten out of hand, but I suppose it keeps your men on their toes. Certainly you may withdraw the men covering my wife. Anything else?"

"No, Sir. Thank you, Sir. Goodnight!" He saluted formally and marched back towards his trees like a drill sergeant, cursing himself for his own weakness. He had betrayed his commanding officer by deceit, knowing full well where his duty lay. He had failed the test of military integrity. It was a bitter pill. He felt ill.

They watched him disappear into the woods, then turned for the house, arm in arm. Chirlo shook his head.

"That man has got to be the most pompous ass in the entire army. I believe he is becoming paranoid.

Felina held his arm tightly. "He may be all of that Pedro, but he is also something else."

"What else could he be?" They went inside the house and shut the door.

"He is a gentleman—a perfect gentleman."

15

1973

Corbin watched the clouds whipping past. From the first class promenade deck, they were so low it appeared the ship's tall mast might snare their progress. He looked around the deck grimly. The other wooden lounge chairs were vacant. He was quite alone.

Charles Corbin faces the elements alone and freezes to death on the high seas, he thought and pulled the blanket further up to his chin. The gulls had vanished from their soaring vigils at the stern of the cruise ship the second day out of New York, leaving the churning spume and trail of periodic garbage for the Gulf Stream to handle. He decided he had been a fool to let Affleck talk him into such a predicament in the first place.

"A World cruise on the S.S. Orient—only for the most discriminating traveler!" The multi-colored brochure promised every exotica: "soft music, mellow evenings sailing the velvet waters of the seven seas in your own luxurious floating palace where every whim or desire is catered to by a staff of superbly trained experts."

As he had flipped through the pages, listening to Don's sales talk with half an ear, he noticed the trip took one hundred and twenty days.

"It says here the trip takes four months!"

"What is time, Chuck?"

"Spare me the prose." He tossed the colorful pamphlet back on the desk and returned to gazing out the office window at the new building Corning Contractors was pushing past the seventh floor, lifting itself by a fragile spider webbed crane, perched on top of the next floor as it completed work on the one below. He had been gazing at it for five months.

"Well, anyway, give it some thought," Affleck said, returning to his office next door. Corbin continued staring out the window.

Everyone was trying to promote him into doing something, going somewhere—anything to get him out of their hair. He couldn't blame them, really; he was useless the way he was. Since losing Peggy, something in him had died. The fun was gone, the thrill of the commercial chase no longer held his interest, so he had returned to the office, rolled his chair around to the window and began cogitating. The frenetic pace of the business charged ahead around him, but without him, under Affleck's direction. He had been surprised at Don's ability, running everything in a much more efficient manner than Corbin had thought possible, and without complaint or criticism over the disinterest shown by his useless senior partner. And Corbin was useless; he knew that. Somehow, he couldn't seem to get himself started again—on anything.

After the first six months of doing nothing, he spent the Winter puttering around the house getting in Hughette's way and reading dozens of the hundreds of books Peggy had acquired over the years from her various book clubs. He had often scorned her for being such a sucker on the new hardcover editions, which, with their colorful paper dust jackets, filled several rows of shelves in the study. By Spring he had become bored with reading. Elizabeth had left him alone, phoning rarely. He had given her the keys for the Laurentian cottage, and on weekends during the winter, she used it continuously, first with Affleck and Rina (until Rina learned of her pregnancy and was forced to abandon the ski runs), then later, with an assortment of girlfriends from the office. Corbin heard little of the various boyfriends who drifted in and out of her life, nor did he care.

Before he knew it, Summer school vacation was upon him and he was considering a series of questions posed by the children. Peter, nearly eleven, and growing out of all his clothes, had demanded, "Where are we going for our vacation Dad?"

It was odd how he had always been *Dad* to his son, but *Daddy* to his daughters. The thought of going anywhere hadn't crossed his mind.

"You speaking individually or collectively?"

"What do you mean?" Peter asked puzzled, and looked at the girls sitting on either side of him on the sofa. It was obviously a nursery delegation which had already planned its attack with considerable care and was not to be thwarted by adult doubletalk.

"Never mind." He put the afternoon paper down on the leather ottoman and eyed the trio of junior conspirators gravely. "You have something in mind?"

"Sure do, Daddy!" Emily said brightly. Peter elbowed her in the ribs, and she pouted and fell silent. It had been agreed he would be spokesman for the group.

Alice looked solemn. "We thought we'd all drive across the country in a mobility home."

"You mean a mobile home?"

"A house trailer sort of thing that isn't a trailer, 'cause it runs by itself with its own engine," his son elaborated.

"Yeah, and it has a roof rack for a boat and one of those ski racks on the back for our motorcycles and everything," Emily gushed, jumping off the couch with the large foldout she had been sitting on, explaining pictorially the advantages of buying the thirty thousand dollar land cruiser. She plopped herself on his lap and opened the display.

"See! Isn't it super—there's our motorcycles!"

"You don't have motorcycles."

"I know, Daddy, but when we get the trailer we'll have to get them to fit on the back," she said logically. "An' there's where the boat goes—on top, see?"

She pointed a pink finger at the inverted punt strapped to the luggage rack in the picture.

"It's a land cruiser, not a trailer," Corbin told her. "And it's very expensive." He looked at the pictures on the sheet with interest. It was a massive highway machine containing every possible comfort, built with luxurious conservation of space, even to color television and full stereo, slipped-in behind a cupboard. Peter and Alice drifted over to lean across his knees, watching his facial reaction for some sign of approval.

"What do you think, Alice?"

"I think it'th a good idea, Daddy. We'd all love to thee the country." Her brown eyes were very solemn. "Of courth it'th expenthive, but we've all thaved our money an' we'll help you pay for it—we dethided."

"And when did you all decide on this particular proposal?"

"Last year before Mommy went to the hospital. It was her idea, really—Mommy's, I mean. She said if she was feeling better she could go with us," Peter said sadly.

"But she wath too thick to go and thaid to athk you nexth summer—this ith nexth thummer, Daddy—tho can we go?" And so it had been decided by the simple logic of a seven year old girl.

A white jacketed steward appeared from the gangway at the far end of the deck carrying a three note xylophone and leather bound knobby wood striker. He leaned against the wind, his hair and jacket blowing, as he made his way over to the lounge chair.

"First call for lunch, Sir!" The wind whipped the words across the shuffleboard court, to the leeward rail and out to sea.

"Thank you, Steward," Corbin replied, not moving.

The man smiled perfunctorily, and continued on to the doorway into the enclosed lounge.

He decided he might as well go and see what they had on the luncheon menu. It was something to do. He crawled out from under the blanket. He'd read on the ship's bulletin board there was supposed to be a movie during the afternoon. Perhaps he would go and see it. He sauntered back to his outside cabin on B deck and went in to wash up. There was a note on the floor which someone had slipped under the door. It was written on ship's stationery: *"Dear Mr. Corbin. Please forgive my presumption, but are you the same Charles Corbin who used to live in Tamiami?"* It was signed *Patricia* something or other. Indeciferable handwriting. At the lower right hand corner of the nautically monogrammed page were copperplate printed letters, *CABIN B36*. Corbin's cabin was *B31*. The even numbers ran along the other side of the vessel—the windward side for the moment, on the ship's present course. He tossed the letter on the small writing desk in his cabin, deciding to forego the windy trip to investigate Patricia whatever-her-name was in *Cabin B36*. He washed his face and hands then made his way down to the first class dining room.

Technically, there were not first or second class passengers on the world cruise; each was supposed to be equal in his use of the provided facilities. However, by some coincidence, passengers who had purchased the luxury suites on *A* and *B* decks were assigned to eat in the ornate uncrowded dining room on *B* deck, while the others, on the lower single room cabin decks, were shunted into the crowded central dining room deeper in the bowels of the ship.

Herman Slitzman, his table companion, was ordering his selection from the menu when Corbin sat down.

"Good morning, Mr. Corbin. It's a Catholic day. We are having fish—or poisson—as they call it here." He had a thick Jewish accent and the florid face of a man suffering from extremely high blood pressure.

"Kosher killed, I hope, Mr. Slitzman!" Corbin smiled as he sat down. Slitzman insisted everything he ate be in harmony with his religious convictions, as the ship's owners had promised him when he'd stepped aboard. The first day out of New York, Corbin had kidded him gently on creating such a fuss over the beautiful baked ham, which served as an example of the culinary excellence passengers could anticipate in the weeks ahead. Mr. Slitzman had been properly outraged and made a terrible scene, sending his already dangerously-high blood pressure rocketing to the top of the Sphygmanometer scale. The ham had been replaced swiftly with a more acceptable compromise.

"Salmon do not require Kosher killing, Mr. Corbin," he remarked and handed the menu across the table. He waggled a fat finger at him sternly. "Take big care you don't go making me mad already, or I'll be moving to another table; then where will you be, hey? You'll have to sit and sulk during mealtimes on your own!"

"It's too late, Mr. Slitzman, there's nobody in the room dumb enough, besides me, to put up with you at mealtimes." He gave the steward his order and sat back smiling at his new Jewish friend. "How's the market this morning?"

Mr. Slitzman spent his mornings and afternoons sitting in the semi-darkness of the financial lounge, watching the overhead ticker tape crank out the endless rise and fall in the fortunes of Wall Street. It was one of the amenities provided on board and the main reason his physician, Dr. Norenblatt, had been able to persuade his delinquent patient to take the long ocean voyage before a major coronary settled the fortunes of the Slitzman family once and for all. Mr. Slitzman rolled one hand from side-to-side.

"So so, Mr. Corbin. So So. The bond market is recovering nicely."

"You mean the suckers are lining up again," Corbin said sarcastically.

"Ah, you don't believe in bonds, Mr. Corbin?"

"As a rule, no; government bonds, never."

"And may I ask why?" Mr. Slitzman removed his two small vials of pre-luncheon pills and extracted the necessary tablets.

"Government bond issues are certificates guaranteeing the confiscation of the investor's money. Have you ever heard of a government repaying its debts in the purchasing power, in which the gullible innocent public bought its bonds, Mr. Slitzman?"

He popped the two pills into his mouth and downed them with a sip of water, then looked at Corbin speculatively. "I didn't know you followed the bond market, Mr. Corbin."

"I don't, Mr. Slitzman, but I have studied the process of elected government carefully."

They both laughed. It seemed, after three days of polite table conversation, they had found a common meeting ground.

"I couldn't agree with you more, Mr. Corbin."

"Call me Chuck, Mr. Slitzman."

"Then you call me Herman—Chuck." They grinned at each other self-consciously as the steward appeared with the hors d'ouvres. "Wine gentlemen?"

"Yes, I think a dry white wine would go well with the salmon—how about you, Herman?"

"Good suggestion, Chuck."

"I'll bring the wine steward." The polished English accent departed to find the gentleman in question.

"Funny thing about Limies—ever notice, Chuck, even their waiters got class?"

"I've noticed—like their country, broke, beaten, bloody, but unbowed. Personally, I find them all a pain in the neck. They're too tongue-in-cheek for me, Herman. I had dealings with some of them once—never knew where you stood."

"Ah—you mean they were polite, but never were they giving the show away?"

"Exactly."

The wine steward bowed himself into the conversation, allowing the huge gold key hanging from his neck to dangle ceremoniously over the table an instant, then swing back to his royal purple waistcoat as he straightened.

"What is your pleasure, gentlemen?" he demanded, handing Slitzman the wine list. They discussed the relative merits of the vintages, finally selecting a light Rhine Valley white wine.

"See what I mean, Chuck? The schmuck's a wine waiter and does he ask—whaddy'wanna drink? No? 'What is your pleasure gentlemen'." He mimicked the accent badly, making Corbin laugh. "They always make me feel like a gonnif—even the damned waiters. I went to England on a trip in Fifty-six with my wife, God rest her. Never so glad to get home in my life." He reflected for a moment. "Lorna loved it though, said it made her feel like real class."

They were silent for a moment, each lost in his own thoughts.

"Your wife dead, Herman?" Corbin inquired.

"Since 1963. God rest her soul. She was a good woman. She gave me three sons and thirty-eight years of paradise." He smiled, the fat lips tugging his face, yet his eyes were sad. "Such a loss after thirty-eight years."

"I know how it feels—I lost mine three years ago—cancer. She took nearly a year to die. It was horrible."

They stared across the table at each other, and noticed the misting of the opposing eyes, then looked out the window together at the white-topped spume crowned rollers lumbering across the ocean beside the ship, rising and falling with a majesty of purpose and power.

"So what did you do today, Chuck?" The moment had passed; their eyes met in the present.

"Not a damned thing. I laid on my duff on the rear deck all morning trying to keep from freezing my ass off and wondering what the hell I was doing on this boat in the first place—and in the second place, how I could get off the damn thing when we hit the first port."

The wine steward returned with his chilled paraphernalia on wheels and presented the bottle, label first, to Mr. Slitzman.

"Never mind the razzle-dazzle, waiter, just crank the sonofabitch open and pour it—if it's sour, we'll send it back."

Corbin laughed loudly, silencing the murmured conversation at the other tables.

The wine steward followed Mr. Slitzman's instructions to the letter and departed. The fat man held his glass aloft: "To a happy voyage, Chuck, and to the happiness we both have lost and will never find again."

They touched crystal rims and drank.

The steaming poached salmon arrived, and Mr. Slitzman looked up at the young steward seriously. "Tell me, waiter, are you sure it's been Kosher killed?"

They had started out on their great adventure during the last week of June, fighting their way across town through the stream of American tourist traffic pouring into the city from the South. Corbin had been hesitant about taking the children alone with him, but in the end, after Hughette had refused to join the safari, decided to plunge off across country on his own.

The vehicle was enormous, square nosed, slab-sided and as long as a commercial road trailer, but surprisingly easy to handle on the highway. From the comfortable driver's seat, looking out the huge picture windows, Corbin felt it was much the same as riding around while seated in his living room at Rockwood—except, instead of the garden and river view, he was watching the road flash beneath him at basement level. The children were enthralled and spent the first hours rushing around the interior, laughing happily at the absurdity of using the bathroom, refrigerator and television set while rolling down the highway. Once he had cleared the narrow city streets and swarming traffic, gingerly gauging the passing distances required' for clearance from vehicles as well as road signs and poles, he felt much more comfortable.

They followed the Ottawa River Road westward to North Bay, on the shores of Lake Nippising. Once they had passed beyond the Atomic Energy Plant at Rolphton, it was all new country which he had never seen before. By then, the children had settled down, the girls sitting on either side of the dining table working at their coloring books, and Peter sitting beside him up front on the swivel passenger seat, gazing out the window at the rolling landscape, continuously replacing itself before them.

"Want to play car poker?"

Peter came out of his trance. "How do you play it?"

Corbin thought back to his own youth when his father had taught him to play the silly license game. "Same as poker—only instead of cards, we use the license numbers on every car—one car for me, then the next one for you."

Peter squinted ahead to a slow moving stake truck with three sevens on its plate. "Okay, I go first." They drew up on the empty trucks. "Three sevens!" Peter announced.

"I'm theven!" Alice crawled onto the transmission mound between their front chairs. "Can I play too?"

"Yeah, Daddy—me too—I want to play!" Emily shouted, cramming herself in behind her younger sister. So, for the next hour and a half they played license poker while Peter carefully kept score.

When at length they became bored with the game and decided to stop until later, there was a brief fight when the girls accused Peter of cheating. He told everyone his score was the highest, with Alice in second position. Corbin laughed after Peter managed to settle it tactfully by telling them he had fibbed and their father held the highest score, while everyone else came in an equal second. Satisfied, the girls went back to their coloring books until they fell asleep on the padded benches.

"Who actually won?" Corbin asked his son quietly.

"I did—you came in last." He grinned impishly.

"Then why didn't you stick to your guns instead of giving in?"

"Because it wasn't important, Dad—like, if I'm going to fight about something it should be something worthwhile, shouldn't it?"

Corbin nodded. "You're quite right, son, it's all a question of priorities." They drove into the sinking sun in silence until they found a quiet rest area to park for the night.

He spent a full hour over lunch with Herman Slitzman, exchanging anecdotes and becoming better acquainted with the New York broker. Slitzman was a second generation American. His father had come from the Ghetto of Warsaw, where he had been an apprentice tailor with a flair for needle work on the ancient Singer Treadle, and had produced—or so he had told his son in later years—the most stylish clothes in Warsaw. Herman had grown up in Hell's Kitchen, fighting his way into the respect of his elders and contemporaries by a combination of brute strength and brute intelligence. His elders admired the latter; his contemporaries respected the former.

He had started out his financial career as a loan shark with the tough kids on his block, using the pennies earned from working in his father's shop for the bankroll to get his six-for-five operations started. He was selective in his choice of customers. Unless they were successful thieves in their own right, he refused to deal; of course the first prerequisite was his ability to hammer them into submission with his fists if the juice money was not forthcoming at the end of each week. Young Herman developed his scorn for investment principle early. To him, the only thing that mattered was interest. Pennies began to grow into dimes and quarters, the quarters into dollars, the dollars into hundreds, then thousands, so that one day when his father finished the last stitch in life and his mother sent him to call the Rabbi, Herman was able to bury the old man in a style rarely seen among the inhabitants of Hell's Kitchen.

"After that we moved to a better neighborhood in the Queens," he told Corbin over their coffee. "Yah! I'm not supposed to drink this stuff. Dr. Norenblatt keeps saying to me—'Herman, you drink coffee, you die soon.'" He grimaced, then smiled as he took another sip of the gorgeous brew. "So I say to Dr. Norenblatt— Julius, I say, 'the only reason I live maybe is to keep you in that Park Avenue penthouse? Better I should die already and save my medical bills.'" He set the cup down on its china saucer and sighed. "Maybe he's right; maybe like Nebuchadnezzar, he sees the handwriting on the wall, so he thinks I'll send fat Herman off on a world cruise so maybe he'll die away from New York and he can tell everyone, 'See—I told him not to drink coffee'."

He said it sadly, but his eyes twinkled behind the thick glasses. Corbin laughed.

"You'd better get back to the big board, Herman; the whole market could have gone to hell while we've been sitting here talking."

They left together, Corbin appearing almost skeletal alongside the lumbering waddle of the overweight Slitzman, fully a head taller than himself. They paused in the central hall, where the four corridors from both sides of the ship converged into an airy lounge festooned with comfortable leather sofas and rubber plants. The Purser's Office and ship's bank occupied one corner of the area.

"Until dinner, Chuck!"

"Until dinner, Herman!" Corbin agreed, then watched the big man waddle away down the far corridor to the electronic financial display from Wall Street.

He went over to the bulletin board. The movie wasn't scheduled to start until one-thirty. He read the list of other activities designed to keep the passengers amused—swimming lessons, bridge lessons, lottery on the ship's log for the day's distance, a ping pong tournament, and a handwritten note tacked to the bottom of the sheet announcing tennis lessons had been cancelled for the day due to the "inclement" weather. He smiled at the word. How like the English! It was blowing up a gale outside, but as far as the Brits were concerned, it was just inclement.

He smelled the perfume beside him before sighting its wearer out of the corner of his eye. He turned toward the woman slowly.

"You will notice they have cancelled the tennis due to inclement weather. I hope it doesn't ruin your day?" He appraised her swiftly as he spoke, stopping to gaze at her wedding ring. She looked like a clotheshorse out of the *Vogue* magazines Peggy used to leave scattered about the house and would never throw away.

She gave him a breathless smile and asked in a throaty voice, "You didn't answer my note?"

"Patricia, ah . . ."

"Kirkpatrick."

" . . . Kirkpatrick. No, Mrs. Kirkpatrick; actually, I was on my way round to knock on your door now." "How wonderful. Shall we go together and see if I'm in?"

"After you." He bowed foolishly, following her outside into the teeth of the gale. Her dress whipped up to her waist and she smoothed it hurriedly, holding it against her thighs, but not before he had seen the pair of magnificent gams. He trailed her into the cabin, a duplicate of his own, only in reverse, and glanced around for some sign of Mr. Kirkpatrick.

"Your husband is at the bar?"

She shrugged. "Probably. Either in Lauderdale or the Tamiami Country Club. Drink?"

"Yes, thanks. Bourbon—you mean you're traveling alone, Mrs. Kirkpatrick?"

"I was until a few minutes ago, Mr. Corbin. Ice?"

"On the rocks—aren't you afraid of being attacked?" He dropped into the chair at the end of the berth and watched her prepare the drinks at the dresser.

"Terrified." She swung around and handed him a fat tumbler. "To sinful living," she toasted, then after a sip, sat down on the bed next to his chair.

"You are the Corbin from Tamiami that married that Vassar bitch who was banging everyone in the neighborhood, aren't you?"

"The same." He said it calmly, but his mind screamed out to protest her words.

"What ever happened to her?"

"We lived happily ever after until 1970 when she died of cancer." He took a long pull on his glass, demolishing half the contents. He noticed the information hadn't affected her in the slightest.

"I'm sorry—I put my foot in it, didn't I Mr. Corbin."

"And you, Mrs. Kirkpatrick, how is life with Mr. Kirkpatrick?" *Whoever in hell Mr. Kirkpatrick is*, he thought. He still couldn't place the cool composed woman in his mind.

"An endless party. My husband is a lush—a rich lush. If he ever lost his money he would be called a hopeless alcoholic, but right now he's still a lovable lush—lovable to everyone but me." She smashed back half her glass too, for emphasis.

"So you took a lonely ocean voyage to put yourself back together in preparation for the next assault, sort of an alcoholic pilgrimage—commendable self-sacrifice, Mrs. Kirkpatrick. He watched her down the rest of the glass in two large gulps. "Offhand I'd say by the time the trip gets back to New York you'll have caught up to your husband—lushwise."

His reflexes had slowed down considerably over the years, but he still felt he should have been able to duck the stinging slap she planted alongside his face.

He stood up and laid his glass on the writing desk. "And on that happy note, Mrs. Kirkpatrick, I bid you adieu and bon voyage!"

He opened the door, his cheek stinging against the cold wind. "Wait! Please wait—don't go! Please don't go!" The husky seductiveness was gone from her voice; she was pleading as she stood up and came over to him, laying the offending palm over his own on the door handle.

"I'm sorry—I'm sorry, Mr. Corbin, I didn't mean to slap you, but you have a way of getting to the heart of the matter very quickly."

He let her lead him back to the chair and push him gently into the seat, then waited in silence as she went to the desk and retrieved his drink. The expression of cool blasé indifference—the *Vogue* look—was gone; instead, he saw the face of a frantic frightened woman, a beautiful face and one to which the years had been extremely kind.

"For starters, I'll make a deal with you, Mrs. Kirkpatrick. If you don't touch another drop of booze this trip, I'll promise to do the same." He waited until she had nodded, then got up and went over to her collection of bottles on the dresser and gathered them into his arms.

"Open the door!" She obeyed and he went into the wind to fling the armload over the rail, then returned to pick up the remains of his glass of bourbon. He threw it overside from the doorway and returned to his chair. She shut the door.

"Now Mrs. Kirkpatrick, can I call you Patricia?"

"Tricia," she told him quietly.

"Tricia—fine, my name is Chuck. Supposing you kick your shoes off, lie down on the bed, shut your eyes and tell me all your troubles."

"What good will that do?"

"Perhaps nothing for you, but a whole lot for me. First, I'll be able to study your gorgeous body without your looking at me, while I learn whether your story is sadder than my tale of woe."

She snickered and kicked her shoes off.

"And if it isn't as sad as yours, what then?"

She crawled onto the bed and stretched out, crossing her legs and yanking at her hemline.

"In that case I'll join you on the bed and you can listen to my sad story."

She laughed, a genuine one. "You don't think such an

458

arrangement might lead to something evil?"

He looked nonplused. "Well, I certainly hope so Tricia, or we're both wasting our time!"

By the time they reached the Prairie's edge, just beyond the Ontario border, they had settled into a routine. It had taken Corbin a full week to cover the distance from Ottawa to the Manitoba border, stopping once for two days to enjoy some fishing at a quiet lake where they unloaded the fiberglass punt from the roof rack to test its seaworthiness. The little boat had been strapped on the Landcruiser when he had taken delivery and the salesman had not explained how the 120 pound craft was supposed to be launched from the wheeled home into the water and back again. The children nagged him the first three days to try out the boat, but he was always able to present the excuse there would be no fun in fishing in any of the numerous lakes they passed, saying they had been fished out by experts long before. On the third day, after passing along the North shore of Lake Superior and through the city of Thunder Bay into the small lake country, he succumbed.

They followed an uneven bumpy logging road off the highway for several miles, stopping finally on the edge of a pretty little lake encased by stunted pine and tamarack. The smooth surface of the water suddenly became peppered with splashes from the eager fish, which, according to Alice, had anticipated their arrival and purpose when Corbin had pulled off the miserable road and parked alongside the shoreline.

"Thee Daddy! They've been exthpecting uth!"

Corbin could find no fault with her logic. He shunted the cruiser back and forth a few times until he had it marble level. The acid test for leveling had become his son's responsibility—he would lay one of his glass marbles in the middle of the dining table; if it remained stationary, the vehicle was level. Usually the damn marble rolled wildly onto the floor and Corbin would have to shunt the cruiser back and forth a few times before Peter would yell, "Hold it Dad! Right on!" Then everyone would cheer and clap their father on the back.

They all climbed out to see the jumping fish, careful to keep the screen door tightly closed; it was the middle of the black-fly season, and although the pests were not a problem during the heat of daylight hours, there were always a few hundred of them lurking nearby, waiting to rush into any human habitation. He climbed the narrow ladder on the back of the cruiser to the roof and untied the retaining straps around the punt, then sat down on top of it to think. He knew there had to be a practical solution to the launching problem. The children were skipping stones along the water's edge, but stopped when they noticed his inactivity atop their wheeled home.

"Aren't you going to pass it down, Dad?" Peter called.

"To who?"

"*Whom* Dad—it's *whom.*" He walked over to the cruiser and looked up at his father with interest, recognizing the problem for the first time. The girls continued skipping stones.

"How 'bout a pulley?"

"We don't have a pulley."

"We have rope. We can make a pulley. Mr. Howden showed us how to cut the weight on anything you want to move by using a pulley arrangement."

"Whom is Mr. Howden?"

"*Who* Dad—it's *Who* this time—he's my math and science teacher. Where's the rope?"

Under his son's careful direction, Corbin rigged a pulley system with the long rope, looping it from the punt to the rear bumper, then back over to the roof rack, and finally, onto the ground, cutting the 120 pounds to a manageable 40. Using the three children to hold the rope, he eased the boat off the roof and lowered it down the back of the vehicle to the ground. They all grinned at the pleasure of their combined accomplishment and dragged the prize over to the water, tying it securely to a tilted tree. Corbin ruffled his son's shaggy head.

"Smart aleck—how do we get it back on the roof now?"

"Same way we got it down, Dad, only in reverse."

"I still think you're a smart aleck," Corbin told him. They all went fishing until the blackflies arrived later in the afternoon.

After supper, they watched television. Reception was poor and it was a rerun, but a cozy way to spend a peaceful Summer evening until bedtime. He bedded them down at ten and went outside to dig a refuse pit for the day's accumulation of garbage and sewage. So far, they had avoided trailer courts or camps where these attachment facilities were provided. He had nearly finished the hole when he heard the screen door slam. It was Peter.

"Why aren't you in bed, young man?" He leaned on the shovel, sweating slightly.

"Thought you might want some help, Dad."

"Okay—I'll buy that. Go get the garbage bags while I connect the sewage pipe."

After they had finished, they sat outside on the folding slat chairs and looked at the peaceful lake. In the cool air there was a warmth to their nearness.

"Are we going fishing in the morning?"

"I guess so, why?" Corbin asked.

"I dunno—I guess I just like fishing—as long as I don't have to clean them."

"You'll clean them tomorrow now that I've shown you how its done."

"Yeah, I guess I will." He grinned at his father in the soft light that spattered the undergrowth with shadow.

Corbin chuckled, but said nothing.

"Dad?"

"Hmmm?"

"Didn't you know really how to make a rope pulley?"

"I suppose I did at one time—but I forgot," he admitted.

"When you get old, do you forget things you learned when you were young?"

"Not everything—just some things, I suppose."

"Boy! I'll never forget the things I learn when I grow up—like this trip—I'll bet I never forget this trip with you!"

"What makes you think so?"

"Because it's fun—like, I mean it's fun being with you. I never knew how much fun until we went on this trip. I'll bet there isn't another kid at school who has as much fun with his Dad as I do this summer."

"Soft soap," Corbin said. He was pleased though.

"No, it's not soft soap, Dad—I mean it. Bet you never went on a trip like this with your Dad when you were as old as me—er—I."

"No son, my Dad was too poor to afford to take me on camping trips."

"Poor or rich, what's the difference? I know lots of fathers who never take the time to go anywhere with their kids—like that ol'grouch, Mr. Crabgrass."

"Crabtree," Corbin corrected him. Denton Crabtree was a golfing nut who spent every free moment trying to improve his golf game.

"Same difference," Peter asserted. "He's still a grouch."

They sat in silence until at last, Peter got up, put his arms around Corbin's neck, and kissed him on the cheek. "G'night Dad, and thanks."

"Thanks? For what?"

He shrugged his thin pajamad shoulders. "Oh, I dunno—just for being you."

Corbin watched him go inside to bed. When he looked back at the lake he realized tears had started in his eyes, clouding the restful view.

Patricia Kirkpatrick's story was about what he had expected to hear, although how much of the hair-raising tales of life with her alcoholic husband were fact and how much developed by a combination of pure fantasy and self-pity, was hard to determine until he knew her better—and possibly her husband. The hour for the afternoon movie was long past when she finally stopped, and regarded him closely from the bed. He was still sitting in the same chair he had taken when her lament began.

"Are you listening to what I've been telling you, Chuck?"

He had shut his eyes, resting them as he listened. She had misinterpreted the rest for sleep. He replied without opening them. "I have digested every perfumed word from your petal lips." He opened his eyes and examined her gravely. "Why did you run away, Tricia?"

She didn't answer him.

"Wouldn't it have been simpler to move out of town, maybe up to Charleston or Phoenix—I hear there's a big migration of women from broken marriages in Florida moving into the desert—must have something to do with the low humidity—keeps the juices evaporating before they start to flow."

She laughed and threw a pillow at him. "You're impossible!" She squirmed herself into a sitting position against the end of the bed, examining him.

"You don't think my problem is too serious, is that it?"

"You don't have any children, do you?"

She shook her head. "I'm what is known as a barren woman—I guess that's part of the problem with Kirk."

"Who?"

"My husband—I've always called him Kirk—pet name—silly really." She brushed back a strand of her black hair. "Having kids might have made all the difference—I love kids."

"Sure you do—along with baseball and Mom's apple pie." He stood up and stretched. "Mind if I use your plumbing—my juices need flowing." He didn't wait for her nod, and went into the small cabin bathroom. He looked at his face as he washed his hands; his eyes looked back tiredly; he tried a forced smile, it didn't work.

When he came back into the cabin she was sitting in exactly the same position, only she had taken off all her clothes.

"Expecting someone?"

"You." She patted the space beside her. She had a lush figure, with breasts just on the point of sagging, but still swelled in the proper curves. Her pubic hair had been shaved. For some reason it made her nakedness seem indecent, seeing the red vertical lips leering at him from the bed.

"It could catch an awful cold that way." He sat down on the bed and laid his hand on the shaven pubus, feeling the tiny bristles in the palm of his hand as he massaged her lightly. The bristles made the whole thing even more indecent. She sighed as he kneaded, and spread her legs. With the motion, he could feel her wetness and worked his fingers into the opening cavity. She began thrusting herself to meet the motion of his hand. Corbin felt like laughing. He had not the slightest intention nor desire to make love to this woman; he was merely a mechanical contrivance to provide her with satisfaction. Her clitoris swelled and his hand grew very wet as she increased the tempo of her hips. He met the new urgency manually.

"For God's sakes, Chuck, are you going to lay me or finger me to death!" she moaned.

When he didn't move, she reached up suddenly and pulled his face into her bristles. With his bristles meeting hers, he brought her finally to a screaming climax. She shuddered and lay back relaxed, holding his head against her belly.

After a few minutes, she asked him, "What was the trouble—not in the mood?"

He sat up. "I've been out of practice—torn ligaments—you know the sort of thing? Coach says I need a lot of deep heat treatment and TLC."

"TLC?".

"Tender loving care." He went back to the tiny bathroom to wash his face and hands. He noticed his eyes didn't look as tired any longer and smiled at the reflection—a genuine smile this time.

Tricia passed him going in as he came out, and grabbed him by the shoulders, pushing her face against his mouth, kissing him hungrily. She stood back.

"Who's going to be your coach for TLC?"

He laughed. "You looking for the job?"

"I don't see anyone else standing in the lineup."

He put his hands on her shoulders and looked into her eyes. "Let me give it some thought, Tricia." He dropped his arms. "I'll see you for dinner."

She ducked around the corner of the bathroom as he opened the cabin door and stepped over the water stop to the deck. "Don't go too far, Chuck—I still have to hear your story." She blew him a friendly kiss. He nodded and closed the door.

He walked back to the afterdeck, his body slanted against the driving wind, and reclaimed the lounge chair. The blanket had either been taken or blown away. The deck was deserted. He decided to sit down anyway. The wind was not that cold; in fact, he decided, it was a warm wind, annoying but at the same time amenable. He stretched out on the wooden chair and contemplated the ocean while he examined his reaction to Tricia Kirkpatrick's invitation.

He had thought of sex periodically over the past three years, but when it came down to pushes and shoves, he backed away with a polite smile. Now he was wondering if he had become impotent. The more he considered that aspect of his recent visit to cabin *B 36* the more alarmed he became. The first time he had gone out with Elizabeth several months after Peggy's death, there had been no thought given to the sexual aspect of their previous relationship, and although he knew she was willing and wanting him, he recognized the lack of arousal when the old subtleties she had used so many times before, failed. The warmth, the affection and understanding were still there, but the sexual part was gone, or lying dormant. Much later, he discovered it had gone.

It was early August by the time Corbin and the children had reached the foothills of the Rockies in time to watch the Calgary Stampede. On an impulse he had phoned the office, inviting Elizabeth to join them. He met her at the airport in the Landcruiser next day. They drove back to their parking site near the fairgrounds and pulled in amongst the masses of campers, trailers and caravans which had arrived from all over the U.S. and Canada to attend the festivities. For the children it was better than a visit to the circus, but without the variety of animals. They had made instant friends with a host of other visiting children and charged off among rows of scattered vehicles to find their companions while Corbin poured a noontime drink for his secretary.

"You're looking fit, Mr. Corbin," she acknowledged across the small dining table. Their conversation from the airport had been restricted by the children, who, although resigned to their father's secretary, regarded her intrusion with youthful suspicion. Corbin had made the mistake of saving her arrival as a surprise. Some surprise!

"Feeling fit. Lots of sleep, homecooked food and plenty of exercise."

"Who's the cook?"

"We take turns—Peter does the breakfast. I do lunches and dinners. The girls do the dishes—some of the baking, too." He added, "When they're in the mood."

"It sounds as if the girls have the short end of the stick."

"Isn't that the way it usually happens?" He looked at her without mirth.

Elizabeth lowered her eyes. "I suppose it is." The door swung open and Peter came in, dragging another towheaded boy in short pants inside.

"Hi Dad, this is Mike—he wants to use the bathroom an' I want a drink."

Corbin nodded. "Be my guest, Mike—second door on your right."

The freckeled face grinned in gratitude, baring a broken front tooth, and hustled down the aisle. Peter went to the refrigerator and poured himself a glass of milk. He examined Elizabeth after the first gulp, his upper lip mustached with the contents of the glass.

"You going to be visiting long, Elizabeth?"

"Mrs. Avery to you, young man," Corbin said sternly.

"Why Peter? Don't you like me visiting?" She made the mistake of talking down to him, instead of at him; the inexperience of dealing with children. Peter's eyes were resentful.

"I guess so," he said sullenly. The double interpretive reply. Corbin picked it up immediately. Elizabeth thought he meant she had his agreement to remain. He gulped down the rest of the glass, rinsed it out in the sink as Mike came charging out the the bathroom, zipping up his pants.

"Thanks, Mr. Corbin." The two boys scurried out the door, slamming the screen.

Inside, Corbin and Elizabeth heard Mike asking Peter, "Hey Pete, who's the girl with your old man?"

"Aw, she's just his secretary trying to move in now Mom's dead." *Out of the mouths of babes.* Their voices faded as they rounded the rear.

"I'm sorry. That was uncalled for. I'll speak to him later." Corbin was genuinely embarrassed. She lay her hand on his arm.

"Don't Chuck. Don't blame him for the way he feels. I don't blame you for the way you feel. It's the same thing—the only difference is that Peter has accepted it—I haven't; at least, not yet."

"I thought, I really thought that . . ." He couldn't form the words.

"You thought we could go back to where we were. You talked yourself into believing it until finally, when you were convinced, you phoned me. Now you know there's no going back." She gave a short laugh. "There never is!"

She was right and he knew it. "I'm sorry, sweetheart—I guess it's still too soon. They sipped their drinks in silence, looking at each other across the inlaid roadmap of North America beneath the clear fiberglass tabletop. He broke the silence of noise and passing voices outside.

"How's Don doing?"

"Great!" They were on safer ground for the moment. "The baby's due any day now."

"I mean the business." He had forgotten Rina's pregnancy, and reminded himself to phone his congratulations when the baby arrived.

"Business is fine. The companies of Corbin are all making millions." She didn't sound very enthusiastic about it.

"Something wrong?"

Elizabeth shrugged and took another sip of her drink. "No, nothing's wrong, in fact, everything is about as right as it could be—that's the trouble. It's so big and so successful I no longer feel a part of it, if you know what I mean? Have you any idea how much you are worth?"

"No, not really."

"Neither do I—nor anyone else, for that matter. It used to be fun to figure it all out at those quarterly meetings, remember? You used to tell Dix and the others how much they were worth. It was exciting—like a roulette wheel; you kept spinning out the winning numbers for everyone. Now, no one mentions net worths. Maybe they're all too embarrassed by the figures."

"Or no longer care. How's your love life?" He changed the subject.

"If you mean am I getting laid regularly, the answer is yes. If you mean am I in love with whom I'm laying, the answer is no."

"What's he like?" Corbin was curious.

"He's a man—like you, but not as rich, handsome or intelligent. Still, he's pleasant company for the lonely evenings. We use the cottage on weekends—I hope you don't mind."

He shook his head. "That's why I gave you the key—the place is yours. I told you that."

"You're not jealous—just a little?" she asked hopefully.

Corbin smiled. "Well, perhaps a little."

"I love you, Chuck." Her eyes filled and she clutched his arm, again.

He patted the clenched hand gently. "I know, sweetheart, and that's what makes it all such a tragedy."

She spent the night in tears in a downtown hotel and flew back to the office on the first flight out the following morning.

He changed into the mandatory semi-formal attire required at dinner and dropped by cabin *B 36*. The wind had died during the late afternoon, and although the heavy Atlantic rollers were still immense, it was possible now to walk at right angles to the deck, instead of a forty-five degree slant. She was ready and waiting when he knocked. He reeled back from her in mock astonishment when she opened the door.

"My God, woman! Straight out of *Vogue*."

"*Harper's Bazaar*, actually. Like it?"

"Woof woof!" He took her arm and escorted her to his table in the dining lounge. Herman Slitzman stood up when he introduced them.

"Like maybe you found an angel, Chuck, while I ruin my afternoon watching Wall Street?"

Gallantly, he held out a chair, placing Tricia between them. When they were all seated, Slitzman appraised her with frank admiration.

"Just the most beautiful woman on the ship, you are, Mrs. Kirkpatrick, and such luck I have you sitting with me!"

"Watch him, Tricia, he's one of those smooth talking New York Jews with a stable full of fillies up at Lake George."

He noticed with surprise she blushed at the compliment from the Wall Street broker. They ordered the full seven course dinner suggested for the sumptuous evening meal. A string quartet in evening dress on a raised platform behind some potted ferns at the end of the room provided selections from Vivaldi, Bach and Mozart, filling the room with comfortable background sound. For a while their conversation was light and amusing, using each other as foils. Tricia kept laughing at the barbed wit dancing between the two men. When the wine arrived, she looked at Corbin accusingly.

He smiled. "Wine at dinner is part of a meal." He poured the sparkling burgundy into her glass.

"Unless, of course, the wine becomes the meal," Slitzman

warned.

They toasted to friends, and friendships, new and old. "Where do you come from, Mrs. Kirkpatrick?"

"Tamiami—near Miami."

"I know the area well. When my wife—God rest her—was alive, we used to spend our Winters at Miami Beach. Kirkpatrick? That's an interesting—Scots and Irish—name. Of course, the best Scots originally came from Ireland. The village kirk was the focal point from the local clan. I suppose your husband's ancestors administered a local kirk—you don't happen to know which one, maybe?"

"No, I don't." She had never known the origin of the name, but was interested in the knowledge the big fat man possessed. "How do you know the origin of names, Mr. Slitzman, is it a hobby?"

He considered the question carefully before answering.

"You will find every Jew is interested in the origins of names, peoples, identities. Heritage is the one thing that separates us all, while at the same time the history of our heritage binds us together."

Corbin looked up from his plate. It was an interesting thought. "My name is French, originally from Louisiana. I've traced my family tree back to 1834."

Herman smiled. Then your origins are probably directly from France or via Canada from the Acadia expulsion in the mid-eighteenth century." He turned to Tricia. "And you, Mrs. Kirkpatrick, what was your maiden name?"

"Cooper, from Maryland. All I know is my great-grandfather fought and died in the Civil War at Chicamauga."

"Cooper, an English name for the man who made the wooden barrels in the local villages. He was an important man. Everyone used barrels. It was a highly skilled trade. Sometimes, if he was an important Cooper, he had a Hooper to help him set the metal binding or hoops to hold the staves in place." He nodded at her, then at Corbin. "You see, the French and English heritage is what separates you, but the history of that heritage has made you Americans." He nodded again, agreeing with himself and returned to his meal.

"And what about your heritage, Herman?"

"Ah, my heritage starts on page one of the Old Testament; in the beginning God created the heavens and the earth. My first ancestor was Adam, a Jewish horticulturist, he was, in the Garden of Eden." They all laughed.

"But your father was Polish," Corbin reminded him.

"Never. My father—God rest him—was a Jew. A Jew can be a Pole or a Russian or even an American, but first and foremost, he is a Jew. A Jew is an ideal, an identity, not a nationality," he explained.

"But you are an American!"

"I am an American Jew, who is American because he was born in America, and pays taxes, but a Jew always—whether I pay taxes or not, or give up my citizenship for some other country."

"Like Israel," Tricia said.

"Like Israel, Mrs. Kirkpatrick," he agreed. "You have been to Israel, maybe?"

She shook her head and glanced at Corbin. "Me neither. I wouldn't go near the place—too many Jews. What chance would a Gentile businessman like me stand against those odds?"

"You should visit Israel if you get a chance. They have made a flower out of the desert." He said it proudly as if he had spent several years digging the sand himself.

"And since 1948 a whole gang of troubles too," Corbin observed.

Herman sighed. "Always where there are Jews, there's trouble; is it Jews that cause the trouble, or is the trouble caused because of the Jews? We are unwelcome everywhere—including the Middle East. But there we fight—for the first time in a long while we will fight to stay. Israel is a part of every Jew now, and yet, what is Israel? It is nothing; scrub desert between the Jordan river and the sea—surrounded by enemies plotting to destroy it." He laughed. "It is worthless as a land. The Negroes have better lands in Africa for sale; rich lands filled with rain, good soil and fresh water."

"Then why don't you buy it and move and let the Palestinians have their godforsaken desert?" Corbin suggested. He had never been able to understand the situation in the Middle East.

"Because it is where we started, and it is where we will end," Slitzman said quietly.

"But Mr. Slitzman, I read somewhere the Arabs said they were there first, so by rights it all belongs to them."

"And the Indians say American belongs to them, the Eskimos say they own the Arctic and the Communists say nobody owns anything, it all belongs to the State. Who is right?" He waited for the answer. Corbin gave it to him.

"Right is might."

Slitzman smiled. "Ah hah! You see, Mrs. Kirkpatrick? The words of a practical businessman. When politics, intrigue and money fail, there is always the power of the fist. My father—God rest him—used to say to me, 'Herman,' he'd say, 'you're a Jewboy. Don't you forget it.' Forget it! How could I forget when I had so many nice Gentile boys ready to beat my head in every time I went out on the street. Now I look along my office wall at all the Israel bonds I've bought, hanging there gathering dust—not interest, Chuck, dust, and I say, 'Herman, you're an old yid with some bucks, so spend a little, spread it around for the other Jewboys to fight with, and keep Israel green—and strong. The Palestinians want their land?' I say to them, 'If you are strong enough, come and take it—if not, keep your peace and leave us in peace'." His eyes softened behind the thick glasses. "You put me on a soap box, already. Now, how can I climb down?" He picked up his fork and began eating.

The string quartet changed pace to a Strauss waltz; Corbin tried to place the tune but couldn't. He had a rotten ear for music and it annoyed him. Herman Slitzman would know, but he hesitated to ask. Several couples were taking advantage of the music.

"Do you dance, Tricia?" The last time he'd waltzed had been with Peggy five years ago.

"Like an angel, Mr. Corbin—you are asking me to dance, or inquiring if I can?"

He stood up. "If you have no objection, Herman?"

Slitzman waved a forkful of food at them. "Go, go! Have fun, make yourselves hot and sticky, see if I care! I'll blow on your food and keep it warm until you get back."

It took a few steps to recapture his form, which, at its peak, had not been that good. Still, Tricia had no trouble in following him and they swirled the floor smiling happily at their accomplishment. "I feel so sorry for your friend—you know, he's dying."

"Oh, how do you know?"

"I heard the ship's doctor telling one of the officers Mr. Slitzman is not expected to last the voyage—his heart, I think he said. He's such a nice man."

"He's all of that. What makes you think any of us will last the voyage?"

She laughed; her face was flushed from the effort of dancing. "I don't know about you, Chuck, but I'm sure I'll last—I'm just beginning to live again."

As they rounded the bend in the highway Peter shouted, "There it is!"

Corbin pulled the land cruiser over on the shoulder and stopped so they could all drink in the magnificent view of the Pacific Ocean stretching out in front of them.

470

"Wow!" Emily was suitably impressed. "You mean it goes all the way to Japan?"

"Not quite; there's a big island blocking the way, but after that it's plain sailing for about six thousand miles," Corbin advised.

"I don't thee any island, Daddy." Alice squinted through the front window.

"It's there—just over the horizon—believe me, the map says so."

"Yeah, Vancouver Island, see?" Peter showed her the Provincial road map they had been following since crossing into British Columbia. He had become a proficient navigator during the trip and spent many hours sitting in the front chair examining the town and city dots, reading their names and speculating on what they were like. He had never realized the country was so big. Neither had Corbin.

They wound down the highway into Vancouver and delivered the Cruiser to the Canadian Pacific Railway to ship back to Ottawa by flatcar. After packing enough clothing to last a few days, they rented a car and checked into one of the fancy downtown hotels. The original thought had been to make the return drive through the U.S., back into Canada at Niagara Falls, but after eight weeks of intermittent driving, Corbin had decided to fly back in pampered luxury.

They drove around the Pacific coast taking in the scenery and made a one-day pilgrimage on the car ferry over to the island that blocked the way to Japan. The children had each collected a glass jar of fresh water from Lake Superior, which, with great ceremony, they poured into the Pacific Ocean while waiting at the ferry dock to load the car.

"Will it make the ocean thweeter, Daddy?" Alice asked, holding the empty glass pickle jar.

He smiled. "It can't do it any harm, Darling."

"What do I do with the jar now?" The screaming seagulls, sensing food, swooped down on the splash of merging water.

"Why not save it and we'll put ocean water in the bottles and carry some water back to the Atlantic Ocean?" Peter suggested. They had planned on a similar trip the following year to the Eastern seaboard. Corbin had agreed, knowing the drive would be considerably shorter.

"Good idea," he told his son. "You can merge the oceans next summer."

"What's 'merge' mean, Daddy?"

"It means mix, dummy," Peter told Emily.

"Oh!" It sounded reasonable.

However, they had to wait until they were on the island before finding a suitable pathway down to the water to fill the bottles; the mainland pier offered no access. The following day they flew home in a jumbo jet, first class, awash with luxury, carefully carrying their three pickle jars of Pacific Ocean. Most of their school friends had returned from summer vacations, so the children dropped back into the pattern of their lives smoothly and without complaint.

Corbin dropped into the office to see Don Affleck.

"How's the baby?"

Affleck looked pleased as punch. The boy had been born a few days after Corbin had left the Calgary Stampede. He had wired his congratulations along with two dozen long stem roses to Rina. Unfortunately, the flowers arrived on the day she left the hospital.

"God, they look old and beat up when they're produced for you through that window!"

The red wizened, tight-fisted object cradled in the nurse's arms had given him a start when he had first been introduced to his son. He had wiggled his fingers hesitantly at the tiny form, not all that convinced the bundle belonged to him.

"They all shape up after a few weeks." He looked around the office.

Affleck had left it exactly the way it had been when Corbin vacated it months before. His name and title were still attached to the door.

"Oh, the kid looks much better now—eats like a horse. You visiting or checking on me?" His smile was still the same—too perfect. It would always be the same. He looked fit and thriving on the responsibility he had assumed. Happy, relaxed, confident.

"I came to make sure you haven't been robbing the till." He walked about the office, touching the familiar objects with unfamiliarity, circling the room.

"I think I'm ready to come back, Don." He sat down behind his desk and leaned in the chair, clasping his hands about the leather armrests. Affleck stood in the middle of the carpet, eyeing him speculatively.

"You sure, Chuck?"

He smiled the smile of friendship. "I'm not sure about anything except I can't go on doing nothing. The problem with long vacations is a guy never gets a chance to take a day off for a holiday."

Affleck pulled one of the armchairs up to the desk and sat down. "How was the trip West?"

472

"A return to my childhood. First time I got to know my kids, I mean really know them. Funny thing that you see them everyday, day in and day out and you know they are yours and you love them, but they are objects of affection, not persons. It's only when you live with them—in close quarters for a period of time, I mean—it's only then you realize they are people. Little people, with the same faults, desires and frustrations we have, but in a different perspective. When yours is old enough I'd recommend a cross-country trip in a landcruiser to get acquainted."

"I'll bear it in mind."

"How's Rina?"

"Full of beans—literally. Her mother flew up and gave her some cockeyed story about plenty of frijoles to produce mother's milk for the baby, so now she's eating the damn things every meal. We've cornered most of the city's bean market."

They both laughed.

"And Elizabeth?"

"Quiet after her trip out to see you. What happened?"

Corbin shrugged. "I don't know. Maybe I have a guilt complex. I should marry her, I suppose—do the honorable thing after all these years, but I can't. Christ! I can't even work up enough interest to go to bed with her anymore." He smiled at him ruefully. "What do you recommend, Doctor, an aphrodisiac?"

"She's taking it hard—there's a dark horse on the horizon—insurance broker—you know the scam, fire, theft, and auto, and don't you dare have a claim or we'll raise your premiums, Mrs. Smith."

"You met him?"

"A few times. He's okay, but she's got him wrapped around her finger, so it will never work for a long term policy coverage, with or without the claims. She's waiting for you."

Out beyond the door in the reception room, he could hear the muffled IBM Selectric as Elizabeth zipped through her workload. She had given him a quick tight smile when he had come in, but that was all, then went back to work.

"It may be a long wait." He tilted forward in the chair, resting his elbows on the desk.

"How about business? What's new and exciting?"

Affleck laughed. "What's new and exciting? Do you have a week of free time—It'll take me that long to explain everything—*man* have we been busy!"

"I have all the time in the world—shoot!"

After dinner they bid Herman Slitzman goodnight, and drifted into the main lounge to continue dancing, when the music pleased them; talking, when it didn't. There was a six piece orchestra in the lounge whose repertoire, either by design or intuition, covered the music of the late Forties to the early Sixties, with a touch of Beatles suitably toned-down for the middle-aged dancers. They had switched from wine to ginger ale, inducing a sobriety of conversation while the other guests in the lounge continued raising the decible level as the evening progressed.

"Are you using for divorce?" he asked her out of the blue. They were sitting at one of the small cocktail tables, taking a break between numbers. Corbin's calves were starting to ache from the use of unfamiliar muscles.

She shook her head. "He's too rich to divorce and there's no community property laws in Florida. I'd wind up with nothing."

"Except your pride."

She laughed. "Ever tried living on pride?"

"So it all comes down to a question of money?"

"Doesn't everything, in the end?"

It was the same way he had felt at one time. He understood the feeling. "I used to think so, but then at a certain point you realize you can only drive one car at a time, live in one house, sleep in one bed and—unless you're a glutton—eat three meals a day. After that, money is only a score card in the game of living—not even a good scorecard if you happen to be occupied with something really satisfying, instead of money." He ran his fingers around the top of the empty glass. After six ginger ales he felt awash in the stuff and had refused the waiter the last time around.

"Spoken like a man who has it made. You can afford to be charitable now—like Herman Slitzman with his Israel bonds. What do you hang on your wall, Chuck?"

"Spoken like a true hedonist."

She shook her head, spilling her hair. "I'm not a hedonist. I'm a pretty girl from Baltimore whose ancestors made barrels, struck it lucky in New York as a fashion model, and met a horny lush between wives and managed to con him into marrying me because he had all the things I wanted and I knew I'd never get. Is that so wrong?" she demanded.

"I don't know, is it?"

"It's rotten. You know it and I know it. But that's the way it is and if I had to do it over again I'd probably do the same thing. Anyway, let's change the subject." She looked away from him, out at the redfaced dancers puffing on the floor.

"Where did he get his money?"

"Who?" She looked back.

"Kirk—your husband. Did he work for it?"

"He's never done a day's work in his life, unless you count lugging out the empty liquor bottles. His granddaddy owned a piece of some railway in the West. Kirk collected fourteen million after taxes when his father died. Kirk was an only child—spoiled rotten."

"So were you."

"How did you know that? Being an only child, I mean?"

"It shows—and, you're spoiled rotten."

Her eyes blazed a turgid blue. "My father was a postman, I'll have you know, very little money."

"But what he did have he spent catering to your every whim, didn't he? Modeling school, diction school, makeup school. I'll bet he even put you through secretarial school so you could learn to type and take shorthand against the day you could uncross those gorgeous gams in front of the Big Boss and run off to Hawaii for a whirlwind romance."

She jumped to her feet and announced imperiously, "I think I'll go to my cabin. Goodnight, Mr. Corbin."

He stood up, started to say something, then changed his mind as she spun on her heel and quickstepped past the tables to the exit. The waiter, serving one of the tables nearby, came over with a polite smile.

"Care for another glass of ginger ale, Sir?"

"Why not? Maybe the next round will change my luck."

"Yes, Sir, and if I might make an observation. Sir? Dealing with beautiful women is much the same as the daily bet on the ship's log—not everyone can be a winner."

Corbin chuckled, nodding. "I know what you mean, Steward. Thank God I'm not a betting man."

He knew he had put his foot in it with Tricia. He shrugged mentally, writing her off as one of life's sickies; ruptured reason running to oblivion. She despised her husband because he had never worked for a living. He wondered how long it had been since Patricia Kirkpatrick had done any work herself? He could never understand how people could go through life doing nothing, taking everything, giving nothing in return. The steward came back with another glass of iced ginger ale, setting it on the fiber coaster.

"Will that be all, Sir?"

"Yes, thanks." He signed the tab for the evening's drinks,

resolving to switch to mineral water in the future. "Do you stock *Perrier* or *Celestine Vichy water?*"

"Both, Sir." He took the receipt. "Would you like me to send a bottle of water to your cabin?"

"I'd appreciate it—with some ice. B31. Make it Vichy water."

"Very good, Sir. I'll attend to it."

Corbin decided he would need something for his stomach later to quiet the sickening sweetness of the ginger ale. He remembered, with some surprise, discovering Don Affleck had switched from Bourbon on the rocks to Canadian Rye thinned with ginger ale.

He had been back in harness over a month when Don had invited him over to see the baby. The first thing Rina had presented to her husband when he walked in the door was a Rye and Ginger.

"Hello Chuck! Where have you been hiding?" She bubbled on without waiting for a reply. "It's been ages since I've seen you—Donee is so bad about invitations—have you met my mother?"

Of course he hadn't, so he shook hands with the short stocky woman who suddenly appeared in the living room.

"Con mucho gusto, Senor Corbin," she said, then launched into a long-winded welcome in Spanish until Rina interrupted her and explained of the senior party, "No habla Espanol." Her mother glowered, hurled another burst of Spanish back at her daughter, and left the room, leaving Rina and Affleck laughing, Corbin bewildered.

"She wanted to know why in th'hell someone didn't say something about it before, instead of allowing her to make a fool of herself. She's a good old girl, a real lifesaver for Rina."

"She's a wonderful mother—very proper, she brought me up very proper—isn't that a silly word—proper? Sometimes I say English words and they sound silly when I say them many times—like house, now that's a silly word—say house, house, house—see?" She laughed, sat down, then jumped up again. "Would you like a drink, Chuck?"

"Sure, anything at all is fine."

"I'll get us something—I never drink before supper because it makes me giddy—but Donee drinks like a fish all the time so it doesn't matter . . ." She was still talking as she went out of earshot. Affleck looked across the room at Corbin and grinned.

"She's always like that—happy like a bird and talking complete nonsense most of the time. I keep waiting for the day she changes, then I'll spank her."

"Pray she never does."

"C'mon up and see the sprog." He led the way upstairs to the newly decorated nursery.

The fat baby, Michael Alexander Affleck, was gluggling happily at an overhead mobile of plastic butterflies attached to the headboard. The chubby round face smiled back at the visitors. "See, he likes you."

Corbin was skeptical. "Probably gas—they all smile when they have gas."

"What do you mean *gas*—the little bugger smiled at you—look at him!"

Corbin stuck a finger into the crib. It was seized instantly by a pink fist. The grin remained fixed. He disconnected the tiny fingers gently.

"I still say he needs to be burped." He lifted him out of the crib and flopped the diapered tot over his shoulder and began patting. The baby burped. Corbin lowered him back to the crib, smiling in triumph. "See, smart ass! What did I tell you—*gas*!"

Affleck didn't reply. They toured the upstairs bedrooms until Rina called them. It was the first time Corbin had seen the upstairs of their home. It was similar to his own.

It had been pleasant sitting with them in the living room reliving old memories with gentle laughter, or mocking the pomposity of bureaucrats with whom they had been dealing over the past weeks.

"By the way, did you know Morris Levy is up for consideration as Director of Atomic Energy?"

Corbin hadn't. "He's a good man. He'll do them a good job."

"Yeah, but you can kiss goodbye to any more foreign sales," Affleck said.

"That's got nothing to do with Morris, that's government policy. If policy says sell, then Morris has no choice."

"He's convinced sooner or later one of the countries will refine their waste and blow up the world—he may be right—but again, that's a matter of politics, I suppose."

"Like your friend Chirlo?" Corbin suggested.

"Oh no, Chuck. Colonel Chirlo would never do anything that silly—he's a wonderful man!" Rina jumped into the discussion, defending her country's idol. "Besides, he already has everything he wants—he rules the country."

"I agree; if we could sell reactors to nations that had men like Chirlo running them, there'd be no problem, but what worries Morris is no one knows what people will turn up to replace the Chirlos. However, that's for our children to worry over—not us."

Corbin nodded. "Do you think Michael Alexander Affleck will

be able to handle it?"

Rina jumped up. "Speaking of Michael Alexander Affleck, I feel a certain tightness in the chest—feeding time," she announced. "I'll run up and give him his supper, then we can have ours."

On cue, her mother met her at the door and together they climbed the stairs to the nursery.

"Have you heard from him?"

"Chirlo? Yup. He sent a silver baby cup with Mike's initials and birthdate, along with a short note of congratulations through the embassy. Thoughtful."

"No problems with the reactor?"

"Haven't heard anything on it. We could ask Morris, if you're interested."

"No, don't bother. I was only curious." He held up his empty glass, looking at the small melting ice cubes. "I have come to one definite decision tonight, though. I have decided the taste of Kentucky Bourbon on the rocks is far superior to Canadian Rye and Ginger Ale!"

Corbin left the glass of ginger ale untouched. It was flat anyway by the time the band started playing *Goodnight Sweeheart* for their evening wrap-up. He sauntered out on deck, heading for his cabin. The air was quite warm now; the seas rolling comfortably, black and shiny with only a periodic flash of whitecap sprinkling across the surface. He leaned on the railing and looked down at the frothy water sweeping past the hull, then on an impulse, spit into the darkness. He looked around guiltily, making sure no one had seen him. The open deck was deserted. Above him a few shadow wisps of cloud still sailed aloft defiantly, but not thick enough to hide the ocean's lid of stars. He felt a dull rumbling vibration in his elbows from the wood railing and decided to pay a visit to the engine room and look at the machinery next day after breakfast. He loved the sight of glistening, well-oiled, heavy engines, even if he didn't know how they worked. Peter Colley had always been the one who knew engines, he remembered. It was an art, or knack—a feeling you were born with; either you had it or you didn't. Colley had it. He smiled, recalling their first year in business when Peter kept all those tired engines working smoothly—aircraft, trucks and cars. He had the gift.

As before, he noticed the perfume, before he was aware Tricia was standing beside him. She leaned her elbows beside him. He didn't turn his head.

"We seem to have trouble getting started on a relationship,

478

don't we Chuck?"

"I suppose it's because I'm from the Doctor Samuel Johnson school of thought on women."

"What's that?"

"Women are like Chinese Gongs and should be struck regularly." He turned his head, smiling. "Or words to that effect."

"You don't believe that?" She linked her arm through his.

"I don't know what I believe, Tricia; do you?" She didn't reply. They leaned on the rail, staring out at the inky water.

"Funny how someone can be lonely in a crowd of people."

He could see lights far out across the ocean where the black horizon met the jeweled sky. Another cruise ship, or super tanker? It looked big enough to be a tanker. Distances were deceptive in the dark.

"Like an island," she continued, "you can stand on a street corner in a busy city and still be completely alone—apart—you know what I mean, Chuck?"

The lights from the tanker—he was sure it was a tanker now—appeared brighter when he looked off to one side, then dimmed when he returned to a direct gaze. Night vision. He knew it had something to do with night vision; look slightly to the left or right of an object, but remember there is a blind spot. Where had he learned that? It was a tanker, a super tanker riding very low in the water, passing them, heading for one of the coastal super ports.

"I hate being lonely—no, not hate; that's not the right word—I'm frightened when I'm lonely—not all the time, but when I want to talk, to feel *with* someone—sharing I guess is what you call it. There is no sharing with loneliness—if you share you're no longer lonely. Crazy, isn't it?"

He had read somewhere super tankers never docked, but stood offshore to pick up or discharge their cargo, then moved off, like Vanderdecken, the Flying Dutchman, roaming the oceans of the world, seeking another port they could not enter. How many months at a time did their crews stay on board, or was it years? Loneliness.

She nestled in closer to his body, clinging tightly to his arm. "When I was younger I used to think the best thing that could happen to a person was being on their own. No one to report to, no one to answer to, nothing to answer for. It's fun for a while, I guess, at least it was when I was young. Then you grow old, well, older, and you find you've dug a moat around yourself and there's no drawbridge, so you just stand there in your castle and watch the people passing by all around—they can't come to visit and you can't get out.''

He heard it took the tankers ten miles to stop at top speed. What did they do with them when they grew too old, too tired, too unsafe to make their endless voyages—scrap them? The Dutchman's pact with the devil had been to find a woman who would die for him to obtain his earthly release; the tanker's release would be much simpler—Liberian registry, an incompetent crew, and weakened plating with a medium-sized storm thrown in for good measure. The lonely road to release.

"I had a girl friend once—Minerva Muncie—can you imagine a name like Minerva Muncie? She looked like her name, drab, stringy mouse-colored hair, skinny legs and flat chested. She had nothing going for her—and I mean *nothing*. She wasn't even smart enough to snag a man with money. Married a local kid who worked in a supermarket stacking cans—a stacker! Married him because he knocked her up—first time out the gate and Minerva is pregnant—I mean she was a *loser*. I stopped off in Baltimore on my way to catch the boat and dropped in on them, so we could cry—I could cry on her shoulder about our lot in life. You know what? She has five kids—beautiful kids, I mean—a lovely little house and garden, two cars, and Bill—the can stacker—he's managing four supermarkets in the area—and he doesn't drink anything but beer when he watches television. Some loser!''

She turned, looking at him, then nudged him and smiled when he looked up.

"Hi there!''

Corbin grinned back. "Hi Tricia! Let's go to my cabin and I'll see if I can do a bit better getting into your castle than I did this afternoon. I have my own drawbridge!''

The idea of an executive jet for the company had been Affleck's idea. With their far flung operations in North America, airline connections to some of the out of the way places were few and at times impossible to arrange, resulting in wasted hours or days waiting for weather in some motel.

"You know something about aircraft anyway—didn't you used to run an airline?'' he asked as Corbin glanced over the information package on the DH 125. It showed a comfortable little corporate twin engined jet, with executive seating for a half dozen people, or optional interiors to include a private bedroom.

"It was a cargo operation with tired old piston-driven aircraft—and it was 1960: this is Seventy-two—everyone's using jets. I don't know anything about jet aircraft."

"What's to know? We hire a pilot and co-pilot, subcontract the maintenance and tell them where we want to go and when. Sure beats the airline ticket counter lineup routine. We could give Rick a call—maybe he'd be interested."

The former company pilot had elected to stay in Florida when Corbin moved the operation to Canada. They had sold the little twin Piper Aztec to him for one dollar as a bonus.

"Give him a call and see. He flew jets in Korea. He's probably got himself a new wife and making a bundle in the brokerage business now, but he's worth a try."

But he was interested when Affleck called, and a month later they were zipping about the continent in their new toy. It wasn't as fast as the airlines; in fact, it was 100 miles per hour slower, but for the luxury of being able to come and go as they pleased, it was worth every penny of the investment. But, more than that, for the first time in many years, Corbin and Affleck were out working together again, as a team.

They concentrated on areas for new development and the game of corporate checkers; buying small or medium sized, well established companies, which had become fixed in their ways of operation, with sliding growth curves and narrow-minded management. Some they merged, spun off unprofitable lines in others, but always they reorganized and consolidated after taking management control through the simple process of buying flagging shares on the open market. For Affleck, it was a joy to watch Corbin do what he knew best, and always, when the game ended, CORCAN held control of the board, with two kings facing the uncrowned trapped checkers left by the opposition. It was fun. It was exciting, particularly because they seldom lost a game.

"What do you think about going to the Olympics?" Affleck asked one day out of the clear blue sky. They had just leveled off on a trip back from Denver, a meeting to investigate a cattle shipping operation using cargo jets to the Far East. The promoters, starry-eyed idealists, were looking for a financial partner. Their idea was sound, but, as Corbin observed, what they lacked in money they more than made up for in their lack of business sense. The trip had been a waste of time.

"As a competitor?" Rick had switched off the seat belt sign, so Corbin got up to mix himself a bourbon on the rocks.

"Ha, Ha," Affleck said formally. "Seriously, wouldn't you like to go to Munich? We could check out that paperboard machinery in

Dusseldorf and write the whole trip off as a business expense."

"Want one?" Corbin held the bottle of Canadian Rye. Affleck nodded.

"I'm game—no, wait; I promised the kids the Atlantic coast this year in the land cruiser. He handed the rye and ginger ale mixture to his partner and sat down on the chair.

"Take the kids—there's enough room—you and I, Rina and the three kids. It would be a great experience for them."

"Who's going to look after Michael Alexander?"

"Mother. She's coming up for a visit next month. What do you say?"

Corbin raised his glass. "I say Munich, here we come."

It was light in the cabin by the time they fell back exhausted from their lovemaking.

"My God! Chuck! And here I thought you were impotent! I haven't been laid like that since I was a teenager. Mmmm." She buried her face in his chest, clinging to him ferociously.

"I've been saving up," he said tiredly. Physically, he felt exhausted, but because it was light, his brain told him the time for sleep had passed. A temporary aberration he knew would pass. The last thing he remembered thinking was how he hoped Herman wouldn't miss his company for breakfast.

It was early afternoon when he finally awoke and jumped out of the three-quarter sized berth. Tricia was gone—back to her own cabin, presumably. He went to the bathroom, looking in the mirror as he relieved himself. A middle-aged wreck, puffy eyes, heavy lidded and blue stubbled chin. He gargled to kill the sweet-sour taste of stale ginger ale, then showered, first cold to wake him, then hot to cleanse, and finally cold to close the pores. He checked the mirror again when he climbed out. Much better; in fact the sardonic smile made him appear a perfect satyr. He shaved quickly and sprinkled himself liberally with lotion, enjoying the sting. Satisfied from the mirror his years had receded to acceptable proportions, he went back to the cabin to dress, humming an old love song from the Fifties. When he stepped out on deck he realized he had made a mistake in his selection of wardrobe; the air was warm, very warm.

"Balls!" He returned to the cabin and changed into a pair of white ducks and striped open-necked shirt, opened to provide sufficient view of curly chest hair. He felt rakish when he went back on deck. A satisfying feeling, like smoking behind the woodshed when he was a boy and not getting caught. He began a circumnavigation of *B* deck, nodding pleasantly to the strolling passengers he met as he strode past. Some smiled, some stared or looked at him oddly, trying to place the face above the broad red and white striped shirt. On the second go around, he paused to knock on Tricia's cabin. There was no reply. Miffed, he continued his walk around the deck and then joined the crowded loungers sunning themselves aft. He picked a vacant area and dragged a deckchair away from the scattered groups, then lay down to enjoy the new warmth from the sun.

When the steward turned up he was tempted to order a Bloody Mary, but settled for a large tomato juice instead, something called a Bloody Albert, with all the proper ingredients, except Vodka. It tasted the same as the female version when he sipped it, marveling at the quality of British deceit. He settled back comfortably, watching a quartet of older people playing shuffleboard on the burnished wood deck. Paint outlines for the court were already fading from bright red to pink from the combination of salt spray and sun. He began examining his emotions towards Tricia; light-headed over the accomplishments with her in bed. It had been a new awakening of urges, feelings he had kept suppressed for so long. Was it because of her, or in spite of her that he was ready? He wondered. Could he complete the course with any interesting woman he met now? He swung his eyes around the deck, fastening his gaze on a pretty twenty-five year old in a bikini, lying on her stomach reading a pocket book. Her back was bare. She had removed the top and held the tie strings against her body with elbows as she read. He scrutinized the tight compact rear-end, seeking an outline at the vee between her legs, familiar ridges packed snugly against thinly-stretched material.

For a moment he fantasized going over and yanking off the bottom of her suit. His erection started at the thought. He smiled inwardly. "I'll be damned."

"I hope not—at least not for a while." She had sneaked up behind him and watching with amusement. "She's not your type—too young, too inexperienced. You'd shock her."

Corbin tipped his chin up, looking at her inverted, framed by sunlight. She was wearing a bikini too, even briefer than the monokini rear he had been observing. His erection continued to surge in the tight ducks.

"Christ, woman, what have you done to me?" He crossed his legs casually, capturing the lengthening intruder between his thighs, and turned on his side.

"Awakened the primeval man." She sat down on the lower half of the lounge, pushing herself against his swelling. "Mmmmm—that feels nice. Were you expecting someone?"

She picked up the glass and sipped it. "Bloody Mary?"

"Bloody Albert." He took the glass out of her hand.

"Naughty! Naughty!"

"It's a Mary without the Vodka," he explained, feeling righteous.

"Oh." She squirmed against him. "How are you feeling?"

"Raunchy."

"Me too—can you make it to the cabin without ripping those pants when you stand up?"

"Let's try and see what happens." He lowered a hand deep into his pocket as he stood, clasping the offending member securely, and followed her across the deck to *B 36*.

They made the trip to Munich with the DH 125 in three easy stages. One overnight stop at Iceland, another in London, then touching down at Munich in early afternoon the third day. The children played games with Rina most of the time; Alice and Rina teaming against Peter and Emily, cards, snakes and ladders, even monopoly, which had to be abandoned halfway through the first game when the aircraft hit some air turbulence and hurricaned the hotels and houses off the board. A violent argument ensued when the pieces were picked from the floor as to who owned what. To settle the problem, the monopoly game was put away, each player firmly convinced he or she had won. After that, everyone slept until they landed at Munich.

The second class hotel charged them first class prices for the suites they had reserved on the fourth floor. The manager was apologetic, in an official Germanic way, over the price increase and managed to give a credible performance of sadness over the way the Olympics had driven up the cost of everything in the town and surrounding countryside. Actually, they knew they had been lucky to arrange accommodations at all on such short notice. The streets were packed with people from all over the world when they strolled the city the day after their arrival; gift shops were selling merchandise as fast as knick knacks were placed in windows.

"Ooooo, look Daddy! Look at the beautiful dolls!" They had been walking side streets around the hotel for nearly two hours, and had started searching for an uncrowded restaurant with a free table for six. Corbin paused to look at the window display of china

Dresden dolls peering prettily at them from the showcase; all sizes and moods; some perched on pedestals, other pirouetting motion-lessly on one foot atop music boxes; all were expensive.

"Yuk—dolls!" Peter took a swift glance and kept walking, trying to pull Rina's hand.

"Oh Daddy, let's go and look—please?" Emily started for the door. Everyone followed without protest through the tinkling entrance. Peter, last through, closed the door and stood looking up at the little bell hanging from the frame, watching until it fell silent.

Inside the shop was a fairyland of dolls, horses, coaches complete with coachmen, all done in flawless delicate Dresden china. Miniscule taffeta dresses, lace mantillas, billowy embroidered ruffled slips peeking from beneath velvet ballroom gowns—all started from the sculpturing of a potter's wheel. The girls were entranced and wandered slowly down the rows of showcases, keeping their hands clasped in strict obedience to the numerous placards, which stated, "Do not touch please," in six languages—two of them Oriental. There were three people at the back of the shop, a man and a woman talking with a clerk. Affleck stared, then called, "Jamil! Leila!"

The two customers turned, startled. "Mr. Affleck—Don, is it not?"

They met in the middle of the aisle shaking hands, introducing everyone while the girls continued drifting past the display cases.

"What on earth are you doing in Munich?"

Jamil smiled. "I heard they were holding Olympic Games. I came to watch—you?"

"Same thing. Where are you staying?" He still could not relate the presence of the thin sober Palestinian and his woman to a gift shop in Munich from their first meeting at Chirlo's finca near Tippitaca. Jamil ducked the question.

"We'll be here only a short time—I have to go back to the Middle East—business matters." He made it sound as if he were a gentleman farmer returning to poke at the level of weight gain in his prize hogs.

"We're at the Berghof—you must drop by for dinner," Affleck suggested. "It's second rate, but the food is good. It was all we could get. We've tied up most of the fourth floor."

"We would like that, Mr. Affleck," Leila said with a fake smile, "but we have a short time and Galal has made many appointments to meet old university friends while we're here. He went to Bonn, you know?"

"No, I didn't. Then you must speak German?"

"But with an Arab accent," Jamil admitted. "Leila's right, unfortunately I have made a dozen dinner and luncheon arrangements over the next week or two. Perhaps later in the Games if you are still at the Berghof I could call?"

"I'll be expecting it, for sure."

"Daddy!" Emily squealed from the back of the shop. "Come here an' look!" The clerk, an old man with half moon rimmed glasses perched on the nub of his fat nose and held securely by thin wires to elfin-like ears, smiled benevolently as he watched the two little girls gazing in awe at the Prima Ballerina whirling atop the music box he had set on the counter. The adults came down to catch the performance. The delicate lady, slowing decorously, then spinning with a blur of motion in time to the music, was the most beautiful in the store. They all watched entranced, until the spring unwound and her poetry of motion froze as once more she became a china doll.

"It is the one I like best, too," Leila said, "but unfortunately I have no room to carry her on the airlines."

"We have room—we have our own airplane, don't we Daddy?"

"Do you, how wonderful—is it a nice airplane?"

"Thuper," Alice confirmed. "We play games and everything—it even hath a bathroom."

Jamil spoke to the clerk in rapid German. The old man nodded, then took two boxes from behind the counter and began wrapping them. Jamil said something to Leila in Arabic. She smiled and winked.

"Would you girls like to have one of those dolls each for your own?"

Both tipped their heads up and down solemnly. It was an important moment.

"And you'll both be very careful never to drop them and play with them only on special occasions?"

She received another series of slow nods, then reached for the packages and handed them each a box, laughing at the expressions on their faces—disbelief, speechless amazement over a stranger's generosity.

"Thank you both very much," Corbin said, seeing Jamil peel a sheaf of odd sized notes from his billfold. He knew the dolls were expensive—he could only guess how expensive.

"We have no children," Jamil explained briefly. "Call it a surrogate gift."

Rina nudged the girls not to forget their manners and both echoed their thanks breathlessly.

"Listen, you two—if you don't give us a call at the hotel sometime in the next few days I'll never speak to you again," Affleck told them.

"We'll do our best, I promise. Now I'm afraid we must go; we are late for an appointment. A pleasure meeting you all—Mr. Corbin, Mrs. Affleck." He nodded, taking Leila's arm and moving for the door.

"Which team are you rooting for, Mr. Jamil?" Corbin asked out of curiosity.

The two paused at the door. "Unfortunately, Palestine is not participating in the Games, Mr. Corbin; an oversight; we are rooting for those athletes who come from our homeland, anyway." He chuckled at his own joke.

"The Israelis?" Affleck was shocked, remembering Jamil's comments on the Jews from their meeting in Cosecha Rica.

"Yes, the Israeli team. The group of visitors we came with have great expectations for exciting things to happen to the Israeli team in Munich." They waved goodbye to everyone under the tinkling bell as they left the shop.

Neither Corbin nor Affleck knew what Jamil had meant then. Later, it became horribly clear.

From Lisbon the ship sailed round the Spanish mainland, past Gibralter and into the blue waters of the Mediterranean to visit Marseilles. In Lisbon, they had wandered the streets like two lovers, visiting the tourist sights, eating strange food, visiting strange night clubs where slim-hipped, curved-backed stereotype *Jose Grecos* machine-gunned their heels around black-eyed witches with garlic breath and fingers riveting castanets to the flamenco rhythms, as foreign to the country as the visitors who came to watch. Afterwards, they went back to the ship and made love until, exhausted, they fell asleep in each other's arms. They skipped breakfast as a matter of course, joining Herman Slitzman for the luncheon and dinner hour, regaling him with tales of events ashore, or teasing him unmercifully over his daily financial concerns which were clicked out on the big board in the financial room.

"I've decided you were right, my friend. After Marseilles, I limit my visits to the market room to once a week—Friday, I think. Since leaving New York I have ridden the bear and ducked the bull twice and wound up in exactly the same position I started at when I came aboard two weeks ago. Tch! Tch! I say to myself; I say, 'Herman, you're not being smart. Smart is to wait a week and see what happens. Why sit and worry, giving yourself ulcers, when already there's nothing you can do?' " He looked at the empty place. "Where's Mrs. Kirkpatrick?"

"Getting her hair done. It was the only time the hairdresser was open today," Corbin explained. "She wants to look chic in Marseilles. Women!"

They ordered their meals and sat back looking at one another. Herman leaned forward.

"Chuck Corbin, my friend, I am going to give you the benefit of my senior years and because you are much younger than me you are going to listen."

Corbin said nothing, waiting.

"For two weeks I have known you, now. For two weeks I have known Mrs. Kirkpatrick. We talk, we laugh, we kid and we learn about each other; already we have closed the generation gap. You are no dummy, my friend. I know dummies. I am an old fat Jew coming to the end of his days—alone. You have given me much friendship here, more than I have had for many years and I bless you for it, but still one day the boat will dock and you will go back to what makes Corbin run and I—well, I'll be alone." He sighed, toying with his fork, making little indentations in the starched cloth.

"I see you with Mrs. Kirkpatrick. I see you happy—much happier than when I met you those first few days. I see the look in her eyes and sometimes in yours. It is the same look I saw once in my wife's eyes—God rest her—it is the light that keeps the darkness of loneliness away."

"Why Herman, I didn't know you were a poet!" Corbin laughed uncomfortably.

Slitzman smiled sadly. "Everyone is a poet, my friend—every man is a king—or a beggar, if he chooses. I don't know what your circumstances are, or hers, not that it matters, it's none of my business, but I tell you this: if there is anyway you can manage to hold onto that woman, do it, because as long as that light glows in both your eyes you will be a king."

The steward arrived with their first course, laying out the double plates carefully. Corbin toyed with his food, watching Slitzman eat.

"We are planning on jumping ship at Marseilles and flying home—she has a divorce to settle; I need time to think."

Slitzman grunted. "What's to think, shmuck. Already you want to become a philosopher two weeks out of New York. By Piraeus you'll believe you're the Messiah!"

"He's already been and gone," Corbin countered.

"Ha, that's your side of the story!" He pointed his knife at him. They both chuckled.

The wine steward went through his routine on a bottle of table Bordeaux and waited for the sip of approval from Corbin. When he left, Slitzman held out his glass, his fat face beaming.

"I shall miss you both—especially you, my friend, because I see you as myself already, nearly thirty years ago. I drink to you and to that glowing light which makes all men kings."

Corbin met him at the table center. "And women queens?"

"No my friend, it works one way—only the king may choose a queen."

"Chauvinist!" They laughed and drank the toast.

16

After the Middle Eastern sunshine, Bruner found the British weather depressing. Each time he passed through Heathrow everyone always told him how they had just finished two weeks of super weather and what a pity he had missed it. This trip required a three day layover to keep his appointment, so he had been hopeful, at least once, he could experience the rarity of sunshine. It had been raining off and on since his arrival. It was raining now, although it was difficult to distinguish individual drops from the coarse spray flung past the windows of the hovercraft as it thundered down the Thames to Greenwich.

There were only five other passengers in the forty-odd seats; but then, mid-October was not exactly the height of the tourist season, he reasoned. The hovercraft slowed, passing a large motor launch with empty decks, then increased speed again, hurtling the water. He was still nursing the cold he had picked up in New York the previous week during the knock-down-drag-out battle he'd had with B.J. over the publishing rights to his book. B.J. seemed to think the working relationship with Bruner included first grab on everything his star Middle East correspondent produced, so when "Crossroads in Crisis" went to the publishers and B.J. learned of its predictable success, he began to howl for his pound of flesh, long distance to Amman. Max had flown back to New York to pacify his employer. And caught cold the day after he arrived. It had probably been psychosomatic then, but now, after three horrible days of London rain and fog, it was a real doozer.

He snuffled miserably, yanking out a soggy handkerchief and blowing into the wet rag, then stuffed it back into his raincoat. The only consolation derived from the New York visit was the book, timed to hit the Christmas market, looked like it would develop into a runaway best seller, making a bundle for the author. B.J. had capitulated finally, agreeing Max was, after all, a freelance reporter. Everything else had gone wrong; the cold, the week long battle with B.J., the cold, the publishers trying to get him conned into a lecture tour which he had somehow managed to duck, the cold, and finally his inability to land himself one interesting woman with whom he could spend the night; but that was because of his cold. Then the information, relayed from Amman, that he must attend an urgent meeting in Greenwich on his way home. He had planned on going up State to spend a few weeks watching the leaves turn gold and recover from the sniffles, enjoy the savor of triumph. But no, here he was, a critically ill victim of his own success, braving the elements of the British Isles to keep a mysterious appointment in Greenwich. He sniffled morosely. There was a chance he might contract pneumonia from exposure. The thought made him blanch mentally. He straightened in his seat, taking a few deep breaths to see if he could feel any gurgling in his lungs. The effort caused a minor fit of coughing; two passengers in the seats ahead turned to look, hearing the barks above the roar of the engines. He shook his head sadly, feeling sorry for himself. There was no justice, no consideration given to anyone anymore. It was all either crass commercialism or mysterious secret meetings. No one gave a shit if a person was dying from pneumonia.

The engines slowed as the hovercraft slid onto the sloping cement apron at Greenwich and stopped. Bruner cranked his aching body out of the high-backed seat and followed the other passengers outside into the drizzle. He lugged himself up the steps of the pier and asked for directions to Greenwich Museum. An elderly man at the exit gate explained the sidewalk route and was rewarded with a sneeze and a muttered thanks.

"You should be in bed, Sir, that's a nasty one!"

"You ain't just a whistlin' Dixie!"

"I beg your pardon?"

"Forget it—thanks." He waved and started off, thrusting his

hands in his pockets, pulling his shoulders high to keep the drips from his hat brim from running down his back.

The Museum, formerly a palace, or group of adjoining palaces, stretched out impressively in the grey light of morning behind bright green level lawns surrounded with high black spear fencing. He walked through the main gate and followed the signs past a display of antique cannons into the stone building.

"I'm looking for the bust of Nelson." The uniformed attendant waited until Bruner completed his sneeze before replying.

"Bless you, Sir," he said formally. "Straight ahead, up the steps to the second floor. You'll find His Lordship's bust there—jacket he was wearing too the day 'e fell at Trafalgar with an 'ole in the epaulet where the ball passed in 'im."

Bruner thanked the man and made his way to the stairs.

The room was deserted when he entered. He circled the bust, examining the handsome life-size face of the hero from Trafalgar. A face nearly pretty, with sensuous mouth and finely etched nose and eyes. He began browsing at other artifacts around the room; Nelson's sword; a painting of the Admiral's death—the famous *kiss me Hardy* scene; a tattered battle ensign and other bric-a-brac laid out in symmetrical rows under wide glass viewing cases.

Bruner recognized the limping step before he saw Asher enter. He sauntered back to the Nelson bust and blew his nose loudly in the quiet room.

"Sacrilege!" Asher came up and stood beside him.

"What is, Captain?" He stuffed the damp rag in his pocket.

"Major now, actually—blowing your nose on England's greatest naval hero. It's considered bad form—*frightfully* bad form, as the British would tell you."

"I have a cold. Captain Armiturk said you wanted to see me. What do you want?"

Asher looked around the room, taking in the various objects. "I've heard this is an interesting place to visit—sort of a trip back through memory lane when the sun never set on the Empire—shall we walk?" They began drifting down the room. "By the way, congratulations on your book; I enjoyed it."

"It won't be out for another week."

"I read the galley proofs a month ago. Great stuff, Max." He didn't bother explaining how galley proofs in New York were read by an Israeli intelligence officer in the Middle East. Bruner was galled by the man's apparent ease at obtaining information or material from any point in the world on short notice. He was relieved the limping man with the impeccable English accent approved of what he had read. Actually, according to their agreement, Armiturk was supposed to clear anything Max wrote for publication before it was sent out, however, Bruner knew they were unaware he had been writing the book, and since their prime interest in him was as a news reporter, he had never bothered to clear the manuscript with the Jordanian captain when he shipped it off to New York.

"I'm glad you enjoyed it, Captain—er, Major—congratulations on your promotion. Will this mean I'll be getting a raise in pay, too?"

Asher laughed, clapping Bruner's shoulder, nearly knocking him off balance.

"That's what I like about you, Max, never too down and out to see the humor in a situation. Say, that's a nasty cold you have there!" He backed away as Bruner produced three wet sneezes in rapid succession, then produced the soggy hankey to remove the evidence from his nose and upper lip.

"Thanks Major, now for Christ sakes—I'm supposed to be in bed!" He looked at Asher irritably.

The Israeli suddenly became all business. "Your friend, Galal Jamil, do you know where he is?"

Bruner shook his head. "I haven't seen him since the Munich affair. Don't want to, either—the man is a nut."

"But a clever nut. He seems to have vanished."

"Maybe someone killed him?" Bruner suggested.

"Unlikely. We monitored a call out of his Beirut office from Germany three weeks ago. The voice on the other end of the line told the secretary to inform Herr Jamil an emergency had arisen and the doctor required his presence at the plant immediately."

"That was all?"

"That was all. Jamil left Beirut eleven hours later on Egyptair to Cairo under the name of Gwadi Melsamm with a Turkish passport. Naturally, our Cairo people were advised and covered the airport arrivals. Your friend never left the airport—never went through customs or immigration. He vanished. As far as we know, he's still in the airport."

"Oh, I doubt that, Major. The food is terrible at Cairo Airport." This time Asher didn't smile.

They wandered out of the Trafalgar era and Napoleonic Wars into a larger room with static displays depicting the growth of Britain as a mercantile naval power. The second room, like the first, was deserted, smelling musty and damp. They paused before a fully rigged man o' war sitting in a large glass case. Both leaned against the

494

glass, squinting at the meticulous detail; every cannon, rope block and pulley faithfully reproduced from the original fighting ship. "Royal William. 1734. Armed Merchantman of the East India Company," the bright plaque explained.

"Seven airlines left Cairo that day. He could have transferred to any one of them under a different identity without leaving the transit lounge. The question is, which one did he take—and to where—and who is this doctor?"

They moved down the row of model ships, stopping occasionally to examine one closely. The workmanship was extraordinary.

"Never heard of the doctor—he never mentioned him to me—must be someone he met in Munich—after my time." He sneezed again.

"That's what we think. There may be something in the wind. We'd like to find out what."

"Is that my cue to offer help?" Bruner asked sourly.

Asher stopped in front of a large model displaying the naval dockyards, showing how wooden sailing ships were built in the days of iron men.

"Look at this, Max!" There were several vessels in various stages of construction at the berths along the blue plaster of paris Thames River. Beyond the ships' cradles were large ponds filled with timbers and spars. "I never knew before," Asher admitted, "that they used to store their masts in water to keep them from warping until they were ready for use. Clever."

Bruner was skeptical and disinterested. "How do you know? It doesn't say so."

"Simple—why else would they fill the pools with long pieces of wood? It's obvious."

"Not to me, it isn't." He felt argumentative, wanting to spin the conversation out while he collected his thoughts. He knew exactly what the Israeli was going to ask him to do and he wanted no part of it. He had already ratted once after the Munich Games. He didn't feel like reratting. Asher wouldn't bite, and they moved on past the Woolwich dockyards to the end of the room and started examining the paintings along the wall.

"I'd like you to go home via Beirut."

"Home is New York," Max inserted.

"You know what I mean. Drop in on the secretary—you're good friends, I understand." He glanced at Bruner. "A little wine and dine—I'll leave that to you. Find out what you can."

"Such as?"

"Don't be obtuse, Max." There was a sharp warning in Asher's voice.

"She'll say nothing she isn't supposed to—to me or to anyone else. She's nuttier than a fruitcake—they all are."

"But then again, she might. It's worth a try, isn't it?"

"And if she tells me nothing?"

Asher sighed. "Well, we'll just have to think of something else, won't we? Maybe try to work some information out of his woman. She's got to know where he is and who this doctor friend is who's so important he can make her husband rush off to invisibility on such short notice." He turned away from the paintings, losing interest, heading for the exit. Bruner fell into step beside him.

"Try the secretary first. What's her name?"

"You know her name, Major," he said resignedly. It was no use protesting, he was trapped.

Asher laughed. "Bernadette Boivin—you call her Bernie for some unaccountable reason. Personally, I rather like Bernadette. It has a certain lilt to it. The seductive French. English women appear cold, but they're really very warm; the Americans have women who appear warm but are actually very cold, whereas the French—ah, the French woman appears warm and then turns out to be a boiling cauldron of desires."

"Are you speaking as an intelligence officer, or from personal experiences, Major?"

They had reached the stairs back to the main floor. The Israeli ignored the question.

"I'll be in touch, Max. If you come up with anything interesting, the code word is *Trident*. Can you remember that—Trident?" He stopped at the head of the stairs.

"I'll try," Bruner told him sarcastically.

"As of now your contact through Captain Armiturk is finished. You deal directly with me from this point on, or through anyone identifying themselves with the prefix Trident. Is that clear?"

"You should stay away from these Ian Flemming books, Major, or you'll wind up spying on yourself."

Asher laughed and shook his hand warmly. "It's been good seeing you again, Max. Take in the rest of the Museum now you're here—well, for another fifteen minutes, anyway."

"So you can make a clean getaway in the stolen Rolls."

Asher's laughter echoed up the stairwell as he limped down and disappeared from view.

Bruner went over to one of the hard wooden benches along the corridor and sat down. He felt thoroughly miserable.

Bruner had been followed the moment they had turned him lose after his painful meeting with Armiturk and Asher in the little room at the military barracks in Amman. Predictably, he had caught the next flight out to Beirut and led them straight to the office in that city, and from there to the village in the mountains, when he drove out of Beirut next morning in a rented car. For the time being, Asher felt that was enough information for any justification Colonel Borodam might require in explaining the monthly wages and expenses being paid out of Israeli intelligence slush funds to support the heretofore unfriendly newsman from Amman.

"Are you sure you weren't followed?" had been Jamil's first question when he arrived and began explaining his Jordanian imprisonment.

"Positive. I spent last night in town especially to give anyone following me a dead end."

Akbar came into the big headquarters room and laid his binoculars on the table.

"All clear for miles—not a car in sight." Everyone was relieved.

"Start from the beginning. Tell me everything. Leila, get us all some coffee!"

Bruner started at the beginning with the visit of Captain Armiturk to his apartment, and carried the story through to his release the day before, pausing dramatically at appropriate moments for effect, milking every ounce of drama from the situation. When he finished, Jamil sat back, apparently satisfied.

"So he played possum and heard our first names. Smart Jew. Probably made him an officer on the spot. The Jew loses his whole patrol on home territory, sneaks off to a ditch to save his own ass, and what happens? They make him an intelligence officer—probably gave him a medal, to boot!" They all laughed at the absurdity.

"The interesting thing, though, is the Jordanian Army working with the Jews! That goddamn Hussein is like a chameleon! He probably has a complete Jewish General outfit in his wardrobe." He grinned at Bruner. "You did well, Max. We're proud of you. Now the question is, how do we use your new position as an undercover agent to feed the bastards enough information to keep them happy, you out of trouble and ourselves operational?"

"Now wait a minute, Galal, I'm no undercover agent, I'm a newspaperman." The fun of telling them his adventures was past; now they were talking something far more serious, something which, no matter how things worked out, could never make Bruner anything but a loser. Jamil waved his hand negligently.

"Words, Max, words. You have been hired as a pipeline for information on our activities. What use is a pipeline unless we put something into it? How are you to know whether the information is accurate or not, so long as it's information and continues to flow back to Tel Aviv. If we toss you a few bones to whet their appetites and increase your value, then when we give them some fantasy, they'll believe it. When the fantasy doesn't happen, they'll believe they stopped it. It has all sorts of possibilities."

He stood up and started pacing the room, deep in thought. The others watched until suddenly, he stopped, snapping his fingers.

"I've got it!" He came back to the table and sat down. "We'll use Max as our pipeline to eliminate the opposition in the PLO."

"What?"

"The only time Fateh ever fought together was during the Six Day War and against the Jordanian Army. Doesn't that tell you something?" His eyes were glowing from a kaleidescope of thoughts. No one spoke.

"With a common danger, there becomes a common purpose—a common front against the danger. Don't you see it? Without the common front, what is the PLO?" He gave no one a chance to reply. "A fractured group of idealists, fighting amongst themselves to preserve their own identities. Everyone beating their own drum. Political compromise. No compromise; unified command of the military—individual areas of command; the commercial interests fighting non-commercial interests—intellectuals arguing with activists. Don't you see it?" He looked around the table, puzzled by their failure to grasp the significance of his words.

"And your solution?" Bruner had an idea what Jamil was going to propose.

"Force the fractured groups back into a unified front. Force them through fear of being picked to pieces by the common enemy, while we provide the enemy with the information to pick them to pieces. When the enemy can no longer pick at the pieces, it will be because there are no pieces left to pick—only a solid mass of resistance."

"But Galal, you'd be betraying your own people!" Bruner protested.

"I like it," Akbar said with a grin. Leila nodded in agreement. "I don't know why I didn't think of it before. It's so obvious!"

"We didn't have Max for the pipeline into Tel Aviv before,"

Leila reminded.

"And you haven't got Max for one now," Bruner said firmly. "Are you all crazy? You're asking me to betray Fateh to the Israelis on a selective basis—your selection as to who goes and who stays. First of all, it can't be done, and secondly, I won't do it."

Jamil looked intent. "Oh yes it can be done, Max. Easily. If we leave the central PLO alone for the time being and concentrate on the splinter groups, the so-called terrorists within Fateh, we should be able to get fast results. For example, we can use our organization to investigate and organize different projects, then turn the operational end of the plan over to one of the groups to complete. Max then gets the date of the strike, who's involved, how, where and phht!" He snapped his fingers. "One less splinter group to worry about. The Jews will take over from there. Think of it! With a string of successes against terrorists they'll believe anything Max tells them after a year or two and in a year or two there will be only one independent group left outside Fateh—ourselves. Then Yasser Arafat has no choice—he must woo us or die himself."

"You'll never get away with it, Galal—after the first two or three disasters the other groups will avoid you like the plague," Bruner argued.

"I didn't say we set them up for a fall on every project. For the sake of argument let's say the success ratio is one out of three operations. That's sufficient to keep the program working. Besides, who's going to tell anyone it's a setup—you, the Jews, us?" He laughed. "If you or we say anything, we're dead in twelve hours, and as for the Jews and your limping Captain, they're not stupid. Why would they look a gift horse in the mouth—particularly an Arabian stallion?" He leaned back, a faraway expression in his eyes.

"Think of it. Hijackings, bombings, assassinations, chaos; all of it arranged and controlled by us! It's beautiful!" He snapped back to reality.

"Good, lets get to work on it. Unless anyone has an objection?" He looked squarely at Bruner. Max said nothing. His mind screamed protests, logical arguments against the illogical plan; he wanted to jump and run outside into the clean air, away from insanity, but he knew protest was useless. Jamil had made up his mind and there would be no dissuading him now.

Much later, after Jamil and Leila had left, Bruner appealed to Akbar. For nearly six hours he had listened spellbound to the zig zag of intrigues proposed by the Palestinian leader, each designed to bring down the wrath of the Israelis on the PLO.

"Khala, what he is suggesting is genocide. He may think they're all traitors, but they are still your people. Your own people, for God sakes! Settling old scores is one thing, but using the Israelis to settle them for you is, well, it's monstrous! And he is compounding the crime by betraying your own people!"

Akbar rubbed his chin. He needed a shave. "I think you are taking it out of context, Max. You're losing your sense of perspective."

"Am I?" Bruner doubted it.

"Do you think Hussein is a PLO traitor?" Akbar grinned.

"He is the Jordanian king."

"Don't duck the question."

"I don't know." He threw up his hands. "I don't know anything any more, except this: you are people at a crossroads, a crossroads in the crisis of your fight. I hope you know which road you are taking, that's all."

"And will you be our pipeline during the crisis, Max?"

"Do I have a choice?" His voice was resigned.

Abkar laughed merrily. "Absolutely none! But what the hell, Max, think of the stories you'll be able to write for B.J. and the limping Captain."

Bruner smiled ironically. "Yeah, a great opportunity. Heaven sent!"

He stayed in London another three days nursing his cold and aching joints, lying in the hotel room watching BBC television and drinking hot gin and lemon interspersed with steamy baths. Room service obliged in providing the continuous shuttle of hot lemonades; the miniature gin bottles, he removed from the pay-bar cupboard in his room. He had a staggering bill when he checked out to take the airport bus, most of it from the damn pay-bar. Still, he decided, it was worth it. He felt considerably better in wind and limb when he climbed on the VC 10 to Beirut, than when he had climbed off the 747 from New York. He phoned Bernadette as soon as he checked into the Phoenicia Hotel.

"Hi, it's me—Max."

"Max who?" came the cool reply.

"Bruner. C'mon Bernie, you remember me—Max Bruner?"

"Where are you?" Her voice was still cool.

"Same place as before—room 844. How have you been?" An inane question.

"I'll be right over—wait for me." She hung up and he looked at the buzzing receiver perplexed. "Nuttier than a fruitcake!" He replaced the phone, unpacked his suitcase, then ordered the valet service to pick up his wrinkled suit. Bernie and the valet turned up at the door simultaneously. She marched into the room, giving him a quick smile, and went to sit decorously on one of the chairs until he had finished with the valet.

"How have you been, Max, or should I say where have you been?"

He went over and sat down on the bed, trying to appear friendly; it felt more like wariness. "Around—here and there, you know how it is. I wrote a book, had to go back to the States for a few weeks on the publishing part of it. Stopped in London." He shrugged. "Keeping myself busy. You?"

"Aren't you going to ask me if I want a drink?" she demanded primly.

"Oh sure—sorry—what would you like?"

"Nothing, it's too early. Maybe later." She smiled.

Just like a fruitcake, he thought. "Is Jamil up country?"

"No—he's away, Leila too. They're all away, as a matter of fact."

"Oh, too bad. I wanted to see them. I guess they're visiting the doctor?"

"You know the doctor?" She seemed surprised he did. Bruner tipped his head with indifference, so she could interpret the meaning either way.

"I've never met him. What's he like?" There was no guile in her question.

"Neither have I. I don't even know what sort of doctor he is—physical or physic." I guess he's still in Germany—Bonn, isn't it?"

"Frankfurt, or at least that's where the office is, but I don't think he's there anymore. I think he's abroad somewhere, too."

Seeing him stretch, she stood up and kicked off her shoes and swung her skirt around to unzip, then wiggled out of the skirt, slip and panties. She rubbed her pubis invitingly for a moment, then began undoing the buttons on her blouse.

"Maybe I'll give the Frankfurt office a call and see if I can run them down," he said.

"Oh, do you have the phone number?" She unhooked her bra and stood naked, then wrapped her arms around herself. The air conditioning vent in the ceiling was blowing directly above her head. Max climbed out of his pants and started working his shirt buttons.

"No—don't you?" He slung the shirt on the desk and pulled off his shorts, finally his socks. She came to him hungrily, pushing him back on the bedspread.

"I've never had the number; no one gave it to me. I'm a reception point for everyone, Max. I thought you knew that?" She spread herself, mounted him quickly, gripping his hands, and began the wild ride. Bruner groaned as her buttocks hammered his thighs.

"Of course you are, Bernie; it must have slipped my mind." But she didn't hear him above the sound of her own delighted howls.

When the message from Frankfurt had arrived at Beirut, Jamil sent Leila across the border to Syria and caught the first available flight into Cairo, switching planes at the ramp to Air Algeria. It was the first time Kastenburg had ever contacted him directly since moving to Cosecha Rica. He knew the doctor well enough to know a request for his presence in the Republic was due to a serious problem, nothing less. He was concerned.

For a lesser man, the very thought of unknown disaster can create its own disasters; irrational decisions are made without thought to plan or consequence of action. Over the years, Jamil had disciplined himself to discount the unknown. He had learned to bide his time, analyze each situation in proper perspective before deciding on a course of action. There was no point tilting at windmills when they might turn out simply to be butterflies.

After the message had been relayed to him by Bernadette, he followed a strict evacuation procedure for vacating the camp. For despite the speculative theories by his wife and Akbar, and the curious stares from the other members of the group who were not a part of the Blucher Chemical plan, he refused to be anything more than concerned, in a placid way. Everyone decamped across the Syrian border to a secondary base, while Jamil raced his Peugeot over the mountains to Beirut.

From Algiers he switched airlines and identities again, and arrived in Paris early the following morning to catch the first flight out to Panama, with connections through to Bahia Blanca. He turned up in a taxi at the main gate of the Blucher Chemicals factory next afternoon as the shift change was in progress. There was a short delay at the gate while several phone calls were put through to the administration office, then a company car turned up to drive him inside the compound. He dismissed the taxi. Instead of taking him into the main office, the car passed through the rear gate and along the coastal road to the private residences of the German visitors. He was dropped off at the last house along the row of homes hugging the hillside around the bay.

"Herr Gruber?"

Jamil sized-up the buxom blonde housekeeper as the car drove away. He nodded.

"Doktor Kastenberg asked me to invite you inside and inform you he will be here shortly." She held the door open. "Please." She spoke a country German, softly accented vowels.

"Danke." He went inside, pausing to wait until she led him through the house and out to the patio. He set his suitcase beside a chair and sat down.

"Doktor Kastenburg said you drink tea. I'll make some."

He thanked her a second time, then sat back to watch the tranquil view of the small bay. He sniffed the musty air, absorbing the surroundings: warm humid vegetation sprinkled lightly with salt, creating an air of universal lassitude. He wondered how the group of methodical Germans had adapted to this new environment. Knowing Kastenburg as he did, he thought it more likely the Germans had made the environment adapt to themselves. Like the British, he thought, they were stubborn, unyielding. The only way they could be beaten was by complete and utter destruction; even then, it was a temporary affair and only until they reorganized. It might no longer be the case for the British people, but it held true for the Germans—still. The thought made him feel comfortable, knowing no matter what adversity had befallen their project locally, Kastenburg and his group would see the program through to the end—whatever the end turned out to be.

"Your tea, Herr Gruber." He hadn't heard her return to the patio.

"Ah, dankeshon! What is your name?"

"Hoffer." She set the tray down and removed the cup and teapot.

"Just Hoffer?"

"Hildegarde Hoffer—*Fraulein* Hildegarde Hoffer," she added, accenting the Fraulein.

She straightened up quickly, hearing the sound of a car arrive, stop and door slam.

"That will be the Doktor." She left quickly. Jamil poured his tea. It was too weak. He raised the lid on the pot and poured the contents back to let it steep another few minutes. He cranked his neck around to see the patio doors, then stood up as Kastenburg appeared with another man. The doctor walked to him quickly, hands outstretched.

"My dear Galal, you did make good time, remarkable time! This is my colleague, Doktor Kurt Hauser—my alter ego. Hildy! Bring us some schnapps, if you please!"

Jamil shook Hauser's hand formally, noticing his cynical smile; *one of life's sceptics*, he thought. They grouped themselves about the glass-topped table, sliding the wicker chairs into a conference format. Jamil observed he would be presiding—the first sign of weakness, he thought, uneasily, realizing now he had been brought to advise, not to be informed. Fraulein Hoffer returned with the schnapps and glasses.

"Close the door when you go Hildy, thank you."

Jamil tried the tea again while the other two poured themselves stiff ones from the clear bottle of schnapps. The tea was perfect.

"We have developed a problem here," Kastenburg began. "Colonel Chirlo knows what we are doing underground at the factory."

If he had hit Jamil over the head with the schnapps bottle the effect could not have come close to the shock the Palestinian felt from the words. He kept his face immobile, holding the teacup steady in front of his lips, his eyes faintly curious, determined to maintain his Arab Karamah.

"Oh!" was all he said. It was sufficient.

Kastenbrug removed his glasses carefully and rubbed the bridge of his nose, closing his eyes. "Yes, an uncomfortable indiscretion occurred—a security leak for which I bear full responsibility." He replaced the glasses, pinching the clip back onto his nose. The two Germans waited for the Palestinian to make a comment, say something. Jamil seemed oblivious to the problem and continued sipping tea.

"Doktor Kastenburg is being kind, Herr Jamil, when he says the responsibility is his—it is not. The entire fault is mine."

Jamil noticed the German's face did not appear particularly contrite for having accepted the responsibility of a fifty million dollar security leak. He replaced his teacup and leaned back in the wicker chair thoughtfully, his face impassive. He could understand now why he had been called to chair the meeting.

"Instead of dueling blame back and forth, why don't you both sheath your high-principled swords and tell me what has happened?"

The Germans glanced at each other, deciding who would speak. Hauser leaned forward.

"I have a son. He's been a bit of a playboy most of his life. He turned up here for a visit in '72 and got himself a job with the

504

national television station in San Ramon. He has a facility for languages and a flair for the dramatic—as well as being a ski bum. At any rate, he made a reasonable success out of the new job, liked the country and decided to stay. I must say I was surprised, particularly when he missed his annual ski trek back home. During the course of work with the television station he met Felina Artega. They became lovers."

"What?" Jamil couldn't believe his ears. "Chirlo's wife? I don't believe it!"

"It's true nonetheless, Galal," Kastenburg verified.

"He's a young, very good looking boy, athletic and highly intelligent, Herr Jamil. Frau Artega apparently succumbed to his charm."

"I would call that stupidity, Doktor Hauser, not intelligence."

Hauser shrugged. "Whatever, the point is, it happened." He took a quick drink from the glass of schnapps and licked his lips. "Of course I knew nothing about it for several months, until I received a visit from Major Martinez, Chirlo's chief of intelligence."

"He knew?" Jamil was horrified.

"From the first day. In fact, he withdrew his security men from protective surveillance on Felina Artega the same day so he would not have to report the incident to the Colonel."

The whole thing was beginning to take on proportions of a major diplomatic disaster, Jamil decided. "What did Martinez say?"

"He suggested, very politely, I order my son to return home; that the whole affair, instead of running its usual course in this sort of thing, had reached a point where, very shortly, it would become public knowledge and Chirlo would be the laughingstock of the country. Apparently they had been meeting for a daily session between two and four in the afternoon at Rolf's apartment five days a week."

"The lad certainly has stamina, I'll say that for him," Jamil said wryly.

"He's only twenty-five, Herr Jamil—didn't we all—at that age?"

The Palestinian offered no comment.

"Naturally, I apologized to the Major and said I would insist my son leave the country at once, and of course, reported the whole affair to Doktor Kastenburg."

"It was my fault he remained here in the first place, Galal. Kurt asked for permission when Rolf arrived and obtained his employment. I agreed," Kastenburg interjected glumly.

"So when did he leave?"

"He didn't. He refused to go. That's when the trouble started."
He took another drink of schnapps before plunging back into the
story. "My son told me he knew exactly what we were doing here at
Blucher Chemicals and threatened to report the whole matter to
Colonel Chirlo if any attempt was made on my part to have him
deported."

"How did he find out?"

Hauser shook his head. "I don't know. Maybe nosing around
the house during those first few weeks after he arrived, searching
through my papers . . ."He threw up his hands. "He never explained
how he learned the secret—only that he knew."

"Exactly how much does he know?"

"Of the technical details, underground tunnel, storage pool and
processing engineering, he knows nothing. All he knows is we are
here to build nuclear bombs."

"*All?*" Jamil said sarcastically.

"He doesn't know why or for whom, Galal," Kastenburg
interrupted.

"Only because I assume you never told any of the others
Doktor, until your associate here"—he nodded towards Hauser—
"approached you with the problem."

Kastenburg did not reply. Jamil was correct. Until the problem
with Rolf arose, he had kept silent on the Palestinian involvement in
their program.

"My son and I reached a standoff. Then while Doktor
Kastenburg and I were trying to plan the best way out of our
dilemma, Rolf told his mistress—Frau Artega—what happened."

"What on earth for?" Jamil was astounded.

"Insurance—at least that was the logic he used with me to
justify his actions. If he were thrown out of the country in the
middle of the night, and failed to meet the Colonel's lady, then she
would have a lever at her disposal to remove us. Frau Artega reported
everything to her husband, naturally."

"Naturally."

"From this point I should tell the story, Galal," Kastenburg
suggested kindly, looking at Hauser. He sighed, removing his pince
nez again.

"Last week I had a request to visit the Presidential Palace on a
matter of 'mutual interest', was how the message read. I drove up to
San Ramon the next day.

He knew instinctively the reason for the summons, but had

been quite unprepared for the reception he received when the Colonel's aide ushered him into the high-ceilinged office.

"Doctor Kastenburg, how kind of you to drive up on such short notice." He came out from behind the desk to greet his visitor, ushering him into a comfortable chair.

"I have been hearing good things about your sales efforts throughout Central America. I must say I am impressed. A four hundred percent increase in one year!" He shook his head with admiration. "Unbelievable progress!"

Kastenburg relaxed a little, smiling modestly. "We anticipate a larger increase in sales next year and this year we have doubled our production again."

"Incredible performance, truly something of which your people may be proud."

"We have tried to do our best, Colonel."

"I have also heard some disturbing things concerning your efforts on the coast—as equally incredible as your sales performance." He gave the German a lopsided, knowing smile. "Perhaps you would be good enough to bring me up to date on how far you have progressed with those atom bombs you are making within the plant?" He leaned back, toying with a paperknife, his smile still fixed in its slant.

Kastenburg decided to play the game. "We're on schedule, Colonel. As you can appreciate, it's a slow process."

"Of course, of course. I understand completely. You have an ETC?"

"ETC?" Kastenburg wasn't familiar with the English term.

"Estimated time of completion."

"Oh! Yes Colonel, our first assembly will start in January, 1976."

"So long?" Chirlo was surprised.

"These things take time; there are delays."

"There are always delays in any worthwhile project, Doctor." He set the paperknife back on the desk very carefully. "And what are you going to do with my bomb when it is ready?"

Kastenburg blinked. "I beg your pardon."

A sudden thought occurred to Chirlo. "Or is it bombs?"

"I don't understand, Colonel." The German felt he was beginning to lose control of the discussion, if he had ever held it.

"It's simple enough, Doctor. The bombs you are making in this country belong to me. Since you decided to go into production without my permission, using the safety and location of this country to cover your intentions, I consider it only fair the *bombs*—it is plural, isn't it?" He waited until Kastenburg had nodded, before continuing . . . "the bombs belong to me. After all, you are making all your money on the chemical factory, it's only fair I make something on the byproducts."

"My associates will be most unhappy, Colonel."

"I'm sure they will. However, you may notify them my bombs are for sale, assuming they are interested in buying them in 1976."

He stood up, signaling an end to the discussion. "In the meantime, Doctor Kastenburg, please carry on with your work. I'm sorry to have interrupted your busy schedule."

He walked the German to the door. Kastenburg paused. "Who else have you told about this matter, Colonel?"

"Sensible question, Doctor. At present, only my wife and myself know, plus of course, those in your own organization, but I have had no discussions with them."

"It would be preferable if we could keep this information to ourselves, Colonel," he cautioned.

Chirlo patted him on the shoulder. "I couldn't agree with you more, Doctor Kastenburg. We'll keep it our little secret." He gave him a mocking wink and opened the door.

Frustrated with the situation and angry with himself, the German drove back to the compound.

Jamil listened to the story intently without interruption until the doctor had finished.

"Then he didn't say how his wife obtained the information?"

"No, he didn't." It was a puzzling thought.

"Which means she might not have told him of her infidelity," Jamil thought aloud.

"But he would question her, surely, on where she obtained the information?" Hauser said.

"Not necessarily the right source, Doktor, but I agree—Chirlo would want an explanation on how she came into such information. Where is your son?"

"He left for Zurich day before yesterday. He will not be returning. That I can promise!"

"Skiing?"

"Skiing. Back to his old haunts," Hauser confirmed.

"Felina will be disappointed. She should never have told Chirlo. Your son's strength lay in the threat of betrayal. I'm surprised at Felina. It seems when the choice arose between sex and duty she chose the latter."

They were silent for several minutes, each locked in his own thoughts, exploring possibilities, avenues to follow.

"Soo!" Kastenburg broke the silence. "What do you suggest, Galal?"

"I never make a decision on first impressions, Doktor; such decisions are invaribly wrong. At present the problem of your son Rolf has been eliminated, Doktor Hauser. Chirlo has made it clear he considers the bombs to be his personal property when they are completed, and we may assume, safely I think, he is as interested in secrecy at the moment as ourselves. I suggest we sleep on it and make our decision tomorrow. Obviously one of us is going to have to go to San Ramon and negotiate a final agreement with Colonel Chirlo."

"Who do you think that should be?" Hauser inquired.

"As I said before, let us leave that decision until tomorrow."

A year earlier, in 1973, under cover of night, the newly trained Egyptian Army of Anwar Sadat took up positions on the west bank of the Suez Canal, waiting for zero hour. Huge hydraulic pumps and motors with miles of high pressure lines were poised beside the hundreds of small landing craft. In the Jewish calendar it was the tenth day of Tishri, Yom Kippur, the day of Atonement, holiest of Jewish feasts.

The Egyptians struck; their huge hydraulic water-pressure hoses carved away the soft sand on the East side of the canal, sloping its steep banks to gradual inclines. The landing craft roared across the narrow ribbon of water, touching smoothly on the new shallow shoreline, and the troops poured back into the occupied desert lands taken from them so swiftly in 1967. The war of reclamation had begun.

This was no war of leaderless ragamuffins without boots running from the sight of the Israeli Air Force, but a highly trained, superbly disciplined army rebuilt from scratch, itching for the opportunity to erase its history of failures. The Israelis were stunned by the ferocity of the attack, and reeled back to regroup, playing down their huge air losses from the surface to air missles. Nor did they elaborate on the suicidal tank battles that weaved back and forth across the sands.

Syria struck at the same instant along the Northern border of the Jewish homeland, forcing the Israeli Army to battle on two fronts, but at a time and place chosen by the enemies. Only a quick diplomatic intervention by the U.S. government prevented a catastrophe. After two weeks, when the dust settled, the insult of 1967 had been washed away, the Arab lands reclaimed, and for the first time in nearly three decades, the Israelis had been put on the defensive. The Egyptian Army returned to Cairo in triumph, leaving the uneasy truce once again in the hands of the United Nations and the political promises of an uneasy American government rushing to embrace the victor while at the same time maintaining its embrace on Israel. The Western press minimized the Israeli losses, yet even this was a triumph to the Arabs; a few weeks later, the American home press was complaining bitterly over the amount of weaponry, tanks and aircraft which had been stripped from the U.S. military to replace Israeli losses. The nation was apalled by admissions from military pundits that the country could no longer be considered as combat-ready in case of war; at least until the gifts to Israel were replaced by the weapons manufacturers. Bruner had been as surprised as everyone else in the international press corps, and rushed to Cairo to follow through on the story.

For months he had been feeding Jamil's carefully prepared information to the Israelis via Captain Armiturk, then scooping his own intelligence by being first with the full story in the press. B.J. loved it. Bruner felt like a whore, prostituting his talents in this sort of intrigue. Airport attacks, bombings, endless skyjackings and political assassinations—some successful, most disastrous for the Palestinian participants—he knew about them all. The periodic successes might cause the Jordinian Captain to raise his eyebrows, but for every success by the terrorist groups, two or three disastrous failures immediately followed, and the Captain's eyebrows would lower again. Bruner was balancing himself precariously on a swaying tightrope. With the slaughter at the Munich Games, he had lost his balance.

Jamil decided the Munich project too important to entrust the knowledge to Bruner, and accordingly, had left him in the dark. Armiturk, on the other hand, convinced he was being deceived intentionally, began threatening all sorts of hideous disciplinary measures. The Jordanian turned up at his apartment, unaccompanied, within an hour after the drama at Munich began to unfold. Bruner listened to his veiled threats calmly, satisfied they were nothing more than threats—why else would we have come alone? Finally, he interrupted him.

"Captain Armiturk, go fuck yourself! And while you're at it, tell the Captain with the game leg to go and fuck himself too—I'm through—finished—kaput. You understand? Now get th'hell out of here!" he yelled at the smooth Jordanian.

Armiturk recoiled as if he had been struck, but summoned his composure quickly.

"You will regret having said those words, Mr. Bruner."

"I doubt it. What will you do—shoot me—torture me—starve me? Listen Captain, there is a sealed letter on file at my New York office, along with some registered letters sent from Beirut, outlining every terrorist incident, and dated *three to six days before they happened.* If anything happens to me—*anything*—they will be opened. So you go ahead and arrest me or whatever you want because I'm through with your games—from now on you do your own spying. Now get out!"

He didn't think the Jordanian officer would leave, but he did, closing the door quietly.

Over the next week Max lived in dread, expecting, momentarily, another visit from the man with the gloved steel hand and soft voice, but he never came back. Later, when Jamil returned to Lebanon after the Olympics and phoned, Bruner cut him off sharply and hung up. He expected swift repercussions from that action too, but again, nothing happened.

Weeks later he began to relax, throwing himself into the book he was writing on the Middle East situation. His production of copy for the New York office fell as he devoted more time to working on the book. The Yom Kippur War turned out to be the only thing that saved his job with C.P. When it was over, and he returned to Amman to finish the last three chapters of his epic, he did so knowing the paycheck and expenses from B.J. were secure for at least another six months. The matching funds from Armiturk were of course cut off the day he threw the Jordanian out of his apartment.

Bernadette awoke him in the morning after their night of lovemaking. She was dressed, ready for work. He promised to phone her at the office later in the day. After breakfast he rented a car and drove across the mountains to the old village camp near the Syrian border. As Bernadette had told him, it was deserted. He walked through the houses slowly, examining empty rooms for some clue to where the occupants had gone. Nothing. Disgusted, he climbed back in the car and started on the two hour return trip to Beirut. A few miles down the road he stopped at the village where they used to buy some of their supplies. The owner, an old Lebanese Christian, spoke French.

"Bonjour!" Bruner greeted him in fractured French.

"Bonjour, m'sieu!" The old man squinted with rheumy eyes,

trying to place the face.

Two young women in the store stared at him curiously. Bruner formulated the words in his mind, translating English to French before speaking.

"You remember me? I used to be at the village." He jerked his thumb to the road and direction from which he had come.

A light dawned in the old man's eyes and he nodded his head, smiling. "Of course, of course. You have come back, then?"

"Yes. I am looking for my friends. They are there no longer. Do you know where they go?" He had great difficulty in past tense French, preferring instead to speak in the present and refer to the future. It made the grammar simpler to remember. The old man threw up his hands.

"They left two, maybe three weeks ago, driving to the north—to Syria—perhaps Damascus?"

"Did they saying to you they go to Damascus?"

He shook his head. "Rien—they said nothing, not even au revoir."

Bruner thanked him and bought a bottle of beer, leaving enough money to cover the cost of a dozen with a friendly wink. The old man smiled gratefully as he left the shop. The two women continued to stare. He drove off down the road into the hot airless valley.

He decided he felt better now than at any time since leaving New York. The combination of the rest in London and a hot sweaty evening with Bernadette had turned the trick. He began examining, in retrospect, his meeting at Greenwich with the limping Israeli Major, remembering suddenly the only person who had told him the man was an Israeli had been B.J. The thought startled him. It had been B.J. who phoned about the urgent telegram from—where? He hadn't said and Max hadn't seen the telegram. It had been B.J. who had suggested—or was it an order?—he attend the meeting in England, dragging him off his sick bed to push him onto the PANAM flight for Heathrow. B.J. Bronstein, an irreverent New York Jew from the old school; bluff, uncouth, even boorish, illiterate—no B.J. Bronstein wasn't illiterate, he was a genius at using words; his stumbling sentences were a facade so he could pat his reporters on the arm and say, "Max Baby, write it for me, willya—you do it so good." And Max, or whoever else, would smile with affectionate superiority at the squat man behind the cigar and break his ass to meet the deadline. *Once a Jew always a Jew.* Bruner wondered how long B.J. had been working with Israeli intelligence.

He turned the car in at the hotel and went to pick up his key from the box at the reception desk. The clerk handed him a small note, written on the yellow memo forms the hotel used. The single word was printed in English and very clear: *Trident*. He went up to his room and after splashing cold water on his face, stretched out on the bed to await the caller.

"Then of course, there are numerous oddities throughout the plant world," Ruis explained. "For example, the Arbusus Precatorius or Indian licorice plant, can predict cyclones and earthquakes. It is a small shrub that begins to activate itself as the time of disaster approaches." Jamil was unimpressed. "I see."

He found the damp heat inside the glass greenhouse at the back of Dr. Artega's residence uncomfortable, and wished he had been astute enough to wear a sports shirt for his visit to San Ramon instead of the formal shirt and tie. For fifteen minutes he had been listening to Ruis expound on his profusion of plant life in the large greenhouse. Ruis knew his subject well, that much was obvious, but a botany discussion was the furthest thing from Jamil's mind at that moment. He began, unobtrusively, edging back to the door; Ruis followed, still talking.

"Another interesting species is the Thizanthella Gardneri—only one of its kind—an Australian orchid which grows and flowers completely underground. Of course the reason is simple, it is a plant that contains no chlorophyll. Then there is the Ginko tree—really unique!"

"I'm sure it is, Ruiz, but why don't you tell me about it some other time. Didn't Chirlo give you any idea when he would be arriving?"

Ruis looked disappointed over Jamil's lack of interest in the botanical marvels. He passed the Palestinian in the narrow aisle between the shelved greenery to the open door. Cooler air enveloped them instantly. "He said only to wait—that he would be along shortly."

They went into the sunroom to wait.

"May I order you a pot of tea?"

"No thanks, Ruiz."

The older man studied the younger man idly in silence, a ghost of a smile tracing his face.

"You seem agitated, Galal; is something wrong?"

"Agitated? No—not at all," he replied, answering mental warning lights immediately, readjusting his composure. If Ruiz noticed concern in his manner, how much easier would it be for

Chirlo to discern the same thing? He forced himself to relax, curving his thin lips into a smile.

"It must be jet lag. I live a sedentary life these days and my body clock tells me it's late afternoon, not breakfast time. Old age is creeping up, I suppose."

Ruis nodded understandingly. "On all of us." He glanced up as Chirlo framed the doorway.

"Hello Chirlo! I didn't hear you arrive." The front door was at the other end of the house. Ruis stood up.

"Well, I'll get back to my plants." He could feel the tension in the room as he left the two men alone, closing the door into the greenhouse loudly.

"Hello Galal, I heard you were back." He removed the cheroot from the breast pocket on his tunic and lit it, then leaned against the door.

"Major Martinez is prompt with his information as usual, I see."

"TACA Flight 317 at eleven fifteen yesterday morning; you spent the night at the German compound with Doctor Kastenburg." He blew a cloud of smoke towards the glass panes enclosing the room. "I didn't know who it was until then—but I had guessed." He smiled idly. Jamil remembered the smile; in profile his face looked normal.

"It is an experiment, Colonel."

"You chose a very expensive chemistry set to conduct your experiment—a whole chemical complex, one that is making money, to boot! I'll say this for you, Galal, when you decide to do something, you do it in style!" He straightened from the door frame and folded into one of the stuffed chairs, dragging the nearest ashtray onto the arm. "So tell me, what are you up to—exactly—no bullshit now, I want the straight story."

Jamil sighed lightly, a ploy indicating he was resigned to come clean. Chirlo watched him narrowly through the cigar smoke.

"Kastenburg was my senior professor at University. He worked in Norway on the heavy water project during the German occupation. After the war he joined Bayer. When I saw that nuclear plant of yours and the waste pools, the thought occurred to try and find someone to put it all together. The first person that came to mind was Kastenburg. I gave him the outline of what I wanted and why and he agreed. The chemical production part of the facility is quite real, by the way."

"I know. I've seen the audited balance sheets."

"So the Doctor picked up the Blucher Chemical name from the

owner, I picked up the money to finance it, and the rest is history."

"You picked up the money?"

"Let's say in addition to the capital I had on hand, I managed to interest another investor to come up with the balance needed."

"Who?"

"I'd prefer not to disclose that at the moment, Colonel."

Chirlo shrugged. "Just as you wish, however, I assume that having financed your research, and ongoing theft of the nuclear waste, this *angel* is prepared also to buy the finished product—*from me.*" He flicked a long ash into the silver tray.

"I'm sure the investor would be interested, although I have not discussed the subject as yet." Jamil smiled. "Your ownership only became apparent to me yesterday afternoon, you see."

Chirlo laughed, a deep happy sound. "Galal, you are a rascal! I should have you shot for trying to deceive me. Whatever made you think you could get away with it?"

"It was worth a try," Jamil said modestly. "Besides, supposing you hadn't discovered it, Colonel, think of all the money I could have saved?"

Chirlo roared with laughter; Jamil joined him, chuckling with relief.

"Well now, my artful young Arab, suppose we get down to cases—no lies now—how many are you planning on building?"

"Five," he replied truthfully.

"Why five? Why not ten or twenty?"

"Availability of plutonium waste, Colonel. We have to allow the waste to cool before we can handle it. Kastenburg is just starting to take the stuff now from the outside storage pools. It will be another year before we have enough to make five bombs."

"How in hell are you taking it out of the pool?"

Jamil explained the underground tunnel and replacement of dummy bundles for the hot waste removed from the huge water tank.

"We have an underground storage pool and from there everything is processed by mechanical hands. It's quite safe. The Doctor has done a superb job. Would you like to see the setup?"

"I don't want to know anything about it, officially or unofficially. As far as I'm concerned, we're sitting here talking nonsense—supposition, ifs and buts—nothing more."

"I understand." Jamil was elated. The attitude Chirlo was going to adopt in the affair was the whole key to success of his carefully planned stratagem.

"I am assuming the mythical bombs you might own are for sale, Colonel?"

"Everything is for sale, Galal. It is merely a matter of price." He butted her cheroot.

"Name it!"

Chirlo held up his hands.

"Not so fast; as a farmer I know different grades of cotton bring different market prices. The market depends on a buyer's needs. One year, demand is for long staple thread—the next, thick and shorter—it always depends on the buyer's need. Why does your buyer need these mythical bombs of mine—assuming I had any. And what is more important to me, what is he going to do with them?"

It was the crux of the conversation. He knew Chirlo, for all his ruthlessness and cunning, was still at heart a moralist. To provide a need which went against his morality would be fatal. Jamil chose his words carefully, stroking his opponent's chords of morality.

"You came to me once in Amman and asked for help. I helped. When I came to you for a visit later, again you asked for help. I helped. Now I come to you and ask for your help—not to repay a debt, nor to repay a loan, but because now I need your help and you are the only one who can give me that help." He spoke slowly, sincerely, gauging the word effect by Chirlo's eyes. Satisfied his spear had penetrated the chink in the armor, he continued.

"I won't bore you with all the details of why I think—we Palestinians think—our cause is just, any more than I tried to dissuade you many years ago on your political beliefs when we fought together against Guerrero. However, unlike your cause, my cause requires something more than courage, idealism and soldiers. It requires a threat. A threat that will be recognized universally by our enemies. Your enemy was one man—Guerrero. Mine is Zionism, and that means wherever there are Jews. It means England, America, Europe. It means the world." Once again he paused, watching for a reaction.

"An ambitious undertaking," Chirlo said quietly.

"Perhaps, but it is my version of your war of the flea. We Palestinians are only fleas, with or without the bombs. However, with them, we can become dangerous fleas, impervious to insecticides or scratching. It will be fear from our bite which will force the animal to accommodate our presence. It is not so bad really. After all, what are we asking? Living room on a small part of the tail, or a little area on one paw—part of an ear, perhaps? Surely that's not

516

asking too much, is it Colonel?"

He appeared to be considering the question, weighing it cautiously. "It would depend on whether your fleas intend to threaten the animal or bite it, because it seems to me a bite would be fatal for the poor beast—in fact, fatal for every beast."

"The object of a threat is to gain an advantage. Where's the advantage in using the threat for senseless destruction, destroying all advantages for everyone?" he countered.

Chirlo thought of Licenciado Munoz, the artful little union negotiator, carrying his threats to the brink of economic chaos for the country, then backing away at the right moment when he knew he could extract nothing more. Was Jamil any less of a negotiator than the loyal Munoz, any less a patriot in what he believed? He wondered. He knew Jamil much better than the Licenciado, or at least he thought he did.

"Then the bombs are for you?"

"Yes, Colonel, the bombs are for me, to use as an instrument for negotiation."

"And they will never be used, except for that purpose?" He held up his hand, his face stern. "Before you answer, Galal, I will tell you this: if ever you try to use them or I hear you might be trying to use them for anything other then political negotiation, then I will kill you!" His eyes burned into the Palestinian's face.

"You have my word, Colonel, I will never use them directly or indirectly for purposes other than negotiating my people back to their homeland." He said the sentence softly, slowly, emphasizing every syllable. Chirlo watched him a moment longer, then smiled.

"Good, then I will agree to help—for a price, of course!"

"Of course, Colonel." Jamil grinned. "After all, I am an Arab, and I enjoy bargaining.

It took until lunchtime before the financial arrangements were worked out to their mutual satisfaction. Cancellation of the original bullion debt to Jamil, a further one hundred million in gold for the five bombs, plus fifty-one percent of Blucher Chemicals operation for public ownership. Both men were satisfied at the end of their meeting; Chirlo, because he had no idea he could ask and get so much; Jamil equally surprised at how little he had to give away to get what he wanted. To him the bombs were everything, the money nothing. For Chirlo, it was the other way around.

"You understand of course, Colonel, final approval for the purchase price rests with my investor? I will have to obtain his approval."

"Agreed. But I have no doubt you will be able to convince him on the reality of the situation, in the same way you convinced me, Galal." Chirlo chuckled. They stood up as Ruis came up the steps from the greenhouse, announcing he was hungry and it was time for lunch.

Before leaving the city, Jamil stopped off at the telegraph office to send a night letter to Damascus. It came to eighty-four words—including the address: a meaningless jumble of letters which Akbar would be able to reassemble in a half hour with his annotated copy of the Koran.

Rolf Hauser liked the action around Innsbruk. He had been depressed when he had arrived after a sleepless night on the Lufthansa flight from New York to Frankfurt and spent two days moping around the house licking his emotional wounds, sleeping and eating. Trudi Heller still had not decided whether he was passing through, and needed a place to stay, or if her ex-fiancé wanted to re-establish their earlier relationship.

It had been two years since he had fled her grasp, explaining he needed time to think, before plunging off the skijump into the valley of matrimony. Although he'd kept up a weekly correspondence during the long absence, promising either to return momentarily, or have her fly into his tropical paradise to join him, after the first year she had stopped hoping and regarded his earnest letters simply as interesting mail from an ex-boyfriend. Now, suddenly and without warning, he had appeared on her doorstep, sans skis, but full of enthusiasm for renewing—what? Relationship or friendship? She didn't know. She did know he was tired; the happy, bouncy repartee at the doorway abruptly vanished once he had gained entrance to the house, and he fell asleep on the living room sofa when she had gone into the kitchen to fix them something to eat. She cut off her two current boyfriends, complaining of period pains, and decided to wait and see what developed with Rolf before making any further commitments. She still wasn't certain her flame of passion had been refanned when he turned up.

"Do you want to hear what happened?"

His voice made her jump. She was standing at the sink, cleaning the breakfast dishes, thinking he was still asleep in the guest room. The part about the guest room bothered her. It wasn't like Rolf to arrive at a girl's house and spend the first two nights in the guest room. The room, seldom used now since her mother had died, had been the attic until her father had renovated the space under the high pitched roof in anticipation of the birth of a son that never came. It was a comfortable little brick house in the old part of the city, one of the blocks that had somehow managed to escape the wartime carpet bombings.

"Oh! You frightened me!"

"Sorry." He looked terribly handsome, devil-may-care, when he grinned. His tousled blond hair was nearly white from the sun and the golden tan from the tropics appeared out of place in the overcast weather of October.

"I'm afraid I made a mess of things." He came over to the sink and wrapped his arms around the apron. The sight of the tiny blond hairs on his arms made her tingle. She leaned back, nestling against him.

"Another woman?" She didn't want to hear.

"A married woman—almost old enough to be my mother, at that," he said soulfully.

Trudi was shocked. "Rolf! How could you?" She straightened and turned, looking at him.

"I was mad about her. They threw me out of the country!"

"Because of an affair with a married woman?"

He nodded morosely and sat down at the small table. "She was the dictator's wife."

Trudi laughed, relieved, and took off the apron. She went over to the table and gathered the blond head to her breast, twining her fingers into his hair.

"Oh my darling, what a fool you are!"

He was silent, then pulled her onto his knees and began unbuttoning her housecoat, seeking the closest lush breast. After a few minutes she pulled him out of the kitchen and off to the bedroom to welcome him back properly.

"How do you spell the name?"

"Hauser—Rolf Hauser." Akbar spelled the letters slowly, watching the man write them down, then shuffle away behind the towering aisles of records. He left Damascus at once after receiving Jamil's telegram. There had been no point in trying to carry the Ingram M500 pistol with him on the airline, so he had arranged to ship it to Frankfurt with a consignment of faulty machine parts being returned for replacement the next day, picking the package up from his contact at the airline counter in Munich. It had caused him to lose a day driving to Munich, then back to Frankfurt, but he had a feeling he was going to need the pistol when he located his quarry. The old man in the records office shuffled back to the wicket lugging a heavy book.

"We have three Rolf Hausers, Sir—which one would it be?"

Fortunately the man spoke excellent English.

"I don't know, give me all three—no wait, do you have their father's names?"

"Certainly, Sir, and the mother's maiden name. Our records are very complete, you see."

"Father's name, Kurt Hauser."

The old man studied the list of names. "Kurt Dietrich Hauser; mother's maiden name Schell, Anna Maria Schell?"

That's the one!" He scribbled down the address and thanked the man, paying the two marks search fee at the cashier's box on the way out.

He found the house on the outskirts of town, nestled between a block of flats and a small garage specializing in brake linings. The Hauser family hadn't lived in the place for seventeen years. Disgusted, he drove the rented Opel into the service station for fuel. On impulse he asked the man handling the pump if he knew what had happened to the Hausers. The man stared blankly.

"Sprechen sie Deutsch?"

Akbar shook his head. The man shrugged and left the pump to call the fat owner, sitting behind the desk in the office.

"May I be of service, Sir?" The fat man's English was impeccable.

"Hauser. I'm trying to find the family from next door there. Do you know what happened to them?"

"Ah, Doctor Hauser. "Yes Sir, they moved away a long time ago." He scratched his head. "It was after his wife died. He took the boy and moved away. I used to see the boy sometimes. He came in once to fix his brakes two or three years ago—a Porsche—such an expensive car for a young man!"

"Did he say where he was living?"

"No—I'm sorry." He shook his head regretfully. Akbar paid the man for the gas and sat drumming his fingers on the wheel while he waited for him to come back from the office with the change. He'd already checked the area directories for Kurt Hauser. There were hundreds of Hausers, and dozens with the initial K—Karl, Kurt, Kristan, Kerig—there were lots of German names starting with the letter K. He would have to trace them all. It would take days and even then there was no guarantee the son would be anywhere in the district. The fat man returned to the window, handing him the change from his hundred mark note.

"You might try his girlfriend—maybe she knows where the family is living now."

"Doctor Hauser's?"

"No, Rolf. He had a nice girl—rich. She was with him two or three times when he came in. Trudi Heller. Her father was killed in an airplane crash a few years ago—it was in all the papers. The company settled out of court with her for a large amount. A million marks, if memory serves me. It was a famous case. Perhaps you remember it?"

"No, I don't. May I look in your telephone directory?" He climbed out and went into the office. It was there in beautiful clear type *Heller, Trudi,* along with her address and phone number. There was no answer when he dialed. He thanked the fat man and drove off to find the house, following the neat diagram the owner had drawn.

The blinds were drawn in the small house, and there were several newspapers piled on the doorstep. He checked the date of the oldest. Four days absence. He cursed his luck and went next door to inquire of the neighbors. An old woman peeked around the crack of her chained door suspiciously. He smiled politely and explained his problem. She snarled something at him in German, and shut the door.

"Are you looking for someone, Mister Englishman?" He turned to look at the soprano voice standing on the lawn behind him. The boy, about ten, was dressed in short pants. He had skinned red knees and a lunch pail. "Do you live here?"

"With my grandmother. Who are you?" He walked to the step and looked up at the dark-skinned Palestinian with interest.

"I'm a friend of Trudi Heller, but she is away."

"She went skiing—with her boyfriend," he announced.

"How do you know?"

"I said goodbye to them when they left. Are you really English?"

"No, I'm Portuguese. Where did they go?"

"Skiing. I know where Portgual is. We studied that in school."

"Do you know where they went skiing?" He heard the suspicious grandmother open the door behind him, then close it abruptly and fiddle with the chain lock.

"My grandmother knows. I'll ask her." The door opened and a stream of German erupted from the old woman. The boy replied quickly and a see-saw rapid-fire exchange continued for a minute.

"Grandmother wants to know why you want to know where

Trudi went? She is very hateful of English, but I told her you are Portuguese."

Akbar beamed at the scowling woman and saw her features soften slightly. He looked at her directly as he spoke to the boy. "Tell your sweet old grandmother I am from the insurance company who paid the claim on her father's airplane accident and I have to see her about increasing her allowance—inflation, you see."

He kept looking at the old lady while the boy translated, then saw her face open in a smile. She nodded kindly and told him the answer, all the time speaking to the boy. He thanked the young lad and mussed his hair.

"Tell your grandmother *dankeschon* and tell her I hate the English too."

"They killed my grandfather in the war," the boy explained.

"Mine too—but in a different one."

There was no need to preship his pistol to Zurich. He put the case inside the travel bag and checked the suitcase through on his ticket. Swiss customs would never think of embarrassing a tourist entering their monetary haven by asking him to open his bags. Taking something out of the country was different, but Akbar didn't think he would be needing the Ingram after Switzerland anyway.

Bruner was standing at the banking window changing a fistful of Lebanese pounds into Deutschmarks. He could just as easily have waited until he got into Frankfurt, but the effort used a bit of the time he had to waste during the two hour airport layover. He saw the stocky Palestinian moving through passport control beyond the glass barrier. He grabbed his German marks and rushed past the row of people, pushing himself into line behind a long haired young man with a violin case, as Akbar passed through the control point and out into the customs area. Bruner prayed the Palestinian had checked some luggage. The man behind him in line muttered something gutteral in Romansch. Bruner ignored it and trailed the violin case out into the baggage claim. He saw Akbar was waiting for luggage. Bruner cleared the customs desk and went out into the arrival concourse to wait, trying to decide whether to talk or trail the man. He was certain the Palestinian knew exactly where Jamil could be found, but would he tell Max? Bruner doubted it. As Akbar came out the customs room carrying a large folding suitcase, he decided to tail instead of talk. He watched him go directly to the Hertz counter and begin examining the list of vehicles available from the price sheet. There were two couples ahead of him in the line. Bruner walked quickly to the taxi desk.

"Do you rent cars with drivers by the day?"

"Yes Sir."

"I want one—now." He yanked out a fistful of German marks. "Here—on deposit. I'm a newspaper reporter following a story—a confidential story." He produced his I.D. and passport. "There is a man over at the Hertz desk renting a car; see him? Short? Stocky Arab?" The dispatcher nodded conspiratorially. "Give me your best driver. I want to follow that Arab wherever he goes."

"Where's he going?" the man asked in a whisper.

"I don't know."

The man walked around the partition in the booth and made a phone call. Akbar craned his head back and forth between the dispatcher's legs behind the partition and the Palestinian who finally reached the Hertz girl, and began filling in the paperwork for his car. The dispatcher emerged smiling.

"I have just the driver you want. He's on his way over now. Two minutes—that door!" He pointed around the corner of the booths, and began writing down the particulars of Bruner's passport and press card.

"I have some luggage checked through to Frankfurt on Swissair 345 coming off Middle East Airlines. Can you intercept and hold it until I get back?"

The dispatcher glanced at his watch. "I'll try. If I miss it, I'll have them send it back from Frankfurt on the next flight. Sign here!"

"Great—I appreciate that!" He signed the short form without reading it and looked over to the Hertz counter. Akbar was nodding at the girl as she explained walking directions to their lot.

"I'll wait outside on the curb. Thanks again." He went outside and stood, watching the stocky Palestinian stepping quickly down the walk away from him to the end of the terminal building. A black Mercedes roared up to the curb and stopped. The driver leaned across the seat and opened the door.

"Bruner?" He was young with a steep angular face and chiseled nose.

"The short dark man walking across the road with the tan foldaway bag—stick to him like glue," he ordered as he climbed in the cab beside the driver. The car was moving before he had closed the door. The driver parked beyond the exit ramp for the rental lot and waited, watching through his side mirror. Bruner twisted his head, scanning the rows of cars. He couldn't find Akbar.

"The blue Cortina backing out at the near end," the driver said. Bruner saw it, a dark blue, four-door sedan; average car, average color. He turned to the front and watched as it passed. The driver slipped into gear and began to follow, keeping well back. They left the airport congestion and swung onto the highway.

"Do you have any idea where he is going, Herr Bruner?"

"Name's Max—none."

"I am called Gus—for Augustus." He glanced quickly at his passenger and smiled.

"Okay Gus, let's see where our fox will lead." He settled back in the seat, watching the sedan moving carefully through the traffic, exactly within the speed limits prescribed by the periodic road signs.

Beyond Zurich, they skirted past the open waters of the Zurichsee, following the highway to the end of the lake, then swung onto the road for Chur. An hour passed, then another. Beyond Chur the traffic thinned and Gus dropped back so the sedan was visible only during brief periods of the straight stretches of road. They passed into the canton of Graubuden adjoining the Austrian border, winding through the mountains, until suddenly, as they neared the town of Davos, Gus announced, "I think this is his destination—*look*, he's slowing!"

The sedan stopped at the edge of the highway a few hundred meters short of town. As they passed the Palestinian, Bruner saw from the corner of his eye that Akbar was studying the town through a pair of binoculars.

"Find a parking stop with some other cars, Gus. We'll wait for him."

The Swiss driver took an open space on the main street and slid into the curb.

"Is this a ski resort?"

The driver kept his eyes on the port mirror. "No, a health resort, mainly. There are some ski runs in the area, but it is mainly for the dry air that people come. Tuberculosis and other illnesses. There are several sanitariums."

The town's streets were bare, but on the hillsides and mountains snow lay whitely, stretching off to the Weissfluh peak less than ten miles to the northwest.

"How high?"

"Davos? Five thousand feet."

"No, the mountain."

"Oh, the Weissfluh!" He tipped his head down to look at it. "Nine thousand, I think—here he comes!"

The sedan passed them slowly, pausing at the lighted intersection until the red had changed, then moving on down the street. They followed until, at the far end of town, Akbar pulled into one of the hotels. The *Raushaus* was a pretty three story building with a large balcony encircling the second floor. They watched him remove his suitcase and lock the car.

"Do you want to stay here?" The driver pulled the Mercedes into a parking spot across the street, down further from the hotel. Bruner considered the question.

"Could I rent a car here?"

"Unlikely—a taxi, but not a car. I can check."

"No, never mind. Let's find a couple of rooms nearby where we can look and see what he does—wait! He's coming back!"

They watched as the stocky Palestinian glanced down the street, then opened the Cortina and threw his bag in the back.

"Where does this road go?"

"To the Austrian border—about fifteen miles away—or if you stay in Switzerland, it circles the mountains back to Chur."

"Good. He's not going to Austria with a Swiss rental, and he's not going back to Chur, so my bet is he asked them inside for directions to a specific place. Let's find out!" They waited until the sedan had passed, then climbed out and walked back to the hotel.

"We may lose him," Gus warned.

Bruner smiled as they entered the hotel. "Or we may find out exactly where he's headed."

———————————

Colonel Mummar al Quadaffi's eyes bored into Jamil's face, searching. They were eyes that were almost black, yet there were tiny yellow darts around the irises, yellow flashes of light.

"This Colonel Chirlo—can he be trusted?"

"He needs the money for his country."

"You are sure of this, brother Galal?" The yellow lights danced.

"I'm sure. He will take nothing for himself—like you Sir, he is an idealist."

"He is like me?" His voice was sharp.

Jamil avoided the question. "Like you and unlike you. But this much I know, when you meet you will discover there is much you have in common."

"One hundred million?"

"In bullion."

"In bullion," the Libyan leader agreed. "Twenty million for each bomb, plus the fifty I have already given you—thirty million each! How do you know they will work when we get them?"

The Colonel had already been swindled by an array of commercial sharks from Europe and the Far East. His most recent experience had been the purchase of a boatload of night vision binoculars from a French group at premium prices. His agent in Madrid had paid the cost of the shipment without checking the contents of the packing cases. When the shipment arrived, they turned out to be standard binoculars available at the Sukk in Tripoli. He had ordered the agent in Madrid executed as an example to others who might be tempted to take advantage of his munificence in the future.

"We could insist on test firing one of them—our choice of a random selection—before payment," Jamil offered, knowing the idea to be impractical.

"Of course! Proof before payment. Sensible business approach. I approve."

Jamil felt his emotions sag, never believing the suggestion would be accepted. He tried a counterattack.

"Of course, we must be prepared to accept the criticism which will arise if we test fire one of the bombs."

"Of course. Think of the reaction. Everyone wondering whose it is. Is it mine? Is it yours? Or is it your Colonel Chirlo's? How many more are there—who has them—where are they—it will drive them crazy! You make demands—I make demands—Colonel Chirlo makes demands—everyone threatening to use their power, but who are they to believe?"

He gave the Palestinian a tight-lipped smile. "Good thinking, brother Galal. I will order Major Hassan to represent me—a full authority—take him with you when you're ready."

"Major Hassan?"

"Good man. One of the Council. Of course I have other sources I am exploring too." He nodded vigorously. "The Jews have them, you know; secret underground factory in the desert; all from the Americans, of course. Balance of power." He banged his palm on the desktop for emphasis. "We must shift that balance. I will shift it. If the Chinese refuse"—Jamil knew they already had—"then the Germans will sell or the Italians, or the French—yes, the French would sell their souls for a song." He curved his thin lips. "It is only a matter of time, only a matter of time."

On his trip back to Beirut, Jamil felt uneasy. He should never have suggested the idea of a test firing. He knew Chirlo would balk at that sort of performance. If the bombs were to be an advertised threat, what was the point of proving their capability? That would be the argument. It was a delicate problem. In any case, he decided, he had a full year before the subject would have to be broached with the bearded man of San Ramon.

The political unrest in the Lebanese capital was another source of concern. He knew it was only a matter of weeks before the country would erupt in a serious conflagration between rival factions of Moslems and Christians. It might be wise to close the office now and transfer everything to Damascus before the lid blew off the country. As the 707 swung in over the beachfront by the luxury hotels and lowered its wheels, sinking to the airport, he decided he would speak to Bernadette before flying on to Damascus.

She was in the office when he phoned from the airport, announcing his return.

"Any word from our missionary?"

"No, Max Bruner turned up for two days then left. He wanted to see you."

A warning light flashed in Jamil's brain. "Stay there. I'll be at the office in a half hour.

He pushed his way through the mob at the front of the terminal and hailed a taxi. Bernadette was filing her nails when he came in.

"We're moving to Damascus. Start packing."

She looked up, startled. "Everything?"

"Everything. Now, tell me about Max; what did he say?— exactly—think back—try and remember every detail!"

Bernadette stood up and smiled coyly. "Every detail?"

"You can eliminate the bedroom details," he said dryly. He stood watching and listening as she walked about the room pulling out drawers, removing papers, documents and other trivia, all the while talking of the two days Bruner had spent in the city. Finally, she stopped and turned to him.

"Why are we moving?"

"Do you want to stay and watch the country blow up? You're sure that's all you discussed with Max Bruner?"

"Everything, except the doctor—he said he knew the doctor too."

"Which doctor?"

She shrugged. "How should I know. The same doctor you know, I suppose. The one from Frankfurt whose office called here for you the last time."

Jamil was stunned. *Of course,* he thought, *they have the phone tapped! But at which end, Beirut or Frankfurt?* He was betting on

Beirut. He stopped to help her pack the piles of papers in some order.

"Go find some boxes. I want to be out of here tonight!"

There were three German license plates in the parking lot of the Menglehof resort when Akbar pulled the blue Cortina in off the private road. He shunted the sedan into a vacant spot close to the exit from where he could leave quickly with a minimum of entrapment. One of the German cars, an Audi, maroon-colored, had ski racks on the roof. He glanced in the car window on his way to the hotel. There was a woman's sweater and a man's raincoat lying on the back seat.

"Guten Tag, mein Herr!"

"Sorry, I don't speak German—my name is Cortera, Hector Cortera from Lisbon. I have reservations," he announced, feigning tiredness.

A formally dressed clerk behind the desk checked his list once, then twice, finally looking up in surprise. "Cortera?"

"Hector Cortera from Lisbon. It was arranged by my office several weeks ago."

"I'm sorry Sir, but we don't seem to have your name. Are you alone?"

"Yes. You mean you have no space?"

"Space, yes, but it is reserved for guests who will be arriving on the weekend."

"Oh well, that's no problem. I'll stay until the weekend then, instead of the full week." He reached for the register book, plucking the chained ballpoint from its holder.

The clerk hesitated, started to reach for the register, then changed his mind, raising his brow slightly. Akbar ignored him and began filling in the blank space under the row of names, scanning the page as he wrote. There was no Heller or Hauser shown. He paused in writing to hand the clerk his Portuguese passport. While the man glanced at it, he flipped to the previous page and scanned the names swiftly. They were near the top of the page: *Rolf Hauser, 204; Trudi Heller 206.* Adjoining rooms! The clerk looked at him severely and dragged the ledger back to his side of the counter. "Very well, Sir, I'll give you 217 until Friday checkout." He slipped the passport into a drawer and hit the desk bell a solid ring. "Dinner is at seven."

He trailed the young porter up the stairs to the second floor and down the hall to the last room on the left. The man waved him inside casually and accepted his tip with equal aplomb. He spent a minute explaining how the catch on the double thermopane doors onto the balcony worked before leaving. Akbar sat down on the bed chuckling and slipped off his shoes. He stretched out on the bed, gave a long luxurious yawn, set his mental alarm for six-thirty and dropped off to sleep. In a few minutes he was snoring loudly.

"Do you know that man at the table next to the window?"

Rolf glanced across the dining room, seeing the swarthy, casually dressed man eating alone. For an instant, their eyes met. The lone diner looked at him strangely and smiled. Rolf averted his eyes.

"Never saw him before in my life."

"Well, don't look now, but he's left the table and coming over here," she whispered.

"Pardon me, aren't you young Rolf Houser?" Akbar asked in English.

Rolf looked up at the dark beaming face and nodded. "Yes?"

"I thought so—it's been years! Well look at you"—the man stood back slightly—"all grown up and married. How is your father?"

"Very well, thank you, Sir. I'm afraid I don't remember . . ." he began.

"Of course not, how stupid of me. You were only a boy at the time. I'm Hector Cortera. Your father and I did a great deal of business in the old days—chemical solvents for industry in Portugal. I was with the government in those days; went into private enterprise afterwards. I haven't seen your father for—let me see now . . ." He squinted his eyes over the effort of recalling a mythical past, then relaxed his face. "Well, anyway, over ten years ago."

Rolf switched into Portuguese. "My father is abroad now, in Central America, working with Blucher Chemicals of Frankfort. He is well and happy. I left him a short time ago."

"I see. Very interesting." Not comprehending, the Palestinian replied in English, dumbfounded that the boy was fluent in the foreign language. It was something Jamil had overlooked in the telegram. He kept the smile fixed firmly on his face.

"Well, be sure and give your father my regards when you see him—nice meeting you again, Rolf; you too, Mrs. Hauser." He nodded at Trudi, then summoned one of the few Portuguese words he knew, "Obligado," and beat a swift retreat back to his own table, furious at the turn of events. They watched him strangely as he sat down, smiled at them again and began eating his salad.

"Who was that?" Trudi spoke nothing except German.

"Said he was a friend of my father's from Portugal—knew me

when I was a boy."

"Oh!" She saw a peculiar look on his face. "What's wrong?"

"I don't know, but something's wrong. He speaks English with an Arab accent and cannot speak or understand Portuguese!" They looked at each other uneasily, then the waiter arrived to take their order. When they glanced across the dining room a few minutes later the table of Hector Cortera was empty. "Probably went back to Lisbon to learn the language." Rolf laughed.

"Or to Zurich to attend the Berlitz school!" Trudi snickered.

Unconcerned, they started their meal. Sitting alone at the next table, Gus, the Mercedes driver Bruner had hired, watched the passing events, speculating idly on how the young couple with whom the Arab had spoken fitted into the scheme of things. He wiped his mouth with a napkin and signaled for the check.

"The couple is registered as Trudi Heller and Rolf Hauser from Frankfurt," the driver repeated. "Does that mean anything?"

Bruner had turned on the motor and heater to keep the chill out of the Mercedes. "It might—how old are they?"

"Man is early twenties, the girl about the same. They were both surprised when he spoke to them." Gus waited for instructions. Bruner was puzzled. Nothing made sense, unless the couple were from Blucher offices in Frankfurt. It was a possibility. He would have a talk with them later, when he was sure Akbar would be asleep. From experience he knew the Palestinian was not a night owl. Bruner's midnight typing at the camp had always been a source of irritation to Akbar, who retired two hours earlier. In the mornings it worked the other way, when the Palestinian leaped out of bed at dawn and began annoying Max with his chatter.

"Let's go back to Davos and find a hotel for the night. We'll come back at eleven and pay your couple a visit."

Gus nodded. "You're the boss." He put the car in gear and drove around the parking lot, out to the highway.

"I hope you don't mind spending a night away from home?"

"Mind?" The driver laughed. "This is the most exciting thing that's happened to me since I drove the French President to the airport in 1969."

"Good. It may get more exciting before the evening's out."

Akbar lay on the bed smoking a cigarette, his fifth since returning from the dining room. He was wide awake, waiting for the minutes to pass, waiting until the young man and his girlfriend were back in their room. His watch showed 10:00 p.m.; time to check again.

He carried the ashes in his palm along with the cigarette butt to the toilet and flushed the debris away, then put on a pair of rubber-soled slippers. He took the Ingram from under his pillow and screwed the eight inch silencer onto the snub-nosed barrel. After turning out the light, he pulled the curtains aside, slid open the glass door and stepped out onto the balcony. The air was chilly, the night clear and bathed with stars.

Akbar crept around to the front of the hotel, past drawn curtains in the corner rooms. Crouching against the side of the building, he waited until a group of people had crossed the parking lot below and driven off in their cars. Along the row of glass doors into the rooms he counted seven pools of light spilling across the wide wooden walkway. The fourth and fifth were from the rooms occupied by his targets.

Akbar approached the first window and peeked in. The room was deserted. He sped across its flood of light to the second. A man was sitting in an armchair reading a book while his wife was putting her hair in curlers on the bed. He could hear her talking in low tones to her husband. Akbar lowered himself to the decking, then wiggled slowly across the space, keeping his body close to the window step. Light from the next room flooding the balcony waned, then vanished abruptly as the occupant pulled the curtains. He stood up and crossed to the next lighted room. It was empty. He could see the suitcase lying on the bed in exactly the same position it had been when he had made the trip an hour earlier. He padded softly on to the next room for a quick check. They were there! Quickly he drew back, crouching in the semi-darkness between the two shafts of light.

Trudi was laughing over something young Hauser had told her. Akbar turned his head slowly, looking inside. Hauser was waving his hands in front of her face, inscribing an arc in the air. She sat on the bed looking up, laughing at whatever it was he was telling her. He tapped on the glass lightly with the tip of the silencer and waited. Conversation inside the room stopped. He waited. He heard the latch mechanism turn on the glass door, and thumbed the safety catch on the Ingram. Young Hauser's head appeared, looking down the balcony.

The Palestinian raised his pistol in the shadow. As the handsome blond head turned to look in his direction he blew it to pieces in a one second burst with a stream of hissing nine millimeter slugs from the automatic. He sprung to his feet, pushed the spurting red corpse aside along with the sliding window and leaped across the open space to the bed, fingers outstretched to stifle the scream rising from the horrified girl. He connected, bowling her backwards, his fingers locked onto her windpipe. She fought him like a demon clawing the air and raked her nails uselessly across the back of his leather jacket. He whipped his arm free of the pistol and slid his hand beneath her back, holding her tightly, then pushed the head until he heard her spine snap. She went limp.

Akbar stood up and felt the pulse. Trudi Heller was still alive—just. He sighed, and leaned forward, pressing his thumb and forefinger against each cartoid artery, barricading the brain blood until her heart had ceased to beat. He went back to the sliding door, picked up Hauser's corpse by the feet, and dragged it into the center of the room, then went back to check the area for footprints in the pools of blood covering the varnished decking. There were none. He slid the door closed and drew the curtains, then went into the bathroom to wash the blood splashes from his clothing with a hotel towel. He took great pains to make sure he cleaned every speck of bloody evidence away, then thoughtfully, left the towel to soak in a sink full of cold water. He went back into the bedroom and checked both pulses again. *Still dead*, he thought, smiling to himself.

Searching the girl's purse, he found the car keys. Hauser's pockets were empty, except for a handkerchief and small change. There was a bundle of banknotes, marks and francs, in Trudi's purse, but he left them. He was interested only in the car keys. One last check around the room; he switched off the lights and opened the door into the hallway boldly and began talking. "I'll let you get some sleep—see you in the morning!" He shut the door. The voice cover was unnecessary. The corridor was deserted. He walked quickly to his room at the end, and went in to change his clothes and pack.

It was nearly eleven when he slipped out on the balcony and checked the grounds below. Satisfied there was no one about, he tossed the bag over the railing, then lowered himself carefully, until he was hanging by his fingers from the balcony grillwork. The drop was less than eight feet from the lawn. He landed alongside the bag and froze, listening for sound, watching for movement. Nothing. He picked up the suitcase and sauntered around to the parking lot.

As he drove the maroon Audi with the empty ski-racks down the driveway heading for the Austrian border, he passed a large Mercedes turning off the highway. Both cars dipped their headlights considerately. The driver of the Mercedes waited until the Audi was clear before starting up the hill to the hotel parking lot.

Kastenburg put his arm on his friend's shoulder sympathetically. "I'm sorry Kurt, truly sorry. We should never have let him stay here in the first place—then, we should never have let him leave."

"But why? He would never have told anyone—and the girl too! Why the girl?"

Kastenburg shrugged. "The possibility existed he might have told her. Who knows?"

Doctor Hauser was silent, his face drawn, tight with sorrow. He had expected something to happen, but not so swiftly and not this way—and all because of a woman! He had been sure that by getting the boy out of the country and home to familiar surroundings the whole thing would blow over—be forgotten. He had been wrong, terribly wrong. Colonel Chirlo's revenge had been swift and exacting.

"Of course it might have been on orders from the Palestinian. Did you ever consider that?"

Hauser looked at him reproachfully. "The Palestinian?" The thought hadn't entered his mind since he received the news that morning from the Swiss police. "You don't believe seriously the Palestinian gives a damn whose wife my son goes to bed with, do you?"

"No, I suppose not."

"It was an assassination arranged and completed by that bastard Chirlo—and if its the last thing I do, I'm going to *kill* the schweinheund!" He clenched his fists in frustration and anger, pushing the sorrow in his breast aside.

Kastenburg was startled. "Now Kurt, I forbid you to do anything stupid until this project is finished. One thoughtless action now will affect us all. We can't afford any more problems with the man."

"I didn't mean tomorrow, Heinz."

"Promise me you will do nothing until our work is completed—on your word of honor, Kurt!"

Hauser looked at him and nodded. "I promise—until our work is completed. But then, my old friend, Colonel Chirlo belongs to me!"

"Agreed." They shook hands on the bargain.

"Now let's get back to work.

17

1975

"Yoo Hoo! Mr. Corbin!" She came running across the front lawn, clopping through the soft grass on the new uncomfortable pedestal shoes; young busybody with jiggling breasts, unharnessed under a loose wool sweater. The National Film Board had lots of them on its payroll: bright, young, liberated women making their lifestyle into a part of every film script, all terribly avant garde. If someone suggested running around with shaven heads because it was *in*, they would obey without question. Corbin broke away from the two people he had been speaking with; engineers on the sound system.

"Yes, Mzzz Stewart." Lona Stewart was how she had introduced herself earlier in the day—Ms. Lona Stewart, with the accent on the *mzzz*.

She came up to him and stopped, waiting for the twin balloons under the Siwash sweater to settle down. "I'd like to change the camera angle on the front lawn for the intro fade-in, bringing the sign in on a pan, subliminally, if that's okay with you?"

Corbin hadn't the slightest idea what she was talking about. "Whatever you think best, Mzzz Stewart. You're the boss."

She tilted her head and looked at him archly, trying to decide whether he was putting her on or merely being accommodating.

"Right! That's what I'll do then." He looked at her rump, swinging under the tight slacks as she walked back to the camera crew lolling around the sound truck.

"Hard to decide whether she needs it kicked or spanked, isn't it Chuck?"

He turned, laughing. "Hello Morris! Sarah, I see you made it."

"What are you doing standing on the front lawn, selling programs?" Levy looked around the grounds, seeing hundreds of clustered officials, visitors, politicians and freeloaders gossiping in the warm summer air. Beyond the lawns, the white and black marble buildings spiraled a sprawling staircase towards the sky.

"The Reach of the Unknown" had been the theme the architect, Matasma Yoshima, had created, using the low odd-shaped modules as huge stepping stones rising in a sweeping curve in tune with the hill behind.

"I still think they look like a cluster of toadstools!" Sarah said.

Levy looked at his wife, exasperated. "What you are looking at is the creation of genius, for the creation of genius—personally, I like it, the whole thing. It's the most impressive piece of original architecture I've seen in this country."

"I'm glad you like it," Corbin said. He was proud of the achievement. His idea, his concept, his genius.

Herman Slitzman had given him the idea. The bonds for Israel; their frames gathering dust instead of interest because a fat old New York Jew believed in an ideal. It came to him suddenly on the way home from Marseilles with Tricia. On the stopover in Orly he had picked up a two day old *Wall Street Journal.* He had kissed her goodbye at the gate for her flight to New York, then wandered the concourse waiting for the Air France to Montreal. He had been so engrossed in the paper he had started wandering away from the booth without paying the three francs until the clerk hailed him, "Oie, M'esieu! Trois francs, s'il vous plait!" Others nearby looked up from thumbing their magazines and smiled knowingly. Corbin laid five francs on the counter and went off to find a seat along the wide aisle.

It was a small box ad. "Wanted: inventions, ideas, business opportunities—we have money to invest. Your choice—joint venture—loan—partnership—buyout." There was a postal box number for the unsuspecting mark to mail in his vision for examination by the experts. He read it several times. It was not unlike hundreds of similar advertisements he had glanced over in every major newspaper. In another box ad, "Money wanted: for million dollar ideas . . ." which went on to suggest, in veiled terms, how the idea was comparable to planting money trees in your own backyard. Both items were nonsense, of course. He knew this from his own experiences over the years, fending off hair-brained investors and their inventions, or pseudo-fiscal management consultants whose wisdom extended to a post graduate course for an M.B.A., looking for someone to put them to work making mistakes with other peoples' money until they gained sufficient experience to handle their own. But that was beside the point. Here was a need that could never be fulfilled.

Supposing . . . By the time he had cleared Montreal customs and caught his flight into Ottawa he had figured it all out. He took the taxi from the airport straight to Elizabeth's apartment, went through the front door as one of the tenants was coming out into the blizzard conditions, and took the elevator up to the apartment, lugging his suitcase. He pounded on the door several times, and was at the point of leaving when she opened it. "Chuck?" She stood aside as he marched into the room, dropping his bag as he entered.

"Fix me a drink, will you, Sweetheart, I've got something I want to discuss with you.

"Where's your coat?"

"What coat?" he asked absently, taking off his suit jacket.

"It's freezing outside. This is mid-winter, you idiot!" She couldn't help laughing.

"Snowing too—blowing like hell."

"Chuck, I have company—you can't stay!"

"Company?" He looked at her for the first time. She was dressed in a pink ankle length housecoat. He knew she was naked under it.

"Well, fix him a drink too!" He sat down and loosened his tie. "Supposing, just supposing there was a quiet place outside the city in the country, no industry, noise, traffic, only trees, hills and peace. Got that?" He didn't look at her; he was visualizing the plans he had made a few hours earlier over the North Atlantic.

"Chuck, please—this is very embarrassing. Can't we talk about it tomorrow?" She drew the strings of her housecoat tighter, waiting.

"Now, in this place we buy all the land around a center point for five miles in any direction so no one will ever build anything on it—ever. Peace, we've got to have peace and quiet. Of course there will be a good roadway in—but a winding road, none of these super highway things—you know the type I mean—comfortable winding road. Now the buildings; they must be unique, unusual, blending with the surroundings—color, design, function—yet still comfortable."

"Chuck Corbin are you going to leave or do I have to throw you out?" She was getting mad.

"Don't interrupt, this is important. I figure the completed package should run around a hundred million the way I want to do it."

Exasperated, Elizabeth went over to the small bar and began making his drink, but for the first time since he arrived, she was listening to what he said. He waited until she came back with a glass of bourbon on the rocks and sat down opposite him, adjusting the housecoat carefully over her knees.

"Thanks! Now—and get this—we open with a big splash requesting the experts to join us. Full media coverage, including the States."

"Which experts?" She still hadn't caught the drift.

"Experts in everything—law, finance, business, agriculture, engineering, chemistry—you name them, we want to hear from them."

"Why?"

"To join us, for Chrissakes—aren't you listening?"

"Sorry." She still didn't understand.

"The deal is simple. You're a first class engineer, Mr. Jones, but you're in a dead end job with a giant corporation or government or whatever. Here's what we're going to do for you: you get a living wage, access to all our facilities and technical knowledge, laboratory, consulting relationships with those within your own engineering field—or any of the other fields you require; all you have to do is produce." He looked at her, his eyes glowing.

"Mr. Jones, you get twenty-five percent of any development you can turn into a commercial reality. How's that grab you?"

"It doesn't." She looked blank. "I don't understand."

"*Jesus Christ*, Elizabeth, what's *wrong* with you? You're losing your grip! The place is a huge think-tank to develop and organize commercially viable ideas submitted to us by people who have ideas but not money, ability, management or business sense to turn them into reality. We take fifty-one percent of the action for a ten year minimum with a buyout agreement in advance. The originator of the idea gets twenty-four percent and the man or men and women who put it all together take the balance. We make it into a non-profit foundation so there will be no taxes on our fifty-one percent, plowing all our profits back into the central fund to repay original investment costs plus expand our financial base for other ideas."

Now she understood, and leaned forward as her mind began to analyze what he was saying. "But isn't it self-defeating? I mean if eventually you lose your personnel in the think-tank because they buy you out and go on their own, you'll run out of staff."

"It'll never happen. Where else in the world can the brightest and best find a place to develop their own ideas or those of others and go into business for themselves supported by experts as bright as they are? For everyone who leaves, there will be a hundred waiting to fill the vacancy."

"It will be expensive."

"Sure it will—at first."

"There will be losses, mistakes in judgment!"

"There is in any business—but if decisions are made by our experts for their own self-interest, there won't be many. Remember, they own twenty-five percent of the project?" He could see the curve of her breast where the housecoat had fallen open, and felt his senses tingle. He smiled at her. His sabbatical was past. "Like it?"

"It's—it's mind boggling! It's like having control of a government-sponsored program for new development based on sound commerical principles run by competent people with a vested interest in success, instead of a lot of half-witted bureaucrats wasting the taxpayers' money. I think it's sheer genius!" She came over and put her arms around his neck, kissing him happily.

He pushed his hands inside the housecoat and around her back, drawing her to him tightly until she could feel his erection against her tummy.

She froze. "My God! Larry!" She wriggled free and stood up, adjusting the tie-strings again.

"Who?"

"Larry—he's still in the bedroom waiting for me!"

Corbin lifted himself off the sofa and went around to the bedroom. He knocked lightly, then opened the door. The room was in darkness. The man lying under the covers propped himself up on one elbow, looking at him foolishly. His top was bare.

"Hi Larry, I'm Chuck! Elizabeth will only be a moment. She has to dress and pack a few things to take home with her."

"Home?"

Corbin chuckled. "Oh, didn't she tell you about us?" He drew Elizabeth into the bedroom with one hand and switched on the light. "We're getting married at the end of the week so I thought she might as well start getting used to her new home now. Hope you don't mind."

Construction started as soon as the frost was out of the ground. Heavy earth moving equipment rumbled into the middle of six thousand acres he had purchased quietly during the preceding winter months. Everything that had not been created by the Almighty was removed—those were his instructions to the contractors. Houses, barns, sheds, fences, silos, windmills; everything vanished into heaps of rubble to be carted away for landfill at other locations around the sanctuary.

They studied the architectural accomplishments of the innovative minds from all over the world before selecting the pint-size Japanese genius to put together the plans for the buildings he wanted. They spent most of their time together arguing the finer points of architecture versus the economics of building structures, Corbin pounding the table to emphasize his point on how he wanted something done, Yoshima hissing back, always in the negative; yet, the finished product left them both beaming.

Affleck was amazed at Corbin's transformation and stood as best man at the simple wedding ceremony for Elizabeth and his partner, while Rina wept buckets. The children were wary in the beginning, particularly during that first week. They circled their proposed stepmother cautiously, sniffing for indications of compatability. The girls took to her just before the wedding. Peter kept himself aloof for several weeks after the official honeymoon ended until the incident with the hit-and-run driver who killed Tomboy, the family cat.

Coming home from school, the children invariably met the sleek fat animal as they walked up the drive; Tomboy would leave his comfortable winter quarters in the garage, racing out to meet them, then, like any feline, pretend the whole thing had been a mistake and proceed to ignore their arrival, looking at everything in sight except the objects of his affection. On special occasions, Tomboy had been known to run across the road to greet them early, but this usually occurred in the summer months. For some reason, one afternoon the cat decided on a winter greeting, and without looking, charged across the road, heard a car, stopped, started, stopped, then galloped uselessly on a patch of ice as the vehicle rolled over him. Elizabeth saw it from the window, and ran out to shepherd the three wailing children off the street. Peter carried the dead animal into the garage and laid it tenderly on the wood pile, then looked in wonder at Elizabeth when he realized she too was weeping over the loss of their pet. He threw his arms around her and for a while they cried together. Later, after phoning the police department to trace the license number, she drove the three children over to the address and knocked on the door. The offending weapon, a blue Cutlass, was parked in the driveway. Elizabeth recognized the driver when she opened the door.

"Good afternoon, Madam! This afternoon when you drove over our pet without stopping or apologizing I thought it was one of the most callous and unfeeling actions I have ever witnessed. I just dropped by so the children could meet a real bitch face-to-face so if and when they run into another some day they will have something to compare to you. Goodbye!"

They marched back to the station wagon and drove off. Peter was speechless with admiration. Before supper, he told Emily privately, "Wow! Mommy would never have had the nerve to do that! Did you hear it? She called her a bitch!"

"Whath a bitch, Peter?" Alice inquired.

"Someone who drives over cats!" Emily explained succinctly.

After that, Elizabeth—and they all called her Elizabeth—became one of the family. Even Hughette accepted her as major domo.

The gala opening—which was the way the newspapers reported it later—of the toadstool staircase—as Sarah Levy called it—ended with a huge outdoor buffet supper. The consensus of the five hundred guests was that *Bayana*, which is what Corbin had called it, would be a huge success. The name had come originally as a suggestion by the architect, Yoshima, who, in addition to his other accomplishments, was a scholar of Greek mythology and suggested the name from the mythical Bayan of the Hundred Eyes. Corbin had preferred Icarus, the boy whose father had covered his body with wax and applied feathers so he could fly towards the sun. It seemed appropriate, rising to the heights of the heavens using the imagination of man, until the architect explained that the particular story had a disastrous ending, when, as Icarus neared the sun, the wax melted, the feathers dropped out and he plunged to his death. As a compromise, they settled on Bayana.

"Happy, Darling?"

He looked at her in the glow of the huge barbecue, and smiled. "Like a bird."

"I'm proud of you."

"I'm proud of me too." His face glowed with satisfaction as he reached out to touch her.

"Here, here, none of that now!" Affleck worked his way into the firelight from behind them, leaving the groups of shadowed forms holding white paper plates. "Well, I've got to hand it to you, when you first proposed it, I thought you'd flipped out. Now I think it's the best thing—the best idea you ever had. Congratulations!"

For some reason the compliment, coming from Don Affleck, embarrassed him. He changed the subject.

"Have you seen our staff roster?"

"Seen it? We've got more brains per square foot during office hours than the Houston Space Center during a launch!"

"And the ideas are pouring in from everythere—it's incredible!" he said happily.

"There's only one thing wrong!" Affleck's face became serious.

"What's that?"

"What do you do for an encore?" They laughed.

Rina joined them. "Are you laughing at me?" She was pregnant again, and feeling awkward.

Affleck kissed her. "Who else do we know that could make us all laugh, my lovely Hertz girl?"

The baby was born four months later while Corbin and his wife were off on a world cruise which they joined in Marseilles; the same ship, different companion.

On the day Bayana Donna Affleck was born to the retired Hertz girl in Ottawa, Lt. Colonel Lev Asher was interviewing another Hertz girl on active service in Zurich.

"That's a pretty detailed description of someone you saw only for a few minutes, Miss Reutger."

It wasn't that he doubted her word, but he wanted to be absolutely sure where the dividing line lay between the helpful imagination and accurate detail.

"You don't believe me?"

He held up his hands, fingers spread in protest. "I didn't say that. But it has been over two weeks since you saw this man, and memory sometimes can play little tricks without our realizing it."

She smoothed her skirt, and considered his challenge to her description of the smiling stocky Arab gentleman who had rented the blue Cortina sedan the police had found abandoned near Davos. She recalled the events vividly.

"I guess it was because I had just come on shift and we don't get that many Arabs renting Cortinas; they usually go for the limos or have their own cars waiting for them." She shrugged. "Anyway the police asked me all these same questions three days after he took the car, so it wasn't that long after the events I first told someone this story."

Asher stood up. He had read her report in Debrisay's office that morning. The inspector had been cautiously cooperative. Cautious, because he could not afford to let a double murder by person or persons unknown get blown out of proportion, less the country's tourist business suffer; but cooperative, because, in a sense, Asher was a fellow police officer and like himself, a Jew.

"Well, thank you very much for your time and trouble, Miss Reutger. I'll let you get back to work. I'm sure you have better things to do than sit in here answering my silly questions."

He grinned apologetically and stood aside, opening the door from the little office back to the rental counter, and followed her out. He gave a friendly wave of thanks and sauntered into the office shop to consider everything he had assembled on the case thus far. It still didn't make much sense.

Bruner had lied to him of course, when he said he didn't know the Arab's identity, but then Bruner was scared. Scared to death. He had finally run him down in Amman. He remembered poor old Max had nearly fainted when he opened the apartment door and saw Asher standing there.

"Hullo Max, where th'hell have you been?"

The two week silence annoyed him. He walked in and sat down, stretching his bad leg out comfortably. "Well, what's new and exciting?"

It had taken nearly two hours to worm the story out of him; everything he needed to know, except the identity of the Arab. Bruner kept insisting the only reason he had decided to follow the man was because he had seen him once in Lebanon talking to Jamil and thought it might be worth a lead. No, Jamil had not introduced them, he had only seen him once.

"So here you are between flights, sitting in Zurich Airport on your way to investigate a doctor in Frankfurt, when you get side-tracked, accidentally, by an Arab you saw once five years ago—you *think*—talking to Jamil. You follow him in a chauffeur driven limousine to a sanitarium, where he murders two people and vanishes. No wonder the Swiss police thought you probably did it, using the Arab as a decoy. Any idea who the two people were?"

Bruner shook his head. "When they let me out of jail I went straight to the airport and got the first flight back to Amman. Do you want a drink, Major?"

"Colonel, actually—no thanks."

He waited for the usual sarcastic comment from Bruner on his promotion. Max acted as if he hadn't heard and went over to fix himself a glass. Asher watched him curiously. The newspaperman was nervous, that much was obvious; almost on the point of panic, as if he were expecting a visit.

"Are you waiting for someone, Max?"

Bruner looked at him quickly. "Who?"

"You tell me!"

"No, no one that I know of." He went over to his chair and stood, leaning across the back. "I'm sorry I couldn't find anything more for you. Maybe your people will do better," he suggested hopefully.

"Maybe. We'll see." There was no point in pressuring him further or he might disappear altogether, and Asher still had plans for Bruner. He pulled his leg into the proper position for the least amount of pain and stood up.

"I'll see if I can sort it out for us, Max. You'll be here?"

Bruner nodded. "Sure, where else would I be?"

The tall Jew paused by the door. "By the way, you know the Beirut office has been closed down—two or three weeks ago. They cleaned everything out and vanished."

"No, I didn't."

"Which means Jamil has returned."

"Has he?" Bruner's face blanched.

"He phoned the girl from the airport. I've heard the tapes. When our man checked the place next day it was empty. Any idea where they might have gone?"

Max remembered the old man at the tiny store in the village near the camp. Jamil and Bernadette would be in Damascus now with the rest of the group; Akbar too.

"No, Colonel, I haven't the slightest idea."

Asher smiled and waved goodbye. He knew Bruner was lying. After arranging around the clock surveillance with Jordanian intelligence, he caught the first flight into Zurich to pick up the trail.

He ordered a second cup of coffee from the matronly Swiss who passed his spot at the counter. Inspector Debrisay had shown him copies of the telexes to the German government, translating their contents word by word, then the replies from Bonn. He knew the man, Rolf Hauser, was the son of Doctor Kurt Hauser and that both father and son had been in the little banana republic of Cosecha Rica together for the past two years. The father working for Blucher Chemicals, the son working at the National Television station. The son leaves, and a week later he is dead, along with his girlfriend; killed by a professional Palestinian assassin. It made no sense.

He was certain the woman, the girlfriend, had been killed because she was with Hauser at the wrong time. Those phone calls from Frankfurt, where everything had started, could be verified as coming out of the Blucher Chemicals office by copies of the long distance charges from the telephone company—but only if that is where the calls had in fact originated. If they had come from some other location, he was stumped.

He resolved to leave at once for Frankfurt. *If they were Blucher Chemical calls,* he thought, *then Hauser could be the doctor. If Hauser is the doctor, then Jamil knows him. And if Jamil knows him and was with him, it means Jamil was in the banana republic on or about the time young Hauser left.* He stirred his fresh cup of coffee absently. *But why would a Palestinian terrorist be interested in a German doctor working in a chemical company in Latin America?* It would take him weeks to unravel the mystery and a great deal of money for travel expenses. He wasn't at all sure Brigadier Borodam would approve, either the time tied up on the investigation, or the money he would have to draw from Central Fund to pay the cost. The whole thing was too vague yet to make any positive assertions, and worst of all, at no point along the way was there any evidence of a threat to the lives of Israeli Nationals. It was pretty thin. He left the half-filled coffee cup and limped out to the phone booths to call Tel Aviv for permission to continue on to Frankfurt. The thought occurred it would be a good idea if he could get Sgt. Kronig to join him. With the cold Winter weather in Germany and his bad leg, he knew the investigation could take twice as long as it should. With Kronig doing the legwork, he could spend his time on the telephone plotting the course of events.

"Hello! Asher here, Sir." He adjusted the receiver and began to make his pitch to Brigadier Borodam in Tel Aviv.

Defense Headquarters is an imposing grey granite building in downtown Ottawa. All day long and well into the evenings, green uniformed members of the Canadian Armed Forces march in and out past the heavy glass doors. Army, Navy, Air Force—the uniform is the same: dark forest green, like most of the country, with flashes of gold or insignias setting off the drab uniformity of dress. There are some civilians, and a few enlisted men, but they are the faceless mass of people who make the gears within the defense structure mesh and are therefore unimportant. The green uniforms with the golden stripes are in charge.

On the seventh floor, Corporal Winston, Photographic Analysis

Grade 3, pushed his chair on the roller casters away from the scanner and scratched a small pimple on his neck. He was nineteen and the sebaceous turmoils of puberty were hanging on to the bitter end.

"Sergeant Collins!" He looked around the tables for his superior.

Collins was sitting at one end of the long table piled high with eight-by-ten photographs, talking to the luscious new dispatcher transferred in two days earlier. She was twenty-three, or so her *Form 744* stated. Winston had read it carefully the day before she arrived, sighed and tossed the card with her small square photo aside, knowing he was too young for a play. Then, when she turned up—wow! Talk about lack of photographic resolution! Of course, Sergeant Collins had moved right in like a hound dog and for all young Winston knew was probably already banging her. It was a real piss-off being nineteen.

He stood up, picked the photograph he had been studying off the scanner and ambled down the aisle between the rows of Grade 3's and 4's hunched over their scopes, checking out their various photographic piles. Bob Norman goosed him as he passed behind his chair; Winston slugged him on the shoulder affectionately without pausing. The Sergeant and the gorgeous piece of stuff were laughing over some joke as he came up.

"Well?" Sergeant Collins put on his severe authoritative look, reserved for special occasions like inspections by Lieutenant Bonnycastle or Captain Harmon . . . or impressing gorgeous new dispatchers.

"Sorry Sarge. This one here—it's a BB 113." Photographs were classified under a secrecy code. BB was almost an A classification, and A was top-secret. He handed Collins the curled picture. The sergeant glanced at it quickly and looked up.

"So?"

"It doesn't make sense. There's a change from the original BB 113." He leaned forward slightly, peeking down the dispatcher's dress front. *Shit! She's wearing a bra.* He started getting a hardon anyway.

"Pull the BB 113 file, Miss Whitelaw." The Sergeant was suddenly all business. The dispatcher went off to central records to find the folder.

"You have the original, Winston?"

"At my desk."

"Let's look at it!" Collins got up and followed the Corporal back to his space. He banged Bob Norman's nose into the scanner as he passed, making it look like an accident.

"Oops, sorry Bob!" Collins said nothing. He took the original photograph from Winston and held it up alongside the newer one, studying both carefully. The kid was right, there was a variation. "Tracks from a wheeled vehicle—looks like someone tried to sweep away the evidence, eh?"

"But it doesn't make sense, Sarge." He pointed across Collins' arm to the tracks. "See, they start mid-fenceline there, and run around the edge of the reservoir over to there. There's no tracks in or out of the compound from the gate or the fenceline."

Collins recognized the place now. A nuclear waste storage pool for one of the CANDU reactors at some place in South America—or Central America; he had never been able to sort the two geographic areas out in his mind.

"This the last one in?" He turned the photograph with the mysterious tracks over and answered his own question. A date stamp showed it had been taken the previous week by photo reconnaissance. The other picture, dog-eared at one corner, bore a 1973 date stamp. The dispatcher came back into the huge room lugging a brown accordian folder.

"Over here, Miss Whitelaw!" Corporal Winston called.

Collins snapped the rubber attachment banding aside and pulled out the stack of photographs, then sat down, clearing a space for himself on the littered desk. Slowly, he went through the set one-by-one; quarterly aerial reconnaissance shots of the nuclear waste storage pools at Punta Delgado. Everything appeared normal until he reached the last three in the series. The tracks were there again, but slightly different in appearance; in the second to last photograph they had vanished, then in the last picture, the one taken the week before, they were back again. He slipped the two track prints under the magnifier and studied them. Winston was quite correct; they had been made by tire marks from a wheeled vehicle of some sort. Narrow track, wide tires—soft tires with no tread. He sat back considering the evidence.

"Good work, Corporal. I'll mention your name in my report to Captain Harmon." He stood up and scooped everything into the folder. "Carry on!"

Winston watched Miss Whitelaw's ass roll seductively as she followed the Sergeant back to the desk at the end of the aisle. He just wished Bob Norman would reach out and goose her too as she passed his chair—but he didn't.

547

"Okay Morris, let's have it—what's your problem?" Affleck gave Levy his perfect smile.

"You're guessing. How do you know I have one?"

"Hah! Some guess. You phone me at exactly nine and suggest lunch, then offer to pay the tab—*that* was the giveaway. You're too tight fisted to take anyone out to lunch on your own so its got to be on the expense account; since you're not sufficiently corruptible to cheat Atomic Energy Commission on expenses, ergo, this is a business meeting."

Levy laughed. "You should have been a lawyer." He dropped his napkin on the table. "Okay, you're right. It's business. We've had a red light from Punta Delgado. I thought you might be able to help —knowing the people down there. We don't want to start making nasty noises if there's nothing to get worked up about. On the other hand . . ."

"On the other hand, if there is, you want to know about it now."

"Exactly."

"Okay, let's hear it." He pushed himself away from the table and crossed his legs comfortably. The noontime rush had started to thin the occupied tables nearby. Levy presented the full story he had received from Defense Headquarters the day before, written in the dull dry language of factual reporting, without embellishment or comment. Two photographs had indicated the fact someone or something had circumscribed 809 feet with soil disturbance around the nuclear waste storage pool. There had been no suggestion, observation or theories offered, only the factual interpretation of photographic evidence. Affleck listened to the story, glancing from time to time at the report Morris had handed to him, as if in some way the answer lay on the white page between the typewritten lines. When Levy finished, he looked across the table expectantly.

"Any ideas?"

Affleck handed back the memo. "Have you seen the photographs?"

Levy shook his head.

"It's pretty bare-bones information to get worked up over, isn't it?"

"Is it?" He scratched his cheek. "I phoned the photo interpreter down at Defense Headquarters—a Sergeant Collins. His opinion, and of course it is only an opinion, is the tracks were made by a narrow gauge vehicle using low pressure balloon tires, and that the marks between the two pictures differed substantially—as if someone tried to sweep away the evidence of their movements, missing a few sections along the way."

"Which could mean whoever it was is working at night with no lights," Affleck extrapolated.

Morris nodded. "Exactly what I thought."

"I agree. There's probably a rational explanation for the whole thing. But do you see the problem, Don?"

"You want a bird-dog to go down and sniff around the marshes just in case the ducks turn out to be wood decoys, before issuing a formal request for an investigation at ambassadorial level and everyone makes fools of themselves."

"On the other hand, if you should discover that they are live ducks, and not decoys, you must return to the blind at once and let the hunter decide on a course of action."

"I think you'll find the ducks are decoys, Morris."

"I hope so. After this Argentina business and the publicity over the Korean sale, all we need is someone to come charging out of the marshes waving a red flag on how unsafe our inspection safeguards are—the whole business could come falling down around our ears."

Affleck laughed.

"You can laugh, Don, but I'm the one that will get it in the ass."

"I wasn't laughing at you. I was thinking of how Rina had been pestering me for three years to spend Christmas holidays at home in the sun—it looks like she had finally managed to persuade me!"

Morris grinned. "Thanks, Don. I appreciate it."

"For queen and country!" Affleck said solemnly, placing a hand at his heart.

"It's not your country and she's not your queen." Levy stood up, taking his check stub and American Express card off the plate.

"You're wrong, Morris. If your Sergeant whatshisname at Defense Headquarters is right, this is a problem which is going to affect us all. There are no citizenships or countries—no kings or queens or presidents—just a lot of people in a very small world," he said seriously. "If India could do it in 1974, why not Cosecha Rica in 1976?"

Morris met his eyes for an instant. "Why not indeed?"

It was always hot inside the radiation suit; not uncomfortable during the first part of the work, the ride down the long tunnel to the hatch room, but after that, it was sheer hell. He realized now they should have designed air conditioning systems into the oxygen supply packs in addition to their breathing supply. It would have meant they would have been able to work in comfort instead of pouring the perspiration out of their boots at the end of each recovery operation. It was incredible the amount of liquid the body could expel during these three hour sorties out to the storage pool; they were actually ankle deep in their own fluids when they left the hot room to undress.

It was dangerous too. There was no way of keeping the thick glass face plates cleared from fogging. Trying to work at night always required extra caution because the smallest mistake could mean disaster; trying to work in the blackness behind the foggy face plates was next to impossible; yet, somehow they had done it. The sweep-up of wheel tracks from the electric dolly finally had to be abandoned after missing sections of the evidence because of this inability to see. Now they took turns going back in ordinary coveralls the next night after a removal, and swept the tracks meticulously clean.

There was, of course, always a danger someone would see the marks during the daylight hours, but he had studied the schedule of waste deliveries from the nuclear plant to the pool for months before they started recovery operations; like a government paycheck, the self-propelled crane from Punta Delgado lumbered down the tracks only on the fifteenth and the last day of every month, carrying its swaying load of expended fuel bundles and lowering them carefully into the storage pool along with the others.

Dietrich slowed the vehicle as the lighted hatch room at the end of the tunnel started to race dangerously towards them. He pulled smoothly on top of the duel white lines and switched off the motor. Everyone climbed out and waddled to their loading positions; Dietrich waited by the little car.

"Ready?" Sauve's voice came in from the bulky suit standing by the control panel. Through the headphones, his voice resembled the reception from an early radio broadcast of the Thirties, scratchy and flat.

Dietrich nodded inside his headpiece—a pointless gesture, since the helmet was immobile.

"Ready!" Sauve punched the panel button and with a whirring of machinery the two channel ramps swung down from the roof, extending in length as they dropped, stopping at last directly before the two white lines on the floor.

Dietrich unhooked the cables from their retaining shackles on each ramp and fastened them to the two hooks on the chassis frame between the front wheels. He waved at Sauve to take in the slack.

Another motor rumbled, the cables tightened, the car moved forward, paused on the lip of the ramps, then began climbing slowly towards the roof at a precarious sixty degree angle. Sauve stopped the motor before it reached the top. Next, he lowered the hydraulic ladder from the roof, extending its telescopic legs between the ramps. Kraus joined Dietrich as the steel ladder posts reached the concrete floor and guided them into the recessed lock holder sunk in the cement.

"Lights!" Sauve's tinny voice came into their helmets. Suddenly they were in darkness. Dietrich began to climb the ladder, Kraus directly behind him. Above them the hatch dome was bathed in red light, then Berger lowered the beam down the ladder, illuminating Dietrich's hands. It followed him up the narrow web to the top, then stopped. He clipped his safety belt to the last rung and reached for the inner wheel lock. He spun it. Next, Berger's beam followed Dietrich's hands over to the wheel lock for the main exit hatch. The light remained until there was no further movement from the second wheel, then, abruptly, it went out.

At the top of the ladder, Dietrich pushed the small circular lid open a few inches, paused, then swung it back, disconnecting his safety belt, climbing out into the starry night. He looked around quickly. Everything was black and peaceful. Kraus joined him, and a few moments later, Berger appeared. They waited by the small hatch until Berger emerged, then closed it softly.

"Thirty seconds to lift!" the tinny voice said. They waddled away, towards the pool, fat black snowmen with shiny glass faces, turned and waited. They were beginning to perspire from the few minutes of effort.

"Lifting now!" It was surprising how silently the main exit hatch opened; the tremendous power of the subterranean motors. The two thousand pound cover rose softly, smoothly, like some giant clam, until it reached a thirty degree angle, then stopped. Sometimes bits of dirt and gravel would slide a few feet, but generally the disturbance was slight.

They waddled back to the front of the black opening, waiting.

"Launching now!" Outside in the night air with the muffled sound of the breakers a few hundred yards away, the deep grumbling cable motor was indistinguishable from the ocean. The nose of the dolly appeared at the lip of the opening, then stopped. Dietrich climbed into the driver's seat, pulled the handbrake, and started its engine while the other two disconnected the cables. When they stepped aside he gunned the motor and rolled out onto the ground.

Berger and Kraus laid the cables inside the ramp, then climbed aboard the vehicle.

As they drove off, the clamshell started closing. Dietrich skirted around the pool to the far side, near the railway tracks and stopped. Now the sweaty work began. The collapsible crane was a miracle of engineering design; at least Dietrich thought so. He had designed it. Weighing just a shade under two hundred pounds and built of thin tubular black stainless steel, the parts fitted together with the precision of a Swiss watch. Assembled, it could raise a thousand pounds with the lifting arm extended twenty-two feet past its base line. Even Doctor Kastenburg had complimented him on the achievement.

Swiftly they untied the parts from the dolly and carried them over by the pool. They began their assembly. It took ten minutes to put it together, string the pulleys and ready the unit for their evening's work. Dietrich lugged the first case load of dummy fuel bundles over to the hoist and set it carefully on the cement coping along the pool's edge. Everyone finished their chores simultaneously and looked at each other. They were ready to start work.

Dietrich swung the crane arm out over the water, steadied it, then signaled to lower the cable. The big hook dropped through the dark surface with a small splash and sank from view. He waited until the flourescent mark on the cable touched the water, then signaled Kraus and Berger to stop. Kraus joined Dietrich, and together they slipped the glass-bottomed viewing tub into the water, and turned on its floodlight. Instantly, the narrow beam illuminated the pool bottom.

The containers all looked alike; except for their curved cable handles, the genuine ones were dull black; the replacements, which had been substituted over the past months, glowed eerily under the water light. There were only four of the genuine articles remaining at the bottom of the pool. Dietrich could see the hook sitting a few inches above and to the left of one of them. He motioned to Berger to lower the cable, slowly, slowly, then waved him to stop. Perfect. He gently pulled the hoist retraction backwards, watching it nuzzle the dull cable handle on the first box of fuel bundles. The hook slid by. Missed. He began extending the travel; the hook turned slightly, and slipped neatly onto the handle. He motioned Berger to take up the slack, then bent down to help Kraus lift the viewing tub out of the water. They went back to join Berger. Pulling together, they lifted the dripping container clear and swung it in a full arc around to the dolly, then lowered it onto the rear platform. Dietrich waddled over to disconnect the hook. He tied the container down on its bed. They had to move fast now. The bundles were hot, and would get hotter the longer they remained out of the water. They swung the dummy container into the vacant position at the bottom of the pool, then pulled the cable hoist in swiftly. A few minutes later they had the whole crane unit knocked down and packed back neatly on the little vehicle. Now they could barely see through the face plates and their feet felt squishy in the lead-lined boots. Dietrich climbed into the dolly and headed back to the tunnel hatch.

Later, in the shower room, after they had shed their contaminated radiation suits, they laughed and clapped each other on the back. It was over. They had completed the last load. Doctors Kastenburg and Hauser watched their antics from the other side of the thick safety glass. They were smiling too.

"If I didn't know Berger as I do, Heinz, I'd swear he was having an affair with young Dietrich!"

"Ach Soo." Kastenburg chuckled.

The ship was in Rio when Corbin received the telegram from his partner. *"Red light at Punta. Morris suggested we holiday in the sun 20th to New Year. Love, Rina and Don."*

Nineteen words. He slipped the message into his jacket and joined Elizabeth and the others, who had signed for the tour up the Sugar Loaf by cable car. He handed his wife the flimsy note once they were seated in the bus.

"Punta?"

"Punta Delgado. It's some problem with the nuclear plant," he explained.

"I'm guessing Morris asked Don to go down and investigate some rumors—if they were rumors."

"Serious?" She looked concerned. The bus door closed, then with a hiss of releasing air brakes, they moved through the dockyard and out into the frantic Rio traffic, weaving towards Sugar Loaf mountain, rising baldly beyond the beach at Copacabana. Corbin was thinking. "It could be serious, then again it could be a conspiracy between Rina and Sarah Levy to get Don to take her back home with the kids for the holidays." He smiled as he looked over. "I hope it's the latter. I'll try to phone tonight, and see what's going on. In any event, my love," he patted her hand, browned from the long sunny ocean voyage, "it would take hell to freeze over before I'd agree to abort this trip. We have until January 29th when the boat docks in New York. We can worry about Morris Levy's problems after that!"

She leaned over and kissed him. "I love you, Charles Corbin."

"I know, sweetheart—ain't it a drag?"

In Amman Max Bruner received a telegram the same day from his employer. It was even shorter. *"Return New York immediately. Urgent discussions. B.J."*

He had started a second book, "The Doctrine of Donkeys." It was more an exercise to vent his frustrations and anger at being trapped in the see-saw between the Israeli Colonel and Jamil than any sense of literary achievement. But, as he began to get into the second chapter, his personal conflicts started receding as the objectivity of a professional newspaper reporter took over. It could develop into another important work, he decided. He tore up the rubbish he had written in the first chapter and began again; then the telegram arrived. He realized the reason for the urgent meeting: the final ultimatum. Get to work or get out! He couldn't fault his employer on that. He hadn't sent a single line of copy out to New York in weeks. His deposit monies from the Colonel were still coming in, and although it had been over a week since the limping man had left his apartment, he was certain that source of money would dry up shortly too. As he packed, he considered the possibility of leaving for good, taking everything and high-tailing it back home. He could work the lecture circuit for a year or two, finish his second book and, who knew what . . . it might be turned into a movie, or a TV special . . . anything was better than sitting around the Middle East caught between his own personal fears of reprisal from warring factions. He packed everything, delaying his trip an extra two days in order to arrange shipment of the bulky items he wanted to keep. When he left for the airport, the apartment was bare.

The New York streets were packed with porno shops, porno theaters, porno panderers and Christmas shoppers, walking hurriedly through the light skiff of snow that had fallen during the day. It was good to be home. He checked into the Travelers Hotel and took a cab over to the office.

"Well, you took your fucking time getting here!" B.J. roared, crashing out of his office after the girl had announced the late visitor. "When I said *urgent*, I meant *urgent!*" Magically the cigar rolled across his lips, then clenched to a stop on the other side of his fat face.

"I had to pack—sorry," Bruner said weakly.

"Yeah, yeah, Middle East heirlooms—one book and you're a prima donna already!" He turned like a Mark IV on one tread and stormed back to his office, then stopped by the glass door, realizing

Bruner wasn't behind him.

"Well!" he yelled, "whaddy' want, Max, an invite?"

Bruner walked into the cluttered room and dropped to a chair, watching B.J. warily. He was exhausted. He had been sitting in airlines for thirteen hours and awake for twenty. He felt punchy.

"Have a cigar!" B.J. pushed the rosewood humidor at him. It was a command, not an invitation. Max obeyed. The fat man behind the desk waited until his employee had the long black stick glowing properly, and had taken his first mouthful of mild flavored smoke.

"Great cigar, eh! That's real Havana, Max, none of that phony muleshit and burnt rope they're selling now days—I have *a friend*," he added modestly with a wink.

B.J. always had a friend. Bruner nodded cautiously, allowing himself a tight smile. His dulled mind began to work, pushing aside the fuzziness of thoughts. Something was wrong. B.J. hadn't brought him back to fire him at all, there was something else in the wind. He braced himself.

"You're a good man, Max, one of the best reporters I got. An' that's straight scoop—no bullshit! You got that booze problem licked on your own a few years back an' since then you've never looked back. I been proud of y'boy."

Bruner knew he and B.J. were the same age. It was the buildup for the attack; he understood the man too well to be wrong.

"We've had our ups and downs, haven't we—over the years I haven't agreed with your approach on everything you've written. But I always let it go just the way you wrote it, right?" Bruner prevented himself from replying by taking a long pull on the Havana.

"In fact, you might say I made you what you are today, right?"

This time he had to answer. "Why don't you get to the point, B.J. I'm too tired for compliments on my writing abilities."

The big Jew scowled at him for an instant, then softened his features. "Can't pull the wool over your eyes, can I?"

"Not so far."

"Okay, then I'll lay it on you, straight out and flat." He placed his cigar stub on the ashtray.

"You've met Colonel Asher, Max. Tell me what you think of him."

So, the name of the limping man was Asher, Bruner thought. He felt himself go cold.

"I think he's a very dedicated Israeli intelligence officer." He was on the verge of asking why, then decided there was no point because B.J. was going to tell him in due course anyway.

His employer nodded in agreement. "A very dedicated officer. He's come up through the ranks quickly. Smart. Smart like a fox. A real gentleman."

It wasn't quite the noun Bruner would have used to describe his tormentor, but he kept silent.

"He likes you, Max; did you know that?"

Bruner couldn't believe the man's gall. "Gee, B.J. that's sweet of him. I'm sort of fond of him too," he said sarcastically.

"He thinks you're real folks."

Bruner decided, even for B.J., this was laying it on a bit thick. "Look, can we get to the point. I gather Colonel Asher has been in touch with you and wants to have another mysterious meeting in Greenwich at the Nelson bust, or is he going whole hog this time putting it on top of the Admiral's monument in Trafalgar Square?"

"Max boy, what's eating you?" He positively cooed concern. "This isn't like you."

Bruner waited. B.J. pursed his lips, considering a different attack.

"He needs your help, Max, he's asking for it, he needs it badly."

"Well, at least that'll be a change. The last time, he locked me up for a month and knocked out two bicuspids."

It wasn't true exactly; it had been the Jordanian who had slugged him, but at this point Bruner was in no mood to discuss the finer points of his captivity. B.J. shrugged his fat shoulders apologetically.

"Fortunes of war. He didn't know you then, Max."

"But he does now, is that it?"

"Will you help?"

"In a word, B.J.—no."

"You're being unfair. Your job, your assignment isn't finished. What sort of a newsman leaves his assignment unfinished?"

"I've become a non-combatant, an advocate of peace, a conscientious objector, a coward. I want to live to enjoy my old age."

The glass door opened suddenly and there was the limping colonel in the flesh and smiling. Bruner groaned.

"Hello Max, glad you could make it. Have a good trip over?"

He came in, closed the door and sat down, straightening his leg manually. Bruner squirmed uncomfortably in his chair, wishing he could vanish. It was too late. They had trapped him.

"The answer, Colonel Asher, is no—*no*."

The Israeli ignored him. "I picked up the trail in Zurich, Max, the day after we had our last chat. The dead man was Rolf Hauser, son of Doctor Kurt Hauser, from Frankfurt. The woman was his girlfriend. Pity about the girl. I went to Frankfurt and checked with the local police. Doctor Hauser works for Blucher Chemicals in the Republic of Cosecha Rica. The telephone records of Blucher Chemicals' Frankfurt office show numerous calls made to Jamil's office in Beirut." He paused.

"Interesting," Bruner observed, and it *was* interesting all of a sudden. "Go on; what else did you find out?"

"The Doctor's son had been back from a two year visit with his father only a couple of weeks when he was murdered by your friends. Now I ask myself, why would Jamil want to murder the son of a German chemist in Switzerland, and why would the office of the German chemist be phoning Jamil's office in Beirut? Any ideas?"

Bruner was fascinated. "Is the doctor a Jew?"

Asher shook his head. "He was a card carrying Nazi in the old days."

"What's the story in Cosecha Rica—Have you checked that out?"

"No, not yet. I thought maybe you could help me out on that . . . if you will?" he added.

Bruner stood up and began to pace. "He never said a word at any time about Latin America." He stopped. "No, wait a minute! Jamil did say something once about working in Central America for a few months, during the military takeover in some country; a popular revolution by some local hero—let me see if I remember the name . . . ."

"Chirlo?" Asher suggested.

"That was it! Chirlo—Colonel Chirlo!" Bruner agreed.

"He's the President's son—son-in-law too, as I understand. Complicated business."

"You know him?"

"Wouldn't know him if I fell over him, Max. Latin America isn't my forte, I'm afraid."

"Nor mine, Colonel." He looked closely at the Israeli. "You didn't want me to go to Cosecha Rica by any chance, did you?"

"I don't see why not. There's no war down there. I give you my word Jamil is in the Middle East and you can probably count the number of Arabs and Jews in the country on one hand. Think you can handle it?" He made it sound as if he didn't really care one way or the other.

Bruner thought about it as he sat down. He picked up the rich Havana again.

"Why me? You're the intelligence expert."

Asher glanced at B.J. "It's a matter of finances, Max," B.J. explained quietly. "The colonel can't get the clearance for funds to go south and spend days or weeks chasing down leads without some proof to his superiors that there is a threat to Israel."

"Is there a threat?" Bruner looked at Asher.

"I don't know. There may be nothing, in which case the reluctance by my superiors is fully justified. On the other hand, there may be something afoot which concerns us vitally. So your employer has generously agreed to foot the bill to send you down to investigate on our behalf—and of course, on his own. There might be a story in it."

"I see." Now he did. He should have been smart enough to know B.J. wouldn't have paid the cost of an airline ticket from Amman to New York for the privilege of firing him face to face when he could do the same thing in a night letter for less than five bucks. It was an intriguing proposition. He had never been to Latin America.

"What exactly do you want me to do, Colonel?"

"Attaboy Max! Knew I could count on you."

"Now wait a minute, B.J., I haven't agreed to anything yet."

"Goddamnit, Max, stop fucking me around! I'm assigning you to Cosecha Rica and that's it!"

"I'd like to know several things," Asher interjected quickly. "First, you can start with Doctor Hauser—why is he there and what is he doing and why was his son there for so long? Is there still a relationship between Jamil and this chap Chirlo, or with Chirlo and Hauser? Finally, are there any apparent Arab or Middle East interests within the country? Think you can handle that?"

Bruner knew he could. It was a straight reporting job on interviews with the principals. Simple stuff, but interesting because of his own personal involvement.

"Do I get a raise, B.J.?" It was worth a try.

"A raise? You shmuck! For weeks you sit on your ass in Amman and send me zilch, now you want a raise already when I tell you to go to work!"

"Okay, don't get huffy—I only asked."

"Well don't." He plucked the cigar butt from the ashtray and stabbed it between his lips.

"Whom do I report back to?"

"Who th'hell do you think you report to, dummy—me, the guy that's paying your bills!"

It was good to see B.J. revert to form; for some reason it made

Max feel more comfortable with the man.

"Okay. Again, I only asked."

It took Affleck a full two days before he could escape the clutches of his in-laws for a visit to the Punta Delgado site. He didn't want to appear in a rush to visit the place, knowing full well if anything strange was taking place, his sudden appearance would be noticed instantly. He borrowed his father-in-law's car on the afternoon of the second day, casually suggesting he thought he'd drop over to the nuclear plant to look up some of his pals.

They held him at the gate until someone had the guard describe the visitor over the phone, then he was permitted to enter. Things had tightened up since his last visit. He was agreeably surprised, after the casual way people had come and gone during his tenure.

A young man met him at the door and handed him a visitor's badge with a film strip.

"Are you expecting radiation in the administration building?"

"Rules, Senor Affleck. Everyone on the premises wears a strip."

He followed the officious young man past the reception desk and down the corridor to a door marked "Privado Securidad," and was ushered in with a polite smile.

"Hello Don, I heard you were back for the holidays!" It was Ballinger—he'd forgotten his first name. The man was a twerp, a petty nuisance who had somehow managed to worm his way into a permanent job when local government takeover became official and the construction crews departed for home.

"Hello Ballinger. You holding the security fort now?"

"Right on, Don, right on." He looked immensely pleased with himself.

"Who's in charge?"

"Numero Uno is Doctor Manuel Dorando, Ph.D. Mexico City, Cum Laude. He's away at a conference in Argentina."

For some postgraduate work?" Sarcasm was lost on Ballinger.

"Hell no, they've just started getting their nuke on stream— didn't you hear about it?"

"Who's numero secundo?"

"Slinky Slavez—foreigner from Bulgaria or Hungary—some place like that."

"But he did manage to get through grade school?" This time Ballinger caught the sarcasm.

"Doctor Kortig Slavez, Ph.D., University of California, Berkeley,

I think." He pawed the rotary file at his desk to the S divider, flipped through a few cards, then looked up. "Yeah, Class of '54. Everyone calls him Slinky, though." He didn't explain why.

"Is Slinky in?"

"Sure Don, do you want to see him?"

"It would be nice if you could arrange it, Ballinger."

"Sure thing—no trouble at all." He went to his desk and made the arrangements.

Affleck noted when he got the Doctor on the phone, Ballinger became appropriately servile.

"Yes Doctor Slavez, he's here now. Yes Sir, I'll bring him right up."

He put the phone down and looked up with a big smile.

"There you are, Don, Slinky says he'll see you. Follow me!"

Affleck trailed him out to the stairs and up to the top floor where the executive offices were located. Ballinger knocked softly and went in.

"Mr. Donald Affleck from CORCAN, Ottawa, Canada," he announced grandly.

Affleck entered the room and went across the carpet to meet Dr. Slavez.

"Thank you, Mr. Ballinger, that will be all," the doctor said firmly as he shook Affleck's hand. The hand was thin and boney but the grip firm.

"Mr. Affleck, a great pleasure—please, won't you sit down?"

Slavez came around and joined him in another chair on the informal side of his desk. Both glanced over at the door closing behind Ballinger. Slavez grimaced slightly and Affleck laughed.

"A prize example of a horse's ass, Doctor Slavez. I'm surprised he's still here!"

For an instant the doctor looked nonplused, then burst out laughing. He had a deep resonant laugh which sounded strange coming from such a small body.

"So you know our Mr. Ballinger from the old days?"

"One of our employees—not a very good one."

"Now he is chief of our security—how the minutiae have risen, Mr. Affleck!"

"They always seem to manage it somehow."

They were silent, sizing each other up, liking what they saw.

"How can I be of service, Mr. Affleck?" He pronounced his English words with a Slavic accent, mastering the consonants masterfully.

"Nothing in particular, Doctor. I'm here with my wife, visiting her family—my in-laws—and thought I'd escape for the afternoon to do an auld lang syne.

"Auld lang syne?"

"See if the place had fallen apart since I helped build it."

"Oh, I see. Yes, of course—returning to the scene of the crime!" They both chuckled.

"How are the outside storage pools standing up? We built them as an afterthought."

"No trouble I've heard of. We've had several breakdowns on the railway crane; difficulties with bearings on the turret swivel, I understand, otherwise everything is functioning smoothly and well." Slavez seemed satisfied.

"Glad to hear it. How 'bout leaks around the pool base?" Affleck suggested.

"Leaks? No, we have an evaporation problem from time to time. The automatic leveler has never failed to keep the surface height at proper depth."

"Good. Would you mind if I took a look around the place, Doctor?"

"For auld lang syne?" Slavez smiled.

"For auld lang syne."

"I'd be delighted to show you around, Mr. Affleck. Shall we go?" He stood up.

"After you, Doctor Slavez," he said politely, rising with his host.

Hauser passed the binoculars back to Kastenburg. "How long have they been there?"

"A few minutes only. Sauve saw them from the records office; he was in picking up a file. Who is the one with Slavez? He looks American." He raised the glasses, readjusting them for his own eyes.

Two men were standing on the lip of the pool near the far end. They were pointing at the water, moving their hands. Counting!

"They're counting the containers, Kurt," Kastenburg said quietly. He continued to watch, seeing the back of the little doctor's head nodding as he consulted a notebook—at least it looked like a notebook. The two turned away from the pool and walked slowly out by the edge of the rail tracks. Slavez was talking. The other man appeared to be listening, his head bent low to catch the words from the short man . . . or was he looking? The tall man stopped and bent down on one knee, examining the ground.

"I think he's looking for something, Kurt."

Hauser strained his eyes across the fence and beyond to the two small figures. He could see the tall one straighten up.

"Photographic surveillance follow up?"

"Impossible!" Kastenburg lowered the glasses. "What could they see?"

"Wheel tracks."

"There aren't any!" He lifted the binoculars back to his face. Now, the tall man was zig zagging down the wide stretch of ground between the rail tracks and the pool, coming towards their fence line. It took several minutes to cover the area; they came up to the fence and stopped. The tall man seemed interested in something Slavez was telling him about the Blucher compound, pointing to various locations. The tall man nodded, then both returned, walked back unhurriedly to the car, and drove out through the gate. Slavez climbed out to lock it. When the rear end of the Jeepster disappeared down the road beside the fence, heading back to the nuclear plant, Kastenburg lowered the glasses. He rubbed his eyes and looked at Hauser.

"Get on to Slavez and find out who the American is and why they are here."

"I think we should give it a few days, Heinz, before we do anything. If it's an investigation, we don't want to do anything to warn them that we suspect."

Kastenburg rolled the neck strap around the hinge on the binoculars, thinking. "I wonder," he mused. "They didn't come anywhere near the hatch." He set the glasses on the table. "They counted the containers—not an unusual interest from Slavez' standpoint." He faced the window, staring over at the pool, his hands clasped behind his back. "One of them bent down to look at something. What? Then they crossed back and forth looking at the ground until they reached our fence line. Then they went away." He turned suddenly to Hauser. "It's the criss-crossing that worries me. Everything else has a logical reason—except that." He plucked the pince nez from his breast pocket and clipped it to his nose.

"You're quite right, Kurt, we'll make no approach to Slavez for a few days. In the meantime, I think I'll go up to San Ramon and have a talk with Colonel Chirlo. This is something I think he should know."

They finished supper; it was always a treat when their father took time out to eat with them. Chirlo walked back to the sunroom with the three to play games of charades they'd discussed during the meal. He was at the point of arranging places and rules when the maid announced Major Martinez was waiting for him in the library. The children groaned.

"I'll get your mother to sit in for me."

"It's not the same—she won't let us cheat!" one of the twins chimed.

"Neither will I, her father said severely, standing to leave.

"But you never catch us!" young Pedro protested, "so it's legal, isn't it?"

Chirlo paused and gave his youngest son a mock glare before leaving the room. The youngster did have a point, he thought. On the way through the house he asked the maid to find Felina for the children's game.

Major Martinez stiffened respectfully when he entered the room.

"Sit down, Martinez." Even seated, the Major was at attention.

"I have a complete report, Colonel." He waited.

"Well, get on with it!"

"Donald Affleck arrived at Bahia Blanca three days ago with his wife and children by private jet to spend the holidays with the family de Felipe . . . ."

"Who?"

"Don Arnaldo de Felipe, Colonel; he is the father of Rina, father-in-law of the Canadian, Donald Affleck," the Major explained.

"Go on."

Yesterday afternoon he went to the offices of the Nuclear Electrica Nacional to visit friends—according to Don Arnaldo. He spent three hours with Doctor Slavez—Doctor Dorando is away in the Argentine—touring the site. They finished with a short visit to the outside storage pool; according to Doctor Slavez, Mr. Affleck was concerned with possible water leakage from concrete cracks at the pool. It seems proper curing of concrete is prolonged by its immersion in water. Mr. Affleck was interested in how his construction efforts had stood the test of time."

Chirlo made a mental note to look into this point.

"As to their weaving walk to the fence line of Blucher Chemicals, Doctor Slavez stated his guest was examining the area for apparent soft spots in the ground which might indicate water leaks. Earlier they had had some discussions about water levels in the pool dropping due to evaporation; Mr. Affleck thought it could be due to hairline cracks in the cement. Doctor Slavez said they could find no evidence of soft spots along the area they inspected." Martinez stopped.

"Anything else?"

"No, Sir."

"And Affleck has not gone back to the place since then?"

"No, Sir. He has been with his family at Bahia Blanca. They are having a reunion for all the relations this evening. You were invited."

"I was?" Chirlo had received no invitation.

"Senora Affleck forgot to send out the guest list."

Chirlo laughed, remembering the scatterbrained woman Affleck had married.

"Good work, Major. Keep Affleck under surveillance until he leaves. Private jet, eh? I must see it. What is it?" He was planning on a ten place Jetstar for himself as soon as the transaction with Jamil had been concluded. Martinez looked blank.

"I don't know, Sir. I can check with the Air Force and find out, if you wish."

"No, it's not important, Major—merely curious."

"The pilots are staying at the Hotel d'Oro. The Captain is Mr. Rick Rogers, co-pilot . . ."

"Rick Rogers!"

Martinez looked startled. "You know the man, Colonel?"

"Describe him."

"I have his tourist card and photograph here." He opened the thin briefcase and searched the interior. He handed a small card to Chirlo, who glanced at it quickly, then passed it back. He recognized the man who had sold him the two C47 aircraft in Miami which he'd flown to Cuba in 1963 for the assault on Guerrero. Was it sheer coincidence? He wondered.

"Yes, Major, I know him, or knew him a long time ago. He sold me some airplanes."

"Shall I have him watched?"

"Don't bother. They were excellent machines—both of them—as a matter of fact, I might say that in a way you owe your present job to that man." He gave the serious Major a lopsided grin.

"Yes, Sir," Martinez said uncuriously. He replaced the visitor's card in his briefcase and withdrew another.

"Do you know this man, Colonel?"

Chirlo looked at the portrait of the man stapled to the upper right hand corner.

He shook his head. "No—should I?"

"He arrived this morning from New York. He is a newspaper

reporter with C.P. He phoned Doctor Hauser for an appointment to interview him on the death of his son in Switzerland."

Chirlo sensed danger; the light velvet movement up the back of his neck; cold probing fingers startling the scalp.

"Young Hauser is dead?" He was surprised.

"Apparently he was murdered, together with his girlfriend in Switzerland a few weeks ago."

"Do you know why?"

"No, Sir." Martinez had not thought the matter important enough to warrant the expense of phoning the Swiss police. It was an ocean away. He had been thankful the matter had not occurred within his jurisdiction, knowing the ramifications which might evolve in an investigation exposing the Colonel's wife to scandal.

"Follow it through, Major. I want a full report. I sense Doctor Hauser is not a friend—at least towards me."

He had gone to the German compound the week before as a guest with Felina to attend their Christmas party. Of the group of Germans and their families, only Hauser had been cool, snubbing him on at least two occasions that he remembered, probably more, but he had been unaware of the rest, deciding to ignore the man. There was no point in causing friction.

"Yes, Sir. The newsman is real. I checked with his New York office. As a matter of interest, he is also a celebrated author on a book about the Middle East," Martinez elaborated.

"The Middle East?" Chirlo felt the tingling on his scalp again.

"Yes, Colonel. He has lived in the Middle East for many years."

"Around the clock surveillance on him, Major." He stood up, dismissing the intelligence officer, accompanying him to the door.

Afterwards, he went back to his library and took down the volume CA - CU of the encyclopedia, turning the thin pages to CEMENT. He stood, scanning the pages until he came to the paragraph on *curing*. He read the section slowly, then closed the book, sliding it back into its place on the shelf. The information on prolonged curing of cement immersed in water was correct. The threat, visualized by Doctor Kastenburg, faded into the background; the concern now had been replaced by someone named Max Bruner from New York. He went over to his desk and picked up the phone and dialed 0. He pulled the number out from under his cigar box, waiting for the telephone to stop its intermittent buzz. A male voice intercepted the fifth buzz.

"Operator!"

"This is Colonel Chirlo. I want a priority call, classified and secret. Is that clear?"

"Yessir. Where do you want to call, Colonel?"

"Damascus, Syria."

Doctor Kurt Hauser relaxed a little more after meeting the reporter. The man Bruner, a German American, he noted with satisfaction, had a typical open-faced honesty and cynicism typical of anyone in the business of gathering and reporting information told to him by others. Hauser could appreciate that point of view. He shared the same feeling himself.

"Have you lived here long, Doctor Hauser?" They were sitting on the open veranda of the main lodge, Bruner, drinking in the tranquil surroundings along with a glass of excellent Scotch. He had sized the German up at once, a Fatherland type, when there had been a Fatherland, laconic cynicism hiding a shrewd mind. They had been sitting together ten minutes and he had, so far, kept the conversation well outside the purpose of the interview. B.J.'s first order to a news reporter: "Remember, an interview is like wooing a virgin— you gotta get 'em to relax before you slip it in."

"This will be my third year, Mr. Bruner."

"Call me Max."

"Very well, Max. Good German name."

"Father from Westphalia. Will you be staying—permanently, I mean?"

Hauser shrugged. "Who knows. I used to like the country, but I miss the Fatherland. This really is a cultural wasteland, even if it happens to be located in Paradise."

"Your son obviously agreed with those sentiments." He slipped it in smoothly, then took a sip of Scotch.

"Yes, he liked it here too. He had an excellent job with the national television company. My boy had a proficiency with languages. Complete mastery of Spanish—I can barely speak the language now, myself." He sighed. "Yes, Rolf was a good boy. He might have settled down here permanently if he had kept his zipper closed."

"His zipper?" It was a German expression, the English translation obscure.

"His penis in his pants."

"Oh, I see."

"He was very handsome. Women fell all over him. It was his downfall." Hauser was talking so easily, relaxed, as if he was relating an interesting story about a colleague.

"That is why he left?" Bruner suggested.

"That's why he left—or escaped. Yes, *escaped* is a better word. He escaped to his death."

"A woman?"

"A married woman."

"But surely that's not a crime. I think, if I remember correctly, the French call it 'un affair du coeur.' A perfectly understandable situation in a civilized world."

"Hah! You call this country civilized? The woman was the dictator's wife!" he snarled.

Bruner's eyes widened in surprise. "Whew! The man they call Chirlo!"

"Chirlo!" He spat the name, then gulped his drink to the bottom of the glass.

Bruner fell silent, watching two sandpipers dancing near the water's edge, darting away from the small rollers until each wave began to slide back and the birds could chase the thin water, nibbling at the specks of edibles slipping across the wet sand. He wondered: was it a game, or a meal?

"So Chirlo discovered a lovers' tryst." He kept his eyes on the sandpipers, feeling Hauser thinking beside him, trying to decide whether or not to continue discussing this subject of his son. Minutes passed. Bruner thought his moment had fled, then, "No not exactly."

"I see."

"But somehow he found out—it was common knowledge in the Capital at the time."

"The beginning of a scandal—a cause célèbre!"

"Precisely."

The sandpipers flew off suddenly, darting beyond the trees near the dock. The curved beach was deserted. There was another pause. This time Bruner decided to prompt.

"So he was asked to leave—quietly."

Hauser nodded. "I asked him—no—ordered him to get out immediately. I felt if he remained he might be in danger." He looked at Bruner angrily. "And I was right, as you have learned." He nodded, agreeing with himself. "Like a fool, I sent him home to Frankfurt instead of . . . ." He stopped, his anger fading, replaced by sadness. "All I did was to arrange things for him to be murdered in Switzerland instead of here."

"You mean Chirlo did it?"

"Who else?"

Bruner digested the information. He didn't know enough about vendettas of Latins to accept or reject the Doctor's thesis. In America the unfaithful wife syndrome was now almost society's norm and resulted either in reconciliation or divorce; seldom murder. Chirlo tells Jamil his problem. Jamil calls on Akbar to take care of it—for old time's sake. It was just bizarre enough to be real, he thought. Colonel Asher would be disappointed.

"A nasty man to cross, by the sound of things. I'm surprised you're still here, Doctor, after such a tragedy." It was the only thing that didn't make sense.

"I'm under contract. Naturally I have considered requesting a transfer."

"Naturally." But has he? Max wondered.

"Yes, the scarfaced Colonel is a ruthless man, utterly ruthless, merciless, bloodthirsty. You know the story of the heads in the hatboxes?"

"No, I don't believe I do." The steward slipped in between them, replacing the two empty glasses with full ones. Hauser picked up the refill without acknowledging its arrival to the steward.

"He cut the heads off two men in the last Dictator's army and mailed them to his wife in hat boxes. It happened back in 1962 . . . ." He related the tale with relish, confirming his earlier remarks of Chirlo's brutality. " . . . . then had the audacity to send the Dictator a postcard from Cuba informing him he would be back for his head too!"

Bruner listened, spellbound. It was a great story. "And did he?"

"Oh he came back, all right, with a bunch of Middle East mercenaries. They overthrew the Dictator in two years. But no, he never cut off his head. The man was shot during a public meeting in San Ramon—some say it was a CIA plot, others a communist conspiracy; frankly, I think Chirlo arranged the whole thing himself." He sat back in the wicker chair, surveying the ocean front.

"And the mercenaries, what happened to them?"

"Palestinians—you know the type—guerillas—they went home before it was all over, so I've been told. Their leader left too. I heard one of them is still living here. Married a local girl."

"The leader left?"

"It was practically over—he drops back now and again to visit."

"Galal Jamil." Bruner heard the quick intake of breath as he said the name.

"You know him?"

"Heard of him. I lived in the Middle East for a while." He could see the Doctor's lips tighten, the easy relaxed manner of the past hour vanishing with a blink from the cautious blue eyes.

"I'm surprised your Chirlo persuaded the Palestinians to come over here and fight at all. I'd always been under the impression it was Jews, not Latins they were interested in killing!" He laughed lightly, saw Hauser's face relax, but only slightly.

"The only Jew I've met here is one we've got working for us— he's our general sales manager, but he's from San Salvador. I suppose there are some around—they usually are where there's money to be made. No, Jamil and his men didn't come to fight Jews, they came to fight for Chirlo and they won. Now, if you'll excuse me, I have to get back to the plant. We have a toxaphene run scheduled at four and I should be on hand."

Hauser stood up, draining his glass. "Please stay and finish your drink, Mr. Bruner. I'll tell the gate guards to let you out. Its been a pleasure meeting you. I'm sorry I couldn't be of more help, but as you see, the story is not particularly newsworthy—certainly not in America." He smiled wryly. "Of course if you tried to print it here you'd wind up losing your head to a hat box."

Bruner stood and shook hands, thanking him for his time and trouble, then watched him stride back through the lodge and out the back to the parking lot. He signaled the steward over to his chair.

"Do you speak English?"

"Yes, Sir, and Spanish. May I be of service?"

"The general sales manager for the company—do you know his name? I understand he's Jewish." The steward looked blandly disinterested. "Yes, Sir, Mr. David Liebe is the company's general sales manager."

"Where would I find him?"

"Through the office, I would imagine. He does not reside here." The man paused. "Will there be anything else, Sir?"

"No, no thank you." Bruner sat down. The sandpipers had returned to their ocean game. He wondered again: were they the same birds, or different ones playing the same game?

Hotel d'Oro
Bahia Blanca
Cosecha Rica, C.A.

Dear B.J.:

I have decided to write, rather than phone or use the telegraph office here, which is monitored closely by Chirlo's secret police. The reason for my reluctance will become apparent as you read. In the first place, I do not believe there is anything worth bringing Colonel Asher down here to investigate. The Davos murders were done as a favor to Chirlo by Jamil after the Dictator discovered Rolf Hauser had been shacking up with Felina Artega, Chirlo's wife and mother of three. Sensing danger to his son, Doctor Hauser ordered him out of the country to—as he thought—the safety of Germany. Chirlo was enraged by the boy escaping and contacted Jamil, who was in the country at a time on a personal visit (they are old friends from their association in 1962 when Jamil provided Chirlo with the mercenary cadre to start his revolution down here). Chirlo probably asked Jamil to help him settle the score with the younger Hauser, Jamil turned the matter over to one of his group, giving the necessary information to locate the boy, and the rest is history. I think that is all there is to it, frankly.

As far as the Jewish question here is concerned, there isn't one. I spent an enjoyable two hours with David Liebe, the sales manager for Blucher Chemicals, after I spoke to Doctor Hauser. Liebe is an American who settled in Salvador in the Fifties while on his honeymoon because he liked the country, then went into the insurance business which, apparently, was wide open at the time. He joined Blucher's when they went into production down here and needed a white man who knew the country's language and the people. He says he has done very well, and other than the odd bit of friction from some of the neo-Nazis among the German contingent at the plant, is getting along with everyone and quite happy the way things have worked out for him. He told me there are a few Jewish businessmen in San Ramon and one or two of the towns, but none of them have had any trouble. They are so few they have only one temple and rabbi serving the entire country! The rabbi, Doctor Eskol, is in the States attending a conference, but I intend to see him when he returns, at which point I'll come back to N.Y.

My pagan Christmas has been delightful and I shall look forward to celebrating the universally accepted New Year in the lush surroundings of sun and sea while you freeze your ass off in New York. Look for me around the tenth of January. Happy holidays. Max. P.S. I am doing a story on this Chirlo character. He's straight out of the Middle Ages, from what I've been able to gather in talking to various people. Sort of a cross between St. Ignatius of Loyola and Attila the Hun. I hope you'll like the story.

Mr. and Mrs. Kibbi Kassim followed the line of passengers through the immigration booth at the airport. A young officer glanced at them briefly, then stamped their Algerian passports, and removed the tourist card from the back of each booklet. He scanned the spaces quickly, checking that they were properly filled, then waved them through to the customs tables in the next room for baggage examination. Once inside the big room, Mr. Kassim headed directly to the nearest pay phone to make a long distance call to San Ramon. Mrs. Kassim waited by the examination tables until her husband was finished. After a few minutes he joined her with a nod and they cleared their two suitcases through customs. They hailed a taxi at the front of the terminal and drove off in the direction of Bahia Blanca.

"Major Martinez speaking!"

"Major. I want your men withdrawn from the Max Bruner surveillance immediately. Is that clear?"

"Yes, Colonel."

"Within the next fifteen minutes. Can you do it?"

"Yes, Colonel." He waited until he heard the disconnect click before replacing his red phone on its cradle and flipping the intercom at his desk console.

"Sergeant Zito, get me Captain Padilla in Bahia Blanca." He glanced at his watch. One minute had elapsed. The Major drummed his fingers on the desk until the console phone rang.

"Captain Padilla speaking!"

"This is Major Martinez. Where is Bruner at this moment?"

"Hotel d'Oro, Sir."

"You will withdraw your men from him at once. You have ten minutes to do it."

"Yes, Sir. Ten minutes. Goodbye, Sir."

Martinez put down the receiver gently and scratched his head. He was used to Chirlo making strange requests from time to time. Generally the reasons became apparent later. The reasons were none of his concern; his function—only function—was to obey orders. He looked at his watch. Four minutes had elapsed. Padilla was a good man; Martinez knew he would meet the deadline, for whatever reason the deadline had been set. The Major pushed the affair from his mind and returned to his paperwork.

Mr. and Mrs. Kassim checked into the Hotel d'Oro, claiming their reservations at siesta time. The main lounge and pool areas were deserted, as were the corridors when they were shown into their room on the fourth floor. They remained in their room for the rest of the day. Shortly after sunset, they ordered dinner from room service, then, after eating, pushed the trolley of empty dishes out into the corridor. Then they made love and slept until well past midnight.

Mrs. Kassim awoke first. Her husband was snoring quietly, peacefully. She rubbed her fingers lightly across his cheek. Instantly he awoke and turned on the bed light, then picked up the phone.

"This is Senor Kassim. Could you tell me if Senor Bruner is back in his room yet?"

"I'll ring . . ."

"No! Please, if he has retired I don't want to wake him. Could you check and see if the key is in his box—he was to be out late, attending a party."

"One moment, please."

Mrs. Kassim got off the bed and went into the bathroom. The hotel operator came back on the line.

"No, his box is empty."

"315 is empty—you're sure?"

"Senor Bruner is in 407, and his box is empty. Would you like me to ring his room now?"

"No thanks. It's late. I'll call in the morning. Goodnight!" He hung up.

Downstairs in the deserted lobby, the desk clerk looked at the dead receiver bewildered. "Foreigners!" He laid the phone down and went back to the *Hustler* magazine one of the maids had found cleaning rooms on the second floor. It was on the Church's forbidden list, which made it doubly exciting to read, although he wasn't doing much reading.

A few minutes later Mr. and Mrs. Kassim slipped out of their room and closed the door quietly. Number 407 was across the hall four doors down. They stepped silently along the tiled hallway, stopping in front of 407 to listen. There were night noises within the building, mingled with a humid smell from the tropic night outside. Mrs. Kassim held out the little blue flight bag. Her husband reached in and removed a small leather tool case. He snapped it open and took out three short steel probes, then went to work on the door, crouching while he labored. It had a simple locking mechanism. After a few seconds picking, there was a distinct click and the door opened with a slight push. He rose cautiously, fingers sliding up the open space between door and jam, searching for the chain lock. He pulled his hand back and glanced at his wife. Bruner had not used the chain. He stuffed the probes in his pocket, then slipped into the room. Mrs. Kassim followed and closed the door. Bruner stirred in bed uneasily, but his breathing remained deep, unhurried. Mr. Kassim crept to the side of the sleeping form and studied the reporter for a moment. Bruner was sleeping on his stomach, one arm cradling his head, his face turned away from the window's dim light, laddered by the Venetian blinds.

Mr. Kassim braced himself on the balls of his feet, raised his hand and swung its stiffened edge down on Bruner's neck just behind the mastoid bone.

"Window!" he whispered to his wife. She sped across the room to close the French doors behind the blinds, then pulled the drapes to turn the dim light into blackness. Mr. Kassim switched on the lamp, rattling the phone as he fumbled for the knob on its porcelain base. The receiver jiggled, but remained secure on its cradle.

"Check the room!" Mrs. Kassim began rummaging through the contents of drawers and suitcases, flinging clothes and papers onto the floor as she went. Her husband watched a moment, then turned to work on Bruner.

First he stripped and rolled him to a spread eagle position at the center of the bed. He ripped the sheets away and tore them into strips, knotting them into thick bindings. In succession, he tied the ankles and wrists to the corners of the bed supports. Then he stood back to examine his handiwork for an instant, ripped a small piece of sheet into a gag, balled one piece to handkerchief size and stuffed it into Bruner's mouth. He forced his mouth open, sticking a longer strip between his teeth, then tying it behind his neck. Mrs. Kassim stopped her search for a minute to read the carbon copy of a letter taken from one of the folders in the briefcase.

"Here's something!" He took it from her and scanned it swiftly, reading Bruner's letter to B.J. mailed out the previous day.

"Colonel Asher!" He looked at his wife. "Do we know him?"

She shook her head. He looked over at the unconscious reporter, pondering his next move.

"What do we do?" she asked.

"Shut up! I'm thinking." He walked around the bed and reached down to feel Bruner's pulse. It was light, but steady.

"The letter clears us from any implication!" his wife said.

"I know." He still held his finger on the pulse.

"If he dies, there will be an investigation," she added.

"He has been working for Israeli intelligence. He has betrayed us all. Fool!" He raised his stiffened hand and swung down, this time with a terrible force. When he checked the pulse again, it had stopped. Max Bruner was dead.

"Replace everything exactly as it was, neat and tidy."

He began untying the bed sheet bindings from the corpse while his wife went to work rearranging everything in its proper order. He worked Bruner into the pajamas and lugged him into the bathroom. He arranged the body between the toilet and the sink, leaving the head to loll near the rim of the bathtub. It was a poor looking accident, but he knew it would be accepted without question. They remade the bed, bundled the torn sheets into their arms and after opening the windows and turning off the light, slipped back into the corridor back to their own room. It took twenty minutes to flush the pieces of torn sheet down the toilet one small piece at a time.

Captain Padilla wandered around the room, taking in the various inconsistencies he saw. The two policemen remained standing at the door, afraid to enter without proper authority. It should have been a local matter, a hotel guest dying at the d'Oro; it had happened before. This time, for some reason, military intelligence was interested in the dead man.

"You're sure you touched nothing?" He looked squarely at the two men.

"Nothing has been touched, Captain. Just as you see it, is just as we saw it," the smaller one said respectfully. His companion nodded.

"The maid touched nothing either?"

"She was too frightened, Captain; she ran away and called the housekeeper."

Padilla pursed his lips. It was all too neat. Men weren't like that; everything set out in orderly fashion—shaving gear, files, papers, even the dead man's clothing folded into the cupboard and drawers just the way his own wife did after their maid ironed everything. He went into the bathroom and looked at the body lying grotesquely in rigor mortis and bent over to examine the bruises behind the right ear near the base of the neck. He checked for signs or other marks or injuries. There were some slight bruises around the wrists and ankles which might have been caused by tight socks and rubbing from starched shirt cuffs. Possible, but unlikely.

Padilla straightened up and rubbed his nose reflectively; try as he might, he could not visualize how the man could have fallen while standing between the sink and the toilet and hit his head on the side of the bathtub. It was possible, but again, unlikely.

He went back into the bedroom and picked his way through

the papers, billfold, briefcase and other articles laying on the desktop. The papers were in English. He could understand some of the words, but not enough to make sense of what he saw. He went over to the bed and sat down, bouncing lightly on the mattress, then peered between his legs, lifting the spread to look under. There were some white threads scattered on the floor near his heels. He picked them up and looked at them curiously, then pulled the spread back from the pillows and felt beneath the blanket.

"One sheet is missing!" he said to no one in particular.

"Si, Capitan," the small man replied from the doorway, because he felt he should.

Padilla twisted the threads between his thumb and forefinger, thinking. He picked up the telephone. "Connect me to Major Martinez at El Tigre Fortress."

The once a week morning breakfasts with his father-in-law had become a tradition. The old man was in fine fettle this morning.

"Well, my boy, there's one thing to be said about the calamity of being a child—it toughens you up for the calamity of being a parent!"

They all laughed. Felina had been telling her father about his young granddaughter, who had burst into tears the previous night when she finally learned that she would never catch up in age to the twins. Felina had explained that for every year she grew in age, they too would grow and age, so she must always be the youngest of the family. The child was crushed by the thought. Ruis began to relate another anecdote concerning Felina when she had been the same age, but the maid interrupted.

"Con permisso." They stopped talking. "Colonel Chirlo, Major Martinez is at the door and wishes to speak with you."

Chirlo stood up and dropped his napkin on the chair. "Save it till I get back, Ruis—I'll only be a minute."

Major Martinez stood in the hallway looking immaculate and uncomfortable.

"Morning, Major!"

"Good morning, Colonel!" He clicked his heels and saluted. Chirlo held out his hand, ushering him into the living room.

"Something to eat, Major—coffee?" he inquired as they sat down.

"No thank you, Sir, I have already breakfasted." He glanced at the two doors into the big room, the one they had entered and the closed door leading beyond the room to the pantry and kitchen.

"My surveillance group was withdrawn as ordered yesterday. Sometime during the night Max Bruner died." He spoke very softly.

Chirlo got up and went over to the open door. He looked at the seated Major.

"Of natural causes, I hope," he said quietly, closing the door.

"It depends on what you mean by natural, Colonel." He stood up and waited until Chirlo had sat down again, before resuming his own seat.

"Any evidence of violence?"

"His room was immaculate. He was found, dressed in pajamas, in the bathroom where he had apparently struck his head—here!" He pointed to a spot behind his own ear. "A faint or fall, perhaps a heart seizure—or a blow. The field of choice is open to selection at this point."

He looked at his superior's face, watching for the nuances he would be expected to follow. Chirlo considered his selection carefully.

"How old a man was Bruner?"

"Early fifties, Colonel."

"Married—next of kin?"

"Only a sister—according to his tourist card."

"Physical condition?"

"Flabby—a bit overweight."

"Hmm." He stroked his beard. "Did you know, Major Martinez, the number one killer in America is heart disease?"

"I was not aware of that, Colonel."

"Probably due to the fast pace of life they lead; always working under pressure, too many sleepless nights, too much alcohol, cigarettes—tension. Tension is what finally does it. One day the human pump refuses to push any longer. Tragic."

Major Martinez knew he had received his orders. He arose.

"I'm sure Doctor Carvello will provide a written report confirming that diagnosis, Colonel, after his autopsy is completed."

"You will notify the American Embassy after the autopsy of the death of one of their citizens?"

"I will, Colonel."

"With suitable comments from the Bureau of Tourism for the man's sister, and our offer to bury his remains in the cemetery of her choice—at our expense."

"It will be done." Martinez saluted at the front door.

"Keep me informed, Major." He watched the thin uniform

march down the stone steps back to the staff car. Chirlo closed the door and went back to the breakfast room.

"Sorry for the interruption, Ruis," he said as he sat down. "It seems some newspaper man, an American, had a heart attack and died at the Hotel d'Oro last night. Martinez wanted to follow proper procedures for arranging things."

He spread his napkin back on his trousers and reached for the coffee pot.

"Couldn't the man have waited until you got to the office, my boy?" Artega demanded.

Chirlo shrugged. "You know Martinez, Papa!"

"I think the man is an idiot!" The doctor bit into a piece of toast.

"True, but a very loyal officer." Chirlo creamed his coffee.

"And a perfect gentleman," Felina added, "always a perfect gentleman."

Chirlo smiled at his wife, then looked at Ruis. "Come on now, let's hear your story!"

18

For as long as Athens had existed, so had the Port of Piraeus. For several thousand years Piraeus had been the front door to the golden city of Pericles, Socrates, Plato, Aristotle and, in later years, Aristotle Onassis. When the magic of wings replaced the time consuming effort of ocean travel, it became necessary to build an airport to serve the cradle of democracy. For the new gateway to the golden city, the Athenians bowed to tradition and placed it at Piraeus. In older days the seaport teemed with shipping, commerce, and cutthroat business practices, developing into headquarters for one of the largest mercantile fleets in the world. Greece, like England, was a seafaring nation; but unlike England, depended upon the sea to administer the thousands of islands which comprised the Hellenes. In addition to voyaging for purely commercial reasons, the sea became the highroad of the Peloponnesian homeland.

Dimitrious Zaglaviras came from one of the small islands in the Kotakas group, Mindrinos. At one time the Zaglaviras family had owned the entire island, commerce, shipping, real estate and the 3400 olive trees on the southern slopes of the mountain from which the island was named. But that was before the arrival of the Turks. In a land where recorded family history can be traced in the thousands of years, conquest by the Ottoman Turks in the fifteenth century was considered a fairly recent event. Stripped of their wealth and holdings, the Zaglaviras' devoted their considerable energies to manning ships, instead of owning them for the next four hundred years, until the Ottoman collapse. With a certain amount of luck, cunning, foresight and downright dishonesty, the fortunes of the family Zagliviras began to rise once more, until the disaster of World War II.

Shortly after the lightening invasion of the German Wermacht to stiffen the spines of their Italian Allies who had been brought to a standstill by the ferocity of the Greek Army, a German naval E boat arrived under the command of Lt. Hans Spiedel. He swung onto the dock, followed by sixteen naval marines, and announced to a muted gathering of townspeople that he was taking command of the island in the name of the Reich.

Dimitri Zaglaviras was, at the time, a shrewd young man of eighteen who had thus far managed to avoid military conscription in either army or navy, owing to an imaginary ailment which made it impossible for him to do any physical work because it caused him to faint. He was just the man Hans Spiedel was looking for to act as liaison between the islanders and the new German garrison.

For some inexplicable reason, young Speidel (he was twenty-one at the time) held the younger Dimitri in awe. It was perhaps the realization of history that created their bond: a man whose family had owned an island for three thousand years and now owned nothing, and a lad from Danzig whose antecedents were at best obscure, appointed to spearhead the thousand year Reich on the same island. And it did become a bond. Speidel learned a passable form of Greek while Zaglaviras mastered the German language in the same fashion he acquired English and Italian—listening to others. By 1945 his German was as pure Danzig as Speidel's Greek was pure German.

After the war ended, Lt. Speidel decided there was little point in returning to the Fatherland. Dimitri agreed. Together they stripped the garrison of its supplies and equipment so that when the Royal Navy inspection team arrived and was told the two converted E boats moored at the new island dock were the property of the Zaglaviras shipping interests and claimed as booty, the British officer shrugged his shoulders and motored back to his destroyer.

They flogged the supplies and equipment in Piraeus during the following months, while at the same time building a sizeable trade in commercial and passenger traffic between the islands and mainland. The attempted communist takeover after the war passed them by. It was easy to retreat to their haven on Mindrinos whenever there appeared to be a threat to their commercial ventures, and wait until the situation blew over, rather than becoming involved themselves. While the fortunes of others rose and fell with the vagaries of politics or commercial excesses, Zaglaviras and Speidel continued to thrive. They were not above turning a drachma diddle on the side to augment their business during leaner times, or indeed during fatter times, if the sum was high enough. So, when a thin, well-dressed Palestinian dropped into their office along the Piraeus harbor three days after the New Year, asking to speak with them privately, Dimitri was interested.

"Excuse me, I'll see if my associate, Mr. Speidel, is in the office." He left the intense thin man waiting in the reception room and disappeared into the labyrinth of offices to find his associate.

Speidel was in the middle of a complicated smuggling negotiation with three Turks from Salonika. He beckoned Speidel out of the room.

"What is it, Dimitri?" he asked testily. Negotiations had reached a critical point with the Turks. It was never wise to leave customers alone to talk among themselves once the formal bargaining was under way.

"I have a Palestinian in the front room. He says he wants to buy five tankers. He has cash!" He said the words with wonder. No one had cash when they came to deal with the House of Zaglaviras. It was always a matter of barter.

"Cash?" The importance of the three Turks was instantly forgotten by Speidel.

"Cash."

"Wait for me." He went back into the conference room to excuse himself and suggest the smugglers reconsider their last position while he tended to a serious family matter which had just arisen. The Turks were most understanding, and promised to wait, misinterpreting his departure as a sign of weakness.

He came out of the office grimly. "This better be good, Dimitri. That's a million drachma deal sitting in there with those bandits."

They walked together down the winding hallways back to the front office. Originally the building had been a cheap waterfront hotel some enterprising sailor had decided to turn into offices. He had been murdered in a dice game, so his heirs had leased the premises on a floor-by-floor basis to various nefarious tenants on a first-come first-served basis; pay in advance and no questions asked. The building was continually raided by the police. The Zaglaviras' offices meandered about the third floor. There was no fire escape.

"Mr. Jamil, may I present my associate, Mr. Speidel, our special projects manager," Dimitri said smoothly, allowing the euphemism to stand on its own. Speidel lunged through the doorway at the Palestinian with an outstretched hand, hastily cranking in his initial wide smile to compensate for the tight thin face with which he was presented.

"My pleasure, Mr. Jamil!" Jamil said nothing. Zaglaviras rubbed his hands, although it wasn't cold.

"Shall we retire to my office?" He led the way behind the movable partition, down another hallway to one of his offices. The offices were furnished for mood and effect—depending on the scam: sparse, luxurious, modernistic, decadent, military style—whatever desired impression the partners wished to create. With Jamil, Dimitri decided on the military effect, sensing a disciplined brevity about the slim man. He stepped aside gracefully, showing him into the room. Jamil paused to look around before taking a chair. The room looked like a military command post complete with handcrank field telephone and rifle rack. The Uzi's in the rifle rack were real, but the telephone had been built in Munich in 1943 and looted from the Mindrinos garrison during the closing days of World War II; it was inoperable. They all sat on the frayed canvas camp chairs and looked at one another expectantly.

"I wish to purchase five vessels complete with crews," Jamil began.

"Of course—you came to the right place, Mr. Jamil!" Speidel interrupted unnecessarily.

"Four of the ships required are to be tankers in the ten thousand ton range; the fifth vessel, an ocean trawler equipped for a five thousand mile voyage."

"I think you would be making a mistake on the tankers, Mr. Jamil; these small tonnage vessels are useless for commercial . . ."

"Mr. Spediel, would you kindly keep your advice and opinions to yourself until I have finished speaking," Jamil said evenly. "I have taken a great deal of trouble to investigate your company and have chosen it because I understand you perform specialized services with no questions asked. If this information is inaccurate, I will leave at once and find someone who can provide such services—or at least is willing to listen to what I have to say without interruption."

He waited for either partner to say something. They were silent. Zaglaviras was starting to sweat lightly at the forehead. Speidel looked hurt. Jamil let the pause linger purposely, using its silence to light a cigarette and exhale a cloud of blue smoke into the battlefield surroundings.

"As I was saying, the fifth vessel is to be an ocean trawler with a five thousand mile range of operation. This will be the headquarters vessel to be occupied by myself and a few guests. It should be adequately equipped for a half dozen passengers, but only for stark comfort—not luxury. I want minimum crews on the tankers. Enough men to operate each vessel, nothing more. Questions?"

Speidel and Zaglaviras looked at each other. Speidel raised a finger.

"When do you want these vessels, Mr. Jamil?"

"Ready for sea by May first this year."

"You're not giving us much time."

"No? That's too bad, because over and above the costs involved I was planning on paying you each one million American dollars for this May first deadline as a bonus, however, if you feel you cannot meet the deadline . . ."

"Nonsense Dimitri, of course we can meet the deadline, Mr. Jamil!" Speidel broke in. He wished sometimes his Greek partner would leave negotiations to him and concentrate on the operational end of the business.

"I didn't say we couldn't do it—only that it wasn't much time!" Dimitri protested. "It takes time to find ships—time to equip them—survey them—hire crews—provisioning; everything takes time, Mr. Jamil!"

While he spoke his mind was zipping along the quays in a dozen Mediterranean ports pinpointing the rusty hulks of uneconomic ten thousand ton ships. He knew where there were dozens of them, pushed out of service by the huge new super tankers with twenty times the tonnage. Ocean trawlers were more difficult. He remembered there were a couple of good ones in Rotterdam . . . "However, I am sure we will be able to meet your needs by May first."

"Then you accept?" Jamil confirmed.

"Absolutely!" Speidel spoke up. "We will go to work on it straight away—won't we, Dimitri?" His partner nodded.

"Right away."

"Good." The Palestinian reached inside his breast pocket and drew out an expensive pigskin wallet. It was filled with new American banknotes. He counted out fifty one thousand dollar bills and laid them on the folding table between them.

"This is my deposit for travel expenses and evidence of my sincerity, and . . ." he paused significantly . . . "to insure your total silence on this matter."

He stood up. "I will contact you again in four weeks time. I shall expect you to have the ships located and ready for my prepurchase inspection." He started for the door. "I know you will not fail me." He gave them a very tight smile.

Speidel hopped out of his folding chair and opened the door. "I'll get you a receipt, Mr. Jamil." Dimitri followed them into the hallway.

"No, Mr. Speidel, I will not require a receipt from you now or in the future."

He led them back to the front reception room and through the main entrance, then stopped with his hand on the door.

"But if either of you try playing any little games with me, I will kill you both."

Dimitri Zaglaviras and Hans Speidel stood motionless and silent, looking at one another for some minutes after their new customer had departed.

"God, it's cold!"

Morris Levy laughed as Affleck climbed into the warm car and slammed the door.

"And why not? It's Ottawa and it's Winter!" He pulled away from the main entrance and turned onto the street. "Where do you want to eat this time?"

"Same terms?"

"Same terms," Levy agreed.

Affleck thought for a moment. "Too far to the Chateau; let's hit the nearest Chinese joint."

"How about the Golden Dragon?

"It's your expense account. By the way, Merry Christmas and a Happy New Year!"

Levy glanced at him and made a face. "Wise guy." They drove through the cold air feeling secure in the toasty interior. "You have anything concrete for me, Don?"

"Yes and no. I'm not being facetious, but that's the answer. I'll give you the facts. You'll have to decide on the content." He began outlining the results of the investigative part of his trip to Cosecha Rica while Morris drove towards the commercial area of the city and swung into the parking lot alongside the Golden Dragon. It was the best spot in town for Chinese food, but terribly expensive and very crowded with the noontime rush. They had to stand in line to wait for a table. Affleck continued his story while they waited, bringing

584

the account up to his visit with Chirlo by the time they were guided to a table. They ordered two specials and two beers, then sat back.

"So there was nothing at the site?" Morris prompted.

"Nothing. No marks, tracks, nothing was disturbed anywhere along the area shown on that aerial photo. I walked the whole space between the tracks and pool right up to Blucher Chemicals' fence line."

"What about Doctor Slavez?"

"A square shooter. A gentleman. I'm positive he's straight—straight as a ruler. He is really the one running things down there with Dorando off in Argentina. I can't comment on Doctor Dorando one way or t'other; never met the man."

Their beers arrived and they sipped the foaming glasses, chilling themselves within the warm room.

"I gave Chirlo a call two days before we left. He was supposed to come to a family party, but Rina forgot to send out the invitations. I was quite frank with him, of course, even showed him the photos. Didn't faze him in the least. Told me he'd get on to his security chief and have a full investigation immediately."

Levy cringed. "You told him our suspicions? Don, I thought we agreed . . ."

Affleck waved his beer stein. "Nothing to worry about, Morris. I didn't run in with an accusation, waving a bunch of photographs. I left my visit with him purposely until the end to impress the importance you placed on the matter—an inquiry, nothing more. Stop worrying. His feathers weren't ruffled!"

The Chinese waiter arrived with the special and scattered the various bowls, plates and sauces about the table. After he left they dipped into the assortment, filling their plates.

"Anyway, he said he'd look into it and we spent an hour talking about old times." He lifted a forkfull of the Chinese mess to his mouth and began eating.

"So we have to wait now until he finishes his investigation?"

Affleck shook his head and swallowed. "No. He turned up next afternoon in Bahia Blanca with a man from Blucher Chemicals; a Doctor Kastenburg. I met them at the airport. Chirlo wanted to examine our DH 125. He's thinking of buying an executive jet of his own. Anyway, it seems they had a problem over at Bluchers'. They had been storing piles of chemical barrels along the fenceline next to the pool. Periodically, some of the labels would blow off and drift across the fence—you know, too little glue, heavy rain?" He took another mouthful. The food was delicious.

"So they went into the area to pick up the papers?" He had to wait until Affleck finished chewing.

"That's it! They lifted a light dune buggy over the fence with their cherry picker, the one used to pile the drums, and drove around picking everything up." He laughed. "Apparently it happened three or four times until Kastenburg saw them at it one day and raised hell. After that they moved all the barrels over to the other fence. The yardmen did it all on their own, and dusted away their tracks after each expedition."

"Did you interview the yardmen?"

"No. They were fired on the spot."

"Were there any barrels along the fence line?"

"Nope. When I was there it was a clear view across to the Blucher offices—they moved everything the previous week." He returned to his food.

Levy mused over the information. The story could be true. It was certainly a plausible explanation for the tire tracks. A dune buggy. Of course, with low pressure tires. He felt better about it, certain there were no commercial dune buggies equipped to do much more than drive around the empty pool yard picking up chemical labels. Affleck had already stated the count on the fuel bundle containers was correct, so maybe it had happened exactly the way it was explained. He smiled at Affleck.

"I'm glad you know people in high places. We might have wound up making fools of ourselves."

"That's still your choice, Morris. I said yes, and no. Yes, that is what I learned from my visit, but if you ask me am I convinced the story—the explanation—is true beyond any reasonable doubt, or do I have proof the story is true, the answer is no. So, yes and no. Take your pick." He went back to his food. It was surprising how quickly Chinese food cooled. It had to be eaten at once. Levy hadn't touched his own plate yet. He was still digesting what he had heard from Affleck.

"Were it not for the fact you know this Chirlo, I think I'd be ready to order a formal investigation. However, at the moment I'm prepared to accept the yes as final word on the subject." He slid a fork into his plate.

Affleck gave him his perfect smile. "But what if it is no, Morris?"

Levy held his fork poised. "In that case I feel confident you will give me your word to return immediately to your friends in high places and find out just what in th'hell is going on." He filled his mouth with lukewarm bean sprouts and beef chips.

Affleck laughed. "That's what I love about you, Morris—the only pessimist I know with an optimistic viewpoint. Why don't you shut up and eat your lunch—it's getting cold.

B.J. chewed his cigar as he reread Bruner's letter a third time. The phone pad, pressing on his ear, felt moist by the time the overseas operator came back to him.

"Colonel Asher is on the line, Sir. Go ahead!"

B.J. set the cigar on his ashtray. "Lev?"

"Hello, B.J. How's the weather in New York?"

"Snowing—so what else is new?"

"The sun is shining in Tel Aviv."

"Yeah, I can imagine. I got a letter in from Bruner a few minutes ago. I'll put it over the telex when I hang up. He's drawn a complete blank. No Jewish problem in the country anywhere; in fact no more than a couple of dozen in the whole region. Young Hauser was apparently having an affair with the Big Man's wife and when El Supremo found out, the kid split for home—Germany."

"I see. Where do the Arabs fit in?"

"This guy Jamil and the Big Cheese were revolutionary pals in the old days. It seems he called on Jamil, who was visiting at the time, and asked him to knock the kid off—for old time's sake. Bruner guesses Jamil called in one of his boys to track the kid down and nail him. The story ended in Switzerland."

B.J. changed the receiver to his other, cooler ear. "Not much help, I'm afraid."

"Glad I didn't try and override the people here. Thank Max for me when he gets back, and of course, I am grateful to you, B.J. You have been very generous."

"Ain't it the truth! I'll get the letter on the wire to you right away. See y'round."

"Goodbye, B.J., and thank you again."

There were a few people on the dock when they approached the East River pier. It was cold, a damp rawness in the air, with a speckling of snow out of an indefinite sky. They watched the two tugs fussing about the ship, swinging it gradually broadside against the current, nudging the white vessel slowly towards the dock.

"There's always an excitement when we dock—have you noticed?" They were leaning on the rail, seeing the distance between ship and shore closing, squeezing the garbage-strewn black waters out towards the bow and stern. Corbin looked down at the few men standing by the samson posts ready to receive the docking lines. They were dressed in navy pea jackets and looked cold, not excited. He pointed at one of the groups clustered on the dock around the covered gangway.

"They don't look as if they're ready to start dancing with joy."

She waited until the ship's horn had snorted twice at the tugs, before replying. "Maybe they should—at least they could keep themselves warm."

He reached his arm out and huddled her into his dufflecoat. "Back to the cold."

A thin weighted leadline swung out from the bow and was picked up quickly by three men near the post on the dock. They began dragging the dripping cord up from the water, slowing as the thick manilla rope to which it was tied emerged.

"Back to the cold," Elizabeth agreed.

Another lead line arced out from the stern and the trio tending the other samson post repeated the performance, dragging the huge rope in to tie the ship to the wharf. Other lines went out, first midships, to the gangway crew, then from the quarter and three quarter positions along the side of the ship. Gulls screamed and wheeled in the grey light.

"It's been a hell of a trip!" The ship's horn gave a long blast, answered immediately by both tugs as they disconnected their lines from the vessel and backed away. They could hear the ring of bells from the open door on the bridge two decks above them. "Finished with engines." Beneath their elbows the wood railing stopped its throb; metal deck plating ceased to vibrate. The voyage was over.

"Let's get our stuff, Mrs. Corbin. It's time to go home."

She smiled and kissed him on the cheek, then arm-in-arm, they went along the open deck to their cabin.

"I'm glad you could make it, Colonel Chirlo."

"How could I resist, Doctor Kastenburg. How often does one get to see the assembly of an atomic bomb?"

They stepped into the elevator. Kastenburg waited until the doors had closed, then locked them from the inside.

"Security," he said unnecessarily, pushing the panel button.

The small elevator trembled and began its descent.

"There are three levels below the ground pad, Colonel; in all we have one hundred fifty thousand square feet hidden from view. This of course includes our storage pool as well as the refining process, although we channel some of the plumbing up into the plant—coolant—power source—water—air-conditioning—plus circulation piping. The circulation plumbing is the main item. It takes miles of piping to run the refining process—there wouldn't be room for all of it underground."

The elevator stopped. Kastenburg unlocked the door. Chirlo followed the doctor down the pale green corridor beneath the flourescent lighting. The air was dryer and much cooler than at the surface, almost chilly, with a faint background hum from the air conditioning motors as they changed the air; dragging in the moist humid sweetness from the surface, sterilizing, laundering, picking out the dust particles, then forcing it one hundred feet beneath the concrete floor of Blucher Chemicals. Kastenburg opened the door at the end of the hall and went inside.

It looked like the inspection area in a maternity ward of any hospital where the anxious father stands on one side of a glass partition and looks across at the masked nurse holding his new infant, to a backdrop of pink and blue bundles lying in the cribs. In this case the glass was much thicker and instead of cribs and a nurse, there were a series of silver metal tables covered with paraphernalia: flasks, cannisters, tools, steel tubes and other objects. Hanging from the ceiling, evenly spaced across the room, were three mechanical pairs of claws, dangling motionless.

"Everything ready, Kurt?"

Doctors Hauser, Sauve and Berger were dressed in white smocks, seated at a table when Chirlo and Kastenburg came into the room. Hauser stood up.

"Yes, Heinz. We're ready."

He looked at Chirlo as he spoke. His voice was casual, but his eyes were hostile. Chirlo ignored the look. He couldn't figure the man out, and had given up trying.

"Good, then let's get started."

Hauser took the pilot controls for the mechanical hands in the center; Sauve and Berger went over to their positions on either side.

"Colonel, if you will come up here with me."

Chirlo followed him up on the elevated platform to the console desk and stood watching as Kastenburg took the only chair. He began flicking switches, lighting the viewing screens.

"Each hand has a television camera on its tip which is produced on these six screens. We can go up to six thousand power on any one camera, turning it into a microscope if we need to examine something closely. It's usually kept at a normal visual power unless we're doing delicate work," he explained.

Each screen displayed a portion of the tables in the room behind the glass.

"Over here," he pointed, "are the readouts for the hot-room; temperature, humidity, REMS, pressures . . ."

"REMS?" Chirlo said.

"Stands for *Roentgen Equivalent Man.* A scientific term for the measurement of radiation levels. The room in there has a fairly high radiation level—not as high as you have over at the reactor, but high enough that we must monitor it carefully. That door over there behind the tables is where the fuel bundles were brought in when we removed the uranium oxide for reprocessing. That's when we contaminated the room." He smiled at Chirlo momentarily. "The waste then went through that conveyor hatch beyond the last table into the next station, where the separation process started."

"And the end product was the plutonium," Chirlo said.

"Packed in those canisters on that table." He pointed to the third screen in the row.

"And the other waste after the plutonium was removed? What happened to it?"

"Processed into low REM glass bricks. Quite safe. We have it buried in a concrete vault under the third level."

He punched the keys on the computer console; figures and letters flashed onto the scanning screen above the keyboard; meaningless jumble.

"I am programming the mechanical hands to remember every manual move made by their human controllers so if we make a mistake and have to retrace our steps, the computer will do it for us. And of course, after assembling our first bomb, the computer will know how to do the others on its own."

"You haven't made a dry run yet?" Chirlo asked uneasily, visualizing the mechanical fingers fumbling them all into oblivion.

"We have made many dry runs—as you call them." He punched a few more keys and concentrated on the monitor screen, watching the numbers flash across in tidy rows. "In theory, we have made fifty bombs already, Colonel Chirlo. Without incident. Ready to start?" He called down at the three men on the floor.

Berger and Sauve looked up and nodded. Hauser met Chirlo's eyes through the reflection in the glass. "Ready!" he said without turning his head.

"Program is running now." Kastenburg pushed a green square cube button on the computer bank. The reel-to-reel tapes on the upright modules behind the platform started turning, recording the memory of the scene. Mechanical hands flexed and stretched above the tables, then set to work, guided by their human counterparts.

"Plutonium 239 is produced by bombarding uranium neutrons in chain reactors like the CANDU here at Punta Delgado. The melting point is 639.5 degrees centigrade and it boils at 3235 centigrade. Between room temperature and melting point it undergoes five separate changes. It therefore has six different allotropic forms—you know what allotropic means, Colonel?"

"The ability of any substance to exist in more than one form."

Kastenburg glanced at him, impressed. The man was no fool. "Precisely. Doctor Hauser and Sauve are removing our PU 239 now from their separate canisters—the critical masses required for explosion—and placing them at either end of that long tube." He pointed to a miniature iron lung stretching out nearly five feet across one table. It was opened in two halves, like a casket; the center portion hollow, with wires hanging from the spherical ends attached to a maze of circuitry and miniature machinery inside.

"The critical masses are inserted in either end of the cylinder— they must be exact; too much and we have a slow burn reaction on our hands as the masses *feel* the nearness of each other—too little, and we wind up with a dud when we trigger them to meet."

They watched the silver white plutonium being lowered slowly into the end of the canister by Doctor Hauser. There was a tension in the room, a breathless quality of anticipation; preparation for disaster, if matter should triumph over man. Then the tensions dropped away as the mechanical claws released their small cargo and rose above the table.

Doctor Hauser's extended hands picked the second canister from the side table as Doctor Berger's metal hands slid in beside to assist. Again, the tension started building as the insertion process was duplicated at the other end of the cylinder.

"It looks like a coffin, doesn't it?" Chirlo observed.

Kastenburg said nothing, keeping his eyes riveted on the television screens. Suddenly, he reached out and touched the FREEZE button on the console. The mechanical hands froze, locked by the computer.

Hauser looked up apologetically. "Sorry, Heinz. Rerun it. I'll hit it higher next time." He turned.

The men on the floor stood back from their positions as Kastenburg keyed out the program reverse sequence, then stabbed the START button. Slowly the hands reversed their motions, until the canister was back on the table and free.

"Shall we wait for a minute until everyone settles down?" On the floor, the trio went over to their desks talking quietly.

"What happened?" Chirlo demanded.

Kastenburg pushed the chair back and removed his pince nez, rubbing the bridge of his nose.

"Doctor Hauser lifted that canister at the wrong point. There was a chance it might have tipped going into the—as you call it, coffin. Unlikely," he hastened to add, "but a chance. In which case we might all be needing coffins."

He lowered his voice. "Since his son's death, he has been terribly upset. I'm afraid the loss of the boy affected him more than any of us realized at the time. He's a good man, Colonel. I might say a brilliant man." He replaced his glasses. "But then I suppose we are all brilliant. But it is not our brilliance that causes concern, only our human weaknesses."

"Affecting some more than others."

"Yes, Colonel." He looked at Chirlo strangely. "Some of us more than others."

"Yes, Colonel Asher, what is it this time?" Two staff officers stood up from their desks and left the room discreetly. Brigadier Borodam glared up from his desk like a bulldog.

"The Max Bruner affair, Sir."

"What's he want now—more money? Can't have it."

"No, Sir. The man is dead."

Borodam's blue chin pointed threateningly, his jaw muscles tensed, then relaxed. He laid down the pencil he had been holding. "Sit down, Lev." Asher obeyed.

"He died in a hotel in the Republic of Cosecha Rica, December 29th or 30th. Supposedly a coronary in the bathroom."

"Supposedly?" Borodam's eyes were bright.

"I haven't seen the coroner's report on the autopsy, but my informant states that it's the official report presented to the American Embassy."

"What was he doing in Cosecha Rica?"

"I sent him there to investigate the father of the murdered boy—Hauser; you remember the case? Double murder at Davos?"

Borodam remembered. "I thought we had agreed to drop that business."

"No, Sir. You refused permission to fund any further

investigations. I took the liberty of utilizing my informant—Bruner's employer, actually, Mr. B.J. Bronstein of C.P. news in New York—to provide the funding in an unofficial capacity. Bruner was sent down on the basis of a followup story for his wire service."

"You think he was murdered?"

"I'm sure of it."

"Why?"

"I don't know—I have a feeling."

"A *feeling*!" the Brigadier barked. Asher reached into his file and withdrew the telex he had received from New York the previous week and passed it to Borodam.

"He wrote this letter the day before he died."

The tough intelligence commander read it quickly and pushed it back.

"That would seem to be conclusive." He watched Asher return the sheet to his file.

"I don't see how it affects us. Either the story is true, in which case there is every likelihood the local strongman discovered your man Bruner was on the trail trying to dredge up the whole affair, and had him executed locally, or he did indeed have a heart attack."

"But supposing the story is not true, Sir?" Asher persisted. "Supposing the Hauser story given to Max Bruner was given by Doctor Hauser under duress—given to Bruner in order to allay suspicions on the real reason for his son's death?"

Borodam considered the argument a moment. "To what purpose?"

"To keep him from discovering the real reason."

"Which is?"

"I don't know, Sir," he admitted.

The Brigadier studied his subordinate's face speculatively. He liked Lev. Asher had become the replacement son for one he had lost in an air force training accident, although he never would admit such a thing to anyone. Asher had done brilliant work. He was a natural intelligence officer; keen brain with a piercing curiosity and an ability to discard dead end leads before they became obsessions. He wondered if this situation with the newspaper reporter was becoming an obsession.

It was so unlike the young Colonel.

"What is it exactly that bothers you?" he asked kindly.

"I know it sounds ridiculous, Sir, and goes against every precept of good intelligence, but I am as certain as I am sitting here this whole business isn't even the tip of the iceberg. The tip is still below

the surface. Don't ask me why—but that's what I feel. It's a feeling."
He shrugged helplessly. "Idiotic, isn't it?" he confessed.

"I'm glad you realize it, Colonel."

"Maybe I need a few days off. I'm becoming paranoid." He allowed himself to smile.

"Take them—make it a week."

"Yes Sir!" He saluted.

"Oh! And if you can give me one hard fact on which to hang my hat, I'll reconsider the Bruner business for a full investigation. Now get out of here, Colonel, and stop bothering me!" he growled, the blue chin jutting threateningly.

Asher paused by the door and looked back at the fierce Brigadier hunched behind his desk like a khaki bear.

"Yes Sir!" He smiled, and limped out.

"There has been a lot of criticism recently, Mr. Corbin, about the Bayan project. People are saying it's a huge ripoff designed to make more profits for CORCAN, your own corporate conglomerate. How do you feel about this?"

Walter Kiddell's face faded on the screen to be superimposed by Corbin, looking slightly ill-at-ease and hot. The kleig lighting of the studio had pushed temperatures into sauna range.

"The Public Asks," a weekly pot-boiler program originating from the CBC's Ottawa studios, delighted in putting public figures on the griddle, then trying to singe them severely with Walter Kiddell's probing brands. It was unrehearsed, live and lovely to watch. There were no political favorites, and no topic was sacred. The public asked the questions by mail—thousands of letters every week—then the current most controversial item was chosen by the program director and the individual most responsible for the subject was approached to appear on the network. The program had made and broken many men and women in government, industry, medicine, the arts and private enterprise, and woe to the person who refused to participate. Refusal was aired publicly, immediately making them suspect of the most heinous crimes. It was great newscopy, coast to coast.

"I'm not sure I understand your word, *ripoff*—do you mean it in a literal sense, or as a descriptive adjective?" Corbin asked blandly.

He saw Kiddell become wary, cautious. "You tell me, Mr. Corbin!"

"Tell you what, Mr. Kiddell?" Inside, he was laughing—two could play the same game.

Now Kiddell seemed flustered, the rugged handsome features

tightened, the camera pulled well back to pan the two men seated on either side of the circular table, set with teacups.

"Tell the public just what you're up to," Corbin continued. "Explain these allegations. I think you owe your audience at least that much!"

"Wait a minute, Mr. Corbin, the public makes the allegations on this show, you do the justifying." It was weak, but it would have to do for a start, Kiddell decided—perhaps he could knife his guest later on in the show.

"I disagree, Mr. Kiddell," Corbin said evenly. "Bayan was set up by private subscription, funded by private capital and is operating under private enterprise. To say it is a ripoff, or that I owe the public an explanation on the allegations made against the company is nonsense; you know it, I know it, and the public knows it. So why don't you stop trying to make sensationalism out of the imaginative ravings of a bunch of uninformed, ill-advised people. Rambling accusations which are without foundation or substance."

He held up his hand when Kiddell started to interrupt. "Let me speak—I assume that is why you asked me to attend this program—to hear what I had to say?" He paused only long enough to wait for a verbal denial, then continued. The camera zoomed in on his features.

"Life has always been pretty good to me, Mr. Kiddell—a combination of good luck, good management, good associates and an ability to foresee opportunity when everyone else considered that opportunity to be too risky to chance, or a pipedream. I took the chances, and I won—here, in the States, abroad." He tugged at an ear lobe. "But I've always felt if you take something out of this life, you should put something back into it. It's only fair. For years you fight your way to the top of material success, then suddenly, you discover you are standing on the summit. The climb is over. You have two choices: sit on the mountaintop and admire your own achievements, or reach down and try to help others to reach the summit too. Bayan was my concept on how the latter could be achieved. It's not perfect. It's not absolute. And maybe it isn't the best way to go about it. But it's one hell of a lot better than any other method I've seen so far in the public or private sector, Mr. Kiddell!" He smiled mischievously. "However, if you have a better idea, I'd like to hear it. Maybe we can incorporate it into what we are doing at Bayan."

"The question was: Is Bayan a ripoff?" The camera zoomed in on Corbin's face once more.

"That's right," Kiddell agreed.

"A ripoff because new ideas and new projects being developed at Bayan from other people's brains or suggestions are being taken over by CORCAN?"

"Exactly." Kiddell finally felt he had his man at bay.

"I suppose it is a ripoff, Mr. Kiddell. We take someone's idea or invention or proposal at Bayan and develop it with them, bringing it up to a point where it becomes a commercially marketable item or system, then we go into production with whoever is interested in the terms of production under our licensing agreements.

"CORCAN is one of three hundred and eighty private and public companies with whom we are putting Bayan's efforts to —in dollar values to date, CORCAN's interests are less than one percent of the total commercially viable operations produced in Bayan."

"And that is your ripoff?" It was Kiddell's obligation to clarify the point.

"Obviously."

"But where is the ripoff, Mr. Corbin?" He had a sneaking suspicion he was being led down a garden path.

"Why the government is being ripped off, Mr. Kiddell! Instead of being able to waste millions of dollars in taxpayers' money developing useless ideas, using a bunch of bureaucratic business failures who are completely out of touch with commercial reality, they now must stand by and watch Bayan take this business away from them. It's a disaster for them. All those super incompetents sitting around the city here with nothing to do anymore and no chance to expand their little make-believe empires. I tell you, Mr. Kiddell, it's a tragedy!" Then he laughed at the handsome square face across the table.

Kiddell staggered along through the rest of the show until the two minute signal to end flashed on the teleprompter, then Corbin laid him away, jumping in for the last word. With his eyes glued to the clock he shut out Kiddell by raising his own voice.

"I'm sorry if I have disappointed a lot of you people out there tonight. There is no juicy scandal or gigantic swindle involved in what we are trying to do at Bayan. It is very simple. If you—any of you out there—have a good idea in business, art, or any worthwhile field, please send it in to us. I give you my word it will remain your property entirely until you and we come to a satisfactory arrangement. If the idea is unacceptable we'll send you our reasons why, with suggestions on how you can rework or improve it, then try us again. We're trying to get this country and its people moving through individual creativity—not through government handouts—government is to govern, make laws, collect taxes, not get itself involved in the private sector. Show me the government business enterprise anywhere that can stand on its own feet and compete with the private sector without props or deficit financing. Government is run by a bunch of lawyers, for the most part. How many of you know any successful businessmen who are lawyers or vice versa?" He smiled into the lens candidly, and glanced at the red second sweep hand on the studio wall clock.

"So far we haven't had a failure at Bayan—nor a complaint from any of the people, people like you, who gave us the privilege of helping them to help themselves. God gave us each a brain to use in order to create. Unfortunately only a few of us were lucky enough to wind up with the wherewithal to make our creations reality. I was one of those lucky ones. I'd like to share my luck with you."

The timing was perfect. The camera dolly began backing away for a pan hold while the credits were flashed on the screen. Kiddell nearly missed his wrapup cue before the station break. Corbin waited until the red eye on the camera went out, then stood up and stretched his hand out to the interviewer.

"Great show, Mr. Kiddell. Loved every minute of it. We must do it again sometime soon. Now, if you'll excuse me, I think my wife is waiting." He walked out the door to meet Elizabeth coming from the control booth. They left together.

As they drove home along the slippery streets she kissed him suddenly.

"What was that for?"

"Because I loved the interview, even if Walter Kiddell didn't."

"Thanks, but it was still a pointless exercise. In six months it will start all over again. Some other sorehead will get the bit in his teeth and demand an investigation on Bayan using a different approach."

"You knew it would happen?"

They slid a few feet as he pulled up to a stoplight. He sighed. "I suppose so, but there was always the hope I might have been wrong this time."

"You? Wrong? Never!" she told him loyally.

He moved across the intersection, building speed slowly on the slippery pavement. "I was wrong about you," he reminded.

"Let's just say it wasn't that you were wrong, Chuck, just that it took longer than usual to make up your mind."

With a laugh, he agreed.

They reached the outskirts of the city just as the sun dropped behind the tall apartment buildings and the minarets boomed out their prerecorded call for evening prayer across the rooftops. Perhaps a few of Alexandria's teeming millions might answer the call, but to Akbar there was only indifference to be seen from the throngs of people along the streets. He had never been to Alexandria and regarded the passing surroundings through tourists' eyes.

The airline flights between Cairo and the Egyptian seaport of Alexandria still had not been reinstated, so it had been necessary to drive the slow three hours through human and animal hurdles to reach the coast. Flights had been suspended during the Nasser era when trigger-happy anti-aircraft batteries along the air route kept shooting down the Russian Illuyshins operated by Egyptair. Aircraft identification had not been one of the Army's strong points during the Nasser years.

"You wanted the Officers' Club?" Akbar looked at the driver, startled. It was the first time the man had spoken since asking for gas money on the outskirts of Cairo.

"Yes, the Officers' Club," he agreed.

They turned east near the city's center and followed a wide boulevard past the crumbling magnificence of enormous houses once owned by the very rich in a happier time, when the very rich existed in Egypt. Spacious weed-filled lawns, scraggly hedges, and aged trees surrounded the huge ornate homes, now turned into government offices, flats and community centers, their decay reflecting the absence of pride of personal ownership.

The Officers' Club was the exception to the rest of the street. Formerly a royal residence, when royalty existed, it had advantage of disciplined labor and meticulously maintained buildings and grounds. Two gigantic white marble lions growled menacingly in unison at the dilapidated taxi as it turned in the driveway and stopped before the main entrance to the building.

"The Officers' Club!" the driver announced unnecessarily.

If he had been French, he would have said 'Violà!' as if he had built the place himself.

"Wait for me!" He reached out the window and opened the door from the outside. The inside handle was missing from the old Mercedes diesel.

"For how long?"

Akbar smiled at him and stretched for his little suitcase in the back seat.

"Until I return, Hadji!" He called him pilgrim after noticing the religious paraphernalia along the car's dashboard. The driver had obviously been to Mecca, and was proud of the fact. He slammed the door and went up the wide steps into the building.

Two armed spit and polish soldiers met him at the top. "Your business, Sir?"

"Commander Al Thani. My name is Khala Akbar."

"One moment, Sir." He went inside a wooden guard post built alongside the top of the steps and picked up a phone. The second soldier looked at Akbar and smiled.

"Palestinian?"

"From Jerusalem." The soldier in the booth replaced the phone and came back.

"You are expected, Sir." He saluted and opened one of the wide brass-flanged portals.

"Please wait in the lobby—the Commander will be with you in a few minutes."

Akbar went inside to wait.

The lobby, or lounge area, was originally the main hallway for the huge residence. It was long and wide, beautifully furnished with carpeting and paintings. It had the pungent smell of aging wood and leather combined with the mustiness of time. There were a number of double doorways leading from the wide hall into rooms. He could hear music, laughter, and from one, further down on the far side, male voices were singing to piano accompaniment.

"Khala Akbar?" Akbar turned his gaze to the voice.

"Commander Al Thani?" he inquired politely, then shook the uniformed officer's hand.

"There is a writing room we can use to talk privately." He led him down the hall, then through one of the open doors. In one corner two young Army captains were playing cards, while another man in mufti was writing a letter at one of the ornate desks along the wall. Al Thani nodded to the card players as they passed and continued on to the back of the room. He waited until Akbar was seated on the deep red leather sofa, then settled down beside him.

"Can you get a leave of absence for five months, Commander?" Akbar did not mince words.

"Starting when?" Neither did Al Thani.

"At once."

"Very difficult. Is it important?"

"Critical."

"For whom?"

"For the Cause," Akbar told him softly.

"In what capacity?"

"To command an ocean trawler and supervise four oil tankers."

"Where are they?"

"We haven't purchased them yet. We are waiting for you to examine them first—make certain they will be seaworthy; we do not want problems later. The sellers are thieves, of course."

"Of course. Sellers usually are," Al Thani agreed.

"When would I be able to return to duty here?"

"July first."

"Give or take a week?"

"No, July first, exactly," Akbar repeated.

"Papers?"

"Passport, clothes, papers and money are in the suitcase." He touched the handle on the bag at his feet. "Your name is Mustapha Awani. Libyan."

Al Thani said nothing. He was thinking.

"Jamil would like you to meet him in Rotterdam next week—February fourth at the Schulmud Hotel. He will be registered as Kassim—Amer Kassim from Iraq." He looked at the gold braid on the naval commander's sleeve and picked off a piece of white lint. "Of course if you cannot arrange it, he will understand."

Al Thani looked down at the gold braid. "If everything works, how many Jews will die?"

"If everything works, Commander Al Thani, more Jews will die than all of us have killed since 1948 when they stole your home in Jerusalem."

Al Thani's eyes glowed with the thought. He stood up. "Tell Jamil—Amer Kassim—that Mustapha Awani will meet him at Rotterdam on February the fourth!"

Female tears always unnerved him, particularly those of his wife. He didn't know how she learned about the death of Rolf Hauser, but she had discovered it that afternoon, and sobbing her heart out, retreated to her room. He couldn't understand that part either. Why the young television newsman's death should affect her as it did? Was he missing something? He sat alone in the library, a thin cheroot hanging absently from his lips. It was late and still he continued puzzling over Felina's performance.

Almost as if the boy had been her lover, he thought. "Her lover!" He said it aloud. "Of course!" He stood up quickly and left the room, turning out the lights as he went. He climbed the stairs two at a time until he reached the first landing, then stopped.

Confrontation would damage her pride—even if she did admit to the affair—and he knew she could never admit to adultery with a twenty year old during a confrontation. He started up the rest of the steps slowly. It would, he decided, be better to allow her the time to get over the loss, and confront her at an appropriate moment. He stopped again in the hallway in front of their bedroom. During all the time they had been married, never once had he been unfaithful. It hurt him to think she had been the one to break that bond. He leaned against the banister along the hallway wall; something they had installed to keep the children's sticky fingers off the wallpaper. He decided to say nothing to her about it—ever. He would let her tell him in due course, in her own time.

But supposing she never admits to anything? He reflected . . . *Too proud to tell the truth, too fearful to tell a lie?*

He removed the dead cheroot from his lips and went into the bedroom. She was lying in bed, reading a magazine, glasses perched on her nose, shielding the red-rimmed eyes.

"You feeling all right?" He began undressing.

She tossed the magazine aside and pulled off her glasses. "I'm fine, Pedro." She met his face through the mirror on the dressing table. "Did you order his execution because of me?"

Chirlo paused before replying, finishing unbuttoning his tunic. "No, I did not order his death. I did explain the problem of his knowledge to Jamil when he was here. I assume Jamil ordered his execution. I never asked."

"I thought it might have been you." She sounded relieved. Chirlo continued undressing.

When he came back from the bathroom in his robe and sat down on the side of the bed, she took his hands and held them to her face.

"You knew we were lovers?" Her eyes filled with tears.

"Not until tonight," he admitted.

"But you suspected?"

He shook his head. "The thought never entered my mind at any time, Little One." He slipped his hands to her shoulders, playing with the straps holding the nightdress. "Are you angry with me?"

He avoided her tearful eyes. The sight was painful. "No."

"What then?"

He searched for the right word—there were so many from which to choose. He chose simplicity. "Hurt." He slipped the shoulder straps down her arms, baring her breasts. He had not noticed it before, but they were beginning to sag.

He fondled her, then brushed his lips across one nipple.

"I'm sorry, Pedro," she sniffled.

He rolled the hardening nipple in his lips.

"I know you are." Gently he pushed her back on the pillows, then worked the nightdress down her body under the sheet until she was naked. There were a craze of tiny white-lined stretch marks below her navel, and some of the skin was lose and flabby; this too he noticed for the first time.

"It won't happen again—I promise." She breathed the words as he fingered her pubis gently. She felt the comfortable moisture flowing.

He spoke softly. "As we grow older, seeing our youth has fled, we want to reach back and grasp those early years—if only for a few hours, and with someone else."

She spread her legs, letting him work his fingers into her smoothly, and closed her eyes.

"But those yesterdays have vanished, Little One. They are gone forever, so don't promise me it will never happen again. Promise instead that when you do—you'll tell me. That's all I ask."

She held his curly greying hair, felt his beard tickling her thighs, his tongue probing.

"I promise, Pedro," she moaned, "and this promise I will keep."

19

February 1976

Rotterdam's industrial harbor area covers nearly thirty thousand acres. The city, at the mouth of the rivers Rhine and Maas, is the watergate to the North Sea. It is the second largest city of the Netherlands, but the largest and busiest seaport in the world for tonnage of goods handled. Sixty percent of that tonnage is crude oil feeding the five refineries at the harbors of Botlek, Europort and Maasvlake. These in turn feed the voracious appetites for fuel on the European Continent. The ocean trawler *Specht* was tied up at one of the supply docks for support shipping in the harbor of Botlek.

Dimitri Zaglaviras picked them up from the hotel with a hired car. He nodded respectfully when Jamil introduced the Libyan marine surveyor, Mustapha Awani, as they pulled away from the Schulmund.

"A great pleasure, Mr. Awani," Dimitri murmured.

Mr. Awani grunted, then settled back in his seat to watch the scenery.

The morning was filled with fierce sleet and driving wind sweeping in from the coast, hurling hats, flapping billboards, slashing at the pavement and car windows. They drove in silence; Zaglaviras in front with the driver, the two Palestinians in the rear. Traffic into the Botlek district was heavy, everyone driving cautiously behind wipered windows. Dimitri turned in his seat.

"We will stop and pick up Mr. Van der Zlapp. He is waiting."

"Who is Mr. Van der Zlapp?" Jamil inquired.

"The owner's representative." He kept his head swiveled a moment longer to see if there was any objection, then turned back to the wipers. A few minutes later the driver angled into a workers' residential area and threaded his way through a maze of narrow streets, stopping in front of one of a row of identical houses. He hit the horn. A face appeared from around a lace curtain in the downstairs window. A few moments later, a figure in a sou'wester and seaboots emerged from the door and trotted up to the car. Zaglaviras slid over against the driver, who looked annoyed as the sou'wester climbed into the front seat.

"Guten Tag, Mein Herren!" Mr. Van der Zlapp gave everyone a dripping smile. They drove on.

"We have to speak English, Mr. Van der Zlapp. My friends do not speak Dutch or German," Zaglaviras said sharply.

"Of course, Mr. Dimitri, then we speak English, ja—no problem speaking English."

He turned his dripping hat and smiled at the two dark suited men in the back seat.

"Zo you want to buy der *Specht*?" He had his head turned to an impossible angle.

"We would like to examine it," Jamil told him.

"Why are you selling it, Mr. Van der Zlapp?" Awani inquired.

"Bigger boat. Mr. Dorfmann, he buys bigger boat; more power, more range."

"Dorfmann Ocean Salvage?" Awani was familiar with the company. The Egyptian Navy had used the Dutch salvage company on two occasions in the Mediterranean.

"Ach zo! You know Mr. Dorfmann's company? Goot. Respectable man. Respectable ship." He finally gave up straining his neck and faced the front, but continued talking.

"I was master of *Sprecht* for six years. Built here in Rotterdam at Van Cleeman shipyards in 1970. Very modern, very powerful. Very seaworthy. You'll like." He nodded the rain hat, flicking water on Jamil's knees.

They drove along the quays and turned in on one of the access roads to the docks, and parked the car at the Dorfmann jetty. There were two ocean salvage tugs tied alongside each other by the pier; beyond, lay a yellow and green painted trawler with the letters "SPECHT" on its bow in capitalized Gothic. Van der Zlapp led the

604

way from the car. The driver climbed out with the others, looked at the sky, shivered and climbed back inside. He wasn't in the trawler market—buying or selling—and had seen enough of them to skip wasting time enriching his experience further.

"I'll wait until you are through."

There were two men on board when they entered the deck salon. The salon served as combination mess hall, chart room and office. The galley and pantry, from which the smells of recent breakfast still drifted, lay beyond. The two man shore crew stood up from the mess table, still holding their tea mugs, and greeted Van der Zlapp respectfully.

He spoke to them in Flemish. Both smiled self-consciously and looked over at the Palestinians. Awani went over to the chart table and pulled out the wide thin drawers, riffling the new chart piles.

"De Nort Sea and Baltic to English Channel and Azores. Complete," Van der Zlapp told him. "Come, we will make tour."

He led them up to the wheel house first, pointing out the instrumentation, gyrosyn, compass, radar, radio shack and signal flag locker. Most of the flags had never been unwrapped from their original packing, Awani observed. He looked through the thick circular storm glass on the bridge down the length of deck to the high snub bow, noting the neatly coiled ropes, new paint, absence of rust. The hawser cables were well greased and looked new—at least the rain kept him from detecting any frays. He turned away to look at the radar scope. It was a Decca Unit. Its rubber eye-piece was well worn and rotting with salt and age.

"Still working?" Awani touched the top of the unit.

"Ja. Like a germ."

"Charm," Zaglaviras corrected him, unabashed.

They went back down to the salon cleared spotless of plates and litter during their few minutes on the bridge. The two crewmen were gone. They followed the forward gangway from the salon down into the crew's sleeping quarters; small compact cabins berthing two men on either side of a central passageway. Jamil counted sleeping places for twelve men. At the end of the passage, Van der Zlapp opened a door into the chain locker and turned on the light. They crowded in to examine the pile of steel links crammed in the small area; chains that fed the bow anchor into the sea. Judging from the condition of the steel links, it was rarely used, Awani noted. They climbed back up to the salon, through the galley and pantry to the after-lounge and messroom for the master, mate and two engineers, each with his own private cabin leading off from the lower passageway beyond. The rooms were larger and more comfortable, although only the master's stateroom had its own head and shower. The other three officers, like the crew, shared a common facility.

Jamil had seen enough. It was ideal in size and appointment. The engine room and deck machinery he left for the professional naval officer to inspect. He sat down on the oak chair at the head of the mess table. The master's chair. He tried to tilt it back, but it was securely chained to the floor from the seat. He watched the other three go back through the galley to the engine room steps running off the side of the pantry.

"Three access doors to engine room—one inside—two on deck," Van der Zlapp explained as he descended the steel steps.

Zaglaviras stood by at the bottom, watching the two seamen examine the glistening turbines. From their conversation he knew Awani was an expert. He was glad he had not tried to play any games with the grim-faced Palestinian sitting up top in the officer's lounge. He would let Van der Zlapp do the selling for him. The man simply reeked of honesty and marine integrity. They had plotted the price together the evening before. Three hundred thousand American dollars, and Dimitri would scoop fifty of it as a kickback commission for getting the price old Dorfmann had been asking unsuccessfully for eight months. The vessel was worth around two hundred tops, but the Greek knew the Palestinian would pay the third as extra premium to have what he wanted. It was, after all, he reasoned, going to be their flagship for whatever they had in mind.

The tankers would be a little trickier. He had found four ten thousand tonners two days after Jamil had left him in Piraeus. They were tired and rusty with rotten hulks; sitting in the backwater of the Bosphorus. He had seen them once years before on a smuggling trip with opium gum from one of the towns along the coast in the Sea of Marmora. When he called his contact in Izmir to learn if he knew their present condition, Lakim Bey agreed to fly over to Istanbul and examine them for his old friend—for a price. Dimitri wired the money from their Zurich account and sat back to wait. He nearly missed the Olympic flight inter-Amsterdam; Lakim Bey phoned just as he was leaving with Speidel for the airport.

"Mr. Zaglaviras!" Dimitri jumped and looked up the steps. Jamil was standing at the top, a hand on each railing. "I wonder if we could talk about those tankers while Mr. Awani is inspecting the machinery?"

Jamil had never told Chirlo the necessity for proof the bombs would work. Proof before payment. When the Libyan President had ordered the test originally, the Palestinian had felt certain the mercurial Qadaffi would change his mind several times during the intervening months, depending upon the political pose he might decide to adopt at the critical moment. The critical moment had now arrived and if there was to be no delay on the July Fourth plan for the bombs, and a test was still necessary to insure the payment by the Libyans to Chirlo, then the time had arrived to settle the issue. He had not foreseen the roadblock put in his way by the presence of Major Hassan.

Hassan was a typical Libyan squarehead; stubborn, unimaginative, poorly educated, but blindly obedient to his master. The difficulty in dealing with a fool, Jamil discovered, was the necessity of becoming a fool as well, in order to communicate.

"I realize what the original instructions were, Major, but I don't want either of us to make the mistake of assuming these instructions still apply, and later be blamed for failing to reconfirm the instructions," Jamil said patiently.

The Major appeared to be weighing this logic. He picked up the memo again and read through it. "Article four states that payment will be made upon proof the nuclear devices will work; this will require selecting one of the five at random and exploding it." He looked up. "Those orders are very clear, Mr. Jamil. Nowhere does it say anything about our re-checking to see if the President wishes to countermand these orders."

God! But the man was stupid. Jamil tried again. "Exactly my point, Major Hassan! Don't you see it now? The Colonel had many things on his mind when he wrote that memorandum. We have had many political changes over the past year. If we explode one of the bombs we might plunge the country into an embarrassing position internationally. Perhaps the Colonel overlooked this possibility."

"The Colonel overlooks nothing. Everything is planned. It is our duty to obey."

Jamil couldn't believe the conversation was taking place. He decided on another tack. "If I were to talk to the Colonel for a few minutes, Major, possibly I could clarify this issue."

Hassan scanned the magic memo again. "It says nothing here about my arranging for you to talk to Colonel Qadaffi. Article two states Major Hassan of the Revolutionary Council will assume the responsibility of discharging the orders of the President." He read the words slowly, like a man who is troubled by the written word. "That makes me the man in charge of making the final decision, doesn't it?" he asked almost with wonderment.

Jamil gave up, exasperated. It was hopeless. "Very clear to me, Major. You are the man in command. You have the ultimate responsibility for the decision. We must abide by your orders. No doubt about that." He examined the Major's black eyebrows. They went in a thick straight line across the top of his eyes without narrowing above the nose. Simian.

"What are your orders, Major Hassan?" he asked respectfully.

He could see the Libyan's square head begin to swell.

"You will explode one of the bombs, Mr. Jamil. I will trust you to make the random choice and notify me as to the exact date. Then, I will inform the President. If he wishes to alter his orders, he will do so in his enlightenment at that time."

Jamil thought, *Shit! Another trip to Cosecha Rica!* Aloud, he replied, "An enlightened decision, Major Hassan. I'm surprised I never thought of it myself."

He stood up and bowed respectfully. "Allah Maak!"

Commander Al Thani watched the pilot boat parallel the *Specht*, slackening speed as it moved alongside. The short burly harbor pilot waved to him once, then jumped across the narrow width of water between the boats and into the arms of two sailors. The launch increased speed, widening the distance between the ships, then dropped away as it swung into a fast turn and headed back to the safety of the waterway.

"Steer two five zero!" he told the helmsman, then rang the engine room for speed. The *Specht* heeled slightly, the engine beat increased, then bow and engines settled on a constant direction and vibration as the trawler pushed through the cold waters of the North Sea towards the English Channel. Al Thani tapped the barometer inside the wheelhouse. It was steady. He scanned the radar scope. There were a few small blips; fishing boats near their two o'clock position working in a cluster and one very large echo from what was obviously a super tanker coming up the channel for Rotterdam's Europort.

They would pass well clear of immediate shipping.

Later, when they entered the compressed sea between England and France, he knew he would have to remain on radar watch continuously. Although Channel traffic was supposed to keep to the west when southbound, and on the French side when northbound, invariably some ships ignored the rules and plunged willy nilly through this heavily traveled area, oblivious to common sense or safety.

"If anything exciting happens, call me!" he told the young Dutch helmsman. He had hired a scratch crew through Van der Zlapp for the voyage to Tripoli. They were all good experienced hands and spoke fluent English.

"Ay Sir. I'll call you."

Al Thani went below to the main salon and picked up the roll of charts he had laid on the bulkhead when they sailed. He removed the rubber bands from each and spread the mass of papers across the salon table.

"Steward!"

"Sir!" The pantryman cook stuck his head out from the galley.

"Some hot cocoa—you have any?" He looked at the lad, smiling.

"Not ready, Sir. Coffee, no cocoa. I can make some."

"Good. Do it. A big pot. I never drink coffee—make sure you don't scald the milk, now!"

"No Sir!" He disappeared back through the doorway. Al Thani pulled off the first map and took it over to the chart table. He smoothed its curling edges into the metal guides on the table top and sat down on the stool.

The map was a detailed replica of the water courses running into the Port of New York. Depth soundings were marked in fathoms; miniature numbers scattered everywhere. The land areas were blank. Even the Statue of Liberty was missing from Liberty Island; only the shoreline bearings to the radio beacons were marked. Al Thani picked up a set of chrome dividers from the cubbyhole and spread its needle points, starting from Pier 34 on the East River, then marked a small pencilled x at each needle point while swiveling the dividers down the river, past Liberty Island and out to the approaches of Long Island Sound.

He worked quickly; a professional navigator plotting a ship's course for the captain he had yet to meet, of a ship he had yet to see.

The trouble with Benton Mossbart was, he talked too much. Talked as if the only thing he was interested in hearing was the sound of his own rich baritone. Maloney worked away on his doodles, scratching arrows and spears over the yellow pad on the boardroom table. He glanced briefly at the rest of the Centennial Group, saw they were all drinking in Mossbart's baritone as if the man was one of God's appointed, and went back to his doodling.

Sycophants he thought. *A bunch of goddamn sycophants.* He lined in the tail feathers for the arrow he had been working on at the moment and wished he'd never been assigned to the New York Port Authority Centennial Project. It was all bullshit, as far as Maloney could see.

"And so, gentlemen," Mossbart said solemnly, "the tall ships will leave their Bermuda haven and set sail for the New World. At twelve noon on July the Fourth they will begin their journey up the river past the lovely lady with the torch—the tall ships from another era, visiting the tall buildings of the New World—dipping their white billowing sails to honor our two hundred years of accomplishment."

He paused, his eyes staring out through the double glass windows across the parking lot to the terminal warehouses and beyond, through the blowing snow, almost as if he could see the procession arriving five months too early.

"Mr. Mossbart!"

Everyone stared at Maloney, surprised the cocky Irishman with the bright blue eyes and curved briar would have the nerve to interrupt their prophet's revelation.

"Yes, Captain Maloney, what is it?" Mossbart did not like being interrupted in the middle of a vision.

"Do you think we can get on to the crowd control problem and leave the tall ships to find their own way to a safe haven? I don't mean to rush you, but the Commissioner is expecting a report from me this afternoon by four. If we're going to have six million people standing along the banks watching your billowing sails with the President of the United States among them, the police department would like to have some information on those areas you're designating as viewing points." He tapped his pipe into the yellow glass ashtray. "That's if it's not too much trouble, Mr. Mossbart."

Al Thani sipped the mug of cocoa absently while he rechecked the notations and figures on the chart. Satisfied, he slid off the stool and slipped the New York harbor map out of the metal guides; it sprung into a partial roll. He took it back to the pile of charts on the salon table and picked up the next one.

"Captain Awani!" He dropped the chart and answered the call from the wheelhouse. The helmsman pointed a finger out the glass. A huge tanker, riding low, was bearing down on them.

"Starboard fifteen," he told the helmsman. "Is that the same one we saw earlier?" He went quickly to the radar screen. It was.

"Idiot! What the hell is he doing on this tack?"

"Fifteen starboard on Sir!" The helmsman spun the wheel, centering the bow on the new course. They stood in silence watching the monster grow, its blunt bows pushing twin avalanches of foam and sea aside as it headed toward the deep channel into Rotterdam. It passed a quarter mile on their port side. Al Thani studied the superstructure with the glasses.

Liberian—naturally. Looks deserted too. They're probably all sitting around in the mess dead drunk while the ship is on autopilot. He went back to the radar scanner and studied the green flourescent screen a full minute.

"Port twenty!"

He continued to study the screen, balancing himself easily as the wheelhouse tilted when the helmsman spun the spokes, turning on the new course.

"Hold that for thirty minutes, then return to the original heading." He looked over the seaman's shoulder, watching the gyrosyn compass repeater settle down.

"Twenty port on Sir!" the young Dutchman said unnecessarily. Al Thani nodded.

"Keep your eyes skinned!" He returned to the salon and picked up the discarded map. He took it over to the chart table and slipped it into the guides, spreading it flat, then picked up the dividers.

The port, like the City of Montreal, is on an island, sitting in the middle of the St. Lawrence River, eight hundred miles from the sea. It is the beginning of the St. Lawrence Seaway, an inland waterway which ends 2342 miles upstream at Duluth, Minnesota, at the western end of Lake Superior. It is the longest inland waterway for deep sea shipping in the world. Al Thani's interest, however, did not extend beyond the Port of Montreal. He spread his caliper needles, dropping a base point in the middle of the half-mile channel separating Montreal Island from the Islands of St. Helena and Notre Dame. He picked the Jacques Cartier Bridge spanning the river to the mainland as mile zero, then began swinging the needles downstream towards Quebec City, making notations as he went.

Corbin slipped off the ski tow and joined Elizabeth at the top of the run. It was a perfect day for skiing; cloudless skies, no wind, and still cold enough to keep the snow crisp, while not cold enough to freeze body extremities. They walked over to join the group of brightly uniformed skiers, waiting at the starting point for the run down the trail to the valley.

"It's all right for you to shrug your shoulders, but I haven't seen the Olympic Games. You have!" She continued the discussion started at the bottom of the slope while waiting for the chairlift.

Elizabeth wanted to rent an apartment and move to Montreal during the two months the games were in progress. It would mean Corbin commuting between Montreal and Ottawa; an idea he found distasteful.

"We can see it all on television, Sweetheart. Complete coverage. In the comfort of our living room. Why fight the crowds and go through all that drama to sit in a bleacher? Besides, you can only watch one event at a time. With television we can see all the events as they happen, continuously."

She considered this reasoning. "Well, then let's at least be on hand for the finals. The Queen and Prince Phillip, Prince Charles, Prince Andrew and Princess Anne are going to be there and I do have my sense of British loyalty to uphold," she said self-righteously.

"Bullshit!"

She made a face at him, and pushed herself off the crest, past the starting flag. Corbin waited a few moments, then poled himself down the slope after her. The air sang in his ears and stung on his face as he rocketed through the powder snow, chasing the blur of his wife's yellow ski suit a few hundred feet below.

He pulled up beside her in a shower of snow at the bottom. "Okay, pest, I'll make a deal with you. July first to the tenth we go to Montreal and see the Olympics. Deal?" He raised his Polaroid glasses, then stuck out a mittened hand with a ski pole dangling from it.

"Deal," she replied. Their mittens met and the two poles clanged together.

"Colonel?"

Asher looked up from the letter he was composing from the code book. "Yes, Sergeant Kronig?"

"I've got a reply back on that Doctor Hauser that might be of interest, Sir."

Asher set down his pencil and pushed the code book to one side.

"Let's have a look at it."

Kronig came the rest of the way through the door and kicked the panel shut with his heel. He came over and gave the letter to his leader.

"Doctor Gerdbaum handles the Nazi files for Bonn," he explained when he noticed Asher's puzzled look at the printed German letterhead.

"So, what's it say?" Asher could neither read nor speak German.

Sergeant Kronig was fluent in six languages.

"Oh, sorry Sir. I forgot. I'll make up a translation." He reached for the two pages of typing.

"Never mind. Do the translation later. Give me the gist of it now."

"Yes Sir." Kronig cleared his throat and began to read. "Mein Herr"—he looked over the sheets—"that means 'Dear Sir' . . ."

"The gist, Kronig, for God's sake, just give me the gist!"

The sergeant looked chagrined. "Yes Sir!" He scanned the first paragraph. "Well, Doctor Hauser is listed as a neo-Nazi with Doctor Gerdbaum's organization. He was one of the first group of scientists selected for the Norwegian heavy water project after the occupation of Norway. He remained as one of the—"

"Heavy water?" Asher interrupted.

"That's what is says, Colonel. Heavy water." He looked back at the letter. "Heavy water," he confirmed. "What is heavy water? I thought all water weighed the same until it was ice, then it became lighter by volume."

Asher made no comment; he was thinking, trying to remember something. Kronig continued reading and translating, relating the life story of Doctor Kurt Hauser as contained in the files of the Nazi intelligence section and garnished by Doctor Gerdbaum's branch of investigators. The story ended in 1967 when the ongoing political affiliations of Kurt Hauser appeared to provide no further interest to Doctor Gerdbaum. Kronig folded the two pages neatly and stood waiting for some comment or instruction.

"Deuterium," Asher said softly.

"Yes Sir."

"Heavy water is deuterium."

"Oh, I see. Deuterium," Kronig echoed.

Asher leaned back in his chair, smiling. "Sergeant, I think you've just solved a mystery."

"I have?" He tipped forward in his chair, and stood up.

"Is the Brigadier in his office this afternoon?" he asked, starting for the door.

"I believe so, Sir."

"Good. Get that letter translated at once—two copies. Send one to the Brigadier." He paused at the door. "Bloody good work, Kronig. Bloody good work!"

The Israeli Sergeant was so surprised he forgot to thank the Colonel for the compliment before he was gone.

Asher limped down the corridor to the elevator and stabbed the button. Now, he thought, he had something Borodam couldn't ignore; something tangible, real, a basis for fact. He crammed himself into the elevator between three noncoms who backed against the sides respectfully, giving up their conversation as well as their spaces. Asher nodded to them curtly as he turned to face the closing doors. For the first time, Hauser's presence in a tiny Latin American republic was making sense. He got out quickly on the sixth floor and started down the corridor for Borodam's office. He met the Brigadier coming out into the hallway with two full Colonels.

"Sir, may I speak to you for a moment?" He blocked their passage.

"Hello, Asher. You know Friedman and Poltz?" The two officers nodded. Asher seemed to remember Poltz from an intelligence briefing somewhere. Friedman he had never met. He shook hands with both and turned back to Borodam.

"I have something concrete on that Bruner business." Borodam's browns began to furrow into a scowl. Asher rushed on. "It seems Doctor Hauser was assigned to the German heavy water program up in Norway during the war. Deuterium production for the atomic bombs they were never able to build in time. Now he's in Cosecha Rica." He waited for the surprised look. It never came.

"So?" Asher couldn't believe the lack of interest.

"So General, Cosecha Rica has a nuclear generating plant, one of the Canadian CANDU type reactors which uses heavy water deuterium. They've had it for several years."

"So?" The scowl was deeper now.

"That is why Hauser is working in Cosecha Rica. He knows heavy water. He knows nuclear physics and he knows how to manufacture atomic bombs."

"You have proof?" The two Colonels appeared interested.

"I have proof that he was working on the Norwegian project for the Nazis.

"That was thirty years ago when he was a young man, Colonel. I mean do you have proof he is working at building nuclear bombs in Cosecha Rica?"

Asher's face fell. "Well, no Sir. Not yet. We haven't got that far in the investigation. I only received the background information on Hauser from Germany a few minutes ago."

"So you leaped to the conclusion Cosecha is the new Nazi arsenal for atomic warheads. Really, Colonel!" Borodam scowled at him, exasperated, then walked away down the hall to the elevators, the Colonels trailing his wake. Poltz looked back and winked sympathetically.

Asher waited until they had left the floor, then went into the Brigadier's office.

"You just missed him!"

"No I didn't, Sabra, I just met him and he cut me dead—stone cold dead." He slumped into the chair in front of the secretary's desk and straightened out his leg. "I made a fool out of myself," he told her glumly.

"Anything I can do?"

"No, nothing. I wish there were. What I probably need more than anything else right now is a swift kick in the ass. My brains are scrambled with this Bruner thing."

"Lev, you're not still worrying about that?"

He nodded, then told her about the letter from Germany; and as he talked he realized where he had made the mistake. He should have waited until he knew more about the Blucher Chemicals operation in Latin America; who were his associates; what were they producing; was it a front for something else? He had handled it badly. He couldn't blame Borodam for his reaction.

"I'm positive there's a connection between everything. Hauser, Bruner, Jamil, the Palestinians, Chirlo, the CANDU reactor, somehow it all fits together, and somehow—I don't know how yet—but somehow, I'm as certain as I'm sitting here we are all in great danger because of it."

He wiped the earnest serious look from his face and smiled. "So, tell me I'm crazy!" She didn't return the smile.

"No," she said slowly. "I don't think you're crazy at all. In a disjointed way it all makes a lot of sense, at least to me. But then I'm not the intelligence officer in this office. If you want my advice, for whatever it's worth, I'd follow it through. If you're right, sooner or later something concrete is bound to turn up. At least if it turns out you're wrong, you'll have the satisfaction of knowing the answers!"

He stood up and leaned over the desk, then kissed her soundly.

"T'hell with the Brigadier! I'll follow your advice." He grabbed her phone and dialed his office.

"Sergeant! Get on the phone to Bonn. I want to know the names of all German nationals who have gone to work with Blucher Chemicals in Cosecha Rica since 1973. Professional background, terms of employment, the works. Got that? Good. Next, get on to the American Embassy and find out what they can get us on the Blucher operations in Cosecha Rica. When you've done that, send a telex to our Embassy in Ottawa—no wait. I'll do that part myself."

He set the phone into Sabra's open palm. "Thanks."

"Cost you a dinner." She replaced the reciever, as Asher started for the door. He looked back.

"Do you think you could stand a dumb intelligence officer that long?"

"Try me, Lev." She studied his face, a ghost of a smile crinkling the corners of her mouth.

"If I didn't know you better, I'd say you were on the make, young lady!"

"I am." Now she was smiling.

"In that case, I'll meet you at reception at five-thirty. We can go to your place first while I watch you undress."

"The word is *change*—into civilian clothes." She laughed.

"I like undress better." He chuckled, then closed the door.

Morris Levy saw the young man sitting in the general waiting room reading a newspaper when he passed through to his office. The man was the only one waiting.

"Mr. Levy!"

Morris stopped, then turned around. "Yes?"

The man folded the newspaper as he stood up. He had looked taller sitting; standing, he appeared compact, muscular, with a calm face and confident eyes. The receptionist looked at both men inquiringly. The young man walked over to Morris, then lowered his voice.

"I am Epsen from the Israeli Embassy. May I speak with you privately? He smiled apologetically, then raised his voice to normal conversational level. "I know you're a busy man, Sir, but it will take only a few minutes of your time."

Levy nodded. "Hold my calls, Mrs. White."

Levy walked with him through the corridor beyond the reception doors into his office. The man stood watching while Morris shed his overshoes, then hat and overcoat onto the coat tree.

"Can I take your coat, Mr. Epsen?" The young man slipped off his fleece-lined duffle and passed it over.

"Boots?"

"I left them out front."

"Well, sit down, Mr. Epsen. What's on your mind?" Levy went to his desk and sat down.

The young man remained standing. "First, Mr. Levy, this is not an official visit, nor should it be construed as such; just one Jew talking to another Jew, if that's okay with you?" Levy looked at him evenly.

"I'm a Canadian, Mr. Epsen."

The young man smiled. "So am I, Mr. Levy, that's why I'm here." He waited for the information to sink in, then went on. "However, I am not here as a Canadian talking to another Canadian, or an employee of the Israeli Embassy talking to a Canadian Jew. I'm a Jew talking to another Jew. Just so there's no misunderstanding. By the way, is this room bugged?" He looked about the walls absently.

"Bugged? Now why should it be bugged?"

The young man shrugged. "I don't know, Sir, I just asked. Okay?"

"As far as I am aware, Mr. Epsen, this room is not bugged. Now perhaps you'll tell me what this is about?"

"Sure thing." He started pacing the carpet slowly, lightly, like a ballet dancer. "Our Ottawa Embassy has received a request from Israeli intelligence in Tel Aviv to check out the CANDU reactor given to the Republic of Cosecha Rica in 1967."

"1969, actually—before that, it still belonged to us. What do you want to check out?"

Epsen shrugged. "Anything you can tell me—unofficially, of course." He continued his slow pacing.

The pacing annoyed Levy. He wished the young man would stay in one place so he wouldn't have to keep swiveling his head, following him.

"Officially or unofficially I can say the unit is working extremely well. It was one of our earlier designs, smaller than the new CANDU 600, but equally as efficient. Cosecha Rica was a sort of test bed for the bigger CANDU system—"

Epsen stopped suddenly in front of the desk and held up his hand, interrupting the sales pitch. "That's not what I meant, Mr. Levy."

"I don't understand." Morris was bewildered.

Epsen came over to the desk and laid both palms on its edge. "To your knowledge, Mr. Levy, have there been any irregularities since the reactor was installed in Cosecha Rica?"

"Such as?" Morris was wary.

"You tell me! Anything out of the ordinary? Something someone might have said? An incident requiring investigations, or clarification? Anything?"

Levy stood up. "Would you excuse me, Mr. Epsen. I have to make a call in the men's room." He patted his torso as he came from behind the desk. "Kidneys!" he said significantly. "I'll just be a minute."

Epsen sat down to wait.

Morris walked quickly out to the front desk. "Mrs. White! Get me the Israeli Embassy. I'll take it on the phone there!" He went over and sat down in a chair by the rubber plant while she searched for the number and put the call through. He picked up the phone on the end table when she nodded at him.

"Good morning, this is Morris Levy calling from Atomic Energy of Canada, may I speak to your Charge d'Affairs?"

"Mr. Stacker is not in the office this morning, can I help?"

"How about Mr. Epsen, is he in?"

"No, I'm sorry, Mr. Epsen will be out until noon. I can connect you to Mr. Perlman. He's Mr. Epsen's superior."

"Do that, please—the name is Levy." He fingered the smooth thick leaf of the rubber plant while he waited. Minutes passed, then an accented voice introduced itself through the receiver.

"Conrad Perlman here, may I help you Mr. Levy?"

"Did you send a Mr. Epsen over to my office this morning?"

"I did."

"Would you describe him for me?"

"Short, muscular, dark hair, about twenty-eight, wearing a sheep-lined duffle coat."

"Thank you, Mr. Perlman." He hung up and went back through the doors to his office.

Epsen watched him return to the desk; his eyes were inquiring. "Well, Mr. Levy, did I check out okay?"

Morris felt guilty as he sat down. He smiled self-consciously. "You did. Mr. Perlman verified your visit and gave me your description. I'm satisfied you're real."

Epsen appeared neither pleased nor displeased by the news. Levy looked at him for a few moments.

"Officially, we have had no incidents, irregularities or anything out of the ordinary since the CANDU was given to the Cosecha Rican government. However, unofficially, I can tell you we made an investigation recently to check some irregularities which appeared on one of our routine photo reconnaissance pictures."

"And what was the result of that investigation?"

"Negative. I was satisfied with the explanation offered at the time."

"When was this investigation, Mr. Levy?" Epsen asked idly.

"Over the New Year."

"Ours or theirs?"

"Theirs—last week in December to the first week in January. As I said, it was an unofficial visit; one of the men responsible for construction of the reactor who had lived several years in the country, married a local girl and was on more or less intimate terms with the government people down there. Had he uncovered anything significant, I would, of course, have instituted an immediate, formal, in-depth investigation."

"You asked this man to go on your behalf—unofficially?"

"I did—as a friend. I've known him for more than ten years. I was prepared to rely on his judgment. Still am—for that matter."

Epsen stood up. He looked very relaxed.

"This photograph, what did it show that aroused your interest?"

"Some wheel tracks bordering an outside storage pool for nuclear waste."

"I see."

"Apparently the tire tracks were made by a small dune buggy that was lifted over the fence from the chemical company which occupies the premises next door, so they could drive around and pick up some paper labels that had blown off a few of the chemical barrels stacked along the fence line. It turned out to be nothing."

Epsen began pacing, more slowly this time. "I take it, then, their chemical company's property adjoins the storage pool sight?"

"It does."

"Blucher Chemical Limitada."

"Oh, you know them?"

"Not really, but I'm learning all the time." He stopped in front of the desk.

"Okay, Mr. Levy, so your emissary was satisfied with the explanation given to him as to how the wheel tracks appeared in the photograph. Now tell me, who was it that gave him this explanation —the government, or Blucher Chemicals?"

"Both—I mean the emissary met with senior government officials who investigated the inquiry, then a day or two later brought him together with the managing director of Blucher's, who provided the explanation after he had done some internal checking himself. I understand several yardmen were dismissed from the company as a result of the incidents."

"*Incidents* or incident?"

"Plural. There had been other instances of tire tracks in earlier photographs which had been overlooked at the assessment center before the latest photo evidence was picked out. The center then went back over all their earlier pictures and found wheel tracks from other overflights."

"May I have a copy of these photographs?"

"For what purpose, Mr. Epsen? The incident is closed," Levy said defensively.

Epsen began to pace again. Morris could see he was thinking, assembling words of persuasion. "If a further investigation—unofficially, of course—provided you with new evidence something was amiss at the waste storage site—or pool, as you call it—you would like to know about it, wouldn't you, Mr. Levy?"

"There is nothing amiss. I am already satisfied."

"I'm not." He stopped before the desk again. "There are a number of other pieces of information that I have, which, when coupled together with what you have told me, make it imperative an in-depth study of the whole affair be started as quickly as possible."

He leaned over the desk, his earnest eyes staring into Morris'.

"There is an excellent chance Blucher Chemicals was set up as a front, first to steal your nuclear waste, then to refine it on site, and finally, to use the extracted plutonium to construct atomic bombs. Okay?" He paused, then straightened up.

"If it is true, and I don't say that it is, we don't know, but if it is true, then I think you, I, the government and Tel Aviv have a right to know before it gets out of hand."

"Really, Mr. Epsen! I don't know where you're getting your information, but I can assure you I'm quite satisfied with the results from my own sources. What you are suggesting would place a friendly foreign government in a compromising position—to say nothing of our own government—and might very well result in making all of us look like raving lunatics!"

"Then, Mr. Levy," Epsen said quietly, "it comes down to deciding whether to open a new unofficial investigation and wind up looking like lunatics, or, doing nothing and perhaps winding up looking like fools."

He went over to the coat rack for his duffle and slipped it on.

"That choice, of course, rests with you. Okay?"

They pulled the soft armchairs in a semi-circle around the blazing fire; the three of them sat watching the red and orange weaving warmth fill the soot-black opening in the fireplace. No one spoke for several minutes. Corbin glanced at the painting above the mantle. It was his favorite, by Frederic Remmington; a huge prairie landscape at twilight; in the distance, on a rise, the lone figure of a cowboy standing in his stirrups looking back and waving his hat to someone just before he cleared the rise and disappeared from view.

"S'long pardner!"

"What?" Levy looked at him.

Affleck tipped his chin to the painting. "It's the name of the painting," he explained.

"Oh! The painting." Morris looked up at it too. "Yes, very nice. Remmington, isn't it?"

"Remmington," Corbin confirmed.

They lapsed into silence, all three staring above the mantle at the solitary cowboy.

Morris Levy had felt himself starting to panic after Epsen left. He had thought of a dozen clever things to say afterwards and a dozen questions he could have asked the young man. But it was too late. He realized later he had been tricked; tricked into giving up what information he had, yet nothing from Epsen in return. Of course, if Epsen had wanted to give any information he would have, Morris reasoned. So, having failed to ask the man for the additional knowledge, he had justified his oversight by deciding he probably would have obtained nothing from Epsen anyway. After a half hour debating on his best course of action, he phoned Affleck and explained the problem. Don suggested they meet at Corbin's after work and discuss it. Now, with dinner finished, their wives chatting in the sunroom, they reflected on a course of action after Morris went over the details of his strange meeting that morning with Epsen.

"What puzzled me is the Israeli interest in the affair. It doesn't make sense," Morris said.

"Wasn't there a Palestinian in Cosecha Rica when you were there, Don?" Corbin asked suddenly.

"Yes—why yes, Jamil—Colonel Chirlo's old revolutionary buddy!"

"There's the Israeli interest." He looked at Morris. "As I recall, this Jamil character and his wife that Don met were a pair of real anarchists, so it might follow the Israelis have had some dealings with them in the Middle East; have heard about the recent trips he or his wife made to the country; knew there was a nuclear reactor on site and put it all together as an item worth investigating; probably just an inquiry; sub rosa at this point, of course."

Levy nodded. "That would make sense." He brightened momentarily, then his face fell. "And I, like an idiot, had to tell him about the wheel tracks and get him further intrigued by the whole thing. I should have kept my mouth shut."

"Why?" Don asked. "You've nothing to hide. It may not be public knowledge, but there was an incident, it was checked out and proved to be nothing more than a yardman's error. I think the fact you did tell him the whole story should set their minds at rest."

"I don't," Corbin said flatly. "I think he will report back to Tel Aviv and within the next few days an Israeli intelligence officer will be sent to Punta Delgado to investigate. Do the Israelis have an Embassy in San Ramon?" He looked at Affleck.

"No."

"They don't need one, Chuck, they can work through the American Embassy," Levy observed logically. "Which then brings the Americans into the picture and another sub rosa investigation by them over the same ground. The ripples are certainly spreading, aren't they?" he said glumly.

"Are, or *will*, Morris?" Corbin suggested. "My own opinion—for whatever it's worth—is that you write a full report to the Minister, sticking strictly to the facts and your appraisal of the events after Don returned last month, then sit back and wait to see what happens."

He stood up and turned his back on the fire, warming his bottom.

"Either the Israelis will find nothing and it will all blow over, or they will find something and start raising hell on an official level. Either way, your ass is covered because you have already notified your Minister."

He felt sorry for Levy. The faithful civil servant scientist caught in the game of politics, see-sawing between his loyalties as a government employee, his responsibilities as the director of the Atomic Energy Commission, and his loyalty as a Jew. Corbin didn't envy him one bit.

"Of course you could always resign and go back to M.I.T. as a lecturer." He smiled, then moved away from the fire; the heat along the back of his legs had become uncomfortable.

Morris looked at him earnestly. "Tell me, Chuck, tell me honestly. Do you think Chirlo and those Palestinians might be trying to build a bomb?"

Corbin shrugged and looked at Affleck. "Probably, but then isn't everyone these days?"

Commander Al Thani saw Dimitri Zaglaviras as he came through the passport control wicket of the air terminal at Istanbul. The Greek was standing beside a tubby little man in a light blue shiny silk suit, scanning the faces of the passengers emerging through the frosted glass doors. He stuck a smile on his face and moved forward swiftly to greet Al Thani the moment he saw him emerge. The tubby blue silk suit moved with him.

"Ah! Mr. Awani! Such a relief to see you safe and sound again." He sounded genuinely relieved, as if the million dollar bonus had nothing whatsoever to do with it.

"May I have the honor to present my old and very dear friend, Mr. Lakim Bey."

The phosphorescent suit moved into position and extended a collection of fat ringed fingers, which Mr. Awani shook dutifully, but without comment.

"Such a pleasure to meet you at last, Mr. Awani," Lakim Bey beamed. "Such a pleasure!" he reconfirmed, withdrawing his hand. "If you will follow me please, I will lead."

He spun on his heel with a surprising agility and threaded them through the baffling babble of passengers, hawkers and gawkers to the bedlam outside the main entrance.

A huge muscular Turk with fierce mustache shoved a half dozen people out of the way to make a path for them over the last few yards to Lakim Bey's Lagonda touring salon. The mustached chauffeur flipped down the running board step with a practiced foot and opened the wide door with a flourish. The three men climbed inside its comfortable interior. Awani settled himself into the quiet plush surroundings as they drove out of the turmoil of the airport to the quiet peace of the countryside along the Sea of Marmora.

"Such problems to get exactly what you wanted, Mr. Awani," Dimitri ventured. "Yes, Mr. Awani, such a problem." Lakim Bey's English was very good on pronounciation, but weak on sentence structure. He was more at home in Greek.

"You have the specifications and surveyor's report?" Awani demanded.

"Specifications, yes; surveyor's report—unfortunately—no," Dimitri apologized. He looked across the wide space from his jumpseat at Lakim Bey for further explanation. The Turk wiggled his shiny bulk around on the seat so he could look at Awani without turning his head.

"No surveyor report, Mr. Awani. No time. Shortage notice."

"In other words, the ships are a quartet of rust buckets which no respectable surveyor would accept responsibility for signing as seaworthy," he said curtly. "Give me the specs.

623

Zaglaviras reached up and tapped the window. The chauffeur pulled the knob on his side down and slid open the pane. The Greek said something to him in Turkish; the man felt down beside him on the seat and brought up a small briefcase, which he slipped through the opening in the window, then slid the glass closed—all without taking his eyes off the road. Awani took the case and dragged out the moldy papers. The last surveyor's report was dated August, 1953, when the vessels had been taken over by their new owners, Petrocean Supply of Liberian registry; there was the appropriate local address for the owners, a postal box number in Ankara. Awani began scanning the specifications of the four tankers. For the next half hour, no one spoke as the big car swayed down the road at moderate speed. He looked up suddenly.

"Where are we going?"

"Near Izmit. Ships stored near Izmit. Safe harbor," Lakim Bey said.

"It would have to be. They haven't operated since 1958. Are you sure they're still afloat?"

"Oh very funny joke, Mr. Awani! Good joke!" He laughed politely, his little piggy eyes squinting at Zaglaviras. The Greek laughed too, and slapped his knee.

"That's a good one, Mr. Awani—are they still afloat? Ha, ha, ha!"

They settled back into silence while Awani continued wading through the papers. When he finished, he replaced the piles into the worn leather briefcase and set it on the carpeted floor, then sighed and looked out the window to watch the passing Turkish country-side. Its poverty reminded him of Egypt, except the soil of Egypt was richer; the poverty of the people was the same.

As they crested a hill he saw them—four rusty hulks at anchor in a small bay. He marveled at how they had managed to get them through the narrow cut and into the cove. There was no room to turn once inside; to leave, they would have to go out through the narrow cut, stern first. The touring car slowed, then turned off onto a narrow road for a cautious descent to sea level.

The road had been unused by vehicular traffic for a long time. At places, the rocky sides had crumbled away, making the descent even more precarious than it first appeared. They all hung onto the hand straps while the heavy car bucked and swayed its way to the bottom, and drew up by the concrete pier. In comparison to the road, and rusty hulks riding high out in the small bay, the pier looked positively modern. Its samson posts were heavy black iron, imbedded in concrete. A large wooden rowboat had been dragged up on the pebbled shore and chained to one of the pier stanchions. The chain was covered with padlocks.

"Why all the locks?" Awani asked curiously as the chauffeur scrambled down on the shoreline to unlock the boat.

"Everyone loses key. Saw off link, then hook up with new lock. When keys lost again, more sawing. Another new lock," he explained.

"Who owns the rowboat?"

Lakim Bey shrugged indifferently. "Who cares! I have only key to fit last lock now." Turkish logic.

The chauffeur pushed the rowboat into the water and led it around the pier to the trio standing on the deck.

"Oars?" Awani asked.

"We have motor in trunk car." Lakim Bey took the chain from the Turk and waited while the huge man went to the Lagonda. He unbuckled two leather straps on the back and raised the trunk lid.

The outboard, a British Seagull, caught on the first pull and they slid smoothly over the calm water towards the tankers, less than five hundred yards away.

The ships were moored by both bow and stern anchors and joined together midships with heavy insurance cables. Their hulls were barely separated by rubber truck tires, some of them badly worn. There were large circular patches of bare metal along the hulls where the tire fenders had rubbed the rust scale clean, giving the effect of gargoyle eyes peering between the spaces separating the vessels. Awani had the chauffeur make a slow tour around the outside hulls first, then between two of the ships, which were far enough apart to permit their boat passage through the pair of towering rusty sides. As they came out the sterns of the tunnel, Awani signaled the Turk to stop the boat so he could check the rudder posts and exposed propellors on each of the vessels. All were rusty, but appeared secure and fuctional.

"Let's go aboard!" he suggested.

The chauffeur started the *Seagull* and brought them around on the far side, then shut off the motor as they came alongside a dangling rope ladder. It was new, the wood steps unmarred by wear. The Turk tied the rowboat to the ladder and stood aside while Awani began the long climb to the rail. Once he had swung himself over the top onto the deck, the others followed. Lakim Bey's suit was wrinkled badly and its owner puffing mightly when the two Turks clambered onto the steel deck. The chauffeur propped him up against the rusty railing and straightened out his master's rumpled clothing, watching his face anxiously. Lakim Bey recovered his breath and pushed the man aside.

"Come, I lead your tour."

Hours later, as the sun dropped behind the cut of the bay, they finished the inspection. The lovely silk suit was in shreds, and all four men were filthy from grease and yellow dust. They climbed back down the ladder to the little boat and headed for the pier.

"Well, what do you think, Mr. Awani?" Zaglaviras asked anxiously.

"Splendid vessels, aren't they?" Lakim Bey wheezed.

Awani said nothing until they had landed, dusted themselves off and returned to the Lagonda. It was dark when the huge Turk started up the narrow road for the highway. The big headlamps from the touring car made the escarpment appear even more frightening than during the daylight descent. Everyone breathed a sigh of relief when they gained the top and turned onto the pavement.

"I think those are probably four, of the most unseaworthy rust buckets I have ever had the misfortune to see in my entire naval career, gentlemen. They should have been scrapped twenty years ago."

In the dim light he could see Dimitri's face fall with disappointment.

"However, there is an outside chance with a hundred hard working men with steel brushes, paint, and grease guns, they can be cleaned up to look presentable. Whether or not their engines will work, or the steering motors turn the rudders, only Allah can tell at this point."

"Everything will be in working order—I guarantee it, Mr. Awani," the Greek promised fervently.

"You're going to have to guarantee it, Mr. Zaglaviras, because both you and your partner, Mr. Speidel, will be the captains on two of the vessels when they back through that cut and head out to sea!"

20

March 1976

Everyone stood out on the front lawn to watch the Jet Ranger sink slowly onto the painted stone cross set into the grass. The two skids touched the exact center of the cross lightly, then the helicopter settled to rest. The children waved excitedly as Chirlo and Paco went out to climb aboard the machine, ducking their heads unnecessarily when they approached the whirring rotors. There was plenty of clearance to stand upright, but it never seemed enough, no matter how many times they walked under the blades. Chirlo nodded to the Air Force captain when he and Paco had strapped their seat belts, then waved out the window to Felina and the children when they lifted up and out over the city in the bright morning sunlight. He watched the landscape slip by as they crested the mountains and started the long slow descent towards the coast and Punta Delgado.

Jamil's phone call from Damascus bothered him. The bombs would not be ready until some time in late April, early May, so why the sudden urgency for a meeting? Had the financiers changed their minds? He shrugged mentally. It made no difference. *He* controlled the bombs. *He* controlled the country. Either they met the terms or he kept the bombs. It made no difference.

"Are you feeling ill, Colonel?"

Chirlo looked over at Paco and smiled. He reached across the space between them and patted his knee.

"No, my friend. I was thinking on a problem—exploring the alternatives."

"Ah, politics." Paco nodded knowingly.

"In a way, but not so much politics as human nature. Human nature is a funny thing. Have you noticed?"

"Sometimes." Paco loved being with him when he went into one of his reflective moods. It made him feel closer, close like in the old days at La Esperanza.

"The most illogical things are logical and vice versa." Paco looked at him blankly. Abstract theory was not his strong point. Chirlo expanded the thought.

"We are enchanted by the splashing of a fountain—infuriated by the dripping of a tap."

Paco laughed. That comparison he could understand.

The Ranger met the coastline four hundred feet above the waves and curved toward the Blucher Chemicals complex, settling while it flew along the shoreline. As it reached the broad lawns in front of the white administration building it slowed to a stop, then hovering, sank slowly onto the grass, kicking out lose bits of sand and clippings in a wide circle.

The windows along the front of the building were filled with faces when they climbed down onto the lawn. Chirlo looked at the windows and waved, then started across the lawn for the building. Kastenburg came out to meet him with Hauser, Jamil, the two scientists and Leila walking behind. Chirlo was surprised to see Leila. It might turn out to be a social visit, after all, he thought, or else the Palestinian needed a reinforcement to spread balm for whatever the purpose of his visit turned out to be.

"Colonel, glad you could make it." They met, then paused as the Ranger lifted off the grass and slid quickly over the fence toward the air base at Bahia Blanca. They watched it leave, then walked together into the building, Paco trailing the group.

"He didn't tell me you were coming too!" Chirlo said to Leila. "Felina will be pleased. You must come up to San Ramon for dinner tonight."

He held her arm, steering her through the doors into the elevator. It was all idle chatter until they reached the boardroom, then before anyone had sat down, Jamil announced, "Colonel, we have a small problem!"

"Too big to solve or too small to ignore?"

"The financier requires proof that the bombs will work before making payment."

"An interesting development, Galal. Why don't we all sit down and discuss it further?"

They scattered themselves around the long table. Kastenburg met Chirlo at the chairman's position, paused, then took one of the side chairs, bowing to his determination to maintain control of the meeting. A minor point to Kastenburg, but to Chirlo, knowing the value of appearances, however slight, it was imperative that his position be shown as the ultimate authority. Everyone sat down and looked at the bearded man in the khaki bush jacket.

"So, your purchaser wants proof that Doctor Kastenburg's creations will go bang. It seems to me if we oblige the gentleman there will be nothing left for him to buy, or am I missing something?"

Kastenburg coughed uncomfortably, politely, then removed his pince nez.

"As I understand it, Colonel, the purchaser would like to see one of our units detonated to verify the capabilities of the other four."

"Capability or potential?" Chirlo asked carefully.

"Well—yes, I suppose it would be potential," Kastenburg agreed. He replaced his glasses.

"I don't remember our discussing anything along these lines, Galal."

"True. It was a recent decision by the purchaser," Jamil admitted.

"An unfortunate decision." He looked at each of them in turn. "How would you propose to provide this evidence, and more important to me—where?" Chirlo decided to keep his options open until he heard the full story and understood the proposal Jamil and Kastenburg obviously had agreed upon.

"The idea of a test is feasible, Colonel, an explosion offshore—fifty to a hundred miles clear of our coasts, a remote controlled firing. It would be quite safe," Kastenburg observed.

"What about local shipping in the area?"

"Not a problem, really; once we get beyond twenty-five miles we'd be past the coastal shipping and traffic down to Panama. There's nothing much beyond that until the Lesser Antilles—several hundred miles further east. Of course we could position the firing platform in the Atlantic beyond the Antilles, but I don't think that is necessary."

"What about fallout?" Chirlo inquired. He knew the bombs

would be dirty.

"West or East of the Antilles?" Kastenburg asked.

"Or North or South—what difference does it make, Doctor—there will still be fallout. It has to come down sometime."

"You seem very concerned for the welfare of your neighbors, Colonel," Hauser observed, keeping his voice neutral; the cynicism was in his eyes nonetheless. Chirlo looked at him.

"I am. It is one thing for us to play our little games and destroy ourselves. It is quite another to extend the play to innocent bystanders—and without warning to them. I will still live here after you've gone back to Germany, Doctor Hauser," he reminded.

"Doctor Kastenburg has told me ninety-five percent of the fallout will descend in the Eastern half of the Atlantic if we perform the test fifty miles offshore; east of the Antilles, there is a possibility some of the material might settle along the African coast."

Jamil spoke up. "At fifty miles from our coast, the fallout will carry over the Antilles and out into the Atlantic."

"Tidal waves?" Chirlo inquired.

"Four to eight feet along this coast. It would be negligible among the islands. I am proposing a surface explosion to keep water movement under control. A few boats may be washed out to sea along the coast if they haven't been pulled up on shore high enough, or properly secured."

"Concussion?" Chirlo wanted an answer to everything.

"None in the islands. Very slight here," Kastenburg asserted.

"And the costs?"

"Costs?" Kastenburg echoed.

"A twenty million dollar bomb is exploded, Doctor—someone has to bear the expense." Chirlo looked at Jamil for the answer.

"It does not affect the end price, Colonel. Four bombs, or five bombs, the price remains the same."

There was silence in the big comfortable room. Everyone looked down the table at the Chairman. He removed a thin cheroot from his tunic pocket, tapped one end with his thumbnail absently, then stuck it between his lips and began searching his pockets for a light.

"So, it seems our original agreement is to be changed." He found the lighter and flicked the butane flame across the cigar tip. "From a simple straightforward construction project to deliver five bombs to be used as a threat for intimidation elsewhere in the world, and in complete secrecy as to origin, we have created now a nuclear blast a mere fifty miles off our shores and notified the world we have become a nuclear power."

He held up his hand as Jamil and Kastenburg started to interrupt.

"Then too, I ask myself, why it should be necessary to prove anything if the ultimate use for the bombs is to threaten—or has that position changed, as well?"

He drew a mouthful of cigar smoke from the cheroot and blew it at the ceiling.

"You must admit, Colonel, with one of them detonated, there will be no doubt in anyone's mind that the others will work; the threat will have been proven as being real—whereas the other way there would always be a doubt . . . ." Jamil said smoothly.

Chirlo considered the point. It made sense. The difficulty was his own position within the international community. He could imagine the furor which would descend on the little country the day they made the test. He was satisfied Kastenburg's estimates of fallout and tidal effects were accurate—at least as accurate as was possible with a professional guess. Then too, there was always the chance such an explosion would provide a certain degree of political leverage for his own position in the world; long term financial aid from other nuclear powers. India had gotten away with it. Why not Cosecha Rica? In the final analysis, who would interfere? The Canadians would be upset at the violation of their treaty, but what could they do? Like India, Cosecha Rica was a sovereign nation, a democratically elected republic. His government was certainly as democratic as Indira Gandi's. Yes, there were advantages to be gained, and in reality, very little to lose. He decided it was worth the risk.

"I don't like it, Galal—I don't like it one bit!"

"But Colonel, the request is reasonable. Surely you can't object to demonstrating that the machinery works?" It was the first time Chirlo noticed a desperation creeping into the Palestinian's voice.

Jamil, he remembered, had never been a very good chess player.

"No, the request is reasonable—in fact I'm surprised no one brought the subject up before now—but it was not in our original agreement. I dislike making changes in agreements. I find it has a tendency to get out of hand; more changes later, then changes on the changes." He gave him a lopsided grin. "Where does it end?"

The Palestinian said nothing.

"Why don't we give Colonel Chirlo time to consider his position, Galal?" Leila spoke up for the first time since they had entered the room. "After all, we must remember he has to make changes in the agreements he made with the Canadian government," she said sweetly.

Chirlo laughed and stood up. "Touché." He stubbed his cigar into the nearest ashtray. "The meeting is adjourned while I consider my position." He went over to Leila and Jamil, laying a hand on each shoulder.

"If Doctor Kastenburg will phone Colonel Moroz at the air base to send the helicopter, I'd like you both to come back with me to San Ramon, unless you have other plans."

Jamil stood up. "We are at your disposal, Colonel. Thank you for the invitation."

"Splendid, then that's settled. Paco! Look after getting their luggage out to the helicopter when it arrives."

"They have been staying at the guest house, Colonel," Kastenburg explained. "I'll send a car for their things." He went to the phone.

Later, while they were waiting in the front office on the main floor for the Jet Ranger's arrival, a trio of men in business suits came through the front door from the parking lot, obviously company employees. They saw the group of visitors with Kastenburg and Hauser and nodded respectfully. The older man in the trio paused, and looked at Chirlo curiously. Kastenburg introduced them.

"This is our reason for Blucher's success, Colonel, Mr. David Liebe, our general sales manager.

Chirlo's eyes met Liebe's. "Mr. Liebe? Haven't we met before?" He spun a list of faces through his mind, trying to match the facial characteristics. He was positive he had met the man before, but a long time ago; the face was younger then, a fuller head of hair. Liebe smiled.

"I was thinking the same thing, Colonel, but for the life of me I can't imagine where it would have been—we don't move in the same circles." They shook hands.

"Here comes your transportation, Colonel!" Kastenburg announced.

They went out to meet the helicopter. David Liebe watched them walking across the lawn. He scratched his head, then joined his two junior salesmen.

"You know the Colonel, Senor Liebe?" one of them asked.

Liebe laughed and slapped the younger man on the back. "Never met the man in my life, but you know for a minute there I could have sworn I sold him an insurance policy a few years ago!"

This time Asher was confident of success. He went through the papers in the folder one more time. The Canadian letter was still pretty thin, but the fact photographs did exist to prove the wheel tracks would make up for their lack of physical presence. It could all be checked. He glanced at his watch. The appointment with the Brigadier was still thirty minutes off. He had kept his voice very formal when he called earlier in the day requesting the meeting with his superior, purposely avoiding the matter to be discussed, although he was certain Borodam knew. There was very little Borodam didn't know. How the hell he had learned about his affair with Sabra was still a mystery to Asher. The report from the U.S. Embassy had been the most detailed of all, right down to the background of Kastenburg's housekeeper and the fact she was acting as stand-in mistress, as well as cook. He shook his head as he read about it. German efficiency. Make everything count. Never a wasted motion or emotion.

"Colonel!" Sergeant Kronig saluted as he came through the door. "I have confirmed the reservations on El Al's eight-thirty flight to Rome with connections through to . . . ."

"Sergeant! There's no need to announce it to the whole building. It's unofficial at present."

"Yes Sir," Kronig replied in a softer voice and dutifully shut the door.

"Here is the equipment list you requested. Everything is on inventory. I spoke to Corporal Mestner in the supply office. He promised to have it all together by the time we leave." He laid a sheet of paper on the desk, next to the open file folder.

"If we leave, Sergeant, if we leave. I still have to talk to the Brigadier," Asher reminded.

"But Sir, I know he will agree now. Why even I can see now we should go to Cosecha Rica, and if I can see it, I'm sure Brigadier Borodam will see it too."

Irrefutable logic from the noncomissioned ranks. Asher looked at him and smiled. "By God, Kronig, I hope you're right!"

They towed a pair of work barges down the coast from Istanbul by tug and, after worming their way through the narrow cut into the bay, tied them alongside the first ship, *Petroprince.* They raised crawl nets first along the rusty hull, then the swarms of Turkish and Greek workmen clambered aboard with their belongings to find themselves berths throughout the ships. For the first few hours there was bedlam. Several knife fights took place on the deck of the

Petropacket, the second ship in line, when workmen's investigations found it to be in the most immediate livable condition; everyone wanted a berth on board the best vessel.

Abdullah Haki, the Turkish pirate Dimitri had hired as foreman, soon straightened matters out, after knocking a few heads together, then flinging the unconscious bodies overboard. Revived by the water, the knife fighters swam back to the barges. One drowned en route. Haki shrugged indifferently.

"Either he should have learned to swim or handle a knife—he was no good as a fighter, no good as a swimmer—better to be rid of him."

Dimitri acquiesced with a polite smile.

Haki sorted the mob into six man groups, appointing a Greek to boss five Turks, then a Turk to boss five Greeks.

"This way they all hate the boss, instead of each other. Work like mules. You see!" he explained with a huge grin.

The crews were sent off with steel brushes, chipping hammers and penetrating oil to clean up the first tanker. Living quarters were assigned to the work parties on the ship they would be working. By mid-day, they had freed up the donkey engine on the deck of the *Petroprince* and were using the ship's loading boom to lift the heavy equipment and food supplies on board. When night started creeping across the hills, they paused to eat from the temporary galleys set up on deck under floodlights, then went back to work until midnight amid much grumbling.

The following day the engineering staff arrived in three cars, bumping their way down the precarious narrow road from the highway. They were supposed to be the best available in Istanbul, according to the promises given Dimitri by Lakim Bey. They looked like Barbary pirates to the Greek, blending beautifully with the deck gangs when they came on board the *Petroprince*. Zaglaviras greeted them at the crawl net.

"Salaam!" Their leader smiled.

"Yassou takanis!" Dimitri replied in Greek, shaking hands with the skinny bald chief engineer whose name was Yakalaminayandok—at least that's what it sounded like when he introduced himself.

"But everyone just calls me Yak—Chief Yak," he added, with a significant wink, then turned and began screaming in Turkish at his twenty-man crew. They dispersed into the bowels of the ship, lugging their tool boxes awkwardly. Yak turned back to Dimitri and gave him another wink.

"Lakim Bey says you need four chief engineers for ships. That right?"

Zaglaviras nodded. "You interested?"

"Me?" He laughed. "Me, no, but I pick four good chief out of workcrew for you. How much I get on their wages?"

"Fifty percent in advance." Dimitri knew how the system worked. "Do they have papers?"

Yak laughed and pointed at the hatchway into the engine room where his mob of cutthroats had disappeared.

"All chief engineers with papers. Every man. Problem in Turkey not papers. Problem no jobs."

"I'll need second and third engineers too."

"Same percentage on wages as chiefs?" Yak looked at him slyly.

"No. Thirty percent on the seconds, twenty on the thirds. You know the rate as well as I do," the Greek chided.

Yak tipped his narrow brown hairless head. "You boss."

A rivet gun started up along the deck, making further conversation impossible. The Turkish engineer smiled, baring his long brown teeth, and left the deck for the engine room.

Dimitri went over to the port rail and leaned his elbows on its rusty piping, surveying the chaos in the bay. One of the barges was being towed over to the pier to pick up additional equipment which had come in by road. Four men were working over the electric diesel generator on the other barge tied alongside the ship, while another group was busy loading the remnants of the last shore load onto a rope cargo net. On deck, the donkey engine clattered and the bulging cargo net, hanging from its slender rusty cable, came up the side of the tanker and over the railings to the distribution point forward. Already the pile of supplies on deck was reaching mammoth proportions; all of it carefully cordoned off and guarded by Abdullah Haki's stores men, who looked very much like sumo wrestlers at first glance. Dimitri was hopeful pilfering would be kept to a minimum by the four Turkish giants. The loaded net dropped to the deck near the pile of supplies and the work crews swarmed across the crates and boxes to carry them off. One man hooked the empty net onto the dangling hook and waved at the donkeyman. The engine clattered again and the net swung over the side to the barge below.

In spite of the apparent chaos, there was a growing orderliness to everything, Dimitri observed thankfully. By the following day, progress would be measurable and he would have some idea how long the job would take to complete. A smell of kibi drifted down on him from the deck galley aft and reminded him he had eaten nothing since the previous night. He straightened from the railing, brushed the yellow rust flecks off the elbows of his boilersuit, and sauntered towards the smell of food.

The mountain air of March was the clearest air of all in San Ramon. By April, small farmers would start burning their corn stalks throughout the country, filling the skies with a grey pall of haze, reducing visibility by two thirds and changing the sky from blue to hazy yellow. For years, the Department of Agriculture had tried to persuade them to plow their harvest roughage into the land, giving back some of the fibrous substance being continually taken from the soil, but without success. Chirlo had signed several edicts making the burning of fields a punishable offense. It had changed the farming patterns of larger land holders who could read the edicts, but the poorer illiterate small farmers continued to clear their fields in the same way their fathers and grandfathers had been doing for four hundred years. The yellow haze in April was thinner than ten years before, but not by much.

"It's turning cold. Shall we go inside?" Felina suggested and stood up. They had been sitting on the patio talking since mid-afternoon, when the helicopter had deposited Chirlo, Paco and his two guests on the front lawn and fluttered away. Doctor Artega and Ruis arrived an hour later after Felina called her father about the surprise arrival.

The little Doctor bustled up the steps from the driveway and waved.

"Well, well, Jamil! Have you come to invade or recruit?"

Jamil shook his hand gravely. The President had aged since he he had seen him last. His hair, still black in places, had become wispy, his face creased and deeply lined, and he now carried a cane, although it appeared to be more of a stage prop than a physical necessity. He waved the cane out towards the city before sitting down.

"Look at that view. I tell you, m'boy, you've got the best of the city without being in it."

"You're jealous, Papa." Felina laughed. "He hates to have to look up the hill in order to see his grandchildren," she told Leila.

The conversation had been light, amusing and filled with old memories of times and events now long passed, until at last Ruis asked the obvious.

"Why did you come so far this time, Jamil?"

Chirlo cut in before the Palestinian could reply. "He came to check on his assets, Remember, we owe him some money, Ruis?"

"You mean we haven't paid that loan back yet?" Artega asked, startled. He had taken little part in the country's economy or finances for years, preferring instead to leave everything to his son-in-law.

"No Papa, we still owe him the debt," Chirlo said.

"But that's disgraceful, my boy!" He sounded shocked. "It should have been repaid."

"There is no need to excite yourself, Don Luis, we are making the necessary financial arrangements for repayment now. In fact, that is the purpose for my visit. Leila came along to supervise." He smiled. "Excellent thought." He reached over and patted his liverish hand on Leila's knee.

"Women should always travel with their men; keeps their man out of trouble."

"Or vice versa," Felina observed, looking at her own husband affectionately.

The conversation remained on the subject of finance and economics until well after dark, when Felina suggested they decamp for the house and dinner.

Chirlo touched Jamil's arm, holding him back from the rest.

"You remember our agreement? Your promise the bombs will never be used except for threat?" he said quietly.

Jamil looked at him and nodded.

"And I told you that if I found you lied to me I would kill you myself?"

The Palestinian's hooded eyes watched unblinking in the demi-light from the house.

"Now I ask you again, my friend, will those bombs be used for anything other than a threat?"

"No." He said the word emphatically, without hesitancy.

Chirlo looked into his face a moment longer, then appeared satisfied.

"You may tell your German doctor I will agree to a test under the circumstances discussed this morning. However, I want to know the date well in advance. There will be a number of political preparations to make to coincide with the blast."

"A tentative date of May 15th at dawn was suggested by Doctor Kastenburg, Colonel, if that is agreeable to you?"

Felina called from the door. "Pedro, come along before you catch cold standing out there. You too, Galal!"

Chirlo waved at her and started walking slowly across the dark flagstones.

"I'll accept May fifteenth, unless you notify me otherwise before May first. But remember this, Jamil, if the bomb goes off at dawn on May fifteenth, I want to see you and your purchaser here in San Ramon before sunset on the same day or I will be very cross."

"We will be here, Colonel, never fear," the slender Palestinian replied softly.

"I never do, Jamil, as you well know!"

They met Felina at the door and went in to join the others.

Corbin kissed Elizabeth as he came into the house, shaking the thawing March rains from his Aquascutum.

"Where have you been? Morris Levy's been calling here every hour since lunch, and then Don called a few minutes ago. He sounded worried."

He hung up the raincoat. "Morris always sounds worried."

"Not Morris, it was Don that sounded worried," she corrected.

"Oh!" He headed for the phone table in the hallway. Peter was discussing a school project over the line with a friend. Something to do with whales.

Corbin cut in. "Sorry to interrupt this erudite exchange, but this is an emergency. Will you both hang up please, right now!"

The two clicks were almost simultaneous. He tapped the cradle to get a dial tone, then called Affleck.

Rina answered. "Oh Chuck! Isn't it exciting! They're here now —all of them."

"Who?"

"Morris and the three Israelis—one of them is the Colonel! Don's talking with them. When are you coming over? We've been waiting for you all afternoon. Where have you been?"

"I'll be there in ten minutes." He hung up and went back to the closet for his coat.

Elizabeth looked at him oddly. "Trouble?"

He slipped back into the wet raincoat. "According to Rina, it's exciting, so it can't be too serious, sweetheart." He kissed her as he opened the door. "I'll be over at Don's if you want me—shouldn't be long."

"I'll hold supper off for another hour!" But he had already gone.

She watched him back the car down the drive and turn off towards the Affleck's.

Corbin had a strange feeling in the pit of his stomach. A feeling comparable to standing at the race track watching the horse he knew

638

would win, heading down the stretch still in the pack, while he stood bewildered, holding parimutuel tickets on one of the losers. It was an odd sensation. Rina met him at the front door when he drove up.

"Where have you been all afternoon?" She took his coat.

"At the airport, National Research Council. They've been doing some wind tunnel tests."

He went into the living room and stood by the doorway, taking in the scene.

A big square-faced Salvic man in his mid-thirties nudged the older man sitting beside him on the sofa, who stopped talking. Everyone turned to look.

"Chuck!" Affleck jumped up and came over, dragging him into the room by one arm. "We've been trying to find you all day!"

He led him over to the group. "This is Colonel Asher of the Israeli Army intelligence section."

Asher pulled his leg in and stood up. "Mr. Corbin, a pleasure. This is Sergeant Kronig, and Mr. Epsen of our Embassy here in Canada."

Morris Levy remained seated, watching the formalities of introduction circulating around his head.

The early alarm he had felt when Epsen arrived at the office that morning with the two Israelis in tow became a numbness of inevitability once he had listened to what they had to tell him. First he tried to call Corbin at BAYAN, then at home, before permitting the three visitors to leave the waiting room for his office. Failing to reach Corbin, he phoned Affleck next and caught him just as he was leaving for a conference downtown. Don promised to come straight over. Only then did he call Mrs. White and ask her to escort the three visitors into his office. Epsen introduced the tall limping Colonel Asher, the colonel introduced his sergeant. He listened without comment for an hour while Asher explained the purpose of their visit—unofficial—and his personal fears concerning the situation in Cosecha Rica. Then Affleck arrived and everything became easier. Don smiled them off into side-line discussions about the situation in the Middle East, the Geneva talks, anything but the purpose of their visit, until it was time to go out for lunch, whereupon he suggested they all drive over to his house for an informal buffet.

The lunch and subsequent talks on world affairs wasted another three hours, until at last, the polite Colonel with the beautiful English accent realized he was being given the runaround. Affleck had just launched into a lengthy story on the Conference of the Sea results, extending fishing rights in North America from twelve to two hundred miles—a subject dear to his heart with CORCAN's eleven fishing trawlers operating on the East coast—when Asher interrupted him.

"Excuse me, Mr. Affleck, but are we waiting for someone else to join us before we can begin discussing specifics?"

Morris Levy looked uncomfortable.

Affleck just laughed. "Now I know why they made you an intelligence officer, Colonel! I'm being that obvious, am I?"

"Not in the beginning, Mr. Affleck," Asher admitted, "but now, well . . . ."

"I'm trying to find my business associate, Mr. Corbin. I think he should sit in on any discussions—a matter of courtesy. He is the man who got us the contract to build the Punta Delgado nuclear plant. I think we should wait for him. If it's any consolation to you, Colonel, he's the only one so far who shares your opinion of what is going on down there. Wouldn't you prefer to wait for another ally?"

"This is not a matter of alliances, Mr. Affleck, but one of investigation," Asher told him tersely.

It was at this point that Rina had come into the living room to announce she had reached Corbin and he was on his way over.

After the introductions were complete, Corbin purposely selected a side-chair and adjusted himself into the circle in such a way to command a full view of everyone's face without having to move his head.

"Well, Colonel Asher, what brings you to the land of ice and snow—and rain?"

Asher told him, repeating the story given that morning in Morris Levy's office. It was also the first time Affleck had heard it. Asher kept his voice flat, unemotional; leaving little doubt in his listeners' minds he believed every supposition he made would prove to be correct. He finished by saying, "I understand you agree with me, Mr. Corbin?"

"Not exactly, Colonel. Of course I don't have the background richness in the affair that you have obviously acquired, but I don't doubt for one minute there is something strange going on at the reactor at Cosecha Rica. However, as to whether or not it is a threat to Israel, or world security, as you suggest, that is still a matter of conjecture. But I do agree you should be given every assistance in your investiagation, assuming of course we all understand the assistance is being provided purely as private citizens and unofficially."

It was exactly the way Levy felt, but it sounded much better coming from Corbin.

"Then we can count on your cooperation?" Asher looked around the room for dissident faces.

"Provided you agree to keep it unofficial, Colonel," Morris reminded.

"That may be difficult if what I believe to be true turns out to be just that."

"In that case, Colonel, it is your duty—*our* duty—to press for a full public investigation," Corbin agreed. "By the way, how deeply are the Americans involved in this?"

"At present, slightly. They provided us with dossiers on all of Blucher Chemicals' foreign personnel—mostly German scientists. I intend to visit the Embassy in San Ramon of course, when we arrive. In a sense, they are our Embassy liaison in the country too."

"But, unofficially," Corbin said.

The Israeli smiled. "Yes, Mr. Corbin, unofficially."

"We seem to be doing a hell of a lot of things unofficially, don't we?" Levy observed.

"It's just as well." Affleck grinned.

Asher took out a notebook from the inside pocket of his tweed jacket and flipped it open. "Fine, then we're all agreed. The first things I'd like to have are copies of those aerial photographs along with the report that accompanied them." He looked at Levy.

"They're at my office. I'll give them to you in the morning at nine."

"Thank you, Mr. Levy. Next, this chap Chirlo." He took out a pencil and looked at Affleck. "I understand you know him better than anyone else here. What can you tell me about him?"

Affleck considered the question carefully, then loosened his tie and leaned back in the armchair. "That's a pretty tall order, Colonel. Perhaps we should start at the beginning when I first met Chirlo. To begin with, he is a man who single-handedly led the popular revolution that took over the country. In a world of pygmies, Chirlo is a giant!"

Commander Al Thani lifted his nose and sniffed the air curiously. "Which one of you is wearing perfume?"

Speidel and Zaglaviras, knowing each other's habits, looked at the two Greek captains seated on the hotel bed. Aphendoulus in turn looked at Gonidas. The latter lowered his eyes.

"It is not perfume, Mr. Awani, it is shaving lotion."

Mr. Awani lowered his nose. "I see. Interesting fragrance, Captain. Sort of a cross between orange blossoms in spring and water buffalo in heat."

Captain Gonidas' olive features paled at the insult, but he said nothing. Mr. Awani stood up and went over to the window, opening it pointedly. The sounds of traffic from Athens Square drifted up the six floors to the room from the street in front of the King George Hotel. He came back to his chair and sat down.

"My organization is engaged in an experimental type of operation which involves utilization of small tankers for transportation of bulk liquids other than crude petroleum. Contracts for this work are under negotiation at present, but we are confident that by the time our vessels are ready to sail, they will be confirmed. The area of operation will be confined to the North Atlantic between Europe and America. Hopefully, if our experiment proves financially rewarding, the company will replace the older ships quickly with newer, faster and more modern vessels of the same type and size. We have already made preliminary inquiries to this end with a Japanese shipyard for prices. However, first we must prove our efficiency to the board of directors of the company before any final arrangements can be made for new equipment—and that part—the efficiency part—is up to you, gentlemen."

He looked at them blandly, pausing for any comment before continuing. Dimitri and the two Greek captains looked entranced; Speidel appeared skeptical.

"Because of the nature of the cargos you will be carrying, timing is the criteria for our success."

"Timing?" Speidel asked.

Mr. Awani nodded. "Timing." His eyes met the German's and held them. "Numerous chemical byproducts have a tendency to produce a synergistic action when exposed to air, light, heat, even the steel plating in an oil tanker, if they are not handled properly. Results could be disastrous. As you can see then, timing for taking on or discharging these chemical cargos is critical. If we arrive in port on time, our liquid cargo is as safe as sea water. But, if we arrive late—even a few minutes late, in some cases—that same cargo could become sulphuric acid!" He stared at Speidel until the German lowered his eyes.

"I have a question, Mr. Awani, Sir!" Aphendoulus spoke up.

"Well?"

"What does synergistic mean?" he asked politely.

Mr. Awani looked annoyed. Zaglaviras turned to the Greek captain. "It is the quality of an end product produced when two substances are mixed together, causing the strength of the two to be-

642

come many times stronger when they are combined than when apart."

He could see the stupid Captain still didn't understand. He put it another way. "Like mixing Uzo and wine, Captain."

Aphendoulus' eyes widened as the light of comprehension dawned.

"Ah! Like mixing your drinks." He laughed and turned to Gonidas, who was still smarting from the insult to his choice of shaving lotion. Gonidas nodded at the allegory without smiling.

"Who will pick the crews?" Speidel asked.

"I understand the engine room officers and men have already been selected." He looked at Zaglaviras for confirmation.

The Greek nodded. He had flown in from Istanbul that morning, so had not had time to explain this point to his partner.

"As far as deck officers and A.B.'s, you can make your own selections—either from among the work crews in Turkey, or pick your own local men. The main thing I want to impress upon you is my criteria for efficiency. Efficiency and timing. I will not tolerate slackness. Is that clear?"

Speidel nodded. He liked Mr. Awani's sense of disciplined efficiency. The man was obviously a competent seaman like·himself. It gave him a good feeling to know he was working with an expert while earning his million dollar bonus. The thin-lipped Palestinian he had met in Piraeus reminded him of a rattlesnake; mindless cruelty without purpose and knowing nothing about the sea.

"Jahwol, Herr Awani! Perfectly clear!"

"Good. Now as to wages, I am prepared to pay your men twenty-five hundred American dollars per month to start, if that is satisfactory." He looked at Gonidas and Aphendoulus, knowing it was twice what they expected. Both captains gulped and nodded, speechless at their good fortune.

"However, if either of you fail me on timing for port arrivals, I'll have your guts for garters!" He stared at them another moment, then his face relaxed. He stood up. The four other men in the hotel room stood with him.

"Well, gentlemen, will you all join me for luncheon? I understand the King George dining room is second to none."

In another hotel room two oceans away, David Liebe was unpacking his suitcase in Tegucigalpa, Honduras. He had arrived on the late flight from Bahia Blanca for a meeting, the following day, with executives of *Tabacalera Hondurean*, the country's cigarette monopoly, which was having severe nematode soil problems in the rich tobacco growing areas in the Province of Olancho. Blucher's nematode formula had been tested during the previous year with satisfactory results, and now the government was contemplating a large purchase of the new chemical for the 1976 crop year, provided the farmers' cooperativa agreed to the purchase. His mind was in the process of organizing his presentation to this meeting of divergent interests on the following morning, when there was a knock at his door. He paused with the unpacking and answered the door.

"Good evening, Mr. Liebe. My name is Lev Asher. This is Sergeant Kronig of the Israeli Army. May we speak with you?"

Liebe was so surprised at the appearance of the two men he had noticed two hours earlier on the flight from Cosecha Rica, he could only gape. The two men stood pleasantly by the door, waiting for permission to enter. They seemed in no hurry for Liebe to make up his mind, prepared it seemed, to stand in the corridor all night if the situation demanded. He came suddenly to his senses.

"Sure, sure, come on in."

He cleared his suitcase off the bed to provide an extra seat. "You guys sure it's me you want to speak to—I mean, I've never been to Israel—you are from Israel?"

"Tel Aviv," Asher confirmed. Kronig dropped onto the bed, bouncing lightly.

"Yes, Mr. Liebe, it is you we'd like to talk to, if you don't mind?" He sat down, then pulled his weak leg into a leisurely position and looked up apologetically. "Old war wound—a bit cliché, I'm afraid, but nonetheless true."

David Liebe sat down and waited.

"I'd like to keep this meeting confidential, if you will—at least for the time being. If that is agreeable?" Asher began.

"Sure. Anything you say. What's this all about?" He was genuinely intrigued, flattered.

"What can you tell us about Blucher Chemicals?"

David Liebe knew he was on solid ground. "Blucher is the largest manufacturer of agricultural chemicals between Panama and the Mexican border. At present, we are producing fifty-seven different products for use . . . ." He stopped speaking when he noticed Asher shaking his head.

"Not what I meant, Mr. Liebe. My apologies—perhaps I didn't make myself clear. I am interested in the puzzling things at the Blucher factory; things that are not known by the public. For example, why is all the top management German? Why do they live in their own private compound, rarely venturing into contact with the local people—even on a social basis? You see what I mean?"

"No, Mr. Asher, I'm not sure I do." Liebe's voice became guarded. "Supposing you tell me why you are interested in this sort of thing?"

"It is part of an investigation we are conducting into the death of Rolf Hauser—Doctor Hauser's son. You know Doctor Hauser, of course."

"Of course. Tragic affair. A skiing accident, I heard."

"You heard wrong. He was not skiing and it was no accident. It was murder, plain and simple. We think we know the people responsible for the act, but before laying any charges or leveling accusations, we must be certain of our facts. Background facts. Do you know this man?"

He held up a four-by-five glossy of Kurt Hauser. It was a blow-up of the photograph from his German passport. Liebe nodded.

"Doctor Hauser," he confirmed.

"What does he do at Blucher Chemicals, Mr. Liebe?"

"He's one of the directors."

"Yes, of course, but what does he do as a director?"

"I'm not sure I—oh, I see, you mean what does he work at—what's his job?"

"Exactly."

"Well he—let me see now. He works up on the third floor office when he's in—the rest of the time I suppose he's in the plant. I don't really know; I rarely run into him on my job. Sales and engineering staff don't mix too much, if you know what I mean," he offered weakly.

Asher pulled out another photograph. "Know him?"

"Sure. Doctor Berger."

"What does he do?" Asher asked.

This time Liebe stopped to ponder the question before replying. "You know, I never thought about it before, but I don't know what any of the Germans do at the plant—except Doctor Kastenburg. Dietrich, Hauser, Sauve, Berger, Hoffman, Scharst—they all keep pretty much to themselves. You know, come to think of it, I'm not sure any one of them even have an office at the plant—except Hauser and Doctor Kastenburg." Liebe sounded surprised by his own information.

"So what do they do, then—no office—no apparent job—not in the plant—not in the administration building—maybe they sit in the sun all day at the German compound?" Asher suggested ironically.

"Germans sitting in the sun all day! Latins maybe—Germans *never!*"

Liebe reflected a minute. "No, they work there, all right, but I'll be damned if I can tell you what it is any of them do."

"Have you ever noticed unusual amounts of chemicals brought into the factory—I mean chemicals not normally associated with production of the agricultural chemicals you produce?"

Liebe thought for a long time on that one. "Once—this was a long time ago, mind you—when I first came to work with the company, I remember seeing several thousand gallons of nitric acid in one of the storage tanks; it was during my first tour of the facilities with Doctor Kastenburg."

"Nitric acid?"

"Yes. It's used sometimes for breaking down metals or oxides, but is used mainly as a solvent or cleaning agent on metal corrosion—at least in my experience. We seemed to have an awful lot of nitric acid at that time, and I remember mentioning it to Doctor Kastenburg."

"What did he say?"

"As I recall he said the Head Office in Frankfurt had made a mistake in ordering their initial supply request—misread a decimal point, I think he said, and it was cheaper to store it than ship it back to Germany."

"Is it still there—in the storage tank?"

"No." He thought about it a moment. "No, Mr. Asher, it isn't, come to think about it. That particular storage tank is now used for liquid ammonia."

"So you sold the nitric acid?"

"No, I didn't. To my knowledge it was never sold. If it had been, particularly in that volume, I'm sure I'd have know about it," Liebe told him.

"So what happened to it?" Asher inquired.

"I really don't know." It was apparent the missing acid bothered him.

"Are you a chemist, Mr. Liebe?"

"No, my only technical knowledge is what I've managed to pick up as a salesman in the agricultural chemical business over the last fifteen years. As a salesman I have to know a bit about the product; how it's produced, mixed, packaged and so forth—hardly an expert chemist."

"Tell me, Mr. Liebe, let us suppose for a moment you had a large quantity of uranium oxide that you wanted to process into a variety of other products; let us—for the sake of the argument—say you had stolen the uranium oxide from the waste storage pool next door to Blucher Chemicals factory—what would be the main ingredient you would need to break that uranium oxide into its various byproducts?"

David Liebe replied without a moment's hesitation. "Nitric acid."

———————————————

"Colonel, this is Major Martinez. I'm sorry to wake you, but there is some information which has just come into my hands which I think you should examine."

Chirlo set the phone on the edge of the bed and turned on the bedside lamp and glanced at the clock. He retrieved the phone.

"Martinez, do you know what time it is?"

"Yes Sir. It's two thirty-six in the morning."

Chirlo glanced back at the clock. It read two thirty-one. There would be no question but that the Major's wrist watch was more accurate of the two time pieces. He cleared the fuzziness from his brain. "Well, what is it?"

"Would you switch to scramble, Colonel?"

"Major, I'm in my bedroom!"

"Yes Sir. I'll wait."

"This better be good Martinez!" He set the phone down, slipped on his slippers and made his way through the house to the library level. He was wide awake when he sat down behind his desk and picked up the phone, switching on the scrambler.

"Very well, Major, let's hear it."

"Two Israeli nationals arrived on the morning flight from Miami. Colonel Lev Asher and Sergeant Mikhail Kronig. They were met by a car from the American Embassy. They drove first to the nuclear plant at Punta Delgado, then on to Blucher Chemicals. They stopped in front of both locations on the highway and examined the areas with binoculars. They then drove to the Embassy here, where they remained until late afternoon. At three-fifteen we monitored a call from the Embassy to Blucher Chemicals. The voice asked for David Liebe, the company's sales manager. Blucher's informed the caller that Senor Liebe had left the office early because he was taking an evening flight to Honduras. A few minutes later, the same voice called the LDRA reservations office and confirmed the Liebe booking of flight 223. The voice then made round trip reservations for Lev Asher and Mikhail Kronig on the same flight to Tegucigalapa. At five forty-two the Embassy car drove the Israelis back to Bahia Blanca where they boarded the LDRA flight to Honduras at eight-thirty this evening. I took the liberty of sending Captain Padilla on the same flight. Padilla has just reported that David Liebe was followed to the Hotel Grande by the Israelis, who booked a double room on the same floor. They then made contact with Senor Liebe at ten-fifteen, remaining in his room until one-fifteen. There was a room service order which arrived at midnight containing servings for three people. Captain Padilla is awaiting further instructions."

After a long pause, Martinez inquired. "Are you still there, Colonel?"

"Yes Major, I'm thinking. Stay on the line." He set the receiver down and searched the humidor for a cheroot. It was empty. He tried the drawers, they were locked, the key upstairs in his pocket. He swore under his breath and went out to the living room thinking of this new twist of events.

If the Israelis were in the picture now along with the American Embassy, it meant a whole new perspective to his plans. Somehow, Liebe and the two Israelis had to be isolated. It had to be done while they were out of the country. If I wait until they return it might be too late. The American Embassy car would be down at the airport to meet them when they returned. The Israeli Colonel would certainly advise the San Ramon Embassy of his arrival time back at Bahia Blanca.

He found a packet of cheroots and stripped the cellophane as he went back to the library. *On the other hand*, he thought, *it might be a grave mistake isolating the Blucher sales manager. He would, of course, return when he finished whatever business had taken him to Honduras. There would be time enough to isolate the man, if it became necessary. Kastenburg can work out that problem. Maybe an extended sales trip to South America on behalf of the company?* He paused to light the cigar, then picked up the phone.

"Major, I want you to take personal command of this situation. Priority one. If you get any backtalk from anyone have them call me. Do you understand?"

"Yes Colonel."

"Pick four of your best men, put them in civilian clothes and arm them to the teeth. Call the Air Force and have the Jet Ranger sent up to meet you at El Tigre immediately. Go to Tegucigalpa tonight. Land on the football stadium in town. If you have any problems with the local authorities tell them it's a military exercise. Get into the Hotel Grande and bring those two Israelis back with you. You'll have to leave three of your men behind. They can get back on the bus. Make sure they have the necessary papers and

648

money."

"What do you want done with them when I get back?"

"Incommunicado in El Tigre Fortress until further notice. Keep them safe and comfortable. Under no circumstances are they to be hurt. Give them anything they ask for—except freedom."

"Very well, Colonel. I'll have them here by dawn."

"And Major, remember, I want them safe and sound. No gunplay, nothing the Hondurans can cite as a political incident!"

"I'll remember that, Colonel. Anything else?" Martinez' voice sounded suddenly alive; anxious to get started.

"Yes. These two men are not sniveling Jewish carpetbaggers. They're soldiers. Tough soldiers, who have probably plenty of combat experience, so treat them with respect."

"Yes Sir. I've had a little combat experience too, if you'll remember."

"I do. That's why I'm telling you to be careful. Good luck, Manuel."

It was the first time in all the years he had served El Chirlo that Major Martinez had heard the Colonel call him by his first name. He was so surprised he forgot to say goodbye and was left staring at the dead receiver in his hand.

When Asher's eyes snapped open with the click of the light switch it was already too late. There were four of them in the room; short dark Latins with machine pistols, the thick-barreled silencers levelled at the two Israelis on the twin beds.

"You will dress please, one at a time and very slowly."

The slight pencil-mustached leader spoke softly in broken English. He was wearing a blue Air Force coverall like the rest of the group. Asher glanced at Kronig, and shook his head quickly, sensing the bunched muscles on the opposite bed, ready to spring into the quartet. Asher knew he would be dead before he left the sheets if he tried. Kronig relaxed.

The Israeli Colonel began dressing slowly, then stood up.

"Turn around and place your hands behind your back, Colonel Asher." One of the blue coveralls laid his pistol on the dresser and came over to slip on the handcuffs, pinching them tight, then stepped back.

"Now you, Sergeant Kronig—and slowly, please!"

Kronig ignored the order and dressed quickly, then turned his back obediently and placed his wrists across his rump. The handcuffs were snapped on—just.

"Use the other pair!" The leader told the man in Spanish. "He has thick wrists."

Kronig winced when the second set of steel bands were slipped over the bottom part of his huge wrists. The handcuff man began packing the Israeli's suitcases and toilet articles, working quickly. They waited in silence while he straightened out the beds and checked the room for any missing pieces of personal property, then went over to the dresser and picked up his pistol.

"We have a taxi downstairs at the fire exit off the main lobby. I will lead the way. You will follow exactly four paces behind, any closer and you will be shot. Is that understood?"

Asher nodded. The leader opened the door, paused to see that the Israelis were following and the procession left the room Indian file, the last man picking up the two suitcases, flicking off the light and closing the door behind him.

They turned down the corridor to the emergency stairs beside the elevators, then through the swinging doors. Slowly the group descended the five floors to the side exit into the street. The taxi was waiting; another blue flight suit lounging by the car's back door holding a pistol.

They drove quickly; Major Martinez, Captain Padilla and the driver in front, the Israelis in the back, squashed between two men with pistols stuck against their bowed heads as they leaned forward in the seat, trying to ease the pain of the handcuffs.

"We are taking you to a helicopter, Colonel. It is nearby. My orders are to bring you back dead or alive—preferably alive, but dead if it is necessary," Martinez said without turning his head a fraction.

Asher was silent. The handcuffs were too painful for engaging in discussions at this point.

A few minutes later they slowed and turned into the dark deserted stadium and pulled up beside the blue and white helicopter. Rotor blades began turning as the car stopped. The first grey light of the new day touched the Eastern skies as they climbed out of the car. Asher and Kronig were pushed outside under the whirling rotors, pausing while one of the men applied wide strips of tape to their eyes and mouths, then led them into the Jet Ranger. Martinez watched carefully while the two Israelis were strapped into the forward seats of the passenger cabin. Padilla and two of the men who had flown in with the Major stripped off their blue coveralls and stuffed them into a canvas bag, together with the pistols, knives, and leather saps they had carried with them on the expedition. Captain Padilla climbed back in the taxi with the two men in civilian dress.

He waved at the Major, then drove off across the wet grass to the gap between the bleachers. Martinez waited until the car had disappeared, then turned to the open side on the helicopter. The two guards were seated directly across from the Israelis, pistols trained at their taped faces.

"No window gazing, you two. Keep your eyes on them; watch their feet in particular! If either one makes a move—kill them both!" he called out loudly and unnecessarily.

"Si Major!"

Martinez slid the door closed and latched it, then climbed into the front seat beside the pilot.

"El Tigre Fortress, Lieutenant, if you please."

The young officer nodded and reached down for the collective pitch control and throttle.

"Yes Sir!"

The engines whined mutely; the comfortable craft with its uncomfortable cargo shivered, paused, then rose into the new day quickly, curving towards the mountains that ringed the city; a blue and white night beetle speeding for home to beat the morning sun.

Major Martinez yawned, then settled back in his seat for a snooze.

21

April 1976

Commander Al Thani was standing beside Akbar talking when Jamil and Leila came out from the customs inspection room. They embraced one another.

"Success?" Akbar seized Leila's suitcase.

"Complete success! May fifteenth at dawn!" Galal told him triumphantly.

Akbar laughed happily. "Won't Hassan be pleased."

They went through the airport mob and out to the car. Al Thani took the wheel of the Fiat Sedan with the Libyan plates. Major Hassan had obtained a CD—corps diplomatique—crest for the vehicle, which, together with the security sticker on the windshield, allowed them to drive everywhere and break any traffic law in the country with impunity.

"How are the tankers progressing, Commander?" Jamil leaned across the back seat. He was anxious for a progress report.

Al Thani grinned at him through the rear view mirror. "The *Petroprince* will be sailing next weekend for Piraeus. The *Petropacket* should be ready the following week. *Petroprincess* will take the longest—we are doing a complete boiler change. Rusted through, I'm afraid."

"But will they all be ready in time?" Jamil's interest was in results, not explanations.

"I can promise you that by June first the four of them will be in Piraeus, provisioned, crewed and ready for the sea."

"Captains?"

Al Thani laughed. "I've got two Greek beauties—Gonidas and Aphendoulus. Both of them lost their tickets last year for smuggling heroin out of Turkey. They're exactly what we wanted."

Jamil settled back in the seat. "And our two pirates?"

"Dimitri flew back to Istanbul a few days ago. He'll be bringing the *Petroprince* into Piraeus. Spiedel is rounding up deck crews locally with the two captains. Everything is under control, Galal." He smiled with the assurance of his own competence.

Jamil looked at Akbar. "Well, Khala, how do you like living aboard the *Specht?*"

Akbar made a face. "I prefer sleeping on dry land with open spaces."

"Believe it or not, he gets seasick tied to the dock!" Al Thani laughed.

"I'm not used to the motion," Akbar explained.

"Didn't you ever ride a camel?" Leila inquired.

"It's not the same sort of motion," he said defensively. "A camel's motion is predictable. Who can predict motion on the *Specht?*"

Akbar had no love of motion. Al Thani had met him in Tangier when he touched in for fuel and water during the trip from Holland. After the initial excitement of touring the trawler, he announced he was feeling out of sorts and retired to his cabin. The Egyptian Commander saw him only once after that during the rest of the voyage into Tripoli. Akbar was not a sailor—either at sea, or tied alongside a jetty.

Al Thani drove through the outskirts of the city, then turned down along the harbor front, following the winding road that followed the storage sheds to where the *Specht* was berthed. They parked the car and went on board.

Al Thani took Leila and Jamil to their cabin aft. The spacious quarters were designed for the chief engineer, a duplicate of Al Thani's, located across the narrow aisleway. The master and chief engineer's quarters, however, had the disadvantage of being positioned next to the lazarette and steering motors, located under the decking. In rough seas, when the steering motor worked the rudder continuously, keeping the ship on course, occupants of the two aft luxury cabins sometimes wished the designers had built their quarters nearer midships. Noise and vibration was the price paid for comfort. He explained the shortcomings to them after Leila had nodded her approval of the new surroundings.

Akbar lugged their suitcases into the cabin and dropped them on the bed.

"Where do you live, Khala?" she asked.

"Midships. Right over the center of gravity where the motion is least—thank God!" He grinned. "Next to the galley and main salon. Which reminds me!" He looked at his watch. "It's chow time," he said solemnly.

"Chow time?" Leila echoed.

"Noonday meal—if you're interested. Actually, the food's quite good. I got a Lebanese chef out of one of the hotels when the Dutch boys went home," Al Thani told them.

They followed him forward to the officer's salon. The table was set; the galleymen greeted them anxiously. "This is Pierre Lascoeur. His father is the chef at the Bristol in Beirut. He was second chef at the Libya Palace Hotel—where I stole him—right Pierre?"

Lascoeur smiled self-consciously. "Yes, Commander." He looked at Jamil and Leila. "I hope you will like my cooking, please— please be seated!" He bowed them to the mess tables and waited until they had slid themselves into place around the white linen, then disappeared into his tiny kingdom.

"What about the rest of the crew?" Jamil asked. "Where did you steal them?"

"Major Hassan collected them. All Libyans, of course. Two are from his secret police, which is amusing. The chief engineer is an Algerian, Mohammed Bakir. He was at the French naval shipyards in Oran back in the old days. Knows his stuff. The *Specht* is a vacation for him." He nodded approvingly. "All in all, I would say we have a good crew."

Lascoeur reappeared with a silver tray and four plates of crab salad beautifully arranged in arabesque design, using garnish and lettuce leaves, spaced with slivers of hard boiled egg. He served them proudly, then stood back.

"Voilà! Bon appetit!"

Jamil looked at his plate, then raised an eyebrow at the chef. "What am I supposed to do with this, Pierre, photograph it, or eat it?"

Lascoeur looked immensely pleased.

"What's the trouble, David, you look ill?" Kastenburg's blue eyes stared out through his rimless spectacles.

"Nothing Doctor. A touch of flu perhaps—maybe something I ate last night. I'm fine, really I am," Liebe protested.

"I hope so. This is a very important tour you're making for the company. We don't want you starting out as an invalid. Now then, when you reach Buenos Aires, the first man to contact . . . ."

Liebe was only half listening to the instructions on his six week itinerary for the South American sales tour. He was looking at the German doctor now as the personifcation of everything evil that he knew—a rabid Nazi fanatic burning his people in gas ovens of Belsen and Buchenwald—a mad scientist working in Norway, racing against the defeat of his country to blow up the world—the insidious fanatic, planning for years, waiting for the appropriate moment to emerge and continue his ghastly work. But David Liebe was a loyal employee. The other half of his mind rebelled against what he had been told by the British Jew who called himself Asher and the Slavic featured man named Kronig, who said little or nothing during the three hours they had spent together in Tegucigalpa. They had promised to contact him after his meetings with the Tabacalera executives and the farmers' co-op, yet when he returned, they had left the hotel —left without bothering to check out. The desk clerk was angry when he had informed him of this lack of consideration in notifying the hotel management. Puzzling. He waited one extra day to see if they would call, then flew back to Bahia Blanca. A week passed and gradually he had dismissed the affair from his mind, until Saperstein called him one evening at home, to inquire if David had heard anything further from the two Israelis after meeting them in Honduras. Liebe was flabbergasted. He poured Saperstein a cold beer and sat out on the veranda with him, discussing the affair.

"How does the American Embassy fit into all .this?" he had asked.

"We don't—officially. It was a liaison request from the State Department. You know the sort of thing—hold their hands and point them in the right direction when they arrive, but keep well back from any confrontations. We sent out dossiers on all the Blucher Management for State in Washington a few weeks before. I didn't think anything further would come of it at the time—you know, normal curiosity by the Israeli government. Then, when this Colonel Asher and his moose turned up and gave us the poop on what they were working on, the Old Man began to get real interested, if you know what I mean."

Saperstein sipped his beer thoughtfully. "We suggested he start off with interviewing you—you know the sort of thing—local Jew on site. The fact you were heading off to Teguc was just a co-incidence; in fact, they had only arrived here that morning. I met them when they got off the plane." He looked across at Liebe in the dimly-lighted veranda. "The plan was to fly back with you when you finished your meetings."

"How much did he tell you?" David inquired.

"Exactly what he told you."

"Including the nitric acid?"

"Nitric acid?" Saperstein looked blank. Liebe took twenty minutes to explain the bare-bones of his discusssions with Asher. When he finished, Saperstein seemed thoughtful.

"The pieces keep adding up, don't they? Building blocks of evidence that our Israeli Colonel might just be right on the money!"

"Then where is he now?"

Saperstein shrugged. "Quein sabe—who knows? These intelligence birds are a strange lot. Super secret types; never tip their hands in advance. For all we know he may have split for Tel Aviv to make a full report on his findings—a sort of interim report before continuing, if you know what I mean."

"He might at least have said goodbye and thank you, to you people too. Not very businesslike."

"No, but then as I said, they are strange birds anyway." Saperstein stood up and drained his beer glass.

"Well David, nice talking to you. I've got a meeting at the airport—some VIP's from AID coming in tonight on the nine-fifteen. I'll slide off and meet 'em." He set his beer glass down on the screen ledge and opened the door.

"See y'round, buddy. If that Colonel or side-kick happens to call, give me a jingle, will you?"

Liebe nodded.

"G'night then, David. Thanks for the beer!"

The screen door slammed and Saperstein sauntered out to the black pool car parked at the curb and drove off. The following day Kastenburg invited Liebe into his office to announce the six week sales trip of the South American Republics.

"Now David, when you finish in Caracas, your next stop will be Bogota; you'll have to backtrack a bit here, get into Baranquilla on the Atlantic coast, as well as Cali on the Pacific. There's a good market potential in both locations. The agent I have suggested—it's in your itinerary outline there—" he pointed to the folder Liebe was holding—"is an old friend from Bayer Chemicals in Cologne, Doctor Meyer. He runs an interesting—"

Liebe cut in suddenly. "Doctor Kastenburg, is this trip really all that necessary? I mean, aren't we biting off a bit too much at one time?"

"Aren't you interested in new business, David?" Kastenburg countered.

"Of course I am, but we've spent the last few years getting our toehold in the Central American market. We're just starting to make progress carving ourselves a good slice of the total sales volume. Wouldn't it be more practical to concentrate our efforts—my efforts —locally in this area, before running off South?"

"You object?" The German doctor's blue eyes were ice.

"Not to the idea of expanding our market, just the timing, Sir."

He removed his glasses and polished them carefully. "Why do you think West Germany has the largest financial reserves in the world today? A country which was flattened first, then divided in two less than thirty-five years ago?"

Liebe said nothing. He watched Kastenburg clip his glasses back onto his nose and repocket the handkerchief.

"I'll tell you why, David. It's because we have the ability to perceive the future—a gift of business prophecy, if you like. A German businessman's sense of where an advantage lies is rarely faulted in the world community."

He made himself sound like one of God's chosen people, Liebe thought with disgust.

"My intuition—teutonic intuition"—he rolled the quartet of t's around his tongue luxuriously—"tells me the time has arrived when we should begin first overtures to the markets south of the Panama Canal." He raised his slim hands off the desk. "If I am wrong, then you can tell me—I told you so—I give you permission for that," he said with a smile, "but I think—in fact, I'm positive—you will find my assessment of the potential is correct. Completely correct."

It couldn't have been more obvious the German had made up his mind. Further discussion would be pointless.

Liebe sighed. "You were saying Cali and Baranquilla."

Kastenburg smiled warmly. "Yes, Cali and Baranquilla!"

In the first days after his arrival in El Tigre, Asher felt certain Chirlo would make an appearance, if only for the sake of satisfying his own curiosity; the whole business was now perfectly clear. Jamil had financed Kastenburg for Blucher's in Cosecha Rica. Chirlo was stealing the nuclear waste for the Germans to make bombs. It was probably a fifty-fifty partnership between the Dictator and the Palestinian. The one needing the bombs for expanding his country's borders in Central America, the other attempting to reclaim his in the Middle East. Beautiful. While here he sat in a medieval dungeon complete with dripping water and rats, powerless to do anything other than pace. He stood up and resumed pacing. Six steps in one direction, six steps in the other. It was a big cell, easily large enough for another seven men. The other beds had been removed, recently removed, he noticed, the day he arrived. The bed, mattress and blankets were clean and comfortable, and so far, they had changed the sheets and his clothing five times since his arrival, all of it returned immaculately pressed. Six steps in one direction—six steps in the other.

The food, too, was excellent. He was being fed three times each day when the elaborate menu tray was slipped under the door into the two-way trap lock by whomever it was that watched over him. He had never seen the man—or was it a woman? He could hear the breathing on the other side of the locked steel door when he opened the trap at mealtimes, but nothing was said. It was pointless to talk, he had reasoned, certain the guard or guards would be unable to speak English, and his few words of Spanish were hardly substantial enough for any discussions. On the fourth day he found a neatly typewritten note in English on his breakfast tray, together with a cheap ball point pen clipped to the paper.

"Please list your toilet, reading and writing requirements, together with any suggestions how your menu or comfort may be improved within your cell."

He had written quickly for a list of toilet articles, several books, including a copy of the Torah, and a suggestion they produce some disinfectant and an extra pail of water so he could keep the smells of the honey bucket under control between exchanges. By the time he had finished, his breakfast was cold, but his spirits uplifted nonetheless. It was obvious they—he—whomever—meant him no harm; that he was simply being kept on ice—until—until what? Six paces in one direction, six paces in the other. He passed the note back, keeping the pen during the exchange of trays through the trap at noontime. At supper, everything he had ordered was sitting on the steel floor of the door trap when he opened the panel on his side. Another typewritten note attached to a pocketbook edition of the Torah with a new paper clip, said, "Please indicate any further requirements as they occur. Unfortunately the only copy available of the Torah is in English. Trust this will be satisfactory. Please clear trap and shut your door for your supper tray." He followed the instructions and heard the other panel open in the hallway, then close. He removed his evening meal. He fell asleep late that night after reading through one of his new library selections. He hoped Sergeant Kronig was receiving the same sort of courteous treatment. He felt sure he was. Six paces in one direction, six paces in the other.

Now it was mid-April, April seventeenth! He stopped pacing and went over to his calendar and crossed off another day. The paper was damp, and the ballpoint tore a piece out of the date box as he made the careful x. He examined it critically, then decided he would have to draw himself another calendar; the present one was almost mush in his hands.

"Twenty-one days!" he said aloud. "Three weeks—nearly a month!"

He replaced the limp paper with its numbered squares on top of the pile of paperbacks beside the bed and returned to his pacing. Surely by now, he thought, Borodam would be wondering what had happened to him; phoning the Canadian Embassy first, then the American Embassy in San Ramon, then—*then* what? Six paces in one direction, six paces in the other.

He probably didn't need the tug, but now that it was here and he would have to pay for it anyway, it might as well be used, Dimitri decided. The main thing was to get the damn ship out and away so the hordes of idle gaping workmen lining the railing on the *Petropacket* anchored alongside would get back to work once the show was over. The barge crews and shoremen were equally at idle ease on the pier. In fact, no one was doing a damned thing in the whole bay except watching the first ship getting underway.

"Ship is ready to proceed, Captain!" the Turkish mate informed him as he came into the wheel house.

The mate had been hanging over the bridge wing watching the lines being disconnected from the *Petropacket*. Fortunately, the air and sea were calm in the bay, so there was no chance of the narrow space between the two vessels closing.

Dimitri rang the engine room, then whistled through the brass communication pipe.

"Ready to proceed, Chief. Slow astern." He turned to the helmsman. "Center wheel. Steady as she goes." He pulled the ship's whistle two short blasts. They were answered immediately by the tug. "Bring in the anchor," the mate yelled in Turkish through the bullhorn outside the bridge, repeating the order.

The *Petroprince* trembled as the partially exposed propellor blade, turning slowly at first, began to thrash the calm waters. Forward, the anchor winch started clanking links through the hawser pipe, straining the dripping rusty chain across the deck and down into the chain locker below; the towing cable aft to the tug tightened, stretched, vibrated its wetness in a three-second blur of motion, then stopped. Slowly, the *Petroprince* began to move.

Seagulls, swarming in the air above the ships, settled back on the hills around the bay to watch and listen to the roar of approval from the cheering voices of workers on the other tankers and shoreline as they watched their efforts slide past the other ships—slowly gathering speed—heading for the narrow cut of water.

"Anchor clear!" the mate announced.

The forward deck engine sounds died. Dimitri went out onto the bridge wing and looked aft, then walked quickly through the deck house to the other wing. The clearance through the cut appeared to be the same on both sides.

"Keep your helm centered!" he told the helmsman again. The Turk at the spoked wheel scowled but said nothing.

Fucking Greeks, he thought, *always excited over nothing.* He removed the scowl quickly when Dimitri glared at him. They were starting to pick up speed too quickly. Zaglaviras went to the telegraphs and rang "Stop engines." It took fifteen seconds before the answer swung back on the indicator. He blew into the voice pipe as the engines stopped the churning propellor.

"Listen Chief, when I ring the telegraphs, I want an instantaneous reply—got that?" He recapped the tube without waiting for an argument, and went back to the bridge wing.

The distance from the steep cliffs to the port side of the ship appeared the same as before. He stood watching as they passed through the narrow opening; the crumbling slabs of sheetrock seemed close enough to touch. An illusion. The steep porous surface was peppered with recesses and filled with debris where flocks of seagulls nested. Thousands of beady eyes watched the *Petroprince* slip through the cut, out into the Sea of Marmora, then swing its blunt bow westward in a slow arc, disconnecting the stern cable from the tug while it turned. The gulls raised, fluttered, and settled when the two vessels hooted at each other as they drew apart; the tug's bow wave creaming as it headed eastward for Istanbul; the *Petroprince*, its single screw thrashing the bright blue water, moving westwards towards the Dardanelles and passage into the Aegean Sea.

It was late. They had been studying the charts for hours since dinner. First, Jamil had examined the courses Al Thani plotted into the four major harbors; New York, Montreal, Rotterdam and Port of London. He could find no fault with the planning, nor with the positioning of the vessels at point zero in each of the ports.

"What guarantee do we have they will be at point zero exactly on time?" It bothered him. A fifteen minute positioning error and the whole plan would be in jeopardy. It would be hard enough to get one of them to the right point on time, but four ships at four different locations . . . .

"Montreal will be the problem one—if there's to be a problem." Al Thani pulled out one of the continental Mercator charts and pointed to where the Saint Lawrence River was at its widest.

"Father Point. This is where they pick up the river pilot for the trip into Montreal; it's another two days sailing. I'm going to give that one to Speidel. He's the type to bust his ass to be there exactly on time."

Jamil agreed.

Al Thani went on. "Now, as to the rendezvous! To prevent any possibility of error, I've decided to have all meeting points along the thirty-fifth parallel."

"Where's the thirty-fifth parallel?" Jamil inquired. Akbar looked equally blank.

"When you clear the straights of Gibraltar you're practically on top of it. We're well ahead of the hurricane season, so the weather should be perfect." He rolled the map aside and pulled out another Mercator chart, this time of the mid-Atlantic. "We meet the Montreal tanker first at longitude fifty west because it will the have furthest to travel. The New York bound vessel at longitude forty west—six hundred miles towards the African coast." His finger traced the thin black line along the thirty-fifth parallel to the neat x on the chart.

"Then we move on another six hundred miles to longitude thirty west where we load the Rotterdam tanker, then on, almost to the African coast, at longitude twenty west for the London-bound boat. Then we proceed back into the Mediterranean and scuttle the *Specht* a few miles offshore from Alexandria, and row ashore, where I report back for work at naval headquarters. Quod Erat Demonstratum!" He smiled to the faces around the table.

"Naturally, I'll be as surprised as everyone else a week later when the news is announced."

"Naturally." Akbar laughed.

"It's a good plan, Commander. I approve," Jamil said.

"There's just one point I think should be changed." Jamil waited. "I don't like the idea of having everyone start out from Piraeus—even two days apart, as you suggested. I think it has an element of risk—unnecessary risk."

"What do you suggest?"

"Start moving them out to different ports two weeks early," Al Thani suggested. "Issue the Atlantic rendezvous orders when they are all apart; keep them from communicating with each other after they sail from Piraeus."

Jamil leaned away from the table and rubbed a finger along his mustache. "Good thinking. Make the necessary arrangements with the foreign ports, for whatever is needed."

"I'll contact the port authorities tomorrow. We'll move the ships up to the western end of the Mediterranean; Palma, Oran, Tangier, and maybe Casablanca for the tanker going to Montreal— give Speidel a head start getting into position."

He began rolling up the maps and charts.

Jamil bid the other two goodnight.

He undressed quickly and went into the shower stall. Leila stripped and crowded in the narrow upright box with him. They began lathering each other under the warm water; urgently, their fingers moved over the sensitive areas of their bodies. They embraced, tenderly at first, then more violently. She climbed onto his thighs, kicking the metal shower door open, then with one arm around his neck she inserted him into herself and hung on, raking her fingernails across his shoulders, working herself against him.

Afterwards, they fell apart, satisfied and exhausted from the effort. Jamil turned off the water and stepped out into the tiny bedroom. The floor was soaked. They dried themselves, then flung the towels on the deck to soak up the water, and climbed onto the narrow bed. She cradled her head under his arm, laying her face against his chest. "It is all going to work, Galal, isn't it?"

Jamil grunted, and reached his free hand over to the locker by the berth for a cigarette.

"I mean, after it's over and everyone knows what happened— how we did it all by ourselves, they will listen to us then?"

He lit the cork-tipped Players cigarette and inhaled deeply. He patted her on the cheek. "They will probably hunt us down and kill us for doing it," he admitted lightly.

"I know. But that part isn't important any more, just as long as they listen to us this time. They've got to listen!"

Jamil gave a dry laugh, bouncing her face on his chest. "Oh, I'm sure they'll do that much for us!"

"I mean if they don't, then the whole thing will have been for nothing. All of the work, the planning, all those lives—nothing." She said it sadly, as if it were a foregone conclusion.

During World War II, Queen Juliana of the Netherlands lived in exile within the safety of the Canadian Capital. In gratitude to the Canadian people and to the City of Ottawa in particular, where she had lived during the five long and painful years that her country had been overrun by the German Wehrmacht, she gave a gift of flowers—tulips, the best and most beautiful from her homeland.

Every April since 1945, when the Arctic air retreats and the fresh Spring winds pour up from the South to melt the snow and ice and warm the land, the City of Ottawa plants the new tulip bulbs given by a grateful Queen from across the ocean. Springtime is tulip time, when beautifully arrayed color combinations suddenly appear everywhere, as if by magic, bathing the city parks, canal banks, and public gardens in the kaleidoscope of flowering wineglass color. Every schoolchild knows the wonderful story of the Tulip Queen who came to visit such a long, long time ago.

Corbin stopped his car along the parkway next to the canal and climbed out. The air was very warm—or seemed to be after five months of winter temperatures.

Well into the sixties, he decided.

There were still traces of icy sludge along the canal banks, but he knew with a certainty of experience they would be gone by late afternoon. He sauntered down to the edge of one of the flower beds lining the parkway boulevard. An older man from the Department of Public Works was clearing away the rubbish which had blown against the low wire fencing during the southern wind which had swept through the city the day before.

"Morning."

The old man paused in his work to look at the man in the flapping raincoat standing beside him. He straightened up.

"Good morning." He examined the sky. "It's too warm for a change, ain't it?" He looked at Corbin. "You lookin' fer sumthin'?" he asked suspiciously.

"Nope. Just stopped to look at your flowers while I wait for someone."

The man smiled. "Beautiful, ain't they? All delicate an—well—

clean an' pure like sittin' there swayin' in th'breeze." He examined them in silence for a few moments. "Too bad they have t'die, though, ain't it? I mean all that beauty, it's so, so . . . ."

"Transitional?" Corbin volunteered.

The man cocked his head. "Yeah, guess mebbe it's that too."

They turned their heads in the direction of a car horn tooting an unconventional series of beeps. A bright yellow Camaro had pulled in behind Corbin's vehicle and parked. The bottom half was filthy with dirt and white-caked salt streaks. Epsen climbed out, checking both road directions before crossing over.

"Morning, Mr. Corbin!" He looked at the Department of Public Works employee quizzically, then decided to ignore him. "Appreciate your stopping off like this—won't take a minute." He drew him away from the flower bed discreetly. The old man watched a moment longer, then went back to work.

"You like tulips, Mr. Epsen?" Corbin asked casually.

"Tulips?" They walked beside the wet curb, picking their way carefully through the water patches glistening in the morning sun.

"We've lost contact with Colonel Asher and Sergeant Kronig."

"We—or you?" Corbin paused to watch a fat robin tugging a twig on the grass. "The rites of Spring, Mr. Epsen." Epsen hadn't noticed the bird, so the remark was as obscure as the tulip comment.

"They were supposed to report back directly to our office before leaving for home—bring us up to date, so we could use influence with the Canadian government to get an investigation started pronto —okay?"

"Why not the Americans in San Ramon?"

"It's a Canadian reactor—we gave it to them—your company built it. Not really an American problem," Epsen explained reasonably.

"I mean, Mr. Epsen, why doesn't the American Embassy in San Ramon tell them to contact you?"

"They've lost contact—we checked last night."

"Tel Aviv?"

"Not a word. Colonel Asher and his Sergeant vanished in Honduras a month ago."

"Honduras?"

"They went to see someone—never came back!" Epsen said defiantly.

It did sound peculiar, even amateurish; expert Israeli intelligence colonel and sidekick vanishing into the wilds of a banana republic without a trace, and after a month no one knows anything.

Corbin stopped, checked the road, then crossed over and began sauntering towards their parked cars.

"So why are you telling me all this?" He was puzzled.

"Thought you might like to help us—unofficially; you see, that's the problem, Mr. Corbin, it's still unofficial. We can't admit to a private government investigation in a sovereign territory based on hearsay."

Which government are we talking about now?"

"Israeli. If it came out the reason for our visit was to check on Palestinian involvement, we might have a backfire at the Geneva talks. You know how the Arabs close ranks and form a solid front whenever there's a threat?"

"My impression has been the opposite; the one area of the world where no one can agree to a solid front on anything—however, have it your way, Mr. Epsen, but please, get to the point—what are you asking me to do?"

"Will you help?"

"I don't see how I can. Intelligence has never been one of my fortes. I think you'd be better advised in speaking to Morris Levy or Don Affleck, instead of talking to me."

"Already did—okay?" He looked up at him as they stopped in front of Corbin's car. "They wanted me to chat with you before committing themselves. Levy is scared shitless—naturally—and Mr. Affleck told me he'd do nothing without your approval."

"Shitless?" Corbin inquired. Presumably, when Epsen spoke to Morris Levy it was Don who was scared shitless; Morris would have been 'Mr. Levy,' while he would have been referred to as 'Corbin'—he noticed that young Epsen always referrred to Asher and Kronig as Colonel and Sergeant. He sighed aloud. He disliked Epsen. He disliked any bureaucratic social climber, irrespective of his brilliance.

"I mean *Mr.* Levy appeared to be upset," Epsen corrected.

"I can imagine."

"You'll help?" Epsen asked anxiously. Corbin was one of the few people he'd ever met with whom he never felt completely at ease.

"You want someone else to go down and sniff around, is that it?"

"Something like that. Someone other than an Israeli—someone we know isn't going to disappear," Epsen explained.

"So why don't you go yourself—you have a Canadian passport?"

"I suggested that, but the boss doesn't think I have enough juice to make it down there on my own—okay?"

He watched Corbin open the car, then lean on the door frame, regarding him.

"Okay, Mr. Epsen, I'll give it some thought and call you, but I think this whole business is starting to get out of hand; first Don runs off down there, then your two intelligence officers, now you want to form another safari. I don't understand why you people can't bite the bullet and make a public request for a U.N. investigation, instead of fiddle-farting around like a bunch of schoolboys." He shrugged. "However, that's your choice, not mine."

He slid into the front seat and closed the door. Epsen stood aside as the car moved off. He started to wave, then put his hand down quickly when he saw there would be no return wave from the man in the car.

"But Major Hassan, the bargain is bullion for bombs on May fifteenth!" Jamil protested.

"Ah, but if the bomb does not explode on the fifteenth—then what?" the narrow-eyed Major demanded.

"Then, Major, we—you—keep the trawler at sea until the explosion takes place."

"That might be weeks, Mr. Jamil, months, perhaps never; you expect me to bob around in the ocean like a cork waiting for an explosion that might never happen? I have better things to do with my time than take sailing lessons from your Commander Al Thani."

"Colonel Chirlo will be very unhappy with another change of plans."

"He has no alternative but to agree—who else can he sell to? The Mexicans?"

He coughed out a laugh at his own joke, then stopped suddenly when he saw the Palestinian was not amused.

"My mind is made up, Mr. Jamil. The boat will stay in Tripoli until the bomb has been tested. You and I will fly in to see Colonel Chirlo May fifteenth as you promised. If the explosion occurs on time, I will order the harbormaster here to release the *Specht* immediately," he promised solemnly.

"It will mean a two week delay in getting your bombs, Major Hassan." Jamil knew it was useless to argue further with the idiot.

"Two weeks—four weeks—what's the difference? The bombs will keep until they reach Tripoli and Colonel Chirlo will wait, until the bullion reaches Cosecha Rica," he said logically. "We're not going to use them, Mr. Jamil, merely put them into our ammunition depot, then tell everyone what we have. It is a gesture in public relations—as Colonel Qadaffi told me confidentially." He lowered his voice deferentially.

Jamil stood up. "I shall inform Colonel Chirlo of the expected two week delay on the bullion."

"You will not!" Hassan said. "You will say nothing until we arrive there on the fifteenth!"

His close-set eyes reminded Jamil of a ferret, beady, hostile, dumb. "You give the orders, Major. It is my duty to obey." He bowed, leaving the Major with a pleased look on his dark face.

He held his fury and frustration in check until Akbar joined him and they left the building together for the car. It was boiling hot despite a light sea breeze ruffling the cinnamon trees lining the parking lot.

"Problems?" Akbar sensed misadventure in the meeting with the mad Major.

"Two week delay—or as the brilliant Major put it so succinctly— the boat will stay in Tripoli until the bomb has been tested. Fucking idiot!"

They climbed into the oven-like Fiat, easing their backs against the scalding vinyl in stages.

"Will we make it in time?"

Jamil paused before putting the key in the ignition. "I don't know—we needed that two weeks. It's going to be tight—very tight. Let's go talk to Al Thani."

He started the car. "It gives us thirty-five days instead of fifty. Tight, my friend, very tight."

The American Ambassador to Cosecha Rica looked around the library familiarly, then sat down. He gave Chirlo an imperceptible nod.

"You and I seem to have a propensity for informal discussions, Colonel."

"Sometimes it's the only way to get at the root of the problem, Mr. Collins. Drink?"

"Thank you. Scotch and water."

He watched Chirlo pour two generous portions, handing him one.

"To the villain!" He held up his tumbler.

"The villain?"

Chirlo smiled. "Yes, Mr. Collins, to the villain who dwells deep

668

within us all."

The Ambassador grinned. "I'll drink to that, Colonel!"

They touched glasses, then sipped the Chivas Regal. Collins set his drink on one of the coffee table coasters.

"About a month ago two men visited our Embassy; members of the Israeli armed forces, Colonel Lev Asher and Sergeant Mikhail Kronig. They were picked up at the airport by our Mr. Saperstein on the day they arrived, spent a few hours at the Embassy office, then were driven back to Bahia Blanca for the evening flight to Honduras. They haven't been heard from since." He paused, watching Chirlo sip his Scotch, then set it on a matching coaster beside his glass.

"I was wondering if you knew anything about their disappearance?"

"Their flight did arrive in Honduras?" Chirlo asked.

"Yes, and they checked into their hotel at Teguc. They were meeting someone."

"Have you notified the authorities in Honduras, Mr. Collins?"

"Yes, and our Embassy. Both investigations drew a blank. The men simply vanished during the night. He reached for his glass.

"And why would you think I could shed any light on this mystery of yours, Mr. Collins?" Chirlo asked calmly.

Collins sipped his drink, then set it down. "I thought you might have heard something. You have unusual sources of information." He turned his eyes away from the bearded figure on the sofa, glancing across the room to the bookshelves.

"The Israeli Colonel told us a fascinating story during the short time he was with us, almost an Alice in Wonderland tale of intrigue, to be perfectly frank."

"I wasn't aware Alice got herself involved with intrigue while she was visiting Wonderland, Mr. Collins."

"True, up to a point; but she did get herself involved with a demented Queen who ruled the land as a complete autocrat—the Queen's favorite expression, as I recall, was 'Off with his head!' " He brought his eyes back to Chirlo. "When anyone displeased her."

"The advantages of dictatorship, Mr. Collins. Demented or otherwise, the Queen ruled the country." He recovered his glass from the coffee table. "But as I remember the story too, didn't the Mad Hatter insist there was no room at the table when Alice turned up for the tea party? Hardly intrigue, Mr. Collins, more a biased decision based on territorial prerogative." Chirlo took a sip of Scotch, letting the smooth mellow fire rest against his tongue before swallowing.

"Or do you disagree?"

He waited for Collins to reply. The Ambassador merely lowered his eyes.

"Of course, Mr. Collins, if Alice had brought tea and cakes to the party instead of trying to muscle in on the Hatter's action, she might have received a different reception. AID is always welcome at any tea party by the host, from whatever quarter it is offered."

Collins said nothing for several moments while he reassembled his thoughts after his shattered allegory. "I had nothing to do with my government's refusal to give you AID, Colonel. That decision was made long before my arrival."

"I thought we were talking about Alice in Wonderland, Mr. Collins."

"No Colonel, I was talking about the disappearance of two Israeli intelligence officers."

The *intelligence* part slipped out accidently. Chirlo seized it. "Ah, so they were intelligence officers as well! I find that a bit upsetting, Mr. Collins. Intelligence officers from a foreign country not properly accredited to our Republic holding secret meetings with your Embassy, then vanishing into the mountains of Tegucigalpa without a trace." He raised his eyesbrows in surprise.

"It was not an official visit, Colonel."

Chirlo barked a dry laugh. "No? Well I am pleased to hear that, Mr. Collins. I would hate to think of your Embassy as a hotbed of foreign conspiracy. No doubt your Israeli friends will turn up in due course? Have you tried the brothels in the district? I understand they have two or three new ones—a syndicate, operating girls out of San Jose—thirty day turnover, I'm told. Now that's what I call progress! Think of it! A new face every month—why, when I came here, I remember—but then, of course that was before your time, Mr. Collins."

The Ambassador looked at him icily. "Are you suggesting I visit the brothels, Colonel Chirlo, or look there for the Israelis?"

Chirlo shrugged. "Just as you prefer, Mr. Collins." He took another drink from his glass, lowered the contents to less than half, then holding it by the base, flicked his thumbnail against the rim. It echoed a purity of sound. "Crystal!" he announced. "We bought the set in Italy during our honeymoon."

"Are you interested in what the Israeli Colonel told us at the Embassy?"

"Not particularly. I dislike the thought of being party to confidences between conspiring nations." He set the glass down. "Of

670

course, if you wish to take me into your confidence . . . ."

He regarded the Ambassador owlishly, a slight smile tugging the corners of his lips. The older man on the sofa seemed to be considering whether to play the gambit, or retreat while his honor was still intact.

"Nuclear bombs!" Collins told him in a hushed voice. "It has been suggested you are making A bombs down at Blucher Chemicals, using plutonium waste from the Canadian reactor." He regarded Chirlo. "True or false?"

"False! The reactor is not Canadian, it is Cosecha Rican; it was built by the Canadians."

"Semantics!"

"As for Atom bombs by Blucher—I am not an expert in the field of nuclear physics—but if you are serious about this charge—and I am assuming it is a formal charge you're making against my government, then the place to start your investigations would be with the management of Blucher Chemicals. If you will be good enough to table a formal note to me in the morning, Mr Collins, I'll prepare a formal reply in writing through our Ambassador at the U.N. and commence an immediate investigation"—he waved Collins down when he tried to interrupt—"always remembering that should such an investigation turn out to be groundless, based on nothing more definite than an afternoon's chat with two Israeli intelligence officers who have mysteriously vanished in another country, your government is prepared to compensate the shareholders of Blucher's and their customers for financial and punitive damages."

Collins looked at him. So, there it was. The bearded Colonel had thrown down the gauntlet; all he had to do now was pick it up. He glanced away uncertainly, trying to decide whether or not to call his bluff. Or was it a bluff? He swung his eyes back to Chirlo, examining the bearded face. It was expressionless. If he levied the formal protest, and he was wrong . . . God! What a mess to be in!

"I'm not accusing you of anything, Colonel—please don't misunderstand me—that's why I came to see you informally—like the last time."

"I see." Inwardly, Chirlo breathed a sigh of relief. The joust was finished. He'd won.

"At this stage I can't see how my Embassy is in a position to make a formal complaint, or request investigative action—certainly not until the two Israelis return to provide us with something more substantial than—than—well, as you put it, an afternoon's chat on their suspicions. I'd be the last one to want to rock the boat on our personal relationship."

Chirlo stood up. "Quite right, Mr. Collins. No one wants to rock the boat."

Epsen was elated. He checked his tough image in the long wall mirror, tightening his lips into a thin straight line, squinting his eyes. Tough, he thought. "Fuck me, but I look tough!" He grabbed his suitcase from the bed and left the bachelor apartment, patting his breast pocket for the new Canadian passport in the shiny calfskin folder he'd bought that morning. He took the elevator to the underground parking area. Two girls got on at the eleventh floor and examined him with interest. Epsen put on his toughest face and stared them out of the elevator on the main floor. The girls giggled as the doors closed.

In the basement he marched swiftly through the tunneled aisles of parked cars to the space where his Camaro was nosed against the grey concrete walls. He slung the bag onto the front seat, then slid in beside it. It had been a real break for him; a one man trip to Cosecha Rica to investigate just what in hell was going on down there. Okay! He squealed the Camaro, charging the automatic doors, timing the rooftop passage under the slow rising door with split second precision as he thundered up the ramp into the street and roared off towards the airport.

He had a feeling all along Corbin would balk at the idea of going down to check things for himself. That Corbin was too fat a cat to waste time picking the fly-shit out of the pepper in a banana republic when he could be sitting on his ass in Bayan turning his millions into more millions. Why should he give a shit if some Latin or Arab blew up the Middle East? It was no skin off his ass. Levy, of course, was a real weasel—it figured. Big Time Operator running a big time bureaucracy, trying to sound as if he knew what he was talking about, while all the time running scared of his own shadow. Affleck was the one that had nearly blown it for him. Affleck was prepared to go back again. Thank God the Ambassador had vetoed the idea. "Mr. Affleck has already been tried and found wanting in his assessment of the situation, so I feel that what we require now, Epsen, is a new, unbiased touch—which is why I have selected you. It's not official yet. Not until Brigadier Borodam approves, but I'm sure he will," the Ambassador said kindly. "We're much closer to the scene of events than he is."

Young Espsen had been on pins and needles for three days waiting for the approval from Borodam in Tel Aviv. Then, it came! The

672

sonofabitch in Tel Aviv actually read his dossier and said okay! He still found it difficult to believe his good fortune. "When Barney Epsen hits them in Central America, they're going to know what hit them!" he said aloud, squirting himself between a city bus and mail truck into the clear road beyond. Right off, he decided to steer clear of the American Embassy—that had been Colonel Asher's mistake, he was sure. No, he would play it real cool from the moment he climbed off the airline. He had a perfect cover story and no one to worry about except himself, and as far as Barney Epsen was concerned, there wasn't anyone who could take better care of Barney than Barney—he'd had lots of practice; he'd been doing it all of his life.

"I understand the Embassy sent that boy Epsen down to look around for those two Israelis?" Corbin looked down the table at Morris Levy and laughed.

"What do you mean, 'You understand?' You mean you phoned up and asked what they had decided to do?"

Levy colored, looked at his wife, and said nothing.

"What two Israelis? Who is Epsen?" Elizabeth demanded, sensing she was being left out.

"The ones that came to visit Don a few weeks ago—you remember, when he missed supper and you called—tall, good looking man with a limp and an English accent?"

"And in that order," Affleck observed, smiling at Rina. "Pass the butter, Rina, and stop talking so much. It was supposed to be unofficial."

He took the plate of patties from her and slipped two onto his side plate.

"I'm speaking unofficially. Anyway, one was a Colonel and the other a Sergeant; ugly looking man; something about Palestinians—nuclear plants—you know?"

"Oh, I see."

"Epsen was the man from the Israeli Embassy here in town. A Canadian from Port Hope. He visited me at my office," Levy explained.

Sarah Levy stared at her husband. "You never mentioned it to me, Morris." She made it sound as if he had been unfaithful.

"You never asked, my Sweet," he replied with a smile.

"So, what's the story—c'mon, tell me what happened," Elizabeth ordered.

Corbin looked down from the head of the table to Morris. "It's your tale of woe, Morris. Tell her—unofficially." He smiled.

Levy set his knife and fork down on the plate and recounted the story. The rest kept eating, except Elizabeth, who picked at her food idly, hearing the story for the first time. When Morris was all through, the food on his plate was cold and the others had finished eating.

"So what happens now?" Elizabeth asked.

"Presumably, Epsen arrives in Cosecha Rica and disappears like the two Israelis, whereupon they'll be phoning us again for another bright idea. Pass me your plate, Morris; I'll give you some fresh."

Levy handed his plate down the table, hand to hand, past his wife. Sarah set it down alongside the roast. Corbin stood up to carve more of the warm meat.

"I don't think that's very funny, Chuck!"

He glanced at his wife. "Neither do I, but that's what's going to happen. Can you imagine anything dumber than sending a pissheaded kid down there to tangle with Chirlo? Christ he'll devour him with a single gulp!" He lifted the thin beef slices onto Levy's plate and sat down.

"Unless there's nothing for Epsen to find," Levy reminded.

"Nothing to find, Morris? Of course there's something to find! Why do you think the two Israelis disappeared? Because they decided to desert the army? I said a long time ago Chirlo was up to something. Now I'd be willing to bet on it. As far as Epsen is concerned, the lad may not know it yet, but he's already a dead man." He looked about at the shocked faces—all except Affleck's.

"Shouldn't we do something, Chuck?" his partner inquired.

"Like what? Send flowers to the Israeli Embassy and Port Hope when they report his disappearance?" He laughed humorlessly. No one else laughed. "Look here! I didn't send the kid anywhere. I told the Ambassador to request a full investigation through official channels. Don offered to go again on his own. What more are we supposed to do?" He looked at Morris. "It's almost as if you Jews have a deathwish. How about some dessert? I understand Hughette has made us a baked Alaska."

———————————

"Another beautiful vessel, Captain," the harbor pilot told Dimitri as he signaled "Finished with Engines." They walked out on the bridge wing and leaned against the outer rail, looking over the bridge of the *Petroprince* tied alongside. The railings on the new *Petroprince* were close enough to reach out and touch.

"Two beautiful vessels!" the harbor pilot corrected.

"Two piles of junk!" Dimitri said morosely. The main shaft

bearings on the *Petropacket* had been smoking badly two days before when they passed through the Dardanelles. He had dropped the rpm's to 'Slow' then 'Dead Slow' while the chief engineer bathed the scaled worn bearings with oil to get them into Piraeus. Now, three weeks work would be required before the ship was ready for sea. God alone knew what would go wrong next!

"But still a good quality vessel in spite of her years," the pilot affirmed. He was waiting for the usual five hundred drachma tip from the master, and was prepared to discuss the beauties of the floating rust buckets all afternoon, if necessary, to produce his reward.

"What are you planning, Captain?" he inquired politely.

"Planning?" Zaglaviras glanced at him quickly.

"For your tankers?"

"Oh! Sorry, it's confidential. The owners have special plans for the four vessels."

"Four?" The pilot added two more five hundred drachma tips into his mental deposit box.

"The other two are still in Turkey making ready for sea," Dimitri explained. "They'll be coming in next month."

"I have a friend who knows a reliable provisioner. Most of the regular ones here are thieves, you know Captain. I would be happy to introduce him to you."

Dimitri thought, *I'll bet you would.* Aloud he told him, "Thank you, pilot, but the owners have made provisioning arrangements already." He couldn't figure why the man was lingering with him on the bridge, then he remembered the tonnage tip. Stupid of him. He had been busy fretting over main shaft bearings, waiting for the pilot to go. He stood back from the railing.

"If you'll drop by my cabin, Pilot, I think I have an envelope for you."

The leathery face broke into a large grin. "Well, what a pleasant surprise, Captain! You certainly know how to treat a poor harborman!" He followed Dimitri down the gangway to the next deck and into the master's quarters.

Asher was doing pushups when he heard the footsteps in the corridor outside his cell. He paused at number thirty-four, listening. There was a jangle of keys, one being inserted into the door, then Chirlo entered. The door closed immediately and the lock clicked. Asher went back to his pushups, finishing the last sixteen of the fifty set.

Chirlo walked over to the bed and sat down, watching him. The

Israeli stood up.

"Fifty in the morning and another fifty before bed, Colonel. With all this good food you've been sending in I've begun to develop a bulge. May I join you?"

He sat down on the bed beside him. Wordlessly, Chirlo removed his cigar case and offered Asher one of the thin cheroots.

"No thank you. I don't smoke."

Chirlo nodded. "Mind if I do?"

Asher chuckled. "It's your prison!"

When the cigar tip was glowing satisfactorily, he looked around the room, taking in the sparse surroundings. He fixed his eyes on the pile of paperback books, then reached over and picked up a few, glancing at the titles.

"You have eclectic tastes, Colonel Asher."

"I'm a curious man, Colonel Chirlo."

"Yes, so it would seem." He placed the books back on the pile. "I used to do a lot of reading once. I rarely find time for such luxuries now."

"Why not change places with me? You'd have an idyllic situation—no distractions whatsoever."

Both men laughed. They had taken an instant liking to each other. Both felt it; a camraderie between men—equals. It was something women never understood.

"I must compliment you on your choice of kidnappers. The thin man with the mustache is a real professional."

"Major Martinez—my intelligence chief. Yes, he is good, isn't he?" Chirlo agreed. He looked for an ashtray, then remembered where he was and flicked the ash on the stone floor. "Been with me for years."

"You should promote him."

"Difficult. Colonel is as high as we go here. If I promote him, then I'd have to promote myself to keep ahead." He gave Asher a lopsided grin.

"Pretentious?"

"Very."

"But he's happy being a Major?"

"Oh certainly—ecstatic!" Chirlo agreed with a pull at his cheroot.

"I am pleased." Asher stretched his weak leg out. It was beginning to throb from the awkward position on the bed.

"Wound?" Chirlo inquired politely.

"Superficial."

"But gives you constant pain?"

"Only in certain positions."

"Pity."

"No, lucky!"

"How so?"

Asher laughed. "I might have lost the leg!"

Again they both laughed.

"By the way, your NCO, Kronig, is in fine form. Going to kill everyone when he gets out."

"Good old Kronig. When do you think he'll be getting out?"

Chirlo shrugged. "Shouldn't be more than a few weeks to process the release papers; his and yours."

"I see. Bureaucratic red tape. We have the same problem in Tel Aviv. It's monstrous how inefficient office staff can be on paperwork."

"I knew you'd understand, Colonel."

"Oh, I do, Colonel. I hope Sergeant Kronig will."

Chirlo stood up from the bed, pushing himself up, using the angle iron frame as a hand hold.

"I'm sure you'll explain it to him, Colonel Asher." He flicked the half-smoked cigar into the honey bucket expertly. It sizzled when it hit the liquid inside. Asher remained seated as Chirlo went to the steel door and tapped it.

"Yes, Colonel Chirlo, I will!" he promised.

22

May 1976

Barney Epsen spent a full week lounging around the bar of the Hotel d'Oro in Bahi Blanca making himself as inconspicious as possible, attempting to learn whatever he could, which, thus far, had turned out to be nothing. Most of the hotel guests were transients from other countries spending their last night on the coast to be close to their airline departure, instead of chancing a drive down from Sam Ramon at the last minute and missing their flight.

At the end of the first week, he exchanged the d'Oro bar for the Prado cocktail lounge in San Ramon, with equally frustrating results. Either no one knew anything, or no one was willing to talk to the tough looking young man from Canada who couldn't speak a word of Spanish. Epsen was beginning to get desperate for action—anything—in order to justify his failure to date. It was the barman at the Prado who gave him the first concrete idea since his arrival.

"You mean you spent the first week on the coast, Mon, and never went fishing?" The barman was a negro from Bluefields, Nicaragua. To him, fishing had been a way of life since he was a little boy.

"Nope," Epsen confessed, "didn't know there was any fishing around Bahia Blanca."

The barman laughed, exposing a pink tongue and rolling his

eyes at the white fool across the counter. "Why, Mon, deys got de best fishing on de coast down dere now with hotted water from de nuke at Punta Delgado! All de warm water pours out from de point and de fish he just love it, Mon!"

Epsen cursed himself for being such a fool. Of course! The perfect cover! He tossed back his glass of warm ginger ale, gave the black barman a generous tip, and marched out to the reception desk to check out.

By sunset he had checked back into his old room at the d'Oro in Bahia Blanca and was downstairs waiting at the bar for a visit from a man with a fishing boat for charter. The man, a sleazy looking American by the name of Smythe, turned up late, drunk as a lord. Epsen wrinkled his nose with disgust at the filthy apparition in tattered white ducks, holed sandals and four day's growth of beard.

"What took you so long, Mr. Smythe?"

"Important business matters," the American grunted, sliding onto the stool beside him, ordering a double Old Crow.

Epsen waited until he had downed it and ordered another before broaching the subject of the boat.

"Sure, I got a boat, son, what d'you think I'm doing here?"

Epsen preferred to ignore the obvious retort.

"Best goddamn boat around—*The Boticelli*—hundred bucks a day, plus."

He drained the second Old Crow and smacked his lips.

"Plus what?"

"Plus expenses—you know, gas, oil, booze."

"What about food?"

"Sure you can eat too, if you want. There's a propane stove on board. Full line of fishing equipment—best money could buy. I spared no expense, I can tell you. Ask anyone about old Dick Smythe's *Boticelli*. He then turned back to the counter and ordered another double Old Crow.

"Where is she?" Espen asked.

"Who?" Smythe had already checked the room for females on his earlier sweep.

The Boticelli, Mr. Smythe. Isn't that what we were talking about?"

"Oh! Down at the wharf—the customs wharf. Know where it is?" He sipped the third glass cautiously.

"No."

"Well, that's where she is. You interested?"

"Yes. I'd like to hire the ship for a few days' fishing."

"Hundred bucks per day, plus."

"Yes, so you said. I'd like to leave in the morning."

"Can't. Boat's impounded by customs." He sipped some Old Crow.

"For how long?" Epsen was exasperated.

"Till I pay the wharfage fee for this year. Eighty bucks."

Epsen was relieved. He pulled out a hundred dollar travelers check and signed it over to the drunk on the next stool. "Will that cover it?"

Smythe looked at the green paper, rubbing his thumb and forefinger across the numbers. "Is it a real one?" he asked suspiciously.

"Real?" Epsen couldn't understand what he was driving at. Smythe held it up to the dim light, squinting at it professionally. "Lovely workmanship. Has the watermark colored thread fleck too. It'll pass," he announced as he folded it in half and slipped it into his torn shirt pocket. "The Aduana's a pal of mine. Anyway, he's too dumb to notice the difference." He called for another Old Crow.

"Mr. Smythe, the travelers check is genuine—I assure you!"

Smythe looked at him and winked knowingly. "Sure it is, son. I'll pick you up at the front door at six in the morning. Now then, what are you drinking?"

Epsen bid him goodnight and went up to his room for a bath.

In the morning he found Smythe in the hotel lobby stretched out on one of the leather sofas, snoring loudly. The night clerk looked grateful when he went over and shook the sleeping figure. The red-rimmed eyes opened very slowly, testing the light.

"Yeah what d'y'want?" he croaked.

"It's six, Mr. Smythe. We're going fishing—remember?"

The man swung his filthy sandals off the arm of the sofa and stood up with a groan. "You gotta drink?"

"No. There's a drinking fountain over there." Epsen pointed.

Smythe groaned again. "I want a drink, not a bath. Let's get out of here!"

Epsen followed him out the front, trailing him down the street towards the docks.

"Pity to waste a perfectly good boat!" Hauser observed. They had finished loading the heavy silver cylinder on board shortly after dawn. The crated bomb had looked immense when they hoisted it onto the back of the pickup at the plant and driven out the rear gate to the German compound. Out of its crate and in the main deck lounge on the Grand Banks cruiser, it seemed to have shrunk in proportion.

"We'd be leaving the *Dolphin* behind, anyway," Kastenburg said. "At least this way it's put to use." He stood up with Hauser, watching the others secure the retaining cables to the fastening rings poking up through the rich deck carpeting.

"We had a lot of good times on this boat." He looked around at the comfortable surroundings, remembering the fishing and coastal exploration trips over the long months away from home they had all enjoyed. Sauve stood up.

"Finished, Doctor."

Hauser went over and toed the cables, then tried rocking the cylinder on its mounting. It was rigid. He nodded at Kastenburg. The Director looked at his watch. They had been up all night.

"We shall sleep till noon. Then leave at three."

They filed out of the lounge and off the cruiser to the pier, then wandered up the pathways to their houses.

Fifteen minutes later Doctor Kastenburg was fast asleep, cradled in the arms of Fraulein Hoffer. Hauser waited until he was certain everyone was asleep before driving back to the plant. He had an important visitor waiting; a professional assassin from Uruguay.

"I thought you wanted to go fishing? There's no fish up this way!" Smythe told him sourly. He had been nipping on the bottle of Old Crow since they cast off from the customs dock. It was nearly gone. Epsen lowered his binoculars.

"I'm examining the shore, Mr. Smythe. Do you mind?"

Smythe said nothing and went back to his bottle. Beyond the straight shoreline in front of the Blucher Chemicals plant, there appeared to be a series of small coves where the land rose steeply from the beach. The *Boticelli* idled along at an easy five knots. It was a beautiful ocean cruiser, not at all what Epsen had expected to find when Smythe led him onto the docks. Perfectly maintained, it had a high superstructure and racing lines making it appear shorter than its fifty-foot length. At a hundred dollars per day—plus—it was a bargain.

"Stop!" he called out to Smythe.

"What!"

"I said stop, damnit—*Stop!* Are you deaf?"

Smythe shut off the motor. "What the hell's eating you?" He climbed through the front transom and stood on the forward deck, looking up at Epsen in the conning tower.

Epsen said nothing. He was studying the bay with its array of spectacularly constructed cottages and main lodge, and the sleek Grand Banks cruiser tied to the dock in front of the last house.

"There's a boat in there!" He lowered his glasses.

Smythe stared up at him, shielding his eyes against the glaring sun. "Are you feeling all right?"

Epsen looked down from his perch. "Who's boat is that, Mr. Smythe?" He pointed across the water. Smythe turned to look.

"It's the *Dolphin*. Forty foot Grand Banks with twin diesels. The Germans from Blucher Chemicals use it for fishing. Why? Wanna buy it?"

Epsen climbed down the ladder to the deck. "Can we go in there?"

Smythe scratched his grey stubble.

"I dunno. Why?"

It had dawned on him finally that the expedition had nothing to do with fishing.

"Because I want to look around. Okay?"

Smythe looked back at the cruiser in the bay. "The beach is all private property, y'know. We'd have to stay offshore."

"Fine! Do a slow circuit close to shore past the boat." Smythe nodded and vanished through the transom to start the engines.

They motored slowly into the bay, cutting close to the shore as they passed the sandspit forming the bay's natural barrier against the ocean. Smythe watched the depth sounder closely. The bay was very shallow. He slowed the boat almost to a crawl. Epsen studied the cottages. They seemed deserted. Two men were standing on the front veranda of the lodge. One of them looked like a waiter. He swung the glasses past them and followed the rest of the houses nestled against the hill until he reached the last one in line; it was the biggest and most elaborate of the group.

"Kastenburg's," he said aloud with certainty.

He lowered the glasses to the small pier, examining the cruiser. Through the large windows on the salon deck he could see something inside reflecting from the sunlight. A big silver object!

He went to the transom quickly.

"Drift alongside that boat. I want to go aboard!"

Smythe shook his head. "Private property. By rights we shouldn't even be in the bay."

He kept his eyes on the depth indicator. They were coming up on the pier gradually.

"Mr Smythe, will you please shut down the engine and drift

into that boat or I'll kick your face in! Okay?"

Smythe looked at Epsen startled, then saw the tough looking young man tense and knew he was deadly serious.

"Okay, okay, son, it's your funeral. Calm down!" He waited a few more seconds, then switched off the motor.

"Get forward and grab the boat hook, will ya?"

Epsen obeyed. Smythe's timing was perfect. They came to a stop alongside the Grand Banks with less than four feet separating the hulls of the two vessels. Epsen hooked the long pole end onto one of the *Dolphin's* guard rails and pulled the *Boticelli* against the fenders. He dropped the boathook and jumped aboard.

"Wait for me!" he called to Smythe, then went around to the salon entrance aft.

Hauser had only just returned to the lodge when he saw the cruiser stop at the mouth of the bay. He went out on the veranda to watch. After a few minutes he saw it start up and swing in towards them. He phoned Dietrich and Berger immediately, waking them out of a sound sleep, then called Kastenburg. By the time they had all dressed and armed themselves to meet behind the boathouse at the end of the pier, the man Hauser had seen climb onto the *Dolphin* had been aboard nearly ten minutes.

All recognized the *Boticelli* and its owner. Before Kastenburg had purchased their Grand Banks cruiser, they had chartered Smythe's boat on several occasions for a day's fishing. The small man in the *Dolphin* came out on deck and waved at Smythe to come aboard. They could hear an argument beginning to develop between the two, then clear as a bell, the young man said the word . . . "bomb." Kastenburg looked at his trio.

"Well my friends, it appears our little secret is out. Kurt, I shall rely on you to see they do not leave the bay alive," Hauser said.

"Dietrich! You take Smythe. Berger and I will handle the other one. If either tries running—kill them both!"

They came out from behind the boathouse and walked slowly towards the *Dolphin*, their Schmeissers leveled at the boat.

Smythe saw them first and froze, then raised his hands over his head. The man on the *Dolphin* whirled, saw the three men advancing, then yelled at Smythe, "Start the engines!"

"One move from either of you and you're dead!" Hauser roared. The birds around the bay rose in a crescendo of beating wings, frightened by the outburst. The man on the *Dolphin* obeyed the order, keeping his arms slightly in front and above his waist where they had been located when he decided to run.

He smiled at Hauser ruefully. "Okay?"

"Still nothing on the radar sweep," Hauser announced. He looked at his watch. "Twelve minutes left."

The helicopter was scheduled to pick them off the boat at 3:00 a.m. He sighed.

"I'm starting to get tired, Heinz." He sat down on the heavy fishing chair anchored on the *Boticelli's* fantail. It was a comfortable seat, much like an airline captain's, with safety harness to keep the avid fisherman on the boat while he played the big ones for the hours it took to tire them.

Taking the *Boticelli* instead of the *Dolphin* at the last minute had been Kastenburg's idea. It had taken an hour to unfasten the cylinder in the main salon and lug it out on deck to the railing, then another fifteen minutes to angle it up to the back of the flying bridge on the *Boticelli*, where it fitted snugly crosswise on deck. Fortunately, they had the mast boom on the Grand Banks to help them with the lift. Another fifty minutes were wasted looking for fuel to top the tanks on the commandeered vessel when it was discovered Smythe had too little on board for the seventy-five mile offshore trip to the blast position. Fortunately, the extra speed from the *Boticelli* more than made up for the time lost in arranging for its use.

"I'll turn on the beacon," Kastenburg said, and went to the bridge.

The Jet Ranger pilot was to home-in on the cruiser with his ADF tuned into the appropriate frequency, supposedly a straight east-west line between the radio beacon from Bahia Blanca, and the weak signal emitted from the boat. The German switched the audio on for a few moments, listening to the steady transmission of dots and dashes, then flipped it off and went back down to join Hauser at the fantail in the other comfortable fishing chair.

"We're on the air now," he said as he sat down. "You're right, Kurt, I'm getting sleepy too."

"Busy day."

"Very busy." They watched the moonlight shimmer the small waves, listening for the sound of jet turbines from the West, hearing only the lapping of water against the hull.

"How are our passengers?" Kastenburg asked.

Smythe and Epsen were tied back-to-back in the master's cabin below deck.

Hauser chuckled. "Snug."

"Too bad about Smythe. I liked him."

"Yes. Harmless type, really. Pity he had to get himself involved," Hauser agreed.

"Yes. Pity. I wonder who the other one really is?"

"Hard to say. Certainly does a lot of talking."

"Israeli?"

"Jew."

"Same difference," Kastenburg observed.

"No great loss."

"None whatsoever."

They stopped talking. Listening intently, they heard the sound of jet turbines growing quickly from the West. Both men stood up and climbed to the flying bridge. Hauser picked up the Aldis lamp and aimed it in the direction of the sound, flashing the shuttered white light in a series of Morse signals for the letter *B*. One long, three short, one long, three short, over and over again. Then he saw the Ranger suddenly take shape beneath the stars; it was very low, coming slowly towards the *Boticelli*, a bos'ns chair dangling from the open side door. He set down the Aldis and waited for the pilot to position himself over the boat.

Kastenburg went to work rapidly. First he removed the inspection panel atop the cylinder and laid it carefully aside. Then he reached into the mechanism to start the timer; a twelve hour miniature clock with a solitary red hand. He checked his watch, then twisted the red needle knob to the figure 2. He stood up and waited, watching Hauser slide into the spinning chair under the rotor's air blast. Hauser waved at the pilot and the Ranger; chair and Hauser rose quickly into the darkness. Kastenburg went below to the lower deck, through the hatchway into the master's cabin. Smythe and Epsen were still sitting in the middle of the floor tied to each other. They glared at him.

"Goodnight, gentlemen!" He shut the door and climbed back to the flying bridge just as the helicopter moved slowly over the top, lowering the empty chair. Kastenburg went back to the cylinder and turned the arming switches, checking off the procedures aloud as he followed the pattern sequence. When finished, he pushed the red timer and bent over to listen. The ticking of the mechanical clock was barely audible. Kastenburg straightened up smiling. Carefully, he slipped the cover plate back onto the cylinder and twisted the butterfly Zuess fasteners into place.

He walked back to the dangling chair, and after removing his pince nez and patting them comfortably into his handkerchief pocket, slipped his bottom onto the canvas seat, locking his arms through the support cables. He looked up and waved, then chortled with delight as the *Boticelli* began to fall away below him, and he was swept out to sea, rising slowly towards the stars.

For the first hour after silence had descended on the fishing boat, Smythe and Epsen worked frantically to free themselves. Earlier, when Epsen had told the old drunk they were sitting with a nuclear bomb, he had been inclined to dismiss the whole thing as the ravings of a young lad with a highly developed sense of imagination; mad German scientists, secret processing factories under Blucher's, uranium waste thefts; the whole thing smacked of an Ian Fleming novel. However, the longer he thought about it, and the more sober he became—and he was *very* sober now—the more he began to have a queasy suspicion the tough looking Epsen was telling the truth. Maybe there *was* a bomb on board! It had certainly looked like a bomb—or an iron lung.

An ex-naval officer, he had faced the possibility of destruction at sea on a dozen occasions by an unseen, and in some cases, unknown enemy. The first step in counter-offensive was a matter of keeping control of the situation; not to panic or create a secondary situation, perhaps even worse than the primary difficulty. When the Schmeissers had been trained on him he didn't argue, and when he was taken below with the young tough Jewboy and tied against him, he did nothing to protest or give cause for the captors to change their minds on the idea of keeping them out of harm's way. The fact they had been checking every fifteen minutes during the long voyage gave every indication the safety of the two prisoners was a prime consideration in the scheme of things. Now, after over an hour of complete silence, he was beginning to have second thoughts.

"Time we got out of this mess, son."

Epsen twitched behind him angrily. "You dumb sonofabitch, that's what I've been telling you since this morning!"

"All right, don't get excited. I've had to piss my pants too. Let's try and stand up."

It took several minutes to work into a position where this was possible. Once on their feet, Epsen complained, "Lean back a bit, you're lifting me too high!"

Smythe obliged the shorter man. "Fine, now let's ease our way over to the door and see if it's locked."

Crabwise, they moved across the cabin in small steps, and tried the door. It was open!

"Now, next step is going to be to get ourselves up the gangway. You go first, I'll come up backwards. At least we'll be at the same level going up the steps."

It took ten minutes and two painful falls before they gained the main deck salon. They crabbed their way over to the galley and worked at one of the drawers, the one where Smythe kept the galley knives. Even with the drawer opened it was impossible to retrieve one of the blades without shutting the drawer as they reached for the knife. Smythe pulled the drawer out and spilled its contents onto the deck. Then they worked their way down into a sitting position and felt for one of the wooden handles. It was a slow, time-consuming process, conducted with much cursing and bitter complaint, as each cut himself on the invisible blades. Finally Epsen shouted in triumph, "I've got one! It's a paring knife, I think!"

He worked it around in his palm, driving the point into Smythe's wrist. Smythe flinched. "For Christ sakes be careful!" He felt blood pouring from his severed artery.

Epsen wiggled the point onto the thin ropes that held them together and began sawing weakly; his fingers numb, refusing to answer the speedy mental requirements from the brain that directed them. It took a long time to cut through the rope. They loosened the cord quickly. Epsen turned to look in the dim light at his partner.

"Tourniquet, son—tie my wrist, will you?" he asked weakly. The deck was covered with his blood, still pumping from the severed artery.

Epsen flexed his fingers, trying to regain sensation, then grabbed a piece of cord and wound it tightly onto Smythe's arm above the elbow. He used the handle from one of the larger knives to tighten it, inserting the point on the dull side of the blade between the rope and flesh to hold it in place. The bleeding stopped. He grabbed the old man under the arm pits and dragged him outside on the fantail deck. Smythe's eyes were closed.

Epsen peered down at him. "You still with me?"

"Still with you, son." He smiled feebly, but didn't open his eyes. "You'd better check out that bomb of yours, hadn't you?"

"I'm on my way, okay?" He scampered up to the flying bridge, taking the steps three at a time. In the East, the first flushing glow of the new day broke across the quiet sea. Epsen saw the evil looking cylinder lying across the bridge deck. It was already light enough to see the beads of moisture from the morning's dew. His eyes hit the four Zuess fasteners holding the inspection cover. As he reached for it, he thought, "No sweat . . . access door, stop the timer . . . Piece of cake. Oka . . . ."

The digital clock on the bedside table clicked.

"Good Morning. From CBC News, here is the world at seven with Rex Corning and Owen Bogden."

Corbin's mind began its journey into consciousness. He rolled over, dragging the sheets with him. His wife, familiar with the morning procedure, clutched her half of the linen defensively.

". . . explosion of the nuclear device occurred several miles offshore from the small Latin American Republic with no prior notification to shipping in the immediate vicinity. Authorities here state the device was, in all probability, a dirty type of atomic bomb in the 20 kiloton range and that any fallout should drift well out to sea with prevailing westerly winds, before settling on the ocean. Ships in the anticipated fallout area are being warned . . ."

Corbin was wide awake now, sitting on the edge of the bed.

"That sonofabitch!" he said aloud. The radio was still talking.

" . . . the Canadian CANDU nuclear reactor was installed in the Republic under an aid program to provide nuclear energy for underdeveloped countries. Officials from the Atomic Energy Commission, the authority responsible for ensuring the reactor was used for peaceful purposes, have refused to comment on the situation until they have studied it further. The last CANDU reactor violation took place in 1974 when the Republic of India exploded a nuclear device . . . ."

The telephone cut across the newscast. Corbin plucked it off the cradle.

"Corbin here."

"Chuck! Have you heard the news?" Don Affleck's voice was excited, worried.

"Yeah. I'm listening to it now. What's happening?"

"The Minister has scheduled a meeting at nine. He told me to call you. It's a real baddie."

"Okay Don, thanks, I'll see you at nine." He slammed the phone back on the side table, then looked angrily at his wife.

"El Chirlo, that sonofabitch! He's done it!"

Paco arrived with the coffee tray and set it onto the smooth polished surface of the big low table. He placed the cups and saucers out in front of Jamil and Hassan; Chirlo waved his own away.

"It was hoped, Major Hassan, you would be arriving with the

bullion—that was our agreement."

Jamil looked at the stupid Libyan in his rumpled suit with disgust and waited until he had finished slurping his coffee.

"I told the Major you would be unhappy with the additional delay, Colonel, but the Major is a very persistent fellow, aren't you, Major?"

Hassan looked uncomfortable. "A thousand apologies, Colonel Chirlo, but I must obey my orders. I promise the ship will sail from Tripoli today. I swear it!" He slurped some more coffee for emphasis.

Chirlo looked grim. "Then we will have to wait, won't we?" He glanced at his side. "Paco! Make arrangements for two adjoining rooms at the Prado for our guests—and a car!" He turned back to Hassan. "You might as well take in the sights, now that you are here, Major!"

Paco lowered his eyes obediently, then bowed himself out of the room.

Gerrard Petain, Minister of National Energy, Mines and Resources, was a soft-spoken patient little man, rarely given to anger or fits of temper. At the moment he was purple with rage.

"Modsie Corliss! Monsieur Levy, you mean you had these photographs last fall and did *nothing?*"

"Not exactly, Minister. Mr. Affleck voluntered to visit the site and returned with a full report," Morris explained.

"Which of you is Mr. Affleck?" the Minister demanded, looking at Corbin.

Don spoke up. "I am, Mr. Petain." He had already been introduced a half hour earlier when they had first arrived on Parliament Hill and were ushered into the Minister's spacious office.

"But of course, Mr. Affleck." He swung his eyes from Corbin. "Not much of a report, was it?"

Affleck shrugged. "It was as I saw it."

Corbin interrupted. "Mr. Petain, why don't we stop wasting time accusing one another of blame and concentrate on the remedial action. I think we are all agreed, Mr. Levy was wrong in not notifying you directly, however, he did send in a report three months ago—you have it there—" He leaned across the desk and pulled out the letter Petain had slipped back into the pile of correspondence, handing it to the little man. "The fact you chose to ignore the assessment, maybe missed seeing it during your busy schedule, is also beside the point."

Petain's eyes narrowed a moment, then relaxed when he realized Corbin did not intend to point the finger of guilt in his direction.

"Nor does it make the slightest difference now that you are making a formal protest through official channels, demanding the return of your oxide waste. Short of a physical invasion of Cosecha Rica, and dismantling the Punta Delgado facility, you haven't a hope in hell of getting Chirlo to do a godamn thing except send a polite reply stating your protest is being taken under consideration. So we are right back where we started when we came in here an hour ago." He sat back smiling at the Minister. "Or do you disagree, Mr. Petain?"

The little French-Canadian considered his choice of words carefully. Although he held a doctorate in engineering from the University of Montreal, he'd learned English as a teenager, much too late in life to perfect the flat Canadian accent. He was fluent in both languages, yet capable of proper pronounciation in only one. The fact annoyed him.

"One then assumes, M'sieu Corbin, you have some plan to propose—a solution to our dilemma." He spoke very quietly, like a perfect government minister.

Levy looked at Corbin hopefully. Sitting like an errant schoolboy at the seat of power was not his idea of happiness. Morris disliked politics and all it implied. For him, the explosion that morning was no different from the one India had set off, nor the one that would happen in the Argentine, Taiwan, South Korea, or any of the other nations in receipt of Canadian government generosity. If he had been able to push his views years before when the policy decisions on this insanity of export were being formulated, things might have turned out differently. Now it was too late, and no amount of bridge-mending or hurried policy adjustments were going to change the inevitability of disaster. This was a certainty he knew. He was tired of being held accountable for the stupidity of others; a pawn for pandering politicans, like Gerrard Petain, the Honorable Minister from the riding of Chateau Neuf. What did he know about nuclear fission? PU 239? Fallout and the spreading evil? Nothing. Did he really care, or was his present mood one of political self-preservation? Hell, he thought, he can't even speak English properly.

"Yes," Corbin began, "I have a suggestion you might consider, Minister. I suggest that Mr. Affleck and Mr. Levy accompany me at our company's expense to Cosecha Rica at once for a personal investigation and direct approach to the dictator, Colonel Chirlo. If he has exploded one bomb—it is a test; he has others for use by himself or for sale to others. Four people have gone down to investigate over the past few months—five actually, if you include the news reporter who died of a heart attack. No one has returned to date, except Mr. Affleck. I think the reason is obvious. Where Don is concerned, Chirlo will do nothing to violate their previous friendship."

Affleck interrupted. "I think you're putting that a bit too strong, Chuck! I know the man, certainly, but as far as our being friends—hardly friends."

"Friends!" Corbin said emphatically. Petain looked intrigued.

"What exactly do you hope to achieve, M'sieu Corbin?"

"Probably nothing more than coming back alive—which in itself is an achievement. However, there is always a chance . . ."

"It would have to be unofficial," the Minister cautioned.

Corbin and Affleck laughed in harmony. Even Morris Levy ventured a smile. The Minister looked annoyed. He disliked English language jokes that went over his small, well-groomed head.

Shortly after eleven, the army trucks pulled up on the pier under the solitary arc lamp by the gangway. Without ceremony, the drivers hopped down and went around to the back of each truck to unhook the tailgates. Four soldiers dropped from the rear of each vehicle. A captain in charge waved a paper casually at Akbar as he came down the gangway to meet the new arrivals.

"Comander Al Thani?"

The Palestinian shook his head. "He's below deck sleeping."

They met where the wooded gangway touched the pier.

"Wake him. I have his sailing orders."

Akbar raced back on board. The soldiers began unloading small heavy wood boxes out the rear of the trucks and lugged them aboard the vessel, piling them along the foredeck.

Al Thani came on deck with Akbar. His hair was dishevelled and he was still in the process of tucking his shirttails into his pants.

"Commander Al Thani!" The officer saluted him from the pier. "I am Captain Awbari, Sir. I have your sailing orders and cargo manifest."

Al Thani waited at the head of the gangway for the Libyan to come aboard. He read through the clipboard carefully.

"Five hundred and fifty-two boxes!" he said with surprise.

"Yes, Commander, at forty kilos per box. A little over

twenty-two thousand kilos in all."

"Very well, Captain. Have your men pile half by the forward hatch—the other half by the after hatch."

He signed the original documentation on the clipboard in the space above where his name had been typed, tearing off the carbon copy for himself.

"Call Jaber to break the hatches open," he told Akbar. "Top off the fuel and water. We'll sail as soon as they've loaded the boxes on deck. Check the amount before they're stowed below."

He handed the Captain his clipboard. "Thank you, Captain. I'll order my men to assist—can we form a line to move the cargo on board faster?"

The Libyan bowed. "You are most generous, Sir."

He waited until the first four men coming up the gangway lugging boxes had passed, then returned to the pier.

"Twenty-two tons of bullion!" Akbar breathed. "That's one hell of a load of gold!"

Al Thani smiled. "Less the weight of the boxes."

"It's still a hell of a lot!" Akbar watched the soldiers pile their loads neatly on top of the other square boxes, then went below to tell the Libyan first mate to roust the crew.

Leila was awake when he knocked on her cabin door. "Sailing orders?" She stood aside to let him in.

"They're loading the bullion now; clearance papers signed. Time for me to go."

"I'll miss you, Khala." She smiled at him affectionately.

"You too." He grinned, and kissed her on the forehead, then looked around the cabin.

"I wonder if the accommodations on the *Petropacket* are any better than this?"

Leila laughed. "You'll know tomorrow."

"Allah Maak, Leila." He studied her, paused, started to speak, then left abruptly.

Forty-seven minutes later the Ocean Trawler *Specht* slipped her mooring lines, and with diesels throbbing, headed out into the Bay of Sidra. Akbar stood on the pier beside the Libyan Army Captain watching the vessel's outline shrink, fade, then vanish across the water. He picked up his suitcase and duffle bag, pushed them into the back of the first empty truck, then climbed up over the tailgate and joined the four soldiers. Captain Awbari checked the gate hooks and looked in. "Where can I drop you off?"

"Any hotel will do, Captain—so long as the bed doesn't rock."

The soldiers laughed.

"Don't be defensive, my boy. I'm your father, Pedro, remember?"

Chirlo smiled at the old President, then lowered his eyes. "I'm sorry, Papa. It's been a busy day for me."

They were alone in Artega's study. After getting rid of Jamil and Hassan, he had faced the wrath of the Canadian Ambassador and the American Ambassador, plus a host of newsmen from the local wire services; Major Martinez had phoned to say hundreds more of them were pouring into Bahia Blanca by airline, private charters and executive jets. The three major U.S. networks were supposed to be on their way from Miami with complete sound and camera crews; telex protests from all over the world were still flooding into San Ramon. Local newspapers, however, were strangely silent on the whole affair. They were waiting in the wings, Chirlo decided; waiting to see which way public sentiment would flow. It was an odd feeling for the local news editors; a situation requiring an opinion on international morality, something that transcended borders or local political beliefs. Overnight, Cosecha Rica had become a nuclear power. No one knew quite how to handle the responsibility.

He finally left his office, slipping out the rear entrance with Paco to avoid the throngs of people waiting in the square outside the Presidential Palace. He was unsure whether they had come to cheer, or censure, his accomplishment—if that was the proper word.

"Where to, Colonel?" Paco asked onced they were in the car.

"Chirlo had to pause and think. The only sanctuary that came to mind was Doctor Artega's house in the Colonia. "Let's go visit Don Luis and hear what he has to say."

Ruis met him at the door, and saying nothing, ushered him into the study, where Artega was engrossed in an old leather bound book. He set it aside and removed his glasses when Chirlo came in.

"Ah! Are you on the run, or is this an official visit, my boy?"

"I have come to seek wisdom from the Seer on Olympus because the Seer seldom descends onto the plains these days," Chirlo said sarcastically.

He heard Ruis close the door behind him. If there was to be a family squabble, Ruis wanted no part of it.

"Sit down, my boy, and tell the old Seer your problems. I hear you were responsible for that big bang this morning."

Chirlo obeyed, dropping into a chair opposite the old man.

He told him the story—everything—holding nothing back. He

made it sound defensible. It was then Artega told him not to be defensive. Chirlo began to relax, unwind a little, realizing his mentor planned neither to criticize nor argue with him.

"You still plan on going ahead with the sale to Jamil?"

"I must, Papa. We need the money."

"Despite the dangers—it is the Libyans who are buying them, isn't it?" he asked quietly.

"Yes, the Libyans; it's their bullion we're getting. Their ship will be here in two weeks." He looked at his adopted father earnestly. "Jamil has given his word they will never be used."

Artega looked at him mildly. "Never, Pedro? That is a long time, isn't it?"

"I told him I'd kill him myself if he betrayed his promise."

"Quite proper too, my boy—that is, of course, always assuming you can find him afterwards."

They were quiet a few minutes, each lost in thought.

"Strange," Artega sighed, "when a good man does a good deed, the world pays no attention. When a wicked man does a good deed, the world pays a little attention. But when a good man does a wicked deed, the world is delighted and lives for the vicarious pleasure of condemnation."

"Have I been wicked, Papa?"

"That, my boy, only time alone can tell."

Except for the usual amount of sensationalism connected with any international news story, the political aftermath of the May fifteenth blast was negligible. There were, of course, numerous high-handed threats from various quarters of the world; two U.S. Senators grabbed the headlines for three days, demanding the President invoke the Monroe Doctrine and send in the Marines to topple the Chirlo regime; Idi Amin offered the neighboring republics his army, air force and secret police to defend their borders from the threat of imminent invasion by Chirlo's communist mercenaries, whatever that meant; and in California, a self-proclaimed minister of the gospel stated everything had been foretold in the Book of Revelation, which created minor stirrings among ecumenical circles in the Baptist Southern States.

Chirlo was unavailable for comment. He gave no interviews, spoke to no one, and had, for all intents and purposes, dropped from public view—to the amazement of everyone concerned. The amazement changed to unease as the days of aftermath passed. People began to wonder if it was a lull before a storm; a marshalling of unseen forces preparing to battle a hidden threat. No one knew. Everyone wanted to know. President Artega began making public appearances after a long absence from the spotlight. People were surprised how he had aged; yet the old fire was still there; the artful play on words, the double entendre, the skillful debater—until someone asked him about his son-in-law, or the country's responsibility for a new spread of nuclear proliferation, then President Luis Artega would draw himself up to his full five feet, glare at the questioner, and state resoundingly, "No comment. Next question!"

The DeHavilland 125 with Corbin, Levy, Affleck and their wives arrived at Bahia Blanca the day after the meeting with Gerrard Petain in Ottawa. Hotel space was at a premium at the coastal city and in the nation's capital; both locations packed with newsmen, foreign government officials and the curious. In the end, they all moved in with Rina's family, who had plenty of space and were delighted to see their daughter and son-in-law for a second time in less than five months.

On their second morning, the three men settled on the comfortable wicker chairs on the veranda and planned their campaign for investigation.

"I think Morris should concentrate on the Punta Delgado site. He has the authority for entrance and if we can get an estimate on the amount of waste the German's have lifted out of the pool, we'll have a handle on how many bombs our friend Chirlo has in his arsenal," Corbin suggested.

"You want me to go after Chirlo?" Affleck asked.

Corbin nodded. "He's all yours. Go up to his house on the hill, or wherever it is, and haunt the front door until you get in."

Affleck smiled. "It's on the top of the hill."

"The amount of stolen waste doesn't indicate the amount of plutonium processed nor the number of bombs constructed, Chuck," Morris said.

"But it will give us an idea at least," Affleck said.

Levy nodded. "An idea—a guesstimate. How about the chemical company? Shall I try my luck there, as well?"

"Let's wait and see how far you get on the first project," Corbin advised.

"What about you. Where are you going?" Don inquired.

"Me? I think I'll slide up to San Ramon with you and nose around the hotels. I have a feeling if our friend Jamil is the man behind this business, then he's bound to be close at hand."

"Maybe right here in Bahia Blanca?" Morris suggested.

"We'll let the girls cover the town here and the highway out from Blucher's—alternating four hour shifts."

Affleck laughed at Corbin. "Provided Rina can keep her mouth shut in a parked car alone for four hours at a stretch, you mean."

"Sarah says they've located a trailer at Choluteca for rent. I understand they've decided to park it off the side of the road near the entrance to Bluchers; you know, three, horny middle-aged schoolmarms on sabbatical." Levy smiled.

"Anyway, that's the cover Elizabeth dreamed up." Corbin shook his head, laughing. "Heaven help them all if someone takes them up on it."

Akbar was perfectly content on board the *Petropacket*, tied alongside the Marco Polo pier at Casablanca. His cabin was comfortable and spacious. The food was excellent, the temperature ideal; but best of all, so far, the ship hadn't moved a single millimeter since he'd come on board. For someone with a queasy stomach, Akbar resolved, there was nothing like shipping out on a tanker. The only difficult part of the past week had been Speidel's persistent pestering of him for sailing orders. Every morning, every noon, and every evening before bed, there was the inevitable polite tapping on his door and the German would enter smiling.

"Ah, Herr Akbar. How fortunate I caught you in."

It was an absurd opening, because Akbar rarely left his cabin except for meals.

"You did not by any chance hear about our sailing orders?" Speidel was like a nervous cat, waiting to leave port. The million dollar bonus was payable only after the first trip. The sooner it started, the sooner it would end; the sooner he could retire to the lovely little resort he had found in Bavaria. He hadn't discussed this matter with Dimitri, deciding there was no sense bothering his partner with personal details at this point; besides, Dimitri probably had personal plans of his own.

"No Captain, no word yet. When I hear, I'll let you know." Akbar was getting exasperated with the German. Sailing orders for each of the four Petro tankers were sealed inside individual envelopes hidden in the lining of his suitcase.

"You are sure the owners know how to reach you, Herr Akbar?" Speidel was bewildered by the Palestinian's lack of concern about their departure time and constant confinement aboard ship; impossible to receive word from shore while the man laid around his cabin all day and night waiting for the next meal, he thought. Akbar grinned.

"Don't worry, Captain, when the owners want me, they know where I can be reached." He patted his comfortable bed significantly and winked. "Right here, or on the mess deck!"

Corbin lowered the overseas edition of the *Miami Herald* just enough to permit his eyes to scan the lobby chairs and sofas. The man was still sitting in the same chair, staring at him; a pleasant slight figure with a baby face and innocent eyes.

Corbin raised the paper again to block the view.

He had been at the Prado for a week, scouring the city and its other hotels for some clue to Jamil's whereabouts, certain if he could attach himself to the Palestinian when he found him, he would be able to catapult into the midst of the intrigue. The baby-faced man had begun trailing him three days earlier, perhaps even before that. Corbin didn't know for certain; he had first noticed him three days ago. He was Latin American, but not Cosecha Rican; he had heard the man speaking to the desk clerk and recognized the accent from his own brief experiences in Central America when he and Colley had run their airline. This man's accent was from South, not Central America; a softer, slower, better enunciated speech. He lowered the paper again, much lower this time, exposing his whole face. Baby face smiled and nodded. Corbin set the paper aside.

"Do I know you from somewhere, Senor?" His own Spanish was atrocious from years of neglect and required a constant search for the right word.

The man came across the carpeted aisle. "Con permiso?" he asked, then dropped into the chair alongside Corbin. "I am Vicente Cardenal Ramon Da Gama, at your service, Senor Corbin. If he had been standing, he would have bowed.

"From?" Corbin asked.

"Montevideo, Uraguay."

"You know my name?"

The innocent eyes widened. "From the desk clerk calling your name, Senor Corbin, and from the messages you left at the other hotels around the city, looking for Galal Jamil."

It was Corbin's turn to widen his eyes. "You have been following me, then?"

The man smiled. "Since the day after you arrived."

"Why?"

"To give you the information you are seeking." He sat back in the chair, surveying the lobby . . . "in exchange for a small favor."

"Why didn't you approach me before?"

"I had to be certain of my bargaining position first. You might have found Jamil by yourself, in which case I would have had nothing to offer," he said logically.

"But now you're sure I will not find him."

"Quite sure," De Gama replied. "Or else by now you would have found him." He swung his guileless eyes to Corbin. "So, Senor Corbin, you introduce me to Colonel Chirlo and I will introduce you to Jamil. Is that not a good bargain?"

Corbin laughed. "I don't know Chirlo, Senor De Gama, but if an occasion ever arises where I'm about to be introduced to him, most certainly I'll contact you. Now, where is Jamil?"

"You are not the Charles Corbin whose company built the nuclear generating plant at Punta Delgado?" Da Gama's eyes lit with amusement. "And did not your business associate, Donald Affleck, live here for two or three years supervising construction? Why, Senor Corbin, of course you can introduce me to Colonel Chirlo!"

Corbin didn't know who the man was or where he had obtained the information, but he chuckled at his audacity. "All perfectly true, Senor Da Gama, however, I have never met Colonel Chirlo."

"Then now is your chance to remedy the omission, Senor Corbin. And introduce me at the same time. Agreed?" It seemed a perfectly reasonable sort of request.

From the sofa Corbin watched the legs swinging past his eyes below the overhead buzz of conversation; strolling legs, bare, in skirts or dresses; marching legs encased in uniform pants; walking legs covered with blue denim.

"What is your business, Senor Da Gama?" he asked.

"I do favors for people—favors for a price."

"What sort of favors?"

"Like telling you where to find Galal Jamil. My price is your introducing me to Colonel Chirlo."

Corbin laughed. "Very well, Senor Da Gama, you have my word, I will introduce you to the Colonel. As a matter of fact, my associate, Senor Affleck, has been trying to find him for the past week. He is not home, or if he is, he's not receiving visitors."

"I know. I tried to visit him myself." The Uruguayan seemed satisfied with Corbin's pledge for an introduction at the appropriate time.

"Galal Jamil is registered in the hotel here under the name of Martin Banke—room 1027. There is another man in the adjoining room who is registered as Juan Gonzales; they arrived together on the morning of the explosion."

"How do you know all this?"

"I was at the airport clearing a package through customs and saw a friend of mine meet them. My friend drove them to San Ramon. After they had met with Colonel Chirlo, my friend drove them to this hotel," the cherubic Uruguayan explained.

"This friend of yours wouldn't happen to be a German scientist working at Blucher Chemicals, would he, Senor Da Gama?"

The innocent eyes widened momentarily. "Why yes, Senor Corbin, how did you know?"

"Intuition." He studied the gallery of legs again. "Your German friend didn't mention what Jamil and this other man came to Cosecha Rica to do, did he? I mean, besides meet the Colonel?"

"No, Senor Corbin, unfortunately he did not. However he did say they would all be leaving together."

"Leaving together—you mean the German is going with them?" Corbin's mind began racing.

"Plural, Senor Corbin—*Germans*. All the Germans are leaving with Jamil and his friend by boat. It is after they have gone I want you to introduce me to Colonel Chirlo." He smiled apologetically. "I have no wish to disturb the Colonel while they are all so busy."

"A passenger liner?"

"The boat? No, I understand it is a small boat, like a fishing trawler, according to my friend."

"Interesting method of travel—close to the waves, that sort of thing." He thought a moment. "You don't know when this boat trip is supposed to take place, do you, Senor Da Gama?"

The Uruguayan smiled. "Soon—in fact, very soon, Senor Corbin."

"How soon?" Corbin was insistent.

"The day after tomorrow, according to my friend." One pair of legs stopped in front of the sofa. Corbin recognized the belt buckle.

"Hello Don!" He lifted his gaze to Affleck's face. Sit down. I'd like you to meet a Uruguayan from Montevideo, Senor Vicente Cardenal Ramon Da Gama."

Affleck shook hands and remained standing.

"Any luck?" Corbin asked his partner.

Affleck shook his head. "Nope, nothing. The place is still surrounded and Artega told me he hadn't the foggiest idea where his son-in-law could be found—bullshit, of course. I'm sure he knows exactly where he is, but that's the official word. It's almost as if they were all waiting for something to happen," he mused.

"Like maybe the arrival of a boat?" Corbin suggested.

"A boat?"

"Yes. Senor Da Gama and I have just concluded a business arrangement. In exchange for my introducing him to Colonel Chirlo—when you locate him—he has told me Jamil and a friend arrived here on the morning of the offshore blast; were picked up by a German scientist from Blucher's and driven to a meeting with Chirlo. Afterwards they checked into this hotel with adjoining rooms on the tenth floor, where they have been laying low ever since. The day after tomorrow a fishing trawler will arrive to pick Jamil and his friends up, together with all the Germans at the Punta Delgado plant, and they will sail away into the pages of history."

Affleck looked incredulous. "What is the name of the boat?"

Corbin looked at Da Gama. "What is the name of the boat?"

"*Specht.* It is called the *Specht,*" he said. Whereupon, Don Affleck sat down on the nearest vacant chair.

Al Thani's eyes popped open in the dark cabin the moment the bridge phone began to buzz. He grabbed the receiver from the wall above his head.

"What is it?"

"We've made landfall, Sir. Bahia Blanca is dead ahead about twenty miles. Sea is calm, wind light and variable. The local time is zero four thirty-one."

"Thank you. I'll be right up." He slipped the phone back on its hook, then swung his feet off the berth and stood up, stretching.

The trip had been uneventful; a fuel and water stop at Tangier, then clear sailing in smooth seas all the way across the widest part of the Atlantic. They were right on time for the end of the month deadline he had promised Jamil—in fact eighteen hours early, he thought with satisfaction. He went over to the wash basin and rinsed his face with cold water. There was a knock at the door.

"Come!"

"Good morning, Captain." Pierre smiled. "Your breakfast is ready," he announced.

"Good morning, Pierre. Set two places, will you, and wake up Madame Leila and ask her to join me?"

"But of course, Captain."

Al Thani stripped his shirt and reached for his razor. "Have you ever been to Latin America, Pierre?" he asked suddenly as the Lebanese chef started to leave.

"No Captain."

"Me either." He studied his reflection in the mirror. "I understand the women are very beautiful—very willing."

Pierre smiled. "Ah Captain, but then all women are very beautiful and very willing—it just depends on the man!"

Al Thani laughed into the mirror.

"Go and use your charm on Madame Leila and leave me to my beard! It's too early in the morning for French philosophy."

"Not French, Captain, Lebanese!" Lascoeur reminded as he shut the door.

Al Thani began lathering his face. He was reaching for his straight razor when the door opened and the Libyan first mate came in unannounced.

"Commander Al Thani, we are in sight of land!"

"So I've been told." He began stroking his lathered whiskers expertly, balancing the blade pressure in tune with the throbbing engine vibrations. The Libyan waited uncertainly at the doorway for further comment. He disliked the Egyptian and felt he should have been made captain of the *Specht*. It was, after all, a Libyan vessel.

"I'll hoist the ensign." He started to leave.

"You'll do no such thing, Jaber. Just hoist the quarantine flag." Al Thani paused, razor in mid-stroke. "And hereafter when you want to come into this cabin you will knock first. Is that clear?"

The Libyan looked sour. "Yes, Commander Al Thani." He slammed the door.

Al Thani continued stroking the blade, clearing the soap and stubble. When it came time to dispose of the Libyan crew, Jaber, he resolved, would be his own special project for elimination.

23

Early June 1976

Chirlo spent two weeks with Paco, living on the farm at La Esperanza. Paco drove to Tippitaca each morning to pick up food supplies, newspapers and the latest bulletins from Major Martinez' dispatch riders, who brought the papers of state into the sleepy town daily before siesta. Even Felina did not know where Chirlo had gone; only Artega, Martinez and Paco. People from the villages around the finca shared the secret, but they were closemouthed, rarely venturing beyond the farm boundaries. His secret was safe.

He spent the time horseback riding, reading and playing chess with Paco, a game for which Paco had begun to develop a proficiency after the across-the-board beatings he'd received from Chirlo over the years. The seclusion had in fact turned out to be a holiday, the first in many years. He had an affinity for La Esperanza; the place where everything had started and the place where it would probably one day all end. He decided he'd like to be buried up in the hills overlooking his hacienda, the hills where the old base camp had been located in the brutal battle against Guerrero. It was strange, but when he had spoken to his father-in-law about it one day in jest, the old President grew wistful and told him it was where he too would like to leave his earthly remains.

"Colonel! Paco is coming—with another man on a motorcycle!"

The maid rushed into the living room excitedly, wiping her hands. He got up and went around the veranda to look. Paco stopped to open the gate while the dispatch rider, without decreasing his speed, simply slipped through the narrow opening used by the farm animals. By the time Paco had the gate open, the rider had slid to a stop under the veranda and dismounted. He looked up at Chirlo and saluted.

"My message is verbal, Colonel. 'The *Specht* arrived this morning at six.' That is the end of the message."

Chirlo came down the steps as Paco drove up in the car.

"The fool wouldn't tell me what he wanted, Colonel!" Paco glared at the dispatch rider.

"Take him to Bahia Blanca in the car, Paco. Wait for me at the pier entrance. I'm taking his motorcycle." He reached out and pulled the rider's scarf from his neck, then began winding it around his chin and throat. The young corporal removed his blue crash helmet with its goggles and handed them to Chirlo.

"How much fuel?" Chirlo asked.

"Enough to get you to Bahia Blanca, Colonel. Maybe to San Ramon."

Chirlo patted him on the shoulder. "Good. I'll try not to wreck it." He cinched the helmet straps under his chin and lowered the goggles, giving the rider his lopsided grin.

"Will I pass muster, Corporal?" The young man didn't know whether he was supposed to agree, laugh, or refrain from comment. He coughed.

Chirlo swung onto the saddle and kicked the starter, rocked the bike off its stand, then with a wave, roared off towards the gate. The dispatch rider stood watching with Paco; instead of driving through the opened gate, Chirlo chose the narrow cowpath between the upright poles alongside. He thundered between them without slowing and slued onto the road, shifting into high gear for Tippitaca.

"I didn't know the Colonel could ride a motorcycle, Senor Paco!" The rider was impressed; he knew how close together the poles were from the handlebars.

Paco laughed. "Neither did I!"

Martinez had plucked Jamil and Hassan out of the Prado during breakfast. They left the hotel together; Martinez dressed in mufti, driving the innocuous grey VW with a crumpled right fender. Jamil sat in front with Martinez, Hassan by himself in the rear. No one spoke until they were outside the city, working their way down the curving broad highway to the coast.

"Is Colonel Chirlo joining us, Major?"

Martinez nodded. "Si Senor, I have notified the Colonel."

Jamil looked to him for further expansion on the subject, waiting. A mile passed, then another.

"You have notified the Colonel of what?"

Martinez glanced at the Palestinian. They looked very much alike—thin, dark, black eyes, straight black hair. "The *Specht* arrived this morning at dawn."

Jamil sat back. Reticence was something he understood in subordinates. They left the high country and descended down onto the coastal plain where the highway became straight and even.

"Senor Jamil, do you know an Israeli Colonel by the name of Lev Asher?"

Jamil, who had been musing on the problem of his tanker meetings at sea, was startled by the interruption to his thoughts.

"Lev Asher?" His mind spun a moment. "No. Why? Should I know him?"

Major Martinez said nothing. Another two miles rolled under the VW.

"He knows about you, Senor."

Jamil decided to play the game with the reticent Major, waiting until they had arrived at where the road met the Pan American Highway in front of the airport, before reopening the talk.

"Israeli intelligence officer with a game leg?" Martinez drew up to the stop sign, then swung down the highway for Bahia Blanca.

"That's the man."

Jamil grunted. "Is he here?"

"Visiting," Martinez replied with alacrity.

The Palestinian became alarmed. "You mean he's in the country?"

"With his Sergeant—Sergeant Kronig." Martinez treated him to one of his rare smiles. "Quite secure, Senor Jamil. He and his sergeant have been visiting with us in El Tigre Fortess since late April."

The Palestinian laughed. "You're a fox, Major—a real fox! Does he leave on the *Specht* with us?"

"You'll have to discuss that with the Colonel, but I think not."

When they pulled up at the entrance to the government wharf and stopped the car, Hassan was snoring loudly. He awoke immediately when the motion ceased.

"Where are we?" The two men in front ignored him.

Martinez rolled down the window as Captain Padilla walked

over. He was in civilian dress.

"Good morning, Sir."

"Has the Colonel arrived?"

Padilla shook his head. "No Sir."

"Security?"

Padilla straightened under the low roof, pointing. "I've sealed off piers six and seven, using troops from Colonel Ramirez' batallion at the airport. The six convoy trucks are standing by at the motor pool with drivers. They can be here in fifteen minutes."

"The crew?"

"Still on board, Major, except for the Captain, who came ashore to the harbor master's office under escort and made arrangements for fuel, food and fresh water."

He leaned down to the open window. "The Captain is very angry, Major."

"Good. We'll let him stay angry a while longer. Open the gate!"

Padilla waved to the soldiers standing in front of the high steel mesh slider blocking the access road into the wharfs.

Beyond the gate, they passed more soldiers guarding the area who watched suspiciously when they rumbled past on the heavy pier planking. The *Specht* was tied down at the far end of the wooden wharf. A squad of uniforms with weapons scattered near its gangway. Martinez drew up in front of the NCO in charge and stopped. The sergeant recognized the terrifying little major climbing out of the VW. He saluted smartly. Martinez nodded. He waited until Jamil and Hassan joined him.

Shall we go aboard?" Jamil walked over to the gangway.

Martinez bowed politely. "After you, Senor."

Corbin and Affleck left San Ramon immediately after the Uruguayan had given them the expected arrival time for the mysterious fishing boat. Da Gama waved them off when they checked out of the hotel, reminding Corbin once more of his promise to introduce him to Chirlo once the boat had sailed.

"Where will you be?" They were standing by the revolving doors in the lobby.

"Right here, Senor Corbin—probably sitting on the same sofa— you won't forget?"

Corbin stuck out his hand. "You have my word on it!"

They drove first to their wives at the strategically placed trailer in the open field outside Blucher's main gate. It was Elizabeth's watch; the other two were preparing supper when they drove up and parked on the grass outside the broad picture window looking out of the tiny living room. Elizabeth blew them a kiss as they climbed out of the car.

"Where's Morris?" Affleck asked as he came in.

"Went to town for food. Shouldn't be long. You staying for supper?" Sarah demanded. There wasn't enough for two more mouths and it would mean another trip back to Bahia Blanca.

"No. Pack everything. We're finished here. We're going back to the hotel."

While Corbin and Affleck related their experiences at the capital, they started a fury of packing.

"So, we will spend the next couple of days in idle luxury waiting for our boat to arrive. When it does, so will Chirlo!" Corbin told them.

By the time they had decamped and returned to Affleck's in-law's in Bahia Blanca, it was dark. Don Arnaldo de Felipe, although glad to see his daughter and son-in-law again, as well as their friends, was beginning to wonder if some form of insanity had taken hold of them all; first they arrived begging accommodation, and then the men disappeared for days on mysterious trips, leaving their women to sit in an old house trailer in an empty field alongside the highway. It was very perplexing. He was afraid to ask how long they planned to remain this time for fear they might change their minds suddenly and disappear again. That night he had a private talk with Rina. She chattered like a magpie, but told him nothing.

The following morning, Corbin, Affleck and Levy sauntered down to the docks and spent the day nosing about trying to figure which of the old wharfs would be the one used by the *Specht*. They decided only one offered security, isolation and privacy—the main government dock behind the customs warehouses. When they returned to their selection next morning and saw Captain Padilla with his swarms of soldiers guarding the mesh gate into the dock area, they knew their guess had been right.

"What do we do now?" Morris asked. So far, he had been the only one to accomplish his task. He had found the phony waste bundles at the outside storage pool after persuading Doctor Dorando to examine one of them. At first, the managing director of Nuclear Electrica Nacional had been horrified by the suggestion, then later, realizing it was only a matter of time before the place would be crawling with an official investigating team from Canada, provided every facility in an effort to reach the truth about the pools. By the time Levy left, and the tight-lipped and steely-eyed inspection team arrived from Ottawa, Doctor Dorando knew the exact number of missing waste bundles, the amount of oxide waste removed from them, and roughly how much plutonium had been extracted by his German neighbors next door, as did Morris Levy. Enough to make a half dozen twenty kiloton bombs.

"We wait and see what happens," Corbin said. They drove on past the gate and down the road, paralleling the customs shed.

"Stop!" Affleck shouted. Corbin hit the brakes.

"That Volkswagen we just passed! Jamil was sitting in the front seat—I'm positive. Turn around!"

Corbin obeyed, shunting into a laneway, then easing back onto the street.

"Look! See, I was right. They've stopped at the gate!" Padilla was leaning on the front window when they came by; Jamil, his head cocked down beside the driver, listening to the conversation.

"Yeah, that's Jamil, I remember him from the doll shop in Munich."

They drove past as the soldiers opened the sliding gate for the VW to pass through.

"So, the clans are gathering. Chirlo should be next." Corbin considered. "It's a cinch they'll want to keep it all private. My guess is everything will be arranged on the *Specht*.

"Why not at Blucher's?" Levy asked. "I understand they have a private dock there."

Affleck turned round in the front seat. "Couldn't get the boat in—not a deep sea vessel. The shoreline along that part of the coast is very shallow, particularly in the bays. No, the first meeting will be with Chirlo, Jamil, and whoever is on the boat. My bet is the Germans will come to the boat later—they won't all go to Blucher's."

"Somehow we've got to get onto that goddamn dock—and the boat—to see what's going on."

They turned the corner at the end of the street as a blue-helmeted military dispatch rider swung wide around their car, leaning his motorcycle at an impossible angle, then hurtled past.

"Idiot," Morris swore. "I think you're dreaming about getting on the ship. If the number of soldiers at the gate is any indication of their security, the dock will be knee-deep in soldiers." They drove around the block, thinking.

"Let's park a half block from the gate and wait to see what happens. Maybe we'll come up with a better idea," Affleck suggested.

There was no argument on the plan; in fact, no one said anything. Corbin drove around the block and slid to a stop under a huge eucalyptus tree, then turned off the motor. They were in the shade, less than five hundred yards from the dock entrance. Through the open windows of the car there was a smell of ocean, soil and fish—not at all unpleasant.

The large wooden crates had been marked "GAZ CYLINDROS" in large black lettering, and then underneath, in a series of smaller red letters, "PELIGROSO." The crates had been sitting outside the factory in one of the chemical storage sheds for two weeks; a precaution in case the test blast brought immediate search and discovery of Blucher's underground premises, on the theory that if the angry foreign investigators rushed into the factory, the four crated nuclear bombs could be shipped out the front gate by truck with a regular delivery of agricultural chemicals. It has been an unnecessary precaution. Chirlo's crack mountain troops turned up in battalion strength on the morning of the blast to surround the premises, but only to keep anyone unauthorized from getting in, not to prevent the Germans or plant workers from getting out.

During the first week, the German wives and families went home, one group each day on the PANAM flight to Miami, until only Fraulein Hoffer was left with the cooks and stewards at the compound's lodge. It was suddenly very quiet along the hillside where the beautiful bungalows nestled in the trees beneath the sun.

Major Martinez phoned Doctor Kastenburg five minutes after he had received notification from the harbor master at Bahia Blanca that the *Specht* had requested permission to enter port. Kastenburg called the others and they had their last breakfast together in the main lodge before packing the few personal things left in the houses and driving off along the private road to the factory. Fraulein Hoffer and the two cooks and stewards cleaned away the breakfast plates, made up the bedrooms in each of the vacant residences, then packed their own suitcases. They passed through the factory in the Land Rover on their way to the airport just as the four crates were being loaded onto the back of one of the company stake trucks. Fraulein Hoffer waved at the group of Germans standing around the truck; only Dietrich waved back and the Land Rover went out the main gate and off down the highway. When the last crate had been loaded, Hauser dismissed the driver.

"You can pick the truck up tomorrow morning at the government wharf. I'll leave the keys under the gas pedal."

The man nodded, giving the German a peculiar look, then went over to hitch a ride with the crane operator, who was driving back to his equipment parking area near the storage tanks.

"Sauve, you ride up front with me and Kurt. The rest of you climb in the back," Kastenburg told the group.

Dietrich jumped up first to receive the suitcases, then pulled Berger and Kraus onto the platform. Hauser swung the tailgates closed, and hooked them into position.

"For Christ sakes, drive carefully, Kurt!" Dietrich called through the wooden trellis. Berger laughed. "Quit snivelling. You'd think we were sitting on a bomb!"

They laughed. They felt lightheaded, happy, their spirits soaring as they drove out of Blucher's main gate for the last time, heading for the docks in Bahia Blanca.

"Five hundred and fifty-two boxes, Colonel!" Major Martinez reaffirmed. He had counted the pile twice after opening ten at random as they came off the boat. Inside each box, packed carefully in excelsior, the gold bars gleamed dully. To Martinez they looked like the huge pieces of Swiss chocolate he had seen once at Christmas time in one of the better stores in San Ramon. The first two he opened took his breath away; the golden bars and what they represented in wealth was as much as he could bear. By the fifth box he became more blasé.

"I'd like to look at that one, Major!" Chirlo was standing with Jamil, the Libyan, Al Thani and Leila, watching the unloading. Martinez lugged the heavy bar over to the group and laid it on the wood planking by his feet. Chirlo squatted down and examined the bar.

"Knife!" Martinez trotted over to one of the soldiers and removed the bayonet from the scabbard hanging on the man's belt. He handed it to Chirlo.

Carefully he scraped off the top of the bar. The others formed a circle around him, watching the performance intently; even the screeching seagulls swooped lower, missing nothing.

Fine soft slivers curled back from the knife strokes. He wiggled the bayonet point into the center of the brick, twisting it. He bored into another spot, then another. Finally, he sawed off one corner, lifting the pyramid shaped nugget off the blade before it dropped. He stood up and handed the bayonet back to Martinez.

"It looks real," he observed, studying the small piece he was holding.

"Quite real, Colonel. You have my word," Hassan insisted.

"However, Major Hassan"—Chirlo pocketed the nugget and

looked at the Libyan—"official confirmation will have to wait until Doctor Kastenburg arrives with his test kit."

"You doubt the integrity of the ingots, Colonel?" Hassan demanded, bristling.

Chirlo shrugged. "Why not? You doubted the integrity of the bombs!"

They watched the rest of the boxes being unloaded in silence, then waited while Martinez made his count.

"All correct, Colonel!" The Major saluted.

"Bring in the trucks," Chirlo told him.

"Where are the bombs?" Hassan demanded quickly when he realized what was happening and the first of the convoy rumbled onto the wharf. He had visions of the little boxes being spirited away with nothing to show for them but one of Chirlo's enigmatic smiles.

Chirlo looked at his watch. "Doctor Kastenburg will be along shortly, Major. I wouldn't concern myself if I were you. I am loading the boxes now, but I am not accepting delivery until Kastenburg has checked the random samples."

"Then you don't trust the Libyan government?" Hassan was horrified.

"No," Chirlo replied evenly.

"I consider that an insult, Colonel!"

"Stop acting like a goddamn fool!" Jamil hissed at the Libyan, and walked away angrily to watch the solders handing the boxes into the trucks.

The bullion was nearly loaded when the stake truck from Blucher Chemicals pulled onto the end of the wharf and stopped. Chirlo followed Hassan's gaze.

"It appears your bombs have arrived, Major," he said absently.

The Libyan walked quickly down the boardwalk to see for himself what was on the truck. "You have my bombs?"

The German doctor looked at him icily, pausing an instant to examine the cheap baggy suit the Libyan wore, then walked on to greet Chirlo. The others in the truck remained where they were, waiting for the army convoy to finish their loading and depart.

"Doctor Kastenburg! Good day to you! Ready to sail away?"

The doctor smiled at Chirlo warmly. "As soon as we've loaded our cargo, Colonel."

He looked over at the row of opened boxes Martinez had selected for testing.

"Only ten?" Kastenburg inquired. He had a bottle of acid and an eye dropper in his suitcase in preparation for the ritual of checking on the bullion's purity.

"Ten will be enough, Doctor. The Banco Central in San Ramon is going to be checking the whole shipment before closing time tonight. *Specht* will still be within range if I should have to fly out for a discussion with Major Hassan on any shortages."

Kastenburg smiled. "Ach! Colonel, you have thought of everything!" He nodded approvingly. "Who is Major Hassan?" He looked at Jamil, then Leila.

Jamil jerked his thumb back to the stake truck. "He's the one crawling onto your truck."

Kastenburg looked. "Oh that one! He's a Major? Tsk!" He nodded to Chirlo politely. "I'll get my bag."

The remaining closed boxes were loaded into the trucks, then the last vehicle in line started its engine and began backing slowly down the pier, past the Blucher stake truck, followed by the others. Doctor Kastenburg returned with his suitcase to begin the test. It took only a few minutes. Chirlo watched the performance with interest.

"What is supposed to happen, Doctor?"

The German chuckled without looking up. "If it's real, nothing." He squeezed the dropper full of acid onto the yellow metal. "See. Nothing. It's real."

As he finished checking each box, Major Martinez motioned the soldiers from the last truck to recap the tops and load them. Finally, Kastenburg straightened up from his squatting, repacking the glass jar in his suitcase.

"Quite real, Colonel. All quite real, I assure you."

Chirlo nodded.

As the last truck backed off down the pier, the Blucher stake drew up alongside the *Specht*. Major Hassan leaned over the side while the three Germans clambered down with their suitcases.

"Colonel Chirlo! These crates contain gas cylinders, not bombs —they don't even *look* like bombs!" His face was angry.

The Germans had been pulling his leg for the past ten minutes; they laughed like schoolchildren at Hassan's stupidity and stood beside Chirlo, clapping at the Libyan's idiotic remarks. Even Chirlo was laughing when the furious Major climbed down from the truck.

Akbar paid the taxi driver with all the Spanish coins he had left in his pocket, then retrieved his bag from the back seat while the man counted the pesetas. The amount was far in excess of the fare.

"Gracias! Gracias! *Mil* Gracias!" The driver kept repeating his thanks as Akbar walked down the dock past a Liberian freighter unloading pallets.

The Balearic Islands seaport of Palma, Majorca, teemed with shipping. It was basically a tourist vacation spot and the ragged coastline reflected this main source of income from the variety of yachts and floating palaces moored beneath the pink stucco villas around the island. It was also an extremely difficult place to reach by air on short notice.

Akbar had left Casablanca the same night the telegram arrived from Jamil announcing the *Specht* had docked in Bahia Blanca.

"I have your sailing orders, Captain Speidel," he informed the elated Speidel a few minutes after the bicycle messenger left the ship. He handed over one of the four envelopes he'd removed from the lining of his suitcase. The German ripped it open and yanked out the single sheet of paper. He looked at Akbar.

"What is this?" He gave the sheet to the Palestinian.

"June 15, 1975, 0600 GMT Lat 30 North. Long 50 West," Akbar read aloud. He handed the sheet back to Speidel. "It seems clear to me, Captain, you're supposed to be at that position on June 15."

"What for?"

"How should I know?"

"It's near Bermuda!"

"Is that bad?"

The German studied the sheet again, searching for some hidden meaning amongst the words and numbers. "But I don't understand, Herr Akbar!" he protested.

Akbar shrugged. "Neither do I, but I'm sure the owners know what they are doing. Why not do as they order and find out what it's all about?" He left the puzzled Speidel staring at the brief sailing order and went off to his cabin to pack.

Later, on the dock, he sat in a taxi with the meter running until he saw the *Petropacket* casting off her mooring lines, then drove to the airport for the evening flight to Tangier.

Aphendoulos hadn't appeared in the least puzzled by the strange sailing order for the *Petroprince.*

"Oh yes, Sir. Latitude 36 North. Longitude 40 West. I know exactly where it is," he agreed, as if ordering an old tanker into the middle of the Atlantic was the most normal thing in the world to him.

From Tangier, Akbar took an Air Algeria flight into Oran, but after sending the second Greek Captain on his way with the *Petro-*

power, he ran into a snag on airline connections to Palma. It took an extra three days on a circuitous route into Algiers, then Paris, where he overnighted on a bench in the new Charles De Gaulle Airport, then another night in Barcelona before squeezing himself onto the crowded Viscount for Palma.

He went up the deserted gangway on board the *Petroprincess* and walked into the wardroom. The deck and engineering officers were having lunch.

"Ah! Mr. Akbar! Welcome to sunny Spain!" Dimitri stood up to greet the Palestinian warmly, then introduced him to the rest of the men seated around the table.

"You have news for us?" he inquired hopefully. He was as anxious to get started as Speidel had been. Akbar handed him his envelope. The Greek's reaction was similar to his German partner's.

"That's all?" he asked in disbelief.

The Palestinian nodded. "That's it, Captain. You'll find out the rest when you arrive on location. I've been ordered not to go with you."

He patted his tummy significantly, giving Dimitri a wink.

The Greek laughed. "Ho ho? So you are not a sailor, Mr. Akbar?"

Others at the table snickered. Akbar looked self-conscious.

"I learned a long time ago, Captain Zaglaviras, my vocation did not lie in the direction of the sea. However" . . . he sniffed the air a moment, smelling the roast lamb on the sideboard with its aroma of herbs and garlic juices . . . "I may be on the way to revising my opinions about the sea. The menus afloat always seem to be so much superior to anything I've discovered ashore."

He pulled out an empty chair and sat down, arranging the linen napkin neatly over his knees, then gave them all a huge smile.

"I do apologize for the delay, Colonel Asher, but the release papers arrived only a few minutes ago," Major Martinez said smoothly. "The red tape on something like this is incredible. You'd never believe the trouble we had with central records."

"Yes Major, Colonel Chirlo explained it some weeks ago," Asher said dryly. He and Sergeant Kronig were both sitting in Martinez' small office waiting for the return of their passports. Martinez passed them over the desk.

"There you are, gentlemen. I noticed your tourist visas had expired, so I took the liberty of renewing them for another thirty days —we wouldn't want to have you held up at the airport going through departure control, now would we?" He offered them a thin smile.

"I take it then we are free to leave, Major?"

"Free? Why of course, Colonel, you have always been free to leave at any time. May I drop you off somewhere? The airport perhaps?" Martinez stood up.

"No thank you, Major. We'll just stroll around a while and enjoy the sights."

Asher and Kronig rose together. Martinez sat down. "As you prefer. Good day!"

The Israelis went down the long, cool hall in the daylight of freedom. Two guards on the main gate looked at them disinterestedly when they passed the entrance to the sidewalk in front of the forbidding grey building. They walked along in silence, down the hill, past vacant lots with scrawny dogs and bits of paper, breathing freedom.

"You all right, Sergeant?" Asher inquired without looking at him.

"Yes Sir. I ate well, rested well and learned some Spanish from a book."

"You know why we've been released?"

Kronig didn't, so he waited for his Colonel to explain. "Whatever the reason for our detention, that reason is now past."

Kronig still didn't understand. "What was the reason, Sir?"

"That, Sergeant Kronig is what you and I are going to discover before the day is out."

From the parked car they watched the army trucks enter the dock and the gate slide closed. No one came or left for another eighty minutes, then the Blucher Chemicals stake truck turned down the far end of the street and stopped at the gate.

"Look at the cargo!" Affleck muttered. They watched the truck go through to join the army convoy. "Four crates. Four bombs?" Corbin suggested.

"What else?" Levy demanded.

"Hardly conclusive."

"But why the armed trucks?"

"For the cargo on the *Specht*," Affleck said logically.

"Which is?" No one replied. After another fifteen minutes wait, Morris said, "I don't like to mention this, but I have to take a leak."

"Wait! Here come the trucks!" They watched them come out onto the road one after another and park alongside the curb.

"There's one missing!"

"That's what they're waiting for."

"I still have to pee."

"Quiet Morris—pinch it off. I need one too—this is important," Corbin muttered.

More minutes passed. The missing truck appeared, paused behind the last one in the parked row, then the whole convoy drove off. Corbin started the car and followed. He dropped Levy off on the main street.

"Have your pee, then get back to the gate and see who comes out—we'll follow the convoy!"

Morris fled down the street towards the hotel restroom.

They trailed the trucks all the way to the Banco Central in San Ramon and saw the small heavy boxes being unloaded on their third circuit around the block.

"Gold for bombs," Corbin observed.

"Six truckloads of it," Affleck breathed. "Chirlo's no piker, I'll say that for him. What do we do now?"

"Somehow we've got to stop the *Specht* from sailing." He drove past the bank again to reaffirm what they'd seen on the previous circuit, then drove off for the Hotel Prado to call Morris.

But the *Specht* had already sailed.

"Sailed?" Corbin was incredulous. "Morris, are you certain? It's only been three hours since we left."

"Left about thirty minutes ago. The soldiers pulled out and I walked onto the dock. The gate was open. There was a big trawler heading out to sea three or four miles away—the Blucher truck is still sitting on the wharf. It's empty."

"Didn't anyone come out besides the soldiers, Morris?"

"Yes, two cars. That Volkswagen we saw—same driver but a different passenger—only one. A big man with a beard. Then a sedan with two plainclothesmen inside."

"The bearded man was probably Chirlo," Corbin said resignedly. "What about the dispatch rider—the man on the motorcycle?"

"One of the soldiers rode out on it behind the Volkswagen. It wasn't the same man that rode it in, though, Chuck. He wasn't wearing a crash helmet—a smaller man."

"I know, Morris—Chirlo must have rode it in from wherever he'd been waiting. Where did the Volkeswagen go?"

"I don't know Chuck; I was on foot."

"Shit!"

"I'm sorry, Chuck."

"Not your fault. I should have thought to get another car. Okay Morris, stay put. Good work. The trucks, by the way, were carrying bullion. We followed them into the Central Bank. You can be sure the *Specht* was carrying bombs. I'll phone you later—explain to the girls." He hung up and went back over the conversation with Don.

"So the motorcyclist was Chirlo!" Affleck laughed. "It figures."

They spent the rest of the evening trying to decide on the next course of action.

"Shouldn't we tell the Embassy?" Don suggested at one point.

"A waste of time. By the time they got off their collective asses and contacted Ottawa for instructions that trawler would have arrived at its destination."

"Then the American Embassy!" Affleck persisted.

"Same thing applies—only they'd probably take longer to react. Remember, they're not officially involved. Shit! Somehow we've got to find out where that boat is going and stop it before it arrives. Think of something!"

They fell asleep thinking, until the next morning when Senor Vicente Cardenal Ramon Da Gama knocked on their door and invited them to join him for breakfast.

Affleck and Corbin stumbled around the room waking up, while Da Gama sat on the bed and watched with amusement. Later, during breakfast, he broached the subject of the promise he had come to collect.

"When might my introduction to the Colonel be arranged?"

Corbin smiled. "Just as soon as I can find him, Senor Da Gama. First we have to find him, then you'll be introduced. You don't happen to know his whereabouts?"

Da Gama nodded. "Certainly, Senor, the Colonel has returned to his house on the hill. He came back last night in an old Volkswagen with a crumpled fender, driven by his chief of security, Major Martinez. This morning I imagine he will go to his office in the Presidential Palace."

He pointed out the window across Bolivar Square. Corbin and Affleck looked at each other in surprise.

"Are you sure, Senor Da Gama?" Affleck asked.

"Sure he went home last night—not sure he will be at his office, but it seems logical."

They had to agree it did. Affleck stood up.

"In that case, let me walk across the square and see if I can get an audience with the great man to introduce you both."

1320 nautical miles at sea east of Bahia Blanca everyone crowded on deck to watch the sights as the *Specht* entered the Martinique Passage between the Windward Islands of Dominica and Martinique. Beyond, the broad Atlantic stretched unimpeded to the coast of Africa.

"Take a good look, gentlemen, it will be the last land we'll be seeing for at least two weeks!" Al Thani told them. They drank in the spectacular sight of the two islands on either side; Dominica, lying to the South, its green mountains soaring four thousand feet into the clouds, a rain forest jungle set in an emerald sea; then to the North, Martinique, with its towering volcano still smoking gently above the cultivated fields and orderly vegetation, a French maiden perpetually enjoying the summer sun. Slowly the islands drew astern until only the spire of the Pele Volcano was left smoking on the horizon.

The Germans started drifting back to the main salon inside the deck house. Jamil and Al Thani touched Kastenburg's arm. "A moment Doctor," the Egyptian commander said politely.

They walked over to the rail to watch the water boiling past the hull.

"The next watch change is at sixteen hundred. I suggest our action start then, if that is agreeable with you?"

Kastenburg nodded.

Al Thani went on. "Jaber is mine. I'll take him when he arrives to relieve me. Galal will take care of the helmsman, Broganik first, then Kammeh when he comes on watch."

"That leaves Leila to kill the second cook and radio man, and your people to look after the three deck crew and engine room staff," Jamil told him.

"I think we should wait until all deck crew are topside before hitting those in the engine room. It gives us more hands to work with. Leila, Galal and I can cover you from the wheelhouse if anyone comes out of the deck hatch." Al Thani made murdering the ten Libyan seaman sound like arrangements for a shipboard paperchase to keep his guests amused during a boring trip.

"What about Hassan?" Kastenburg looked directly at Jamil. There were flecks of spray on his pince nez.

Jamil's black eyes narrowed. "Major Hassan will be in his cabin taking his usual afternoon nap before stuffing his face at supper. I will visit him there, Doctor."

"Good. Then it's agreed. Four o'clock. I will advise the others. I hope those pistols are reliable, Galal!"

They straightened from the rail. Jamil barked his dry laugh.

"The very best money could buy!" The trio went into the deckhouse to rejoin the others in the main salon. Al Thani continued through to the wheelhouse.

As the hour for the watch change approached, one-by-one the Germans made their excuses and slipped away to their cabins. Major Hassan left shortly after.

"Wake me at six!" he told the Lebanese cook.

"I'll wake you, Major!" Jamil interrupted. "I'm going to be back working in my cabin."

He watched Hassan march out, then checked the remaining Libyans in the salon. The helmsman, Kammeh, was reading an old newspaper in a chair by the passageway into the wheelhouse; two engine room oilers sat playing cards at the rear of the big room. Jamil winked at Leila and stood up. He sauntered past Kammeh and opened the door up to the wheelhouse. Closing it behind, he pulled the thick green night curtains carefully across the small window, then quietly crept up behind the helmsman, Broganik.

Al Thani turned his head, saw Jamil, then glanced at the helmsman. He nodded his head slightly. Jamil sprang from his crouch, knocking the man to the deck, his arms locked around the Libyan's neck, pushing until it snapped and the body went limp. Al Thani dragged him by the feet to the side of the small bridge. The brass chronometer on the wall showed four minutes to watch change. Suddenly the door from the salon opened and Kammeh called, "Hey Aziz!"

Seeing no one standing at the wheel, he came up the steps quickly to investigate. Jamil's hand slashed out from behind the chart desk as the man came into the room, shattering his Adam's apple to pulp. He caught him before he fell back through the open door. Jamil dragged him inside by the shirt front, then strangled him.

"Take the wheel—I'll deal with Jaber!" Al Thani ordered. "Hold it steady on zero seven two." Jamil obeyed, grabbing the idly turning spokes before they drifted off course.

Al Thani waited at the starboard entrance onto the deck where he knew the Libyan captain would appear. The brass chronometer had its regulation eight bell chime as Jaber opened the side door onto the bridge. He froze when he saw the two corpses lying on the other side of the wheelhouse. His jaw dropped in surprise. Commander Al Thani smashed it closed with his fist, lifting the Libyan into the air. The man collapsed in a heap in the middle of the open doorway. Al Thani dragged him inside the deck house, then stood up and drove his heel into Jaber's face, stamping it into a bloody mush. Jamil shook his head with disapproval.

"Sloppy, Al Thani. Very sloppy." He looked at the mess on the deck. "Not only that, Commander, the man is still alive."

The Egyptian looked down at Jaber, growled and put an instep across his throat, balancing himself lightly with the other foot as he choked air and blood from the unconscious body. Jaber died.

Jamil relinquished the wheel, shaking his head. "Not only sloppy, my friend, but unorthodox as well."

Al Thani smiled. "But oh! So satisfying!"

The Palestinian nodded grimly and went below to the salon. Leila was gone. The two oilers were still sitting at the card table, although now both were dead. He went on into the pantry. Pierre, the Lebanese chef, was cowering in the galley, staring at the splattered brains from his Libyan second cook spread across the door of the white refrigerator. A soft-nosed nine millimeter bullet had blown his head apart, dropping him to the floor beside the oven. Jamil stepped across the corpse and patted Pierre on the shoulder.

"You didn't happen to see my wife pass through?"

The Lebanese looked at him in terror.

"No? Well never mind, she'll turn up eventually." He started down the steps to the officer's messroom, then looked back. "We'll be short a few for dinner tonight, Pierre—better get that cleaned up!"

The Lebanese chef began to cry.

Jamil passed into the aft cabin passageway. Dietrich and Berger appeared at the engine room door. Both looked pale. Murder was not their business.

"They're all dead down there!" Dietrich said loudly, then checked his voice as he remembered Major Hassan sleeping in the cabin just around the corner.

"Splendid, Herr Dietrich!" Jamil said in German. "Now why don't you go back down and bring up the bodies. We don't want to leave the engine room in a mess."

He waited until they left before continuing to Hassan's cabin.

He knocked lightly and went in. The major had just removed his boots in preparation for his afternoon nap.

"Ah Major. I'm glad I found you still up, you must come on deck—there is something I've got to show you. It's a breach of security if I ever saw a breach of security. Quickly, now—there's not a moment to lose!" He gave his voice the proper sense of urgency.

Hassan jumped back into his boots and rushed through the doorway and down the corridor to the after deck, Jamil right behind him. The major opened the door cautiously and peered out, then wider, and stepped on deck, looking around quickly.

"Where?" He looked bewildered.

Jamil walked past him swiftly to the taffrail and leaned over, pointing to the waters churning up in a hum from the ship's twin screws.

"Here. Look for yourself!" The major ran over to see, leaning far out, peering down into the turbulent water. Jamil flipped him into the green foam, then returned to the deckhouse without bothering to look back. He knew Hassan couldn't swim, so what was the point?

Asher was fuming. He slammed the phone, stood up from the bed and began pacing the carpet of the hotel room. Sergeant Kronig watched him from the window chair. Nine paces up the room to the door, nine paces back to the window. So far, he thought bitterly, the only thing he'd been able to alter after their release from El Tigre was to increase his confinement from six to nine paces.

"That Ambassador says we must be patient, Sergeant," he told Kronig as he arrived at the window and turned back for the door.

"Didn't he tell you that yesterday, Sir?"

Asher waited until he had completed his turnabout at the door before answering.

"Yes, and the day before, and the day before that!"

Kronig watched his limping Colonel thoughtfully. Although it was not his station to criticize a superior officer, the results of their efforts since release from Chirlo's dungeons were hardly spectacular.

First they had gone straight to the American Embassy where the horrified Ambassador heard the full story of their kidnapping and incommunicado incarceration at El Tigre. Then Mr. Collins provided them with an updating on local events since their disappearance. Morton Cuddy, new CIA agent-in-charge, filled in the blank spots. Asher listened attentively, realizing every fear he'd imagined had come to pass.

"So what are you doing about it?" he demanded of Cuddy.

"We're investigating. Actually, our hands are tied officially; the Canadians have sent an inspection team down and confirmed the missing waste from that outside storage pool—enough to make a half dozen bombs, it seems. Colonel Chirlo refuses to discuss the subject with anyone—officially or unofficially. That's where it stands."

"What about the German scientists and Blucher Chemicals?"

"What about them?" the Ambassador asked.

"Good God, man! They stole the waste and made the bombs—aren't you going to do anything about it?"

"Please, Colonel Asher," Collins protested, "this is an internal matter between Blucher's and the local government on the one hand, and an external matter between the local government and the Canadians on the other—it's not in our interests to get involved. I have received very clear instructions from the State Department to adopt a hands-off, wait-and-see posture until the situation becomes clear enough for us to formulate a policy at the official level. We have filed our formal protest. Now we must sit back and see what develops."

Asher looked at him incredulously. "You mean you're doing nothing at all?" Even Sergeant Kronig swallowed in disbelief.

The two Americans said nothing.

Asher stood up. "Well, by God, gentlemen, *I'm* going to do something!"

Cuddy looked skeptical. "Oh! What?"

The Israeli thought a moment. He was so surprised by the turn of events he hadn't begun to formulate a plan yet.

"First, I'll contact Brigadier Borodam for instructions."

Collins stood up too and patted Asher on the shoulder. "Very sensible, Colonel—no point in creating an incident on your own. Let your superiors make the decisions. I have found that always to be the wisest course. Keep your nose clean. If you like, I can transmit your report to Tel Aviv as soon as it's prepared . . . through Washington," he added.

Asher caught the drift at once. If he expected any help from the Americans, everything was going to have to be funneled through Ambassador Collins and the State Department in Washington.

"Thank you, Mr. Collins. That would be very helpful." He used one of their offices and in three hours had a detailed report prepared for Borodam, outlining his own recommendations. Cuddy promised to send it out as soon as they had encoded the nine pages.

Asher and Kronig went over to the Prado and checked in to await the reply and instructions from Tel Aviv. They were still waiting.

"Let's go and have breakfast, Colonel!" Kronig suggested brightly. He was hungry. Asher's pacing didn't help. The Colonel obeyed the Sergeant. They went down to the coffee shop.

Corbin recognized the limping Israeli the minute he entered the room of clattering dishes and chatter. Asher paused at the entrance searching for a table, then caught Corbin's wave, said something to

722

Kronig and came over, the huge Sergeant following behind.

"Welcome to the sunny South, Colonel!" Corbin stood up, "You down here slumming? Rumor has it you and your Sergeant deserted!" They shook hands and sat down, crowding Affleck and Da Gama to one side of the small square table.

Affleck's visit to the Presidential Palace had been fruitless, although he did get to speak with Paco a few minutes. He sensed the restraint in Chirlo's faithful aide during their short talk, yet it was better than nothing.

"As you know, Senor Affleck, the Colonel has been away from the office for over two weeks and has much work to catch up on before he can see anyone—even old friends. Perhaps His Excellency Doctor Artega could see you?"

Affleck gave him his gleaming smile. "No, Paco, you rascal, we both know that's a waste of time. It's Chirlo I want to talk to, not the President."

"I'll tell him, Senor Affleck, but he's very busy."

"You already told me that. When do you think I could see him —when he's not busy?"

Paco looked around the big waiting room. The crowds of international reporters had thinned out considerably since the beginning of the events in Cosecha Rica. Old news is stale news. But, a few dozen diehards still clung to the belief they would be lucky enough to grab a personal interview with the Dictator and provide the exclusive followup story to shock the world. They pushed and shoved their way into Paco's line of sight, striving for recognition.

"I cannot say, Senor Affleck. But I will promise to tell him you're here."

"Waiting at the Prado," Don added.

Paco smiled tiredly. "Waiting at the Prado. Yes Senor. I'll tell him. I promise."

He walked back across the square to where Corbin and Da Gama were sitting on a public bench.

"No luck, I'm afraid. I spoke to his man Friday, Paco; he promised to let Chirlo know I was sitting at the Prado waiting." He sat down at the end of the bench. "I guess we wait."

They studied the pigeons perched on Simon Bolivar's statue in the square. They cooed softly at the passersby, one or two fluttering down occasionally to check for bits and pieces of paper which indicated food. It was very peaceful; even the traffic around the square seemed quiet.

"You think he will call, Senor Affleck?" Da Gama asked.

Corbin looked at Don. "Well?"

Affleck shrugged. "Probably, once the heat's off. There's still a pile of newsmen trying to get at him. Chirlo's never been one for publicity."

"But you're not a newspaper reporter, Senor Affleck!" Da Gama observed.

"No, I'm not. If I was maybe I'd have an idea what would make more sense than sitting on our butts over at the Prado waiting for a call."

"Give it a few days. We'll see what happens," Corbin suggested.

Affleck nodded. "I'll hit Paco again in the morning, and keep bugging him twice a day until we get some result—it's a cinch Chirlo isn't going to stay hidden forever."

"Maybe we could drive up to the house tonight?" Da Gama said.

"It's worth a try," Don agreed.

"Meanwhile, that goddamn *Specht* closes on its destination!" Corbin said angrily.

They sat in silence, thinking, watching the pigeons, then strolled back to the hotel.

"So, here we sit, Colonel Asher, waiting for the great man to call!" Corbin told him in conclusion.

"Have you spoken to anyone about this?"

"You mean about seeing Chirlo, or the bombs on the trawler?" Corbin asked.

"The *Specht*."

"No one—what's the point? We'd run into the same brick wall you did at the American Embassy if we went to see the Canadian Ambassador. Besides, we have no proof."

"Neither did I when all this started last Fall, but I was right," Asher said emphatically. "Just as right as you are about those four crates and the gold bullion! God! Spare us from fools and politicians!" He reached across the table, grabbing each of their arms with strong fingers. "We're on our own now. Are you with me?"

"With you?" Affleck asked.

"I will take Sergeant Kronig with me and go find the *Specht*. You stay here until you get to Chirlo. I'll phone you every evening between nine and midnight your time." He started to rise. "And we haven't much time."

Corbin interrupted. "Wait a minute, Colonel, before you rush off. We have our company jet down at Bahia Blanca. If you take Morris Levy and our wives back to Canada for us, you can keep it as long as you want."

It was a generous offer. Asher sat down. "What type?"

"DeHavilland 125 with long range tanks—it'll cross the Atlantic —we've done it before."

"Mr. Corbin, you're a Godsend! I accept with thanks. When can we leave?"

"As soon as you can get to the airport. I'll phone down now and tell our wives to start packing. Do you have a car?"

"We'll take a taxi."

Affleck piped up. "Nonsense, I'll drive you down—have to pick the girls up anyway and explain things to my wife. Let's go."

Asher grabbed Corbin's hand again with both his and shook it warmly. "Thank you, Mr. Corbin, we're very grateful."

"Yeah, I know—I'm a Godsend. Colonel, take care not to get lost again. We'll wait for your calls." He sat down with Da Gama, watching the Israelis and his partner leave the coffee shop.

When they had gone, the Uruguayan turned to him. "Forgive me, Senor Corbin, but my English is poor; exactly what was that all about?"

Corbin waved the waitress in for coffee refills and the bill. "The Prodigal Son, Senor Da Gama."

"The Prodigal Son?" the Uruguayan repeated, still none the wiser.

"He that was lost, has been found, Senor Da Gama—it's about a Jew in the Bible."

Far out in the mid-Atlantic, the *Specht* cruised through the dark waters under a cloudless starry sky, idling along at a bare ten knots. From the wheelhouse, Al Thani watched the three Germans knock the wooden pegs into the slots around the hatch cover to prevent the canvas top from flapping. He reached up to the panel above his head and killed the floodlight as they left the forward deck, carrying the wooden mallets. It took a minute for his eyes to adjust to the darkness and starlight.

The Germans had taken over the crew functions with surprising adaptability for a group of scientists and slide-rule engineers. Al Thani had explained the barest of information to his middle-aged crew before they grasped quickly what was necessary to run the ship safely and efficiently. They were becoming as good as experienced seamen. All in all, he was immensely pleased with his new scratch crew; with the Libyans long-gone for shark bait, the vessel also had the advantage of being far less crowded below decks than when it sailed out of Bahia Blanca two weeks before.

"Good evening, Commander!" Kastenburg entered the wheelhouse from the side door. "Lovely night."

Al Thani smiled at the German. "Morning, actually Doctor."

He turned, looking out the windows. "Are we on time?"

"If the *Petropacket* is in position, we should sight her at dawn—in about three and a half hours," he added, glancing around at the glowing dials of the chronometer on the bulkhead. "Everything primed below?"

Kastenburg nodded without turning his head. "The timers are set to seventeen hundred hours Greenwich, July fourth—twelve noon local time in Montreal and New York; late tea time in London and Rotterdam. Four bangs. Phsst! Fourteen million people." He said it softly with satisfaction.

"Fourteen million!" It was the first time Al Thani had heard the magnitude of intended destruction. "That's bigger than Hiroshima and Nagasaki combined!" The immensity of it stunned him.

"Not really." Kastenburg turned from the window, then leaned back on the sill. "Nagasaki's bomb was just a small twenty kiloton blast—like ours will be—detonated from eighteen hundred feet. Unfortunately, we'll only be able to have ours a hundred feet above ground zero in the crosstrees of the tanker's mainmasts, so our effective concussion will be considerably less." He smiled. "But I assure you, it will be enough—*quite* enough—for our purposes."

His pince nez glowed a moment, catching the dim green light reflected by the compass repeater. "Do you like the sea, Commander?" the German asked curiously.

Al Thani shrugged. "When I was younger, it was my first love, my mistress; now, well, this mistress became my wife and a man grows tired of wives, doesn't he?"

"I have decided I like the sea, Commander. It's a pity man is destroying it."

"But man destroys everything eventually, doesn't he, Doctor?"

"Including himself."

"Including himself," Al Thani agreed.

Kastenburg removed his glasses, then rubbed the bridge of his nose. "I wonder why that is, Commander?" He replaced the pince nez.

It wasn't a question to which there was an answer, as both the German and Palestinian knew. Kastenburg walked past the helm to the steps down to the salon.

"Goodnight, Commander Al Thani."

"Goodnight, Doctor Kastenburg."

Three hours after leaving Corbin and the strange silent baby faced Latin in the Prado coffee shop, De Havilland executive jet—*Able, Echo, Zulu*—was crossing the San Pedro Sula VOR at twenty-two thousand feet above the Republic of Honduras on its way to Miami and Ottawa. During the refueling stop at Butler Aviation in Miami, Asher went into the guest lounge and phoned Tel Aviv. With the time difference, Borodam was at home, in bed. Asher advised the night duty officer of his whereabouts and intended plans. The duty officer knew nothing of any report forwarded from Washington through channels and sounded surprised that the missing Colonel and his Sergeant were still alive; Tel Aviv had written them off, listing them officially as "missing." Asher cursed Ambassador Collins and hung up angrily.

Next he phoned the C.P.I. offices in New York and asked to speak to B.J. Bronstein. He gave his name and told the girl on the switchboard it was an emergency.

"Colonel Asher! How ya doin', pal? What's up?"

"I'm in Miami, Mr. Bronstein. This is an emergency. I can't explain it now, but I'll phone in four hours and give you a rundown. In the meantime, can you check out full particulars on a ship for me?"

"When do you need it?" B.J.'s voice was all business.

"When I phone back from Ottawa."

"I'll do my best—shoot!"

"It's an ocean trawler named *Specht*"—he spelled the letters out slowly—"under Libyan or Liberian registry, I'm not sure, probably originally Dutch or German, but recently purchased by new owners. I need the company that sold it, the company that bought it, who handled the transaction—in fact, anything you can get. A photograph would be helpful too."

"It's too late for the Lloyds office in London, but I'll try their branch here. Call me from Canada." He hung up.

Asher went back to the plane. Rick Rogers stood by the door waiting for him.

"All set, Colonel?"

Asher smiled, "All set, Captain." He started up the airstairs, then stopped. "I know this is asking a lot, but do you think you could arrange to carry on from Ottawa to Europe?"

"Tonight?"

"Yes."

"Whereabouts?"

"I'm not sure yet. Either Schipol airport in Amsterdam or . . ." he shrugged. "I'll have to let you know in Ottawa after I make a phone call."

"Is it important?"

"Terribly important, Rick—I wouldn't ask otherwise."

"Okay, Doug and I can take turns sleeping, I suppose."

Asher patted his shoulder. "Good man." Rogers followed him aboard and retracted the stairs.

It was still light when they landed in Ottawa two and a half hours later. Asher bid Morris Levy and the wives goodbye, then rushed to the first telephone booth he could find inside the terminal and called B.J. It had been only three hours since the Miami call, but there was a chance.

"Hi Colonel—you're early! I got it! You have a pencil?"

"I don't need one—go ahead."

"Motor vessel *Specht*, built by Van Cleeman yards Rotterdam in 1970 for Dorfmann Ocean Salvage, Dutch Registry. Present master Cornelius Van der Zlapp, 324 Ofert Zoom Street—crazy name for a street, eh?—324 Ofert Zoom Street, Botlek."

"Botlek?"

"Yeah, it's a suburb of Rotterdam—one of the harbor areas, the local Lloyds guys said."

"That's it? No new owners?" Asher was puzzled.

"None shown so far. Of course if they sold it recently there'd be a delay on the filing notice. The London Lloyds may have different information, but their New York office still shows it as Dutch registry. What's all this about, Colonel?"

"I think the *Specht* was purchased by Jamil and his Palestinian friends to pick up four nuclear bombs in Cosecha Rica last week. It left Bahia Blanca, after unloading six truckloads of gold bullion and taking four large crated cylinders on board. I've got to find it before it arrives in the Middle East."

"Oh my God," B.J. said softly through the earpiece.

"Mr. Bronstein, can you get a photograph of the *Specht*?"

"What! Oh, no, they don't have one on file here. Are you going to Holland?"

"Yes, in a few minutes, as soon as the plane's refueled."

"Okay Colonel, listen, I'm going to send a *most urgent* out to all our men in Europe and the Middle East to stand by for instructions. I'll call Peter Reichman in Amsterdam to meet you when you land. Which airline are you on?"

"I'm not. I've got a corporate jet on loan from CORCAN, a DH 125, Canadian registry, CF-AEZ. I don't know what time we'll get into Schipol, though."

"Don't use Schipol airport—go into Zestienhoven. It's closer to Rotterdam . . . ." He paused. Asher could almost hear the mental wheels turning through the receiver.

"Okay, Colonel, here's what to do. Reichman's still in bed, so I'll wait until six a.m. their time, then phone him. He can do a complete rundown on the *Specht* and its master—including a photograph, if he can find one. I'll have him check air traffic control for your arrival time. Leave it to me. You get started."

"Thanks, Mr. Bronstein. Oh, and by the way, until we find *Specht*, please, no publicity."

"And after you find it?" B.J. was, after all, still a newspaperman at heart.

"Then I want you to tell the world."

In former days, the British government ruled the Northern coasts of Somalia from their Colonial office in London. Somalia guarded the approaches into the Red Sea and Suez Canal, on the southern shores of the gulf, in the same manner British Aden guarded the Northern gulf coasts. That was before Nasser closed the Suez Canal. Aden became the Republic of Yemen, and the British Protectorate of Somalia was incorporated into the Republic of Somalia in 1960. Parliamentary form of government lasted until 1969 when a Russian-backed revolutionary dictatorship seized power as part of the overall Russian plan for control of the African Continent.

Somalia was no bargain. Eighty-five percent of the population was illiterate, and prior to 1973, there was no written language depicting the strange nomadic tongue. The Moselm nomads which populated this arid barren land with its equatorial heat and humidity, regarded the intrusion of any foreigner with deep suspicion. It was exactly the reason Doctor Waddi Hadad had chosen Somalia as his new base of operation for the training of terrorists for the PFLP (Popular Front for the Liberation of Palestine).

The training camp outside the new seaport town of Berbera was even more difficult to reach by air than the island of Majorca. The air flight from Mogadiscio, the nation's capital on the southwest coast, was irregular and inefficient. Consequently, Akbar was three days overdue on his agreed arrival time. Doctor Hadad was not pleased.

"I dislike tardiness, Brother Khala. It displays a lack of discipline. A slovenly attitude. Sit down!"

Akbar obeyed, removing his smile. There was no point in arguing with the legendary Hadad over the impossible traveling gymnastics he had made during the past week. He glanced around the sweltering room, a corrugated steel sweat-box stirred by a huge overhead fan with slowly revolving blades. The air buzzed with flies.

"You have a comfortable place, Doctor," Akbar observed politely.

"Are you trying to be funny? The place is a hell-hole. However, it has the one advantage of complete privacy. I take it you're here to discuss your diversionary action?"

"Yes Doctor."

"Then the primary action has been successful?"

"I have been informed that it was."

"By Jamil?"

"By Jamil," Akbar confirmed.

Hadad snapped a quick nod. "Very well, what do you want?"

"A skyjacking."

"Very original," Hadad said dryly. Akbar pressed on, bending to pick up his briefcase and remove the contents of the plan.

"Except, with this one we want you to hold the aircraft and passengers from June 27th to July fourth." He opened the file on his knees and removed the top sheet. "The plan calls for taking over Air France Flight 139 out of Athens on the morning of June twenty-seventh, flying it to Benghazi for refueling, then on to wherever you decide is the best location to hold the plane and passengers until July fourth."

Hadad reached for his desk calender. "The twenty-seventh is a Sunday. What about airport security?"

"I've made arrangements for a wildcat strike that day starting at six in the morning. Security will be lax. The Greeks are a lazy lot."

"And at Benghazi?"

"You will be expected. Arrangements have been made," Akbar confirmed.

Hadad set the calender down and stuck his hand out, waiting for the file of papers. Akbar laid it on the opened palm.

He riffled through the pile quickly, then withdrew a photograph. "This is the equipment being used?" He held it up.

"The schedule calls for one of the new air buses operating on the Tel Aviv/Paris run."

"Hmm, we've never highjacked an airbus." He dropped the

black-and-white glossy and went through the rest of the papers, aircraft layout plans, fuel specifications, operating manual for the aircraft, emergency procedures and safety exits.

"Am I permitted any leverage?"

Akbar shrugged. "Whatever you wish, Doctor—ransom them for money, propaganda, prisoner release, anything you want—just so long as the aircraft and passengers remain hostages until July fourth."

"One week," Hadad mused. "Two hundred odd passengers and crew to feed and house. You're asking a lot."

"But it will be worth it when you hear what we have planned for July fourth. I promise!"

"Very well, Brother Khala. It will be done as you say." He stood up. "Now, let me show you around our little camp. It's much better than what we had in Jordan, or Lebanon, for that matter."

They went outside into the blazing sun, walking towards the first prefabricated nissen hut. The air was stifling.

"You won't bring the air bus here?" Akbar said hopefully.

"No, not here. Uganda perhaps, but not here."

A small green lizard scuttled across their path and vanished into the yellow grass.

"You can deal with that syphillitic lunatic?" Akbar asked in wonder.

Hadad laughed. "Even syphillitic lunatics have their uses for the Cause, Brother Khala!"

Peter Reichman was standing with the customs officer at Zestienhoven Airport when they landed. It was late afternoon and Western Europe was in the grip of the worst heat wave in living memory.

"Colonel Asher! I'm Peter Reichman, C.P."

He was a stocky, rumpled man in a damp suit and curled shirt collar that stuck to his neck. Asher shook his hands.

"Good of you to take time out to meet us. Any news?"

Rogers and the co-pilot came past. "I'll get us refueled, Colonel, and wait in the lounge till you're ready to leave for town."

The two pilots looked completely bushed; red-rimmed eyes with dark circles. Asher waved as they passed. He had slept most of the way over, waking when they landed at Goose Bay, Labrador, and again at Kafavlik, Iceland, during the thirty minute fuel stops. Sergeant Kronig, on the other hand, had slept across the entire Atlantic.

"Yes, Colonel, I found Cornelius Van der Zlapp. He still works for Dorfmann Ocean Salvage. He told me that he sold the *Specht* personally to the Libyan government through a Greek agent named Dimitri Zaglaviras from Piraeus. They—that is the Greek and Libyan surveryor—turned up here in February to inspect the ship and bought it the next day. Van der Zlapp arranged a ferry crew for them to sail the vessel to Tripoli. The Libyan, a man named Awani, commanded the *Specht* when they sailed. I interviewed two of the crew who went on the trip; they confirmed Awani was a professional seaman."

They walked slowly towards the executive pilots' lounge and stopped by the door.

"Did Van der Zlapp ever have any dealings with this Greek Zag-*whatshisname* before?"

"Zaglaviras, Colonel. Yes, he has done a little business over the years with both the Greek and his German partner, mostly buying or selling salvage. Van der Zlapp said they're both unsavory characters."

"The kind that would do anything for anybody for a quick profit?" Aksher asked him.

"Precisely, Colonel." Reichman opened the glass door into the lounge. "I have a photo of the *Specht*—an old one, when she was first commissioned." He drew it out of the brown envelope he carried and handed it to the Israeli.

Asher studied it a moment, then gave it back. Reichman handed him another paper. "This is the address of Mindrinos Ocean Enterprises, S.A., in Piraeus, operated by Messrs Zaglaviras and Spediel."

Asher took the paper and folded it into his shirt pocket. "Mr. Reichman, I wonder if you would do one more favor?"

"Name it."

"Take the photograph of the *Specht* to the Israeli Embassy at the Hague and have them transmit it to Brigadier Borodam's intelligence section in Tel Aviv—open transmission with no message. Can you do that for me?"

"Certainly, but they may be closed now."

"Then make them open up—use your newsman's cunning. Tell them it is a priority one transmission. Use my name and explain the circumstances to the Ambassador himself if you have to. If they need confirmation, have them call Brigadier Borodam on the scrambler."

He watched Reichman write the instructions in shorthand scrawl on a tattered notebook with no cover.

"Can I take you into the city?"

"No thanks. You get started for the Hague. We'll make our own arrangements here. If I don't see you again, Mr. Reichman, my apologies and profound thanks for your help."

He shook the newsman's hand warmly.

"If you don't mind my asking, Colonel, is there a story in all this?"

Asher laughed. "Isn't there always a story?" He ushered Reichman to the parking lot exit and bid him goodbye, then went over to the phone booths beside the desk, where Rick Rogers was making servicing arrangements for the aircraft.

He called Tel Aviv, person-to-person for Borodam. This time he got through.

"What th'hell are you doing in Holland, Colonel?" the Brigadier growled.

"Kronig and I are on our way to Greece."

"Wonderful holiday weather, I understand," he said sarcastically.

"Sir, there is a priority one transmission coming through to you sometime tonight from the Hague—photograph of an ocean trawler, the *Specht.*" He went on to explain the full story of his captivity, release, American Embassy visit, the Corbin and Affleck meeting, and the loan of the DeHavilland to track down the four crated bombs; then capped it off with the information Reichman had just delivered to him. It took a full thirteen minutes at long distance person-to-person rates, but Brigadier Borodam didn't mind a bit.

"Good work, Lev! *Bloody* good work! Thank God you're safe! I was worried about you. Sabra too—we thought . . ." He checked himself, suddenly remembering he was speaking to a junior officer. The old tone returned. "I'll deliver copies of the photograph to Naval Headquarters immediately after I get them, Colonel. With six patrol boats sitting in the straits of Gibralter, that trawler doesn't stand a chance of getting those bombs into the Mediterranean. We'll board them."

"They may not be for Libya. They may head for Casablanca."

Asher had considered this possibility.

"Except for the gold, Colonel. No, that boat's heading for Tripoli. The Libyan madman isn't likely to spend a fortune on nuclear bombs to give to someone else. Call me from Piraeus!" He paused. "And Lev—take care of yourself." He hung up abruptly.

Asher smiled inwardly at Borodam's inadvertent affection. It was mutual.

He clattered the hook on the phone box to recover the operator, then called Corbin at the Hotel Prado in Cosecha Rica, charging the number to the Israeli Embassy in the Hague. The connection was clearer than his previous call. Corbin was delighted by the information on the *Specht* and Borodam's plans, but had nothing to report himself. There had been no summons from Chirlo for a meeting.

"By the sound of things, Colonel, Chirlo isn't that important anymore. The action is where you are!"

"Perhaps, Mr. Corbin; perhaps not. We'll know better after I get to Greece. I'll call tomorrow night."

He got the operator back on the line and gave B.J.'s number in New York. "You want me to charge this call to the Israeli Embassy too?" she inquired.

"No. Make it collect." He caught the publisher at home and quickly brought him up-to-date on events.

"Great work, Colonel! I'll phone our man in Athens to meet you on arrival."

"I don't know if my pilots can stay awake that long."

"Lazy bastards! Goddamn executive pilots don't do anything anyway except sit on their asses pushing buttons!" B.J. growled and and rang off.

He hung up and looked around for Rogers. Kronig, Roberts and the co-pilot were sitting together on one of the sofas waiting for him to finish the calls. He went over to them. The pilots looked up at him with bleary eyes. Asher stopped, trying to decide how to couch his request.

"Look here, you two, I don't quite know how to say this, but we have to go to Athens tonight."

Corbin grabbed the phone. "Hello, Corbin here!"

"Senor Corbin?" It was Paco calling for Don Affleck. He handed the receiver to his partner.

"Hello Paco—I thought you'd forgotten me."

"No, Senor Affleck. I did not forget. Colonel Chirlo says he will be happy if you visit him now."

"What time?"

"Now—right now, if you can spare the time."

"I'll be right over." He slammed the phone down. "Bingo!" He grinned at Corbin. "Chirlo's waiting to see me." He started putting on his jacket.

"Perseverance pays off—by Donald Affleck." He watched his partner smooth out his shirt front and adjust the tie in the mirror.

"I'll ask Da Gama to come up and wait with me until you call back."

Affleck paused by the door. "He may want to put off seeing

734

you till later—I'll do my best, though."

They waved casually to each other as he went off for the appointment. Corbin strolled over to the phone and called Da Gama's room.

Paco was waiting in the big reception room when Affleck arrived at the Presidential Palace. The large room with its rows of uncomfortable ornate Spanish seats and sofas lining the walls, was deserted. Affleck's leather heels echoed loudly as he walked across the terrazo. He looked about the empty room.

"Your newspaper reporters appear to have vanished, Paco!" He smiled at Chirlo's faithful metizo.

"Si, Senor, only the Presidents are left." He waved his hand at the rows of stern-faced oil paintings hanging from the walls, immortalizing those responsible for the ordered chaos of the Republic since Simon Bolivar rode into San Ramon; even Guerrero was there, his fat face glaring down beside a recent painting of Doctor Artega.

"The Colonel is waiting."

He ushered him through the double doors into the Presidential office, then closed them softly behind him.

"Hello Don!" He came from behind the desk, greeting him with an embrace. "Sorry to keep you waiting. Things have been unsettled —no doubt you've heard."

"I've heard."

"Sit down. You're the first outsider I've seen since all this happened." They pulled two plush armchairs away from the desk, then sat, facing each other.

"I understand your partner Mr. Corbin is with you over at the Prado."

"Waiting to see you."

"With a Uruguayan named Da Gama—who is he?"

Affleck laughed. "Still on top of everything, eh, Colonel? I don't know who he is—probably a newspaperman—but he did us a favor and we promised him an introduction to you if it could be arranged." Affleck's face grew serious. "You are wrong, you know that?"

"Wrong?"

"Very wrong—not because of breaking the safeguard treaty with the Canadian government—not even for swiping the waste from the storage pool—that was very clever, by the way; but because you sold four bombs to the terrorists. That was wrong."

Chirlo took out a cheroot and lit it slowly. "Five bombs, actually—the first was a test requirement."

"Was it worth it?"

"In terms of payment received for the country, yes. This is a poor country." He blew a smoke ring. "I want to make it a rich country; not super rich like your country, but rich enough so my people can lift their heads with pride and say 'We did that.' Rich enough to have more schools, more new roads, houses, sewage, electricity, industry. All this takes money, my friend. A man can have courage, the knowledge, the ambition, the strength and the will —yet, without money a man can produce nothing except dreams."

"You are avoiding the central issue, Colonel Chirlo—the terrorists will use those bombs, and when they do, you will have to bear that responsibility. You have created a lot of enemies by your action."

He gave Affleck his lopsided smile. "I find the emnity of enemies sometimes much more dependable than the friendship of friends." He leaned forward and laid his hand on Affleck's knee. "The Isrealis have their bombs at Dimona, paid for by the Americans; now the Palestinians have their bombs, paid for by the Libyans. Do you think that unjust?"

"But the Israelis will never use theirs unless attacked to the point of conquest," Affleck protested. "The Palestinians will use theirs to get what they want—there is a difference; surely you can see the danger?"

Chirlo shrugged. "In the nuclear chess game there is always danger someone will forget the rules and sweep the pieces from the board, but if Cosecha Rica had not supplied the bombs, in a year or two someone else would have—France, Germany, Canada—someone. Then they would make the profits on their initiative, instead of us." He patted Affleck's knee. "In any case, don't worry, I have Jamil's word the bombs will never be used except for political gain."

Affleck laughed. "And you believe that?"

Chirlo sat back in his chair, looking stern. "I have known Galal Jamil much longer than you, Don. We fought together; without him I could not have won the day. When a comrade-in-arms gives me his word, I accept it."

"And if the comrade-in-arms lies?"

"Then I kill him," he said emphatically.

"Then, Colonel Chirlo, I think you will have to kill Galal Jamil!"

24

Night was gathering her skirts and fleeing the dawn when Al Thani spotted the *Petropacket* riding high in the distance. He swung his binoculars along the lighted horizon, searching for other ships. There were none. He rang the fire bell, shattering the early morning silence, penetrating every living space on board the *Specht*. After thirty seconds of bedlam, he switched it off. The first crew members stumbled on deck a minute later, looking up at the wheelhouse, bewildered. Al Thani pointed to the horizon. Then they understood. In a few minutes, everyone was on deck peering at the growing bulk of the tanker as the distance between the *Specht* and the *Petropacket* closed across the waves.

With the trawler hidden by the backdrop of the western darkness, Speidel sighted the *Specht* when it was less than five miles off his port quarter. He had been sitting on station nearly a week, steaming slowly each night for two or three hours to move back into position for the dawn. It was a good exercise, although he had begun to have doubts about the sanity of owners who would waste money on wages, food and fuel for an empty tanker to float uselessly in the mid-Atlantic for six days. Still, he reasoned, it wasn't his money, and obviously there had to be some sort of plan which made it all worthwhile. He walked into the wheelhouse.

"There's a trawler bearing down on us, helmsman—probably our rendevous for further orders. Keep her steady as she goes."

He rang the engine room telegraphs, ordering slow ahead; it was much easier to maneuver two ships at sea when both were underway. Speidel went back to the bridge to watch.

The trawler began a wide circle, turning in behind the tanker, then slowing as it drew abreast a few cable lengths away. Through his glasses, he could see the people on the foredeck of the smaller vessel, read the name on the plaque, and saw Jamil standing beside Al Awani on the trawler's smaller bridgewing. Al Awani was holding a bullhorn.

"Captain Speidel, this is Mr. Awani!" The metal voice filled the air above the waves. "Lower your scrambling net and steps; we will tie alongside! We have a cargo transfer for you."

The Greek crew on the tanker appeared, lining the rails drawn on deck by the sound of the bullhorn. Speidel waved that he understood, then leaned over to call his Bosn' on the lower deck.

"Prepare to receive their lines, Bosn', scrambling nets and stairs! Put the crew to work unshipping that cargo boom on the port side!"

The Greek Bosn' tipped a hand to his forehead, then began shouting at the seamen who was leaning on the rails.

The space between the ships narrowed slowly, then the weighted lead lines swung up from the trawler fore and aft, arcing onto the tanker's deck. The ships were roped together snugly. Speidel rang *Stop Engines*, then went down to meet Mr. Awani at the gangway.

"Good morning, Herr Awani—and Herr Jamil—and . . ." Speidel stood aside as Kastenburg, followed by Hauser, came up behind the other two familiar faces. No introductions were offered.

"We have a chemical sonar safety cylinder on board the *Specht*. The owners wanted it delivered to you before sailing."

Speidel glanced overside at the activity around the forward deck on the trawler where the main hatch was being unbattened, the canvas tarpaulin snapping in the morning breeze.

"Chemical sonar safety cylinder?" Speidel repeated. "What is that?"

As previously arranged, Kastenburg stepped forward, speaking in German.

"It is an invention of mine, Captain—and I am afraid I must take the responsibility for this delivery delay." He lowered his eyes self-consciously. "There was a strike at our factory in Mexico, and"— he shrugged—"two weeks delay. The owners were furious and gave orders to meet you at sea instead of Casablanca. Unfortunately we will not be able to have the bridge instrumentation installed until you reach Montreal." He shrugged again. "But it can't be helped. These Mexicans, you would not believe the problems I had!"

The others watched Speidel's reaction closely, tensed for argument. There was none. The German Captain smiled gratefully. "Not to worry, er, ah . . . ."

"Doktor Graub, Captain, Hans Graub from Munich," Kastenburg interjected, bowing politely.

"Doktor Graub, a pleasure, Sir. So it's to Montreal we are sailing? Good. No problem at all. I'll have the Bosn' break open the dunnage hatch." He turned to give the order. Kastenburg held his arm.

"That won't be necessary, Captain. We can mount the unit now on the forward mast if your welder can make a jury rig to hold it securely."

"Now?" Speidel was surprised.

"I want to have it mounted in position before you leave for Montreal. Electronic specialists from the Canadian government will meet you when you reach port and complete the wiring from the unit into the bridge."

"It's a government project?"

Kastenburg nodded. "Top secret. There are certain operational requirements relating to your Montreal arrival which Herr Awani will explain in detail. The main thing is that after years of research, our chemical sonar unit is being accepted—on a trial basis—by an international government." He rubbed his hands in triumph, smiling at Speidel.

Al Thani stepped forward. "I suggest we go to your cabin, Captain Speidel. I'll go over the sailing orders with you."

Speidel looked around uncertainly, then nodded. "Of course, Herr Awani, this way please."

Jamil and the two German doctors went forward to supervise cargo transfer from the *Specht*. The donkey-engine for the loading boom started a chugging clatter, winding in the slack cables on the port boom; slowing, suddenly straining as the cable tightened on the capstan drum, lifting the long boom off its deck cradle. Speidel followed Al Thani into the master's cabin, closing the door.

"Who is that Doctor Graub, Herr Awani?"

"Ah, Captain Speidel! He is a genius—one of the true geniuses in this world."

They sat down. Awani opened the shipping orders and passed the papers to the German. "As you will note, Captain, because of international implications about the cargo you will be picking up at Montreal, your orders call for strict radio silence—that means complete and total silence at all times! I cannot overstress this point to you; if word of our program should leak out, even by inference or suspicion, the whole contract could be placed in jeopardy. You must not use the radio!"

Speidel glanced up from his papers. "Of course, Herr Awani. I understand."

"Next, the matter of timing. You will notice you are scheduled to be by the Jacques Cartier Bridge at exactly twelve noon local time July fourth. See that you are on time!"

Speidel unfolded the St. Lawrence River charts, then followed the course plot slowly with a forefinger past Quebec City where the river narrowed, and down to Montreal. He had never been on the Western side of the Atlantic.

"Good." He looked up. "No problem, Herr Awani—no problem at all. I will be there on time."

"Not too early—not too late—it must be exact, Captain. We want to prove our dependability. There have been questions raised already about using these old vessels instead of buying new ones. The government will be watching our performance carefully."

"Please, Herr Awani, when I tell you I will be by Nun's Island in Montreal at twelve noon local time, July fourth, then that is where I will be; I give you my word as a German officer!"

Alexi Scarpos, C.P.'s man in Athens, was waiting at the airport that evening when Alpha Echo Zulu landed after two vicious bounces and taxied to the ramp. Kronig looked at Asher uncertainly on the second bounce, then relaxed when Rogers apologized over the cabin loudspeaker.

"Sorry back there! My depth perception was a little off on that one!"

Except for catnaps across the Atlantic, the pilots had gone twenty-seven hours without sleep.

A groundman with glowing red lights in both hands waved the corporate jet to a parking place in the small visitors' area beside the terminal. The engines whined down.

"Now, before we leave, Colonel, I want to lay it on you like it is, okay? This aircraft isn't going anywhere else tonight until we've all had twelve hours sleep. Agreed?" He waited by the exit for a reply.

Asher nodded sympathetically. "Agreed, Mr. Rogers."

The pilot smiled, then unlocked the door and airstairs. Scarpos was standing at the bottom of the steps with a pair of customs and immigration officers. He watched the four men descending, looking at their legs. When he spied Asher's limp, he came over and introduced himself.

"I have reservations for you at the Akadimos in Athens; four separate rooms on the third floor—as soon as you finish customs and immigration."

They followed the uniformed officers into the building. Scarpos had a thick Macedonian accent. It suited his fierce looking face and bristling mustache. He snarled at the officials in stacatto Greek; the airport officers started moving more swiftly after the outburst.

"Government officials!" he spat. "Lazy bastards, all of them!"

"Were you able to get a line on Mindrinos Ocean Enterprises, Mr. Scarpos?"

The C.P. man laughed. "They're well known to the local authorities here. Real bandits; but real artists! They smuggle, steal, plunder and rob everyone blind they deal with—a great pair!" His voice was tinged with admiration.

"Then they're in town?"

"No, both Speidel and Zaglaviras left port a few weeks ago with some tankers they were converting into chemical carriers. Liberian registry—naturally."

"Oil tankers?" Asher echoed. It didn't make sense.

"Yes Colonel, old ships. You know, the type they used back in the mid-fifties before the Suez closed—fifteen thousand tons, or thereabouts?"

The Israeli took back his passport with its entrance stamp, paused while the customs officer put an unnecessary chalk mark on each of their suitcases without opening any of them, then walked through the mezzanine and outside to the parking lot. He was deep in thought.

The business with the tankers was a mystery. Were they connected to the *Specht?*

"Who owns the Liberian company that owns the vessels?" he asked suddenly.

Scarpos shrugged as they packed themselves into his old Buick.

"Hard to tell. I'll phone B.J. to check with the New York registry office. It will probably turn out to be a bearer company with shares held by some attorney in the Caymans—that's the usual way it's done with oil tankers these days; everyone can then shrug when there's an accident."

He started the car and backed out of the lot, driving off towards the city.

"When are they due back?"

"No one seems to know. We can find out better in the morning. Their office was closed when I got down to Piraeus this afternoon, so this is all secondhand information from a friend of mine in the harbormaster's office."

"Did your friend say where the tankers were headed?"

"Different ports—they all left at different times; Oran, Tangier, Casablanca, Majorca."

"There were four tankers?" Asher asked. "I thought you said two?"

Scarpos gunned the car around a smoking diesel bus blocking their route.

"Speidel and his partner sailed on two of them. The other two were captained by local men."

Asher turned in the front seat. "Did you hear that, Sergeant? *Four* tankers?"

There was no reply. The three men in the back were asleep, snoring peacefully. The pilots, sitting on either side of Kronig's huge bulk, had their heads resting comfortably on his massive shoulders.

"Yes Major!" Chirlo leaned against the desk in his study, adjusting the phone to his ear.

"I'm sorry, Colonel, there is no reply yet from the Uruguayan Embassy in Panama on my request."

"Did you try calling Montevideo on the passport number?"

"Yes Colonel. They said such information must originate from their nearest embassy—in this case, Panama."

He didn't like it. He had asked Affleck to invite Corbin and the Uruguayan to join him for an informal dinner at the house, a gesture of hospitality to an old friend; besides he wanted to meet Corbin anyway; there was something about the name that bothered him. The man Da Gama was still a mystery. He called Martinez as soon as Don left the Presidential office and asked for an outline on the man. The Major had nothing; he was a tourist who had entered early the previous month from Panama, labeling himself as "business-man" on the tourist card handed in at the airport. He had spent his entire time at the Hotel Prado, a great part of it with Affleck and Corbin. Perhaps he was a businessman after all? Chirlo disliked meeting people for the first time without knowing something—any-thing—about them.

"Hmm. What's he look like?"

"Baby face—harmless looking. He reminds me of a typical son of wealthy parents who has never done physical work, Colonel."

"Very well, Major. Let me know tomorrow if you get anything on him from Panama."

"Yes Sir. Goodnight Sir."

Felina came into the room, trailed by the twins, as he hung up.

"Dios! I hate those instruments!" She laughed at the phone. They had disconnected the line when Chirlo had vanished to Esperanza to stop the ringing. It had been reconnected the previous day. The twins went to their section of the bookcase to pick a selection for their bedtime story. Through the open windows came the sound of a car; Paco stopping down the driveway with the guests. A car door slammed, then two more.

"Quickly children, our dinner guests are arriving!"

They seized their books and scurried from the room, pausing to give Chirlo a kiss on the way out.

Husband and wife watched them gallop up the stairs to their bedrooms. The front chime rang. Felina crossed the tiled floor and opened the door.

"Hello, lovely lady!" Affleck stepped inside, kissed her on the cheek, then handed out a bouquet of long stem roses—yellow, her favorite color.

Felina giggled happily as everyone stepped inside. Affleck introduced Corbin and Da Gama.

"Why don't you all go to the library while I get these into water?" Felina suggested.

She waited until they had gone into the comfortable room, then started for the kitchen, up on the next level of the rambling house. She had barely entered the kitchen, to give the main instruction, her arms outstretched with flowers, when she heard a shot—*small caliber, 32 or 38 special, no silencer*—her mind raced. She dropped the roses and ran. There was another shot. She screamed, racing for the study. She hit the hallway the same instant Paco came running in the front door, his pistol drawn. He pushed her aside and down roughly, then crept swiftly to the open study door. He peered cautiously around the edge, then sprang into the room. Chirlo was lying on the floor, face down, blood streaming from a head wound on the temple. Affleck and Corbin had Da Gama pinned by his arms and legs on the sofa. The Uruguayan was struggling like a demon, grunting from the effort. Paco walked over and smashed the butt of his pistol across the back of Da Gama's head. The struggling ceased. Felina crawled to Chirlo and cradled his head on her lap. His blood began staining her dress. Corbin and Affleck stood up from their quarry. Paco knelt beside his Colonel, taking his head gently from the wailing woman sitting on the floor who was rocking back and forth in anguish. He lifted the head and examined the wound professionally, then probed it with a finger. Felina screamed, pushing him away.

"Stop it!" he shouted loudly.

Felina froze, opening her mouth in surprise. Paco smacked her across the face twice. The hysterical eyes came into focus.

"The wound is superficial. He will live. Go get hot water and plenty of towels—alcohol too—go now. *Go!*"

She stumbled to her feet and ran from the room. Paco lowered Chirlo's head gently to the carpeted floor and stood up. He smiled briefly at Affleck, nodding.

"He will live. It takes more than a badly aimed assassin's bullet to kill my Colonel," he said with satisfaction.

He plucked the phone off the desk and dialed a number. "Major Martinez, this is Paco, please switch to scrambler." He waited until the Major told him he had, then continued.

"Colonel Chirlo has just been shot by Da Gama, the Uruguayan. No, it's superficial—a creased temple, nothing more. He will be coming around shortly. I suggest we keep the information to ourselves. I am holding Da Gama here until you arrive." He waited, nodding. "No, Major. It seems Senor Corbin and Senor Affleck saved the Colonel's life." He hung up.

Felina came running back with the maid, carrying a basin of water and armful of towels. Paco took the basin. Everyone knelt beside the unconscious form on the floor. Felina soaked a towel, wrung it out, then gingerly started patting off the blood around the wound. Paco grabbed it.

"Give me that! Have you forgotten your training, Senora?"

Swiftly he swabbed the blood away from the wound, then took another wet towel and pushed against the bloody crease, soaking up the flow.

"Now the alcohol!"

"I forgot it!" She looked helplessly at the men. Corbin went to the liquor cabinet and yanked a bottle of vodka from the rack. He uncapped it and gave it to Paco, then stood staring down at Chirlo in fascination, watching the vodka being poured into the open wound, dripping from the side of the bearded face, flattening the hair with wetness, flattening it to reveal the facial bone structure beneath the hair. He blinked in disbelief, rubbing his eyes, then shook his head, clearing the images being conjured in his mind. It was impossible! He knelt down again beside the big prostrate form, studying the face. His scalp tingled. He patted down the beard, holding his hand against some dry facial hair missed by the vodka. He felt giddy—felt like laughing, crying, jumping, screaming.

"My God in Heaven! He's Peter Colley!"

Chirlo groaned and opened his eyes. He had a splitting headache; the room was swimming with faces.

"Those fucking Mexicans!" he mumbled . . . "and I'll bet they stole my money belt. Shit!"

Images cartwheeled through his brain, the million circuits closed in a kaleidoscope of colored shocks. His eyes began to focus; faces peering over him, strange faces, foreign faces—all but one. The one was familiar. Two separate express trains hurtling toward the future on parallel tracks, one labelled *past*, one labelled *present*. Their whistles shreiked in anguish for the single track ahead, then, unavoidably, they met in a screech of tearing metal, exploding in a shower of realization and became as one.

Chirlo looked up at Corbin and smiled weakly. "Hello Chuck!" A waterfall of memories cascaded over the dam; the wheel, motionless for so long, started turning under the deluge of buried history, resurrecting the past and present.

"Imagine seeing you here!"

The moss-laden submerged paddles of the water-wheel broke through the dark surface into the light of realization, a constant turning towards infinity.

"It has been a long time!"

Asher drove down to Piraeus the following morning with Sergeant Kronig in Alexi Scarpos' noisey Buick. He let Scarpos handle the interrogation of the Greek staff members in the Mindrinos office maze until he was satisfied all the stories he was getting cross-checked with each other. They went back to the car.

"I guess the story about the tankers is real, Colonel. They bought them in Turkey from an agent for a third party, moved them to Pireaus for crewing, then delivered them to the various ports."

"Then why aren't they back from the delivery? Isn't it a bit unusual for the owners of a shipping company to make their own deliveries? Why didn't they hire two more captains and stay here? I could understand if all the ships went to the same place, but they didn't. There's something missing somewhere."

Scarpos considered the questions a minute, then started the car.

"The employees say no—both partners have made deliveries in

the past—usually Speidel; sometimes both have gone—but you're right, Colonel, everyone admitted it was unusual for them both to be away this length of time."

He pulled from the curb and drove slowly down the harbor highway. The area was crowded with tourist buses discharging mobile cargos onto the sleek looking tour vessels that sailed the Aegean on various one to five day cruises. With the departure of the Greek Colonel's regime, the tourists had returned, secure in the knowledge the new Karamanlis government welcomed the sight of short pants, skirts and bikinis with more rational perspective than their severely conservative predecessors.

"Where do you want to go now, Colonel?"

"How hard is it to find out when they sailed from those ports in Spain and Morocco, Mr. Scarpos? More important, where were they bound?"

"A couple of days, I guess, although I think you'll find its probably a North American destination, maybe South America." He glanced at the Israeli. "You look worried?"

Asher smiled. "I am, rather. Tell me, is it mandatory for a vessel sailing from a port to state its next port of call?"

"No, not mandatory, but most ships indicate where they're bound on the shipping declaration; of course, that doesn't mean they will go there; there's just space on the form requiring an answer."

"Let's go back to the hotel and wait. See if you can learn where those four were headed when they left their last ports."

Scarpos turned away from the harbor, back on the road for Athens, trailing one of the empty glass-topped tourist buses, that blew clouds of smelly, black diesel exhaust fumes over the Buick.

"It may take a few days before we hear from all those ports," the C.P. man warned.

Asher shrugged. "So we take a couple of days off and visit the sights. How about the Parthenon, Sergeant? Have you ever visited the Parthenon?"

He looked around, but Kronig was asleep.

Asher called Borodam when they returned to the hotel, confirming the departure of the six Israeli patrol boats to Gibralter that morning at dawn. He explained that he would wait in Athens until Scarpos received word on the tankers' destination.

"I don't think they're related, Colonel," Borodam told him.

"I don't know, Sir. Four crates—four tankers—it's too strong to be coincidence!"

"I still can't see the Libyan madman turning them loose to

someone else after he's paid for them; it's not his style—one or two, maybe, but not all four. Hell, he only *has* four; that's his whole arsenal! Anyway, follow it through if you think you should.

Later, Asher phoned Corbin and learned of the assassination attempt by the Uruguayan and the fact that the dictator of Cosecha Rica had been an amnesiac and Corbin's business partner seventeen years earlier. Asher was incredulous.

"Are you certain?"

Corbin laughed. "No question about it, Colonel. Chirlo is Peter Colley, my partner from Miami days."

"Another Canadian. God Almighty! You people are the worst troublemakers I've ever encountered—bombs—dictatorships—and yet, you know, I liked the man the moment I met him."

"Peter's a likeable fellow."

"But not to everyone, apparently."

Corbin explained. "The assassin was hired by one of Blucher's German scientists on the *Specht*—Hauser. It seems Hauser thought his son had been executed on Chirlo's orders."

"And was he?" Asher was intrigued. He thought so too.

"Peter denies he had anything to do with it. Thinks it was probably arranged by Jamil to keep the son from talking about the bombs—the son knew about it—overheard his father talking—or found some paperwork the old man was working on. Anyway, Peter's fine. How are you making out?"

Quickly, Asher brought him up-to-date on the tankers.

"Then that's it! The tankers are picking up the crates from the *Specht* at sea, then proceeding to different destinations to blow themselves up!" he said excitedly. "Good work, Colonel!"

Asher was thunderstruck. *Of course!* That was exactly the plan—it had to be! He had been too stupid to see it, while all the time it had been staring him straight in the face. But where would they blow up and when?

"Of course, it's still only a guess, Mr. Corbin."

"A guess, my ass! Wait until I tell Peter. Colonel, you've got to find those tankers!"

"Any idea where to start?"

"You're the intelligence officer. It has to be a seaport with a big city. Take your pick—Sydney, New york, Tokyo, Rio, Miami." He paused. "Yeah, I see your point, where do you start?"

"Give it some thought, Mr. Corbin. I'll call back tomorrow. Right now I'm going to phone Tel Aviv again."

Borodam would have to persuade the major powers to conduct

an air search for the tankers before it was too late.

Peter Colley listened gravely to the information from Athens. "I've been a fool!" he growled. "I should have known the man was a snake." Since the attempt on his life, he had remained at home, sitting in bed, savoring the joy of remembering; a large adhesive covering the newly acquired gouge on his temple. It would develop into a smaller scar than the one on his face, Doctor Artega informed him, although much deeper. On impulse, he shaved off his beard, making him a stranger to everyone in the house, except Corbin. Felina approved, however, saying it made him look much younger.

The partners had spent the first day by themselves talking, remembering. "So the two million dollar insurance policy provided the foundation for everything?"

Corbin nodded. "Everything."

"How much have you made, Chuck?"

Corbin shrugged. "Hundreds of millions—I don't really know. There comes a point when you're no longer interested."

Colley sighed. "And all this time I could have come to you for what we needed here." He looked sad. "No one would give us credit—nothing."

"Well, amigo, your worries are over now—you've enough to build this place into Utopia if you want to spend the time." Corbin laughed. "In fact, I may just move down and help you do it." He got up and went over to the wide picture window to gaze at the panorama of the city, mountains and sky.

"You don't have to feel obligated, you know. After all, you're the man that made it; you always had a way with the buck."

Corbin swung around suddenly. "We started out as partners, we'll finish as partners. Half of everything is yours. No arguments." He turned back to the window. "You know, Peter, I created a research organization called Bayan. It's produced a surprising number of new ideas—new technology. We could begin setting some of the pilot programs up down here, then later, develop an export market; small products, labor oriented for unskilled workers, then train them—develop more sophisticated machinery—you know what I mean?" He was talking to himself really, musing through a host of possibilities to help the tiny country.

In his mind's eye he could see the city growing, neat new colonies on the slopes around the existing town; he noticed a reasonably flat plateau a few miles to the north. Why, with a little grading and proper machinery, it could be turned into a new international airport. The ideas started coming faster.

"By the way," Colley said, "whatever happened to that girl?"

"What girl?"

"You remember her, Chuck. The young one from Vassar that drove you nuts. Peggy something."

Corbin turned back to the bed and smiled sadly. "I married her, Peter. She gave me three beautiful kids, then died a few years ago—cancer."

Colley nodded, understanding. "She grew up."

"We all did." It was at that point the long distance call from Asher was relayed over from the Prado switchboard. Colley heard one half of the conversation. It was enough. He climbed out of bed and started dressing before Corbin hung up.

"Where are you going?"

Colley continued putting on his clothes. "First I'm going down to visit my father-in-law and turn over the ship of state. Then you and I are flying to Athens to meet Asher. I owe that man a favor and" . . . he paused to turn and smile his lopsided grin . . . "I owe my friend Jamil a debt; I intend to see it's repaid."

Four days later they arrived in Greece. Lev Asher was gone.

The Israeli Colonel had waited two days in Athens until he was satisfied the patrol boats were in position and no word would be forthcoming from any of the ports to which Scarpos had wired for information.

Then he flew to Majorca, spending a day scouring the waterfront for information. Finally his luck changed. A warehouse-man who managed the storage sheds along the dock where the *Petroprincess* had been berthed remembered the tanker clearly and her Greek Captain, Dimitri Zaglaviras; in fact, he had spent time on board the ship drinking with him during off-duty hours.

"Then one day a short stocky man—an Arab I think—arrived in a taxi with the sailing orders. He had lunch and left."

"Did you see him?" Asher demanded.

The old man stopped talking and pulled the Israeli back from the path of a forklift tearing down the wharf with a load of bales. He screamed at the driver in Spanish, ordering him to slow down, but the rumbling loader had sped beyond earshot.

"My excuses, Senor. But they drive too fast—I am always warning them—these young men we get now—terrible. They think they're driving at Le Mans." He stopped to collect his thoughts.

"Oh, yes, the Arab . . . I met him of course when I came aboard at noon for a drink. Captain Zaglaviras was very happy to be sailing. He had been waiting two or three weeks." The old man nodded his approval on the vessel's departure.

"You don't remember where he said he was going, do you? The clearance papers state T.D."

"To Be Determined—yes, they put that down sometimes when they want no one to know their plans. You know—competitors?" He laid a finger alongside one nostril and winked.

"So the destination was secret?" Asher confirmed.

"Oh no, Senor! Captain Zaglaviras didn't know where he was going—just a point out at sea somewhere in the Atlantic. Meeting someone, I suppose—another boat." He sniffed and wiped his nose on the back of his sleeve. "Nice man, Captain Zaglaviras."

"And the Arab, did you get his name when you were introduced?"

"Oh certainly, Senor, his name is the same as the ancient Moorish hero—Akbar—that's why I remembered it. They conquered Spain once, you know—the Moors, I mean—Arabs—same thing." He sniffled again.

They thanked him and walked back to the rented car.

"Do we go onto the other ports, Sir?" Kronig inquired. He was beginning to enjoy jet travel in the corporate DeHavilland.

Asher put the car in gear and pointed them back to the airport. "No, Sergeant. The other three will have the same T.D. departure clearances, and I'd be willing to bet every one of them is meeting the *Specht* at sea to transfer those bombs. No, we now go back to Tel Aviv and see the Brigadier."

Brigadier Borodam took the lecture platform in the war room. The Defense Minister, Army, Navy and Air Force Chiefs of Staff filled the first row of chairs in front of the platform. Behind them, sitting in less comfortable classroom chair wing-desks, were an assortment of civilians and other officers from the three services, as well as representatives from the American and British Embassies. Colonel Asher sat at the back of the room.

"Gentlemen," Borodam began, "we have given the code name *Thunderclap* to this operation—hopefully, it will prove a misnomer." No one smiled. "At this moment, somewhere out in the Atlantic, four old tankers are each being loaded with a nuclear bomb." He snapped a cricket clicker in his hand and the lights went out.

A projector, hidden behind the wall at the back of the room, flashed the Petro class tankers onto a wall screen. The image was blurred an instant until the projectionist focused the lens, then the four vessels appeared with clarity.

"Upper left, *Petropacket*. Upper right, *Petroprince.*" Borodam's pointer shadowed the screen as he indicated the ships' identities.

"You will notice they are all roughly the same in appearance." He clicked the cricket. The tankers slid away into blackness and the *Specht* appeared, the photograph Asher had received from Peter Reichman in Rotterdam.

"This is the trawler *Specht*. Libyan registration, Libyan crew. It left Bahia Blanca, Cosecha Rica, on the afternoon of June 1, 1976 with four nuclear bombs in its hold. Destination, unknown. At top speed, taking the most direct route, if it were heading for the Gibralter straits, it would reach the Mediterranean in twelve days, roughly the thirteenth of June." He clicked the cricket. The lights returned as the screen went blank, a white wall above the blackboard.

"On the morning of June eleventh, D Flotilla of our navy took up station in the straits of Gibralter. They have been covering the area on regular two hour sweeps ever since. To date, the *Specht* has not appeared. The reason is obvious. The trawler has been busy meeting the tankers to transfer its cargo of bombs. When the transfer is completed, *Specht* will enter the straits heading for Tripoli. We will board her at that time and learn where the tankers are headed."

"Brigadier Borodam!" The Defense Minister raised his hand casually. "I gather you believe this transfer is taking place somewhere in the mid-Atlantic."

Borodam nodded. "A theory, Sir. We cannot be certain."

"My point exactly. The Atlantic is a big ocean, south, north, central—which part?"

"Our theory is north of the equator, but south of the fortieth parallel, due to the operating range of the *Specht* and the sailing time of the tankers themselves. We know when the tankers sailed. We know how much fuel each had in its bunkers. We know how much fuel the *Specht* took on in Bahia Blanca. Our theory is that the targets for the ships are the largest seaports on the eastern coasts of the North American Continent and/or the largest ports on either side of the Atlantic, north of the equator."

The Defense Minister nodded. "And just when do you expect to see the *Specht*, Borodam?"

The Brigadier turned to the blackboard and picked up a piece of chalk. "If the trawler met the tankers as a group, transfer could have been completed in one day. That would add on to its arrival time in the straits—June fourteenth or fifteenth. However, if the trawler met the tankers separately in four different locations, it would add another five or six days to the total sailing time from Central America—bringing it into the straits June twenty-first or twenty-second." He paused significantly.

"And since June fifteenth has already passed, we can assume now that *Specht's* arrival date will be June twenty-first or twenty-second—anytime between now and the day after tomorrow."

Borodam surveyed the room, watching the men scribbling furiously in their notebooks.

"Question?" He acknowledged the American liaison officer in the middle of the third row.

"Yes Sir." The American stood up. "Do you have any dope yet where the tankers are heading—I mean specifically?"

The Brigadier shook his head. "None—other than what I already mentioned. However, we know the vessels will have to touch port before July tenth operating at normal fuel consumption speeds. Obviously they will reach their destinations well before July tenth when they run out of fuel. Our guess—theory—is they are programed to arrive simultaneously at four different ports sometime between July first and fifth."

"Boston, New York, Baltimore and Maimi, for instance?" the American said as he sat down.

"Or Lisbon, Le Havre, Southampton and Rotterdam—take your pick!" Borodam smiled grimly. "Until we know, we have to assume every major seaport is in danger."

He turned to the blackboard and drew down a retractable wall map, hooking it to the edge of the chalk bar.

"Israel will assume responsibility for capturing the *Specht* and providing information on the destination of the tankers. However, Israel has no long range patrol aircraft, so we look to you for help to find the ships at sea, intercept, board them and defuse the bombs." He picked up the pointer.

"My planning staff has provided this suggestion for the airborne surveillance; one hundred mile sweeps every eight hours around the clock until the ships are located, starting at the equator and moving north to the forty-fifty parallel."

He moved the pointer between the continents. "East to west,

west to east."

"Do we have time, Borodam?" the Defense Minister inquired. "That's an enormous area!"

"Twenty-seven hundred nautical miles, Sir. Twenty-seven sweeps—nine days for one aircraft or one day for nine." He paused. "Disregarding downtime for crew changes and refueling, of course!"

The Defense Minister appeared satisfied.

"Every tanker over ten thousand tons must be identified. Question?"

"Britain and the Low Countries are above the forty-fifth latitude, old boy. What did you have in mind for us?" Brigadier Brock-Norton, M.C., D.S.O., represented the British Embassy. He and Borodam were good friends. Both had attended Sandhurst.

Borodam smiled. "North-south sweeps of the English Channel from Jutland to the forty-fifth parallel every day; same thing for the western approaches—daily sweeps from Land's End to the Orkney Islands working westward over the Irish sea to the fifteenth meridian west. You'll need four aircraft."

The Englishman nodded, satisfied.

"Who is going to pay for all this?" someone asked from the back of the room.

Borodam laid down his pointer. "Why don't we look at it as a cheap insurance policy, because if we don't pay our premium cost now, we're going to have one hell of a claim on our hands if any of those tankers arrive and blow up."

Flotilla Commander Zeke Gerdbaum nodded his permission to the signalman to come up on the open bridge. He took the yellow sheet from the youngster and read the message line pasted to its center, "RETURN GIBRALTER FOR THREE PASSENGERS." He looked up surprised.

"We just left yesterday!" He shook his head. All right, Shev, make it, 'ACKNOWLEDGED, AM PROCEEDING NOW'." The signalman scribbled on his pad.

"Make to the other patrol boats, 'AM RETURNING GIBRAL-TER. D14 WILL ASSUME FLOTILLA COMMAND. ACKNOWL-EDGE.' Make sure you get a reply from each of them."

He tossed back the lad's salute then turned to the Cox'n. "You heard the man—wheel it back to Gib!"

The helmsman spun the spokes. Zeke rang for increased power. The patrol boat lurched ahead with a muffled roar, heeling into a tight turn for the Spanish coast and Gibralter. Zeke pulled his peaked white officer's cap down tightly so it wouldn't blow away in the forty-five knot breeze and went back to his comfortable swivel chair next to the deck compass.

The French built Israeli patrol boats were not made for long sea voyages; their prime function was hit-and-run or close offshore patrol support for the navy. Except for fuel and provisioning at Gibralter, they had been out now for nearly two weeks. Initial excitement of the venture had begun to pall, not only for Gerdbaum, but for the other captains in the flotilla as well. They had thundered out of Tel Aviv at dawn on June eighth, heading for Crete, their first refueling stop on the twenty five hundred mile trip to Gibralter. He had been jerked out of bed at three in the morning by two security officers who rushed him down to naval headquarters to see the flag captain. It sounded like a real flap. However, the flag captain handed him a package of photographs—photocopies, at that—of a Libyan ocean trawler named *Specht*, and ordered him to meet it in the straits of Gibralter.

"You will stop, board and seize the vessel if it attempts passage into the Mediterranean," Captain Shaliman said.

"In international waters, Sir?"

"Those are your orders." The Flag Captain was not in the habit of repeating himself.

Zeke rushed around the city rounding up his off-duty officers and crews and managed to make the dawn deadline with six minutes to spare. The complete orders, when he had time to sit down and read them once they were underway for Crete, were more puzzling than the verbal instructions given him by the flag captain.

The Libyan trawler was thought to be carrying contraband—in crates—although it didn't specify the size or shape of the crates. Inside the crates were steel cylinders—it didn't state what the steel cylinders were supposed to be or what was inside them, or indeed, if they were what naval headquarters had decided was contraband. He gave it to his number one to read to see if David could find something Zeke had overlooked. His lieutenant handed it back with a blank look.

"They're getting nuttier and nuttier up at headquarters, aren't they, Sir? Comes with not having enough sea duty to keep them busy." David Hamman was twenty-two, his commander twenty-seven.

"What I can't understand is why they didn't ask the British to intercept it out of Gib. Why us?" He folded the orders. "However, I suppose we'll find out when we reach Gib."

But, they were no wiser when they put into Gibralter on the

third day. The British naval dockyards had been expecting them when the little flotilla arrived at the harbor, and turned over the necessary fuel and provisions without comment, but no one appeared to know anything about their mission.

Zeke spaced his boats across the twenty mile width between the Spanish and Moroccan coasts, taking up position as ordered, and waited for the *Specht* to appear. They had been there ever since, cruising slowly back and forth along the straits in unending monotony; two hours west until they were abeam Tangier, then two hours east until they were abreast Europa Point, Gibralter. Commander Zeke was certain even the monkeys on Mount Tarik were laughing at them. They had left the harbor that morning, replacing Lieutenant Mordecai's D16 on the blockade line; it had been Mordecai's turn to spend twenty four hours shore leave in Gibralter.

The D10 cleared the breakwater into the harbor and reduced power, cruising slowly south to the dockyards. He conned his boat alongside the D16 and stopped its engines. Three men were standing on the deck of the D16. With Mort Dielman was the Israeli contact man from the Madrid Embassy who had been supervising things in the British colony since they arrived. The three men shook hands with Mort and jumped across the narrow space between the boats. Dielman waved up at Zeke, then turned and walked down the gangway from the D16 to the dock. Zeke signaled for *Slow Ahead Both*, then warped his boat past the D16 and swung back to the harbor's mouth.

He examined the three arrivals on the deck below curiously. They were older men, on which the mantle of authority rested easily. All were dressed in civies, Zeke noticed with disapproval. He was always wary of older men dressed in civies; invariably they turned out to be politicans or senior naval officers and it was difficult to say which of the two species was worse. In appearance, each of his passengers was dissimiliar. One looked like an American businessman on holiday, the second an English diplomat complete with limp, but it was the third passenger that held his eyes: he was bigger than the other two, powerfully built, with greying curly hair and a long terrible scar running from one ear to the mouth along the left side of his clean-shaven face.

Once they cleared harbor, Commander Zeke turned the D10 over to his number one and went below to meet his guests in the tiny wardroom. All three stood up when he entered.

"Commander Gerdbaum. I'm Colonel Lev Asher, intelligence section, Tel Aviv." Asher greeted him in Yiddish and produced his

I.D.

Commander Zeke glanced briefly at it; he had heard of Asher. "These two gentlemen are my friends." He switched to English. "Mr. Peter Colley and his associate, Mr. Charles Corbin."

They all shook hands and sat down. Asher continued.

"We believe your trawler will turn up sometime during the next seventy-two hours—which is why we are here. You will instruct your other captains to stand clear when the *Specht* is identified. Boarding parties will originate from this boat. I want no shooting unless it is strictly in self-defense."

"We don't have enough men for boarding parties, Colonel Asher," Commander Zeke protested.

"In that case, you have my permission to take them from other members of your flotilla."

"We'll put into Oran for fuel and water," Al Thani said. "I want to bypass Tangier this time. Anyway, we have enough to make it to Oran."

"You expect trouble in Tangier?" Kastenburg inquired.

"Not in Tangier, Doctor, in the straits of Gibralter—if there is any trouble, I'd just as soon we be through the straits and into the Mediterranean."

"The straits—when do we reach them?" Hauser demanded.

"We'll be abeam Tangier tomorrow at midnight. By dawn we'll be well into the Med. Then Alexandria on the morning of the twenty-sixth in time for prayers—once we get ashore."

He smiled and sat back satisfied.

"One week later we will all be horrified to hear of the latest outrage to humanity perpetrated by those frightful Palestinian terrorists!"

Everyone sitting around the mess table laughed.

The tanker loading had gone off without a hitch. Speidel and Zaglaviras were so anxious to obey orders they questioned nothing; all the two partners could see was their million dollars apiece in gold at the end of the voyage. The other two captains were so thankful to have employment, neither considered for an instant questioning the purpose of their mission—or, if they had, kept it to themselves. The strange crew of the *Specht* cheered in exaltation as they watched the *Petroprincess* drop astern, her propellor churning the tanker northwards for the English Channel, and Rotterdam.

Pierre Lascoeur was ordered to prepare a magnificent dinner to celebrate their success.

The President of the United States closed the file on his desk and picked up his phone.

"Get me the Chairman of the Joint Chiefs of Staff."

He waited thirty-five seconds.

"General, this is the President. Operation Thunderclap may proceed with my blessings—and hopefully, those of the Almighty."

The Chairman of the Joint Chiefs of Staff called the Air Force Chief of Staff. He had to wait only twelve seconds.

"General, you may proceed with Thunderclap now. It's official. Good luck!"

The Air Force Chief of Staff phoned Lowry Air Force Base in Colorado for the General commanding the Air Force's worldwide MAC-Military Aircraft Command. He got through in seven seconds.

"Hello, Harry! The word is go on Thunderclap. Get 'em moving and get results!"

Harry picked up the hot line to McDill Air Force Base at Orlando Florida. It was answered instantly.

"Colonel Travis, Sir."

"Hello, Tug. Drag your boys out of the fart sack. We have a go on Thunderclap. The OP's order will be on the teleprinter to you in a few minutes. I'm moving relief crews to Dakar, Casablanca, Torrejon and Shannon for you. They'll be in position by the time your group arrives. Take it cool, Tug."

The line went dead.

Three hours later, eight huge C141 Starlifters trundled down the taxiway to the active runway, their sagging wings glinting in the humid late morning sunshine. One-by-one they swung ponderously into position and thundered off, climbing towards the southeast for the long, long journey across the Atlantic to Dakar, Senegal, on the west coast of the African Continent.

"You will remain with Khandi in Bahrain until your flight leaves. Stay out of trouble!"

Doctor Waddi Hadad looked at the five he had selected for the diversionary operation. Three Palestinians, two Germans; it was a nice balance, although the German girl, Gabriele Kroche-Tiedemann, worried him a little. She was an excellent soldier, but the loss of her lover, Bernard Hausman, the previous month at Isreal's Ben Gurion Airport, had left her sorrowing in grief, mad for revenge. Hausman had been sent in from Vienna with a suitcase bomb set to explode when the bag was opened. It was the only way Hadad could figure to get rid of the twenty-five year old German who had become a nuisance. Unfortunately, only Hausman and an Israeli security officer were killed in the explosion when the suitcase was inspected, Hadad had been sorry to learn, but at least he had rid himself of the problem. Gabriele had begged Hadad's permission to join the Athens operation. Reluctantly, he had agreed, after extracting her promise no one was to be summarily shot on board the air bus during the skyjacking—at least not until it had landed in Entebbe.

"You have reservations on Singapore Airlines Flight 763 out of Bahrain, which gets you into Athens early Sunday morning. Jaber will meet you at the airport."

"Do we take the equipment with us, or pick it up in Bahrain?" Wilfried Boise, the German, had been assigned the job of cockpit commander once the air bus was secured.

"Jaber will have everything ready for you to pick up in Bahrain from Khadni. The machine guns are in Athens now." Hadad stood up from his deck. He was a short balding man with a nervous habit of running his palm across the top of his forehead, as if checking for new growth.

"I've decided to use the release of comrades as the reason for taking the plane. We'll ask them for everyone, the Archbishop, Okamoto, Namri, Darwish—all of them." He rubbed his forehead vigorously.

"When you reach Entebbe release everyone but the Jews—heart patients, pregnant women and so forth are to be dropped off in Benghazi. We have been promised full cooperation by the Field Marshal, but I'm sending a backup force in from here to give you a few more relief hands to work with." He stopped rubbing his head. "Anyone have any comments?"

"Yes Doctor. One question: can you control the Field Marshal from here?"

Latif was a good friend of the Doctor.

Hadad laughed. "No one can control His Excellency, but we have over three hundred Palestinians running his government now, so I'm sure he'll behave." He shrugged.

"But if he doesn't—kill him."

"Bridge!" Lieutenant Mordecai glanced over at the lights from Tangier nestled on the black horizon. "I have one dead ahead, Sir. Range twelve miles and closing. The image is the right size."

The radar operator reported from the scan in the radio room below deck.

"Right!" Mordecai raised his glasses and peered out across the bow of the patrol boat. He had it in a moment. He adjusted the glasses.

"By God, Benny, it's a trawler and it looks like the *Specht!* Here, take a look!"

His number one focused his own glasses in the direction Mordecai and pointed.

"You're right—it's the Libyan and moving like hell is after her—must be making twenty knots or better!"

Mordecai signaled the radio room. "Sammy, make to D10; target ten miles west my position closing. Standing by. Give them a course to intercept if you have them on the scope."

"I have them, Sir. D10 is bearing red four five—about sixteen miles."

Mordecai turned to his number one. "Well Benny, it looks like we're finally going to see some action!"

He pushed the buzzer for *Battle Stations* then went back to his comfortable command chair to wait for orders.

Al Thani recognized the Israeli patrol boat when it thundered down on them from the north then swung alongside less than half a mile off. He turned around and yelled down into the main salon.

"We have company. Israeli navy boat!"

Jamil dropped his cards and rushed the steps into the wheelhouse. He looked around, blinking his eyes. "Where?"

Al Thani pointed. "What do you want to do?"

The Palestinian thought rapidly. "What's their firepower?"

"Torpedoes, depth charges, missles, cannon, machine guns—you name it. We wouldn't stand a chance."

Al Thani knew about the French built boats from the last war with Israel. He had a lot of respect for them.

"How many men?" Jamil demanded.

"Enough." Al Thani squinted ahead. "There's two more—and another over there—I'm afraid we're surrounded."

"Will they board us?"

Al Thani sighed and rang for *Stop Engines.* "They didn't come this far to provide us with escort back to Tripoli."

Jamil went below to the salon to tell the others. They were gone. Everyone was standing outside on the port railing, watching the patrol boat slipping slowly alongside as the *Specht* lost its headway. A searchlight flooded the trawler. Behind the whiteness a voice announced unnecessarily, "We are coming aboard. Remain on deck."

Moments later the D10's fenders bumped the *Specht's* hull and a swarm of Uzi-toting seamen scrambled over the trawler's railing. They looked very tough. The young officer called out, "Who is the Captain?"

The Germans and Jamil and Leila backed away as Al Thani came down the deck from the wheelhouse. "I'm the Captain."

The Israeli officer stepped forward and saluted Al Thani politely.

"Good evening, Captain. My apologies for stopping your ship, but I have been given orders to search this vessel."

Al Thani looked suitably outraged. "On the high seas? This is an act of piracy! On who's orders?"

"Mine!" Everyone turned to look at the three men climbing over the railings from the D10. Asher opened the door into the salon. "My orders, Captain. Everyone inside!"

They all filed slowly through the doorway into the main salon and sat down, glaring at their captors. Hauser's mouth fell open when he saw the shaven face with the huge scar in the salon's light.

"Chirlo!"

Peter Colley gave him a lopsided smile. "Your Uruguayan missed, Doctor Hauser." He touched the scab at his temple. "But only just. You were foolish to believe I killed your son. If you had asked I could have told you your friend Jamil made those arrangements."

Hauser's jaw sagged again; he spun his head sideways, looking at Jamil. His face grew hard. The Palestinian looked away.

"Well Colonel, I see you finally got around to having a shave. I must say I preferred the beard to the scar."

Corbin walked to the back of the salon and leaned against the bulkhead, overseeing the proceedings in the crowded room. Colley came over and joined them. Asher took the center of the floor once Al Thani had sat down.

"We are searching your holds for contraband, Captain," he began.

Al Thani started to rise in protest, then stopped and sank back to his chair when one of the seamen thrust an Uzi barrel in his face.

"You loaded four nuclear bombs on board this vessel on June first. We want them."

Al Thani laughed. "Do you now? Well, we don't have any bombs on board—although I haven't checked the holds lately."

Commander Zeke stuck his head in the door. "The forward

hold is empty, Colonel. We're checking the aft one now."

The salon was suddenly very quiet; the clumping feet along the deck passageway drifted in from the procession of Israeli seamen running aft to the cargo hold. Everyone started smoking. Colley lit a cheroot, Jamil and two of the Germans chose cigarettes, and Doctor Sauve brought out his pipe. Doctor Kastenburg began polishing his pince nez.

"The bombs are gone, Colonel," he said quietly and replaced his glasses. "Long gone." He sat back smiling comfortably. "But I'm sure you'll hear about them again."

Asher looked at him pleasantly. "We assumed as much—but you won't mind if we check anyway, will you?"

The German raised his shoulders slightly. "Suit yourself."

"Jamil!" Everyone turned to look at Peter Colley. "Does the name *Petroprince* mean anything to you?"

He saw the Palestinian's hooded eyes widen slightly.

"How about the *Petropacket*? Ever hear that name before? No? Maybe the *Petroprincess*?"

Leila leaped to her feet. "He knows!" she screamed. "They all know!" She looked around the room wildly. Jamil started to stand up, reaching to calm her, when he saw Hauser's movement from the corner of his eye. He dropped to a crouch reaching for his pistol. He was too late. The German's nine millimeter bullet hit him in the face. Leila grabbed Jamil's pistol and fired wildly at the German doctor, then turned the pistol on Colley.

"You—you," she spat, "you did it all!"

The Uzi gunner in the doorway cut her in half with a single burst. Everyone ducked the buzzing, ricocheting bullets, everyone, except Asher and Colley. They smiled at each other.

There was a rushing of feet on deck outside and Commander Zeke charged through the door, followed by other seamen. He looked through the pall of cordite and tobacco smoke at the bodies on the carpeted salon floor and the crouching figures of the Germans behind the furniture. "Everything under control, Colonel?"

"Completely under control. Nothing aft?"

Zeke shook his head. "Nothing—they've trans-shipped at sea. Both holds are empty."

"All right. The blitzkrieg is over, gentlemen, you can go back to your seats!" Asher told the Germans.

"So, you've put the bombs on the tankers. Now all we have to find out is where you sent the tankers—anyone want to give me a hint?" He surveyed the silent room of frightened faces.

"No?" Asher reached beside him and took the Uzi from the sailor. The barrel was still smoking. Slowly he removed the clip and reached for a new one from the seaman's belt, then inserted it with a snap.

"When I was a little boy in England, we used to play a game called 'eenie-meenie miney-moe'—ever hear of it?"

The Germans stared blankly.

"Here's how it works." He began explaining the childish game.

Hauser interrupted. "I'll tell you where the ships are going, Colonel."

"Like hell you will!" Al Thani's aim was much better than Leila's. Hauser dropped to the floor, a bullet through the heart, his eyes wide open with surprise.

Al Thani was dead before Hauser hit the carpet, a single bullet in his forehead. Asher lowered the machine-pistol and looked back at Colley.

"Nice shooting!" Colley blew the smoke from the Walther's barrel and pocketed his firearm. "Why doesn't everyone remove their temptations and give them to me. Maybe we can keep what's left of this meeting intact until we leave?"

Peter Colley moved around the room, stopping in front of each German with his hand extended invitingly. He passed the weapons over to the sailors who went with him around the salon. Kastenburg was last. Colley passed him by.

"You don't think I'm armed, Colonel Chirlo?" the German sneered.

Colley turned and smiled. "I don't think, Doctor, I know. Your type never is; you always find someone else to do the dirty work." His eyes swept the room.

"Now before Colonel Asher has to continue his children's games, why don't one of you tell us where the four tankers are headed and when they're set to blow up?"

"New York, Montreal, London and Rotterdam. Seventeen hundred hours Greenwich. July fourth."

"Schweinheund!" Kastenburg spat at his associate.

Asher gave a sigh of relief and lowered the Uzi. "Thank you, Doctor Sauve. You've been a real brick."

The men in the *Specht's* salon sat looking at one another in silence long after the patrol boat had thundered away from the drifting trawler. Finally, Kastenburg stood up. "Well, gentlemen," he surveyed the blood and bodies in the shattered room, "does anyone know how to steer this thing to shore?"

Singapore Airlines Flight 763 taxied up to the ramp at Athens Airport shortly after six a.m. and began deplaning passengers; those destined for Athens, and those in transit for connecting flights. The transit passengers were waved through customs and immigration without a baggage check into the transit lounge. For a number of passengers ticketed to Paris on Air France Flight 139, it would be a long wait. The Air France air bus was not scheduled to leave until noon.

Mr. Garcia and Mrs. Ortega, passengers from Bahrain, sat quietly, reading through an assortment of magazines they purchased from the kiosk in the lounge. They were printed in English. Neither Ortega nor Garcia understood any Spanish. Two young Arabs, passengers also on the Air France flight, sat at the far end of the lounge, apparently sleeping. According to the reservations list, the two Arabs were identified later as Fahim al-Satti and Hosni Albou Waiki. During the late morning, Mr. Garcia excused himself and went to the men's room, carrying his small flight bag. The bag was empty. He went into the third cubicle from the end of the row of urinals and shut the door.

"How does it look?" he asked Fayex Abdul-Rahim Jaber, the PFLP's operational commander.

Jaber smiled. "Everything according to plan. The strike will keep the security people busy covering absentees. Take off your coat!" he ordered.

It was awkward with two men inside the tiny cubicle. Quickly Jaber strapped the machine gun onto Mr. Garcia's back, taping it securely to his waist and shoulders with adhesive. "How does it feel?"

"Fine." Mr. Garcia wiggled into his coat, then turned around. Jaber stood up on the toilet seat and examined the hidden weapon critically.

"Walk upright. It won't show. Keep Gabriele behind you when you go on board. The rest of the stuff is in the bag."

They traded airline bags, and Mr. Garcia left the men's room in time to hear the multilingual loudspeaker in the transit lounge: "Announcing arrival of Air France Flight 139 from Tel Aviv."

The *Petroprincess* was four hundred miles southeast of Bermuda when Starlifter 5558 spotted it. The giant aircraft made a steep turn, dropping its landing gear, flaps and dive brakes to bring it down quickly from the fifteen thousand foot altitude it had been maintaining on the sweep. Zaglaviras, inside the bridge, noticed nothing on the aircraft's first passage at altitude, however, when the Starlifter streaked past on the starboard side less than a hundred feet over the water, he was positive the machine was in trouble and was going to ditch. It didn't. It circled again, wagging its gigantic wings slowly as it raced past a second time at two hundred knots, then sucked in its landing gear and climbed away to the west, its mighty engines roaring faintly after it had blended with the sky.

"What th'hell was that all about, Captain?" The deck officer came running up the gangway to the bridge.

"I thought for a minute he was going to land on the ocean."

Dimitri nodded. "So did I. It's one of those big American Air Force cargo freighters. I've seen them at the base in Athens." He shrugged. "Probably got bored on the way over, saw us down here and decided to raise a little hell to break the monotony."

As the Starlifter regained its fifteen thousand foot sweep altitude, Major Dehman, the aircraft's commander, pressed his mike button.

"Bermuda control, this is MAC triple nickel eight ball." He waited a few seconds until Bermuda had acknowledged interest, then continued.

"Roger, Bermuda. I have a positive I.D. on the tanker *Petroprincess*. She's about four hundred southeast your position on a course of two niner seven, making about eight to ten knots." He went on to give the coordinates of longitude and latitude.

"Roger, eight ball, I copy that. Did you try radio contact?"

"Affirmative—no reply on standard or Mayday frequencies."

"Okay, check that. Stand by, one."

Major Denham waited. He scanned the flight instruments idly. He felt pleased with himself. It gave him a real boot to think triple nickel eight ball was the first in the squadron to find the quarry they had been criss-crossing the Atlantic for the past few days. Fortunately, daylight weather conditions had been ideal; scattered clouds and the occasional towering cumulonimbus in the Southern latitudes, obscuring the seas from time to time, but that was all. The cumulonimbus were a pain in the ass if the radar scan picked a ship echo out from under any of them. It required dropping down beneath the thunderhead into pelting rain to check visually the type of vessel. None of them had turned out to be tankers. The rest of the time, the airmen, positioned behind the pilot's seats in the cockpit of the empty aircraft, had been covering the empty sea with binoculars through the aircraft windows, kept awake by Lieutenant Hollis— "Screaming Hollis," as the men now called him. Tired eyes scanned the sea in thirty minute shifts during each seven hour sweep, breaking the monotony only to drop down to examine the tankers they found at close range.

"Eight ball, this is Bermuda Control."

"Eight ball here—go."

"Headquarters advised, continue your sweep and good work on the tanker I.D."

Dimitri was in his day cabin when the bridge phone rang over his berth. He went over from the desk and answered it. "What is it?"

"We have another airplane circling us, Captain; looks like a seaplane this time—propellors." The second officer manned the bridge during the eight to four watch. "Wait a minute, I think he's going to land. Yes, he is Captain, he's landing!"

"I'll be right up."

Zaglivaras grabbed his jacket and ran out on deck. He saw the seaplane hover above the waves, then thump across the tops a short distance, before slowing abruptly to settle in the water. Zaglaviras took the steps up to the bridge three at a time.

"Stop engines," he yelled when he reached the wing deck. "Standby to lower a boat!"

The Air Force SA 16 Albatross taxied along slowly, keeping a safe distance from the ship. A roof hatch opened and two men climbed onto the wing center of the bobbing aircraft. Both wore orange life vests. Dimitri studied them through the binoculars. They were young men. One of them raised a bullhorn.

"Ahoy *Petroprincess!* Do you speak English?"

Dimitri went into the bridge and picked up their own loudspeaker. It was an antique with a long trailing cable.

"Are you in trouble?" he called out across the water.

"Negative. But you are. We wish to come aboard."

"I'm lowering a boat now. Stand by."

Dimitri walked back inside the bridge. "We're in trouble? What sort of trouble? We haven't been trailing anything, have we?"

It was a tanker habit to discharge waste oil and filthy seawater before reaching port. Along the North American and European coasts there were heavy fines levied on the masters of those vessels who got caught.

"Nothing Sir!" the second mate affirmed.

Zaglaviras dropped the loudspeaker into its rack and returned to the bridge wing. The crew was still working on the port davits trying to unscramble snarled lines to lower one of the ship's lifeboats. He looked across at the Albatross. A door on the side of the hull opened and a man tossed a yellow bundle into the sea on the end of a rope; it blew into a six man dinghy. Another followed the first. Lifejacketed sailors piled into the dinghies. Everyone carried weapons, Dimitri observed uneasily. There were two older men, civilians, sitting in one of the yellow boats. They left the Albatross and motored quickly towards the tanker.

"They even have their own outboards!" the second mate said in astonishment. He had come out on the wing to join the Captain.

"Tell those idiots to stand fast on that lifeboat—I can see we need more boat drill. Christ, we'd be at the bottom before they got the damn thing launched!"

The second mate went below to find the Bos'n. "Tell them to see if they can manage to lower the boarding steps without fouling the lines!" Dimitri called.

The two dinghies pulled alongside the platform at the bottom of the boarding steps and everyone tumbled out of the crafts, clattering up the steps to the deck of the *Petroprincess*. They looked very alert, obviously anticipating trouble. Suddenly, there was a thundering scream and everyone looked up as a formation of Phantom fighters zoomed over the vessel and swept back into the sky, circling the ship.

"Are you the Captain of this ship?"

Zaglaviras nodded dumbly at the young major holding a forty-five automatic.

"Where are you bound?"

"New York."

"For arrival July fourth, twelve noon, right?"

"Right."

"Do you know you have a bomb on board?"

"A bomb?" Zaglaviras was incredulous.

"An atomic bomb—these gentlemen with me are here to defuse it." He turned in the direction of the two civilians. Dimitri clutched the railing.

"I don't understand. We have nothing on board—no cargo—nothing."

The major looked skeptical. "You trans-shipped a crated cylinder at sea a few days ago from a trawler called the *Specht*, didn't you?"

"Yes, but that was a chemical sonar device brought in to us from Mexico for use with the cargo we're picking up in New York."

"Where is it?"

"On the forward masthead," he said weakly. The group of seamen and two civilians left them instantly, running to the forward deck.

"That chemical sonar, Captain, is the atomic bomb!" the Major told him gently, reholstering his forty-five. Whereupon, Dimitri Zaglaviras fainted.

25

JULY 1976

"Still no word on the last tanker?" Borodam demanded.

Asher shook his head. "Nothing. They've swept the area straight through to the forty-fifth parallel and down the Saint Lawrence River. The *Petropacket* has vanished. We've notified all ships at sea in the Gaspe to Cape Race but nothing. I think it's gone down somewhere. Zaglaviras said they'd been having trouble with the shaft bearings before it sailed."

"In which case there'll be one hell of an underwater explosion somewhere July fourth. I can't understand why the German isn't listening to his radio!" the Brigadier remarked.

The two Greeks, Aphendoulos and Gonidas, had radioed their position within hours of the emergency broadcast from the BBC to report in. Once it was apparent the tanker captains knew nothing of their cargo or the purpose of their voyages, advisory notices had gone out every hour to the ships telling them they were in great danger and to report their position to the nearest oceanic facility. *Petroprince* and *Petropower* had notified British Coastal Command within four hours after the first broadcast. Both vessels were boarded in the Bay of Biscay less than a hundred miles from each other.

"The orders were complete radio silence under all circumstances, Sir. You know what the German mentality is when it comes to taking orders?'' Asher said sadly.

Borodam nodded slowly. "Yes, I can remember. All the same, even with a German captain, I can't imagine the rest of the crew allowing their vessel to go down without some call for help.''

"Unless it blew up,'' Asher suggested.

"Possibly. Well, in any case, we'll know where it went down July fourth. In the meantime, I want a tight lid on everything until we get this Entebbe thing sorted out. General Gur is certain they'll kill everyone once they know the primary objective has failed. So far the stalling has worked in our favor. Operation Thunderball goes at midnight July third. The good Lord willing, we'll have everyone out by dawn.''

"I'd like to be going,'' Asher said.

Borodam smiled at him affectionately. "I'm sure Dan Shomron would like to have you, if it wasn't for that leg of yours. Yonni Netanyahu has been given the field commander's job; he'll make full colonel if he survives.''

"Yonni's a good man.''

"So are you, Lev. You moved mountains against my wishes to follow this thing through from the beginning. If I'd listened last Fall, things might have worked out differently. Then again, maybe not.'' He stood up behind the desk and stretched luxuriously, scratching his chest.

"What happened to your two friends?''

"Chirlo and Corbin? They're back in Canada now, I guess, watching the Olympics.''

"Good men, both of them. I'll ask the Premier to send a letter of thanks when this is all over.''

"They'd appreciate it, I'm sure. I couldn't have done a damn thing without them.''

"B.J. Bronstein too.'' Borodam stopped scratching.

"B.J. too. Still waiting impatiently for his story.''

"He may never be allowed to publish it.''

"He'll understand, Sir. He's that way.''

The office door opened and Sabra came into the room. I'm leaving now, Sir.''

Borodam glanced at his watch. "Good God! I'd forgotten all about you sitting out there. My apologies.'' He smiled benignly. "Perhaps Brigadier Asher will take you out to dinner tonight to make up for it.''

Asher stood up. "Brigadier?''

"Yes Lev, a reward for Operation Thunderclap. They pushed

me up to Major General." He lowered his eyes modestly, out of character.

"Congratulations Sir!"

Asher had trouble crossing to shake Borodam's hand with Sabra's arms wrapped around his neck kissing him.

"Now get out of here you two and leave me alone. I've work to do!"

"Goodnight, General Borodam. Shalom!"

"Shalom, Brigadier Asher."

Colley had telephoned Felina from Heathrow before taking off for Canada, telling her to catch the next flight to Montreal.

"But Pedro, whatever for?" She sounded bewildered. "What on earth is going on—where have you been?"

"I'll tell you about it in Montreal. You're coming to see the Olympic Games. When you know your flight number, phone Don Affleck from Miami. He'll meet you at the airport."

He gave her the CORCAN phone number and hung up before she could provide him with any more questions to answer.

They all met next day at the Hotel Bonaventure. Montreal was jammed with visitors.

"How in hell did you get reservations?" Corbin asked Affleck.

"Magic!" He winked, then gave them his pefect smile. "The management has been led to believe we are interested in buying the hotel."

Corbin and Colley laughed. Rina was aghast. "But that's dishonest, Donnee. That's terrible. I mean, what will you say when we check out?"

"He'll tell them he changed his mind," Elizabeth said logically. "Let's eat, I'm starved."

They went through the rooftop of the hotel to the dining room.

They were sitting in the grandstands watching the swimming events the following day when Corbin suddenly announced his idea.

"If we were to take a computer profile at Bayan on the weather and ocean currents from the time *Petropacket* left the *Specht*, I'll bet we'd be able to trace a fairly accurate plot on where the ship might be today—tomorrow, or on July fourth."

"I don't understand," Colley said.

"I do," Affleck told him. "If the tanker broke down on the first day and started drifting it would follow a definite course, depending upon the various external factors of wind, ocean currents, even the broadside surface area of the hull blown by the winds. It's a hell of an idea, Chuck. Why don't we try it?"

"Can you get all the required input?" Colley was unfamiliar with computers, but knew enough to realize the machines would only reply on the basis of information fed into them. If the input of information was inaccurate or sketchy, the output would be useless.

"I don't know. Let's try," Corbin said. They leaned over to speak to their wives, making excuses for the sudden departure to Ottawa.

It took all the next day to come up with a plot based on the various information they had garnered. The programmers had complained at first, being dragged in to work on a Saturday, but as the information began pouring in from the U.S., Canadian and European meteorological centers, they became fascinated by the intriguing problem. No one told them the purpose for the mathematical exercise, merely that it was a theoretical consideration requested by the tanker industry as a whole.

By nine o'clock that night they had a plot positioning for the *Petropacket* off the coast of Newfoundland. They called Rogers and told him to have the DH 125 ready to leave in the morning.

"Shouldn't we call someone else on this—the Navy, Coast Guard—someone?" Affleck asked on the way back to Ottawa.

"Why? If the plot is right, the ship will be well out to sea when it blows up. If the plot is wrong, we'd look like a bunch of fools for suggesting it in the first place. In any case, I want to follow the Saint Lawrence river from Montreal all the way to Father Point first, to make sure no one has missed the tanker."

Alpha Echo Zulu took off the next morning, July fourth, from Ottawa airport, twenty-two minutes before dawn.

Petropacket had been drifting for days. Speidel had retired to his cabin on the third day after the shaft had seized and told the chief engineer to call him when he had completed repairs.

"But Captain," the engineer protested, "we have nothing to work with!"

"Then improvise, Chief, improvise."

Speidel proceeded to drown himself in Schnapps. They jury-rigged a generator to keep electrical power supply available to the ship, but beyond that, there was nothing further to be done on getting the ship underway again. The deck and engineering staff lounged around waiting for their Captain to come to his senses and radio for assistance.

"No radio communication! We will observe our orders to the

letter."

He yelled at the first mate when the man stuck his head into Speidel's cabin on the fifth day. The German was lying on his bunk surrounded by Schnapp's bottles. The place smelled like a distillery.

"But Captain, we can't get the ship to run!"

Speidel propped himself up on an elbow and roared. "Then improvise, goddamnit—improvise!"

The mate closed the door discreetly, deciding he would have to assume command if the situation continued much longer. The Captain was obviously mad—*quite* mad. He explained their predicament to the chief engineer.

"Fuck him! Stupid Kraut! Tell Sparks to send an S.O.S. anyway. Christ, we could starve to death before that silly sonofabitch comes out of his fog!"

But Speidel, anticipating disobedience to his last orders, left his cabin and staggered into the radio room with a fire axe, demolishing any chance of communication with the world beyond their drifting hulk.

The days passed in uneventful activity. The first mate plotted their position daily at noon. Gradually, they had drifted North, along the edge of the Gulf Stream's northerly flow. They saw a few ships in the distance, but received no acknowledgement to their distress rockets and frantic Aldis Lamp signals.

On July third the mate smiled at the second officer. "With any luck we should see the Newfoundland coast by tomorrow night." He closed the sextant into its box carefully.

"Probably run into some fishing boats before then. They can relay a signal into St. Johns for a tug."

"What about the Captain?" the second mate inquired. Speidel frightened him. He didn't want a bad fitness report sent into Maritime Bureau in Athens and have the authorities lift his new certificate—he had just received it two months before landing his berth on the tanker.

"Fuck the Captain! He'll never command another ship as long as he lives, if I have anything to do with it. Stop worrying, Constantine. I'll cover your ass with the owners."

He set the sextant box back in its drawer and closed it with his butt.

"When I finish my report to the owners, my lad, I'll be the Captain instead of that lush we've got below. How would you like to be my first mate?" He grinned enticingly at the young man.

"So much for my theory!" Corbin said sourly after they landed in St. John's, Newfoundland, to refuel.

"Cheer up. It could have been worse. We might have found the boat and had it blow up in our faces!" Affleck told him carefully. They went into the coffee shop at the terminal building while Rogers looked after refueling arrangements for the return flight. Everyone was talking about the raid on Entebbe by the Israeli commandos. They listened with half an ear.

"They got them out, didja hear?" The waitress asked when she handed over the menus. "This morning at dawn they were all home safe n'sound. Grand, eh?"

They ordered toast and coffee. Colley sighed.

"Well, I guess that wraps it up. Asher will be pleased. It's all been his show from the start, hasn't it? The *Specht*, the bombs, the tankers, now the rescue at Entebbe. He's the real winner in all this."

"I don't think he went to Entebbe, Peter, not with that leg," Corbin told him, stirring his coffee.

Colley waved his hand negligently. "Details—you know what I mean. In the end he came out on top because he had the most to lose."

"If he hadn't, we all might have lost. New York and the American President—Montreal and the Royal Family—Rotterdam with fuel supplies for half a continent—London, with its millions of packaged people. We all would have lost something."

"It was a damn good plan, just the same," Colley said with a trace of admiration in his tone. "The bastard Jamil had it all figured out—came within an ace of making it work, too. Clever." He sipped his steaming cup.

"You call that clever? I'd call it insane!" Affleck said through a mouthful of toast.

"Insane perhaps, but still brilliant. Of course they'll try again. They have to."

Corbin looked at Colley. "Do you believe that?"

"No question about it. They'll try again next month, next year—sometime; they'll have to try again," Colley told him with certainty.

"Buy why?"

Colley shrugged. "Because they have nothing to lose except their lives, and everything to gain. They'll try again for the same reason men like Asher will try to stop them—that's the way they're made; only this time—the next time, it will probably be easier to get the bombs—Argentina—Brazil—Libya—Taiwan—Pakistan—India—how many more countries will be like Cosecha Rica in the next five years?" He looked at his partner and smiled, his crooked face sad.

"It's only a question of time."

"But what about us, what about reason and common sense. Surely in the end that will prevail?" Affleck protested.

"Us?" Colley said absently, holding his coffee cup cradled in his palms. "We'll try to build a better world, because that's the way we're made. We'll use our wealth, ingenuity and powers of persuasion to try and help where we can; argue logic when none will listen to logic or common sense because of their own greed, or fears of political reprisal at the polls from the people—the little people—who are always kept in the dark on everything until the last moment when it is too late to change direction."

There was a shout of jovial male laughter at the counter, followed by a peal of guffawing on a higher note as a second voice enjoyed a mutual joke. Colley looked around at the two men.

"So in the end it will not be us who decide what will or will not happen, but the little people—the stupid people—people like those two over there who still think there's nothing wrong—people like Jamil who believed that everything was wrong and were prepared to die trying to change it." He turned back to the table.

"That, my friends, is who will decide our eventual fate, and I can assure you we will have very little to do with their decision." He paused as Rogers came up with Doug Bailey, the co-pilot.

"All set. The weather's perfect all the way back."

"Sit down and grab a cup of coffee, you two, then we'll go. I'd like to fly along the South Coast on the way home if you have no objections, Rick?" Corbin told him.

"Objection—why should I object—you're paying for the gas!"

Ralph Lundrigan tied his small fishing boat to the crumbling wooden pier in Bingham Bay. His two sons, Jarman and Isaac, jumped off onto the dock. They'd been out since dawn, working the waters outside the tiny bay, searching for the fish that once, not too long ago, had been plentiful. Now the fish were gone; not gone somewhere else, just gone. Gone for good. Huge Russian and Japanese factory ships operating with hundreds of small superbly equipped fishing boats had denuded the Newfoundland coastal waters until there was nothing left for fishermen like the Lundrigan family who inhabited the tiny outport fishing settlements along the bleak coasts of the mighty Forest Island. Lundrigan didn't know exactly who had taken all the fish; some said it was the Russians, others said it was the Danes and Norwegians, along with the Japs and Portuguese. It didn't make much difference anyway, now—the fish were gone.

In Bingham Bay, everyone was on welfare, and there was nothing to sap a man's pride more than welfare, Lundrigan knew. That was why he took his sons out fishing; not because he expected to catch anything worthwhile—they hadn't done that for the past few years—but because it gave father and sons a sense of worth, a sense of purpose, a value knowing at least they were trying.

The three men walked up the rotting wharf towards the unpainted clapboard houses clustered precariously along the granite face of the sloping hills behind the bay.

Seagulls screamed around the cliffs, diving, then soaring above the dark green waters and shoreline spume. Some children were playing on the porch of the first house along the pathway to the Lundrigan home. They stopped their game and laughter and came over to peek at the men between the porch railings.

"Didja get sumpin', Mr. Lundrigan?" a boy asked.

"Nope. Mebbe t'morrow!" The three walked on up the uneven path past the church and general store.

Wally Durkin came out. "Howja do, Ralph by?"

"Notta ting, Walley—mebbe t'morrow!"

Durkin nodded and returned to his tiny store. It was a store with little in it except necessities—bare necessities of coal oil, flour, pork, beans—things that would keep month to month till receipt of government checks by the eighty odd souls in the community.

The Lundrigans reached their house and climbed the steps onto the porch, then sat down. They were breathing easily, despite the long climb. No one spoke. It was a ritual after each day of non-fishing; they sat on the porch, looking down glumly at the bay and beyond to the ocean that had betrayed them.

Suddenly, far out at sea, there was a blinding flash, brighter than the noonday sun, as twelve pounds of plutonium 239 collided within a four foot cylinder. In a trillionth of a second, a billion atoms smashed, vaporizing a square mile of ocean. The fireball flowered, then quickly died.

The Lundrigans blinked their eyes, momentarily blinded from the glare. The ocean rose darkly, wetly in the sunlight, rolling towards the sky, gathering itself within itself as it climbed swiftly, higher, higher and still higher, then began to crown in a purity of white magnificence, expanding as it rose.

Ralph Lundrigan stood up. "Lardy Jesus, old man—wouldja

look at dat, my bys! Them fellars on the mainland gotta be crazy! First dey let th'furriners in to take away d' fish—now dey've come along back again to blow up what's left us!" He shook his head in anger and disbelief.

His eyes caught the glint of an aircraft less than a mile offshore. A DeHavilland executive jet streaking westward along the coast, climbing as it raced the shock waves rolling in from the blast.

Lundrigan pointed. "Look! Oh me sons, wouldja lookee dat! He's d'one what done it—just you bet he'd d'one what done it! Tear-assin fer home on d'mainland!" His eyes were blinded by tears of fury and frustration over things which he knew neither he nor his sons would ever have control.

Far out at sea, the silver-white crowned cloud slowed its rise, then stopped and began to expand its lovely lacy tendrils, reaching out softly, quietly, to embrace the world.

EPILOGUE

.... DATELINE ... *AUGUST 1976, OTTAWA* ... ATOMIC ENERGY CANADA LIMITED HAS CONFIRMED SALE OF CANDU NUCLEAR REACTOR TO REPUBLIC OF SOUTH KOREA ....

.... DATELINE ... *SEPTEMBER 1976, BUENOS AIRES* ... ARGENTINE GOVERNMENT HAS ADMITTED OPERATION OF AN EXPERIMENTAL NUCLEAR WASTE PROCESSING PLANT FOR PLUTONIUM ....

.... DATELINE ... *SEPTEMBER 1976, TEL AVIV* ... ISRAELI GOVERNMENT NEITHER DENIES NOR CONFIRMS NUCLEAR ARMS CAPABILITY AT SECRET FACILITY NEAR DIMONA ....

.... DATELINE ... *OCTOBER 1976, HONG KONG* ... INFORMANTS HERE STATE TAIWAN GOVERNMENT BUILDING SECRET NUCLEAR WASTE REPROCESSING PLANT ....

.... DATELINE ... *NOVEMBER 1976, BONN* ... WEST GERMANY GOVERNMENT ANNOUNCES INTENT TO SELL NUCLEAR FUEL REPROCESSING PLANT TO BRAZIL. ...

.... DATELINE ... *DECEMBER 1976, OTTAWA* ... CANADIAN GOVERNMENT CONFIRMS SALE CANDU NUCLEAR REACTOR TO TAIWAN GOVERNMENT. ...

.... DATELINE ... *JANUARY 1977, CAIRO* ... PRIME MINI-STER ANWAR SADAT TOLD EGYPTIAN CONGRESS HE WAS HOPEFUL GOVERNMENT OF INCOMING ADMINISTRATION WOULD OBSERVE VERBAL COMMITMENTS GIVEN BY SECRE-TARY HENRY KISSINGER TO PROVIDE NUCLEAR POWER PLANTS TO EGYPT....

.... DATELINE ... *FEBRUARY 1977, BONN* ... CHANCELLOR HELMUT SCHMIDT SENDS OFFICIALS OF WEST GERMAN GOVERNMENT TO WASHINGTON TO EXPLAIN HIS COUN-TRY'S POSITION ON SALE OF NUCLEAR REPROCESSING EQUIPMENT TO BRAZIL....

.... DATELINE ... *MARCH 1977, TOKYO* ... CANADIAN AMBASSADOR TO JAPAN BRUCE TANKIN STATED HERE JAPANESE GOVERNMENT EXPECTED TO BUY CANDU NU-CLEAR REACTOR BEFORE DECEMBER 1978 ... END

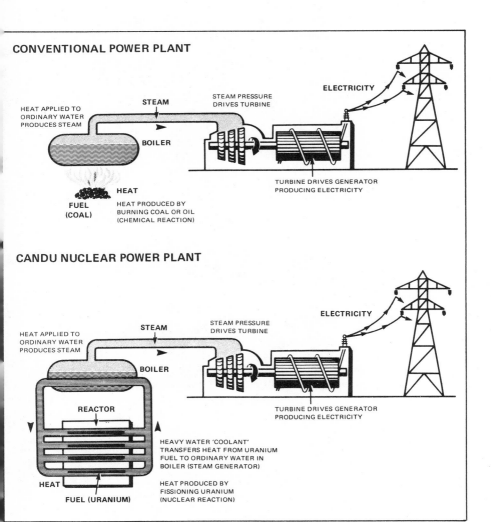

CONVENTIONAL POWER PLANT

HEAT APPLIED TO
ORDINARY WATER
PRODUCES STEAM

STEAM

STEAM PRESSURE
DRIVES TURBINE

ELECTRICITY

BOILER

HEAT

FUEL
(COAL)

HEAT PRODUCED BY
BURNING COAL OR OIL
(CHEMICAL REACTION)

TURBINE DRIVES GENERATOR
PRODUCING ELECTRICITY

CANDU NUCLEAR POWER PLANT

HEAT APPLIED TO
ORDINARY WATER
PRODUCES STEAM

STEAM

STEAM PRESSURE
DRIVES TURBINE

ELECTRICITY

BOILER

REACTOR

HEAVY WATER 'COOLANT'
TRANSFERS HEAT FROM URANIUM
FUEL TO ORDINARY WATER IN
BOILER (STEAM GENERATOR)

TURBINE DRIVES GENERATOR
PRODUCING ELECTRICITY

HEAT

FUEL (URANIUM)

HEAT PRODUCED BY
FISSIONING URANIUM
(NUCLEAR REACTION)

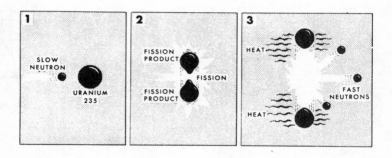

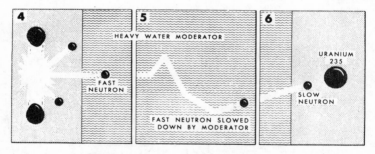

Slow neutron (fig. 1) strikes nucleus of uranium-235 atom and splits ("fissions") it (fig. 2) into fission products which fly apart (fig. 3) creating heat. Neutrons given off at same time are slowed down as they travel through heavy water (fig. 5).

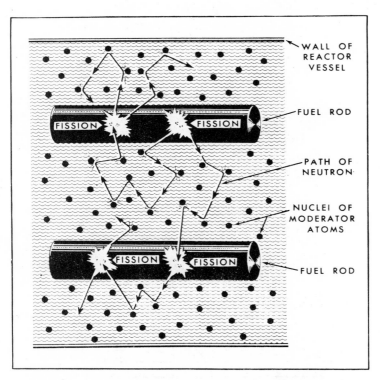

WALL OF
REACTOR
VESSEL

FUEL ROD

PATH OF
NEUTRON

NUCLEI OF
MODERATOR
ATOMS

FUEL ROD

Neutrons given off by splitting ("fissioning") uranium-235 atoms are slowed down (their speed is "moderated") as they bounce against the nuclei of heavy water atoms. Slowed sufficiently, the neutrons will split other uranium-235 atoms and thus maintain a chain reaction.

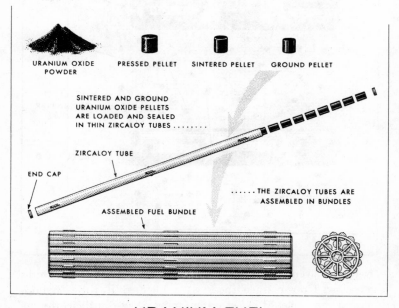

URANIUM OXIDE POWDER

PRESSED PELLET

SINTERED PELLET

GROUND PELLET

SINTERED AND GROUND
URANIUM OXIDE PELLETS
ARE LOADED AND SEALED
IN THIN ZIRCALOY TUBES . . . .

ZIRCALOY TUBE

END CAP

. . . . . . THE ZIRCALOY TUBES ARE
ASSEMBLED IN BUNDLES

ASSEMBLED FUEL BUNDLE

URANIUM FUEL

Reactor Simplified Flow Diagram

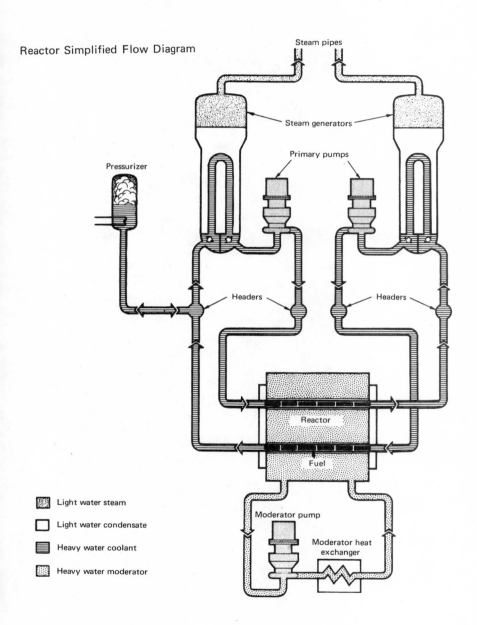

Steam pipes

Steam generators

Pressurizer

Primary pumps

Headers

Headers

Reactor

Fuel

Moderator pump

Moderator heat exchanger

Light water steam

Light water condensate

Heavy water coolant

Heavy water moderator

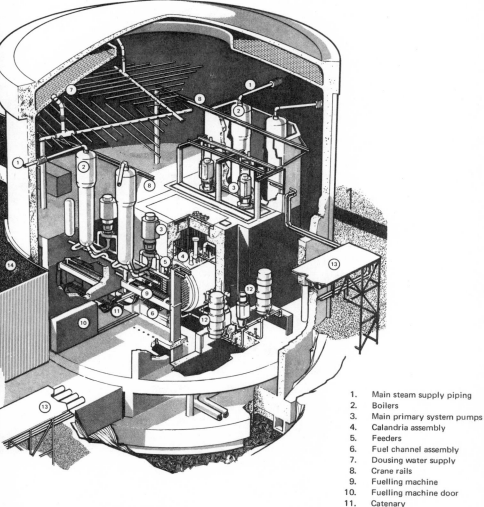

Reactor Building

1. Main steam supply piping
2. Boilers
3. Main primary system pumps
4. Calandria assembly
5. Feeders
6. Fuel channel assembly
7. Dousing water supply
8. Crane rails
9. Fuelling machine
10. Fuelling machine door
11. Catenary
12. Moderator circulating system
13. Pipe bridge
14. Service building

Reactor Assembly

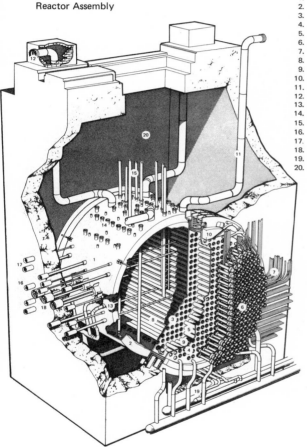

1. Calandria
2. Calandria shell
3. Calandria side tube sheet
4. Fuelling machine side tube sheet
5. Lattice tubes
6. End fittings
7. Feeders
8. Calandria tubes
9. Steel ball shielding
10. Annular shielding slab
11. Pressure relief pipes
12. Rupture disc
13. Moderator inlets (4 each side)
14. Reactivity control nozzles
15. Reactivity control devices
16. Horizontal flux detectors (9)
17. Poison injector nozzles (6)
18. Ion chamber cooling piping
19. End shield cooling piping
20. Calandria vault (light water shield)

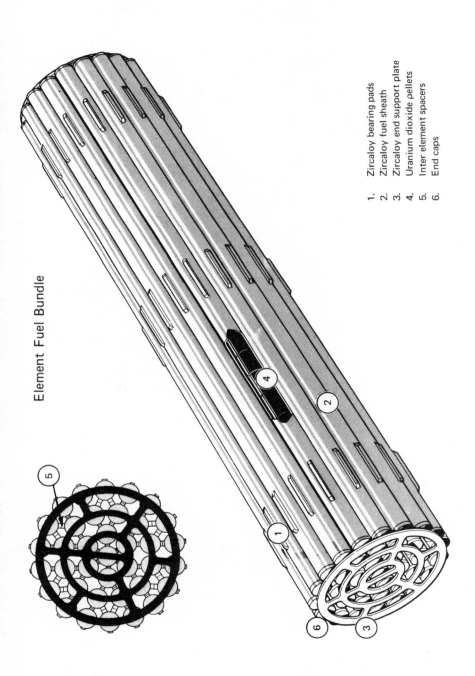

Element Fuel Bundle

1. Zircaloy bearing pads
2. Zircaloy fuel sheath
3. Zircaloy end support plate
4. Uranium dioxide pellets
5. Inter element spacers
6. End caps

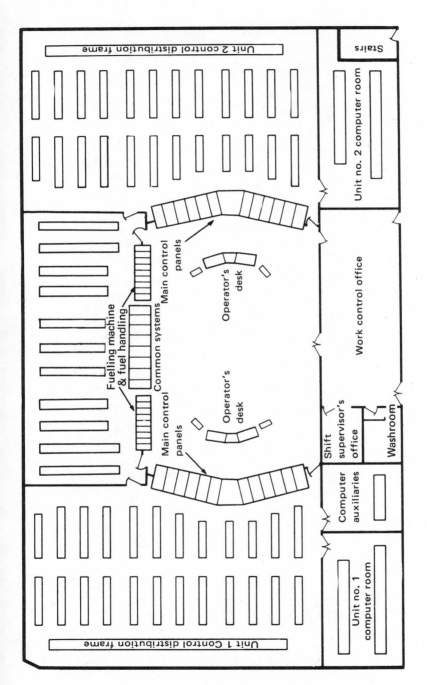

CONTROL ROOM PLAN

INSIDE STORAGE POOL